THE SECRET BOOKS
OF PARADYS

TANITH LEE

THE SECRET BOOKS OF PARADYS

THE COMPLETE PARADYS CYCLE

OVERLOOK DUCKWORTH
NEW YORK • WOODSTOCK • LONDON

This edition first published in the United States in 2007 by
OverlookDukworth, Peter Mayer Publishers, Inc.
New York, Woodstock & London

WOODSTOCK:
One Overlook Drive
Woodstock, NY 12498
www.overlookpress.com
[for individual orders, bulk and special sales, contact our Woodstock office]

NEW YORK:
141 Wooster Street
New York, NY 10012

LONDON:
90-93 Cowcross Street
London EC1M 6BF
inquiries@duckworth-publishers.co.uk
www.ducknet.co.uk

Cataloging-in-Publication Data is available from the Library of Congress

Book design by Bernard Schleifer
Manufactured in the United States of America
ISBN 978-1-58567-984-3 hc
ISBN 978-1-58567-987-4 pb/US
ISBN 978-0-7156-3750-0 pb/UK
10 9 8 7 6 5 4 3 2 1

CONTENTS

The Book of the Damned

STAINED CRIMSON 3

MALICE IN SAFFRON 85

EMPIRES OF AZURE 165

The Book of the Beast

THE GREEN BOOK 215

Part One: The Scholar   217
Part Two: The Bride   237
Part Three: The Jew   265
Part Four: The Scapegoat   275
Part Five: The Widow   287

THE PURPLE BOOK 291

Part One: The Roman   293
Part Two: The Suicide   345

THE GREEN BOOK 337

Part Six: The Madman   339
Part Seven: The Demon   345

The Book of the Dead

THE WEASEL BRIDE 367

THE NIGHTMARE'S TALE 383

BEAUTIFUL LADY 415

MORCARA'S ROOM 437

THE MARBLE WEB 457

LOST IN THE WORLD 475

THE GLASS DAGGER 497

THE MOON IS A MASK 523

The Book of the Mad
Le Livre Orange

Prologue:	Paradise	541
One:	Paradis	545
Two:	Paradys	565
Three:	Paradise	577
Four:	Paradis	587
Five:	Paradys	603
Six:	Paradise	611
Seven:	Paradis	621
Eight:	Paradys	625
Nine:	Paradise	649
Ten:	Paradis	657
Eleven:	Paradys	665
Twelve:	Paradise	687
Epilogue:	Paradis	693

THE BOOK OF THE DAMNED

STAINED WITH CRIMSON

Le Livre Cramoisi

We were young, we were merry, we were very very wise,
And the door stood open at our feast,
When there passed us a woman with the West in her eyes,
And a man with his back to the East.

Mary Elizabeth Coleridge

How fast does a man run, when the Devil is after him?

I was seeing it, but unknowingly, as he came towards me up the cobbled hill, his breath cawing with the effort, his eyes colourless and bright. The afternoon had grown late and the sky rolled with storm clouds. Slanting light, driven down between the cliff-like walls of the Temple-Church of the Sacrifice, gave only greyness to the alleys. I had come from Philippe's séance dulled, and with immeasurable foreboding, dissatisfaction. And into all this, the storm-light, the stony channel, my vision, the runner ran. His arms were outstretched and his long rags streamed behind him. He seemed to have been clawed by great thorns; hair and clothes. I stepped to one side to let him by. I thought him a madman. Instead, he fell at my feet. "Ah," he moaned, as if, thirsting, he discovered water, "*aah*."

I drew back again. His hand clawed after me and gripped my ankle.

"Take your hand off," I said, "or must I make you."

"Lean closer," he answered. "Lean down."

His voice was cultured, and sounded young, though my impression had been of an old man. The hand was elegantly kept, the nails clean and trimmed. Rings adorned it. Suddenly I imagined him some helpless noble creature set on by scoundrels. I knelt beside him.

"Who attacked you, monsieur?"

He laughed. It was an awful noise, as if his throat had been cut. He turned, and I was gazing into his face. It was the countenance of a man in early middle life, no more. How had the other idea got hold of me? And he was handsome.

"Listen," he said, "I have only a moment."

"But –"

"Ssh," he said, soothing me. Then he laughed again, softly. "Young man," he said, "I am *so* glad to have found you. Ah yes. Now I will give you the secret of life. Do you want it?"

3

"Who does not?" I took his words for a joke, though he lay on the cobbles before me.

"You are right. Who does not. Do you?"

"Perhaps."

"Oh, perhaps. Here is my other hand. Open it." He offered me a closed fist. "I can't unclench the fingers," he said. "You must do it."

I was bemused by now. I took his fist in both hands and prised it open, which was not easy. There in the palm was another ring, that burned in the half-light a deep smooth red, like a drop of syrup. Yet the boss, highly polished, had also been engraved. Something insectile it would seem to be.

"There now," he said to me. "Take it."

"This?"

"What else. Yes. Take it." I took it, to calm him, for he was becoming very agitated. "Your name," he said, "give me your name."

"St Jean."

"What more?"

"Nothing more. Andre St Jean. That is all. Let me help you up. Where did you mean to go?"

"Away," he said. And abruptly he was scrambling to his knees; next to get upright. I assisted him as best I could. Then he sprang forward, away from me. I called after him, but he only turned back to me the profile of his madman's face and gave a raw snarl that might have been amused hatred or simply terror. He was old again, an ancient lunatic escaped from some hospital, with bits of wire wound on his knotted hands. He rushed flapping and flailing up Sacrifice Hill, and was gone into the dark stone ditches under the church.

An urge came on me to hurl after him the thing he had given me. What could it be but a gaud of glass, or something much worse. But I stole a look at it again, and it had remained immutable. A huge polished ruby, incised with a snub-headed insect of folded wings. I closed my hand on it in a sort of spasm.

The encounter had unnerved me. I leaned on one of the blind walls by me, my head full of gentle buzzings. What was he fleeing from? Oh, pursuit, of course. His keepers must be after him. Or he had robbed someone of the jewel, and the City police were on his track.

The rain began a moment later, a thousand stilettos flung into the street, over and over. The rain would revive me, probably.

When I heard the shadow, I raised my head. I had expected the pursuit, but not the shape it took.

Two black dogs, lean and long, with jackals' pointing heads, came loping up the cobbles through the rain, slick and wet, altogether like basalt. They barely glanced at me. They went swiftly by, and it seemed to me I felt their heat dinning through the chilly air. After them rode a man on a black horse. He was cloaked in black and cowled against the rain, like a priest. But he, as he drew level with me, paused. Through the water, against the black of the hood, I saw his pale face, and the black eyes that fixed on me and seemed to impel the heart out of my body.

"Did he go this way?"

His voice was quiet, but it reached me easily. It was the voice of music, and its colour too was black.

"Who is that?" I said.

"Don't play," he said. "Answer me."

"Yes," I said. I lifted my hand to point, or to show him the ring, which must be his, but in that instant he turned his face from me, and lightly touching his horse with the spur, set it racing over the stones.

He was gone. The air seemed cold as iron. I wondered if I would follow, to see what happened, if he would catch up to the other. I had a notion now the lunatic fled to the Temple-Church for sanctuary, but that it would do him no good. The desire to go after the rider, to make him speak again, perhaps to insult him or somehow draw him out, was very strong. But I had not liked the look of the dogs he did his hunting with in the lanes of Paradys. No, it would be better to go home.

I was turning down into the old market, when I thought I heard a thin high terrible screaming, far off, back up the hill.

Since ten in the morning I had been in the house of crazy Philippe, where the séance had been held with such pomp. It led to all types of manifestation, attractive rotten things, like death-bed lilies. The furniture had moved, a decanter smashed; a naked ghost-child appeared to prophesy – stupidities that were certainly faked, or induced by the energy of suggestion. But it had left me sensitive, left me wanting, in need of a supernatural completion as in need of food or sex or sleep.

What then had I been a witness to? A running man, a riding man, two striding dogs. And had I even heard those dreadful cries behind me?

I stood in the rain below the steps, wondering if he would come back, Satan, Prince of Darkness, on the night-black mare, the broken body of his victim flung casually across the saddle. But no one came except a woman of the alleys, who wished me good-day, looking slyly to see if I would go after her to her lodging.

Stumbling, shivering, I turned for my own.

Philippe, Le Marc, Russe, and some others stood in the street shouting up at my window.

I opened it, and looked down.

The bell was ringing midnight from Our Lady of Ashes across the river. A howling dark, with intervals of deaf stillness. The candlelight touched their faces oddly, making them look mad or damned, the very things they strove to be.

"Regard him!" Le Marc cried in turn, of me, "death's-head with a book. Come down, corpse, and be happy. Despair is so sensuous, so delicious, it will wear you out."

"He is sulking," said Philippe, "because the little ghost-maiden didn't sit on his lap."

"Go with your legions to hell," said I.

"Later, later."

They clamoured at the outer door until my landlady trudged up the house and admonished me at the inner one. To keep the peace, I descended. And because, of course, I had nothing better or worse to do.

We went to the *Iron Bowl*, and later to the *Cockatrice*, drinking, drinking. The red wine that opens the eyes, and the black brandy that blinds you.

"He's still wearing that ring. Look. Three whole weeks. It must be some token."

"You are a fool," said Russe, going back by the wine to the sombre forests of his blood. "Some cut-throat will have your finger off for that one night, when you're sprawled in some alley."

"The left hand," said Philippe. "He doesn't care what happens to that. As long as the right hand can write."

I gazed at the red ring, the ruby, with the beetle engraved on it.

"Who gave it you?" said Philippe. He smiled. "I know who would like it."

"Philippe, you know everything, why do you bother with us?" said Le Marc.

"*Who* would like it?" said Russe. "The Devil?"

"What Devil?" I said, feeling my blood on its path turn and rise and move another way.

"It is the Devil's ring," said Russe. "I never saw anything so clearly. Let a thief steal it. It will bring you sorrow, and horror."

"What's new?" I said. I put my head on my arms on the table. Philippe stroked my hair, long as the fashion now was in the City of Paradys, and hennaed "Martian" red, since the fashion too was for such colourings. Blond Philippe, a Narcissus, a snow-chrysanthemum from birth, laughed in my ear. "Don't you want to know whose ring it really is?"

"Tell me, you liar."

"A most beautiful woman."

"Liar, liar," I murmured.

"Not tonight, you are too drunk tonight, and it is too late tonight. Tomorrow we will go to her. And you shall return her the ring. The most beautiful woman in Paradys."

"Who is that?" said Le Marc.

"The old banker's wife," said Philippe.

"Oh, I heard of her. Yes. He lets her hold her salon, like the other empress-es of the City. But they are foreigners."

Nearly asleep, I swam through my skull, and sometimes listened.

Philippe and Le Marc half carried me home.

Philippe guided me up the stair and shut the door of my room. He moved about, fingering books, caressing the sheets of paper, some with a single line of prose upon them. "The light drains from the great window," he read, "like blood from a fainting face." He overturned the ink-well, shaped like a gryphon, and with a candle dragged from its socket drew in the ink a cruci-fied Christ, screaming in ecstasy.

"Burn that in the morning," he said. "It will be unlucky."

He sat down on the bed by me, pulled off my shirt and tugged down my breeches. Bored finally by the long caresses, similar to those lavished on my papers, which evoked no sustained response, he concluded his act with a violent introduction and sudden achievement, wracking the house with his groans and cries. He fell asleep lying on top of me, on my back, his white hair getting in my mouth, so I constantly awoke to remove it. Once he whispered again. "Tomorrow, I will take you to her."

A man in a black cowl galloped over and over through my dreams and I was slung across the saddle before him. Near dawn, barely conscious, I too climaxed with a slight shuddering that woke Philippe and caused him to curse and punch me in the ribs.

Before he roused himself I got up, dressed, and left the stinking room.

I went down into the City valley, to the river, coiled like a sliding serpent in the mists of earliest day. The buildings rose like crags from the mist, like hills weathered into oblongs. Birds flew for miles, back and forth.

I thought of casting the ring into the river, but might not some fish swal-low it? And then I, cutting into the prize sturgeon of some dinner at Philippe's house, find the ring again, glowing up at me from the fish's backbone?

I had searched the journals, I had asked everyone, but there had been no mention of a particular body found in the yards of The Sacrifice, or of a phan-tom hunter accompanied by black dogs.

I turned from the river and wandered up towards the tall libraries of the Scholars' Quarter. Philippe would lie in wait for me at my lodging a while, and, as usual, I felt myself done with him for ever, until the next occasion of our meeting.

Two days later, he called on me, at his smartest and most exquisitely dressed. It was mid-afternoon.

"Come to my house."

"As you see, I am working."

"Let me look."

"No."

"Oh you," he said, "like some country girl with her lower parts. Very well. Give me a copy when printed. One more slender volume … Till then, come to my house."

"Go away, Philippe."

"It is tonight," he said.

He had odd eyes, one much lighter than the other. It enhanced his looks, though as a child, he had been disturbed by it. The nurse his dead mamma had got for him had said it was a mark of evil. She urged him on. At thirteen he raped her.

"*What* is tonight?"

"She opens her salon, like a rose."

"Who?"

"That lovely woman I spoke of. The wonder of the City."

It was hot today and hard to work now concentration had been shattered. I laid my pen aside and put my head in my hands. Philippe trailed a flower across my hands, my neck. Presently I got up and followed him out.

Philippe's house stood up against the old City Wall, near the Obelisk, where they had burned the dead in millions during a plague named "the Death." Now a variety of trees rooted out of the stones, casting a wet feverish shade. The elderly house was shuttered, an old thing itself, despising the human lizards who flickered through its lofty rooms: they lasted only a moment, better let them do as they wished.

"How I hate this house," Philippe had said, a hundred times, cheerfully. Now his father was dead, he did everything he wanted there. It was the scandal of the district, but he was rich.

In one of the marble baths I lay soaking, like a piece of statuary dug up from the muck and taken to be cleaned, while one of Philippe's domestics stropped the shaving razor behind the screen. When I vacated the bath-chamber, drugged and stupefied by hot water and balsams, a valet put me into a suit of Philippe's clothes. We were almost of the same fitting, and everything of his might be worn with loose ease by me.

"Oh what a beauty," he said, flitting round me, most malign of the lizards – one better caged.

The light was growing heavier, more solid, slabs of it in the pillared windows and fallen across the road outside.

"Do you want to dine?" he said.

"I want nothing. I want to go to sleep."

"Bloody slug. Come on. Where is that ring – you do have it?"

I had stopped wearing it. It had been in my pocket, *his* pocket now, and I took it out and offered it to him. He skipped away. "No, no, Andre. But you must show it to her."

"Her. This woman. She had better be worth all your trouble."

We went out, and along the street together, two young princes in a democratic Paradys that no longer recognised such beings. But who would know me, anyway. A scribbler. A few had seen my plays, and read my essays and miniature novels in their closets. But I was not in the mode, unlike my hair, and now my clothes. I said things that cut too near, or not near enough their candy bones. (Or maybe only I was no good at my trade.) Three pamphlets of mine had even criticised the City Senate, but they took it in good part. *There* was shame. Probably I would rather have been hauled off to jail, unless I had been.

"Philippe," I muttered, "if I die –"

"Here it is again," he said.

"If I die, see to it – make that wretch of a printer take it all and print it all. Every word. Anything unfinished even, and all the pieces he has refused."

"This ego," he said. "Who will care? If you're dead. Do you think you will?"

"No. But I care now, I care this moment. Promise me."

"Very well. As before. I promise you."

"You. I can't trust you. You never read a line I ever wrote."

"Many lines. Now, how does it go – 'Light leaving a window like blood in a faint' – what was that?"

"Something I can't remember. A dream I think I had."

"Like that other dream. I could make you once. You used to yell louder than I did. I used to listen in amazement."

"You see," I said, "but you don't listen to the *words*."

"When you die," he said, he swung towards me and took me by the neck, by the snowy linen of his own wardrobe, "when I *kill* you, Andre, I will make sure every line of your fretful *oeuvre* is published. Shall I bite through a wrist vein and swear it in blood?"

I pushed him and he drew off.

"This woman," I said, "who is she?"

"I have told you."

"Her name." (Give me your name, the running man had said.)

"Wait, and see."

We walked on, through the thick, tree-interrupted light, as the bells of the City sounded seven o'clock. We were moving west towards the Quarter of the Clockmakers.

"Where does she live?"

"On Clock-Tower Hill."

"Tell me about her."

He said, "Bloodless skin, ebony hair. A pale mouth that seems drawn on to her face, but is not. Eyes like all-blackness."

He had been an artist at one time. It informed his speech, if no longer anything else.

"No eye is ever black. You go close and look into it, the eye is some other shade."

"Not hers, Andre. Ah, such a blow in store: you won't be disappointed."

"And the husband?"

"If he is. Monsieur Baron von Aaron."

"A name after all."

"A foreign name. He's antique. A marriage of convenience."

"Oh," I said. "You have had her, then."

"Not yet. Never, I should think. She isn't to be *had*."

Fashionable strollers patrolled the lower walks of the Wall Quarter, from the Obelisk Gardens to the Observatory. Some greeted Philippe, with flippancy or caution, and whispered when he had gone by. On the Observatory Terrace the tables were out, the gossips, gamblers and drinkers, cards fluttering like red and black pigeons, and the resinous clink of glasses of black coffee and liqueurs. From here, by means of an architectural gorge running through the City of Paradys, you saw the masonry precipices drop down, through coins of roofs and flutes of steps like folded paper, into shadow depths veiled in parks, with little bright sugar churches appliquéd on to a mellow sunset, which shed a glamour now like the lambency of some old priceless painting.

We crossed the Terrace, and went up Clock-Tower Hill, where, thirty metres in the air, the gilded white face stares four ways at time.

The house which the Baron von Aaron was renting was one of the stuccoed piles along the inner shoulder of the hill. A lamp hung over the wrought-iron gate, alight. The gate itself stood wide. We went through, up some steps to the porch, and rang the bell. The house was mildly pulsating with its occupancy, and in the dimming atmosphere, the windows of the second floor were quietly burning up.

A domestic opened the door. Philippe handed him at once a card. That was all. The man, an absolute blank, moved back to allow us to come in, and next, having shut the door, solemnly walked ahead of us. We carried our gloves, and would have carried our hats too, had we been wearing any, straight up the curving stair and to the salon.

The card was given over to another blank at the entrance, and borne away across the room. There was nothing unusual in the salon, but for the strange soft candlelight at odds with the softer deepening radiance of the sunset windows, an exciting, expectant light, that would, as ever, lead you fiercely on to nothing. The house itself all around seemed blind, and echoed. Though fresh flowers had peered from the vases by the stair, the building was not exactly alive. The salon, painted and upholstered in the way of such rich men's rentables, was a pastel, and already filled by smoke. There were groups of men, and a handful of women. Some of either gender I knew, others by sight. No one to be interested in; rather, to be avoided. The cadence of talk was low but ceaseless. Now and then a breaker burst, laughter or an exclamation. Somewhere someone was playing a guitar.

"Be patient, wait," Philippe said to me.

He began to move through the groves of men, the trailing willows of women, accepting as he went a quip, a cigar, muttering, "Oh God, is *she* here?" over some woman he was not pleased to see. White shoulders flashed and white pipes puffed up at a ceiling of plaster acanthus.

Near the long windows was a piano, and leaning on it, the guitar-player himself, strumming away. An oil-lamp of dense crystal rested on a low glass table, and cast its bloom upward. It caught her hand as she took Philippe's card from the attendant, and her face as she bent her eyes on it to glance. Then, it caught her little, little smile, as she set the card down by the lamp, into a petal-fall of other similar cards.

"Madame," said Philippe. He bowed over her and took her hand up again and pressed his lips to it. "I am so glad you allowed me to return."

"It is my husband you must thank."

"Then, I thank him, with all my heart. Madame, may I present my friend."

"Of course," she said. Her lips stretched once more in the little, little smile.

"The writer, Andre St Jean," said Philippe.

"Of whom you won't have heard," I said.

She raised her eyes and looked at me directly, for one entire and timeless second.

"I am afraid that is true."

"Don't be afraid, madame. If it is to frighten you, most of the City would have to share your terror."

But her eyes were already gone. They seemed to gaze down into the lamp, so I might go on looking at them, but not into them. They were perfectly black, as Philippe had assured me. So black the charcoal shadow of the lashes, cast upward by the glow across the heavy lids, was ghostly in comparison, and the black brows also seemed pale. These brows were long, and unplucked, and the lashes long and very thick. In the bloodless face, the mouth was a pale ivory pink, the line of the lips' parting or joining accentuated by the lamp, as if carefully drawn with pencil … Black hyacinth hair, the

kind that thickly and loosely curls; the sheerest shoulders, slender and boneless, above a dark dress. Not a jewel, except the marriage rings which I would
diligently search out when her hands came up again.

"You see, Madame von Aaron," I said, "I don't hanker for fame at all. But
it is at moments like these I wish I had it. If I were known, then you might
look at me with some attention. As it is, what in the world can I hope for?"

I felt Philippe's whole body shoot into lines of overjoyed and spiteful
satisfaction. She raised her face and gave me one more look, a cold look, of
surprised indifference. She did now know what to do about me, or my arrogant sally, and so would do nothing at all.

And I? Having bowed to her, I walked away to a table where the valets were
pouring out white wine. As I drank it, I imagined her say to Philippe, "Really,
my friend, might I ask you, in future, to spare me such acquaintances?"

But she would not say that. He was no friend of hers.

It was the truth, what I had said, so naturally I confronted her with it. The
others would fawn and keep their place. She did not care for anything original, it seemed.

I thought of the sort of women who liked me, some of them even aristocratic. But she was not of their type. She would be tall when she stood, almost
my own height, perhaps equal to it. Neither did I care for her, she was so cold.
Her hands (beautiful probably, it had seemed so) would be cold as ice to
touch. Splendid hair, and eyes. Otherwise, nothing much. She might give the
illusion of great beauty but in fact was not beautiful. Though a voice like the
music of the night.

I remembered that ring, then, the gem of hot syrup in the pocket of Philippe's
brocaded waistcoat, and slipped in two fingers to find it. At that moment someone else entered the salon, and there were loud, acclaiming calls.

Who was this? Who could it be but the husband, the ostensible lord of her
court. The groves were parting to let him by, the men were shaking his hand,
or clapping his shoulder. He was tall himself, but stooped and grey – his
artificially-curled hair, his expensive coat. He paused to sample someone's
tobacco, then shook his old head sadly. The foreign look was exotic in her,
and not quite palpable, but he surely had it, in all of his massive face hanging forward off its skull. A cunning, just, ineloquent face.

He passed me, not seeing me, of course, for who was I?, and went on to
the window and the piano and the lamp. The guitar-player instantly rose to
greet him, and Philippe, who had stayed at her side with four or five others,
hung about there, looking glad and expectant, awaiting the man's notice.
Stalest of all tricks; it was the husband he had come to see, the woman only
a pleasurable diversion encountered on the path.

Philippe now bowed, and shook the old banker's old bankering hand. Was

I to be recalled and introduced again? It seemed not. I had disgraced myself.
I stole a look at her. She was actually plain. Just the eyes, the hair, the grace.
Yes, clever. Women with more made less of it than she. Now her hands rose
to greet her husband too. Lovely hands, and there, the big silver rings, one
with a pale jewel catching the lamp. When should I give her this one, the red
ring with the Egyptian beetle cut in it? Was it hers, this drop of crimson
blood? It was all hers. Everything.

Now the old baron raised his hands and the metallic lace on his cuffs
glinted. He addressed us. Poor old fool, buying *that* for himself – was she a
virgin still? She looked untouched. But knowing, also. Cold all through, or
passion somewhere? (Their wine was potent, a good clear wine like water,
dazzling the lights.) Her skin was fresh and pure as a young girl's, but she
was not a girl. Somewhere in her eyes, a hundred years had looked back at
me. No wonder she hid them so quickly from my discernment. I thought of
lying on her, and what would her skin be like then, and all her textures? Of
reaching through her, deep and deeper, and making her cry, if she ever did,
her eyes sightless and her pale sculpted mouth wide on its gasp for life –

But I did not want her. She repelled me. She was not for me.

"– And I know you will all help me to persuade my modest wife. Now,
Antonina, my dear. The piano, if you please!" He finished in mock severity,
and, in mock docility, she rose and curtseyed to him, and glanced one glance
across the whole now breathless silent room. Then she went to the piano,
opened ready for her. Someone held the stool, seated her, another offered a
sheaf of music. A slight shake of her head, so burdened with its mantle of
hair. Then, her eyes unfixed, looking miles off, a hundred years away, and her
hands straying to the keys of the piano –

The day had turned to dusk in the windows of the room. We might be anywhere, on a mountain that gazed out to other mountains, spires of granite and
quartz in a sea of air –

The first note drew me forward. I was glad, glad to have the excuse of the
music. I went to her, moving forward, forward. They had all come, all pressed
near, yet no one touched me, or impeded me. I reached the piano, and the
vibration of the music purred against my side from her fingers. My glass was
empty; it too seemed to reverberate. She could not see me now. I could look
at, and all through her.

The wine, or the music, had made me drunk, in a wild disembodied way.
I wanted the sounds of it never to stop. I believe she did play for a long while,
entire stanzas of melody and convolutions of development. It was sombre, the
music, scattered by hard white arpeggios, and tumbling white streams of glis-
sandi, and under these the ever-moving river of Death.

When it finished, it had sucked all the strength from me. I leant on the piano and wanted it only to resume, or not to have ended. It was like deepest sleep, in which you dream of making love, always on the verge of ecstasy, to waken fumbling, exhausted and unable.

She rose from the piano, the banker's wife, and the salon frantically applauded her. I clapped her, desultorily, the empty wineglass hindering the gesture. My head ran. I felt nausea. As if, all through the music, I had been having her, and was suddenly dragged away by my hair, and slung out on a cold street before sunrise.

Only I remained by the piano. Everyone else had gone away. In a tiny oval of clarity, I seemed to make her out, standing near the fireplace, where a summer fire was being kindled, holding now a slim white dog, rather like a small greyhound.

Philippe was beside me.

"Well, I had never heard her play before. She's a virtuosa."

I went to the wine table, and took another full sparkling glass, and poured its bright blood into my own.

"What do you think?" said Philippe.

"A cold bitch," I said. "Look how she's frost-bitten him."

"Yes," he said, gloatingly. "Come to a crossroads with me. Let us spill something's blood and invoke the Devil. Make him send us cold her."

"Give her the ring," I said. I managed to find it again and extract it. "That may tempt her to you. If you want her so much."

He looked at the ring. He said, "Is that a scarab, that beetle?"

"The symbol of renewing life," I said. I held it out to him, and abruptly he snatched it, and strode off. I watched as he encountered her. What could he say? The husband was not particularly close, but others were about her. I saw the ruby flame out, as he extended it. It reminded me of something – a spurt of blood in a duel.

Yes, she looked at the ring, but did not take it. How was he explaining his action? There was too much noise in the room to hear. Then, she had turned to me. I stared back at her. I wished I had not drunk so much of the bright wine. She moved, and then she was in front of me, with Philippe, and the rest of her court at her hem.

"Monsieur," she said, "am I to understand you are offering me this?" She laughed, the way women generally do, falsely. It had a special quality when she did it, most unpleasant. "That is surely rather improper?"

"You're mistaken, Madame von Aaron," I said. "I am not a jeweller. My friend brought you the ring to show you. He seemed to think you would find it unusual. However, if you would care for it, I should be delighted."

"He gave me to believe," she said, "you wished me to have the ring." Another slight laugh. "And before witnesses."

"Is it not," I said, "already yours?"

"Not at all. I never collect red jewels. I dislike them."

"Then you had better give it back to me."

Her eyes were never once meeting mine. She avoided my eyes. It was not reticence. There was always something more vital in the room that needed her attention. Yet every time her eyes glided by mine, my pulses jumped. She was less than an inch below my own height. To avoid me took dexterity. Now she looked at the ring.

"Where did you obtain this stone, monsieur?"

"Oh, nowhere of interest, Madame."

"I think it is very rare and exceedingly old, monsieur. Have you never had it valued?"

"Perhaps," I said, "your husband could advise me?"

"Oh," she said. "I don't think so. I am sorry."

She held out the ring. I took it back. Her hand was like ice, and the ring was icy cold from her.

"Grant me five minutes alone with you," I said quietly, "and I can tell you how I came by the ring."

"Oh, really, monsieur." Arch now, truly horrible.

"I won't tell you," I said, "when another can overhear."

"Ridiculous," she said.

"Or do you already know the story?"

Then her eyes did meet mine. It was like some sort of shock of burning searing cold. Black mirrors, black water frozen to iron, trapped under the surface to freeze or drown.

"I think," she said, "your sense of drama is running away with you, monsieur. Of course, did Philippe not say, you are a writer of some sort?"

And turning, she went back to the fireplace and the dog and the husband.

Left alone, I put down my glass and sought the door. I was on the staircase when Philippe came running after me.

He said nothing, till the domestic had let us out into the street. Then he said, "That was her name, before she married."

"What are you talking about?"

"Antonina Scarabin. The scarab. Do you still say it isn't her ring? Someone stole it from her. She'll send you a letter privately, tonight. I'd bet on that. What mysteries. Promise to tell me every item!"

My blood had leapt, sunk.

"She didn't want the ring. I doubt if it was ever hers. And she has nothing to say to me or of me, I'm sure, but the very worst."

"No red jewels, those were her words. No red flowers or fruit, either, in the house, did you see? No red wine. *No* red-haired *men*. No *red*."

"Once a month she must betray herself," I said.

Philippe laughed and sprang in the air, like a cat after a moth. We went down to the *Cockatrice*, then to the *Surprise*. We drank. While Philippe engaged himself with two of the girls, I held another in my arms, kissing and caressing her until she moaned and shivered and fainted into sleep.

I dreamed of the great window again, perhaps more clearly. The long dark wall that had risen out of slumber two weeks before, and the dagger-thrust of casement wounding it. It was in the height of some tower, one sensed an abyss around, and almost primal open spaces, as in the cranium of the sky. The window was petalled by glass, red glass that shaded through maroon and blood and scarlet into crimson and into rose, and finally into the palest rose of all, nearly colourless, and through these panes I seemed to trace mountains far away, but I was never sure. And as the light went, so the colour went, and all form. And so, too, the dream.

She did not write to me, and I did not suppose she would write. I could think of nothing but her. Snatches of the tidal wave of music would return and sweep me under, and in the same way the memory of her eyes and her shoulders, her hair, the sinuousness of her body as she moved across the salon. If I saw a white dog on the street, my heart turned over. I did not dream of her, but waked with the feeling she had been in the bed beside me (that sagging bed with its torn and sallow sheets), her hair spread everywhere and her fingers and lips printed all over me, but I, the fool, not opening my eyes until she was gone. I thought of her, and across the single leaves of parchment, her description was set down again and again, always a little differently.

In a few days I wrote her a letter, and disdaining the bureau of mail, gave it to a runner to deliver. What did the letter say? Not what the prose, the poetry had said, certainly. I had bludgeoned and possessed her body a hundred times, eaten her alive, licked up the juices of her flesh, gnawed her bones, and hanged myself in her hair. But, though she would guess, I could not commit the truth to paper.

"Esteemed madame," said my letter, "Allow me, if you will be so good, a minute of your time in which to tender my apologies. I fear I was discourteous to you. I would be glad to make recompense, and also to discuss with you that ring you saw. I am woefully ignorant on the subject of stones, and should value your advice. I remain your servant, madame, with every respectful wish for your continued health and pleasure in life. A. St Jean."

This, after I had bound her and time after time crucified her with my lust. Well.

She returned no answer.

In a few days more, I walked over to Philippe's house. He would tell me when again the salon was to be opened.

He was lying on a sofa in the inner courtyard, under the plane tree, eating cherries from a china bowl. He looked wan, a wreck. What had he been doing that he had not attempted to force on me?

"Oh, sit, sit," he said, "you wear me out, standing there."

He began to talk about books, knowing quite well, from his sidelong grimaces, what I really wanted to discuss. I watched him eat the cherries and call out scruffy Hans to go and fetch some more for him from the market. Grumbling, Hans set off.

"And what have you been writing, eh, my dearest Andre?"

"Very little."

"Not a single poem? I see you have taken to wearing that ring again."

"And I see you have been sliced again by that senile fool of a barber," I retorted, for his neck linen, on the left side, was stained right through by a blotch of blood.

"How wise you are," he said, "never to let any of them shave you, here. Just strop the razor and get out. And you are always so closely shaved, it's quite a miracle."

"Be quiet. Tell me when she holds the salon again."

"Oh, who?"

"Your banker's bitch."

"Not for some time, I should think," he said. He lowered his eyes, and allowed himself, faintly, to blush.

In the hot afternoon, a surge of heat went through me like the most scalding cold.

"Oh then," I said, "she truly is a fool."

"Ah, Andre," said he, taking my hand, "such amazements – she – oh, she. Do you want me to tell you everything?"

I flung off his hand and he laughed.

"Actually," he said, "for a while, she and I. Even when I took you there. I wanted to see what you thought. You know how I revere your opinion. But she has been in Paradys society less than a month. I met her one day in the Gardens. She was in her carriage, do you see, and the little dog was wanting to get out. So I bowed low and I said, Madame, allow me to take care of your little dog."

My heart lurched and roared. I said, "And what of him? The foreigner. He's complacent, I take it."

"Most complacent. He likes her to have lovers. Decorously, naturally. Like a new dress, or a new string of pearls."

"When do you expect to be replaced?"

He leaned forward. "Kiss me," he said. "Perhaps you may still detect a trace of her. Try for it."

I struck him in the face; it was not enough and I had to hit him again. He sprawled backwards off the sofa, and staggering up, came for me. We struggled in the lacy shade of the plane, and now and then rolled together over its roots. We had fought before, always viciously; continuous bouts of fighting in childhood and adolescence had eventually ended in haphazard orgasm, and so the similarly struggling, thrusting, desperate union of sex. But this time I seemed to want to kill him, and it was only my realisation of it that at last reined me back. I left him lying under the tree, went to the china bowl and scooped out the last of the cherries. I kneeled over him and crushed them into his fair bruised face, his snow-blond hair, and into the muslin of his cravat to stain it and his shirt more thoroughly than the blood. That done, I abandoned him, spitting and weeping with his fury and hurts.

My first impulse, next, was to leave the house. Then I thought better of that. Let the ancestral mound overlook a few more of the antics of this lizard.

I used the third of the bathrooms – cold water in the heat was not amiss – and dressed myself, as before, in one of the more breathtaking of his suits of clothes. His brushes through my red hair then, and his mirrors to show me he had not left a mark on me, but for a contusion along my knuckles. The scarab ring, however, had done him some damage, blacked his eyes and split his lip for him. He was vain. Would he go to her like that, with his prettiness spoiled? Or maybe he would seek her mothering solace in his pain.

Lastly I visited his library and took off his shelves a novel of my own, given him a year ago, the latest finished work I had written. He had never read it, I thought. No, here was a page turned down one quarter of the way in, that had a look of midnight yawning. I'd made him no dedication, I had only inscribed it *Andre St Jean*. ("If I die, it may be worth something, for if I die they will know I was a genius. They will be safe then to do it.")

With that under my arm, and his fine garments all over me, I left the house. I had heard nothing further of Philippe, but I met Hans by the basement step. "Be careful," I said, "how you take him those cherries."

What would she be doing? The single Bell of Prayer was sounding from Our Lady of the Wounded Rose, the shadows lengthening under walls, trees and gate-pillars. At this hour, lying on a sofa as he had done, probably, but indoors, out of the sun. Reading, the little white hound on her lap. Too hot still to play the piano. And no one of any sophistication dined for three hours yet, if at all, since it had become the rage for suppers at midnight, or one or two in the morning.

I reached the von Aaron house, announced my arrival, was let in, and waited. I had thought of assuming another name, but did she even remember the real one?

The domestic came back and said, "Excuse me, monsieur, but Madame is resting, and not to be disturbed."

"Please tell Madame, without disturbing her more than is essential, that I shall remain here, in her hallway, until I have seen Madame."

Off he went again, and back he came again, and conducted me into a downstairs side-parlour. "You may remain if you desire," he said, "but Madame regrets she may have to keep you waiting a long while."

"Tell Madame I will wait as long as is necessary. I imagine," I added, "that eventually your employers will think of moving house, and will then discover me, a skeleton, still propped in one of the chairs. Pray ask Madame which, as I should hate to ruin a favourite by expiring in it."

When he was gone, I poured myself a brandy from the decanter, then another, for I was misgiving and in a cold sweat. God knew, *he* might come down or in, and then I should have to talk to him, the cuckold whose horns apparently I wanted so badly to refurbish.

An hour passed. A small porcelain clock told me the news, chiming sweetly. Did she then remember me, if only as unwelcome? If so, this was a politic ploy, for if she left me to kick my heels a sufficient time, I must get bored, or only hungry, and skulk away. I looked about for something I could disfigure with a secret message, something she must discover with time. If I were able, any more, to write anything, I would have written of her, flayed her with her own self and my delirious fascination with it, and published. Sent her a copy. Let her read at length and in detail, what she had been to me, I the magician who drew every night her soul out of her body, remade it into flesh, and over and over possessed it.

I expected she would never appear, but after five more minutes, I turned, and found her in the doorway. It was an afternoon gown she wore, a robe for reclining, dark, as previously. Her face was expressionless and flat. Was this she? Was she only this, nothing else or more? Her eyes, after a second's black burning, she lowered.

"Thank you," I said, "for coming down."

"I am afraid you have had to wait some while."

"I'm afraid I have."

"It is not the hour for visiting."

Her eyes lifted, looked a mile beyond me. She searched the horizon for something, or someone. But she had come alive for me, by speaking, or only by existing. Yes, she was more, much more.

"You received my letter," I said.

"Oh yes, indeed I did receive it."

"But did not think to reply." Nor did she think to now. I said, "Naturally, I'm no one you would have to reply to. But it would have soothed my remorse."

"You really should not suffer remorse, monsieur, on such slight occasion."

"I offended you. That was enough. So. Here I am again to offend you again, merely by my presence."

"My husband," she said, "is a banker not a jeweller. For myself, I know nothing about jewels, except in a very ordinary way."

"You told me, Madame, the ruby was rare and old."

"Which was all I could possibly know of it."

"I added that, given five minutes alone with you, I would tell you how I had come by the stone. Here we are."

"No," she said, very quickly. "I'm not at all interested, Monsieur St Jean. Please excuse my frankness."

I felt myself go very white.

Walking straight across the room to her, before she could drift away or disappear through the partly open door, I held out my book. It was precious to me, as were all the things I had written; even where I despised their inadequacy there was not one I would disown. Each tore its way from my entrails. Each had shortened my life, killed me with its own especial little death, regardless of any other thing I had ever done with or to myself.

"Please take this, Madame. I'm aware you can't want it, a book by an unknown writer, doubly of no consequence to you. But nevertheless."

"Why should you wish me to have this book?" Her eyes floated over its surface like black water.

"One day you might read it, Madame. In, say, a fit of aberration. And if you had forgotten me sufficiently, you might even enjoy a passage, a sentence, a phrase, here or there."

"Oh my dear Monsieur St Jean. This constant spectacle with which you present us all, of your bleeding body, mutilated by a thousand wounds, pegged out for the vultures and our chariot-wheels always to be at you."

I turned and threw the book, the precious book, onto the table by the decanter.

"I can say nothing to that," I said.

"Indeed," she said. "Do you think I want something that was hurled at me?"

"Give it then," I said, "to your beloved Philippe. I must confess," I said, "that I have rather marred his looks for you, if only temporarily. I hope that will not distress you too greatly."

She stared at me, with all her eyes, then walked by me, crossing the room to one of its windows.

"Are you now resorting to blackmail, Monsieur St Jean?" she asked the street outside.

I was angry with a child's anger, and could only choke it down, which left nothing to be said, for sure.

I thought, in a blinding, sickening horror, You will not escape me. You will not get away. The pin of the pen, if not the lance of lust, will go through you because of me. Redress – I must have something!

She said, "My husband, of course –"

"Of course knows everything you do, and condones it. Ask Philippe, he may tell you some of the things *I* have done. I'd never want to cast stones, Madame."

That uttered, somehow, I walked out, into a place of despair, into an endless down-pouring of hell, not knowing where I went.

All the cafés and the bars of my world would see me that night, and none would be any good to me.

As I stepped paralysed down the hill, someone came flying after me. I started round, and there was the man from the door, bowing, and trying to give me something – a book. Mine.

"Forgotten in my hurry to leave," I yelled at him, "did she say so? *Wait.*"

And drawing out my matches, I struck one, and wrenching the book from him, set fire to it. I burnt it, my book, so precious to me, there before the startled domestic, and a multitude of faces appearing like pale turnips in several windows of the thoroughfare, attracted by my scream of anguish.

It did not burn all through, but most of it was gone, when I gathered up the ashes and the brittled leather, and thrust them on the servant, who was still waiting there patiently, as required.

"Take her that," I said. "Take her *that.*"

He did not argue with me. He clumped stolidly off up Clock-Tower Hill, with ashes in his arms for Antonina von Aaron.

"Antonina, I love you – I cannot say: as I have never loved another thing, for there are other things I have loved so well – the night, the sun, music, beauty itself, *life* itself. Yet all these things I have loved are now valueless to me. You have put out the light. Priestess of darkness, you.

"Antonina, even your name, even the misery you have afforded me, are worth more than anything I ever owned. I would give it all away in exchange for you, even those scraps of a blazing talent, all in fragments, that you would never recognise, but which are all I have and am, and for which, solely, if ever remembered, remembered I should be.

"What can I do? I would murder you, I would cherish you. I would torture you and take you by force, I would lie across your door and die for you. But you want nothing of mine, or of me. Who is he, you say, if you think to say anything: ah, a little second of annoyance. And to me you are everything that exists. The soul of my soul. Black light, by which I see.

"Oh, let me go down and find the waters of forgetful night, and drinking them underground, unremember you. All memory take, your face, your voice, your eyes, all of you, till nothing remain – but still I would be in agony, all of you forgotten, yet all of you unforgettable and with me still, my sin of omission – Lethe leaves me to grieve, though I no longer know why."

This I wrote to her, and much, much besides. But did not trouble her with it.

A month, it seemed to be a month, went by. Days and darknesses. Nightingales sang in the parks, and one night fireworks burst over the city, it was the democratic decade of the Senate, Year Ten of Freedom, a celebration. All Paradys stood in its trees, on its roofs and balconies to watch. I watched. If my heart would burst like one of those gunpowder lights, into stars, falling. Ah, it was not to be.

During the days, I lay on the bed, I slept when I could. At night I roamed the avenues, the squares, the boulevards. I resisted the temptation to climb Clock-Tower Hill, or to scutter lizard-like to Philippe's domicile and hammer on its doors and shutters.

I avoided the women in the places where I drank. Some came mewing to me. I gave them money to go away.

Alone, in my room near dawn, I once or twice tried to summon up a demon, or something dead, to instruct me. Numbed by wine and brandy, burning with spirits, I requested spirits of another kind to come to me. The candlestick, the gryphon ink-well moved, and papers flew about like birds. Heat filled the room, then clinging cold, but all these happenings ultimately failed and went away, leaving nothing behind them but a common mess. The climax of manifestation had not been achieved.

Why should it be so difficult to die, so impossible to live?

My landlady trudged to my door, and asked me if she should summon a doctor.

"Why, madame, are you ill?"

She explained that she was not, but that I would seem to be, I had been screaming in the night again with bad dreams.

"There is a window," I said, "it drips blood, it runs with tears."

I heard them say on the narrow stairs that I was in the process of going mad and should be evicted.

Russe, who had found me at the *Imago*, attended on me from a discreet distance as I spewed into a gutter. When I was done with that, or it with me, he lifted me off my knees, and took me to his own lodging. Here I was placed in a clean bed, between sheets that had the fragrance of new bread and lavender. His mistress kept house for him very nicely. I slept far into the new day in this unaccustomed comfort. Then the two of them came to perch by me, while she fed me milk and fruit.

When he sent her away again, he said to me, "Why do this to yourself?"

I lay in the marvel of the bed, watching the shadows of birds fan over the ceiling. There was a bird in a cage, too, very thrilled with itself and tweeting, not aware of something missed.

"We are each given a life," I said, "do with it as we may or must."

"There are other roads to the sewers and death," he said, "more profitable and more gallant than this."

"Take them, my dear Russe. You are so solemn. Take them."

"Over some woman," he said. "You bloody idiot. You're behaving like some stupid girl yourself."

I laughed, drearily, not without appreciation of his wit.

"This is not being kind, my friend," I said. "Nurture me if you must, or put me out on to the street. But let me do what I am inclined to."

His girl began to sing, charmingly, downstairs in the house. I had never wanted that, the nesting proximity of a shared life. Never. What then had I intended with her, my lady of shadows? Not to leave her with her husband, surely, enjoying her at random? No matter. No question could arise of it.

To make a little conversation with grim Russe, lurking in his ancestral forests, responsible for his fellow men, I said, "And where is my beloved erstwhile companion, Philippe?"

"My God," said Russe. "You haven't heard. Well, you have been hearing nothing, have you, but the sound of corks got out of bottles."

"Heard what?" I thought, He has run off with her. That will be it. It seemed at a great distance. It did not matter.

"Philippe has vanished. Fifteen days now, and sixteen nights. Even the City police are alerted."

I said, "Well, you won't see him again."

"What? Why do you say that?"

"He will be out of the City, over the borders, with her."

"With whom? What do you know of this, Andre?"

"If he purloined her, how could he stay? The old banker might have wanted satisfaction after all. Old bankers are notoriously unpredictable."

"If you are speaking," said Russe stiffly, "of the von Aaron woman, she has nothing to do with this. She is in her house. She holds her salon twice a week now. Most fashionable. Everybody goes there."

The bed seemed to slip away under me, a boat casting off to sea.

"He told me he was her lover."

"Probably he lied to you. She is supposed to be virtuous. Oh come, Andre. Philippe – is *that* what began this –"

I wanted to get up, I was not certain why. I had some notion I should go over to Philippe's house, and that he would be there. Then, since nothing else could then conceivably have happened, I might refind myself also. If I wished to. She no longer seemed a part of me. I had drunk Lethe, all the brandy-black glasses of it, and after all, did not recall her quite. Nearly faceless now, just the cowl of hair, the coals of the eyes – Her voice, murmuring something foul to me.

Russe would not let me get up. His girl ran in and joined his lament. I lay back down again.

In the middle of the night, when they were making love below, and the tweety-bird slept, I got out of the bed of bliss and dressed and crept down the house with my boots in my hand. Someone had polished them, these boots, as I saw by the glow of the moon and the street light outside the door. Polished the boots, laundered all my filthy linen, cleaned and brushed my coat. It was Philippe's coat too, in fact. I had kept it, to go drinking in, to write and weep and vomit while wearing, to die in along some alley gutter. Well, better return it now.

From Our Lady of Ashes came the four o'clock bell.

I shambled towards the Wall Quarter, the old City barricade that once fenced Paradys above the river. Sometimes I laughed at the moon, she looked so like a nun, a priestess, with her bloodless face cowled by night.

The shuttered house too was gaunt in the moonlight. Was it not somewhat like a tall thin skull, eye-sockets, nostrils, cave of mouth with its teeth knocked out. And what about that phalanx of round attic windows above? Of course, the scars of the bullets which had gone through the brain and killed it long ago.

(In a skull then, the lizards played, darting, fighting, resting. And they had stored clothing, swords and books, and a rocking-horse, behind the bullet-holes.)

The bell jangled mournfully. It seemed to echo away over the chasms of the City. Would anyone come, at this hour, to let me in? So frequently Philippe, with the door key, much later than this, would go in to find one of them, Hans or Poire, dozing on the wooden seat in the hallway.

A lamp fluttered up behind the glass. A face pressed itself there, like a prisoner's, staring out at me.

The door was opened.

"Good morning, Hans."

"Yes, monsieur."

"Is he awake?"

"Not here, monsieur. No. Haven't you heard?"

"Oh that. He is here. Hiding from us all. Don't you remember he used to do that, as a revolting child. He hid constantly from his hysterical mother, and the nurse. But I recollect every hiding place."

I came into the house, and Hans allowed it. He looked bovine, and anxious, he looked willful, too, for I was not the master here. I was the impecunious writer, Philippe's guest, and other things.

But then again, I had accustomed them to obey commands.

He stood there stolidly now, feet planted, rela:

"Come on," I said. "We will search him out."

"Yes monsieur," said Hans.

He plodded after me. Very likely he thought I w ing me. For Philippe might abruptly return an Philippe might even be behind it all.

We searched the lower floor first, the two parlours and the dining room. (We would leave the basement area, I told him, the servants' cells, until the last.) Philippe was not there, so upstairs we went. Still he was not found. In the library he did not conceal himself in the curtains or among the volumes. Beneath the massive desk there seemed some chance of locating him, but neither was he there. We ascended to the bedrooms. Hans was tired now, and had begun to remonstrate with me, for the game was gross and silly.

"He's here," I said. "Can't you tell?"

"No, monsieur."

"He is."

Beyond the last bedroom – its canopy investigated, and even the chamber-pot dragged from under the ruching – the gallery led across to the bathrooms at the rear.

The lamp faltered in this corridor, trying to give up its ghost, as disillusioned now as Hans.

"Trim the wick. I mean to find the bastard."

Unhappily, Hans trimmed away, and the light steadied as I squinted into the stone-panelled privy.

A kind of coldness seemed to flow along this upper floor, disuse perhaps, for he had apparently been gone all the while, those sixteen nights. Or some essence of demons had been trapped between the walls, left over from his séance, and from the ghost-girl. But it was like absence rather than presence.

Hans began sneezing nervously.

"For God's sake quiet," I said, as if afraid to disturb something.

Why? Surely Philippe must know we were upon him?

The largest of the bathrooms, the remnant of the bath-house which had formerly stood separate from the rest of the building, raised its marble façade into the lamp-smear. Philippe had favoured this one's round tub most often. I kicked the door wide open, and the watery light fell in.

The sinking moon was there before it, coming sideways through from the vanes of glass in the roof. And there, below, Philippe lay, in the bath.

Hans gave a high, pig's squeal. He did not drop the lamp; habit, presumably, not to break his master's things.

After a long time, I said, "Did you never think to come up here?"

"Oh monsieur," he bleated, "only yesterday – and the maids, to clean – it was always done, every day –"

"Then it seems he came home this evening."

"No, no," he said, panting now and sobbing. "No, not possible –"

"Not through the front door then," I said. I looked from Philippe's uptilted unlistening face, towards the glass vanes. One stayed open. "Climbing on to the roof over the attics," I said, "they let him down through the skylight. How curious. How agile."

He was clothed in shirt and breeches, his coat and linen were gone, he was barefoot. He was white with a solid thick whiteness, like plaster. The density of his pallor, though not its colour, clogged the room, which was like a winter vault.

"Go down," I said. "Get Poire and the others. Send someone for the police." He stuttered, and shook. "Don't take the lamp," I cried out in a ritual fear. He implored me. "Take it then. Christ, there's the moon."

In the cold moonshine then, and alone, I went and looked into Philippe's waxwork mask of plaster. His eyes were shut, and his lips parted. His hair now was darker than his skin. He did not resemble anyone I knew, and seemed dead a year, though it could not have been more than a day.

The bruises and cuts of the beating I had given him were all healed. Only the barber's gash had not gone from his throat, or it was a fresh one. From the puffy dark mottling on his neck, one long dried trickle of blood had flowed out black, running down under his shirt, down to where the nipple had checked it. There was a similar abrasion on the inside of his left wrist, and the sleeve there was stained, plummy, under the moon.

Then I saw – he had not been quite dead, when returned. No, not quite, for on the bottom of the bath, in his blood, the artist had been drawing, as he had once drawn in the spilled ink … I looked closely. I thought I could make out the indication of a horse, slender and running, with a slender hooded thing leant forward on its back – and before that, two slender running hounds –

"Philippe," I said, urgently, as if he would hear me.

What must I feel? I had spent it all, all emotion, all sickness, for her. I was bled out and had nothing over to offer him. Drained like the window of its light, like Philippe of his blood.

I sat down on the floor by the bath, in the coldness of his death, to wait a while, to see if he could catch me up.

Called to a painted hall in the Senate Building, I, with several others, was asked various questions. Russe, my surety, described to the officials, while clerks busily scribbled, how I had been taken sick, and spent a night and day in his home, overseen continuously by himself and Mademoiselle Y –, whom he did not wish to bring into the affair unless it were unavoidable. Philippe could not have been dead more than an hour or so, when found in the bath-house, this the doctors had quickly verified. Besides, the operation across the roof, the lowering through the vanes, these postulated several persons labouring in unison.

One by one, forming into irked and vocal groups, Philippe's friends, amours, money-lenders, debtors, and scavengers extraordinary were sumoned, quizzed, and dismissed to pace the antechambers.

One sensed that, with all the muck that came swiftly to the surface, the murder of Philippe seemed not only inevitable but perhaps aesthetically fitting, to the members of this Senate Investigatory Committee.

At no time did I think I would be apprehended for anything, despite having arrived at an unsocial hour and plainly knowing the exact whereabouts of the body. Such behaviour was too pat for an assassin, or if I were one, they could not be bothered with me. At length, they turned us all out on the street, as innocent. The Committee had got hold of the idea that some enemy from Philippe's past had done the heinous deed, then fled over the northern borders. This was deemed a proper programme. They liked it, and did not like any of us. If a single murderer had been proved in our midst, I think it would have disgusted them, for evidently the itinerary of Philippe's life had not pleased. They desired the whole thing filed rapidly and put in a cabinet.

The death of Philippe was discussed generally after that. Many theories, including that of an ingenious suicide, were aired. At the *Iron Bowl* a fight broke out, and at the *Cockatrice* two more, though the *Surprise* and the *Imago* remained quiet. Indeed, under the black beams of the *Imago*'s medieval roof, they concocted weird scenarios of witchcraft. It was the Devil who rode over Philippe's attics and dropped the corpse into the tub. Had there not been a drawing, in blood, to that effect, all over the walls, ceiling and floor? Better ask Andre, who had found the remains.

When any of them came to badger me, they found me out, asleep, or drunk.

"Well, and are you to grace the funeral?" said Le Marc, who had cornered me at last, partially sober, in a library of the Scholar's Quarter. "You had better go. You may want to write about it later on."

This was quite true. Besides, I had known him almost all his life. I would have to put him to rest somehow, and to see the lid of the coffin's ponderous cigar-box closed on him might be the only way.

What a funeral this was. What a brave quantity of followers. Ancient fragile aunts had come from their towered and chimneyed crannies in the pastoral suburbs of Paradys, supported by equally elderly retainers. They doddered on each other's arms in black lace mittens, stove-pipe hats, and veils. Had Philippe ever met any of them, or remembered them? Relics outliving his disastrous sprint of youth, did they hope to be his heirs? (It transpired that in a way I was, he had left me a quantity of largely unspecified, useless and bizarre treasures from the attics, to be collected by myself at my own inconvenience. A patronising, perfectly suitable bequest. Odd he had made a will. We stood amazed.)

His friends, if such we were to be called, also arrived at the graveyard gate. And, apart from this gathering of vultures, the morbidly curious of the neighbourhood strolled up to take a stare.

The memorial was to be conducted in the Martyr Chapel of the Sacrifice; he was then to be ladled into the ancestral vault behind the Temple-Church.

"Hallowed ground," said Russe, to whom Philippe had bequeathed three huge clocks and a dresser too big for any of his rooms. "But he died godless, of course."

The most savage of the vultures had found dark clothes to wear. I wore the coat I had stolen from him the last time, when I crushed the cherries into his mouth and hair.

The absurdities of his will, as I had heard them out, kept recurring in my mind. The jokes were too contemporary. They would not have worked when we had all grown old. He must have known he would die young.

Trap after trap drew up with its black horses and black ribbons, disgorging more and more derelict aunts. Then at last came the coal-black coach, whose black horses, like the steeds of Pluto, had each a black flame of plume upon its head. The overcast was also turning black. It was a hot and airless afternoon, with a sudden rough, similarly airless wind, that tore between the trees of the burial garden, while the immovable massive hills of the Temple-Church pushed up at the monumental sky. We, whipped and blown about below, were of no importance, but anxious not to face the facts, we went on playing at our rôles. Out came the coffin, nails already firmly hammered home. Supposing he had changed his mind? That would be like him, crashing forth in the midst of the service, cursing and shouting for his valet, in ineffable bad taste.

But the professional porters of death had the coffin up on their shoulders now, and bore it away along the gravel path. The aunts were permitted to go next, then the rest of us. Somehow I walked the very last, an afterthought.

I was not paying much attention to any of it, the stony fields of asphodel, the shaggy bear-like cypresses. The Chapel, with pale windows, lay ahead, and we would all get there.

Then came a noise behind me, another carriage, arriving late, pulled up, horses snorting, passengers dismounting, the gawpers at the gate, with a murmur, giving way. I halted, and turned. Along the path towards me walked the illustrious banker-baron, von Aaron, in darkest, greyest mourning, and on his arm, her feet scarcely touching the gravel, she. I took two long steps back, out of their path, standing as if at attention beside an angel on a pedestal of basalt.

As they went by, von Aaron nodded to me, not looking into my face, but quite courteously, as if out of consideration for my grief. She did not look anywhere, but straight ahead. Her habitual black was augmented by a strange dramatic black veil, like a mantilla, raised on a pearl comb, covering her hair and also most of her face.

When they were gone, when they and the rest of the funeral had quite vanished into the Chapel, I went after. The usher was shutting the door as I stayed him to get in.

A full house. I did not look for anyone, but stood at the back, alone.

The windows had closed with the afternoon's darkness. When the wind clawed at the building, the candles flounced. Quickly, quickly, let it be over with. I rested my head a moment on the stone of a pillar, wondering how many others, overcome by this insidious faintness, might have done so. I must think. But why, and of what?

For example, had that running man come up the very path we had taken, had he reached this place? I considered. Not the Church, certainly, with its sacred altar of sanctuary, not that, for then how could Satan have claimed him. Where, among the angels and gargoyles, the marble praying children and stone wreaths, had the black hounds pulled him down? I had trodden in the face of his ghost. Or imagined the whole episode. Did I find the red ring in a drain?

The Chapel was mumbling now with spoken responses, the words of the priest in a magpie gown of white and black stripe. Everything swung to and fro, like a ship in a sluggish storm. Rain pummelled the windows. The shut doors shook. Another latecomer was wanting to get in. What was out there? What rider on what long-maned mare of the daytime night? Of the endless night, inescapable night, washing round us, which would have us all. Antonina, save me from this dark, this precipice into which I, with all the world, must fall –

Thank God, it was finished. I drew aside again, and let the porters and the cigar-box go out, and the tide of flesh and crêpe, the aunts twittering and sniffling now. And caught in the tide, the cameo of a face under the water of its veil –

The graveyard had become a desert sailed by cloud.

It was an old mausoleum, and it leaned. Through the tilted doorway they took him, and left him behind there. Some of the aunts were now being assist-ed. The smell of aqua-vitae travelled up the slope to me. His friends broke and ran, waving their arms. They must hold a wake now, what else was to be done? Drink the man down.

As the crowd thinned, separated, dissolved, some of it toiling or hurrying past me, I realised the rain had begun.

I stood in the rain, indifferently trembling, and watched the banker talk-ing quietly to the priest. The door to the vault stayed open. She was inside. Did no one think that strange?

Of course, none of them mattered. Props, strawboard things, not real at all.

I walked down the slope in great strides, and went past them and by them, as probably they gazed at me distractedly, and up to the narrow, lopsided door of the darkness, and through.

There was an array of stone boxes, the family of Philippe already fore-gathered, but the coffin, being brand-new, was shining on its slab in the light of the white candles.

She was poised on the slab's other side, her veil off her face, her naked hand lying on the coffin top, with a crimson rose between the fingers. As I entered, she let the flower go. She let it lie there, a drop of reckless colour on the dark. It might only have been her excuse for coming in, but was not even that – what had she said to me? – *rather improper*? To drop the bloody tear of a flower on the coffin of one's salon's mere occasional visitor. A cliché, too, madame, of the worst, and you waited, static as a doll, for me, or someone, to come in and see you do it.

I said, "But you do not like red. Are you insulting him then, madame, his poor helpless body?"

She said, "My husband is just outside."

"Don't be afraid," I said, "the extensive branches of his horns would never let him through the doorway."

"You are so very insolent. Arrogant and rude. You were from the very first. Do you suppose the earth turns around you, monsieur?"

"Around you," I said. "As I see it."

The candles lit her eyes, still veiled always from mine.

"You observe," she said, "how I am placed. I have a husband, and a position in society."

"And a lover, previously."

"There is *nothing*," she said, "for you."

I could not mention that they had murdered Philippe, one or other or both of them, for she would then resort to the former accusation of blackmail. Otherwise everything just said was irrelevant. Neither the slab nor the box was very wide. I leaned across them and slid my hands around her throat and brought my mouth against her pale cool skin. Because she did not struggle, there was nothing turbulent or unwieldy, nothing to ruffle the deathly seren-ity of the tomb. It was also quite fitting that I should kiss her over his corpse.

She let me, did not stay me or cry to implore help, but her lack of resist-ance was itself a stay. Neither did she concede. She had no scent, no odour at all, only perhaps the faintest fragrance in her hair, like the clean fur of a cat that has been out on a chill moonlit night. Her eyes were shut, to exclude me, no concession either there. Then they opened, and I saw them stare beyond me, to the horizon. I had only pressed her lips gently. I set my mouth to her cheek, and temple, and the smooth bone of the jaw beneath the ear. The lobe of the ear held no jewel, but a tiny incision remained in it, for a jewel's piercing. With that, where I had not ventured to part her lips, I allowed my tongue an instant for its curiosity. Then I took her hands and kissed them in their turn, the palms, the strong and slender backs, where the two silver rings pressed against the knuckle-bones, the wrists; they were icy cold, dipped up from some lake within a piano of snow mountains, rinsed in liquid music, over and over, they burned ten freezing notes across my mouth, before I let her go.

"You say to me," I told her, "there is nothing for me, of you. Perhaps not, perhaps not." I, now, did not look at her. It seemed to me that, this being the case, her eyes were fixed on me intently, terribly. "But there's no use your telling me anything, or warning me in this conventional mode. I am beyond any such pale. What you say is meaningless. Do you think I have no spirit, Antonina, that I can be *told*, can be *instructed*, how I may or may not desire you? Do you believe my emotions are so volatile they will simply evaporate at one sensible soulless little word? What am I? Your servant? No. You are in my blood now. You've coloured everything, stained me, just the way blood stains. I'm marked by you indelibly. It will never come out, the bloody dye of what you are. Stained through and through."

Each act, even unfinished, or unbegun, knows for itself its proper comple-tion. I left her at once, and went out, into the air and daylight which seemed neither.

The wet heat almost struck me down, the darkness. Von Aaron was standing solicitously at my elbow.

"Monsieur St Jean, you do not look well."

"How is it," said I, "that you know my name?"

"But you have been so good as to call on us, in company with your friend."

"Yes. I hardly thought it was through my literary glories."

"I must repeat, monsieur, you are not at all well. This shocking business of the gentleman who has died … Our carriage is below. May we have the pleasure of driving you to your home?"

"Why did you come here?" I said. The rain teemed round me, making everything unstable, shifting and falling down; my condition would not matter.

"To pay our respects, naturally."

"Naturally. You should dissuade your wife from wasting flowers on the dead. A silly custom. They do better in the houses of the living, or growing in the ground."

"Monsieur, monsieur, can't I entreat you to reason?" He smiled, encouraging me. A wave of deadly nausea passed through me. I fought it away. On my lips, the touch of her icy fingers still burned ten times over, on and on.

"You are too kind," I said. "Your wife would perhaps not like it, some wretched stranger in your carriage, at such a moment. Good day."

As I crossed through the graveyard, I seemed to see an old man flitting about there, huddling down behind the stones, and two black dogs, slicked by wet, questing without hurry.

On the cobbled alley, I walked in my trance. The rain rushed by, as it had that other day. I felt I might die before I reached the bottom of the hill. There was some sickness on me, some plague, something. Gladly I welcomed it. Come thou sweet night, close mine eyes.

And all the books unwritten. Well, let them go.

And all the songs unsung.

And Philippe in his box, not hearing the rain.

"They're to close up the house."

"Like the damnable coffin itself."

"Boarded. The neighbours are complaining, there are noises in the night. Hoary old Father Mouse-whiskers, that priest, has been asked to perform an exorcism. But is afraid to. Must apply to his Holiness to see if he may."

"The servants meanwhile hold drunken parties in the basement. They don't give a *that* for any phantoms."

"But whatever else, Andre," said Le Marc, "if you don't go there and collect those bits he left you, you will never get them. The bailiff's men are also reportedly to go in. A debt or two unsettled, we are given to understand."

The onset of the soft and tender illness, which for a week now had sustained me with its shadow, had enabled me to resume my life. I would not have to put up with living much longer. So, as with an unwanted love shortly due to depart for ever more, I could afford to be polite. It might take months,

of course, but months   r or two was possibly to be
borne. Every lissom ov   ed me. It was sensuous, fas-
tidious. A weakness, :   the appetite for drink, the
desire to sleep a great v   the limbs was like a lullaby.
I needed only to surren   nk into a delicious nothing
ambient to all the phy   ie invalid's concupiscence
also, febrile, intense, ar   iodate, uncaring of object.
From the depths of sli   awareness of wonderful
dreams, glowing with e1   of me, I was whole. I had
begun to write, an outl   nergised me. Working, I
passed through the outposts of the dulcetly aching messenger of sleep or sexuality, passed through with bright banners of words starting from the pen
almost faster than my thoughts could envisage them. Surely faster than the
ink could set them down. Until undeniable exhaustion at length put paid to
me, snuffed me out and let me free again for that other world inside, beside,
beneath, above, wherever it was, the heaven of my invention, liberty.

In this condition I was amenable too. I would heed, and sometimes be
kind. Now I would get up and hire a carter for a few coppers with his cart,
and go to Philippe's house. I would climb, albeit slowly, up to the attics, and
rummage, and take, and go away again.

Despair, the worst of all the deadly sins, since it is denial of the self, of
the god-in-self, since it is so seductive, like the snow-death, so warm. Ah,
who would tear himself to pieces when he might lie down in such arms, in
comfort, and cease. Bless you, my despair, my dear and loving despair. So
painlessly you take my pain away. Oh Father, by no means dash the cup from
my lips –

The carter was solicitous. The wind was cold today, he said, blowing from
the north. He tucked my muffler about my throat and did up the buttons of
my greatcoat as if I were his child. It was entertaining. On the road where I
was going, scarves and coats were not necessary. He had had a sad life, the
carter, all about which he told me as he pushed the cart, on our journey up to
the Wall Quarter. Dear friend, I nearly said, Why not abandon hope. Why not
do as I do, and escape. Perhaps he had already contracted the plague from
me, if it was contagious. Then again, the thought of him as a companion on
a trip to the Underworld, constantly retelling episodes of his misfortuned
days, as now he did, decided me against his inclusion in my party. One might
ask Charon, of course, to push him off the boat into the River Styx. But you
could not be sure of Charon. I had seen ferrymen like him, plying their
slender vessels through the morning mists along the City river, looking for
fish, or that night's drowning victims, who might offer a gem or a pocket-
watch, or a fine head of hair to hack off and sell the wig-makers. Charon

would be of that sort, maybe. Of some sort, anyway. For I did not suppose only nothing lay beyond the great gate.

I fell asleep as I walked, and the carter woke me solicitously when we reached the house. I reminded him he should wait for me. He did not say, why else had he come?

"Take care," he did say. "You're not looking too well, young gentleman."

The domestics were now all out of Philippe's house, or else hiding under the boards like mice. Not a light showed, though the street was already cast for night. In the west, framed by the alligator scales of the roofs, a red sunset. The dome of the Observatory would appear to have a winged dragon seated upon it, but that was a cloud, or some hallucination. I turned from it in puzzled pleasure, and used the key with which Philippe's executors had presented me.

Inside, the dimming house would soon be black. I would not bother to light a lamp, I should be able to find some candles upstairs. As I ascended, here and there a carnation shaft struck through the shuttered windows from the sky. One such pierced through the ruby scarab, that today I had put on again, red through red, such a colour the eyes were besotted by it. I stopped a full minute, gazing, until the sun had moved. Were her lips as red as that, her cheeks that red, after she had drunk the blood of Philippe? The old stories said so, but I did not credit it, any more than I trusted her hands could ever grow warm.

The Devil, the Devil is in it. But where?

On each floor I paused to rest, supporting myself on the bannister, breathing with a wonderful awareness of air, the machinery of lungs and heart. I bypassed the floor of the bathrooms without a qualm or even a jibe. On the final landing, below the attic stair, something was different. I had begun to breathe in long gasps. My heart beat untidily. My head swam, but it was not from weakness but in a dreadful resurgence of strength.

My sinews, my very skeleton, seemed to toughen. Blood coursed. My eyes went black, then cleared to a sharp perception.

I stared upward, to shadows where the attics began. Then took the steps, opened the door, and went in.

There was the clutter of centuries, much of it older than the house. Every one of the brief lizards had left something, like a pebble laid on a cairn. *Remember* me!

What had Philippe left, then? What had he left for me? Some priceless volumes, some costume bodice of his mother's, crusted with pearls? No, I did not care at all. Already, instantly, across the stacks and mounds, the pillars and tomb-stones of things, I was searching. And there, a round window, shutterless, was burning with the last of the red sky. In its path balanced the wooden rocking-horse, black lacquer, with his fearful grin of teeth, his maenad eyes, and thin blood skimmed on his back from the sunset.

I walked on, stepping around and over things. As I passed him, I touched his rump, to make him go. He creaked and leisurely fell into the motion, sounding like an oar grunting in its lock. Such sins that black horse knew, such confessions. The first taste of lust from the thrust of his hard lacquer saddle between the thighs, the first taste of flight, of getting away, poetry, vision, death-wish, dreams –

Books all over the floors and I stepped on them. Where the Italian chest squared across the window, a movement, too. Then she stood on glass-paned red fire, black-cloaked, cowled like a priest – Yes, the Devil was in it.

I felt her eyes, before I saw them; they drew me forward. If I had been bound, unable, physically, to go to her, my spirit would have gone to her in spite of the flesh, and my heart leapt out of my body. No. There was no need of that. No chain could have held me, seeing her there, her eyes looking into mine.

"I have been waiting for you," she said. Her voice was very low, very dark. It did not seem to come from her at all, but out of the light, the shadow. "Since the funeral, I have come here each evening. Seven days, seven nights."

There must have been a key he had given her. Or did she melt through walls, the way her kind might do – not her *kind*. There was only Antonina.

"Such protestations," she said. "Then to make me wait."

"I was here with you," I said. "I must have been."

"Yes, I think you were. Sometimes, a flicker of the edge of your sleeve, your hair catching a burnish. There, or there. Your ghost. But now, it is you."

There were also books scattered round the chest. Standing on them, careless of them as I had been, had made her taller than me. She stood above me, in the halo of the dying window, like a madonna. I could only just make out the pallor of her face, which I had kissed, the pale mouth, but the eyes, like the voice, were in a separate dimension. They lived and blazed on their own.

I did not ask her why she had changed to me. It was superfluous; besides, only this made any sense. The denial was the lie.

"Your husband?" I inquired, with no conviction.

But she answered stilly, "He will do as I tell him. He is only my servant. He serves me. Him I may tell and instruct what he may desire of me."

"What now?"

"Whatever you wish," she said.

"And you?" I said. "You, oh, you."

She put out her hand and touched me then, first my forehead between the eyes, next the base of my throat, then above the heart. Finally she took up my left hand and touched the ruby ring. I felt each touch, cold flame, like a kiss on my forehead, starting a race in my breast. Even through the stone of the ring, I felt her.

She said, "I divine that you understand, Andre St Jean."

Her eyes held me, close to her, held me far off. I could do nothing to her yet, she would tell me when, and very soon.

"Philippe's not watching," I said.

"I thought that you imagined he might be."

"No. He believed in nothing. No god. Nothing beyond himself as he was. Nothing after death. He's dead then."

"But you believe differently. In God, do you believe in God, Andre?"

"Death is God," I said. "Life is Man. The day we are born begins our love affair with death."

Now, said her eyes.

I stepped up on the books with her and she slipped down to a little height, her head against my shoulder, tilted back, her lips parting. Her hair was like a river flowing through my hands, and the hooded cloak, and under it her skin, only some silken thing between us, and her small, her beautiful breasts –

We slid down beside the carved chest, on to the dust and the books, with the window turning wan and grey above us. We slid into the dark –

(Once, somewhere on the shores of those black spaces, the rocking-horse stirred, settling, as if someone had climbed up on to his back.)

How slow the rhythm, now, the rhythm of Death's River – it was she who guided me, through the deep spirals of the river's course, its deepest pools. Stars filled the attics, splashed on the air.

Ecstasy was always near, it came and went, swelling, singing, widening, never finished, never begun. Her coldness was warm now, like the snow. Her lips which had come to my throat so quietly, had begun to burn. Her lips were fire. She drew me down and down, into the caverns of the night, where sometimes, far away, I heard myself groan, or her murmuring voice like a feather drifting – Her mouth was fire and her body was snow and the cradling night held both of us. The long endless resonant spasms came and went and came and went like the throb of strings, like the circling wake of the slender boat. She was the ferryman. It seemed to me I had not ceased to look at her. That never once, meeting mine, her burning eyes had closed.

It was almost morning, and all the stars had died … Whose face was this, peeking into mine so dolefully? And these damned hands, fiddling with me, worrying at me.

I struck him off. He recoiled.

"Oh monsieur. Christ knows, I thought you were a dead man."

I was lying flung across the volumes and the old carpets of the attics. Above me towered a hill of carven chest, and over there the wooden horse with its mad and pitiless eye. Between, miles up above me, the carter with a candle, and the bloom of false dawn on him from the window.

"I waited for you, monsieur. And then, I confess, I went and got myself a drink or two. A cold study it was, waiting out there. But I thought, Well, he knows what he's about I suppose. But then, having come back, and nothing in the cart, the bell goes for midnight. I knock on the door. No answer. So then I curl up, in my cart, see, and I take a mite of sleep. No trouble. Once some woman passes. I think to myself, Did she come out of the house, now? Is *that* it? But then she vanishes away and I forget her. Then I'm blowing on my fingers for the cold, wishing I could do the service for my toes, and finally I hear five o'clock. Up to the door again, and now it's open. So I think then you meant me to come up, and up I come. What a house, monsieur. Horrible, so dark, and empty. They said in that drinking-place, it's haunted by the young man that died here. Vicious murder. But you know that. Then I can hear a noise. I nearly perish of fear I don't mind admitting."

Through all this I had lain on my back, smiling, my eyes taking in the beams in the pointing ceiling, watching the light begin to return from the dead, the sky deciding if it would put on pinkness or only paleness. What sound could he possibly have heard? Some moan from me, perhaps, sprawled here with my shirt open and my breeches unbuttoned, a ludicrous shambles of some dream I had been having of a woman I wanted to possess.

"It was that rocking-horse," said the carter, "creaking and bucking away. No one on it, unless it was you, monsieur, and you fell off. Well, then, here you are. I reckoned you'd been set on. Blood-stains on your shirt. But there's a bite there, on your neck. That will be a rat, no doubt of it. The house is full of them, all rustling away behind the walls. Now if you'll listen to me, you should go straight to a doctor with that bite. Nor you shouldn't have brought a lady here."

Still on my back, I took out some money, and tossed it to him. He caught it, but looked at me reproachfully.

As he watched me, I sat up and put my clothes to ˙˙   l that spotted my shirt had dried to the colour of rˉˊ   t. It was the way Philippe's blood had appeared to   ˋll.

The carter aided me down all the stairs.

It was true then. Not a dream. Not, not a dre

"And you have a fever, you're burning," the luˌ
ed me.

I had not collected my bequest. The carter, n
Philippe's house with a senechal's attention. Then, s
into his cart, where I lay semi-conscious, euphoric. In ˌ
dled home, to my landlady's dismay.

I threw myself on my bed, clothed and stupid. Let them have the day, any who wanted it. Sleep, let me sleep. Tonight I would go back to her. And she would come to me.

Thinking of her, as she had been for me, all of it rushed up and overpowered me. Down I fell, through the abyss of the bed, past a grinning rocking-horse with the spectre of Philippe cavorting on its back, past Baron von Aaron in a waiter's uniform, past pages of my books, my childhood, past all the hours of my life, seen as when drowning.

Unfinished, the manuscript lay on the table before the window. There was no need to write any more of it. Let me live it now, quickly through, to the last sentence. And there end. Amen.

When I woke again, it was very late. I wakened with the knowledge of having made a grievous error – oh God, the midnight bell was sounding from Our Lady of Ashes over the river. What had I done?

I must get up, find myself clean linen, run across the City to the house –

I remember I reached the table where the manuscript lay. Nothing else.

I woke again, as in a nightmare, somehow on the bed and dawn was returning. Someone must help me now. Some demon or angel. My head seemed full of the galloping of hoofs as I hurried about. But I was stronger. I could wash myself, I could look into the pitted mirror and even pick up the razor with a steady hand.

How long before I could be ready, how long before I could essay the stairs, the streets? My plan was already made. I must go directly to the house on Clock-Tower Hill. She had said, he was her servant, nothing else. The only impediment had been Antonina herself, when she was afraid of me, before she surrendered herself to the truth.

There was straw on the roadway. This meant that someone on that wealthy avenue was seriously ill. They had put it down to muffle the wheels and hoofs of passing traffic, but there was also a liveried man sitting in the gate, to make sure of proper silence, and perhaps to turn away visitors before they jangled the door bell. It was her gateway he was seated in, and he wore the banker's livery.

I went up to him. "What is the matter? Is the Baron unwell?"

"No, monsieur. It is Madame who is very sick."

I gaped at him, and he, more circumspectly, at me. I was dishevelled enough. The day, growing hot, beat down on us both.

"You say – she – Madame von Aaron – is sick."

"Yes, monsieur. Monsieur, please don't go up to the door."

"But I – must – I will inquire of the Baron –"

"Very well, monsieur. I will see to it. Who shall I say?"

I swallowed, my throat seemed engorged and hurt me. I glared at the man haughtily. "Say Andre St Jean."

"Very well, monsieur. One moment."

And leaving his post, he went in and around out of my sight, presumably to a side door. I waited a few minutes, expecting to be turned away, to make some scene there on the pavement before the house, having a picture of running to a window and smashing through it.

Was it a plague, the ancient one called the Death? Had we both caught it, she and I, in the house near to the Obelisk where they had burned the corpses centuries ago? Only a hundred years ago, it had returned, that plague. Cloaked death had stalked the City. The crematory chimneys had turned the day sky black, the sky of night into blood, with their ceaseless smokes – so many of the writers of the day had left accounts of it in their journals.

"Please come with me, monsieur."

The doorman was back. He took me up to the front door, which had now opened. Inside, another man led me over the polished floor, into the side-parlour where I had been shown previously, and there left me.

Would it happen again? She, coming in, telling me she was afraid I had had to wait. And then would I fall on her like a wolf, unable to control either lust or terror? Why did you shut up the house this way? Oh, to be free for you, only for you, she would answer me.

The blinds were down. The room sank in a dull parchment shade. Even the little clock had left off ticking. My hands shook, I paced about. Then the door opened. I turned to it with a stifled shout. The Baron entered.

He looked more frightened than I, that was the first, the only thing I really noticed.

"It is very good of you to call," he said.

I stared at him. We had both gone mad. Dispense with these ramblings then.

"Tell me what has happened –" I cried.

"I regret – an illness, an hereditary ailment. We had hoped –"

"Doctors," I said, "who is attending her?"

"The most capable physicians, of course, monsieur, I assure you. And among our own household, the use of herbal medicine is not unknown – but in any event –" he broke off. He said, with sudden and sinister calm, "You should not be optimistic, Monsieur St Jean."

I clutched one of the chairs. I said, "What do you mean? You'd let her die –"

"Oh monsieur, please. You do astound me."

"Let me see her at once! Where is she? I'll search your house – throw me out and I'll return with the City police. You are not a citizen, Baron. An alien – they can deal with you –"

"Please, monsieur, these threats, these outcries, are uncalled for, and wasteful of your strength."

"You say to me she's dying –"

"I tell you there is no hope at all."

I stood there staring. I stared, but saw nothing, and when he poured the cognac for me and put it in my hand, I drank it down, though it might well have been poison. What did I care for that?

"I will tell you, Monsieur St Jean, what it would be best for you to do. Go away now, and come back, perhaps in the early evening."

"I must see her," I said. I took his arm, his hand, imploring him. "Please, for God's sake –"

"Tonight then, if you wish," he said. "It's not possible now."

"You expect me to go, and leave you to get on with killing her –"

He was so serene now before my ranting. He said to me, "But she has told you my place, has she not?" He withdrew his hand from my grasp, gently. He put his own hand upon my shoulder. "Now do as I say, monsieur. It is beyond any of us, but I'll assist you as best I can, for as long as I can. You have my sympathies."

I laughed. This was what I should have said to him.

"I love her," I said. How vapid, such words. "If you must kill someone, then here I am."

"I know you love her. I have nothing to do with any killing."

Without knowing what I did, I walked towards the door. I could dash up the stair, and fling open all the doors – the commotion of that might finish her, if what he said was a fact. But it was all a surreality. She could not die.

Out in the hallway, I gazed up at the curving stair, and for a moment I seemed to hear the piano being played, above in the salon, but the music only rang through my head.

"There, monsieur," said the kindly placid cuckold. "Now do as I say. Return this evening, or I'll send for you if there is any improvement. But that is of course unlikely. It is improbable."

As he finished speaking, an awful, unearthly, etheric cry tore through the house. The shock of it threw me round on him again, almost taking him by the throat – "What in God's name –"

"That is her dog, monsieur. Howling. The dog knows, monsieur."

It was not until I had left the house, not until I was on the hill again, that I comprehended what I had all this while known. It was I who was the murderer. In the blissful whirlpool of adoring, death-wishing delirium, I had never thought *I* might be the poison. Or had she foreseen – was it that which made her hold me off? That fear which finally brought her to me?

I had no strength now. None. But I would return in the evening, duly as he said. Come back and die with her.

The dim piano continued to play within my skull, and now and then the dog howled there, or voices spoke to me, as if into my ears. The borders between unconsciousness and waking, between dream and reality, had long since given way.

Above the door of the *Cockatrice*, the sign of the scaled, snake-headed cockerel turned its look on you and blasted you to a stump. Then you went inside to the damp and greasy cave, where sometimes only the spits turned, or coloured lanterns were lit in the ceiling, so it became hell. Today it was gloomy.

They had all avoided me, the intellectual riff-raff of the tavern. I was a plague-carrier, I was accursed, and they knew it by instinct. No one I had ever known well was present. I guarded my corner like a wounded dog, and nobody drew near. A meal was served me I did not eat, and wine. Sometimes I wrote a line or two on pieces of paper I had found in my coat pockets. Generally I slept. Time had stopped. The day would not move, it sat there on the sills of the slit-eyed windows. The bells, the clocks, they continually kept striking the same hour, three o'clock, over and over. When would I be done with it?

Then I woke and there was a new shadow running with the spilled wine from the bottle. The windows had pulled closer and day been shoved out. I poured the last glass and took a mouthful. The room was unusually silent, and two men in black were before me by the table. How long had they been there? Were they there now, or did I conjure them?

"Are you real then?" I said, with a flippancy that oddly stirred me.

"You are to come with us," one said to me.

In the cock-snake's cave, eyes glittered out on us. We were an event.

"Sergeant Death, are you arresting me?" I said. "Who sent you, and why must I go with you?" My heart had stopped, I could not feel it beat. "From von Aaron? Is she dead?"

"We do not belong to the Baron. But that is the house. Get up, monsieur."

"Or will you make me?" I said.

"If necessary."

"It will not be." I put down the glass. My heart flickered, it had only been sleeping. I did not feel as I had done. I was alert, I was expectant. What had happened? Oh she was alive. That must be so. She was alive. She had sent them for me. Yes, they were hers, these creatures white-faced in their black. "We'll go then," I said. "as quickly as you like."

I went out jauntily with the death's-heads, one on either side. Plainly, I was a prisoner on my way to execution. Yes, the silken rope about my neck, the dagger of pleasure driven through and through.

People turned to look at us on the streets. The infernal escort, the happy condemned. They did not prevent me when I whistled a popular song of the City, or when I plucked a spray of flowers off a bush growing in a wall, and insanely twirled it. Sometimes I spoke to my guards. I asked them if they had had difficulty in finding me. Not much, they said, my haunts were known. Now one spoke, now the other, but each seemed to have use of the same voice.

From a height, I glanced behind me once, and saw the river, a scimitar of pure metal, white-hot, as the City lapsed in the shallows of the dying afternoon. A boat or two moved on the water, the brotherhood of Charon was out early.

Then they took to the alleys, avoiding the Observatory Terrace, and going around at the back of the tall four-faced clock on the hill, not wanting me to be seen by the influential or the fashionable of the district.

My excitement increased. Sex and anguish were mingled in it, doubt and nervous delight. Most of the straw was swept from the street. No man sat to bar the gateway of the house. I hurried up the steps and rang the bell, and they came on behind me, the two black dogs who had hunted me and brought me soft across the City in their mouths.

The door was opened. I burst in, then stood looking about as if I owned the property.

"If you will go up to the salon, monsieur," said the domestic.

I ran up the stair. I had not felt the paving stones under my feet throughout our walk here. Twirling the flower-spray, I thought, None of them either conducts me or follows me. I am to go there alone. Something pristine in that. Only the purified accolyte may enter the presence of the high priest.

The salon was full of the last flare of sunlight, its blinds raised. All the dazzling brilliance centred in one flaming entity, before the fireplace.

Antonina stood there.

It was not Antonina.

A man in a white satin coat, all in white but for the long black loosely-curling hair that was the Freedom mode of Paradys for both male and female. Her black brows, perhaps a little more thickly accented, her heavy-lidded eyes, heavily and blackly fringed, blackly burning in the pale triangle of the face that was larger and cut with a bolder hand, and as hard now as white granite.

He looked at me, out of a different distance, for he was some inches taller than I. He said nothing, did nothing, only the left arm, leaning on the mantle, the left hand with a pair of white kid gloves in the long fingers – her hand exactly, grown a size or two, a man's hand, elegant, ringless – that gave a little flick, a little omen of gesture.

I cannot say how long this moment lasted, while he looked at me, and I at him, seeing her, losing her.

Gradually I became aware that von Aaron stood to one side, and two other men with him, advisers or lawyers, or merely witnesses. But even then, I could not look away, look at them. My arms had fallen to my sides. They weighed on me like lead. The boom of my heart shook me. And the black eyes went on burning into my skull. That was all there was.

Then the Baron spoke soflty, maybe even timidly, from the wings.

"Monsieur St Jean. I can't prepare you. The news is bad. My wife – we lost her a few hours ago. I see that you already knew it. Well. This gentleman –" He did not go on, I sensed him slip away again, only his mute gaze on us.

Then the man in white spoke to me.

"I am her brother. Perhaps that is obvious to you?"

"Yes, quite obvious."

He nodded, as if I had done something clever, a clever trick.

"And you," he said, "what are you? In my eyes, what are you? It chances," he said, in his exact and musical voice, "that I arrive here and find this. Her husband," he did not glance aside, "will do nothing, but, Andre St Jean, I am not insensible to my sister's honour, or to the cause of her death."

She could not die. I could not proclaim as much.

The light and the dark came with the crashings of my heart, ocean on to rocks.

Well, let him get on with it.

"What do you say now?" he said.

I shrugged, and let the spray of flowers fall to the floor as I did so.

"I will give you my name," he said. "It is Scarabin. Anthony Scarabin. You got hold of a certain ring, I believe. A ruby scarab. Yes, well you will give it back, I will take it back tomorrow, after I've finished with you."

"You mean to kill me," I found I said. "Will it be so easy?"

"Nothing," he said, "easier."

He moved from the hearth. He walked across to me, and with his gloves slapped my cheek, so lightly, it might have been an idle caress. He smiled. Her mouth, changed. And the skin, fine and fresh as hers, but more dry, and roughened by shaving.

"What will you have?" he said.

"Whatever suits you."

"Pistols, then. That is the vogue in your city, I think. Pistols at dawn. Can you come by a gun? How splendid. Will six in the morning be convenient?"

"Most inconvenient. I'm not by choice an early riser."

He raised one of the black brows at me. Cold, as once she had been.

"Don't play," he said. "Answer me."

"I will accommodate you," I said.

He said, "The choice place, I hear, is the wood below the Observatory. Bring your seconds," he said, "I shall have mine."

No one else spoke a word. There was not a noise in the house. Only the sunlight seemed to scrape faintly, as it crept down the windows.

What next? I need only turn and leave the room. It had all been arranged, and now there were things to do besides. How mundane this was. I had not predicted the deadly ordinariness of death.

I would not request that they let me see her body. There was no body. All that remained of her was here, was *him*, this other.

I felt neither exhilaration nor fear. As I walked from the salon, I heard him give a contemptuous little wordless sound, like a note or a chord of music, low down in the register.

Don't play, answer me, he had said that before to me, on Sacrifice Hill. He would know that I remembered him. But then, on that former occasion, when I would have held out the ring, he turned and was gone to his hunting. All this had had to come between. Besides, then, he had only been a demon. *Satanus est.*

I walked away into the city, and found a notary. By his reluctant candle-light I set my affairs in as much order as I could, and allocated such posses-sions as might be of any worth. I had never thought I should do such a thing, or that there would be any margin to do it. For I would be assassinated on the street, or perish in some stupor. Nor was there left me a Philippe, unreliable, impassioned, to take the residue of my writing to the printers, if he ever would have taken it. Would it concern me, in hell or in the grave, to recollect my unpublished works? Who would remember me in a year or two? But in two centuries, who would remember anyone, and in a hundred hundred years, all the paper would have transposed to paste, and dust. All the words, all the con-certos, all the shrieking and the shouts, lost in the void of life. Oh, let it go.

The business with the gunsmith did not take long. The barber's took longer.

It did occur to me that perhaps I might also seek a priest, and make to him my confession. But in the end, I had visualised it so thoroughly I seemed to have done it. And I did not want to go over all my sins again. Instead, I com-posed an ambiguous letter to Russe. I did not call on him. I wanted no one with me when I died but Death himself. He should surely be sufficient.

Having paid my landlady, and told her only that I was going away, I went to bed.

At first I woke several times, choking and panic-stricken. Then I slept deeply. I knew I would wake at the four o'clock bell, and so I did, with a mild surge, as if cast up by a wave upon a beach.

Because I was to die in public, last night my vanity had determined it had better be as beautifully as possible. And so, last night, the barber's shop, with its hirable bath, and then my hair washed and curled and freshly laved in "Martian" henna. From the launderers' came the shirt with all its ruffles starched, the linen and muslin immaculate (Philippe's coat), and so on. Even to the boots my vanity went, and had them polished up again with a rubric molasses to bring out their red.

I had put on the ring. He would have to take it from my hand himself.

The gunsmith's man had been told he must make his own way over to the duelling place, with the case of pistols. But he knew where to go. As Scarabin had said, it was the preferred venue for those who wished to kill each other. The Senate winked at such illegal fights. Who could say what went on, at sunrise, in the thick woods below the planet-searching dome of the Observatory, which saw only space and stars?

The sky looked nowhere near light when I went down the stairs and out into the City. All Paradys seemed to lie dumbfounded under a high black lid. Not a window awake. The street lamps glimmered, drunk to their dregs; many were out. There was a tingle of frost on the air.

Two or three times I paused to drink from a small brandy-flask, a worthless metal thing from which, for a while once, I had never been parted. I was glad of it now. All natural feeling was gone, yet the world seemed far too real, and so insistent. It rubbed its bony sides against me. To die had no glamour left, because the practicalities of its arrangement had revolted me. Yet I wanted it more than ever, with a kind of hunger, and a desperate dread of its complications.

It appeared to me I wandered more than walked, but I had left plenty of time to get there. I even went along a little way by the river, but no slender ominous boat came drifting from the mist.

Then, as I began to climb up into that gorge of masonry, up towards the Observatory hill with the woods lying dark upon its lap, a kind of quickening came again, just as on the stairway of Philippe's house. A terrifying brilliancy, a sumptuous fear. Not the reality I had just stumbled through, but the true reality, dramatically plunging its beak and talons in my vitals, and bearing me up on its wings.

The vault of the night had swung higher, and eastward some rogues had set fire to the sky. I came to the railings and got over them, and walked up the mound of frosty turf, and into the trees.

In the hollow, where it is done, they were waiting. A group of three men there, and there another group of two, where the folding table had been set up and the cases of guns put out. The surgeon sat nearby on a camp-stool, recognisable from his bag beside him, his arms crossed, indifferent. Up on the other slope of the hollow, a couple of carriages stood under the trees. They would have come in by the lane that ran past the Observatory, and would go out again by the same route. I wondered if I should be packed into one of them, or simply left lying, as sometimes happened.

Seeing me arrive, the gunsmith's man was now checking Scarabin's pistols, as one of Scarabin's seconds investigated mine. His pistols had not been hired for the occasion. They looked very white, disembodied, in the twilight. He, too, in the white coat, seemed to float between earth and open sky.

I had forgotten I would urgently *want* to see him, to look at him. I was drawn, pulled over the grass towards him. But suddenly the gunsmith's man got in my way. I tried to put the obstacle aside.

"No, monsieur, wait a moment. There's some irregularity here."

I halted.

"Oh," I said, "What?" I thought he was going to say I must have a friend with me, one at least, but I would rejoin it was a formality and dismiss it.

"The bullet in this fellow's gun – there is only the one, and in the one pistol only."

I looked at him. "Well?"

"Well, it is –"

I said, "Silver?" He nodded.

I put my head down, shuddering, as if I had received a blow, and the gunsmith's man caught at my arm. "Monsieur, you have every right to object –"

"Yes, yes." I dislodged him. I moved on, towards the being in its white coat. If he was an icon, yet the black boots were planted on the ground. Framed in the priest's cowl of black hair, *her* face, unfamiliar and the same, its cruel changed lips compressed. And the eyes, waiting for me.

Overhead, above the trees, the sky had bled out to nacre.

"Are you ready to begin?" he said.

"Why is there silver in your gun?"

"An eccentricity. Humour me."

"I can object to it, the man says."

"But you will not," Scarabin said. "Or are you going to dare to prolong this?"

"Where did you get it, the silver? Since you mean it for me, I have an interest."

"Don't concern yourself," he said. "You will be penetrated only by the very best."

One of the men chuckled, slimily.

"Some heirloom," I said. "Holy silver from some priestly cross."

He stood and gazed back at me, arrogantly, disdainfully.

I said, "There was another before me. What about that one? Or do you think he will be no trouble? Did you always do this service for her?"

The men, his seconds (although I guessed he did not know them particularly, more of the Baron's tribe, perhaps), were faint outlines at his back. Did they realise what we spoke of, and think we were mad?

I said to Scarabin, "I'm sorry now I acquiesced to pistols. That's too removed. I'm sure you were trained to the use of a sword, but I never was, or I would clamour now for two honed blades. I should like to cut that look off your bloody face."

"Such a pity," he said.

I stepped up to him and slapped him hard across the left cheek. His skin was so fair, the blood at once came up like thunder beneath it.

"There," I said. I nearly laughed aloud. The contact with his flesh had energised me. "I am ready to begin, when you are."

"Oh, come then," he said, mockingly.

We walked to the table. His hand settled on the nearer of the white pistols.

"I shall require only this," he said. "You may take both your weapons, if you wish."

"One will suffice."

A man came between us and spoke the litany.

"Gentlemen, your witnesses have been given to understand this meeting is by mutual agreement, and that both of you have made your arrangements suitably. It is understood that the affair can be settled only by a death. Then, gentlemen."

I tasted frost in my mouth, but already the wind of dawning was combing over the sky. Birds sang. A rook's rasping bleat trailed like a flag as it passaged down into the City – I saw only the eyes of the man who must kill me.

" … Paces to the count of ten. And on the count of ten, to turn and fire at will."

The speaker stepped away.

We stood, Scarabin and I, under heaven. Then turned, as instructed, to begin our walk.

"One," said the man who counted, "two … three …"

The cord that bound us drew tighter as we moved further from each other. It tautened, ready to recoil, and plunge us home, breast to breast, eye to eye.

"… Six … seven …"

But here is the day, and soon it will be gone. Here am I, but where, tomorrow?

He is making sure, with his silver. Antonina is the quarrel between us, lying at ease in her white coffin now, a white dead hound coiled at her feet. He would take the ring off my finger, but the electric coldness of his touch I should not feel.

"Ten."

I turned again, in a noiseless spinning roar of lights, and brought up the pistol, sighting along it, not seeing. Just the shining blur of him against the maze of dusk and morning. I moved my arm, letting the pistol tilt, to miss him, and fired directly. In the same second, he also fired at me.

I heard the shot. I heard a tearing sound.

There was an impact. It threw me over and the earth slammed against my shoulders.

This then, was this death? No, he had not hit me. No.

Into the white shield of sky, the elongated dark silhouettes of men came stooping. I lay under water and looked up at them. They wavered and were folded away.

The pain was a spike driven into my arm. There was a rawness in my chest. Ah then, he had hit me. The left arm. I should be able to continue to write. Someone held me, as I lay along the ground, my head was supported. Russe? No, Russe was not with me –

I opened my eyes and the surgeon leaned forward. He peered at me. How insignificant and human were his eyes. "There is nothing I can do," he said to me. "You are a dead man. You comprehend me?" Then, he raised his glance a short way and said to someone, "You have your satisfaction, monsieur. You will forgive my haste. Good day."

He rose up once more into the sky and was gone. They were all gone. There, across the grass, a solitary figure stood, in dark livery, and on a leash, a black dog rippled in and out of existence, a phantom thing, and beside it, another. Their black eyes stared at me. They scented blood.

Who was it held me, then, my head on his thigh, the blood staining his white coat?

"Is it you?"

Not a word came out of me, I thought, but he seemed to hear.

"I'm above your City laws," he said, "and so not afraid to stay."

"To be sure of me. Where – am I hit?"

"In the heart. An astonishment you still live."

I lay above the agony. I could not see him, only the red hair and the red blood, soaking across the skirt of his coat.

"Take the ring," I said.

"Not yet."

"When?"

"Presently."

The tears ran out of my eyes and I did not feel them, or the grief. All my days reduced to *Presently*.

"Go now," he said to me. His beautiful voice, it gleamed, like darkness. "You can hardly remain."

"I haven't any last words," I said. "They must invent them for me.

Someone must. Dying is like the final moments of the carnal act, I suspected so. The intimation, the galvanic tremor that foreshadows it, then the unavoidable giving way, the surge, the sinking. Yes, I was right. Did I die before, to know it?"

But I had ceased speaking long ago. My lips were fractionally parted on the words I had not whispered. My eyes were wide. And then his cold hand came gently to my face, and closed my eyelids down, carefully, as a mother might brush a leaf from the face of a sleeping child. And I was dead.

The bird was tapping on the inside of the shell. I heard the sharp beak, its noise grated on me. Tap, tap, tap.

Be quiet. Let me think.

I was moving now, it was not unpleasant, there in the dark, to be moving. It was the boat, surely, for it was a wooden thing. Hush then, you need only lie still, and let the rocking lull you back asleep.

Tap, tap, tap.

The bird kept tapping at the shell. It sensed daylight. It wanted to get out.

But I did not want the light, only the peaceful dark.

Then the boat jolted, Charon making an error with his oar, or the Styx was choppy today. Well, I might open my eyes, might look to see what this country was like, after all. My eyes would not open yet. Well, there was no hurry. They were shadowy, the riverbanks of Hades, not much to gaze at.

My thoughts, unable to lift my eyelids or operate any part of my body, swam up and down within me. Some sensation had returned, for I felt the wooden planks, and the touch of my own linen against my skin, and my own hair.

Then abruptly the boat fell down. It fell and hit the bottom with a smack, rolling me about, making me move my hands and feet and head as I could not myself.

Thereafter, cessation. And then a reverberating thud against the black air above me.

It was the sound of a spadeful of soil flung in on to my coffin. I had not reached the shadowlands: I was still alive; and alive they were burying me.

I tried to shout. I had no voice. I was not afraid. I lay in the dark, and listened to the earth thudding in to cover me up.

This was a foolish thing. I had only to depart. He had told me, someone I had known, he had said to me, *Go now*. It was so close, the Shadow, the River, so near in all its vastnesses. Anything was possible, there. How had I lost my way?

Tap, tap, went the bird. More earth slammed down. Tap, tap.

When the burial was complete, and the last vague shakings and thumpings of my world had ceased, the vagrant thought in me composed itself. Though the bird continued to irritate me by random flinty pecks, the sheer comfort of this state allowed awareness to be reabsorbed. I abandoned the sensations of my outer skin, and sinking inward again, I glimpsed the threshold I had lost, quite suddenly, so accessible and near – and in that instant the bird's beak ripped through the shell like a knife.

I screamed aloud and my eyes flew open. My hands flew up, and took hold of the flimsy botched coffin, and broke it. It shattered around me and the earth poured in, and like a fish leaping from some depth of water, I drove myself upward. I exploded from the pit in a fountain of blackness, soil and stones and splintered wood. Almost asphyxiated, I kneeled in the broken grave, retching and coughing and choking for air: all the horrors of birth.

The moon rose later, as I was lying there. Next I heard bells telling the hour. Where was I? Some ruinous cemetery, with a little church. A coffin of plywood, and the diggers anxious to be off and drink the money from the job. A pauper's makeshift grave; the only reason I had got out of it.

What city was this? Was it Paradys, or some other place? Did Paradys exist? It had been a dream, maybe.

The moon was so cold, staring in my face. It made something glitter, too, lying near me. It had come up with me from the earth, a silver nugget of some sort. I took it in my hand. It was blunted and tarnished, but surely it had been pure?

To leave the vicinity I had to claw my way through brambles, clamber over fallen tomb-stones – a deserted corner. When I came to the church, the door was firmly locked.

As I stood there, I thought I saw a white greyhound rush across the cemetery. What was it chasing? I turned to see.

Then I heard ordinary voices, and some light began to come, weaving through the thorn trees. Two men appeared, gallants going home from some feast, by way of death's garden. They were drunk. They saw me, and exclaimed. The one with the lantern came up to me, leaned over me by the church wall, holding the light high.

"Now what has been happening to you, eh?"

My voice would trouble me. I spoke very low.

"As you see, something unpleasant."

"Well if your sort will frequent such spots. Why are you dressed like that? Some brute made you, did he? The rotten scoundrel. What else did he do?

He put his hand on my neck, his fingers into my hair. He leaned hard on me. Did I remember these things? Oh yes, long ago.

"What's your price?"

They put the lantern on the ground among the weeds. The first one had me the first, urgently. Then his companion took his turn, and time. When they were done, they left me a handsome sum of money, and as they were buttoning their breeches, the first said to me, "You were lucky, in meeting us. But another night, better be more careful, sweetheart. Go on home now, and put your dress on." The other said, "If she wants to dress herself as a man, I've no objection to it." And he grinned at me before they careered away through the briars under the moon.

I met an old rag-picker, an old bent woman, as I was leaving the cemetery. She stared at me, as the moon had done. "Oh, lady," she said, "oh lady you are in a fix."

"I shall be better soon."

"I thought it was a man," she said, "a boy. But there's grave-dirt in your hair."

"Do you know," I said, "is there a monument near here – a monument of plague?"

"Oh, not far. Don't you know where you are, girlie? Been looking for someone, I suppose, trying to dig him out again. Well, it's a sad world."

"Where is this place?"

"How should I know? Some place without a name. What's my name? What's yours?"

"I – forget – my name –"

"There now. And so it is with that place. All those nameless bones. The headstones weather and wear, if there are any headstones put for them."

"Young men killed in duels are buried there."

"Yes," she snapped, "and old ones, too, that ought to know better."

She raised her threadbare body an inch or so, and held my hand as she pointed away towards the Obelisk Gardens. There were no rings on my fingers. She could only be jealous of my youth.

I crept down the ancient avenue, there was such an ache in my side, under my breast. I pressed my palm over it. My boots were too big for me.

Grass grew between the stones, which were pied here and there from the sheep that had been herded through the day before, to the markets – but to which markets, now? And the Obelisk? Yes, the Plague Monument, I had been asking after. I recalled it. Nearby was the house. The house would help me, perhaps, if I met no one on its stairs …

Further bells rang in the City. I did not note the hour they struck. The night seemed in suspension, between dark and dawn, affording me as much time as I should need to reach my sanctuary.

And truly, like a temple's high altar it was, the house, the moon behind it, the aisle of the street blotted all through by shadow.

Up the steps, and oh, the ache in my heart, I went so slowly, and leaned my forehead on the door. Not boarded up. But locked, as the church had been, and yet I had a key – perhaps? I rifled the pockets of my curious clothes, and found a key which seemed the one I sought. It entered the lock of the door, and mastered it with the formal goodwill of a handshake.

A black chimney, the house, with the spine of the stair ascending. Familiar scents were dying. New smells of vacancy. With the turning of the seasons, damp would come, beetles would eat the wood and mice gnaw through the walls. The house would collapse at last like a dead tree.

I climbed, sometimes stopping to rest against the bannister. My debility was luxurious. If I wished, I could fall down and lie there. Who would ever come to disturb me? Yet I must reach the top of the skull, the attic. Why was that? Someone had left me something – it must be collected, for it was mine.

The attics, when I did reach them, had a familiarity I had missed in the remainder of the house. For instance, I remembered reading the books lying about the floors, and hiding in various parts of the hoard. I had often ridden the rocking-horse. It was on one of these rides, it seemed to me, a child of perhaps nine or ten, that I made the decision I did not want to live as a girl or woman. There had been a contrary example constantly before me, a snow-blond male child of my own age. He had taunted me and provoked me. Always copying him, I was never quite successful, while I remained female. Eventually I took the logical step. I altered. I became what he was: a boy. And later I remained masculine as I grew up. Here I was still in both their clothes, the garments of the blond Philippe, and of the young man who, until very recently (but how recently?) had been myself.

Presently I opened the press where Philippe had stored articles of his mother's wardrobe. She had been a tall, slender woman; we were of a size. The clothes would seem strange to me at first, as my voice had done. But that would not linger. (The fortunate mode of Paradys had outlawed any but the lightest corsetry.) My body itself was a garment only partly recognised. There was a deep stain on the breast of the shirt, but nothing on my skin over the heart. The grime of the burial, too, had been shaken from me; it was mysteriously and satisfyingly gone, which was as well, for there would be no water left in the cisterns of the baths, no soaps in the jars. But here were ivory-backed brushes for my hair, and the pearl-handled nail-clippers. How did I seem now?

My night-sight, sharpened by immersion in the ground perhaps, had been good enough for my wanderings and seekings so far, but, as I bound my waist with a sash, I had an urge to *regard*. There was a candle in the stand I located and lit with matches from a discarded male pocket. Holding my light, then, I went towards the one round unboarded window at the attics' end. There was no other mirror.

And in the black panes I saw my dim reflection, a young woman with a cloud of long and curling hair reddened by "Martian" henna. Nothing amiss with her, just a faint mark to the left side of the throat. I returned immediately to the press and took a woman's lace stock, and wrapped my neck and breast in it.

I had just filled one of the mesh purses with all the left-over items of my male pockets, when I heard, four storeys below me, the house door grate, hesitate, then thunder open.

All the house clanged like a bell, roof to cellars. A fine trembling like a fine dust was left in the air.

Then came footsteps, jumping, stamping, running and stumbling up the house, just the route I had come, but headlong and precipitate.

I took my purse, and the discarded apparel of Andre St Jean, and walked across the attic softly, as the other footsteps blundered nearer, shaking the building to its roots. I left the candle burning on a stack of volumes close to the rocking-horse – as I passed the beast, too, I put a hand on its hindquarters and set it going vigorously. There was a large Italian chest by the window. Lifting its lid, I threw in the clothes, the purse, and got in after them. Here I was again, in my coffin. I lowered the lid of the chest, and the door of the attics burst wide with a crash.

There were two arrivals. They paused as one. Then, through my wooden crate, I heard:

"Look at the candle! And the horse prancing – my God, someone *has* been in this room."

"But no one is here now."

"They say it's haunted, this bloody place. How not, the things that were done here? Oh, perhaps."

I knew both voices. What were their names? One deeper than the other, heavy as if leaden.

"The front door had been unlocked. Can a ghost not pass through a door? Does it need keys, and candlelight? Well, who knows. That fool. Why couldn't he explain himself in his letter."

"Andre is – Andre was mad. He and Philippe."

"It was in my mind, he must do something unwise. The insanity over the woman. Then her death."

"I told you, Russe, I heard them saying at the *Iron Bowl*, there was another duellist's body found in the Observatory woods."

"That's not unusual."

"They buried it, as always – no identity, and no questions. That was before dawn yesterday. But when did he send the letter to you?"

I listened, marvelling. When he said, this second man, whose name was surely LeMar – when he said "dawn yesterday" he meant a morning gone, one day and night. Could it be that I had lain all that great while, deliberating, between ending and resuming, before I moved and flung up from the prison? It had seemed to me to be only minutes.

"It may be Andre has only gone away. They think so at his lodging. This is what his letter implies. But I am perturbed by the reference to a debt to this man, this Anthony Scarabin."

"*Her* brother – Russe, Russe. Don't you see? Scarabin shot him. Andre is dead, and in a grave. We've searched the City. Where else could he be but under the ground."

"Here in this house."

"Yes, *in this house*. We come searching, we see the flicker of a light and rush in – but where is Andre, tell me that. Oh, he is here. He is here, Russe, but not in the flesh. Ah *God!*"

The cry was sudden and full of a kind of gratified terror.

Russe only cursed, in his heavy way.

It came to me the candle had been blown out abruptly, by an invisible agency.

I heard the noises of the flight of that one, that LeMar – Le Marc – all down the stairs again, howling, and out into the street."

But Russe remained, and he said, "Andre? Andre, are you truly dead and truly here?" (I had the desire to answer, sepulchral, from the chest. But he would not know my voice now.) "Ah, Andre, if you are. I warned you. Horror and sorrow, unholy things. You were a fool to meddle with it, Andre. Well, I'll go to the house of the Baron. I will ask him outright. It must be settled."

I crouched amid the chest and heard Russe in his turn go down the stairs. Then I rose up. I started – for the first tide of daybreak was in the window. I could see by it the candle, smoking.

Perhaps Philippe and I had played another game upon our friends.

Of whom had Russe been speaking? This Baron. I must follow the two men, and learn.

The lid of the chest fell, shutting in, conceivably for ever, perhaps, the shed bloodied skin of dead shot Andre. I had the bullet, however. It must have worked its way out like a splinter.

I took up one of the woman's veiled hats, the mesh purse, and a pair of respectable gloves, and went quickly down the house, ignoring the soft cracks and hissings it made at me. I locked the front door, then tossed the key high, at the crowns of the trees growing from the old City Wall.

Andre had known the way to the Baron's house, but I was not so certain. The peculiar light before sunrise showed me the agitated figures of the two men, about a hundred metres up the street. If they should chance to look back, they would think me only some lady of darkness hurrying to her lair, or lady of virtue hastening out to church.

I felt much stronger now. I felt the edge of laughter, but scarcely any pain, under my breast.

And how quaint the lady's shoes sounded on the pavement.

We went downhill, and crossed a terrace, and heard, far below, the City stirring.

They climbed another hill, my guides, with a clock-tower on it. I climbed after.

We came to a street along the hill's inner shoulder, and here memory sharply returned. The stuccoed houses were still asleep and blank as mausoleums, all but one. There was already some activity there. A pair of carriages stood outside the wrought-iron gate, reminding me of another pair of carriages, or the same, under the trees above the duelling hollow. Grooms had been holding the heads of the horses; now a coachman came and got up on the box of the foremost vehicle. Russe was on the pavement, arguing with a domestic from the house. Both spoke intensely, quietly, not to wake the street, Le Marc sometimes joining in, flapping at the house, the carriages, the sky.

Across the road I spied on them, concealed in another gateway.

Le Marc had turned towards the iron gate, now ajar, and the steps. The domestic tried to restrain him. The voice of Russe rose suddenly.

At that moment, the house door opened. Something was coming out. In the twilight, so pale it seemed to float of its own volition, a faceless glimmering shape – but two servants bore it between them. It was a milk-white coffin. Down the steps, the gate opened out for it. A groom pulled wide the carriage door. They eased the coffin into the interior.

It had had its effect, this manoeuvre. Le Marc was immobile, nonplussed. Russe had foolishly removed his hat.

And now the Baron, the banker, von Aaron – I recalled him very well – was coming down the steps. I listened with great concentration, and heard him say, to Russe, "This is not the time, not the place. What is it you can want?"

"We are concerned," said Russe, holding his hat, "for the safety of our friend. Monsieur St Jean. I believe you, or your guest, may be able to help us in the matter,"

"I? How can I do that? Her brother, to whom I take it you are referring, has insisted that the body of my wife return with him to – to a previous residence. I am to follow. As you see, that second carriage is already loaded with my trunk and boxes. There is no time now, to discuss any of this. If you must, you may call on me upon my return."

"When will that be?" said Russe.

"I'm not certain, monsieur. You must excuse me, you really must. I'm surprised, monsieur, at your lack of taste. To accost me at such a moment, almost across the corpse of my wife."

Russe stood, frowning and out of sorts at this reproach.

Le Marc cried, "And the duel? There was one – you admit as much?"

Von Aaron said nothing. From the porch above, a clear voice cut sinuously and crystallinely down, like a fencer's sword.

"If that is your problem, you must address yourselves to me."

There, in his white, white as the coffin, my enemy, gazing at them from his battlements of flawless arrogance and contempt. My heart leapt. The pain of death's memory wracked through it: my heart recollected. And in the purse of mesh the silver bullet, blunted on my muscle, flesh and bone, seemed to jump and scrabble.

"Then," said Russe doggedly, "we do so address ourselves."

The man Anthony Scarabin, descending to the street, said in passing, "I can tell you only this. Your friend caused harm. I therefore shot him, two mornings ago. You will find his grave, I believe, in the derelict cemetery that is generally used for such purposes. And now, if you would move aside."

As if they could not refuse, they obeyed him. Then as he stepped into the first carriage (which contained the coffin), Le Marc bawled: "You murderer!" But Russe took hold of Le Marc's arm. From Scarabin there was no reply. (And from the flat windows all about, not a face squinted out.) The groom closed the carriage door. The coachman unfurled his whip. The horses came to life and sprang forward. With a grumbling jangle, the carriage was off. It bowled along the street, and up on to the crest of it. Watching, each of us beheld it run away, looking weightless as a shadow-ball, around the tower with the clock, and then, taking the downward path, it was gone.

"This is not over with," said Russe.

Le Marc broke out shouting, and just as quickly broke down in silence.

"I shall present the business to lawyers," said Russe.

Von Aaron nodded.

"On my return, I will be at your disposal. But now you must let me get on." He nodded to them, and turned abruptly, marching back into the house. The door was shut by the domestic, who had followed him. The one remaining carriage, humped with its luggage, without a coachman still, and with only the groom beside the horses, waited like a thing of stone, in the stony light.

For a few instants, Le Marc continued to complain and flail. Then Russe had him in hand. Russe declared there was no point in their loitering there any longer. They would go straight down to the Justiciary, and be ready when the doors opened at eight o'clock.

Once they had dwindled from the street, the groom took out of his pocket some pieces of bread and dark chocolate, and began to eat them hungrily.

When I emerged from my gateway, crossed the road and approached the carriage, the groom did not look at me with any special interest. When I opened the carriage door and got into it, he said merely, "Now –" but nothing else. Obliged to keep the horses in check, he did not pursue me, nor call again.

I placed myself on the upholstered seat, adjusted the veil of my hat so that my face was lightly filmed, put my gloved hands on my purse, and waited for von Aaron to come back.

He was not very long. Probably he had only gone in again to evade Russe and Le Marc. Now the coachman also came, and going round, got up on the box. I heard the groom say in an undertone, "Some girl has got into the carriage." The coachman grunted with no amazement.

But von Aaron, when the groom had opened the door for him, froze in the middle of his ascent into the vehicle.

"Who the devil are you?"

"Your fellow traveller."

"This is," he said, still bowed over in mid-entrance, "a private coach."

"Quite so."

"Then please get out, mademoiselle."

"I will not," I said. "You had better get in, instead."

His engraved face loomed before me, at a loss. Then he pulled himself up and sat down across from me. The groom hovered at the door and von Aaron indicated this fact with his hand.

"Must I have you ejected, mademoiselle?"

"Don't consider such a thing." I stared at him through the veil. "I am going where you are going."

"And where is that?"

"After the other. The man in white, and that white coffin. It's perfectly simple. Why delay us both."

His hand went into his cuff of metallic lace and drew out a lace handkerchief. He put it to his brow and lips. His eyes never left me. Finally, he said, "It occurs to me that I know you, mademoiselle."

"Not at all."

"Yes. I've seen you before. I –" Quite suddenly his face grew very white and still. Only the lips separated from each other, and the eyes darted up and down me, up and down. There could be no doubt; I was a woman. He was thinking to himself, was he, that I was some relation of Andre St Jean? A cousin, perhaps, or a sister. At length he glanced away, at the hovering groom, and told him to withdraw and to shut the door of the carriage. The groom did so. He went back into the gateway and stood there looking at us, not much intrigued, surreptitiously slipping slivers of chocolate into his mouth. Von Aaron said, "You will render me your name, mademoiselle, at once."

I lowered my eyes. I replied deliberately, "My name is Anna Sanjeanne."

There was a pause. The difference in the "Sanjeanne" was very slight from the one he had been expecting. It caught and held him, trying it over, licking his lips. The handkerchief fluttered again. I closed my eyes, my hands folded upon the purse in my lap.

"And you –" he said, "you will not get out?"

"No I will not get out."

"God in Hell," he said. He swore. He compressed the handkerchief and thrust it away. Then, he leaned from the window and shouted at the coachman. As von Aaron lurched again into his place, the whip cracked outside and the vehicle juddered. We began to move, rolling forward, the wheels grinding over the stones, as I had seen happen with the first carriage.

Sleep, or faintness, stole over me. I leant my cheek against the seat's cushioned support, my head turned from the Baron towards the other window. The world swam and streamed, all Paradys streaming away. My lids fell again.

Von Aaron said to me from far off, "I shall not, mademoiselle, exchange another single word with you. You must understand this."

"Do as you please," I murmured.

He laughed bitterly, just once.

The jolting of the carriage as it gained speed joined with the furious knocking of my heart. The roar of wheels and hoofs flowed in my brain. Awareness, Paradys, they poured off me together. The City was going, being left behind, as if we lifted into the morning sky. Somewhere, thin and hard and pure as steel, a thread led away out of the labyrinth, at the other end of which there ran before us a blazing gem of white.

The carriage travelled through the day, almost as the sun did. There was only one brief stop.

In the first hours, I saw very little from the window, after the fragmentary passing of the City. Once, after we had clattered across the great bridge that spanned the last northern loop of the river, a vagary of the curving road laid out before me one ultimate vista of Paradys. It rested behind us in a valley of light, glittering there like water, for the day was already growing hot. The towers and domes had melted down into the molten whole. It was a landscape solely, only possibly inhabited. And thereafter, the only bells we heard, the speechless, sweating Baron, and I, were the sheep-bells from the orchards and pastures at the roadside.

Later, the dust came and furred the windows, already shut by glass and sun. We rushed then through a pollinated world, lost in bright mist. When there were woods, the carriage darkened. Here and there a fountain jetted from a rock, or a stream-bed widened, flashing like diamonds.

I slept, or swooned, rising in and out of deep silences to the clash of wheels and the groans of the vehicle. I was not alarmed he would set on me, my companion, that I should be taken up unconscious and thrown out on to the road. He had acceded. He had given in to destiny which had assumed my form.

At noon, the sun was overhead, striking the carriage roof with its spears. I rose from my stupor and lay in another one of unbearable heat and savage excitement. I was proceeding where I must. I was a creature that was itself beyond all transgressions, all impediments. I could revel in that, half-dead in the heat and deathless, as the Baron mopped his face and drank water from a travelling bottle.

Afternoon came, and all things slept but we. Black sheep lay in the shade of colossal oaks. Crows on a parched field stood as if petrified. Blond wheat parted at the wind of our passage, and closed again together like the tines of a fan. Black as agates, the grapes on the vinestocks, among the grey and dusty leaves –

About three in the afternoon, came the halt. There was an inn above the road, and the horses were to be changed. As it was seen to, a man materialised at the Baron's window, and handed in a hamper.

The Baron unfolded for himself a wooden tray, and spread a napkin over his knees. He ate shiftily, then took a goblet from the hamper and a bottle, uncorking and pouring the red wine. Now the glass bulb glowed like a huge garnet. He gulped the glass, spoiling it.

Just before we started up again, von Aaron, discarding the remains of his meal, the tray and napkin, leaned diagonally, across the carriage and offered me a glass of the garnet wine.

"The day is very hot." He apologised for showing kindness or pity, breaking his vow not to speak. But I respected the vow. I raised the veil of the hat, and drank a little wine. A very little – I had no intention that nature should force me to quit the carriage. Though he superstitiously dared not put me out, an independent withdrawal would obviate destiny in an instant.

When I set down the glass, he was staring at me in distressed fear. He shook his head, retrieved the goblet and himself swallowed all its contents. Then, he spoke again. "Mademoiselle St Jean, if you would reconsider. Do you see that inn? It's very pleasant. I have money here – and I must come back this way, and can then … Surely –"

"No."

"Why this stubbornness?" he pleaded. "What can you hope for?"

What indeed? The hope, ghostly, unclaimed, flooded me like fire at his question.

"We were not to converse, I thought," said I. "And you have misremembered my name."

The man appeared at the window for the hamper, and von Aaron pushed it out to him. He dropped a coin in the man's hand. Hamper, wine and waiter moved away.

Perhaps a quarter of an hour had elapsed. The coachman called a query from his box. The Baron shouted out to him to go on. Nor did the Baron evince any want or need to vacate the carriage.

The new horses started forward with all the rush of the old.

Towards sunset, when a pink-geranium glare filled the vehicle, the Baron spoke again.

"I think, Mademoiselle St Jean, that we should talk."

"Formerly, you thought otherwise. You were then correct."

"Mademoiselle – Mademoiselle St Jean –"

"Sanjeanne, if you must."

"This is very ill-advised on your part."

"You believe so."

"This venture. Let me tell you what I conclude. That you have some strange irrational dream of vengeance on your mind."

"Vengeance for what, pray?"

"The death of your brother."

"I have no brothers, Baron."

"The – gentleman whom you saw leaving my house in the City – he is not to be trifled with. You should not – I'm telling you, mademoiselle, you are embarked on a dangerous course."

I laughed. A girl's laughter, it came to me unexpectedly and delighted me a moment.

We plunged on through the radiant pink light, and pines began to come along the road, which rose upward, upward. Then we entered a great vault of geranium sky, with, hanging in it, cliffs and spires of rock, the dark forests boiling over them, and the sun, a transparent burning-glass, only the colour of the air.

As I gazed at it, he said quite crisply, "You will have to cross the northern border, mademoiselle, if you mean to go on with this. Do you have papers?"

But it was the beauty of the sunset which was real. The Baron apparently did not understand about the being of reality, its translucence, its elasticity.

When the sun sank, the forests closed on us. Now it grew chilly. Timelessly time advanced.

It was near midnight, and I was numbed and stiff with cold. I had slept further it seemed, or at any rate, been absent from the carriage where my body journeyed. Now, the carriage had stopped again.

This, and the stealthy movements of the Baron, had alerted me, but I gave no sign. I lay motionless, scarcely breathing, my eyes shut. Soon I heard the carriage door softly opened. Something eased itself out, and then the door was tenderly closed. A footstep on earth. One of the horses blew and stamped, and the carriage rolled and steadied. Nothing more.

I opened my eyes. Beyond the windows the pine trees pressed on the carriage. Between hung the lucid avernal daylight of full moon.

Von Aaron was gone. Not prompted by any natural urge –

Sufficient space allowed, I lowered the window and looked out with care.

The road had become little better than a track, packed earth littered with small shards, through the edges of which the roots of the trees had sometimes clawed. And there indeed was the coachman, box deserted, plodding in between the pine stems to relieve himself.

Ahead, a second carriage stood across the road, blocking the way. It was like a phantom thing; it had no horses in the shafts, and no driver.

I opened my door and got out, the far side of the vehicle from von Aaron's coachman. I walked along the track in the moonday-night, past each pair of black horses, and then across the interval of track between the carriages.

The vehicle which blocked the road had, within its body, a white coffin, whiter than the moon. It rested on the floor where one of the long seats had been removed to facilitate its presence. On the opposite seat lay a pair of pale kid gloves.

I went beyond the carriage, walking now off the track, among the pines. The road dipped up and down, and just over the brow two men stood. I heard the voice of one of them, I hesitated, then stole on until I was some nine or ten metres away.

"Well, you must send her back again. Take her yourself, since I tell you you will be going."

"I think," von Aaron said, "she lacks documents. She could not cross the border."

"Well then."

"This is your last word."

"As you are aware."

Scarabin, tall and slender, a pillar of ice, black midnight of hair poured down his back. The other fawning, placating, angry and helpless. Before them both, the lands of night. The moon rode high, stopping for no one.

"She was sleeping," said the Baron.

"Perhaps."

Von Aaron looked back apprehensively, directly at me, staring into my face, and did not see me at all.

"Do you suppose? But where could she go?" Back again he looked at Scarabin. "I will put her out, if you tell me to do so, Anthony. She would be lost in this place. Let me come on with you, as it was arranged."

"Who arranged it? You. Your constant expositions. Return to that City where you let her out, where you let her do as she wanted."

"I? How could I prevent it – how can I answer you – what terms will you accept? It is *you* –"

They were no longer speaking of me, but of another. Of Antonina.

And Scarabin turned in that moment too, and thrust von Aaron from him.

"I'm tired of listening to this. You have no say in any of it. You'll do as I tell you, nothing more. Now get away, get out of my sight."

But, "There are the horses coming," said von Aaron importunately, point-ing down the track ahead. Black movement from the black pines there. A fresh team of drays being brought for the foremost carriage, to replace others already taken. Some village hereabouts, or some other servitor of Scarabin's.

"Anthony," said von Aaron now, "you may yet need me –"

There was no strategy in overhearing any more. I turned and retraced my way through the skirts of the pine shadow, to Scarabin's carriage. I opened its door and entered it, and shut myself in. There was a vibrancy in the air of it, scentless, tuned and pitched. I put my hands on the lid of the white coffin. How secure? But I had broken one such box already.

I drew up the lid with ease, it had not been secured at all.

Within, in the dark bed of silk, a woman's outline was deeply imprinted. I had known there would be nothing else. I had known that Antonina was not here, not *here*. Instead, I stepped into the silk, and lay down in this shape of her, which fitted me. Then I drew the lid up and resettled it. This time, some jigsaw groove connected with another. It sealed itself above me.

I placed the mesh purse under the folds of my skirt, and crossed my hands over my breast. I had not lain so eloquently or so neatly before.

How peaceful the dark was, out of the strident moon.

In a short while I heard the horses come up, and that they were being backed into the shafts. A man vaulted to the box. Then, the door opened. He came into the carriage, he, Scarabin. I knew him, by his step, the susurrous of the coat he wore, the faint intake and expiry of his breathing. Now he sat, now took up the gloves and threw them down again. Now the beautiful voice called out its order to the driver.

Hoofs trampled and wheels revolved. The carriage was angled and posi-tioned and set northward on the road, and with only this prelude, exploded into a great and nearly maniacal speed. The floor bounced under me. I was stunned by it, by the intimacy of its noise and motion. Then a light gentle impact came above, the click of a boot-heel. Anthony Scarabin had put his feet up on the coffin.

We came to the border.

I was by now hypnotised in my shell. I heard, or felt, the carriage draw up. At the window, muffled voices courteously insisted that the passenger must descend. He did so. Out on the roadway, I heard a man say to him, "And the coffin. Regretfully, we must inspect it." In response I could ascertain only the notes of his voice, no words. But then the door was opened, and rough nervous hands came down on the lid of my shelter.

I ceased at once to breathe; I had learnt this knack in the grave. As the lid sheared off, moonlight and shadow sprinkled me like cool water. A man drew in his own breath harshly, then let it go in a long sigh. I sensed, but did not see, that he crossed himself. Then the lid was awkwardly replaced, grating about until the grooves again engaged, and the dark, my coverlet, covered me.

"Your papers are correct. My condolences. Your sister's death is a great misfortune. Ah, a sad loss, so young. She seems only sleeping."

Scarabin re-entered the carriage. Orders were spoken on the road. The horses broke into their run. We raced across the northern border.

He had carried the box from Paradys for show. He had therefore required papers which noted it. Finding such luggage empty the border's watchdogs might have torn the receptacle apart, but a vacant coffin was no crime, an eccentricity, like a silver bullet ... But full, such a sad loss, the young sister, looking only as if she slept. He knew now he had company.

Would he speak? Would he himself lift off the lid, and should I see that face look in at me, and those eyes?

He might do anything.

He had had melted down the silver of Antonina's wedding rings, that had made the ammunition for his duel with me before. He was inventive, and capable, and quite as fey as I.

Nothing happened for a little while.

Then he called again to the driver, and the carriage halted, the driver dropped down and was at the window.

Scarabin said: "You see this?"

Together they raised it from the floor of the carriage, and I was borne a short distance, as it seemed, from the road.

Cautiously, as I was swung with the coffin in their grasp, I raised both hands and pressed against the lid. I could not in any way shift it. Some trick of the grooved mechanism made the box accessible only from without.

"Here. This will do," said Scarabin, above me.

The coffin was lowered, and let go. A slight fall, yet it jolted every bone of my body. I repressed the urge to laugh at his malice.

I made out their footsteps, retreating.

Then, in another minute, from some way off, I heard the carriage start up and tear away. After that, came a great stillness.

Having spontaneously evicted myself from the earth of a grave, the insoluble problem of the coffin bored me. I lay and did nothing, did not even think of it. I thought only of the carriage bounding along the tracks and roads between the pines. How should I find it? How catch up?

My mind flew after, never lost him. But I never could. Wherever he might go, my dearly beloved enemy, into whatever dim, invisible reach, I must come on him again at last, by design, or by accident. We could not be parted.

I relaxed, I composed myself.

What now?

There was a scratching on the lid of slumber. As I wakened I knew better than to call encouragement. Perhaps some hopeful thief had found me. He would be frightened off if the corpse merrily greeted him. Or perhaps it was some bird at work, or a large insect taking its constitutional along the lacquer.

Then the coffin-lid moved. Brightest daylight entered like a dagger. As I lifted my hands to assist, the lid was abruptly shovelled off and fell away. Against a blinding lace-work of leaves and sky, I saw the pagan beast-face of Satan himself, gazing in at me. A handsome black goat with a long Roman nose, and whorled medallions of horns.

I sat up with a cry of elation, and he frisked away.

I came from the coffin and stood in a young meadow. The spot was fringed by pines, but a wild orchard bloomed between, and here the goats were feeding. The tindery sweet scents of morning sun on clover, the wholesome stink of the herd, were here and there touched by the fermentation of fallen red apples lying in the grass. There was no sign or symptom of any road or track.

I cast off the veiled hat into the coffin, and took up the mesh purse and spilled it over the silk. Like the field-lily, it seemed to me I had no need of items such as money, paper, or matches. So I buried the latter, for fear they might combust and set the land on fire, and left the rest. What a sight it made, the opened coffin on the grass, and the papers and the coins, and the hat. The silver bullet alone I placed in the bodice of my costume.

Then I strayed away over the meadow, among the feeding goats, and picking up an apple, ate the red skin and the white flesh of it.

Possibly I might come on a goatherd. I would say, Where is the road? And he or she, meeting the eyes of Anna or of Andre respectively, would blush and hoarsely inform me there were no roads at all: this was Elysium.

But I met no goatherd.

Light and shade rained down and spangled everything. Then, on a slope beyond the orchard, I found a path after all, not wide enough for any carriage, yet I followed it. What did it matter if I lost my way? I should find it again. Help was always available. And he, like the moon in the sky of night, could not hide himself for very long.

The day was an idyll. I think I never spent such a day. Perhaps I had, as Andre; some picnic or excursion into the hills above the City.

I was all alone in a country that had no human things, only sunshine, trees and wild flowers, only the strands of streams and huge boulders clung with moss. Birds flashed and fluted. And though I saw animals playing and eating, never once did I discern a cot or hut, let alone a village, let alone the mirage of any distant metropolis.

How quickly it came and went.

Noon passed over like a wave, and afternoon, three waves, or more. The sun westered, the world slipped back towards the shadow.

High among the pines, I came on a stone that might have been an altar. Beyond, the forest lessened. Far away, miles away, in a cup of distance, I saw an architectural structure, which I knew from some dream.

Going down the escarpment I lost the view, but found a broad stream, not at all shallow. It wound away northwards, under the trees. Not quite a river, but by the stones, a small narrow boat with one long pole lay tethered and waiting.

Though not underground, the Hadean stream coiled through the trees, and night began to fill the hollows and put out the afterglow. Then a mist did rise, out of secret places in the banks; cold and fragrant. I stood in the boat and poled my way along. Often a fierce current drifted us downward with no labour on my side at all.

Blackness came, and black willows swept to the stream. I poled my way through mourning-veils. The pines seemed more animal than floral. Did they move about when I had passed, with huge soft steps? The mist encircled my thighs, my waist, but rose no higher. And now I myself was Charon.

Suppose this is not the way? Then I will find it at another hour.

Is there time? All time and none.

How wonderful it was, the sense of abandonment. All things gone but one focused goal. And that pristine and sure, whatever was or would be between. Liberty. Truth. To have two names, and neither, to be one being now, and there another, and perhaps no one, perhaps all. Here is the dark, and here am I, *of* the dark.

I followed the graceful stream.

* * *

It came at me suddenly, with an awesome shriek. I could not see what it was, but I raised the pole and swung the length of it between us. The merest collision resulted, but the pole shuddered and the boat pitched. Not quite letting go the pole, I fell to my knees.

From the blackness, two albino eyes, a beak of burning wire. Wings. It flung itself at me again.

Some nocturnal bird I had dismayed, or some guardian of transit.

The feathers of its black wings guttered and ignited as it threw itself at me again and again. Now an eye seared. Now the beak stabbed for my throat or sight. A talon scored my hand. It dashed itself against me, to take the blood, and I let go the pole and seized its neck like a snake's, and broke it.

I hurled the corpse into the stream, the night.

Horror and hell were all around. I had no strength. I had fallen down into the boat and lost the guiding pole, also my only weapon.

Fool, to abandon the reality and laws of the sensible world, to set out on this perilous course.

Now I lay in the boat as in the coffin, less optimistic than then, and only the current drew me on.

I cannot go to you armed then, in armour. When I approach with pride, with a book, a loaded pistol, these are of no avail.

The stream ran fast now, and straight. We plunged out under the open sky. The moon had not risen, yet there it was, down among the trees. The boat sidled to the shore, and rocked there, refusing to continue.

I was following the moon. A land moon, crossing the surface of the earth. She glimmered between the trees. I reasoned to begin with that this must be some man or woman, at last, and carrying a lantern.

The village, to which the moon led me, was deserted. It lay outside a palisade of trees, all up an incline, like fallen stones. As I came out into its grass-grown lanes, among the toppled chimneys, I saw for the first that what flitted along before me was the figure of a girl. She passed through the houses in a way that gave me to suppose she was not solid, not flesh.

Where the derelict village ended, the land opened to a sheet of black mirror, a tarn of water. The girl, a quarter of a mile away from me now, seemed to glide out on to it, bobbing there like a candle-flame, but when I too reached the brink, there was a massive causeway, with huge paving-blocks, well able to accommodate a carriage.

After the causeway and the tarn, appeared the structure I had seen at sunset.

It was a ruin, of course. In the darkness the impression was of solitary standing walls, perforated by round glassless spoke-framed windows, like colossal wheels, similar to those found in ancient churches. Higher than the highest, a tower broke the sky. It was out of all proportion to the landscape, or so it seemed, too tall, like a funnel spun of black night, yet it also was cleft at the top, blasted wide as if by the hand of God.

The glimmer of the ghost-girl went up the shore and in among the ruin like a moth attracted to warmth or light. There was light. I made it out as I drew closer.

In a wall against the tower, a featureless door had been cut, and the ground rose up to it in a flight of steps. Above this door a window like a spiderweb held a sonorous living glow.

The ghost, if she was, had disappeared. No carriage, and no horses, were in evidence. Only the lit window. The tower leaned and the wind of night sighed through its great axed cranium, the alleys of shattered corridors, the window-wheels, as through the fingers of the pines.

I climbed the sunken, uneven steps, and touched the door, which opened.

It was a priest's chamber, perhaps the ruin was indeed that of some religious building. The light came from a pale and leaping fire, and from candles in silver stanchions. There were a few pillars, with a soft, grey-velvet texture, a long table of darkest mahogany, pulled close to the fire, with some objects on it of glass that caught the flames and reflected them down into the wood. Three silver crucifixes of various heights stood on the sculpted mantelpiece above the hearth, and above these, hung a sword in black chains. This was all the room seemed to contain.

I shut the outer door, and advanced across bare flagstones. As I passed the table, a crystal apple on it turned to red amber, then to insubstantial pearl, as the flames brimmed and drained it.

In the farther wall there was an inner doorway, with a dark curtain thrust to one side. Beyond, through the echo-chamber of the great barrel-vault of tower, a sound was tenuously beginning. Was it music I heard, or only some deception, a whining in the coals of the fire, my own blood singing, silence itself?

No, the eerie sound came full upon me now, sweeping down the arteries of stone into the small mouth of the doorway.

High in the tower, Antonina played her piano, as in the rented house at Paradys. She played the carriage-ride, the savage headlong race across the plains of darkness, the rough track, and the race of the pines overhead – she played the slowness of the Hades stream, the languor of relentless willness-ness, obsession and dim night …

Close by, the ghost-girl clung to a pillar. The firelight came and went in her, as in the apple of glass. Did I recall her from some occult tampering in the house of Philippe, some séance? *Was* she a girl, or a crone? She looked familiar, and not so. She throbbed, the whole length of her, to the pulses of the piano. I said to her: "What are you doing here? Your time is over." And she faded to nothing. She was gone.

The piano crashed like thunder. It ascended and rushed down the scale, searching new peaks and abysses of cold brilliance, power and menace. It was not Antonina who played.

Presently the torrent stopped. I turned from the door and retreated to the far side of the hearth. It was a retreat, but not unstrategic. I had remembered a stance Philippe's mother had been wont to take, her back straight, her head slightly raised, her hands clasped together at her waist above the fall of her gown. I assumed it, and when I heard his step, on the stairway, on the flags of the room, did not turn to face him.

He came to the table, but it was between us. From the tail of my eye I saw him now. He was no longer dressed in white. The fire sprang, he dazzled and sank.

"An unexpected displeasure," he remarked. I heard the gentle clink of glass. From a decanter on the table he poured wine into a goblet – red wine, or white? "I would have thought," he said, "under such trying circumstances, you would have had a wish to go home."

"Your domicile is haunted," I said. "Perhaps I'm another ghost."

"There are no such things," he said. He raised the glass and drank.

I turned, and looked at him. He wore black, like a priest. As she had done. The wine was itself blacker than ink, a black brandy or some unknown distillation. Some while since we had been so close. Not since the duel, the day he killed me – but we had been closer then. His eyes bore upon mine like a weight I could not bear. I lowered my gaze. And he said, "But you lack papers, I believe, mademoiselle, and cannot cross back over the border."

"Who am I," I said, "do you think?"

"I don't think about it. Your identity is your own business."

"Your dog, von Aaron, will have given me a name."

"Von Aaron's deductions are usually faulty."

"And so you sloughed him. You would find that easy."

"But you have proved more difficult," he said. "What is it that you want?"

"My revenge on you," I said, "of course. Because you have made me suffer."

"That was your choice."

I raised my eyes and stared at him. I stared into his eyes which were her eyes, as, all along, her eyes had been his.

"You are abusing me as she did," I said. "You're telling me that if nothing is given me I must try to *take* nothing. That I must starve."

"Then take some drink by all means," he said. "You've a long journey before you."

He moved from the table to the hearth, as I moved from the hearth to the table. I reached out to the wine and discovered it was after all a blackish red, it had been reflecting his clothing and his mood merely. It had the taste of wormwood, however, when I drank it.

I smiled, and said, looking into the wine, "You have no husband to hide behind on this occasion. Or do you have some convenient *wife* stashed in an upper room? Is each assault to be different, or are all of them the same? A snake eating its own tail."

"Mademoiselle," he said, "I give you the freedom of all the night. I request only that you leave me this small part of it, my privacy."

"What will you do," I asked, "in your corner of the night? Lovingly dwell on the darkness?"

I put down my glass. Fire filled it, and sank from it. Blood filled and sank from my heart.

I moved around the table and stood quite near to him, though not quite near enough to touch. The flames burned, throwing their flimsy architectures to the roof, and dismantling them again.

"Let me," I said, "enrage and unnerve and trouble you. Let me speak the truth to you, Anthony, to your face for once. No, don't look away. If I have the courage to meet your eyes, at least salute my courage, however little you value or desire it. Are we not, all of us, on a field of battle? I betray myself, I am my own enemy. She gives me to you, in chains, like the sword. You see, I offer you nothing at all anymore, not a book, not a line of prose. You may think I have written this, but if I had or if I ever do, these are words drawn from air, magic, or a dream. Only think how strange it is, that I have formed a whole cathedral out of nothing, where for you the chance is only a pebble, a moment's acute annoyance. All the passionate song stemming from the same fount as your little indifference and dislike. It is you who have made the monster, where I invented beings with wings. Well, I love you. Nothing is changed. I have no more fame than ever I did, or I could offer you the bribe of making you immortal. You'd spurn it anyway, until it was too late to take. Then, perhaps. But who will remember me? And who will remember you?"

At the end of this recital, each of us lowered our eyes. The fire too lowered itself. The night was very still.

"Well," he said at last, "you have had your say."

"And you have kept your silence."

"Go home, mademoiselle," he said. "We are at variance."

"Put me out," I said. "I'll lie across the doorway."

"Oh, please," he said, "must we now have this?"

"You may step over me as you choose, or on me. I would prefer not the latter, but can't quarrel with it if you do."

"There are other measures I might take against you. You're very trouble-some."

"That is the nature of life. Risk and trouble. You may do as you want. And so shall I. To go away from you is, for me, to be annihilated. I've said before, command your own actions. You may not command mine."

He lifted his glass, as I thought for a second to drink, but instead he cast it across the room with tremendous force. It struck some obstacle, perhaps a pillar, and shattered into a glittering spray.

"This then is your notion of a revenge," he said.

"Yours was, perhaps, more conventional."

His hand flew upwards, as if to strike me, but he checked it. In turn, I caught his hand. It was so cold, what could I do but warm it a moment, before it should be snatched away.

"Where is the ring?" I said.

"You will never find that."

"I shall find it. A drop of blood on all this palette of pallors and shadows, in a tower of shadows. Perhaps in the wine?"

"Certainly, look."

"Not there, then."

I let go the cold hand, which withdrew itself.

His eyes, since we had drawn so much nearer, seemed lost in the fiery dark.

I said, "Have I made you hate me yet? That's better than uninterest. I'll give you something in exchange for the ruby scarab, shall I?" I put my hand to my breast and drew out that snub-nosed silver thing. He stared down at it. He did not ask me what it was, avoid or take it, and I did not say, See, even this failed. More lightly than he had thrown the glass, I cast the bullet into the dying hearth.

The fire was hurt, there. It turned a curious red. As I gazed at it, he walked away from me, towards the inner door with the curtain. His footsteps echoed up from the stones. The clash of the rings, when he drew the curtain over after him, repeated itself in the air, the way ripples do in water.

I listened to this noise for centuries.

After the fire had died, I continued to sit on the stones of the hearth. I felt a deathly peace, only that. When the sun rose I must go away. I must choose unreality, for reality, going by the name of the Unreal, would no longer har-bour me. But I was lost at last. Therefore, sit, and await the dawn.

But the night stayed a great time, it was fond of this place.

Having discarded my paper, I wrote with a piece of charcoal from the fire along the stone. All single lines. What I had said to him, and other things.

Also, once I wept. If there was any alteration in Anna's weeping from the raging grief of Andre, I did not notice it. I wondered if the stones of that priestly hall would hold my pain long after I had gone.

Then, dawn came. The spiderweb window changed to silver. Even down the chimney of the hearth the anaemic resin seeped. Suddenly, beneath the curtain of the inner door, there ran out a pool of blood.

I came to my feet. I stared at the revelation. Slowly as if afraid, I went towards the bloody light, stepped into it and stood half a minute, wading. Next, I put my hand on the curtain and drew it aside.

What had been a black funnel, the tower, was now the cavity of a burning rose.

High, high above, just before the top of the tower had broken, hung the wound of a mighty sword, a window petalled by glass ... magenta and maroon, crimson and carmine, blood, scarlet, madder and pomegranate – it *bled*, this glass, every petal, and as it fell down towards the east, the sunrise, it paled through every flushed nuance of roses. Tears of blood – I knew its name, had named it in the City when it formed inside my dreams. Beyond, a horizon of mountains, dim and fine as if drawn with a brush. The very land about was a mountain, which I had climbed unknowingly, within its mantle of pines and water. One only sees such things as mountains for what they are when they are far off.

My foot found the first step. I must approach the window. Through a gauze of crimson light, ascending – such a shaft it was, it too seemed made, the light, of glass. Birds of thin alabaster might have been set in it, or carven fish leaping. I moved upwards through the hollow core. It had a perfume, this colour, like the gardenia incense of some temple. And a sound, a low and sombre drone.

Trembling, the air, the light – I had reached a stone landing, and a gallery. The window seemed suspended, and it was possible, turning here, to touch the glass. Huge drops, they rained, some transparent, some opaque, some translucent – they passed me and went on below. I was dizzy now, the tears seemed to fall in actuality – I put my hand against the panes. But they were not wet. They were cool and dry. And under my very fingers, a creamy stone, not glass at all. I had found the gem from Antonina's marriage rings. Yes, it was true. Still in its oval setting of silver, lacking the band, pushed now into the glass, a single pane. Then I looked up, up the window. And saw there a ruby tear with, incised in it, a beetle with folded wings.

You could look a year and not see it. Or, staring only a second, see in a second. As with any mystery.

I stretched myself, all my height and more. If I had had Andre's stature, it would not have been so difficult. At my back the uncertain railing of the gallery, the drop below. Before me the blood-jewel of the scarab. My fingers sought it and my nails prised at the rim. Let it come out. It was mine. It shifted. It twisted, paused, and fell into my hand. Still in its metal band, it remained a ring. It burned my hand, so cold it was. I slipped it on my finger, which, though more slender than that same finger of Andre's, it seemed to have shrunk itself to encircle.

I turned and went along the gallery and in at a doorway.

The first room was very bare. The piano stood in it. The lamps had burned out, and one tall candle frilled with wax. There was a table with large old books spread over it, a rack of pens, a chessboard with only two or three figures standing or lying on its spaces. The red light of the mighty window had come in. It lit the lettering on the page of a single book: *Benedictus qui venit in nomine Domini.*

The second room, opening from the first, had light of its own, a round eastern window of plain glass. Here, morning was white.

As white effigies lay on the marble of their tombs, so he lay, on the bed. The pillows of it, the covers, were heaped about him like sands, or foam from the sea. He was stranded in the wake of these things, hair spilled, lifeless. His sleep resembled death, was that so curious?

I moved closer. It would be impossible to wake him. I need not be afraid of it. He might never wake again.

The sheet would seem to have been dragged off him by some external agent, leaving the left shoulder and the left arm bare, outflung. The left hand rested, palm uppermost, and open, as if it awaited some gift or some caress. A vulnerable hand. He slept without his shirt.

I stood above him now, and my shadow fell across his face. Without the open eyes, the face was like a mask. I leaned down and touched my lips to his cheekbone and his jaw – with some surprise I felt the rasp of new beard starting against my mouth. The orbs of the eyes moved under their white lids. These were smooth, as the lips were ... The reserved kiss did not wake him. No, nothing could. Nothing, nothing.

Like Psyche, who had searched for her love in hell, I leaned to his flesh. But the onus of the myth had been to dash aside unconsciousness. I was not Psyche, though he might be said to be Love.

He was Love, and he was Antonina. He and Antonina were one thing, as Anna was Andre. Vampires, shape-changers, incubus-succuba – such vacant names.

I drew all the sheet away, and gazed at him as he lay there. He slept on. What might I not do?

I put from me any clothing that impeded me, and slipped into the white bed with him as if into a bank of snow. My skin touched his skin. I fastened my lips to his. His mouth parted under mine. I drew the soul out of his mouth, and in his sleep, unwaking, he moved against me, as if we lay beneath the sea.

Refuse me now. No? You will not do it. This you will do, and this.

I lay over him, curved to his body. In sleep, his excitement had answered mine. We swam together now. So beautiful, my love, you are so beautiful. The strength of you, and all the pain and glamour of your body, your bones, your silver spine arching – now, now –

The white light was cloven, stayed, *Not yet*. As with the first kiss, my lips sought, closed, against his flesh.

Yet, I am she and she is you and you are myself. I hold you and am held. You are my slave, and I am yours. You destroy me, and are destroyed. I give myself and receive myself. We are one thing and all things. And nothing. We are nothing.

I felt and heard him catch his breath. I need not wait any more. I raised my head and cried aloud under the sword of death.

And the cloven light burned, but only like a fire.

As the interior of the coffin had borne her imprint, so the mattress had retained the shape of him. There was no other trace, save for two or three long and curling jet-black hairs.

The interim might not have been sleep. Some blank omission from awareness following the summit and the fall. What had occurred? Ah, was it only that? I left the bed, and hesitantly went about the room.

In the round casement, the landscape was framed, under a high sun. It was midday, perhaps.

There had been some failure. Something amiss, or mistakenly done. Did I remember what it was? I wound the black hairs about my finger, around the scarab ring. I was depressed and weary. I left the bedroom, crossed the chamber with the piano – quiescent in the noon dusk. The great window beyond was a symphony of crimson by day, nothing else or more – I descended the tower with a strange sense of permanence, or memory – not my own, but others. The ghosts lay thick as the shadowy sunlight on everything. In the hall, a woman was busy at the dead hearth. She was scrubbing with her rag, erasing the words I had written there during the night.

I stood and looked at her. What was she? Was she a creature of normal reality, or a phantasm, or had she crawled from some aperture between these states? Her rag made a husky noise. How dared she obliterate the ramblings of my heart's soul? An illiterate, she could not read them, she thought them only the marks of the soot.

"What are you doing?" I said. "Leave that at once."

To my gratification, she did stop immediately. She got up and observed me. She had a quiet, vegetable face.

"Where is he?" I said. "Do you belong to him?" For some reason, I found it hard to speak his name, any part of it. But she nodded now. She was some villager, from some village, a servant. "Well," I said, "where has he gone?"

She stared. He came and went as he pleased. How would she know.

I sighed. What did I want?

A dreadful lassitude, almost a revulsion, threatened me. I had possessed him and it was done. It was no more than a convention. There had been so much poignant drama, did it only end in this unoriginal deed of lust? The storm of orgasm was so soon over. What could one say after it but, Farewell, or, Again and *then* farewell. Or, for ever and ever, Amen, and God preserve all from that Amen. Passion is not self-begetting. It must burn up brighter and consume. It must always be in doubt, and in anguish, and perhaps even in agony – to this, carnal love was nothing. It would be better to die in the act. Such fireworks, and then to go out in the habitual dark behind the sordid roof-tops?

The woman, relieving herself of any duty to make conversation with me, had turned and was going out of the door. I followed her, naturally. She went down the steps, which looked peeled in daylight, and walked along the shore. How was the rest of the scenery by day? I could not have said. It was a place I passed through. The huge tarn of water gleamed, hard as a gem. My eyes were hurt by so much truth-discovering light. I shielded them, and was glad when she went in at another entry in one of the standing walls.

I found us then to be in a sort of kitchen, with long ovens and a wide hearth, fireless now. By the hearth sat a girl with a snow-blonde chrysanthemum of hair. She did not glance at me, she was taking from a wicker bag a baby, only a few days old, and next a leather bottle with a teat. She fed the child from this as he sat naked on her lap. His fine floss of hair was paler even than hers, and one of his eyes was lighter than the other. They had a look of someone I had known, both the girl and the infant. I realised it was a decided resemblance to Philippe.

The older woman now busied herself with lighting the hearth fire. That achieved, she took a broom, of the pastoral sort, a bunch of twigs tied together, and began to sweep the floor, up and down, back and forth, with an aimless determination.

I sat down facing the girl, and pushed back the red hair from my face and shoulders. Hers, cotton-white, straggled all about her.

"Is this child yours? When was he born?"

She glanced at the woman who swept, but that one only went on sweeping. The girl pursed her lips, readied herself, and spoke to me.

"Not mine. Another girl's. But he makes things happen, so I bring him away."

"Makes things happen – what do you mean by that?"

Her skin was lucent. Now she blushed.

"Well, he does."

The child turned then and stared at me. He could not be more than ten days old, less maybe, or a little more. But his odd eyes seemed to look upon me with knowledge and some sly amusement. I had known Philippe when not much older.

"Do you mean," I said softly, clandestinely, leaning forward to the girl and endeavouring to catch her eye, "that things move about when he's in the room – that, say, a candle will blow itself out, or some hanging thing will be swung to and fro?"

She nodded. "And the shuttle goes on the loom." She lowered her lashes. "The priest, he says it will stop as the child grows. It's not a demon, but the spirit is restless."

Behind us, the woman swept the floor, up and down, and round and round.

"But you've come here quite often," I said. "When *he* is here. The master of this ruin."

She smiled. She would not look at me now.

I got to my feet. "You must heat water and fetch it up to me," I said, "for the bath in the upper room. You understand me?"

The child pushed the leather bottle away. He crowed. Ah! Philippe cried, reborn between a peasant's thighs, you see, here I am again to mock and torment you.

But I turned and left the room quickly. I went back along the shore. Light pierced open-work windows like flights of arrows. Walls leaned as if about to come down. Birds were rising from trees on the farther bank; perhaps Scarabin rode there, on one of the black horses. Or were all the horses metamorphosed now to white?

I wondered if the girl would obey me, but when I had climbed up again through the tower, she presently came with two buckets and filled the porcelain bath with scalding water and with warm.

I made her remain in the chamber as I bathed. She was shy, and would not look at me, but she wandered about the room, more surely than I had done, now and then picking up some item, a brush, the razor from its bowl, an ivory pencil-case that lay under the window.

"You're familiar with these things," I said. She did not answer. "And with that bed, also. He's had you. Is that not so?" She darted one glance at me. It was true. Was it jealousy that burned through me? No, it was a pang of horror at the vulgarity of it, that I had only been that, too. A woman had by him, and he, a man I had had.

I dried myself, and put on again the costume of Paradys. There was not a stain on it, not a rent in its soft fabric. And I, stained like the church-glass of the unholy window, immutably, and rent by silver – I was damned because I had failed, had failed.

"Come here," I said to the girl. "Brush my hair now."

She brushed my hair, with long smooth strokes, more nicely than her fellow had swept the floor.

"There," I said. "We're friends."

I stood over her, some inches taller than she. I took her face in my hands and kissed her fresh mouth. He had kissed her, I kissed, deeply, and she leaned against me, letting me caress her, her flower-like skin, her warm breasts. As there had been Anna within me for Philippe, so Andre now sampled this girl on my behalf, for my sake, since Anthony had made love to her. She was like Philippe herself, as the child was. She and I, had by the same one, were, briefly, the same one. And I remembered the exaltation of my abandonment in the sexual climax of desire. Of course, it was nothing of any value at all.

When I let her go, I asked her name. Shivering, her lambent eyes on mine, she said she was called Oula. I wondered then why I had asked. What did her name matter to me?

There came a sharp clangour from below.

"The child!" she cried. And turning from me ran away, out of the rooms and down the tower again. I hurried at her heels. And going by the window of the tears of blood, thought, Passed and repassed and so past. So it becomes a thing of no consequence. I am used to it, now.

In the hall below, the woman had come back to work, with her broom, and had brought the child in the bag. His cobweb mane and anemone arms protruded from the wicker. Meanwhile, one of the three heavy silver crucifixes had been crashed from the mantel. Now another was rising, and wafted through the air, as if weightless. The woman watched it, stopped in her tracks but with no appearance of alarm. The girl Oula called out something in the dialect of the north, another language, which I did not know. The child gurgled and laughed.

Oula ran across the floor and whirled him up. She lifted him high and shook him a little. The miniscule face was vivid with evil glee. The second crucifix too clanged on to the stone floor.

I looked at the broom-woman and shouted: "Take him. Take him out. Do as you're told, you bitch."

She made a vague move towards the girl and the fiendish baby. Just then, the decanter rose from the table. It flung itself at me and instinctively I threw my hands before my face. With a stinging drizzle of lights, the glass smashed at my feet. The liquor spurted up, and I was splattered, all over the fine old gown, as if with blood.

I ran across and pushed my hand against the baby's laughing sneering face. "Yes, I remember the fight, and the cherries. Yes. Enough. Go away and forget. This isn't for you." And the face fell, enviously. Toothless gums tried to bite. "Give him to her." I indicated the woman to Oula as if they had never met. "He must be taken out."

But the child had abruptly lapsed into a sullen exhaustion. It was borne away and put back into its bag. The older woman, having propped her broom on one of the pillars, took the bag, and without a word, plodded to the door and down the steps.

Would she walk into the tarn and sink there, becoming some aquatic animal? No, she simply trod her route along the shore to the causeway. Oula and I, standing in homely fashion in the door, watched her out of sight.

Oula timidly put her hand on my waist. I removed it.

Together we replaced the crucifixes. If they were an iota from their stations it would be sure to be noticed. "Sweep up the glass." She swept it up and took the fragments away.

Drearily I stood before the hearth. What a barren place this was, when he was not in it.

I did not properly believe that Oula's habitat, village or otherwise, existed. She, or any other, evolved and retreated to some secondary plane, inaccessible to me. There was therefore nowhere I might escape to. When he returned, whatever should we do, he and I? With Antonina, when it had been Antonina and Andre, the progression was unavoidable, rushing away downhill, tumbling forward into the pit of delicious darkness. But this. Dear God, suppose it should become domestic?

But suppose too he did not return.

Terror fastened on me. I lay against the hearth in fear and misery. And was aware, through these monstrous concussions, that I was glad of them.

Just after sunset, I heard Oula laughing along the shore. I had been standing under the tower window, watching the light go out of it, to see if this happened in the way I had formerly described. Her laugh came like a flying thing, and flitted round me. Hearing it, I knew Anthony had come back, and was with her somewhere in the ruin.

My eager foreboding drew me across the pillared hall, to the doorway. Here I looked out and saw smoke still tapering from the chimney of the kitchen room.

The tarn was a bath of wine, the whole sky had become a red window, and made all the broken open wheel-windows red, the tower a black fire-iron against incorrigible space.

On the threshold of the kitchen, some colourless flowers lay scattered. Inside, it was an oil on canvas, though not from Philippe's quirky brush. Pale Oula was kindling two hanging lamps, with alabaster arms highlighted, while dark Scarabin stood by the hearth.

As I shut out the afterglow in the doorway, both looked at me and then away. They had formed a liaison against me. I was to be excluded.

There was a table of wooden planks near one wall, and two wooden benches. Here I sat, as if at the *Cockatrice* or the *Imago*. After a moment he took a place at the table across from me, without a word or further look. Oula brought an earthenware jug and set it down, with a glass for him.

"Bring a glass for me," I said.

She went at once to a cupboard and extracted another glass and gave it me.

He took up the jug and to my surprise, poured the drink firstly into my glass. Tonight the liquor was cloudily pale, an absinth that seared the mouth.

During, and after this, we sat in silence, and the girl prepared a meal, moving to and from the fire and the ovens and here and there. Scarabin drank steadily. His expression was lazy, but his face held tensely in against the bones. His eyes were fixed far off. They looked sightless, so densely black, giving no access, having no floor. The mouth was sulky and cruel. In the muddy lamplight, sometimes it seemed to me the face of a handsome man, sometimes of a beautiful woman.

When the food was ready Oula brought it to the table. White meat and bread, and a dish of cheese and apples.

"Sit down," he said to her then. The room quivered at his voice, as if a coin had been thrown into a well. When she only stood by him, he got hold of her and gently pulled her down at his side.

Then, as if she were some clever clockwork doll, he began to feed her. It seemed he ate nothing, only drank the absinth, but her he fed, with infinite persuasion, persistence, and care. The attention, or the food, brought the blood into her cheeks. Even her hair pinkened, appearing to blush a little.

Beyond the door, the dusk had drawn its curtain.

"Why do we eat, Oula?" he said. "Why drink? Could we not do without sustenance, don't you suppose so?" But she had now ceased herself to eat, or he to feed her. She lay against him, her head on his shoulder, sometimes play-ing with the buttons of his coat. Her hands were gracious for a servant girl's, and the nails clean and trimmed. "What is reality after all," he said. "Did we not invent all this, are we not God, any and all of us?" He spread his own ele-gant hand on the table. "I could pass my hand through the wood as if through water. Any man, any woman, could do it. No chains, no bindings. It's a world of chaos restrained solely by the human mind, which then, afraid of itself, steps back and says, see this colossal machine over which I have no power at all."

I said, "She won't understand you. And I already know it." But he ignored me.

Soon after, he stood and drew the girl up with him. He said to her tenderly. "Where now?" And she murmured her laughter. They went away.

The room, in which the fire still crackled, turned cold, solid, and deathly still.

Stars were in the sky above the tarn, I could see them through the doorway, huge stars that blazed too brightly.

I closed my eyes, and saw instead Philippe, a maddened child of eleven years, on the rocking-horse, riding faster and faster, with his head thrown back.

I had nothing to write with. The hag with the broom and rags had finished cleaning off the stones of the hall when I left her unsupervised. Write with my voice then, on air, or with my nails in the plank table. Or with fire, scour the kitchen out with arson.

Plucking three of my own long, curling hairs, I wove them together with the black hair I had found in the bed. (What colour had my hair been, before the "Martian" red of Paradys?) Then I burned the hair together.

Water was sadness, air a vision, earth was thought. But fire, fire was the will.

Since reality and the physical world were only chaos, illusorily subdued, I did not perhaps pass through night along the ground, or through ruined halls of stone. Ascending, what did I climb but the heights of meaning? Certainly the tower had grown taller. High up in it, I was on some rarefied and open summit, where the air was thin and chimed with ice. There were no dimensions, or they were different ones … No, they were the usual ones. A bedchamber lit by a few candles, a man and a woman embracing.

I walked about them, round them, once, twice. They did not (did they?) know I was there. Hungrily they annexed each other with their mouths.

I put my arms over hers, around him, and my hands on hers – and drew them down from his body. Standing at her back, I wrested her quietly from his grasp, and when I had her, putting my mouth to her ear, I whispered, "That is over. What are you doing here?"

She opened her eyes, and looked at me with a somnambulist's smile. Then, in the way of a peasant girl released from some temporary office, she bobbed me a silly little curtsey, and drifted at once across the room. The candlelight made lace, a bridal veil, over her hair. She vanished through the doorway, or only altogether.

He stood and looked at me, already in his shirt, a libertine's face of arousal, the eyes of dreaming death.

"It *is*," he said, "all one. You, or she, will do. Come here, then."

I went to him and said, as he took hold of me, "Not for this. Only I, or you, will do for this," and took hold of him as he had taken me.

The bed received my body like a cloud. How low the candles burned, the room seemed full of a darker sunset ... In the sunset of the cloud, his weight lay on me with the heat of fire. In the hell of ecstasy, the caverns below were flame, and the river molten. Down and down, fall down with me into the underworld of red forgetful night. I am the ferryman. Lethe is all lava. My mouth is at your throat as you press your face against the pillows and your hands clench upon me –

And rising and sinking in the billows of shadow, the light was cleaved to crimson, crimson through and through, a dye never to be washed out, though the wounds of a redeemer might wash away all sins and stains. Crimson, crimson, the caves, the river, flowers and fruit and crystal and blood. Crimson the benediction; the waves, crimson, that never ended and were never begun, and were never begun or ended.

And in the morning, he lay beside me still. He was not asleep; when I kissed his skin it was only faintly cold, all the coldness fading from it. There was no pulse in the wrists, no heartbeat in the architrave under the breast. The texture of his jaw was unaltered, today it would not require a razor – The long lids of the eyes, fast shut, harboured darknesses.

A few drops of blood had spilled on the sheet. Under the left wrist, the blood had left an odd mark, but try as I would, I could not make it seem to resemble or suggest anything.

I had not failed. Things were as they must be. Antonina with Andre. Anna with Anthony. First one, now the other, was lost. To say she or he was dead was a great simplification. The exquisite taste of his blood – did I even remember it? Had she remembered the taste of mine?

I stretched myself along his body, and held him a brief while, reluctant to leave go.

But the room itself, by barely perceptible little shifts of the light, by distilled mutterings of the wood and the bed-curtains, did not permit too long an indulgence. I might grieve if I wished – surely grief was in the order of these new emotions, euphoria and dread, a bacchanal needing no wine – but not here. I must run from here, as from any place in the future where this should elect to happen. Forests, hillsides, city avenues, such a wealth of them should see me in flight from this. What aisles of woods and masonry groves of rooms would shelter me.

As I descended the tower, I recalled my agitation in Paradys, not knowing what I must feel or be or do. I had changed in more than gender. Eventually, perhaps, all these huge sensations would be worn down, or cauterised, and then must come a final act –

But not yet.

I ran along the shore. My pain tore from me like a birth. It pinned me to the earth and crushed me against the sky.

Towards evening I went over the causeway, and down into the derelict deserted village. Which had come alive.

I was not amazed to see it, the grass-grown lanes where now people walked, and the broken windows coined with lights. A shepherd drove his little flock of sheep across the slope under the trees. In the square, where only leaves had blown before, tables were set out, barrels and bottles and platters of food. Women were bringing oil lamps. Three wiry old men crouched near an open fire, one tuning a slender fiddle, one warming a drum-skin just clear of where the spits were roasting rabbits. The third worried a cloth through the notches of his pipes. It was to be a village feast. And there, a stout man in a good coat, with Oula on his arm, and a young man with bulging arm-muscles, and some gossiping wives. A handfasting, was it? Oula and her rustic swain.

I paused on the edge of the ripening lamplight. There would always be helpers. Always to hand, slaves, victims, other characters in the play. One called them up like spirits, and, more reliably than spirits, they came at a need. This – well, it was straight from the etchings and aquatints of the City, the bucolic world as seen through the eyes of Paradys.

When I moved forward, the villagers looked askance at me, but not in an unreceptive way. The stout man, Oula's sire or uncle, came up to me, handing me a russet rose.

"For your hair, mademoiselle. Here you are, for the celebration. You're most welcome."

So I put the flower in my sash and sat at Oula's table.

The beer and the sour potent wine gushed into the beakers. They crammed their mouths with food, and danced madly when the fiddle, pipe and drum struck up a wild and scrambling tune.

All around, the sheer glare of fire on faces, and in the shadows young lovers running off to the fields beyond the lanes.

A tallow moon rose.

Oula danced with her beau, who, presumably, did not care she had been deflowered by the local landowner. The beefy arms swung her round and round. Beyond them, I saw a woman suckling a baby. She looked like no one that I knew, but the child was the child who moved things, and was perhaps possessed by Philippe. Oula dashed by in a dance of skirts.

"Will you honour me?" said the stout father.

I came to my feet. He took my hand and waist, and we danced. It was a paraphrase of the intimate dances of liberty, and rough.

"The one who touched you last," he said. "What has become of him?"

I looked up into the massive face, at its jowls which were hanging forward so earnestly, its uneasy eyes. Was it the face of the banker-baron, was it von Aaron in flighty disguise? He looked younger. He had no metallic lace at his cuffs, he smelled of garlic and tobacco.

"Become of whom?" I asked, as he bore me round in the prancing dance.

"Of *him*. Is it done? Has it taken place?"

"Possibly. If I take your meaning."

"Dear God," he said. He panted from the speed of the dance, and called a jolly greeting to Oula as she sped by. "We are all," he said, between his gasps, "in the mill-race of destiny."

"I don't – believe in destiny."

We plunged so fast now, both of us panted for breath.

"Believe in it. You will perceive it, for all the facts are now before you, or almost all the facts. He hates what he becomes, that is his pleasure, the hate. And to punish the cause, and to avenge it. With her, the same."

"Are you speaking of your daughter? Of a wayward son, perhaps."

"Dance, dance," he cried.

A sustained and ghastly sound shot like a spear over the dancing-floor.

Everything ended. The curvetting dancers turned to stones, and the tiny band stood with its instruments aloft and voiceless, eyes twinkling with terror in the firelight where the skeletons of rabbits lingered on the spits. The drops of the lamps blinked in the scores of stares like tears.

The stout young baron had let me go.

Fear came to me, with an electrifying tingle.

"What noise was that?" I said.

"A dog," he said, "a dog howling."

As I walked away from him, across the burnished square, they watched me go with curious pity, and relief, with distaste, in silence.

And beyond the village? There lay the mirror tarn, and there the causeway, gaping like a bridge of bones under the moon.

I glanced over my shoulder. There were no lights among the trees, where the feast had been, and the dancing.

As my feet met the earth, a strange vitality seemed to course up into me. The dew was down. I was afraid. Oh let me feel and caress the fear. Close as a lover it clutched me.

The night pulsed with fear, all the land was in terror, but where was fear's source?

Up among the forest trees, a pale glimmering. Had Oula run after me to be comforted? Or the ghost, that ghost of some predecessor of my own? How ethereal it was, that whiteness, yet it was neither quite human nor quite ghostly.

There, and there, threading in and out between the poles of the pine trees, there and there –

At once something leapt out, and another thing, two white bolts that flew down the incline, the distance and the dark, towards me.

Two white dogs.

I took my skirts up in my hand, and I ran. I ran towards the causeway, I screamed aloud as I did so. I had seen fear's source. It was two white hounds, lean and long, with jackals' pointing heads. And after them rode a figure on a white horse, clothed in white and cowled against the moon like a priestess –

Sanctuary – where was it? The ruin, the high altar of the crimson window and the white bed stained with crimson. Run, run, never look behind you.

I felt the heat of their desire upon me. I felt the teeth of the hounds rip the hem of my dress and their talons comb my flying hair.

The causeway slammed against my feet. On either side, the water like a precipice. And now, shining there, three white stretching ribbons of fire.

How fast do I run, now the Devil is after me? I am learning, but unknowingly, I have no time to tell. And she is a woman, the Devil, Princess of Darkness, clad in white. She is Antonina, hunting me – I have sold them both my soul.

I can make no noise, have no breath for it, but now I have reached the further bank. I fall against the stair to the tower door, then stumble up and rush on. I do not shut the door at my back. What good would that do?

Through the hall, the silver crucifixes staring down. I am on the inner stair. My heart is divided and beats twice at every blow. I cannot see the window, only a vertical pool of ink.

I am in the bedchamber. The bed, of course, is empty.

I hear my own breathing, like that of some dying thing. Which is apt enough.

And now I stand waiting, facing the doorway. The moon shines through the eastern window, striping the night, showing me all I will have to see. She is on the stair. She is coming towards me. She is Death.

(One day, or dark, I will slide the ruby scarab from my finger. In some graveyard, on some hill, I will find some other like myself, one who comprehends the real nature of reality. Shape-changer. Only then, and if, can I discard this horror and this appalling joy. A finish then. But not now. I am on the wheel with her. I am on the wheel with both of them and both of my selves. The snake devours its own tail. There is nothing domestic in this.)

The doorway slowly changed its shape. It glowed, and whiteness entered the chamber. In the room beyond, a dog shone like zinc, and beside it, another.

In the white cowl, the pale face, and the black eyes fixed on me.

Then she spoke.

"I am his sister. Perhaps that is obvious to you?"

In my terror I smiled. I dropped to my knees.

"I will give you my name," she said. "Before my marriage, it was Antonina Scarabin."

I kneeled at her feet. She came towards me, floating on her own whiteness. Andre struggled in turn towards her, deep within my flesh. She saw him in my gaze and bowed her head. She kissed my mouth, slowly and sweetly, and sank the steel of a dagger, warmer by far than her lips, into my raging heart.

She held me in her arms until I was dead, then gently closed my eyes.

MALICE IN SAFFRON

Le Livre safran

> Every Night and every Morn
> Some to Misery are Born.
> Every Morn and every Night
> Some are Born to sweet delight.
> Some are Born to sweet delight.
> Some are Born to Endless Night.
> *William Blake*

A young girl with pale yellow hair was walking between the wheat fields, her hands at her sides and her eyes cast down. It was very early in the morning, the sun had only just risen, discovering in the sky tall northern hills black with pines, and lower down some black goats in a field busily feeding.

As the girl walked, a man's voice shouted loudly to her. "Jehanine!" Jehanine hesitated, then halted. She looked over her shoulder and saw her step-father, Belnard, riding down the track on his shaggy donkey. At once she sensed not merely trouble, but danger. A brutal, coarse man, strong as a bear, he had beaten her frequently and often abused her in small ways. He was an important person in the area. He had received his own farm and lands for past service had pleased his lord, and Belnard had even ridden with this master, twenty years ago, crossading to the Holy Land, and returned not only with scars, but with certain riches. Having a fancy for Jehanine's mother, Belnard had wed her, though she already had a baby (Jehanine) at her breast. There-after the woman gave birth to several sons and daughters who were Belnard's own. Of these, the favourite was Pierre. Lucently handsome (and as it transpired gifted by God) Pierre had been the joy of them all. Over the years, Jehanine's mother grew sickly. Belnard's proper daughters were sluts, and his other sons swaggering drunken louts like their sire. Beautiful Pierre, in whom even the lord had taken some interest, was now seventeen and gone three months to the dream-like city in the south, to be apprenticed at the studio of a great artisan. He was to become a famous painter, and a prince would be his patron. Meanwhile:

"What are you at, eh, mooning along there?" said Belnard, riding up on his step-child.

"The goats are in the wheat," she said.

"Chase 'em out then," said he.

So Jehanine ran forward into the field, clapping her hands and calling, and scattering the goats away into the pasture beyond. Once there she had a mind not to go back to the path, but Belnard, anticipating this perhaps, had ridden through the wheat after her, and now approached her again under the pear trees.

"Do you miss your brother?" said Belnard, riding along beside Jehanine.

"Yes," said Jehanine.

"Yes. It seemed to me, you and he were always close. Too close maybe for brother and sister. Teach you some tricks, I expect, did he? And you him a thing or two."

Jehanine lowered her eyes and clenched her fists. She was now beginning to be afraid.

Belnard reached up and plucked a pear. But it was unripe and after a bite he spat and threw the rest away. This waste was part of his flaunt of ownership. He could do what he liked here.

"Now, on the other hand," said Belnard, "you and I are no proper kin at all. I'm not your dad. Christ knows what son-of-a-sow got you on her."

Jehanine picked up her skirts and began to run.

With a hearty laugh, not put out, Belnard kicked the donkey into a gallop. Presently he rode the animal straight into the fleeing girl and tumbled her under a tree. Swinging from the donkey's back, Belnard dropped down on her. She tried at first to fight him, but he said smiling, "Don't you raise your hand to me, my girl. Or I'll break your nose. Do you think I can? So, then. Lie still." And so Jehanine lay like a piece of wood. He pulled up her dress and forced her. "By bleeding Christ, a virgin still," he said. In another minute this was no longer the case. "Move," he grunted then, "move, you bitch." So Jehanine obediently moved. He soon finished, collapsing upon her. When he recovered he rose and left her in her blood on the ground. He glanced only once into her tawny eyes that looked now almost as white as her face. "Well not much to that," he said. "Perhaps you'll improve with use. Don't take all day there. There's milking to be done. And don't let any of my men catch you like that. Pull your skirts down, you trull."

Jehanine pulled the cloth down over her thighs and lay under the pear tree watching Belnard ride away. When he was out of sight beyond the orchard, she kneeled and vomited. Then she wept, but not for very long.

That evening, when Jehanine, with her younger sisters and the farm girls, served the men their supper, Belnard seemed to have forgotten what he had done in the orchard. Though it was of slight consequence to him, nevertheless now he had accomplished it, he might wish to repeat the venture. Virgins were somewhat scarce. Of course, too, the act had been a sin. Belnard might feel bound to make a confession and give the lord's priest some money. Jehanine, since all women were besmirched by the fall of the first woman, Eve, would be held largely to blame.

Jehanine's mother whined and complained during supper. Afterwards two of the brothers fought in the yard and returned with wounds. Much later, when the moon rose outside, the farm was full of snoring and sighs as the family and the house-slaves slept. Somewhere off over the hills, a dog, or perhaps a wolf, bayed at the moon. Jehanine lay awake on the edge of the mattress she shared with her sisters, and listened. She thought of Pierre, who had always been kind to her and who, on leaving, had made her a promise. "When I'm rich, I'll send for you. You shall keep my house for me. I'd trust none of the others. But you're clean, and clever. We'll have servants, and you can order them all. When I come home from decorating angels on to the walls of some church, or goddesses in a private supper-room for a prince, I'll lie down with my head in your lap and you can comb my hair and sing to me. I'll give you three silk dresses, Eastern silk from the Spice Lands." "You'll marry," Jehanine had murmured. "Marry? Not I. A girl or two, maybe. But you're the only one I'd want in my house." There had been nothing between them that was sexually familiar, but Jehanine had always been in love with her golden-haired brother. He was the only beautiful thing she had ever known, beyond the natural things, the weather, the country and its beasts, whose beauty harsh everyday use had inevitably spoiled for her.

When she had finished thinking of Pierre, Jehanine thought of her stepfather's rape, and of the fact that he might like to repeat it. Then she listened to the wolf, howling in its ecstasy of lonely freedom.

In the middle of the night, Jehanine got up and put on her clothes in silence. In equal silence, opening the clothes-chest, she took one of her sisters' mantles, for they were of good quality and so more durable than her own. Although she had never really considered the thing she now began to do, in some part of her mind she must have made a plan. She went about it quickly and quietly. She first spoke softly to the big house dogs that lay by the hearth. Then going into the stone larder, she took a slab of bread and another of cheese and wrapped them in a piece of linen. Then she took a jar of milk and drank it dry.

As she left the farm and stole across the dirty yard, by the well and the hen-house and the duck-pond, Jehanine felt neither regret nor anxiety.

She skirted the huts of the labourers with care, because their dogs did not altogether know her and might give an alarm. When she reached the track between the fields, the moon was going down. There was another long hour to sunrise, and no Belnard would be stirring much before.

The track ended and Jehanine came out upon a road, old as the hills and kept in repair by the lord. This was the way Pierre had come, though he had had a donkey to ride, and one of the farm men to accompany him.

Jehanine, however, did not feel a lack. She had known only the farm and the surrounding landscape all her eighteen years. Now she was heedlessly eager to be off, to discover the rest of the world which lay waiting. She turned south, for the road conveniently ran that way. She walked briskly, holding her small bundle of provisions, looking ahead.

By the time the dawn began, Jehanine was well down the valley, and above her, eastward, she saw the humped tower of the village church. The bell was not ringing, for the priest was a sluggard. Inside the church stood a golden crucifix with jewels on it, which the lord had had made with some of the wealth brought back from the Holy Land. In a niche a pale and melancholy Madonna exhorted women to do their duty. She wore a golden crown, also the lord's gift, because she had obviously done hers.

Belnard, too, had relics of the Crossade on show. A great Saracen spear was hung up in his bedchamber, its tasselled sling still dark with blood. Besides, there were some jewels, or so he and the brothers said. Belnard had once announced he would give each of his daughters a jewel on her wedding day. He had been drunk at the time. But he had also vowed to give Pierre something at his leavetaking. This might have been true.

Brighter than all jewels, the sun pierced through the sky.

Though men and women were out in the fields few saw Jehanine, or if they did, apparently reckoned her on some errand. Once past the cultivated lands of the lord, the road went down among the pine forests. An unfriendly place in winter, full of hungry wolves and starveling robbers – or so they said. Bears even sometimes loitered in the pines, not to mention creatures of the Devil. But winter was a way off, and surely the City nearer?

Among some fallow fields, Jehanine heard hoof-beats on the road behind her. She withdrew hastily to the side of the road, but there was nowhere to conceal herself. She was suddenly afraid her step-father might be after her, for it sounded like his donkey – only the lord's sons had horses. She crouched down.

Sure enough, the donkey came clumsily pelting along the road. On its back sat a heavy, hairy boy, not Belnard in fact, but one of the younger sons. He blundered past and reined up, hauling the animal round. He had seen his sister in the shallow ditch. The hood had slipped from her hair and the sun fired it like a pale torch.

"There you are, you cat," said Belnard's son, Jehanine's half-brother. "He said you'd be sure to go this way. When the sluts woke up and found you gone, he said to me, You take the ass and go and bring her back. She's got work to do. He told me something else, too," said Jehanine's half-brother, riding up to her. His shadow came between her and the sun. He slid down from the donkey abruptly, dropping, falling against her and rolling her over in the ditch. "If you did it with him, now you can do it with me."

Jehanine did not struggle. Her eyes went wide and blank. She said, "If you want. But not here."

"Here, here and now," he said, fumbling at her.

"No. The priest may come along."

Her half-brother considered. If the priest did come this way, or the lord's steward, which was also a possibility, Belnard's son would be fined, or pilloried, for they were bloodkin, he and she.

"Get up then, quick," he said. "Come there, where the trees are."

He dragged her over the fallow ground, but not so fast she could not stumble and pick up as she did so a spiky, hand-sized rock from the soil.

As soon as they reached the trees, he pushed her against one, and Jehanine struck him in the face, on the forehead, as hard as she was able. She only stunned him, but he poured with blood, and staggering aside, he fell. Then she ran round him, kicking and beating at him with the stone, now from one side, now another, until his howls and groans ceased and he lay still. The rough vengeance gave her satisfaction, but she was also frightened. Looking back down to the road, she saw no one was there. The donkey had wandered away into a patch of clover. Left to itself it would gladly feed all day, and perhaps be lost. Belnard would think his son had not found the runaway, but continued on to an inn to get drunk.

She was not sure she had not killed her half-brother, though he was breathing. Strangely, it seemed the other inner part of her mind had again been formulating plans, even as she beat him unconscious.

Though he was bigger than she, his clothes in their turn were rather too small for him, being cast-offs of the slender Pierre. She stuffed the loutish boots with leaves and pieces of her own shift, to make them fit, and with a strip of her shift she bound her breasts before she drew on his tunic and sleeveless surcoat. With the innocence of thoughtless knowledge, she also tucked a roll of the material inside his hose – now hers – at the appropriate juncture.

She left him naked under the trees and ran back down to the road. She could not ride, and besides did not dare to steal her step-father's donkey.

The boots, so much too large, would hurt her before the day was done. But the clothes gave an extra freedom of movement, and though she did not care for their odour, this too would help in disguising her.

She had now gone so far on her career she felt the rightness of it. She strode out, her heart was light.

An hour later she left the lord's estate's behind, and came down to the brink of the pines. She had never been so far before. This in itself would be her talisman.

The journey absorbed several days, and Jehanine kept no count of their number. Everything was so unusual to her, the area, her aloneness, the act of her flight itself. By the second day she was convinced that Belnard would not attempt to have her followed further, or that if he did so, she was now immune to his search. The weather was consistently fine, and even the nights, when she slept on the earth, were fraught only with owls.

She walked south, which was quite easy, though the first road vanished on the first day. Later on, there were other tracks, and other better roads. Sometimes she passed through a village, where she would beg for food. Generally they gave her something; the summer had been plentiful. They thought her a boy off to make his fortune. Though her clothes were travel-stained and not new, they were those of a wealthy peasant, and her chiselled features led women to believe she was the by-blow of some duke. Now and then too, Jehanine passed the estate of some other lord, and once a fortress craned above the woods. But she had no difficulties. The land changed again, rolling and swooping, clad in wild flowers and ruined towers, then vineyards.

Finally, she had the luck to fall in with a sort of caravan, the wagons of a tanner and an apothecary, and certain others, making for the City, which was now only one day away.

The apothecary seemed keen to take the boy (who gave his name when pressed as Jehan) into apprenticeship. It was conceivable too that the apothecary fancied Jehan. Nevertheless, the man's advances were mild, and he was inclined to feed his travelling companion, while allowing him to ride in the wagon among the vials and antique bottles, spilled powders and dried scorpions.

"The City is a wonderful place," said the apothecary, boastfully. "You've never been there before? Stick by me, I'll see you don't go wrong. Have another sausage."

In the middle of the afternoon, Jehanine put her head out of the wagon and saw a hilly plain below, awash as if in a sea-flood in the amber light. A river cut the plain in long burning loops.

"There is Paradys," said the apothecary even more boastfully, as if he had built it, pointing into the plain. Jehanine could see nothing but the landscape, then, gradually, she began to make something out. It was like a heavenly city, all hollow arches and disembodied towers, floating on a ring of walls half-way up the sky.

Then the apothecary began to fondle her leg, and Jehanine was forced to round on him with a gruff "Leave off."

"Now, young lad. This is the City. It has got great markets and avenues. We are building enormous churches to the glory of God. We're sophisticated here. Slough your peasant morals."

Jehanine considered her blistered feet. She said, lowering her eyes, "Well, maybe tonight, then."

Having said which, she remained silent as the apothecary's servant drove the wagon across the river, and along a winding road full of traffic, and uphill, and at last through the ring of City walls. Soon they were caught in a jam of carts and mules. Jehan-Jehanine absented herself from the wagon on the excuse of nature, and thus gave the apothecary the slip.

She was now in famed Paradys, without a coin or a scrap of food, clad in her brother's clothes and her sister's cloak, and the shape of a boy, knowing only the name of an artisan to whom Pierre had been assigned. But armed with this, and the meal the apothecary had given her, Jehanine looked about her boldly.

She knew nothing of Paradys, scarcely its title, which was almost as much as Paradys knew of itself.

She wandered a while, carelessly aware of everything, for everything was different from all she had ever known, and consequently she observed it through the lens of familiar concepts, and could by this means discount it. The people pushed and shoved at her like herds. The bulging, craning and leaning buildings, which frequently met overhead in the narrower thorough-fares, reminded her of defiles among the rocks, or overgrown woods. The air, rank or sweet with smells of cooking, perfume, humanity and filth, was only an outdoor variety of the air of farmhouse or hut. Since she had nothing worth stealing, no one attempted to rob her, or if they did, it was performed – and disappointed – without her knowledge. Climbing up the hills of the city, even as the sun began to slide down them, she started to catch glimpses high above her of a massive form, in fact a building that was in the process of birth. Brown walls and skeletal scaffolding towered into the sky. This was unlike anything from experience, and must be one of the churches the apothecary had mentioned when inducing her to sin. At length, remembering a conver-sation between Belnard and Pierre, Jehanine detained a pedlar, at this moment the only creature in sight.

"Is that the great Temple-Church they're making there?"

"Is so," said the pedlar, a tall dwarf she now noticed, the crown of whose head reached to her ribs. "The Temple of the Sacrifice of the Redeemer."

"Then," said Jehanine, "does Master Motius" – the name of the artisan – "live hereabouts?"

"Oh, are you going to be apprenticed to him, or to model for the class? You might buy a ribbon for your sweetheart. Here, look –"

Jehanine pushed the tray aside. She frowned.

"Tell me," she said, in a tone Belnard used with his slaves. "Or I'll tip your tray in the muck and black your eye for you."

"Vicious thing," said the dwarf, skipping back. He grinned. "It's one of the young men you're after. Who is it? I tell you, you won't find him here. He'll be in his lodging. Or in the tavern. I can guide you there, where all the students of Master Motius go drinking. Buy a ribbon for your sister."

"I haven't any money," said Jehanine. "Sod your ribbons."

The dwarf spat neatly on the cobbles between them.

"See that alley? They call that Satan's Way."

"Take it then and go to Hell," said Jehanine. Her male attire, freeing her tongue, pleased her. She went by the dwarf and continued up towards the gaping caverns of the part-built Church. However, to her annoyance, she realised the dwarf was creeping after her. There was nothing lying about suitable to throw. He must be ignored for the present.

Above the alley, circling the Church, a street of decent houses followed an old walled garden. A trough and an impressive well stood in the midst of the street, with steps, and carved figures holding up the well's cowled roof. Something again fluttered in Jehanine's memory. This was the very street where the artisan lived and had his studio.

Jehanine ran to the first house and spontaneously struck the door.

A small panel was opened. A pudgy face looked out.

"What do you mean by it?" a voice demanded. "Be off."

"Wait!" cried Jehanine, her own voice rising to a wail. "Is this the house of Master Motius?"

"It is not. Be off."

And the panel slapped shut.

From the tail of her eye, Jehanine was aware of the irksome dwarf still watching her. She walked across to the well, released the bucket and let it down into the water. As she was hauling it up, another house opened itself, this time by means of a small side-door, and out came a fat woman with an apron and keys at her belt, attended by a boy with a cudgel.

"Hey! What are you doing there?" bawled the woman.

Jehanine leant to the bucket and drank from it. The woman flumped over, the boy at her heels.

"As you see," said Jehanine. "Isn't God's water for all?"

"Indeed not. We pay taxes for it," said the woman. She eyed Jehanine, Jehan to her, with a round eye. "But the damage is done. Pray Heaven you've not let loose some disease in the water." The round eye was now a lascivious eye. Jehanine played her part. She smiled at the woman, and leaned on one of the carved figures of the well. "Lady," said Jehan, "I'm looking for my brother, one Pierre Belnard –"

"Ah!" cried the woman, and threw up her hands. "What a beauty he is. And a proper resemblance. You'll be one of those younger brothers. Not trouble at home?"

"I must find him at once."

"Not here," said the woman. "Master Motius has the 'Autumn Cough,' there was no work today. Though why he can't cure his cough, with all he knows – stop in a moment at the house. My old master's off on his business – always off on something. I'll feed you up, skinny boy. He'll never know."

But, "A drinking-shop …" suggested Jehanine impatiently.

"Well, your Pierre, the naughty one, that's true. Down across the river. The *Cockatrice* is where they drink, bad fellows, and get up to all sorts. You ought to be careful of yourself. Now why don't you come in –"

But Jehan-Jehanine was running on blistered fire-hot feet. Affronted, the woman turned to scold her cudgel-boy.

The dwarf had already vanished from the scene.

Darkness closed on Paradys. But the night City was no worse, no more impenetrable, than a night in the country. This too had its own strange sounds, its own pitfalls, and generally the City gave more light than the forests, hills and fields, which were lit only by fire-flies, fungus, stars and moon. The City moon was made of dull plate, but lower down other luminosities shone out. High round windows in various towers of a college where the students pored late over huge books and parchments, dim bars of light behind iron grills and panes of sheepskin. Sometimes, at the gates of a fine house, or along the river and its bridges, torches flashed on poles. But on the lower bank the hovels crowded to each other in sympathy, darkling, though here and there an occasional fire bloomed on stones in the street.

It had taken Jehanine a long while to find the *Cockatrice*. She had chosen wrong turnings, directions had not always been helpful. Twice, thrice, ladies of the alleys had spoken very ill of her, when the young man she was garmented as refused their services.

Above the inn door hung the sign of a cock with the head of a serpent. Superstitiously, Jehanine would not look straight at it. In the lord's village, only twenty years ago, a man, coming home drunk one night, had disturbed a real cockatrice in the wintry pastures. One glance, and he had petrified to stone. The place was still pointed out, and the stone which stood there, hunched over in terror, ivy growing thick on him.

Having gone under the sign into the doorway, Jehanine was prompted to cover herself, head to toe, with the cloak. Pierre had of course never seen or would ever have dreamed of her in male clothing. She sensed he might in some way be offended.

Just then, men emerged from the inn, arguing. They blustered past Jehanine, partly throwing her against the timbers. Their features and expressions had the inimical alien look which the girl was accustomed to seeing on the faces of fellow human beings. While, at the edge of the night, lit by the opened door, she beheld the tall dwarf lurking in an alley. It seemed he had stuck to her tenaciously through all her wanderings. Jehanine hastened into the *Cockatrice*.

It was a place whose light seemed only to contribute to its darkness. Beams crossed close overhead, below, a fire jerked and spits revolved. Opaque shadows had massed at tables, on benches, or passed her through the ochre gloom. The air too was thick with noise and smells. In such a place, where was her brother?

She began to wade slowly forward, looking cautiously aside into meaningless faces. Beakers clinked or were spilled. Men shouted. Serving girls screeched. Then she heard his laugh, so known, clear and musical and all embracing, across the formless din. On instinct, she swung towards it, almost collided with one of the servers – who cursed her flightily, thinking her after all a male – and got between the tables into an alcove.

Five or six young men sat there, indeterminate in the unlight light, oddly amalgamated by it to an entity. But in their midst, a holy face, sculpted and painted by sun-tan on ivory, and hair gilded by a master craftsman with costly gold-leaf mixed in honey.

"Pierre," said Jehanine.

It was not by way of an address to him, but a magic word, spoken as an amulet.

But hearing it from an unexpected quarter, her handsome brother turned, and stared at her blankly.

"What's this, eh, dear prince?" one of his companions, whose arm lay across Pierre's shoulders, inquired of him. "Fallen foul again of the sorority of the streets?"

Pierre smiled, and shook his head.

"I don't know her," he said.

Struck in the heart, Jehanine stood in silence. For the first time since her escape, she was at a loss. She could see it was true. He did not know her.

"Well, what does she want?" said another of the men. Nearest to her, he caught at her suddenly, squeezing her flank. "We're not ready for your single talent yet. Try us later."

All of them burst out laughing, and Pierre's beautiful laugh rose up again with the rest.

Jehanine shook off her hood in terror. She clutched her hands together at her throat. "Pierre – Pierre –"

"Oh, she's glue, this one."

"Go on, you hussy. Clear yourself off."

"Wait," said Pierre. Now his voice was low and shaken. He reached suddenly across all of them and caught down one of her hands. "*Is it you?*"

"Yes –"

"What in Christ's name – what are you doing here? Am I drunk and dreaming you?" Then, breaking through his guffawing and shoving friends, Pierre came out to her. Ignoring the fresh outcry, he began to drag her away with him, into some darker than dark corner. Vaguely she saw skeins of onions hanging from the roof about them, vaguely she heard all the clamour recede like a rumbling in the earth. "Why are you here, Jehanine? What's happened?"

All of her seemed to give way at once. She wanted only to weep, and that he would take her instantly to some private gentle spot, and comfort her. But something in him, something new and novel, something old and well-known, warned her not to lean on him or shed her tears.

"I couldn't stay," she said. "He raped me."

Pierre only gazed at her. His eyes were wide. What girl was he seeing here before him?

"Who?" he eventually said, without interest, only bewildered.

"Belnard."

"Do you say our father –"

"Your father. Yes. He raped me. And later another of them would have – but I –" something stopped the phrases of how she had used a sharp stone. "What could I do but –"

"Oh, Jehanine," Pierre interrupted her. "What are you saying? As if he'd do such a thing."

And now it was her turn to gaze in astonishment.

"Oh very well," said Pierre. He lowered his eyes, put out that such matters must be verbalised between them. "Perhaps you were unwise with some man. I won't judge you. But to say our father did that to you. That's disgusting."

She closed her eyes. *It is true*, she cried out at him, soundlessly, hitting and clawing at him with her heart as she stood there motionless, defeated once and for all. Ah Pierre. Fair hero, but a man. How could it have been otherwise?

"Well," he sighed. "I must get you back to the farm."

A word, despite everything, sprang from her mouth, like the frogs of witch-cursings in tales. "*No.*"

"Don't be tiresome, girl. I'll have to spend time on this. I'm not best pleased, I can tell you. I have other things to do."

"No – no – let me stay with you. I'll care for you and –"

"*Christ's teeth.* You fool, Jehanine. I lodge in a sty. You can't come there. You must go home."

And as they stood there, among the grove of onions in the dark, the smothered light burned in his eyes, on his hair, and suddenly touched also a spark under his throat. Having glimpsed it, she could not look away from it, though she had no understanding of what it might be – a fleck of mysterious fire, or the eye of some creature clinging inside his tunic.

"No," she murmured again, but her purpose was gone. She spoke now on a dying reflex. But he answered in anger: "Yes, by God. Home you'll go, you damned and stupid sow. Coming here and shaming me like this. Do I want you? Stupid fool, I'd rather hang myself than say you were my sister, flouncing here like some trollop."

And then she saw what the spark of fire, the eye, really was. It was a jewel, a perfect topaz set square into a small crucifix of gold. It was the fabled gem Belnard had promised his son at his leave-taking. A gift for the boy, an abuse for the girl. As with the rape, these harsh words, this betrayal, oh, what else?

Jehanine whispered, "Forgive me, Pierre. What shall I do?"

Her heart had now died, and she felt nothing at all as he brusquely told her. Nor did she listen. The dead have no necessity to heed or to obey.

"What's up with you? There now, ssh. Tell? I'll listen."

Jehanine struck out feebly, but the bending shadow dodged her blow. The shadow moved a space, and leaned philosophically on a wall. It sang: "Fero, fero, fero." Then: "I could have told you. Whatever you are, girl or boy, that sort – they use you up then cast you off. No use begging in this blighted world. Stones for bread, poison for milk, kicks and cuts and cuffs and curses for a kiss."

It was the dwarf, still following her. She supposed he would know about stones and curses. But that did not make her fond of him.

Directed by her brother to sit in a recess at the inn doorway, she had done so, the way a dog follows a command, meaningless in itself, by tone. She could not recall the direction. Other than herself, and a sleeping, toothless crone, the recess was vacant. Beyond, the drinkers came and drank and stayed or went. Pierre had also said he would return and fetch Jehanine, when he was done. Though she had not heard the words, she had assimilated the fury of his irritation.

After a short while, seeing it was ridiculous to remain, she got up again, left the crone and the *Cockatrice*, and wandered away into the City.

Somewhere – unlit houses, perhaps an open square under an arch – she sank by a wall and began to weep.

She did not know why, and assumed the sobbing would quickly cease, as in the past it always had. It did not. Then the dwarf approached.

"You see," said the dwarf now, "the world isn't God's, it's the Devil's. Satan is Lord. You make a grave mistake, calling out to the other one. Think how it hurts him, Prince Lucefiel, the Morning Star, to be passed over."

This blasphemy was gibberish. Jehanine wept. Rising, weeping, she pushed by the dwarf, and wandered into the open arch, and through, and on, and away.

The rain began much later. The moon had set, hardly a lamp burned anywhere. Only bells sounded across the lakes of the night. Then into these pastures and caves of the City, the rushing water crashed.

A curious thing happened. Though she had almost forgotten it, someone still followed the girl, and now she became aware that by following, he *led* – he *drove* her, as the shepherd and the goatherd drive their flocks and herds. She did not understand how this was, yet it had happened. Mindless in her grieving nullity, he had somehow sent her up and down the City, and now she had come through a labyrinth of alleys, in the rain, and so to a long high wall of stone. And then there was a gateway, and thick black doors studded by iron were shut fast in it.

Jehanine entered the gate for shelter and slipped down against the doors.

"Knock," said the dwarf, "and be answered."

"Why have you brought me here?" she said.

"I? Brought you?" He smiled. He had rain for teeth and eyes. "Fero, fero. *Knock.*"

She raised her fist and saw it dimly, like a wet white bone. She knocked on the door.

Presently a grill rustled above. Jehanine did not bother to raise her head or face. She bowed there in the rain. A woman's voice whispered to her. "Demoiselle, what do you want? Do you wish to come in?

Jehanine thought: It will be a brothel.

The voice spoke so softly.

"You are at the gate of the Nunnery of the Angel. I will open the door at once. Don't be afraid."

Jehanine had an urge to drag herself away. She looked about now to try to see the dwarf and to say, He knocked, not I. But the dwarf had disappeared again. Then the door was unlocked and one leaf of it swung inwards. A robed female shape, holding a pale lantern in a staring-pale gorget. A nun.

Jehanine got up slowly, the Bride of Christ helping her, and the lantern enfolded them both and drew them in. Another robed, veiled nun locked shut the gate. Beyond the light was darkness, and the faint adrift dagger of a bell-tower. The rain stopped suddenly.

"Come now," said the lantern-nun. "You're safe at last. Our Lord has brought you here."

Jehanine laughed. God was male, Jesus a man.

Black by night, the structure of the nunnery turned white by day.

Jehanine woke to such whiteness, and the scent of lemons, and the distant female notes of a chant. Such things haunted this place.

In a small wood oblong to the north of the gate lay the six cells available to guests and itinerants, and Jehanine in one of them. Her chamber gave on to a cloistered yard with a well, and two lemon trees. Through an arch in the cloistering was visible a paved inner court, dominated by the church door and the implication of the tower. From the height of this, the bell tongued out mutedly over and over, at its three-hourly intervals night and day, and the nun-bees droned, punctual as the bell, their ghostly songs to God.

As Jehanine had travelled to Paradys, she travelled through a light fever, through sleep and time, to an empty amazed awakening. As previously, she had not counted the days. But the same birds fluted, the same bells moaned, and there rose the same eerie singing.

A young nun stood at the foot of the pallet. Her face was flatly suspended in her gorget. Below, subserviently waited her body in the robe of the order, which was fulvous, the autumn-leaf colour of a yellow fox.

The nun asked Jehanine no pertinent questions. She merely said, "You are here. Do you remember where you are?"

Jehanine gazed in silence.

"The Nunnery of the Angel. You may stay or go, as you want."

"I've nowhere to go."

The nun said, "This is sometimes the case. We ask nothing from you, but you're strong and healthy, perhaps you will perform some small domestic services for the order, in return for sanctuary. Get up now. I'll take you to the refectory. You may wish to pray. I'll show you the chapel. Later the Mother may send for you."

Jehanine, ignorant and uneasy, said, "If I remain, must I be a nun?"

"That is your choice. The order never asks it."

While Jehanine garbed herself in the bounty of the nuns – a shift, linen stockings and garters, a plain gown and worn cloth shoes without heels, the nun stood by like an icon, with averted eyes. (The male clothes had vanished, no comment had been made on them.)

The nun conducted Jehanine from the yard and across the court, past the vault of the church door, into the refectory. The morning meal, served at seven o'clock after the office of Prima Hora, was done. But behind an angled wooden screen at one end of the long room, cup, spoon and platter had been laid on the table. Jehanine felt only an unspecified shame, then, seated, only a ravenous hunger, and devoured the warm porridge and black bread fiercely. While she ate, again the nun stood by, hands folded in her sleeves, her eyes concealed. Her forehead was smooth and her little chin firm and rounded. She could not be more than nineteen or twenty years. Yet she seemed old, set in her ways, perhaps wise.

The jug contained water. Jehanine was disappointed, for the priest at home had drunk beer and milk and wine.

"Are you concluded?" said the young-old nun. "You didn't thank God for the food." Jehanine, whose tragedies far overbore such a minor omission, still coloured and bit her lip. But the nun said, "It isn't needful. But come to the church now. I will show you where you may pray."

The food had made Jehanine drowsy again. She thought that in the church she might conceal herself and sleep once more. Or she might find some crevice in the garden that ran by the refectory and away into an orchard of plums.

Beyond the garden, on the south side of the church, there was a massive cloister, where a fountain was standing dry on the sere sunny grass, but they went quickly through a small door into shadows. Within, the occluded windows of the church were high and narrow, perhaps for purposes of defence. Yet eastwards lay the altar, with metal things burning on it, and above a strange unearthly mirror hung in the dark air. Jehanine had not seen coloured glass before, and it bemused her. She had the impression of movement and force where there was none, only hues glamoured by light – with a wild shaft hammered down out of them, for the sun was now directly behind.

The shaft fell unbroken into the quire, and caught in the slanted pillar of it, a white-robed figure seemed to levitate just above the floor.

Jehanine halted. The figure filled her with awe – she turned instinctively to the nun for guidance. But the nun did not pause, only went gliding on into the nave. Turning back then, Jehanine saw that as the shaft of sunlight shifted and faded, the white image was no longer there.

Nevertheless, on entering the quire, Jehanine stopped.

"What are you looking at?" said the nun. "That is the Great Light."

"What picture is that?" said Jehanine.

"It is the Angel," said the nun, and as she spoke, she made a genuflection towards the altar, bowing knee and head, but also touching her hands to her forehead and breast.

The Angel in the window flamed out of a sunburst of molten brass. His sunflower hair was rimmed by a halo like a coin of new gold, and in his white wings every feather was veined with fire. His gaze fixed downwards, and one foot rested on a shining globe. A sword of fire was in his hand. He was beautiful. It made her think of another ... of Pierre. Jehanine's eyes scorched with water. She turned from the Angel in anger and pain.

A small chapel stood north of the altar. Here the non-initiates might essay their orisons.

Jehanine knelt on the stone floor dutifully. She did not notice anything else.

For a long time she made pretence at humble prayer, then she glanced about and the guardian nun had left her.

Jehanine rose. She had forgotten the idea of sleep. Her skin held tight to her bones. She thought of what she had done and what had been done to her, and that here she was in a kind of prison or trap which she could never leave. She found as she thought of these things, that she looked back towards the High Altar, to see if the shaft of light would fall again out of the window, but the moments of the light were past.

Eyelets of saffron glass, merely, dappled the candlesticks and the cloth. Jehanine, seeing them, thought of the topaz crucifix Pierre had been given by Belnard her step-father.

Then, in a sudden flaming thoughtless and inexpressible trance, she fell to her knees again. She offered up, unconsidered and patternless, her agony. It was neither plea nor prayer, it was not an acceptance. She was no saint, certainly no pure virgin, crowned with the snow roses of martyrdom.

The bell, balanced far overhead, and sounding for the office of Tiers, startled her to her feet. She ran from the church like a guilty thing.

Days passed, leaves that fell, birds that took flight.

Jehanine served the Nunnery of the Angel. She swept its yards and scrubbed its flagstones alongside the girls, some younger than she, of the novitiate. The novices did not aspire to a habit but only wore plain gowns like her own, their hair bound up as hers was each in a bleached scarf. Sometimes they innocently giggled, told stories, or sang gentle sad songs as they worked. One was very pious. Her name was Osanne. She kept herself from the others, sweeping and scrubbing alone, muttering prayers, toiling until her knees were raw and her back stiff, for the glory of God.

Sometimes they would work in the garden among the late-blooming bushes, pruning and weeding, picking plums, berrying, and gathering herbs for drying and flower-heads for pressing. They rinsed linen and tawny robes and hung them to sweeten in the sun. They hauled water from the two garden wells, one of which was ancient and brackish, fit only to wash floors or sluice the privies.

Sometimes the novices went away into the House of the Novitiate, to learn from painted books, and left Jehanine alone. They spoke, even in daydreams, of their bridal, and the white Bride's robe embroidered with gold tears, the marriage once and for ever to their Lord, the Son of God. They were like any girls before their wedding. Half afraid, half lost in love-desire.

Jehanine could not adventure with them. She was not to be a nun. Besides, they were of good birth, these girls, surplus daughters sent away. Jehanine was a peasant, from the north outlands. She could not read, and knew no songs. They allowed her their company, for she was couth enough, and in her tall slender blondness there glittered some truth they sensed but would not know.

Jehanine feared and despised, admired and liked them. Osanne's fanatic hauteur seemed more natural, however, and if anything Jehanine was more comfortable in its presence.

Beyond the thick walls of the nunnery, the City lived and had its being, too. Occasionally some noise came from it, and often the huge stenches of the falling year. Within and without the wall, the weather was the same. Should she wish to re-enter the City, the world, Jehanine had only to say so. But, having done that, self-exiled, she could not return.

Had Pierre ever searched for her? At first it had seemed he might have done, and that he was afraid for her. But swiftly these hopes of love and renewal died. They were simply the pangs of healing. She knew quite soon that she was whole, though now scarred and crippled out of shape.

She was not unhappy. The chores of the nunnery were nothing to the labour of the Belnard farm. The food, though less various and not always so fresh, was sure. And in the house of women, the threat of male wickedness and strength could not intrude.

Now and then, playing their innocent ball or catcher's games in the south garden or the deserted hostel cloister, the novices elected Jehanine as the Boy. She must give judgement, she must threaten. Once or twice they kissed her. In much the same way one found an infrequent garland on the brow of the stone child, perhaps a boy, who held the bowl of the dry fountain.

The Mother had never, after all, sent for Jehanine. Perhaps such orphans were beneath her notice. Jehanine had briefly believed it was the white figure of this Mother, this queen of the hive, that she had glimpsed light-pierced under the window. But on certain days, the Mother would enter the refectory and herself read passages of scripture as the nuns silently ate. Around the edge of the screen, Jehanine saw her, another fox-robe, a proud full face, and plump hands. The vision of light, therefore, unsolved, remained Jehanine's property: all she had.

The garden and the trees turned brown.

Here I have been, then, thought Jehanine, by which she meant she had lived there thirty days or more, though she could not reckon them. A season was nearly gone.

She knew now by ear the call to all the offices, from Matines to the office of the evening star, Hesper, and to Complies which closed the day. She knew three ball games, and certain secular songs of the novices, though she did not sing them. She learned the uses of the herbs from the garden, and, by rote, paragraphs of herbal lore and myth, read from a book by an elderly lay-sister.

Who had she been once?

One twilight, she saw a white-robed woman walking before her down the roofed passage that ran between the church and the House of the Novitiate. At the opening of the passage the white robe blended out and was gone. Nobody was in the hostel cloister beyond. It was, then, a ghost. Jehanine knew fear, and disappointment.

In the hostel-cell where she still slept her few hours each night, she looked about. At a dying spray of vivid leaves in a cracked jar, a cross of wood on the wall and a pallet on the floor, a low straight chest which contained her cloak, and oddments of linen, and had on its top a comb and a small crock of water, in the shallows of which a fly had drowned. Such were her possessions, and two of them dead. She had never had anything much. A doll of her mother's when she was a child that the half-sisters broke, carved sticks and pebbles a boy called Pierre had given her, then retrieved.

The ghost was common to all who could see it. It might harm her but was not hers.

The bell rang for the office of Hesperus.

That night the Mother entered the refectory. She opened the Bible on its stand and read these words: "God so hated His Son, that He gave him to the world that the world might have him."

In a dream, Jehanine was seeing the City by night, and it was like a waste-land of rocks. Nothing moved, no lights showed. The moon hung low. Then in the east there seemed to be a bright star rising, which sent its rays across the roofs, and lit their edges. Brighter and brighter the star became, and then it opened like the petals of a flower, and things rushed out of it.

At first she thought they were insects, then birds, then men and women riding over the rooftops of Paradys. But on the church at home had been some rough-hewn gargoyles, and now she identified the galloping throng – they were demons, with the bodies of men, even sometimes with the breasts of women, but the horned heads of goats and snouts of lizards snapped and gri-maced from their long wild hair. Their bodies were the colour of the tired low moon, and glimmered in the same way. The mounts they rode were of all manners: huge black dogs, winged baskets and poles, or other creatures like themselves –

They were horrible, yet they laughed and called to each other, and filled the air with a robust foulness.

Jehanine, dreaming, had a terror they would see and catch her up, but it was another they took, who had been standing waiting not far off. He leaped to join them, and in a moment he went by Jehanine, mounted on a monstrous beast part pig part bat. He was Pierre, but he did not see her and he rode away with the jolly host of Hell.

"*Jhane!*" cried the dark. "Jhane!"

"Jhane. Wake, Jhane."

Jehanine opened her eyes and rose from sleep to fill them and her body.

Before her, dark on dark, a figure leaned. Jehanine was terrified, then stupefied. No monster, but haughty Osanne, who of all the novices had never before abbreviated Jehanine's name in this way.

"What do you want, dem'selle?"

"Don't call me that. I'm to be a holy sister. Say that. Say, *sister*."

"Sister."

"You trouble me," said Osanne. She sat back now, beside the pallet. She wore a cloak over her shift, but her hair was unbound and coiled all about her restlessly. "Were you dreaming? Stop it. Attend. I want you to tell me why it is you won't come into the shelter of this order? Stubbornness. Your low birth, your unlearning – such things don't matter. Do you love God?"

Jehanine was silent. Osanne breathed more quickly.

"Answer me, girl – *Do you love God?*"

"If I must," said Jehanine. How soft the night. Hell did not ride the roofs. The dream was dying.

"Sinner! Evil sinner. How can God live except by love? Every such word hammers in the nails afresh."

"Demoiselle – Sister Osanne – leave me alone."

"No. I must save your soul. I know it now. God has revealed it to me. Get up at once. Kneel by me here."

"Go away," said Jehanine.

"I'll make you if I must. Stupid girl. Do you want to burn in the Pit for all eternity?"

"What pit is that?"

"Fool. The Pit of raging Hell. The cauldron of live fire where Lucifer is king. The torture never-ending. Didn't you hear the lesson tonight that the Mother read at supper? God loved the world so well he sent his only Son, Jesus, the Christ, to be our saviour."

"But she said –" began Jehanine. She stopped saying it.

Osanne, unheeding, curved forward like a snake, and gripped her, pulling her up from under the cover. Suddenly Osanne had seized her prey. She wound her arms about Jehanine and buried her mouth, hot as the fire of which she warbled, in Jehanine's neck.

"Jhane, Jhane, pray with me now. I'll save you. Dear sister in Christ. You have the marks of goodness on you. So fair, child-like, yet rough like a boy – put your arms about me, Jhane."

Jehanine did so. Osanne fell upon her, and as they floundered on the pallet, enormous waves began to pour upon Jehanine, of alarm and physical pleasure and horror. The darkness of the room, half hiding everything, seemed to make all things foreign, removed and possible. Osanne squirmed and writhed. She lay beneath Jehanine now. She wrapped Jehanine with all her limbs (a demon, mounted), and abruptly let out a hoarse mad cry, a moan, a grunt, and fell back.

"What have you done?" she gasped. She pushed Jehanine away. "You're evil. Dirty and foul. Possessed. A monster – one of the Devil's minions – oh let me go –"

She crawled towards the open air, sobbing and gulping. The room seemed icy cold. How comfortless it would be in winter.

When Osanne, her sounds enfeebled and muted by dread of discovery, had gone, Jehanine dressed herself. She trembled violently as she had not done at the rape of her step-father.

Leaving the cell barefoot, she crossed through the yards into the south garden, and passed over it in the moonless nothing of the night. A small bake-house, now seldom used, stood against the outer wall, and here a tree spread up, already leafless. Jehanine climbed it without effort, pulled herself atop the wall, and looked out not in dream, for the first time in those years of days, on Paradys.

Where the nunnery was situated she had never properly known. Now she saw the locationless gullies of alleys, hills of masonry, no lights, and the stars' cooled clinker. Then she sprang from the wall, into an abyss two-and-a-half times her own height.

She fell into harsh and lumpy softness – a pile of sacks, filled perhaps some by meal, and some by goose-feathers, for elements of such dust and fluff puffed out at her impact.

"Well, you've made me wait," said a voice. "That's the only sly way, you see, that tree, then down. But I'd thought you would be sooner tired of them. Here. See what your friend has brought you."

Jehanine, lying on the sacks, looked up through muffled lantern light, to a grinning face and two hands dangling a tunic, hose, a boot of sheer leather. It was a dream, like the other, and since dreams make their own laws, Jehanine got to her feet and grabbed the dwarf.

"Hey, hey. You can even go back. We'll see to it, we will. But somewhere else first. Put these on. You can't travel as a maiden. I'll look the other way."

Jehanine hit the dwarf across the face. This time, the blow met flesh and spun him. He dropped the samples of male attire, nearly the lantern. Jehanine bent to the clothes, found the complete set, and picked them up.

They were not her half-brother's rubbish. These seemed unworn, garments of a lord of the alleys, gaudy, elegant – what a man might thieve who was clever at thieving.

It was a dream.

"Go over there," said Jehanine. She started to pull up the drawers and hose under her skirt even as the dwarf turned away. She thrust and hauled on the robber's clothes; they were a panoply. She made a bundle of her own, like a discarded skin, and left it rolled into the sacks. In a dream, who would discover it?

"Good! Come then, this way," said the dwarf, skipping ahead.

His lantern suddenly blared out. There was no longer any need of caution.

Jehanine had forgotten the freedom of such clothing, how she had been a boy, a young man, but now her body itself remembered. She laughed suddenly, and the dwarf said, "This way, Jehan. Praise the Prince it's a fine night." They slipped between the alleys, down the long worm-burrows. They passed by loops of the river seen beyond black and rotting walls. Fires burned uncannily between some of the hovels, and now and then a weird-lit face peered at them. Up a cobbled lane two torches volleyed before a house with noisy windows. It was an inn with a swinging sign that showed a ghostly figure with wings – an apparition. The dwarf went through a side-entry and up a spine-broken stair, Jehanine following him. In the corridor, where her head, if not his, nearly brushed the sagging beams, he rapped on a door. It was opened from inside. They stepped into the hollow of a room, ringed by faces. Fat candles were blinking on jugs and blades.

"Here's Fero."

"Welcome to the *Imago*," said the dwarf. Then, to the room at large, "You see, my mates, I brought you him, as I said I'd do. What do you think?"

Jehanine stood stock still. Was this another betrayal? Even in dreams, such might occur. She said, speaking low but loudly, "Who cares what they think. Who does the choosing here?"

There were men in the room and boys. Each was a thief, you could tell at a glance. In every belt at least one knife, in every mask the eyes of wolverines; they wore the dress and ornaments of men who clawed and snatched above their station.

The dream-dwarf, perverse and mad, had brought her to join them. Why should he? Well, he must have sniffed her criminal air.

"*We* choose," said a man from the ring. "But you look agile and leery enough. The dwarf's generally right. He found me, didn't he?"

"Then," said another, "we want the gift, the buying-in."

"Do you know what he means, new lad?"

"I'll tell him what I mean. I mean something precious from him to us. A Judas kiss. A game. Proof. So what's he going to offer up?"

"His own self's enough," replied one.

The dwarf, Fero, idled, sidled from Jehanine's side. Jehanine, Jehan, she-he stood alone, the door at her back, the rowdy inner inn and the black tunnels of night City beyond. She said, "You can have a gift." She felt herself whiten to a skull, they saw it and attended. (But it was a dream.) "I've kindred in the City, one who wronged me. I'll give you him."

"What use is that? Is he wealthy?"

"Not much."

One or two swore. A man came close and put his hand directly on her groin. She moved aside before he could tell he had touched only a cunning bulge of cloth – and bringing up her fist she mashed her knuckles into the base of his nose. As he left her, blinded by tears and roaring, the roomful laughed, commending her. She had seen her half-brothers and her step-father fight. She had learned their tricks, it seemed.

As the blinded robber crouched on the floor, the tangle of his body reminded her of Osanne. Jehanine kicked him in the back, and he fell down.

She said, "What I offer is my brother. I hate him. I can manage things so you'll have him alone. He drinks late at the *Cockatrice*, and perhaps he's there now. His clothes are good, strip him and leave him naked. He's handsome. Do what you like. From his neck hangs a gold crucifix. There's a gem in it."

Her head whirled. She closed her eyes.

Someone caught her by the shoulders, and a cup bumped against her lip. She drank bitter wine.

"What is it, you boy, this vengeance?"

It was the man who had spoken first, and who was also the dwarf's protégé. He apparently liked the look of Jehan and might protect him, so *her*. She pushed his arm off.

"My vengeance is your buying-in wanted gift. What more?"

Because it was a dream, she knew that her brother, beautiful Pierre, would be at the other inn. She knew that if she led them there, they would find him.

The dwarf sat on a table, drinking; he showed no inclination to make up the party, barely any interest, but six or seven of the fellowship were nudging at her now. Together they went down the twisted stair, with a clatter, and out. Jehanine did not know the way back to the *Cockatrice*, they did. They walked in a bunch, bravos, swaggering, not afraid. This was their holding, this trample of middens and slips along the river bank, these rat-holes. Sometimes they were challenged, from a wall-top or hovel's depths, pass-

words were exchanged, whistles or dog-barks, and once, two of the men made
water in a well, to pay out an old score. Then some invisible border was crossed.
The formation of the band altered. They were more wary, and walked two by
two or three, knives to hand.

"No knife of your own?" Jehan's champion put his free hand on her
shoulder. "This brother – did he sour you for your birthright, maybe?" he
asked, continuing the earlier dialogue. "My whoresons brothers did that on
me."

Abruptly the inn of the *Cockatrice* appeared, surprising Jehanine with
recognition.

"Wait here. I'll go to see."

"No jokes," said one, but that was all. She might have known them all for
years, grown with them from desperate infancy like flowers on the dunghills
of Paradys.

She went towards the serpent-cock, boy-walking as her brother's ungainly
boots had taught her to. She spat, under the inn-sign. The inn was hardly awake,
flickering with dying candles. All the drinkers seemed gone but for a sleeper at
the hearth, and a man at his work with one of the wenches on a table.

But it was a dream, and so Pierre must remain. Where had he sat before,
that night she came to entreat him? She could not be certain of the place.

Two men came down a stair. Brushing through the strings of onions, they
yawned and grumbled. They had been with a girl, but she had turned them
out before cockcrow. Old Motius would be aggrieved at their condition this
morning. But old Motius was an intellectual dolt who conducted esoteric rituals, but thought mice ate the unground paint his pupils had stolen and sold.
Motius was in love with Pierre. Oh, yes he was. One look from the lucent
eyes, and the old fellow would probably pay for their harlots out of his own
purse.

As Pierre came by her, Jehanine took his sleeve between her fingers.

He turned, gazed at her. His handsomeness, not spoiled by the debauch,
turned her heart over. Seeing her, he seemed to see a spectre.

He said nothing. His companion said, in wonder, "Your living *shade*,
Pierre."

Jehanine said to Pierre, "You must come with me."

The other student said, "*Oh* no. Come on, Pierre. This is some rogue."

Jehanine stepped in their path. She shoved the student away from her
brother. Being tipsy and fatigued, nor having either the strength of her hard
life, he stumbled back and fell into the hearth, banging his head, landing
among the bones and ashes. He lay there stunned, and presently threw up
there, which caused discontent in several dark quarters of the inn.

While that went on, Jehanine drew her brother after her, staring in his eyes, beckoning to him but no longer touching. He followed, he did not seem to know why.

As they went out through the door, he said. "Who are you?"

"Your sister," said Jehanine. But not aloud.

She led him almost listlessly to the alley where the *Imago* thieves waited. She pulled him by a leash of air. Then, in the alley, she took her brother's hand and drew him forward.

"See," she said to the thieves. A light flared and went out. Three of them leapt at him and flung a sack over his head, shoulders and arms. Pierre struggled. They beat him and he fell and was scrambled away with. They dived and tore a route into a copse of gutted hovels, where ratlets swarmed from their advance.

She stood by, she watched, lamped in the glow of a far-off lightcast – some brothel's beacon – as they removed the garments from Pierre's body, the dyed leather belt and fashionable shoes. At his throat, the topaz glared. They were leaving it till last. Pierre lay moaning, his head still furled in the sack.

"Now what?" said one.

They crowded grinning, and slowly unravelled the cloth from their captive's face.

"Your kin, decidedly." They lifted him over on to his belly. "Do you want him?"

"Incest," said Jehan. Jehan smiled. Then walked off and leaned on a post, not watching finally what was done to Pierre Belnard, turn by turn, by the gang.

But Jehanine heard Pierre scream more than once, a hoarse masculine shriek. She had not cried out at her own rape. Nor had she been so appreciated, for his abusers spoke love-words to her brother.

At length, there was silence, but for the heartbeat of the City, a strange noise Jehanine had begun to hear, compounded of every beating heart that inhabited Paradys. Uncovering her eyes, she noticed that the beacon light had grown in magnitude. Next a cockerel crew deep in the alleyways. Then one by one the bells sounded across the river, closer at hand, the tongue of Prima Hora, dawn.

Jehan's protector, whose name she had picked out as Conrad, shook her shoulder now. He sweated, and his odour was ripe. She moved away from him. "You're proved," he said. "You're one of us. Sin for damnable sin." The others mumbled. "Now do it to him, too."

"No," said Jehanine.

She walked towards the heap of flesh that was her brother. He lay on his side now, senseless perhaps, breathing through his open mouth. He was naked, covered by blood and filth. She leaned down and drew up his head a little by the soaked silk of hair. The dawn was spilling on the world. His eyes spasmed open. He looked full at her, knowing her, if not who she was. It was a look so terrible, so agonised and ruined, so utterly devoid of any hope for help or pity, that it reminded her of the face of the crucified Christ, and she shuddered at it.

"It never happened," she said to Pierre softly. "Such a disgusting thing." Then she said to the others, "I don't want him. I'll have something else." She ripped the crucifix from his throat, and let his face fall back into the dirt.

The gang of robbers eyed her in the revelation of the light.

One indicated Pierre. "Better kill him. Then scatter." To Jehanine he added, "You give that here."

"It's mine," said Jehan.

Turning, Jehan bounded out and up from the wreckage. A running male figure, sprinting westward from the sunrise, towards the note of a bell earlier identified as that of the Angel.

Some of them dashed after Jehanine.

It was a dream: she lost them easily.

It was a dream, but in her hand she held the topaz cross.

Well then, waken now. But waking was not to be had.

She saw the nunnery ahead of her, rising from a tide of flotsam streets. The dwellings were of better quality here, and the river, a road of crystal cut by a ship's mast, was not far away – none of these things had she known before.

She came below the wall where the old bakery was, and saw the tops of the tree she had climbed, two and a half times her height above her. The sacks were gone, but tucked against the stone her clothes lay in a bundle almost as she left them. And down the wall itself, from a bough of the trees, hung a hempen rope. The dwarf had returned again to aid her. For, after all, it was not a dream.

She tied her female clothes to her body, and seizing the rope, climbed up the wall. In the tree, she undid and coiled the rope and took it down with her.

She changed her garments amid the bushes under the tree, in the wetness of the dew, for the nuns would be coming from the church to breakfast, and in the refectory some of the aged lay-sisters would be making the porridge.

As she went however to her cell, accessories bunched in her skirts and excuses ready, Jehanine met no one.

Into the chest she laid all her new possessions. The rope, the male attire, a knife Conrad had awarded her during their trek to the *Cockatrice*. Lastly, she laid the topaz cross upon her pallet. The thong had been broken and lost. She would search out another cord, then she might wear it, under her dress.

Paler than the dawn, the Eastern topaz shone for her. From desert lands by a sea of salt, under the mountains where God had walked, and from whose stones He had carved his devastating laws, from the tombs of prophets and messiahs, from the dazzling shrines of the Infidel, this jewel had come.

She saw again her brother's appalling face.

She put the crucifix away into the chest.

Sister Marie-Lis paused in an arch of the south cloister, as Jehanine watched her. Presently, her hands folded in her sleeves, the young nun floated out on to the plot of grass. The dry fountain with the wild-haired stone child holding its bowl had been garlanded again. The child had a kind of crown of thorns of twisted leafless creeper. Sister Marie-Lis seemed not to pay attention to these things. She came to the opposite arm of the cloister, where the northern girl and three of the novices were sweeping.

"Come here, Jhane."

Jehanine approached. Jehanine's hair was confined in its scarf from which tendrils escaped like rays of winter sun. Otherwise she was decorous, always excepting her looks.

The young nun eyed her, then called the novices.

"Where is the novice Osanne?"

The girls looked about.

"But she's here –"

"She came out with us. She had no breakfast. She sets herself penances."

"The Mother says Osanne is arrogant in her humility –"

"Hush," said Sister Marie-Lis. "It was the duty of Osanne this morning to attend the infirmary."

"Well, she'd be pleased to do it." The infirmary contained sick, senile nuns and vats for boiling soiled linen.

Sister Marie-Lis said, "Our Lord himself had compassion on the sick. On all who call to him."

Jehanine raised her eyes. She listened, and heard Sister Marie-Lis saying:

"Did he not make the world against the will of his mighty father? Did he not risk all and forfeit all that mankind might live? And as he fell, his torch kindled the moon and stars, and the roots of mountains."

Then one of the novices exclaimed, "Why, there is Osanne. She's on the flags on her knees, scrubbing and *suffering*."

Along the length of the cloister, over the parti-stripes of shadow and sun, the mystic figure of Osanne rocked with its rags like a swaying serpent.

"Osanne," cried the young nun sternly, "leave that work and go at once to the infirmary."

Osanne seemed not to hear. Sister Marie-Lis took a step, smooth as if walking on water, towards the kneeling shape. And in that moment Osanne rose. Without a look or word, she went away, passing through the elbow of the cloister, and out of it into the garden. Her dress flashed very white as she vanished.

"That wasn't Osanne, sister!" said one of the novices. "And see – the flags aren't even wet –"

"Hush," said the young nun once again. She found a hand in her sleeves and touched it to her forehead and breast.

Jehanine felt a desire to follow Osanne as Jehan. Or she might bring in one of the thieves, Conrad possibly, and give Osanne to him as she had given – that other –

A dreadful pain tore through Jehanine, unseaming her. She sank suddenly to the ground and lay still. When the novices squeaked and came running, peering into her face, Jehanine covered her eyes with her hands. The young nun had gone away. Then the bell rang: Tiers. The novices fluttered. They must go to church at Tiers, and what of Jhane?

Jehanine got up slowly. What had happened to her was nothing, she was at her monthly bleeding, it was only that.

As the novices ran away, she realised she would not be able to return among the robbers for a few days, for at these times they might scent her, like a bitch, and so learn her true sex.

As for Pierre, they would have killed him, by what they had done, or afterwards with their knives.

She must think of him as dead, and of herself as his murderer. That was all it amounted to.

Going over to Osanne's discarded pail and rags, Jehanine detected a curious but delicious fragrance. It fled in a moment. Kneeling down, she began to wash the stones carefully.

In the succeeding days, Osanne was spied at her duties and devotions continuously, but not consistently. It appeared she must be sick, or that the passion of her faith drove her often to lonely prayer – for in the church they saw her most of all. But on their hurrying in she went away, was gone. She spoke to no one. They said the Mother had sent for Osanne, but it seemed Osanne did not attend the Mother.

"See, *look*. There she goes, she," said one of the novices to Jehanine, as they passed together along the roofed passage between the church's north wall and the House of the Novitiate. The weather was turning chilly, but they carried between them a cask of candle stubs, due to be melted down for new, and this was heavy, heating work. The figure of Osanne flitting before them gave an excuse to hesitate and lower the cask. "Look how white her skirt is, and her scarf. She must bleach them over and over –" the process of bleaching, which intimately involved mules' urine, was disliked; doubtless Osanne would revel in it.

"Osanne!" cried the novice. "Let's run and catch her."

They ran, but did not catch. Beyond the passageway, the hostel court was empty, and the churchyard beyond empty also.

They returned for the cask of candles, and the novice started to talk of her marriage to Christ.

Soon after the bell of Matines, Jehanine dreamed the dwarf came into her cell. He carried a stone bowl on his shoulder, the contents of which – fire – he tipped on to the floor.

"Fero, fero," said he. "Why do you make me wait about under the damned wall?" said he. "Get up and come to the Inn of the Apparition. You know the way. Or you can find it."

Jehanine opened her eyes and the fire and the dwarf were gone. Her female bleeding had ended, and getting up she opened the chest and looked in at the items there, the male clothes and the rope, and the topaz cross.

Soon a long-haired boy came out of the cell and took his quiet stealth across the courts. The nuns were at their disembodied chanting in the church, but in the garden a nightingale, disturbed, whirred mournfully that the summer had died. Here and there, the garden had begun to smell oddly. The stink of the midden had grown less, but the moulder of fallen leaves, where visiting cats had relieved themselves, seemed sharpened by the cold night. The elder well smelled bad, and might require cleansing. The stealthy boy went on, found his tree, climbed it and roped it, and spent himself into the dark City. The cares of a nunnery were for a while no longer his.

The *Imago*, which owed its Latin name to some obscure story entailing the Roman troops once quartered on this bank of the river (when Paradys was but a hedge of huts the other), had not changed: it roared and thumped, and scaling the stair to the upper room, Jehan had slight need of caution.

She did not knock. She flung the door wide. There they were, staring astonished at her. The dwarf she could not see, but Conrad was the first to his feet cursing her. Others lunged forward, but halted. She they thought a he had come back to them. What plot was in it?

"Thief," said the fat man.

"Bloody tricky swine," said the man with the scar down his long nose.

Jehan shrugged elaborately, in the way of young men.

"Did you bring it?" cracked out Conrad.

"What?"

"The jewel –"

"It's mine. I didn't come to act a contrition."

"Get him," said Scar-Nose. There was a surge again, which now faltered on Jehan's high, maybe unbroken, voice.

"I'll find you better."

They cascaded against her, but the vicious rush had become a pawing query. She kicked and pushed them off.

"Who leads this herd?" she said.

"No man. We're one. A brotherhood. An equal share, an equal voice for all."

She supposed then it was actually the dwarf who ruled the gang. She had suspected it. But they were embarrassed to admit the fact, pretended other-wise, and resorted to high-flown phrases of fraternity.

"Tonight *I'll* lead you," said Jehan. "Again."

She was mocked. She took no notice. Where, in her apron and skirts she had no say, now, her breasts bound, and weaponed with cloth in her hose, she had a say, and would say so.

"Be quiet, you pigs. Listen. Didn't I give you nice sport before?"

"And then cheated us."

"What's a paltry bit of coloured glass? It had value for me, not for you." For a second she was prompted to demand if they had knifed their victim, Pierre, her brother. Something stuck her tongue against the roof of her mouth, and when she could speak again she said, "The upper bank of the City, near that great big church they're fussing up. I know a woman there. It's a wealthy house. You'll see how we'll find out its secrets."

The idea of the fat woman, the housekeeper with the keys, who had accosted her in the street by the statue-fountain that first day, had come to Jehan this very morning, as she sorted herbs in the infirmary annexe. That the house was a rich one had been evident. That the woman had charge was prob-able. The master was "old" and "always off on business." Come in, she had urged Jehan.

For a while they debated and said No, but, standing silent in the door, watching them with clear eyes, she brought them round. Conrad declared this boy was a fiend, and another that fiends were lucky to the wicked, and they all laughed and spoke of hair the hue of sulphur, and after that ten of them went with her down the stair, and only three stayed sullenly behind.

Under the wall of the overgrown park, in the sky-sailing shadow of the embryo of the Temple-Church, the thieves stared across at a house Jehan had indicated. And the City bells rang for Laude.

"Stay here then, I'll go rouse the fat dame," said Jehan. "When I'm in the house, Conrad – you come across and wait by the door. No other, till he gives the signal to you."

Jehan ran lightly, dark to dark, to the side door of the house, and shook it. As she had supposed, the boy she had seen was porter there, and in a moment he whined at her through the panels. "Is your master at home?" said Jehan.

"No. Master's off," came the high voice, stupid with sleep and resentment.

"The housekeeper then. Your mistress."

"She's in her bed."

"Wake her," said Jehan in a low and terrible tone.

Through the door, with an uncanny night-hearing, Jehan heard the boy stumble away.

(From the wall across the street rose a mutinous shuffling, and she cursed it down, making no sound or sign.)

Then, above, in a toadstool bulge of the house, the pane of a window lighted. Again, Jehan heard the noises of human things aggrieved.

(Conrad was out, standing by the cowled well. Jehan flung an arm out at him in a gesture of rage, and he lurched down behind the trough, hidden.)

The woman's flat fat tread was descending through the house now. What luck, they were alone there. No other servant even, it would seem, and the old man "off."

"Who's that? Who's there? You rogue –"

The woman's voice was breathy but not alarmed, not even entirely prepared for anger. She might be prone to night callers. Jehan put her mouth to the door and moaned, "Kind lady, let me in for the love of God. I'm known to you – that brother of Master Motius' student, Pierre –" her voice quavered on the name, which was fortunate. "I've been set on, mistress. Robbers. Help me –"

Then great billows of righteous outrage and passion the far side of the door, and bolts and bars being sprung.

Wrapped in her bedclothes, the woman flooded the door alcove. She thrust her candle out, and Pierre's handsome brother, Jehan, stood wilted and swooning in the radiance, one hand to his side, gasping.

"God's vitals. Poor boy. Come in at once. There. Lean on me, as hard as you like. I'm well-cushioned."

"I knew no one else –" said Jehan.

"And what of your fine brother? For shame. And the Master Artisan's pet, too."

"He won't know me. Turned me off. It will break our mother's heart."

"Where is he then, the disgrace?"

Jehan said: "I know no more than you." And staggered.

"Where are you hurt?"

"Only a little."

"Yes, you seem unmarred."

"In my heart the worst."

In the kitchen, Jehan sprawled out in a chair. Her swimming vision told her that the pans were of quality, and the big hearth and its apparatus evidenced many lavish roasts. Instantly the woman had lit another three candles – extravagance, too. Then she used one of her keys, and brought wine. In her own right, the lady was also a thief.

"Drink that now. That'll bring you back. And I'll keep you company in a drop. He's got so much, he never misses the sip or two I take. A mean fellow. Pays me in pennies, works me off my feet. I must live. His poor relation you understand. Kept me from a husband, too, I've had my chances – all lost –"

Jehan tried the wine, thick as velvet, and began to revive.

Jehan asked nothing about the old man and his valuables. No need, for the woman spread the night with tidings, while sometimes patting Jehan's knee. Gold plate sat above, and candlesticks, a chamber-pot with gold handles, a box of money – the one key he stinted her of (no trouble when a dagger-hilt might be used on it)—another of rings and chains, which he hid, as if she would touch it, God pardon him. There was a Bible too, and a book got from the artisan, who was a magician, both with covers warted by gems. And a robe trimmed with bullion, and gloves stitched with pearls – what a treasure trove! – and her without a decent gown for holy days.

Jehan, much recovered, aided the woman to more wine. As it was done, Jehan gave her too a kiss on the cheek, and dropped in her cup a powder of herbs from the infirmary.

"Well now, you saucy boy," said the housekeeper, very much delighted. "I'll begin to think no one set on you at all, you only came here for a naughty reason."

Jehan lowered eyes that, in the smoky light, were gold as any rich man's plate. Boy-like, smiling, Jehan reached out, and gave the fat woman's vast bosom a gentle tweak.

Such shrieks. The neighbours would think her murdered, unless they often heard the sounds, which seemed probable. Then, such a gratifyingly big drink.

"And you only a youthful lad."

"Willing though to learn."

"Well, well. One can't even trust opening the door these nights."

She drank again, in a huge swallow, not noticing the wine, eyes sparkling, breasts heaving. All the potion was gone, inside her. She reached and caught Jehan and pulled him down, massaging at buttocks and thighs. Jehan panted, fondled various mounds, imparted kisses and tasted in the wine-sweetened mouth the bitter tint of herbs, the powerful bringers of sleep –

Before the insistent hands could find out their mistake, they suddenly went sliding off. The fat woman rolled back, her eyes startled and still gaping as the first snore shook her bulk. Then her eyes shut on her. Protesting, snoring, kidnapped by unconsciousness, she cascaded from the chair on to the floor and lay beside a mouse-trap baited with cheese.

Outside in the street, a thief barked. They were growing anxious. As Jehan opened the door, Conrad shouldered through it. He glared at her, then stepped out again. He whistled, the twittering note of a bird, and one by one the others darted noiselessly bat-like over the gap between the shadows.

Conrad and another man caught the door-boy asleep at the stairfoot, hammered him on the head for fair measure and left him sprawled there. At the fat woman lying by the mouse-trap with her legs wide, some of them were tempted. They thought her only dead drunk. Her keys were taken. One mounted her. She quaked under him, gurgling, oblivious, and so was reckoned secure.

Upstairs the gang ransacked the house, Jehan having informed them of what might be expected. Everything was found, even the chamber-pot, and the casket of jewellery, which last had only been inserted in the mattress, a common recourse.

Thereafter, Conrad and others slung their arms about the neck of Jehan, and crowned him with a gold chain from the casket, and poured a cup of white wine over his head to christen him in their fellowship, when once the wine-barrels had been got at. They remained, throughout the acts of carnage and celebration, quiet.

The house, so staid and safe without, was now inside a shambles. Only the kitchen had remained lit, and here at length they repaired, draped in the bed-curtains, toting their spoils, to drink about the laundry heap of the drugged woman.

There was time enough. The City gates would not part until the dawn, still an hour or so away. Even if the old fellow returned, he could not get in the City till after sunrise, and by then they would be gone. What a surprise they had left him.

"How Dwarf will cuss, how Fero will bite himself, when he learns what he missed!"

On the floor the fat woman breathed only in jerks and gutterings. Her face was grey and her lips slaty. The herbs had been generous in amount.

But the wine was good, and, not able to port it, they did not see why they should leave so much of it behind. The drinking went on, and in the middle Jehan sat on the table, looking under her or his lids, not speaking, scarcely-tasted cup set down.

Then the dark that came in at the alcove chink turned to a deep grey light. They roused to be going. They did not want to be seen.

As they stuffed the handy pouches in cloaks, surcoats, loincloths, with loot, there came sounds out of the speechless night. They were the hoofs of a mule that clucked along the cobbles, indeed, of two mules going in tandem.

"Not here," said Conrad, "God's tail, not here."

But the mules picked delicately on, coming closer, coming to the door, and were there reined in. And now voices spoke outside the front of the house. A respectful mutter, an old man's pedantic drone.

"He's rich," said Scar-Nose. "He'll have paid the gate crew to open the postern. Back early, rot him."

"When he's in he'll start a do. The world will come running."

"Then when he's in," said Jehan, "we must stop his mouth."

"I hear two of them, the old rat, and a young."

"Both mouths stopped," said Jehan. She moved from the kitchen towards the front of the house and its large door. "This has a lock. Be ready."

When the large key turned in the large door, the inner space was waiting, lined by flesh.

The old man came through, calling irritably to the porter-boy by name, his grizzled skull and fur-lined garment, his old body, creaking by a few inches from Jehan beside the door. Then, in the gloom, someone whacked him. The blow seemed to split his head across, blackish liquid spurted, and he fell into the vortex of finished deeds without a cry.

Outside, in the twilight, the servant was giving his mule water from the trough by the well.

Jehan called to him softly. "Sieur, sieur." He turned, hearing a girl's voice addressing him so politely. Puzzled, not dismayed, he came towards the door and found it empty and unlit. He was a young man, strong and comely. He stood framed against the dusk, as all their eyes, unseen, fastened on him. Then he moved inside.

Two of the thieves took him at once. But he was not such easy meat as the old one. For some reason he did not shout as he evaded them, but his fists lashed out, his feet. The gang closed with him, and the walls seemed to totter, grunts were audible, now something went over with a thud, and there were oaths. As the battle swung, Jehan moved through it. She lifted her arm, with the knife Conrad had given her, she stabbed the servant in the belly. It was a death blow, but not quick enough. Dazed, amazed, he was sucking in his breath to scream and wake the dead. But Scar-Nose, an able hand, reaching over the young man's shoulder, cut his throat before his voice could sound.

Clambering across bodies, the thieves filed into the street and shut the door neatly. Conrad locked it tight with the key. Glancing at the mules, they rejected them, for they were over-ridden and besides conspicuous. The gang then broke in twos and threes or ones, and fled with bold strides away across Paradys and down, to the river, and over into the warrens beyond, losing all of itself as intended, Jehan with the rest.

The young nun stood in the yard, and coming from her sleeping cell, Jehanine discovered her. The face of Marie-Lis was grave and pure, but had none of the smug melancholy of a true Madonna.

"You weren't in your bed at sunrise, Jhane."

(Jehan smiled under Jehanine's skin. Why, did you come seeking me there?)

"I was about early, sister."

"Yes."

"I was in the garden."

"You came from there. With a bundle of clothes."

"A piece of washing I'd forgotten, sister."

(Careless on this occasion, she had returned late. She had seen the ghostly shapes of two lay-sisters bending over the refectory well, and the phantom nuns wafting in a dawn mist from the church. Now, under her gown, a golden chain, and on the chain a little golden cross set with a topaz.)

"But you roam at night, Jhane," said Sister Marie-Lis.

"Some nights, when I can't sleep. How do you know, sister?"

"Where do you go to, Jhane?"

(Over the wall, into the blackness, into the night. You spy on me, but not enough.)

"To the chapel. Or sometimes I sit in the garden."

"The nights are cold."

"My cell also is cold."

"We must endure, Jhane. We are not worldly, here."

"No, sister."

(And I washed off a dark stain in the dew. I thought of creeping to the other well, but it stinks, there must be a dead cat in it. And at the hostel's well under the lemon trees you might find me. Why are you drawing so much water, Jhane? Dew was best.)

"We know almost nothing about you, Jhane. The Mother has never interviewed you. It's customary, after a time, to inquire if you have come to feel any yearning for the life of a Bride."

Jehanine lowered her eyes.

"I haven't, sister."

"Gaze on the window, Jhane, the Great Light, its petals of saffron and snow. Our Lord fell in his beauty, a shooting star. He brought light into the world. He asks only love."

Jehanine frowned. She said, "You told me, it's never demanded. I won't be a nun."

The air filled with shrieks. In a fashion, Jehanine had become accustomed to outcry. She did not respond, as did Sister Marie-Lis, who whirled about and spun away. Through the arch she went, into the churchyard. The noises came from the garden. Slowly, cautious now, Jehanine followed. She had a vision of the fat woman erupting in at the nunnery gate, rushing through, to stand screeching of villainy under the bare fruit trees. But Jehanine suspected the fat woman might be dead, that all of those at that house, like Pierre, might be dead. She felt neither satisfaction nor distress. She was mostly indifferent, except to a certain tidiness that all the deaths together seemed to present, like duties performed.

The shrieks had ceased. Tawny fox-robes milled about the garden, clotted near the stinking ancient well. Across the turf the Mother was stalking. The nuns parted before her. She towered beside the well, imperious, ever a Queen Bee.

"What is it? Why does this well stink so? Pah! What's in the bucket?"

A murmur. The Mother drew back. She crossed herself and touched her fingers to brow and heart. She did not look in certain health.

Jehanine wandered close, and saw into the inner circle.

"I drew up the bucket, Mother, to look ... I thought some animal might have died in the well."

Jehanine had now approached near enough that she was able to look inside the bucket herself. She saw that it contained some murky water, and in the water a long pale fish with five fingers.

"Merciful Lord," said the Mother. "One of you run and kindle a lantern. It must be lowered. We must be sure."

Two of the nuns fainted, one setting off the other. Yet another hastened away to a withered bush, into which she vomited. The Mother stood like a statue.

The lantern came, and they lowered it on a rope. And then there was a terrible wailing of lament and disgust.

The Mother drew aside quickly from her scrutiny. She said, "I've seen the drowned before, from the river. This is not drowning. It is not a suicide. I must think. She must be raised."

When the Mother departed, and the nuns fell away into groups, Jehanine went to the well and looked down where the lantern still hung. Beyond the fearful stench and beyond the light, a girl's body was wedged far down in the shaft. The water, and time, had acted on it, but also it seemed to have been subjected to fire, and to some cutting weapon: blasted and partly disembowelled it stuck there, mindlessly looking up with the remains of the face of Osanne.

The body was not to be raised. It fell to bits and its entrails poured out.

The Mother, kerchief pressed to her nose and mouth, instructed that logs be thrown in, then oil, and the whole set on fire. She was of course obeyed. At first, dampness seemed likely to wreck the scheme, but then the wood caught. A merry blaze leapt for a while from the chimney of the well, and a ghastly smoke gouted from it.

"I have written to the Father of the order," said the Mother. "Everything is explained. No suicide. I believe our daughter Osanne was struck by lightning. She bore the marks of it. God has gathered her home. We shall make a marker for her, and place it with the tombs of others who had died here in faith."

When the blaze sank, earth was shovelled into the well, and finally stones.

"Thanks be to Christ," said the Mother. She muttered some other brief prayer. She said, "We will pray for the novice Osanne."

All went to the church and prayed for Osanne.

Late in the afternoon it rained, water after fire. The smoke still hung low in the garden, and the evil of the stench remained in pockets.

Supper was a loathsome meal, for which very few had an appetite. The Mother did not appear. The young nun Marie-Lis lifted the cover of a book, not the Bible, but a theosophical work. She began to read to the silent and mostly motionless assembly.

Behind the screen, Jehanine, hungrily eating her black bread and soup, heard the beauty of the voice of the young nun.

"Why then did God so punish His formerly peerlessly beloved Son, made by Him an angel, a winged being of such power and beauty they are to men as men are to the little worms?

"It was in a rage that God did so, as when a favourite child has gone against the parental edict. What will you do? God had asked him. I will create a universe, I will make men in the image of the angels, replied the errant Son. For this, his Father flings him from the sky.

"For in his enormous wisdom, God knows that a world of men created must suffer, firstly the choice of good and ill, and the guilts and torments that attend upon both, and nextly must learn grief and disease, despair and death. God sought, in His compassion, to spare mankind, to deliver it from its very self. But our Lord said, Let them choose. And so he made the earth and peopled it. Then God said, If that is your wish, you I will exile. Go you into the very pit of that which you have made. And for the rest, let there be darkness on the face of the earth forever, that they may not be afraid, through seeing what they are, and what they are at. So God made darkness and it hung on the face of earth. But the Lord, our Saviour, said again, Let there be light. He stole then one flame of the seven divine fires of Heaven. And with this he fell, burning, like the morning star. The sun was lit from his flambeau, and all the stars, and the moon, and all the lights of the firmament. And when he had cleaved through the earth and fallen to the deepest depth of it, that pit too became fire, a furnace that warms the earth's heart – a cleansing flame, the light of knowledge – until the world shall end.

"And for this gift of fire, men loved him. And when he saw their love, the love of those he had created, Lucefiel in turn loved them.

"Later, others of his brethren rallied to the banner of this Prince. They too exiled themselves from Paradise, and fell to earth and under it. From these he chose his captains, and on them his aegis lay as sternly as on his own self, and besides that, the furious censure of God. But to men the Lord gave only one commandment: Know what you are. But they forgot."

When the reading was done, and the chores of the evening were done, Jehanine slept until the bell of Matines. Then she was Jehan, and she ran over the plains of the nunnery, got over the wall, and was gone into the rain and darkness.

Day by day the rain nailed heaven to earth. In the wintry night, the rain sighed and rushed and stamped. It was a curtain of disguise and a deflection of all other noises. It cleaned the spillings from the stones of Paradys, whatever they were.

At the *Imago* now, the dwarf sat sometimes on his table in the upper room. He sorted through the sumptuous trinkets and the coins, and petted the clever thieves, though never Jehan, the cleverest, their leader in his default.

"Jehan is a demon sent to guide us by Prince Lucifer," said Conrad. "Jehan is one of Lucifer's fair knights, a fallen angel. Sulphur hair and cat's eyes. Pretty as a girl, sweet voiced as a girl. And charms the girls, too."

They gave the dwarf all their news, while Jehan sat by, yellow cat-eyes cast down. The dwarf gave them their news back again.

"Three wicked murders at a house near the building Church. An old rich man and his servant in their blood, and the housekeeper poisoned, and every bit of wealth plucked from the place. The little boy can't remember a thing, but he says he thinks a handsome youth knocked on the door and the woman let him in. But the boy's wits are addled since the blow the murderers gave him." Restrained, tense as dogs who have done a cunning trick and wait for bones, the thieves listened and said how bad a matter this was, a shocking state the City must be in when a rich man could be killed for his riches. "And another tale has it, a girl was honey-talked into letting in a young man at her window, but he brings his friends too, and while some have her down, others open the father's coffers. Many drunkards have been waylaid coming from the Snake-Cock or the Blacksmith's Inn, or on the South Bridge. Beaten senseless and their purses, their very boots taken." Oh, a shocking state of affairs, yes, yes.

The nights had been busy. Jehan was full of Mercury and went before them. (Remember how he stabbed the servant in the rich man's house, not faltering?) Oh, they had known him for years, their Jehan. He was one of their own, and theirs, but polished brighter.

Conrad twitched. He had a powerful lust for Jehan. One night Jehan might kill him for it. You may eat the apple but not twine the serpent with the maiden's face.

"Well, Dwarf, you like our antics?"

But the dwarf said, "I'm thinking. Fero, fero. It will be a hard winter. The snow will fall. The river may freeze. Then Yule. And the year's turning. The Janus festival, the Feast of the Ass."

The dwarf stared at Jehan. He had never, plainly, told Jehan's secret. That Jehan had breasts and carried no dagger but the one in her belt, that Jehan lived by day in a nunnery, scrubbing the flags and sweeping the yards. Sometimes she slipped herbs into the drinks of their victims, opium, man-dragoras. The thieves did not suspect Jehan of that, only of witchcraft. Jehan was fey, lucky, a shining thing of Hell. They did not ask him where he went away from them, or where he came back from – he put on animal shape, or wings and flew behind the stars as they went out. He sprang from the ground at the sun's setting. Winter, the time of dark day and long night, that was Jehan's country. They expected great events.

There was no more Jehanine in any case. There was only Jehan by night and Jhane by day, which two names were one, only a letter differently set, if he-she had been able to read or write and had known it.

Yet, as Jhane went about her work, always dutiful to the nunnery, modest and hard-working, again and again the young nun might be noted, standing observing her, or coming near she might say, "Search your heart, Jhane."

"For what must I search there, sister?" asked Jhane meekly. Jehan smiled and waited. In the interim, absconding, Jhane took care to leave during the offices, when Marie-Lis was in the church.

"Come over the river," said Jehan to the thieves. But of this they were wary.

"The watch is fly-thick there now. Since our first visit."

"Follow me then," said Jehan.

The rain clattered like tin pans.

Some glanced at Fero the dwarf to see what he would do. But the dwarf did nothing save finger the columns of coins, an earring of canary beryl. One voice, an equal share – a fraternity, honour among thieves. While, beyond that cross he had taken and not thrown into the communal pile, and the chain Conrad had hung on him for a garland, Jehan took nothing.

All the robber band followed Jehan into Noah's night.

"We must build an ark, quick," said the fat man.

"Agreed. Let's us wicked be saved this time."

Near the South Bridge they beheld a party of tipsy gallants with torches in the rain.

"What now?" said Conrad.

Jehan singled out a young man, blond as the old man's servant had been. Alone, she approached him, and drew him aside from his friends who, in wine and rain not properly aware of his loss, went on over the bridge.

He seemed to believe, when the gang surrounded him, that he had been in conversation with an importunate girl. They took his money and stripped him to his tunic and drawers, like a Roman, and the rain had stopped. The resin torch still burned on his cringing, their jovial circle – his purse had been full, and the coins beamed too.

"He can dance for us," said Jehan. "Can't you?" She raised the torch and looked intently in the robbed man's face. "Let me bring you light. Aren't you glad to obey Christ's command? Look, you've given all you have to the poor." How the thieves giggled. Then Jehan put the torch down to the young man's garment, and up again into his hair. He was wet enough that there was a great smoulder, but also enough flame to send him hopping and screaming over the bridge, and Jehan pranced after him, clapping her hands and singing in a quire boy's voice, to an Eastern rhythm of the Spice Lands. Conrad and one or two more abetted the macabre fun, picking up the song, which had been born of some hot night's Crossade. The rest of the gang paused uneasily, the lower side of the water, not chancing the bridge. Halfway along it, Jehan pushed the youth into the river. Swollen with rain, it would not be happy swimming. Jehan seemed content, and at once returned along the bridge, with Conrad and the others at his heels.

"What shall I do?" said Conrad. "You want me to go over there? Hang the watch, I will, if you want it. Up the hills. I'll go to Hell with you."

"That door-boy at the rich man's house," said Jehan.

"He's a half-wit now. No need to slaughter every one of them."

But Jehan seemed to wish only deaths stacked methodically in the chest of deeds. Glancing in the river, one noticed the blond young man was not swimming at all, had gone down.

"Let me have you," said Conrad.

"No. Don't try."

"One time you'll let me."

"I'll kill you first."

Conrad laughed into the face of night. Much bigger and heavier than this boy, he could pin him now to the stone over the tumult of water. But did not dare.

"You love another," jested Conrad.

"A lovely nun," said Jehan.

"A nun? Where could you see such a thing?"

"I have seen. One night you'll get her for me. Skin like cream and eyes like deep thoughts. A young nun. You can take her, I'll let you."

Conrad licked his lips. He was superstitious. Satan protected his own, and so did the other One.

It thundered overhead, and Conrad winced. The rain resumed. It was cold, it was winter.

They went back to the *Imago* to drink and Jehan to sit watching the dwarf count coins.

Seven o'clock in the frosty morning, not yet light nor yet still dark. The office of Prima Hora was done and Jhane stood at the church door as the nuns stole drifting out, to allow Marie-Lis to witness her there. But Marie-Lis passed by with the sisterhood, not seeming to see her, her countenance remote as ivory.

When the nuns were gone, Jhane went into the church.

A cold iron heaviness hung there. Smudges of light faltered on meagre candles, but nothing was given from the great window, which had become a whorl of leaden quarter-tones. The form of the Angel – Lucefiel – was mostly indistinguishable.

Was it that they worshipped the Devil here, or that Jhane had seen through a mask even they were unaware of?

As she moved along the nave, she saw the pale figure in the quire. It was not Osanne, for the spectral figment – or decoy – that had seemed to be Osanne, had ended its manifestations with the discovery in the well. This apparition was the original, a nun in a pale robe, tall and gracious, her face unseen since lifted in reverence to the blinded window. Jhane walked on, making no sound. The figure did not alter, only the hood or veil slipped back from its head. This nun did not effect either scarf or coif. A lion-like mane of gold hair burst out against the dimness, raying over the shoulders and down the spine.

Was this hair like the hair of Marie-Lis? Was this she? Had she turned into the side passage or the cloister, and re-entered via one of the smaller doors ...

Perhaps not. The young nun was not so tall, and much slighter, surely –

Jhane halted. Something made her unable to approach any closer to the vision. Now the glowing quality of the figure seemed to be flowing upwards into the window – it warmed and waxed lambent. Suddenly colour shot into the glass and it came alive. The sun was rising and had pierced abruptly through the cloud. As the window quickened, Jhane saw that the image of white robe and lion hair was gone.

Kneeling before the Great Light, Jhane bowed her head and slowly touched her hands to brow and breast. A peculiar sensation went over her as she did this, an exquisite intimation, both carnal and spiritual. But getting to her feet, she soon turned her back on radiant Lucifer and all his works.

In the black icicle of the night, some young men coming out of the *Cockatrice* met with a sauntering blond youth. There were exclamations. And a pause.

"Stop! You –"

"What have I done?" said the youth, turning on them two beautiful lynx's eyes.

"No – but you're like –"

"It *is*, I tell you."

"No, not the height or muscle. But a double, certainly."

"Oh," said the youth, not unnaturally curious, "whose?"

The young men from the studio of Motius looked at one another. One of them said, "Well, he's in the sewers –" and was commanded to silence.

"Then I'm like someone," said the youth. "Where are you bound?"

"Come with us, where we're bound," they said, and went off into the icicle with him, to a lower tavern behind a stable.

"Look at his hands, so delicate, and his face. What a model he'll make, our Jehan – you did say to us that was your name?"

"Come to the studio tomorrow. Present yourself to the Master. He'll take a fit, seeing how like – well. Do it anyway."

They petted him, far gone in ale.

"Where is his house then?" *he* said, lolling there sober.

They explained with care the location of the house, and its appearance, and drew maps of the way upon the table in spilled drink.

> *O winter is, the poor birds sing*
> *And hide each head beneath a wing.*
> *So cruel to me my lady is*
> *Like winter snow that gives no ease,*
> *My heart its head beneath its wing,*
> *And winter is, my heart must sing.*

Winter rode through Paradys on a grey horse, a lord in mail and armour, with a vizored helm, and his train behind him. The sky and the bare trees groaned and the honed winds blew. Branches, slates and birds fell down. The snow began to fall. The City blanched. The river froze for vast stretches, and all the wells. Love-songs listed cold hearts, but in the nunnery the nuns wrapped their feet and hands in cloth, the hearths were lit in the refectory and the infirmary, and braziers carried into the church, and quantities of blankets lugged to the sleeping cells. Two of the sick nuns perished, and were put underground. The matriarchal Mother took cold and kept to her chamber where a fire roared day and night. The novices slept two by two for warmth, which was not allowed. (On such freezing nights at the farm, even the unloving sisters of Jehanine had clasped her close.) But Jhane lay alone, cold as a stone, and deep within her body she coiled asleep. She did not fear the winter, it had no jurisdiction over her. And now and then Jehan went out across the wall and reviewed the City of Ice, its turrets and points sewing up an enamel moon, on the surface of which there now showed absolutely a Madonna's mournful face. Over the thick glass of the river by night, muffled shapes dragged secret wares on rough sleds. The ships lay dead at anchor.

And the lovely young nun read in the refectory, above the coughs and snuffles of winter. "In the Book of Esrafel it says this: 'Thus the man who was sent to the Angel asked him, "Were it not better that we should not live at all, since we live in wickedness, and suffer, and know not why?" And I, the Angel, answered him; "Weigh you the height of fire, and measure the tower of the wind, and call here to me yesterday." But the man said, "I cannot." "Believe then," said the Angel Esrafel, "in this manner also you cannot know the guiding intent of the Creator, cannot weigh or measure it, or call it here before you. Yet it is.' " The young nun waited as two or three of her sisters sneezed and wiped their noses sadly. Then she read, " 'Hear, my beloved, says the Lord: be not afraid, nor let your sins weigh you down as the briars cover the field, that no man may travel it. Your sins are finished, tear up the thought of them by the roots. For the field choked by briars is put to the fire to be consumed.' "

The thieves, wrapped fast, and sometimes snuffling like the nuns, came from their bolt-holes to the *Imago* to toast and steam. Once in, they did not incline to go out again. Gold burnt the fingers in such a temperature, the dwarf said so. There he sat, slit-eyed and brooding, saying not a syllable now. But Jehan prowled and some followed. Where there were no pickings to be had, Jehan would crack some costly window with a ball of packed snow, or scratch on doors with his dagger obscene symbols of the alleys learnt instead of letters. Jehan would inaugurate sliding games, which slides might break legs in the morning. And sometimes they would find a vacant house to get into.

On the far side of the river, a weird gleam went up by night, where the torches reflected back from the snow into the wild and chiming air. But it was forbidden, that upper bank. The great market, the great borning church, the house of murders, the enclosing arm of City Wall that held in it slabs the legions had laid there.

"I'll go with you. Up the hills. Who cares," said Conrad. Scar-Nose added, "For what?" The thin man said, "It's cosier there."

Jehan ran over the bridge, through the palings of ice-crystals, gliding where there was the horizontal ice, arms outflung graceful and demoniac.

"Come," said Conrad.

Yet not one of them moved.

The well lit, climbing streets about the market were nearly bright as day, but black mud lay around the houses and torch-poles where the heat had melted the snow.

For Jehan, creature of darkness, it was early, not yet eleven o'clock. With the advent of winter when night began to come down in the afternoon, he sometimes took the risk of evolving during Complies, the completion of the nunnery's diurnal.

As she entered the street of the statue-well, Jehan gave her nothing to feel. She glanced at the house where the fat woman had died, the rich man, the servant. No watch was any longer kept on it. Meanwhile, across the way, stood the other more important house, the studio and dwelling of Motius the Artisan. Seven nights before, solitary outside the *Cockatrice*, Jehan had identified other students of the Master. She had fallen into chat with them. They had seemed stunned by Jehan's resemblance to someone they had known but would not coherently speak of. One had suggested Jehan might model for the studio as a young Patroklos or Dionysos. Jehan had not seemed averse, and so learned the house at which he should present himself.

Through the shutters light showed in the upper storey. Jehan knocked at the door. After a time, a shutter opened. A young man's face, unknown, peered down. "Who's there?"

"Jehan."

"Who is Jehan?"

Jehan shrugged, standing out in the pool of light to be seen. "I was told to come. The Master might employ me as a model, they said. Perhaps not."

Then the youth in the window gave a startled sound.

He withdrew. Voices came together.

(*It is one like Pierre Belnard. Oh me, oh my!*)

Feet bounded down a stair and hands unbarred the door.

A second youth drew Jehan in, shut the door to keep him there, stared at him unblinkingly in the flame of a flinching candle, then said something very fast, a sentence of Latin, unrecognised. "So," added the youth huskily, "you don't vanish."

"Shall I try?"

"Don't mock. Don't speak. Stay there, exactly where I have put you. Wait." And the student rushed away, up the stair once more, the panic-splayed light borne with him.

Jehan stayed, unmocking, or speaking, and seemed to be waiting. Then he moved, went to the stair-foot, and looked up the dark funnel of it. In a moment more he began noiselessly to ascend.

There was now not a twitter, not a mumble, above.

Jehan entered a passage and came to a door, closed, with a keyhole of shouting light. Tickled by such aptness, he knelt to the hole at once, and looked through.

There before him was a morsel of fire-lit chamber, and in it a man stood, lean and old and bearded, stooping a fraction. One hand clutched at his breast, and the other held a chalice of wine, which he was pouring evenly into the flames on the hearth. The sizzling splishery intrigued Jehan, so much so that when it ended, and the man moved from the sphere of vision, Jehan did not react. Then came a motion across the light that indicated someone was returning to spring the door. Jehan was up in an instant, standing aside. As the second student burst out toward the stair, Jehan stepped directly in the doorway and said, "Here I am." Which brought the other back cursing foolishly.

The fine fiery chamber, opened out, was opulent. A hearty meal had been eaten in it at the white-clad table, not long before, and still positioned there were a gilt wine-jug and cups, a dish of yellow plums and apples – in winter Paradys – and two branches of candles that stintlessly burned. Through a part-closed curtain beyond lay the studio, darkened and asleep, but smelling yet of paint grindings, clay, oil and marble-dust. Here Pierre would have been wont to work late, and dine afterwards with the Master, a favourite pupil, as these, too, must be.

But Pierre had evaporated from their lives. Drinking and whoring had undone him in the alleys. Now on the threshold, his double, more exact after an interval, and so more miraculous.

Master Motius now sat in his carved chair by the hearth and stared as the young men did. He was, as keyhole-seen, old, bearded and wore besides a cap to warm his head and a fur-lined mantle in the hot room. And three rings on his fingers.

"You are the brother of Pierre," he said.

Jehan smiled.

"Brother of who?"

The artisan sighed.

"Not," said Master Motius.

"There was some gossip one of his brothers sought him out," said the student who had looked from the window. "That's why he went off without a word."

The second student said, "And this one was at the door, peeping through it, I'll bet. What did he see?"

Jehan looked down at his feet modestly.

"There was nothing to see," said Master Motius.

"Except, you pour wine on your fire," said Jehan.

The artisan said, "That's a Roman custom. We keep the classic formula here. Otherwise, what do you say?"

"To what?"

"To our talk of Pierre Belnard."

"Who is that?"

"You have never met such a young man."

"I?"

"Do you know of whom we speak?"

"Is it possible?"

"He was my pupil and apprentice. He was well-liked everywhere, and well-known."

"For what?"

"Uncivil, gutless, pig-souled dog –" cried the second student.

Master Motius held up his hand. Leaning on the arms of his chair, he rose. "I will show you," said he. He took a candle-branch from the table.

The first student hurried to open the curtain into the studio, and the Master passed through.

"Go in," said the second student to Jehan, threateningly.

Jehan smiled again. He went after the artisan leisurely and the students followed.

The studio was a big vault, where the candlelight collided with angles, drapes and shapes, was smashed and fell down. A peculiar being – a whole, if idealised, skeleton of wood – posed on a plinth, making a mad gesture. There were benches and cold braziers, long tables with parchment, canvas, jars and alembics. Things stood propped or lay prone; things sweated under wet cloth.

The artisan moved through this forest and stopped before the far wall. A small panel of wood had been fastened on it. He raised the candles, though his arm shook a little, from age or feeling.

"This he painted, in his third month with me. It is flawed, he had much to learn. But ah, so perfect also. What he would have been."

Jehan looked at the painting.

Jehanine had never been shown anything the mature Pierre had fashioned, though he had performed some work for the lord of the estate. She could not properly understand the painting, however, for it was not real, not flesh and blood, and did not move. A girl sat under a flowering tree, her fair hair falling round her, and birds fed from her hands, and a faun, and a she-wolf with a cub … But Jehan was distracted somewhat by some strange scuffed marks along the lower wall and the floor. Did the students of Motius also draw on the ground?

"He called this painting *The Madonna of the Innocents*," said Master Motius. He wept. "Marie the Mother, but also the goddess Venus. Sacred and profane. But all beauty is sacred." The tears ran down into his beard like flames, catching the light. "Boy, if you know where he might be – no matter what depths he may have fallen into – whatever sink or vice – I beg you, you must tell me."

"Who?" said Jehan.

One of the students said hoarsely, "He *knows*, Master." He moved towards Jehan. "Shall we make him? I can do it."

"No – no – no violence here. Perhaps he doesn't know. The likeness isn't so marked as I thought at first. We see what we wish to. I have studied men's faces."

Jehan felt the topaz cross slide between his girl's breasts under the binding. He toed the chalky lines on the floor. He smiled and he smiled, and reached out to take the candles from the artisan.

Master Motius seemed surprised but not reluctant to let go of the light. Conceivably, he thought his guest wanted to gaze more closely at the painting, and that this might augur well.

Jehan, clasping the candle-branch, leaned forward carefully, and touched the fire to the wooden panel. A black line ran along the edge of it, and the paint bubbled. She seemed not inclined to burn, the Madonna –

"Oh God!" shrieked the artisan. His old voice splintered, he tottered against Jehan, striking at him, clutching now for the fire, now for the painted panel. Jehan turned and smote downward with the candle-branch. It cut the old man's temple and most of the candles showered upon him, catching webbed in his hair, beard and mantle. As he began to burn, so did the panel on the wall. Jehan stepped back, face composed and serious, the eyes very pale.

The students were running to their master, who writhed on the floor, stunned and crying and alight. As they came Jehan both avoided and met them, and dipping the last candles, with gentle strokes, torched each of them. They seemed highly inflammable, perhaps some constant contact of their garments with the paints and oils. It was very simply done.

Jehan flung the fire away against a hanging bolt of dry material, which flared at once.

The studio was illumined in saffron, and by hopping, dancing, screaming fire-creatures, that tried in turn to come at her, at each other, and which all the while beat at their own selves, until they went down and boiled along the floor.

Jehan dashed from the room. In the outer chamber he took fruit from the dish and snatched up the gilt jug of wine.

Escape was made by a lower window, into a side-slip between the houses.

In the open yard before the embryo of the Temple-Church, Jehan climbed a workman's ladder up a pile of stones, and seated there high in the air, watched all the street come alive in terror as fire exploded from the upper storey of Master Motius' house in one mighty blast. Some combustible in the studio had ignited, it would seem.

In fear for the wooden structures of their homes, men scurried in the street like frightened mice. Jehan, eating plums upon the stone pile, watched. It was like a scene in Hell, until the snow began to fall and, as the cumbersome buckets had not been able to, whisper by whisper, put out the burning house.

He had a fancy for the jug, and kept it by him. Springing down from the nunnery tree with the rope and the vessel in his hands, he found before him a young nun.

"There's soot in your hair, Jhane," said Sister Marie-Lis.

"Then I have been in a fire, demoiselle."

"And this is how you travel the City by night."

"How else?" replied Jehan.

"But you return."

"I found a rope hanging down to the street. I climbed it."

"You are Jhane."

"Presently," said Jehan. He moved towards the young nun. He put his face to hers. She did not resist. He put his hand on her breast. She did not resist. "I know a quiet cell, over there," said Jehan. "We shan't be disturbed. Or here, on the cold ground in the snow."

"You are Jhane," said the young nun again.

Jehan drew back. He lowered his eyes.

"Who will you tell?" said Jhane.

"No one. God sees."

"You worship Satan," said Jhane.

The young nun turned from her and moved away over the snow and vanished through an arch of white plum trees. The ground was too hard to have kept her footprints.

Jhane burned on her pallet. Garbed in fire she rose and ran into the south cloister to cool herself in the snow. She wished the fountain would play. It did so. It played fire. Fire like a golden tree splashed up into the black sky. By its light, she saw it was not a stone child who held the bowl, but the dwarf.

"Fero, fero, I am Ferofax," said the dwarf. "Fire-Bringer. I am a demon. But you're possessed by devils."

"Lucifer, King of the World," said Jhane as she burned.

"His first captains were Azazel and Esrafel," said the dwarf. "They hastened to him, and consoled him, after the fall."

"I am burning," Jhane cried bitterly.

She screamed: "*I am burning!*" And the nuns tied her to her bed in the infirmary where now she lay in the blazing fever.

"I'm burning! I'm burning! Fire! Fire!"

"Lie still," they said.

She hated them, but that was not new, to hate. There was a pain in her groin and her bowels. She saw an old man with a beard tied to a stake, and burning too.

"Pierre!" she screamed.

Ferofax sat cross-legged on the foot of her bed, crowned with stone flowers, eating a lump of paint. *The world will end in fire.*

"It is Yule Natalis," said the nuns. "It is the birth of the Angel as the Christ."

Bells rang.

The Temple-Church rose and hung, unfinished in the sky, with great windows like flame for eyes.

When the pain and fever left Jhane, she was very weak for a long while and lay in the infirmary where the old sick nuns came to die.

"The world is a terrible place," the old nuns said to each other. The City was the world in miniature, filled by lusts and malignities, killings and awful crimes. (Jhane wearily suspected they kept certain secrets and sorry events from her ears, out of regard for her illness.)

There were no novices left. Unfeelingly, they had wedded Christ, as Jhane burned. Christmas was past also. Soon the year would die. New Year would come, and two-faced Janus, an antique Roman deity, would fling open the doors, at the Feast of the Ass.

On the estates of the lord in the north, as everywhere, the Ass Feast had been celebrated with riot. It was the contrary time, the letting of the bung from the cask, when everything must reverse itself, upside down, in order to come right for the remainder of the year. Carts of manure had been trundled through the village, and the unwary pelted. The priest would put on his gown inside out and the bell be rung, for once, but at the wrong hours. Processions roved the fields, beating drums and Eastern tambourines, and a garlanded donkey, though not Belnard's own, paraded about with an idiot or a young peasant girl made king, and riding on its back. You might do anything on the Day of the Ass: all things at their season. By that token, for the rest of the year you could be virtuous.

It had begun in classical times, the old dying nuns said now, disapproving, admiring. A beautiful god on an ass's back, drinking, and ritual, and other things.

Jhane, who had had hideous hallucinations and dreams during the fever, did not discuss the festival. The weather had changed. There had been a thaw (Fire! Fire!), and there was an unseasonable warmth, so a few thin buds spurted from the trees and were chided. As soon as Jhane was able, she resumed her duties and chores. But, having spent so long with the senile nuns, she now moved slowly, ached, must lean often on her broom, sometimes fainted as she scrubbed the flagstones, could not remember easily anything.

Jehan woke, got up and dressed himself. Stowed behind the chest he found a wine-jug, gilded, which he had partly forgotten. He took it with him, along with the cross – which he had only once removed, when ill, for fear enemies might steal it as he raved – and his climbing rope.

He left sanctuary behind without a backward look, and made towards the inn, over the slush.

The torches burned as usual on the cobbles before the gate, but in the upper room, only three or four were gathered together.

They jumped up when Jehan entered.

"Where did you go?"

"We thought you were hanged."

Jehan set down the jug. They gazed at it.

Then Conrad came and grasped Jehan, hugging him close. Jehan eventually pushed him off.

"Tomorrow is the Ass Feast," said Scar-Nose. "Tomorrow we'll rob the world and slit its gullet."

They sat drinking most of the night. Jehan watched them. For the first time, he slept at the inn. When Conrad came slinking to his resting place, Jehan rolled over and laid the knife against Conrad's windpipe.

"When?" said Conrad.

"After the nun."

"What nun?"

"The nun I told you of. There's a dainty nunnery not far off, near the river."

"Never."

"Ask the dwarf. He knows."

"Did you burn the house?" said Conrad.

"A house?"

"In the street where the rich man lived, before we did for him."

"We'll burn the Temple-Church next," said Jehan.

"You're the Devil," said Conrad.

"One of his captains," said Jehan. He laughed softly. "Azazel, Esrafel."

"You laugh like a girl. Your voice never broke. Is that why you hate the whole earth?"

Jehan reached out and fondled Conrad. Conrad fell against him. He whined, struggling forward, labouring. Jehan ceased his attentions, spat in Conrad's face, and went away to another part of the inn to sleep.

At sunrise there was a colossal noise, the clashing of cymbals, pans and pots, the mooing and bray of horns. All the bells jangled. It was Donkey Day, All

Fools Feast. The little madness that held off the greater, hopefully, while God, the Harrier and Destroyer, winked.

The gang of thieves came out on the street along with the rest of the City. Festivals were always fortunate. But sometimes, in the day's tradition, having gained purses and other oddments, a robber might infiltrate a coin into some poor man's satchel or pocket. A day of reversals.

On the bridges they were fishing with mousetraps, and throwing decaying fish back into the river. Huge chunks of ice still wallowed sluggishly by in the water. But the morning was clammy, and drops sweated on the stones and plaster, the foreheads of men.

Processions were going up and down, men with donkey masks, and donkey phalluses strapped to them, ran about shaking rattles, and fake priests in patchwork gave bawdy blessings, while pretend-doctors, carrying jars of leeches and enormous pincers for the pulling of teeth, lunged to and fro.

At Our Lady, over the river, the whores' penance would be enacted, and the thieves went, as if idly, across a bridge with Jehan. A country boy, he had never seen such a thing. "Oh, it's worth your while!"

The City squealed and banged and sang and shouted.

Our Lady was a minor church near the quays, but on the open stretch before, slippery with fish-oil, a mass was being held, with an ass-bishop in a mitre with holes cut for his ears. At each snort and asinine trumpet, the crowd acclaimed the sagacity of the remark.

The whores came from the church presently, in chains, drawing metal balls behind them, but these things were of dented tin and skittered about as the whores screamed with mirth, flinging up their skirts, ribbons in their hair, bare-breasted, some of them.

A cavalcade was coming along the streets, going up towards the market and the Temple-Church.

Jehan pushed towards it, with Conrad and a few others who had not gone after the whores and the tin chains.

Men-devils, next to naked in the muggy day, horned and tailed, and armed with torturer's forks, pranced about a platform, dragging it uphill. On a gaudily painted throne sat the festival's king. The crowds bayed and boomed about him, and he nodded at them his head in its diadem of gilded spokes, feathers and bells. His little feet were stuck in pointed shoes, a wooden sword hung at his side painted with the words: *Rex Urbi*. The wig of flaxen straw framed the handsome, unkind and deformed face of a child. It was Fero, the dwarf.

Jehan laughed with derision.

The dwarf heard him.

"Stop. Your king commands you. I have heard a beautiful sound. It must have been a lark singing."

The platform waddled, tilted, subsided to a halt.

"Every woman turn to your king your face. I'm about to choose a consort."

In the uproar, Jehan stood sneering, and the dwarf pointed at him. "There. That one."

"But, Sire, it's not a woman."

"My command is law."

As he was seized, Jehan did not fight. He hung, contemptuous of them, on the boisterous arms, and was lovingly hoisted aloft. The dwarf caught Jehan and smacked a kiss on to his mouth. "Garments for my queen. You, you. Strip yourselves."

Shrieking, various girls were made to give up various examples of apparel. They trooped in person on to the platform, twining the handsome youth, adorning him in cast-offs and embraces. When they were shooed away again, there was a sudden relevation. Draped in a mantle, a striped sash, and with a knot of ribbons caught through his yellow hair, Jehan was abruptly a girl.

"Sweetest Jesus," said Conrad. He seemed stricken, white-faced, his desire bulging before him. But Jehan did not apparently care. He leaned on the dwarf's shoulder, looking arrogantly about. The glances were unmistakably male, in that young girl's face.

"Will my queen sit?"

"On your head, pig-dwarf."

The crowd applauded with zeal.

"On my lap, dear queen."

"And be got with another babe?" ranted the queen in his high melodious damsel's voice, playing the part now.

"I'll give you another!" offered a male in the crowd. Offers fell fast upon the boy-girl queen. She shook her hair, "I came to Paradys to make my fortune. I came to be apprenticed to a trade."

"Ohh-ho!" volunteered the crowd.

"I meant," shouted Jehan. "to paint pictures of the saints in the great new church. Not sit in a cart and be dighted by a dwarf."

The dwarf caught Jehan and pulled him down across his knees. Jehan laughed, this time lightly and boyishly.

"On, slaves, you vermin. To the Temple. My queen shall paint it."

They careered up the hill, the wineskins jumping through the crowd as if alive. Striving to get one, and to keep up, Conrad lost his brothers. He strove beside the dwarf, took hold of an edge of the platform to help it heave along. He stared at Jehan, who ignored or did not see him, with coals for eyes.

So they poured through the market-place, gathered converts, drove up a hump in the world and into a stone alley, crushed against the walls, the platform tumbling and righting itself in a storm of flesh and confusion.

The outer yards of the Temple-Church, when they got into them, were piled with stones, rubble, bales, ballasts, work-shops, sheds. Architects and menials alike were gone. It was to be their gift to God, the ornament of Paradys, what did it need of protection, the Temple-Church of the Sacrifice of the Redeemer?

Huge and hollow the walls arose: the window-places, finned with iron, gaped. The bones of the scaffolding stood waiting for embodiment, like the Word itself, once. But it had no life, no soul, only its sensed, unborn suspension. The cavalcade swirled about the ankles of future history, and asses defecated there.

"Come now," said King Fero.

"Not I," said Queen Jehan.

"It's a fact," said the dwarf, "my queen here has borne me thirty babes. We must be wed at last."

The crowd brought censers filled with old shoes, and lit them, and the reeking smoke lifted to heaven. The donkey in the mitre was led up, and Jehan and the dwarf were married by it, the crowd itself suggesting the proper words.

"And so to bed," said the dwarf.

"A favour," said Jehan.

"More delay. What is it?"

"Give me the donkey."

"I promise I'm better than the donkey."

"Well, I'll take him anyway."

Jehan, garbed in maiden's robes, intercepted the donkey, tore off its mitre – to yowls of sacrilege – and lifting his skirts, got up on the beast's back. Mildly clocking heels to its sides, Jehan persuaded the animal to a walk. They rode forward, past the king-dwarf, to where Conrad stood in ecstatic petrification. "Wake up. Get up behind me" said Jehan.

"Rebellion," crowed Fero. He drank from a wineskin and toppled over sideways from his seat.

Conrad flung himself aboard the donkey. He gripped Jehan by the waist. "The Devil, the Devil, Satan, Lucifer, death, night," he cursed and moaned, clinging.

They rode off with scant hindrance, the crowd separating to let them by, only cawing commiserations to the dwarf. At its edges, unattended, a pair of drunken men lay on the road.

The donkey trotted now, glad to be out of the press.

They went up a street with an artistic well and a burned house in it.

"Oh Christ, Jehan, Jehan."

Beyond the walled park, some open land ascended. Presently one could see the wave-head of the City Wall above and to the east.

The donkey cantered. Conrad groaned and fumbled at Jehan, who shifted off the thief's hands from the area they sought. Conrad mouthed the smooth neck under the ribboned hair. He sobbed, and spasmed suddenly, giving the ass an unintentional kick that almost unseated both riders.

Having run its length, the donkey pulled up under some trees.

"You've had your pleasure," said Jehan. "Now where are the others?"

"No pleasure. You bastard son of Hell. They were at their own business."

"Just you then, creep-thief. Spraying your lust on an ass's back."

"Shut your damned mouth. I'll kill you."

"No you won't. Now I want that nun."

"I should slit your throat."

Jehan swung from the back of the donkey and hesitated, finding himself sore and stiff. Had he never ridden before? The physical sensation seemed familiar, but he associated it with fear, trouble – putting the thought aside, he pulled off himself in a skein the girls' clothes and the ribbons. Conrad had also left the animal. He sat in the grass under the leafless, untimely-budding trees. He was crying.

"What a fine, brave, bold man," said Jehan. "The artisan cried. Don't burn my house! Don't burn my precious painting!"

Conrad seemed not to listen. "That boy," he said. "I never should have. That boy, your brother. All my life. Sins, sins. I'll burn in Hell. The Devil sent you. We'll be punished, every one. God's wrath. God help me."

"Do you have a home?" said Jehan casually, straightening his tunic.

Conrad wept.

Jehan left him there, and the ass feeding on a crocus. But as he went down across the rough land, towards the wall of the garden-park where once some palace had vaunted, Conrad stumbled after.

"A hut's my home," he said, "in Smith's Lane."

"Good. Then we'll take her there."

"Take who?"

"Christ's Bride. My young nun with the holy face."

"I won't. Don't you fear yourself, Jehan? I won't do it."

"Then take yourself off."

Conrad strode at Jehan's side, head down, sweating.

"To Hell then," said Conrad. "*Noli vade retro, Satanus!* What else did I expect?"

To travel back down through the City was slow going in the festival, particularly since Conrad's sullen gloomy face, and Jehan's purely intent one, urged others to assault them in many ways. The noon bell of the Sextus had rung itself out when they approached the nunnery. Conrad had forgotten it was unknown to him and therefore did not exist. He skirted the wall and the bell-tower, and went along with Jehan to the west side, and past the gate. By day, even while the alleys crouched and the houses stood with their backs to it, the clandestine nature of the place was gone. Anyone might appear, if only to deliver necessaries to the nunnery door. But the bakehouse made an angle in the wall, and beyond that the tree reached over. It had no premature buds, it had not been fooled. Only the rope still dangled from it, ever unseen, unfound – a sorcery of will-power or fate.

"Climb then," said Jehan.

"What?" Into there?"

"Where else?"

Conrad baulked, so Jehan sprang first up the rope, and soon lay along a bough of the tree above, taunting him.

"Is it an apple tree, you serpent?" snarled Conrad. But he grabbed the rope and did climb, getting up into the branches as Jehan uncoiled from them and down into the shrubbery below.

This part of the garden was secluded, the bakehouse wall, the high bushes, screening it in. They crouched there.

Jehan said, "You see that plot, with the plum trees? She'll walk into it in a minute and you'll see her."

"How do you know she'll do just that?"

"She'll have missed me. She'll be coming looking, after every one of the offices, to catch me climbing in again."

"What do you mean by that? Coming in again? Have you been having her here every night?"

"Living here," said Jehan. "They thought me a girl. You've seen what a fair girl I make, when I'm dressed for it."

Disbelieving, believing, Conrad swore.

Then, between the plum trees, a slender nun walked out. She moved towards the wall. When she was less than ten paces away, Jehan stood up.

"Here I am," said Jehan.

The young nun did not speak, her pale face perfect in her gorget and her hands in her sleeves.

"Did you wonder where I was?" said Jehan. "Look, here's a friend I've made in the City." She kicked Conrad glancingly. "Get up and show her." But Conrad would not. Jehan leaned down and pulled on him. He rose then reluctantly, looking at the young nun from the corners of his eyes. She did not appear afraid or angered. Conrad said, stupidly, "Excuse me, sister."

"Yes, excuse him," said Jehan. "He's about to lay harsh hands on you." To Conrad, Jehan said, "Now do it." But Conrad stayed rooted to the earth with the bushes, and now the young nun was turning away. As she went back into the plum trees, Jehan said, "Get her for me now. If she screams, hit her. Cover her head with your cloak. Do it. Or you'll never see me again."

Conrad lumbered out of the shrubs, his mouth forming a protest even as he rushed to obey. The young nun was among the trees and now Conrad was

among them – vanishing. The rest of the nunnery seemed long-dead –
obviously the Feast had not been observed here. Jehan stood and waited for
Conrad to come back over the bare winter plot with Marie-Lis slung across
his shoulder, and after a handful of minutes he did so. He loped heavily under
his burden, breathing noisily, broken twigs in his hair. His cloak wrapped all
of Marie-Lis, but the hem of her habit, which trailed out meaninglessly. Her
head and upper body hung over his back, smothered. "I hit her anyway. To be
sure. And tied her hands with my belt. The blow wasn't hard. She didn't
struggle. Maybe wanted to come."

It was with difficulty and toil that Conrad, unassisted, got the package of
nun up into the tree and down again into the street under the wall, but he managed the feat, for it was similar to thief's work, such removals. He was
throughout industrious not to crack the skull of the prize, nor bruise its bones.
Sometimes he inquired of it how it fared, chuckled when it did not answer.
Conrad on the rope, put himself between it and the wall, Landed, he kissed
it, adjusted it, remarked that it seemed weightier, perhaps the wench had
taken on herself his sins. Remorse was plainly superfluous, now. He turned
briskly and made towards the worst venues of the City, where lay Smith's
Alley, he said.

Further along, they met crowds again, coming up from the river with a
girl attired like a mermaid, and then in the long alleyways, which were
stuffed with drinkers and fornicators. To the curious, Conrad presented his
portable as a besotted comrade. So many strange articles went by in any case
in the arms of others, what odds one more?

A blacksmith's forge dominated Conrad's domiciliary alley, close and
boarded on this day. Behind, sheds and huts leaned on each other the length
of the route, and into the last of these Conrad ducked.

It was a mere space, a sort of absence of anything good or comfortable,
and it was foul. When the door was shut and tied with a cord, the only light
came through a roof-hole. A stirring in one corner indicated a rat, but when
Conrad had lit the single candle-stub, this ceased. Next he let down his
bundle on the bed of rags and fleas. He bent over it solicitously, and began to
fiddle with the folds of the cloak to come at its face.

"No," said Jehan. "Get out now."

Conrad this time definitely remonstrated. The walls shuddered.

"When I'm finished," said Jehan. He sauntered to Conrad and put in
Conrad's hand a coin thieved earlier amongst the crowds. "Go drinking."

"No, you damned imp. This is my house."

"Oh, your house. Your dung-heap, and stinks like it."

"I could have you down. I could cut off your ears, and the rest."

"Go away," said Jehan. "Come back later."

Conrad ranted, and Jehan slapped him suddenly across the lips.

"Go out, or stay and *I* go out. Do you think I'd want her after you'd been chewing on her? Good then. Farewell."

Conrad cursed the world as he left the hut.

The light in the alley was thick and grey, with all the day's yeasty heat panting in it. Jehan shut the door and re-tied it. Then he stood for a while, only looking down at the shape under Conrad's cloak. It seemed not to breathe. It seemed also larger one moment, then to shrink. The candle-end sputtered and would soon go out. If there was gazing to be done, better be quick.

Jehan found himself reluctant. He pictured himself beside the form of Marie-Lis, staring into her face, running his fingers over its sculpture, and then on into the loosened robe, along the statue of her body. And thinking of this, he felt himself swell erect, the weapon at his groin quite ready, having forgotten it was only a roll of cloth not even attached to him, as indeed at other instants of nature, it and he had forgotten.

He strolled to her now, and began to peel away the robber's cloak from the young body of the nun. Some earth fell out on to the floor, and then some broken branches. Then a white hand fell limp against his own and he saw it was not a hand but a piece of damp linen. Jehan stood back, then he fell to his knees and threw himself on the bundle, tearing it apart. Under Conrad's cloak lay a roll of washing, seemingly found drying in the garden beyond the trees. There was a shift filled with soil and muck, finally pushed into a convenient habit, and so brought away as the nun Marie-Lis. Ah, carried with such *care* down the wall. Conrad smiling, Conrad kissing, Conrad ranting he must be first at the rape to ensure dismissal.

A tumult of fury filled Jehan, so violent and tragic it was also true pain. He let out a cry, leapt upright, and was blinded by a rush of blood behind his eyes.

It blotted out everything, and caused him to stumble. As he fought to regain himself, he heard the rat rustling again, widened his eyes – and saw – it was not a rat.

No, it was not a rat at all. But it was between him and the rickety door. Conrad … come back to gloat? The door had been secured. *Not* Conrad – Jehan clenched his fingers on his knife, which might be useless.

The hut seemed to have dematerialised. It had gone to a vast, black openness. Then specks of light emerged out of the black.

The thing against the door was straightening up, and Jehan beheld it was the young nun, Marie-Lis. But she was much changed. Her gorget and veil were gone and her dark hair veiled her instead. An Eastern drapery covered most of her body, but it was thin as water and her breasts were bare, and between them was a golden sign, like a dagger pointing down. Her naked arms were outflung, her feet were set one over the other, and nails of steaming white-hot steel went through her palms, her feet. Her face was serene. In the fingers of her left hand, though it was nailed, tilted a chalice which she now somehow upended fully, and black fluid fell from it, bubbling and smoking. Then she howled. As she made the ghastly ululation, her teeth came visible, and they were like the teeth of a boar.

Jehan gibbered. He could not move, he could only watch.

And now the host were riding, streaming through the black, astride their Hell-mounts, which as they rode, they *used* in other ways, squealing and whinnying, winged and tailed and clawed. Jehan felt the leathery wings clash and scrape about his head in the stench of rutting – and he too howled, in fear.

There was a lightning. It tore everything. The beast-woman on her cross, the raucous riders, Jehan's scream – and fixed them. Every atom hung in black, in bright, in black again. Jehan's eyes died a second time – then he had a view of something – it was as fearful as the horror and ugliness which had gone before – yet it was beautiful, it was *beautiful* – and it was gone – oh what had it been? Some landscape, some palace, some gathering of a Heavenly populace with flesh of pearl and sun-drenched hair – Paradise, or Paradys itself no longer a parody of the parks of Heaven – translated.

Then sight merged back into his eyes. Jehan *saw*. The knife slipped out of his fingers. Intuitively he reached after it, but unable to look, to look away, and he thought, What does a knife count for? And gave it up.

That vast black openness was filled now only by one image.

The man who had entered there wore the garments of a lord, a prince of the City of Paradys-Paradise, and everything was white, so white, while a kind of glowingness shone through it from his skin under the Eastern silk. For his skin had gold in it, and his hair was a rage of gold, a furnace. And his eyes were like the wide golden eyes of tigers in one of the novice's books, which Jhane had once been shown.

Jhane had seen him before, of course. In the church of the nunnery, the white figure untrammelled between earth and air, sometimes static, sometimes moving before her with a woman's gait – or not – disguised as a woman – or perhaps not even that – in a white mantle. And he was a prince. Not a king. Not the world's King. Not Satan, not Lucifer. One of the captains of the fallen host.

Jhane stepped away, Jehan sloughed, everything gone like the knife.

It came to her that she underwent a vision, a religious experience of Hell, but no less holy for being profane.

Jhane's body would no longer allow her to her knees, she seemed to have altered to wood, unbending but capable of splintering. She shut her eyes, but the burning flame of the angel remained imprinted under her lids.

A wonderful aroma filled the void that had been the hut. Her head swam at it, in a moment she would lose consciousness and die, and fiends would bear her to the Pit –

"Esrafel," she said.

"You have called me," he said, "I am here with you."

And no sooner did the voice touch her ears, like no other voice in the world, like music never heard there, than his hands also touched her. (The palms of his hands were golden, as were the soles of his feet in the silken shoes.) The caress seemed to find her forehead, but her whole body was laved in it, even to the tips of her nails and hair.

"I never called you," said Jhane.

"You called me. You did not see that I stood at your side. Which is common to mankind."

"Who are you?" she said, not sure at all if she spoke to him.

"You have named me."

"Esrafel," she said again, "the Angel of the Lord."

"You recognise me as Esrafel," he said. "Then I am Esrafel."

He was winged. She felt the wings enclose her as his voice and hands had done, and the perfume of eternity.

She began to cry quietly on the breast of the angel. Fires mounted through her. She clung to him and begged for release. Her whole flesh seemed sundered, and she too was winged, and as she rushed to the pinnacle of Heaven, she saw his heart blazing like a rose of gold beneath silk and skin, and on the heart of the angel was a scar of an old wound, wounded again, over and over. Then Heaven shattered. She fell. She fell and the stars were made and in the pit of the earth a light, to last until the last of the world, its ending, and beyond, for ever and for ever. So let it be. *Amen.*

Bells were tolling, and only half-aware she counted the strokes. It would be Nonus, the ninth office, three in the afternoon, for there was daylight, but on and on clanged the bells, near and far. It was not an hour or a summons, but the death-bell, sounded from all the quarters of the City.

Jhane sat up in the wretched hut. She had been lying on the flea-ridden bed of rags and itched to prove it. How much time had passed? There had been a wonderful dream …

A man owned the hut; he might return. Jhane rose, and on impulse, shook the soil and twigs from the cloak, and wrapped it about herself. It hid the masculine dress by means of which she had sought protection.

As she walked out into the sallow gloom of the alley, full memory returned to Jhane. It met her like a blow, so she dropped back against the wall, covering her face in shame and distress. But the enormity of what had happened, being insupportable, gushed as suddenly from her. She regarded, in the distance, her days and nights in Paradys, their culmination, and the ultimate and terrible advent of revealing light. She was calm, and under her breath whispered a prayer of her infancy. Through all this, the bells churned on. Who had died? (She thought of the priest in the northern village, and wooden coffins lowered with scant ceremony. Once a son of the lord's house died. That had been different, a hundred mourners on the skyline and the bell at its crying all day.)

At the end of the alley, by the forge – which had stayed silent – she saw a group of beggars sitting in the street, huddled together.

She thought, for no reason she could divine, *I slept too long.*

As she passed the beggars not one of them stirred, and looking at them she saw a single face, its mouth slack and black tongue protruding. The skin was mottled, and there was a smell of bad meat. They were dead.

Jhane went by, and came out into an open square of muddy earth where the houses crushed each other. Smoke went up from two or three chimneys, but otherwise there was no evidence of life. Under the bells a dog bayed ceaselessly. Premonition was total if unnamed. Moving over the square into another of the lanes, Jhane met an old woman and nearly started from her skin.

Jhane said, "You're alive!" The old woman laughed. "Is the City dead?"

"Pestilence," said the old woman. "After the Ass Feast. That's three days. Where have you been?"

"Asleep."

"Done better, you, to have stayed asleep. God sleeps." She craned away and pointed at Jhane. "A man goes to his bed well and at daybreak they find him dead and black. At the festival some were falling down, spewing black blood."

I lay in the arms of a demon.

"Don't come near," said the old woman. "You may have it on you. It comes from a touch, or a look."

"Why?" said Jhane.

"The wells are poisoned," said the old woman. "Full of bodies and piss and curses. It's God's punishment. Perhaps I have it," said the old woman. She licked her hand and smeared the spittle against Jhane's cheek. "There."

Jhane ran away through the alleys of Paradys.

As Jhane fled and wandered through the City, she found Death stalked ahead of her. She began to look out for him, too, personified, some hooded shape. One world had ended for her. Now she was in this other. She had left off dividing reality from dream.

It seemed, soon enough, that the City was on fire. The winter pall from the chimneys and the alleys had lessened, and the wider streets were now full of smoke. Fires were burning on the cobbles, columns of black going up in the still air. Sometimes people darted from the houses to renew the kindling or to throw in aromatics or sulphur. They were plague fires, set to burn the contagion out of the atmosphere. A breath could kill as well as a touch or a look.

Sometimes figures went by Jhane. Robed and cowled, their mouths and nostrils muffled and only the eyes visible, smudged around by smoke, they were like the Death she visualised. They might have been priests going to tend or bring comfort to the sick, or collectors of the dead, but they had a terrifying appearance, looming out suddenly from the smouldering vacuum, under the shadowy cliffs of higher buildings.

The chorus of bells rang continually. Now and then one might fall off, but later it would resume.

Jhane came to the river, which she had instinctively been seeking, though often in circles in the dark. The water had an aspect of stasis as complete as that of the sky. Not a ripple moved, and where any boat lay, it was lifeless as a fallen tree. The upper bank of the City too was lost in smoke, and a cloud rose from it, but without apparent movement.

As she stood there a black procession evolved nearby, a priest with a lantern, many coffins, a flock of carrion-crow mourners.

They passed away over a bridge, perhaps towards the burial ground of Our Lady.

From the houses Jhane began to hear sounds she had not heard before, cries and weeping, and sometimes screams. The dream world was becoming more real. Again she ran away. And having nowhere else, it was towards the Nunnery of the Angel that flight took her.

In her mind, Jhane had a knowledge that she must get in again over the wall, the way the boy had done, the young man who had possessed her, he who was the symbol of all the evil of the masculine species. She felt the horror of casting off the cloak (the thief Conrad's) and being revealed for herself as a male once more.

On an open area between the houses, some carts were being loaded. This time, there were no mourners. All were dead except for the porters, who went about their task jeering and laughing, and sometimes drinking. Elected to such a duty, they did not reckon they could escape the pestilence. "Drink and be merry!" They shouted to Jhane, then two of them gave chase, reaching after her with hands that had just slung the bodies across each other in the carts. But Jhane evaded the men, and they did not pursue her far.

The smoke was very thick beyond that spot, and at the end of an avenue of smoke, the gate of the nunnery suddenly appeared in front of her, and above, the ghost of the tower, the bell tongueless in it.

At that moment, the doors of the gate both began to open. Jhane stood still. The sight of the opening black doors frightened her, making her think of the first night she had come there, and also of the houses in the upper city, the fat woman opening one door, and then the student of Master Motius opening another.

But no one was to be let in this time. It was a group of nuns who were coming out. How strange they looked, their faces in the icon-like blankness with which they drifted into the church at every office. At their head moved the Mother. Her strong, fleshy countenance had altered, it was now gaunt and very pale, an icon like the rest. She glided out into the street, and the nuns of the Angel glided after her. A vague chanting, the note of bees, floated near but did not seem to emanate from them. They came on. They passed Jhane, not seeing her. And she looked at their Madonna faces in perplexity. When they were gone, had vanished into the vacuum of smoke, she realised she had not noticed among them the face and body of Marie-Lis.

Jhane approached the gate and went in through one leaf of the unlocked doors.

The smoke had barely got in here. Jhane could smell incense and herbs and tallow and women – familiar things. She sensed the bell should be ringing for an office – Nonus it would be truly now, perhaps. Her soul had memorised the times. But the tower was mute, and a great quiet lay everywhere – for all at once, all the bells in the City seemed to have stopped ringing.

She went through the outer court, and under the arch into the churchyard. She half turned towards the hostel then. She could go to her cell and hide herself there. Soon it would grow properly dark. Wrapped in her female clothing and the covers of her pallet, and the night, she might be safe. But no, all these layers would only close her more surely inside her own head, where fear was.

The nunnery was a desert. They had all gone out of it. Crossing over the south cloister, Jhane remembered sweeping there with the novices, and the phantom of Osanne with her rags and pail. What had it meant, the death of Osanne? Maybe the nuns had understood, for they had gone about disguising the death very swiftly. Jhane, before she knew what she did, sang aloud a snatch of song the novices had taught her: *Oh winter is, Oh winter is.* "No, no," said Jhane, and the cloister echoed. At its centre the stone child gripped the bowl of the dry fountain. Jhane hurried on. She entered the garden, and stopped immediately, for there was the young nun gathering up washing that had fallen to the ground.

Jhane flew forward. She would cast herself at the feet of the young nun. She must say: I have seen. Save me now, tell me what to do. But at the last instant, the nun turned a little, and Jhane saw that it was not Marie-Lis, but one of the senile sisters from the infirmary. Her wizened face was not an icon. It looked on Jhane, and parting the seams of its mouth, plaintively said to her, "They left me here. Useless. Well, here you are then, too. I shan't die alone."

And the elderly nun sat down on the stone kerb of the poisoned well (in which Osanne had been burned and buried), holding the two or three habits, and the linen things in her lap.

Jhane went to the old nun cautiously.

"What is it?" said the nun. "Can you see me? I can see you."

"Where have they gone?" said Jhane. "The sisters, the Mother?"

"There's a plague," said the old nun. "Didn't anybody tell you? Poor girl. They've gone to nurse the sick and the dying, it's a part of the vows. Pay no heed to yourself, the Enemy strikes us down with his arrows by day and by night. But we must love one another. So the Mother prayed and took them all out, and most or all of them will catch the ailment and perish." The nun was disapproving. "They didn't think of me. I shall die, but it isn't plague, it does-n't matter. Come here, sit beside me. Did you know, this well can't be used any more? One of the novices drowned herself in it."

Jhane went nearer. She said. "Where is Marie-Lis?"

"Sister Marie? I must think. My old head ... Three weeks since the plague came. The night of the Donkey Feast."

Jhane crept close. She sat at the old nun's knee, trembling. Was it so? To sleep three days, or three weeks – she had seen an angel, he had put into her heart the searing light – a slumber of days, weeks, a hundred years, was noth-ing to that. She meant to say, I was granted a true vison: one of the Lord's winged knights came to me. But she said only, "She was the youngest of the nuns."

The old nun said, "Alas, yes. Now it comes to me. It was like the other, the novice, Osanne. But Sister Marie hanged herself."

Jhane now could say nothing.

"In her cell," continued the old nun. "Suicide, a mighty sin. But the Lord understands and forgives. It is a sin only against oneself. Now I know you. You were sick with a fever and they tied you down on the bed beside mine. Well it was that night she hanged herself, for I heard the talk that it must be kept from you, she had been kind to you, and you loved her."

"Never," said Jhane. She leaned her forehead on the old nun's knee and wept silently for some while. The old nun laid her hand gently on Jhane's hair. When Jhane's crying ended, the old nun said, "We have a special dis-pensation, all the City. The priests are dying, or afraid and run off. Any man, or woman, may hear another's confession. Now you must hear mine."

"If you knew what I had done –" cried Jhane. She kneeled up and burst out: "I saw the Angel of the Lord. How can I bear it?"

But the old nun only said. "Be merciful to me, for I have sinned." And then she recounted her confession softly, which amounted to some small jeal-ousies and omissions. When she was done, she smiled at Jhane, then closed her eyes and began to sleep.

She will die in her sleep and leave me alone here, thought Jhane, and had the urge to wake the old nun up. But she looked so peaceful, Jhane did not do it.

Darkness stole over the garden. The fruit trees and the bare plots dissolved into the night. In a while there came up over the wall a straw-coloured moon.

Jhane imagined going back to the church and entering it and flinging herself before the altar and the window. Osanne's ghost might reappear and tell her: "It was your strength that slew me. I got between you and the light. You thrust me aside. It was like the lightning bolt." Or Marie-Lis might be there and say, "I came between you and the light. I removed myself." For Marie-Lis too had presented herself as a ghost, and to Conrad besides, for she had been dead by the Day of the Ass. (Or had Marie-Lis been the tempter, the evil one, the shadow mimicking the light –) But after all, maybe Osanne had only drowned herself in the well and some element in the water had marked her body like burning, and some creature had got down to her and gnawed her belly wide – and possibly Marie-Lis had endured a secret sorrow which she had ended for herself without a notion of Jhane, Jhane's power, or Jehan's crimes. And only Jehan's lust had summoned her back among the plum trees.

The Angel Lucefiel would not descend from the window to comfort Jhane. The Angel Esrafel would not console her ever again. Yet she had seen him.

Yes, she had seen a vision, and now her life must change. No, for it was changed already, she must only accept the change of it. Nor let your sins weigh you down – your sins are finished, tear up the thought of them by the roots. It seemed the other inner part of her mind had again been formulating plans.

There in the garden, by the sleeping, dying nun, Jhane pulled off Conrad's cloak, and all Jehan's male attire. She unbound her breasts, and did not even notice when the penis of cloth was sloughed into the shadows. Jhane took from the old nun's lap one of the habits, and articles of linen. Jhane clothed herself. She covered her head and neck with gorget and veil, her body with the robe of the order, when everything was in place on her, she drew up the topaz crucifix and wore it there openly on her breast.

The old nun still slept.

Jhane took her hand.

Light as a husk, the old nun slipped forward and rested on her. Jhane lifted her in her strong arms and bore her back to the bed in the infirmary.

An hour later, at the office of Hesperus, which was not rung, the old nun died.

Jhane dug and buried her in a shallow grave, in the traditional area. She did not visit the church, before passing on into the City through the gate.

They had forbidden the ringing of funeral bells; they had forbidden process-ions of mourners. Who had done so? None but the unseen Lords of Paradys, her Duke or Prince (and Jhane did not know which), the authorities of the City – most of whom had fled the pest, and sent their orders back with doomed messengers. Almost all the function of the City had stopped, however, and so to cancel funeral rites was nothing. There were scarcely any priests remaining to speak above the bodies. The graveyards were full. Now they dug up any spare land, and piled in the corpses on top of each other, twenty, thirty persons deep. There was no commerce this side of the river. Men lived by what they could get, stealing and hoarding. On the upper bank, some forms were kept, this far, but for how long? The plague seemed fit to withstand them all. The plague was healthy and vital. The Death, they called it now, as if there were no other kind of death in the world, and maybe there was not. Cadavers lay in the thoroughfares, uncollected a great while. They were blotched with black, black boils, and black blood. The dogs, scavenging, refused to eat them. Smoke still rose, the warding fires, and a few vehicles still trundled back and forth. Sometimes there might be a woman at a well, but since the wells were supposedly poisoned, these women were reckoned mad, or already infected – or witches and actually the poisoners, and were liable to be stoned.

It was difficult to traverse the river. The upper City had set the source of the plague on the other bank, fount of all villainy and misadventure, and sometimes extempore guards patrolled the south and west ends of the bridges. It was also pointless to attempt to escape the City, for the roads beyond the walls, rife with infection, fringed with rotting bodies, were also blocked by wagons and carts of which the drivers had perished, dead horses and sheep, while the fields and woods were said to be choked by wildmen who had lost their minds, and by desperate wolves which had come to a feast that, in the event, repelled them.

In the new world, Jhane took her way. Dressed as a nun, she was accorded respect. The female orders of the City had proved valiant and thorough, where the priests had frequently made off with their lives. Even the topaz cross on the girl's breast was not taken from her. What use were riches now? Could you bribe King Death? The plague was everywhere (they said), civilisation was ending. And robbers who thieved food or apparel, let alone gold, they contracted plague from them.

It was simple and easy to tend the sick, when once all barriers were down in brain and heart. In just such a manner, she had found it simple and easy to do harm, to murder.

Not so much did Jhane expect death: she expected nothing. She walked among the victims of the pestilence, unafraid, and in itself this gave them a sort of courage. Jhane proposed no remedy for the symptoms of disease. She offered only her cool hands, into which they drove their nails in agony, which they clasped in dying, and only her quiet voice that murmured nothing impor-

tant to them, and her nun's robe which symbolised divine respite and forgiveness. She heard ten hundred confessions. When hoarse whispers pleaded for
God's grace, she nodded. Her eyes carried a wonderful conviction. She had
done far worse than any of them, or so it seemed to her, and she herself had
been consoled by an angel. That they called the world's Lord by the wrong
name, this she overlooked. It was not, this hour of their death, any time to
quibble.

Though sometimes she glimpsed others religious at similar work, she met
no nuns of the order she had adopted. She met, however, with many forms of
human fear and anger, acted out as if upon a stage. She saw pageants with
banners, and orgies, when beer and naked limbs swilled down the street. She
saw men who whipped themselves with thongs studded by nails, and women
dancing in their skin to the pound of a drum. She saw a death-cowled priest
who screamed that the Day of Wrath had come, and a young maiden embracing her lover's corpse, begging it to kill her with its infection, she would go
with him. Jhane paid little heed. It was the new world. But then again, the
earth, and all things in it, had never seemed familiar or sane to her.

The brown days of smoke, the blind nights, went by. Sometimes a biblical,
yellow-lit cloud stood over the higher City after sunset.

She saw and held children as they gave up the ghost, young men, maidens, crones. She learned all the degrees and stages of the illness, and all the
guises of it. When they should begin for her, she would acknowledge them.
They did not begin for her. Like a weightless feather she floated on the tide
of misery.

"Oh, sister, devout lady, come to the bridge with us. You'll help us? They
can't turn back *you*."

It was in fact a funeral procession, though not clothed in mourning,
which, in any case, most of it would never have afforded. Cartloads of the
dead outnumbered the living. Everyone wept, which was now unusual, for
apathy and despair, the greatest of the sins, had settled on Paradys.

A tall old man stood looking down into Jhane's face.

"We must get over," he said. "There are no places left here. Holy ground.
They must be got into holy ground. Or when the last trumpet's blown, they
won't hear it."

Jhane did not say to the man, It will not make any odds. There is enough
life for all. She did not say, He remembers even the fall of a sparrow. She
bowed her veiled head in assent, as she had recently done whenever any
request had been made to her that she was capable of granting. She led them
towards the South Bridge.

There was a huge bonfire half-way across, uncared for and almost out. Even
so, they must pick through the crackling rims of it, and a black fume rose.

Over on the other shore, some men in mail coats were standing about. They were soldiers, or a company from some lord's guard. One stepped forward, on to the bridge, as they came near, and drew his sword.

"No farther."

The carts rumbled to a halt. Women began to cry and wail loudly. Jhane walked on. As she came closer and closer to the soldier or guard, his face engorged – firstly with fear, and then with amazement.

"You can't," he said, when she too halted, a pace or so from him.

"Yes."

"*No*, sister. Take them back. There's no grave-ground here. *Christ's nails.* They're burning them, that's all. Look east, up there. Those aren't the pest fires. It's corpse fires now. Too many dead to bury."

"Then," she said, "the fires."

"No," he said again. "We're keeping the riff-raff away. We've checked the sickness this side. It's less here. But not if they all come over. They stink of death."

Jhane stood motionless. She looked into his eyes and said, "When I was hungry, you fed me. When I was thirsty, you gave me drink. I was sick and you tended me, in prison and you visited me. The Lord says, Even as you have done to the least of men, so you have done to me."

The mailed man began to cry, just like the people around the carts, but perhaps only the smoke of all the thousand fires of Paradys was in his eyes. He stepped away, lowering his sword. The other men shifted. "Let them by," he said to these others. "What does it matter." They moved, and the carts began again to jolt forward. Another man in mail ran at Jhane and pushed the point of his sword against her breast. The first man came and eased the sword aside. As Jhane went on with the carts, she heard him say, "Can't you see, you fool, she's the Virgin. It's a miracle. We'll be saved!"

As they proceeded off the bridge, the last cart toiled beside Jhane, and when she looked into it she saw the face of the thief, Conrad, but upside down. He was lying across several other bodies, which they had tried to arrange in a seemly way, although this was not possible. The tall old man trod by the cart. He said, "That was my son. He was a wicked sinner. A cut-throat. He started doing evil as a child. I knew then he was lost. Whatever ground he goes in, or if he's burnt, it's the same – he'll be baking in Hell already."

"You're wrong," said Jhane. "A woman saw an angel in Conrad's hut."

The old man stared at her, but they were coming level with the outer yard of the church of Our Lady, and a fearful smell was in the air, worse than all the rest. Between the church and the quay boats had earlier been dragged ashore and set alight. This had laid the foundation of a pyre for multitudes, but was now mostly crumbling, a tower of glowing ashes. From thick smog a ragged priest or two was emerging. One ran forward and waved them away.

"Not here. No more. Go on to the east wall, the Roman wall. Up there." Then he drew Jhane aside. Unconcerned with her now, the death procession moved by, and left her behind. "Sister, I can see you've had the Death, and survived it." Jhane said nothing. "It's plain, you bear all the marks. I too. Look, you see? Like the mark on Cain's brow. There was one good doctor, he gave me myrrh and saffron, and bled me. On the fifth day the boil burst and I recovered. To show my thanks to God, I serve the City. When this is over, this terrible reckoning, I'll kill myself." He paused, waiting to complete his catechism.

"Why?"

"Can you ask? There will be so few of us left alive. The whole world will have to begin again. Besides, God's punishment is so cruel. I'll thank, but I can't worship such a God. I defy him."

"If someone must be the enemy of mankind," said Jhane, "and not Satan, then God, perhaps."

"Blasphemy," said the priest. He laughed. "Stay here," he said. "If you go up there, you may get caught in some building. When the pest comes, the soldiers wall them up alive inside, the sick, the hale, the dead together."

Jhane turned from the priest. He said again, "Stay, pale rose. We have wine in the church." But Jhane slid from him and was gone, climbing up the hills of Paradys, quickly lost to him in smoke.

Over Satan's Way, the ribcage of the unfinished Temple-Church had the look of a ruin, something which had been, but now decayed and fell to bits. A large fire had been built in the midst of the sheds, but it was out. No one was by.

Peculiar noises, often indecipherable, ascended and sank constantly in the City, generally isolated. One such now began in the street that circled beyond the Temple. Jhane came out on the street. It was not as she remembered. The decent houses, the ornate well and trough, the burned house, were in position as before, and yet everything seemed subtly to have misplaced itself. There were no fires here, as if once had been enough, and smoke coloured the air, but only that. Far along the wall of the old garden-park – which had not yet been utilised as a crematorium – mailed riders on thin horses sat under a battered, stained banner. They were directing the actions of some labourers in the process of boarding and plastering over the doors and lower windows of one house.

"Stay away, sister. *It's* here." The man who rode towards her on the sorry horse did not meet her eyes. "The only method to stop it, lady."

Then he drew closer. He leaned towards her. On his face was a terrible invisible unmistakable shadow. He murmured, so the other men should not hear, "I have it. I'm hot and cold, and a pain in my groin. Some live through. I might. I shan't. When this job's done, I'll go up on the waste land, where the fires are. It's like the Pit up there, the damned all crying in torment, and the flames. Confess me? They say anyone can do it, but a holy nun's better if I can't have the priest."

"Yes," said Jhane.

Leaning from the horse then, as if he discussed ordinary things with her, he gabbled his confession, a sibling to so many others she had heard. And when it was over, he added, "And they're on my conscience – the mason in the house there. He was at work on the Temple-Church. His wife and servant were taken out, dead, but then the order came, close the house. It's him and some lunatic son he's got, dying in there and hearing the plaster shutting round them. Better to go in the open. But I don't care. Rot the lot of them. Rot 'em." Suddenly, no longer bothering with life, he rode headlong through the street, going eastward. His men did not pay much attention to him, the labourers none; they were at work on the final window.

"Let me go in," said Jhane to the labourers, when she reached them. They looked at her, then at the mounted men under the banner.

"Trying to earn Heaven, sister?" one of them sneered. "Go on then. It's up to you. If you can squeeze through the window, skinny nun."

But two of the labourers assisted her politely through the narrow aperture, even fisting out some of the fresh plaster. When she was through, they asked her blessing. She rendered it as she had seen the Mother do. Then, she stood in the house and listened to the wood smacked back and the slap of the putty, and watched the light fade.

The house already reeked of the Death, but the odour was customary to Jhane. She climbed a stair and midway up she was confronted by a man – the dying mason. He raved at her, an intruder in his home. He asked her what she meant by it. But his breathing was hard. He coughed fluid into his sleeve.

"Forgive me," said Jhane. "Something made me come in here. I'll care for you. Recovery may happen." She saw that this was unlikely. When he staggered, she supported him back to his bed. He had stopped reviling her. He smiled at her in a frightened and placatory manner, like a sick child.

Presently he said, "Nothing, no chance for me. But the boy –"

"Your son."

"Not my son. I wish I'd had – such a son – still-births were all she could manage, poor bitch. She's dead, poor bitch." He coughed and choked and recovered, and said, "Not long. The boy – might live. He's been sick a while – not this, before. That can – make them stronger to fight – I've seen it before. Before. He's lived through trouble before. Wits – gone – the worst of all – better any crippling – though not the hands –" The mason's speech wandered with his thoughts. He then said, "Having seen what he was capable of, I asked him if he'd train to work in stone – well – he'd drink and go after – that sweetest part of a woman's frame – but he was young. Anyway murdered for it, we thought. Then on Fool's Day, over – the – river – I found him. Some slut had taken him in. Well – he was useless – to her. She told me. She'd come on him – crawling in his blood. Oh the Devil burnt up that house, oh – yes. The Artisan Motius – they said the Devil rode over his roof and hauled him up through a window – all alight. Dead, anyhow. So *I* took the imbecile in. How could I leave him – in her hovel? Perhaps – did him – a bad turn. This fell on us." Then he was feverish and screamed that he also was burning, Fire! Fire! And then he choked and drowned and died.

Jhane went further up the house and came to a small room with a slender bed filling it. On the mattress a young man with wringing-wet yellow hair, writhed and tossed in unemphatic delirium. His skin was blotched by dark-ness, and beneath one arm nested the black knots of the plague. He was how-ever recognisable. And so Jhane looked into the face of her brother, Pierre.

Inside the walled-up house, it was very quiet. The earth, which had formerly condensed to a City, had now become the house alone.

Shortly before midnight, Jhane had managed to drag the heavy corpse of the mason off the bed, and into the chest at the bed's foot. Plague cadavers putrefied rapidly. The chest, of a proper size and air-tight, must serve as cof-fin and burial together. Having sealed the chest – its linen would be useful elsewhere – with its own iron clasps, Jhane went about the floors, seeing if anything else was to be had there. All access to a well was gone, but previ-ously in the kitchen, perhaps the bounty of the law, she had found a barrel of water. There were also some casks of ale. Jhane now searched and discovered a store of candles, kindling, garlic and withered apples, and some mouldering bread, but if there had been any other provisions, someone had appropriated them.

Above, the young man who was her brother strove on between sleep and delirium and death. Jhane had sat by him some hours, telling him at intervals that he would live. It was the only panacea she employed, other than to wash his body with the tepid water, and to moisten his lips. She had rolled him aside also, twice, to ease the soiled clothes from under him, replacing them with fresh. When he cried out or shouted, which happened occasionally, she took him in her arms, responding to all he said, replying, whether he spoke with some semblance of logic or only in nonsense, and whether he might hear her or not. (She had been made aware in the strife of the plague that the sufferers suffered far worse when feeling they were ignored, or that the phantom situa-tions of fever went unstraightened. In certain cases she had also pretended to be wives and mothers, daughters and sons, and the victims – crying for these lost kindred – were deceived and calmed.)

It had not surprised her to come on Pierre. She had supposed him dead, but the world had changed. It seemed to her, although she did not dwell on it, that the moment the angel touched her, Pierre had been reborn. Thereafter the mason accidentally located and rescued him inevitably. Ever since then, some invisible cord had been slowly pulling her towards this spot. Reborn, Pierre could not die again so swiftly. And to attend and comfort him as he fought for life was not an expiation. He had been cruel to her, and she had not forgotten it. But what he had done no longer mattered, whereas her own cruel malice had turned her towards kindness and deep pity. Compared to her own wickedness, Pierre's was of a slight order, and probably he had learnt nothing from it.

Because he would survive, too, Jhane did not attempt any of those remedies which the doctors had practiced before her in a number of scenes of the pest-stricken City. Though the black boils were hard and leaking, she did not lance or cauterise them; she did not bleed or radically try to cool or inflame the desperate body on the bed.

For herself, she took no precautions.

She had always been underfed. She ate the apples, and drank a little ale, and slept in separate minutes, sitting on the floor.

A morning came, blooming up through the upper windows. A day passed, declining down through them. These windows had been left alone as they were too small to provide egress. But they did provide some air, for the smoke seemed less. That afternoon, Jhane heard a distant bell give tongue in Paradys. She had almost forgotten the sound. In a while she realised it was not a funeral knell, but the Nonus, from some church away towards the river. Beyond the window, in the vanishing light, roofs and towers stood in islands among the smokes.

When night returned Jhane took off the topaz cross and laid it under the sick man's pillow. The flash of the jewel as she came from the window had reminded her she wore it. If she had recollected earlier, she would have removed it then and placed it ready for Pierre.

Near sunrise of the third day, Pierre screamed, and the evil pebbles of the Death burst open, freeing him of poison.

When she had cleaned him and given him water, he dropped down into an intent oblivion. After the sun had risen, all that day, she sat and watched his skin begin to clear and change colour, the dark patches gradually leaving it. But the ill-treatment, the assault, the rape, the madness – these as much as the pestilence – had aged him and torn his beauty. Through the empty pane of his unconscious face, Jhane could see now a resemblance to his father, Belnard.

He did not know her. This seemed to her a proof that the insanity the mason had spoken of was leaving Pierre. Sane, he would not accept her presence, he would *reject* her presence – once precursor of such horrors.

"You're good to me," he murmured, and drifted again to sleep. Later he said, "I'm hungry." Later again, he said, "Hunger gnaws at me. There's a snake in my guts. Kind holy lady, please tell them I must have something to eat."

"Not yet," she said. She gave him more water.

He trusted her, drank, and fainted again into sleep.

He was very weak and would die without sustenance. What should it be? Milk, with a little bread crumbled in it, a light meaty broth. She mashed apples to a pulp with water heated at the kitchen hearth, and added a sip of the ale. This mush she fed him, but it only made him nauseous, and brought no strength.

"Who else is here?" he said. "Sister, send some boy to the market. He's sure to go. Give him – "Here he fumbled for coins, and found nothing. "Well, only tell him Pierre asked it." He smiled charmingly.

"Rest," she said. "I'll do what I can." For he had obviously forgotten a great amount, and it was not the time to tell him they were walled up inside a house.

Almost all the smoke seemed to have cleared from the City, but a heavy rain had begun, and sometimes thunder shook the timbers of the building. The street, peered at through the tiny window-place, looked deserted, though once she saw another cart go past below, lugged by a weary man, mounds in it under a covering, and making east. The mason's house had no upper east window. She could not see if the pall of the crematory fires still flooded upward there.

Jhane set about searching the house again. It was true that she discovered items she had not found on her prior foray. In a pocket of the chimney of the great hooded fireplace in the mason's bedchamber was a cache of coins. In a cupboard she came on the tools of builders, a saw and tongs, pick-axe and hoe. In a box beneath rested the mason's level, and some wooden shapes whose purpose eluded her. She unearthed some wine also which, as with the cloves of garlic, was a useful disinfectant: the training of the nunnery. She found, too, parchments with architectural drawings, and three books she could not read, ink-horn and quills, a child's cradle with a cloth doll lying in it, at which she recalled the mason's words of the still-births, and the bones of a dead rat. None of these was of any help to her.

Days and nights washed over the house. Each was its own season, a little year.

Pierre, who had begun to seem stronger, now lapsed. He said, "There's a hard stone under the pillow."

"Not a stone. It's your own cross."

"I haven't any," he said.

"Yes. When you were in the fever, I took it from your neck and placed it there for safe-keeping. Your cross with the topaz."

He said, "My father gave it me." He said, "It came from the Holy Land.

Just the jewel, the crucifix was made for it after. My father was on a great crossade. He killed Saracens. They reject the Christ – as you know, sister. They worship a man. And an angel also – Jabrael, God's Mighty One … Yes, the yellow stone, the topaz, he cut it from some breast-plate of a fallen pagan priest, in a shrine there, or so he said …" He faded and was senseless for a while. Then he woke and said, "But the cross was stolen from me. I *remember* that. I was beaten, and the cross –" Wild with fear he stared at her, struggling not to remember.

"A dream of the fever," she said. "It's over."

Later in the night he said, "I had a sister. She told me lies about our father. How could she do that?"

He had learnt nothing.

"Sister …"

She did, for a moment, start. But all nuns were the sisters of all men.

"Lie quietly," she said.

"Did I – make confession to you?"

"Never. It was not necessary."

"But now."

"Nor necessary now."

"I can't," he said. "I can't."

"Live? Yes."

"The little cross –"

"Yes."

"If I – don't live – take it. No, that's wrong. If I live, take it anyway. For your order, sister."

Now she did not start at all.

"She said, "Some gifts can't be given. Your father gave it you. It must stay with you."

She thought he slept. Then he said, "Will you put the cross round my neck?"

Jhane did as Pierre asked her. The chain, which had been thieved elsewhere, seemed to puzzle him briefly. Then he lay still, thinking of the feel of the cross, the jewel, on his skin.

"That girl I told you about – did I? My sister, Jehanine. She was a harlot in the City. She came to me to show me her degradation, then she ran and hid herself. I saw what she'd become, just by looking in her eyes. I wish I hadn't seen that."

Oh, he had learnt nothing. He must live, it was his only hope. Yet he was dying now.

Jhane walked the house, up and down. She opened again the chests and cupboards, held a candle to the mouse holes, but even the mice were gone.

She felt no hunger, she felt only beyond herself, a vast space hollow as a bell, in which she was; breathing, moving, alive, slenderly hard and sure as a needle. But Pierre was like the dust, like melting snow, like water. He must be remade. He must have food.

In the watery dawn, some men went by. Jhane called down from a window. They took no notice of her. Perhaps her voice failed to reach them, deaf ears or hearts or minds.

Through the dark, the City bells rang once more every one of the offices. At Laude, Jhane went down through the house, to the kitchen. By the glimmer of the candle, she looked into the empty larder.

As her hands were searching over the bare surfaces, she thought very clearly and suddenly of the Angel Esrafel, companion-captain of the Prince of Light. Standing quite still, arms on the shelf, her head thrown back, she closed her eyes, recapturing as it seemed entirely the ecstasy and healing of his embrace.

Then she opened her eyes and gazing before her, she saw what she had been looking for: food. At the revelation of the sight, she was grasped by utter terror. For an instant she rejected the absolute truth, the miracle, as unthinkable. But in another instant, she felt again the touch of the angel. She accepted that the world was altered. She accepted her own power and strength. Terror left her immediately. There was only the hollow of the night enclosing her hard purity, which could not be shaken.

Then, practical, she turned to seek out the means of preparation, and – the training of the nunnery – such methods as there were of care.

"The boy came back from the market," said Jhane. She set the bowl on the floor. Propping Pierre half asleep on the pillows, she began to spoon the broth into his mouth. She was very weak. It had taken an endless time. It had taken years even to climb the stair, but maybe not so long, for the broth was still hot, fragrant with the grains of garlic, the dash of wine, the ripe clean smell of the fresh meat.

At first, he was almost unable to take it. But after he had had some, and slept a while, he took more. There was enough of the food for some days.

At the hearth fire, she kept the cauldron heated, and also burned the stained and ruined linen. The wine and apples fortified her now. When she lost consciousness it was never for very long. She had fainted repeatedly in the beginning, kneeling by her cooking.

Some dream told her she had committed a sin, heeding the angel, but she laughed aloud at it. She was full of joy. She would not bother with the rest.

She knew also that miracles attended upon miracles, and that, before Pierre had consumed all the broth, some means of escape would come to them.

One morning, a colossal thunder-clap shook the whole house. It was a group of mailed men banging on the plaster of the lower house with axes and mallets.

Jhane looked down at them dreamily from a window.

"Sister! How are you faring? Are there any more with you? Any still sick with the pest?"

"One man with me. Neither sick now, but starving."

"You were heard calling, but they said it was a ghost. *I* said, that's the gentle nun went in there, to help the mason. And God will have spared her."

He was the soldier who had sneered at her when she had done so. Now his face was bright and young with happiness.

"The plague's over. It's gone. Old Death's taken himself off."

A chunk of plaster gave way and fell with a crash. The men cheered and hullooed, waving their mallets up at her in salute.

"The young man with me is very feeble," said Jhane. "Please will some of you come in and carry him down."

She left the window and went to Pierre to tell him, but he had heard, of course.

He was handsome today, his looks returning like the spring. Under his tunic, hastily pulled on for the outing, the topaz glinted. He did not know her, but he said, "Sister, my own kindred couldn't have been more tender to me. You saved my life, perhaps my soul. Do you know, I was apprenticed to an artisan. But I heard he died. Well, I'll find one to take me on. God gave me a talent. I must use it, to God's glory."

Then, when a doorway was smashed, and the men came tramping up the stairs, he said, "You have a look of my own sisters, isn't that strange?"

But his eyes were still dimmed over.

It was two of the soldiers, not Pierre, who noticed her own plight.

"Ssh," she cautioned, as another of the men bore Pierre away. "Tell him nothing. Don't mention it when he's by."

"But in God's name, how did this happen?"

Used perhaps to the wounds of war, the two soldiers stayed by her, and renewed the wrappings and bindings. As if seeing the rough staunching by fire, however, for the first, and the protruding sawn bone, so very white, Jhane herself turned ill. When she recovered, she was in the street in the arms of the soldier who had sneered, and now held her like his child. A mild rain kissed her face. "Ssh," she said again.

"How –" he said. "This sacrifice – did you? How –"

"The Lord guided me and gave me strength."

Of such matters legends were made.

They took her to another house of nuns, much depleted since the Death, whose inhabitants cared for her in costive silence. The surgeon, a man who had fled the City, returned and did not credit the tale. This woman had been attacked by criminals in the hysteria and panic of the pest. Confronting Jhane with his verdict, he was pleased by her acquiescence. He prophesied that the upper portion of the limb might grow infected, in which case the work would be to do again, the cut higher, and she might die. He did not fear this death, nor warning her lavishly of it, for it was not in itself contagious.

She heard no more of Pierre, who had gone away with his golden head lying on the newest rescuer's shoulder. She did not give a thought to paintings and carvings which perhaps, by his skill, might come to adorn the churches of Paradys. Or to the love he would effortlessly win, or the jewel Belnard had given him.

Part of her own self had become a part of him, yet even this reverie did not prevail upon her. Recollecting her act, the use of the tools found in the house, the tight-binding and cauterisation, the subsequent preparation of the meat – into which had intruded a ghostly figment of Osanne (whose own disintegrated arm had been raised from the well) – then Jhane herself doubted that she could have performed the deed. She did not at all regret it.

A pain-wrought phantom arm and hand, to the very fingers, remained to her below the elbow. Their presence was so decided that often she would reach out with them, finding with surprise she could not then take hold of things in this way. The phantom was, she knew, the incorporeal arm of her spirit. Unlike flesh, it could not be severed from her.

When she left the nun's hospital they were greatly relieved, for the proximity of a martyr and saint had oppressed them.

Jhane herself was unencumbered. She was already putting from her mind the image of her brother. She did not feel holy. No more than she hugged to herself the mad terror of her crimes did she clasp the greater terror and madness of her act in the mason's house. She did not believe she had been valorous, extraordinary, tested, or kind.

The unlocked doors of the nunnery gate had saved them from being forced, for at some time persons had entered. They were gone now, and there had been no desecration, only a certain amount of human dirt left lying. Nor were there any corpses. Jhane set herself, slowly, to clean the yards.

The milk had turned to curds in the refectory-kitchen, and these she ate, along with such fruit and salt fish as the invaders of the nunnery had not devoured. The water in the refectory well was crystalline.

As she ragged and broomed, the flight of a sudden bird among the empty cloisters, or the flutter of stray sunshine, might cause Jhane to glance about her. But the ghosts did not return.

She would have rung the bell in the tower, but, lacking an arm, it was inconceivable she would be able to do it. She regretted this, the gap where its notes should have sounded oddly disturbed her. She missed also the chanting of the nuns, and sometimes thought she did hear it, but the susurrus was in her own head.

At first she went to the church solely to see what had been done there, and if the great window was broken, but only a little debris had been blown in, and rain, which had formed and dried in pools in the uneven floor. The window was intact. So, on days when the sun shone, and at dawn, Jhane would go to look at the picture, at the Angel Lucefiel, Son of Morning and Bringer of Light, sword drawn and still falling eternally through the sky, the solar halo behind his head, on wings of fire, one foot against a gilded orb. Perhaps it was the daylight which blazed through this image that gave it such reason for her. It was the only artistic form she had ever understood, and the only iconic thing, apart from her doll in childhood, she had ever found plausible.

At night, or when exhausted, Jhane went to her former sleeping place in the cell, in the wooden hostel, and lay down there.

Sometimes she dreamed, on the pallet, that new nuns had filled the stone desert and were at the offices, or hoeing the south garden, while the novices learned from painted books in the House of the Novitiate. It seemed to her this might come to be, and that they would accept her, although she had not been made a Bride, and that it would be very simple to live in this way for a life of years, knowing everything by rote, and beyond the rote, wedded to the certainty of the fact.

Then again, she dreamed that the Nunnery of the Angel had been for centuries a ruin, or that it did not exist, that she had imagined or conjured it. Or that, even though the walls and courts were present, the order had not worshipped Lucefiel, the Christ, but some other.

None of this concerned Jhane. Her dreams were not fears or even questionings. Merely rehearsals of different chance.

She did not attempt – she never had attempted – to count the days. Spring came blustering through the nunnery, and lit the columns and the garden with yellow and white flowers.

As she crossed the south cloister, Jhane saw that the stone child by the fountain had become a dwarf, who got to his feet and bowed and capered, revealing the stone child was there after all, behind him.

"Buy a ribbon," said the dwarf. "Or have you cut your hair and shaved your quaint skull?"

"I have not," said Jhane. "But neither do you have your tray of ribbons."

"True. When you saw me last I was a king. When I saw *you* last, you were a boy. What are you, female or male? Or both – some abomination."

But Jhane moved on towards the church. The dwarf went with her, and entered as she did through the side door into the nave.

It was almost the hour of Tiers, and the sun filled the Great Light.

They regarded it, the nun and the dwarf.

When Jhane sank to her knees, the dwarf was taller than she. He seemed to be considering this. Then he walked forward, between Jhane and the window. And he began to stand up in his skin.

He became Belnard her step-father, he became the apothecary of her journey, and then he became – spreading and billowing – the fat woman with the keys – and then stretching thin and bearded, he was Master Motius, and, getting fleshy and smooth again, the mason, and losing the flesh, Conrad the thief, and folding inwards and out, in a quick succession, pious Osanne, the Mother, the young nun Marie-Lis. And then, he was Jhane herself.

There she stood, clad as she had been in the bounty of the nunnery, in that plain gown, but her hair was loose and savage about her, her eyes gleaming.

"It's very clever," said the real Jhane, still kneeling. "How do you do it?"

"Ah," said the dwarf-Jhane. "That's telling, that is."

And then he rose up and opened into fire and wings and was an angel, all golden, who extended his hand to her, while through the translucence of his garments she saw his heart burning like a wounded golden rose.

Jhane sighed.

"Was it always you?"

"Perhaps," he said, "or not." But she barely heard his words through the music of his voice. Leave yourself, said the music. You may come back to her.

And Jhane left herself, kneeling there on the floor of the church. She lifted with the angel into the sky. She was an angel herself. She was not indeed, *herself*. There was no gender, neither female nor male. Jhane was a winged creature of the light. Above her the sun, below, the earth, which was a round orb, shining.

They flew freely, the two angels. They embraced and sang and communed without speech and touched all things and glorified all things, and *were*.

Jhane will die?

Yes, although not yet.

And the world? Will the world end?

One day the world will end.

When will it end? Surely sin will not destroy it?

Sin will not destroy the world. While the world has sin it cannot end. Not until the world is perfect may the world end. The world is for a purpose. But when the world is perfect and whole, and all things therein, and all mankind, perfect and whole, then the world will be permitted its finish. There will be a great shining, as in the window you see it, the coming of a great light, like fire. And in that time, the world will end, and all life find its liberty.

Life is the dream, said the angel who had been Jhane.

So be it, said the Angel Esrafel. But let it be a sweet dream, at least.

Then Jhane opened her eyes in the church, cramped and chilled, alone, and night was falling in the window.

She could not read or write, and so she could not set down her vision of the apocalypse. It is often the way. This she understood, and that it did not matter in any case.

Rising, she went quietly to the refectory, lit a candle, and ate curds and drank water behind her wooden screen.

"It is Lucifer, Lord Satan, who rules the world," said the priest. "To survive here, we're bound to worship him."

He showed them a drawing on parchment, a rose transfixed by a dagger.

"Remember this sign. We meet here, under the old church. You will be obliged to render passwords. In time, who knows what riches and power we shall accumulate, through the favour of our Master. I myself," he said, "survived the plague. That was his sign to me. God smote me, but Satan raised me to do *his* work and glorify *him*. You're an artist of the City. Who spoke to you of this secret society?"

"Several," said the young man. "But Motius the Artisan was once my tutor."

"The magician? Yes. His house was burned up and flaming fiends carried him to Hell. You understand, there's no escape at last. It ends in fire."

"Hah. Yes." The young man smiled.

"But meanwhile, a life of wishes fulfilled. His servants he never cheats. All the joys of the flesh, full dominion over others. The end is horror, but you may have three hundred years of pleasures before that payment comes due."

Through the heavy frozen passageways they went, into a chamber drawn with symbols, floor and walls and ceiling, where the worshippers waited in silence.

"Should I take off this?" asked the beautiful young artist, indicating a crucifix at his throat.

"No. Why would he fear it? He ousted *that* one long ago. It may amuse him. Leave it on."

The ceremony began. It had elements of a mass, of a communion, and of a christening, for the new initiates were to be sworn and bound, and marked in blood. Three black cocks were sacrificed, and the sooty tapers set alight. Eastern incense smoked from the censers.

Pierre Belnard had once attended such rites in Motius' studio, but been bored by them. His adventures since had urged him back. There were fever dreams which haunted him still, and memories of the Death, and some story he had heard of a nun who hacked off her hand to feed a starving man walled up in a plague house.

As the rituals went on, however, he grew drowsy.

They had said to him, the other living students with whom he had been reunited, that Prince Lucifer would manifest tonight, to greet his worshippers. Now everyone shouted and howled, and Pierre joined in the tumult, lay on the floor when they did, but felt a sensation of distance, and a wish to go drinking.

Then a film of shadow began to hover in the radius of the inner circle, something not to do with candlelight or gloom.

Pierre came awake. He looked intently.

The shadow had an odd glow, dark on lesser dark, turning first black, then to a muddy hue and texture. A being was after all about to appear.

What would Pierre see! The Fallen One, the Angel who had defied God, envious of the creation of man, seizing the world away to corrupt and ultimately to destroy it?

Out of the mass of shadow something rose. It was the colour of a dead moon, glaring dully with a light that was lightless.

The worshippers screamed, calling a hundred names of the pantheon of Hell – those of Satan himself, and of his demon captains – there was some discord, it seemed, over who the apparition was taken for.

But Pierre knew what he saw. He saw the Devil.

It was the body of a huge man, a giant, and the face of a bestial thing. Its eyes were pits of nothingness. From its lips snaked a serpent's tongue. Horned and clawed and tailed. Deformed, blasted. Ugly, evil and pitiless, and *glad*.

This was the vision of Pierre. He dropped senseless on the floor.

In the years to come, his images of paint and stone would reveal glimpses of an awful revelation. His Hell would leap with rending flame, his cyphers of the Last Judgement of Mankind, and World's End, would display Satan in all his might, eating souls alive, while the earth burned.

EMPIRES OF AZURE

LE LIVRE AZUR

From the hag and hungry goblin
That into rage would rend ye,
And the spirit that stands by the naked man
In the book of moons defend ye!
Anonymous: 17th century

In a week, or less, I shall be dead.

Having written this on his card, he handed it to me.

"Why?" I said.

"I'm under sentence of it," he said.

"Again, why?"

"Ah. There's the story."

"I'm expected to listen?"

"Perhaps not. I've left an account, a sort of diary, and various papers. My address, you will see, is on the front of that card, with my name. Are you familiar with the Observatory Quarter?"

"Quite. What I would rather discover is your reason for approaching me in this way."

"Dear mademoiselle, you are a stranger. So far at least, you've heard me out. Those that know me, mademoiselle, won't credit a word."

"I seem to know you better with every passing second."

He smiled, and sat down opposite me.

The name on the card was Louis de Jenier, and the address, as he said, on a street among the steep, stepped terraces and balconied apartments that banked the Observatory. He himself was so handsome that he remains difficult to describe. Elegantly dressed, and with a silk neck-tie, his lavish dark hair was parted on the right side, and his hands manicured. His eyes were of an extraordinary unreal saturated blue, impossible to penetrate, like those of a statue, or, more actually, a doll. Since I had never met him before, I could not tell if he were unusually pale, sickening for illness, or had gone mad. He had come directly to my table through the crowded café, most of which had stared, as they do in the north, especially in Paradis, at his novelty of looks and style. Now he said: "Mademoiselle, let me add that I know you write for the journals, albeit under a male pseudonym. Yes, I've found you out, and tracked you down for a purpose. I gamble on you. I think you begin to be curious."

"Not very, monsieur. I assume someone has threatened your life, maybe after a love-affair. Why not go to the City police, if you have no influential friends who could help you."

"No, no one can help," he said.

When he spoke, a shadow fell, the way it does when a cloud covers the sun. It was not that he sounded fearful or even dismayed. But it was like that moment which comes, for the first time, to each of us. The moment which says "One day, incredibly, I too will die."

And in that instant, as I stretched forward mentally towards him, we were interrupted.

Two men were forcing their way through the café. One called excitedly to him, "Louis! Louis!" But the other, as they reached us, said, "For God's sake, what are you playing at now?"

He glanced at them, with the cruel contempt of a beloved and misunderstood – and so deeply angry child.

"Well, you were boring me rather."

"Excuse us, mademoiselle," the second man said to me, tipping his expensive hat. The other only tipped his eyelids.

"Don't," said de Jenier to me. "Don't excuse them."

"Louis, shut up. Oh this really is too much."

"Hunted down," he said to me. "Well, good-bye. It was a great pleasure to meet you."

His eyes held mine, but conveyed nothing, only colour. Then he rose, and turning aside with the two men, went away in their company.

My immediate impulse was to follow up his invitation. Not today, for when I emerged on to the street, already the dusk was coming down, the blue hour, and along the boulevards they were lighting the lamps, while on the summits of the Sacrifice and Clock Hill the neons of the theatres and the nightclubs had begun to blaze. Tomorrow then, at midmorning. Not too early, for I sensed he would rise quite late, not too late, for then, I sensed, he would be gone.

I had an article to finish that evening, and went to my apartment on the Street St Jean.

At midnight, when, work completed, I turned down the gas, I had already started to have doubts on the other matter. De Jenier might so easily be a poseur.

Next day, rather than seek his address in the Observatory, I attempted to discover his nature from colleagues and acquaintances. A few thought they had heard his name. My editor at the office of *The Weathervane* believed that there was an actor named Louis de Jenier, a southerner, however, obscure.

Daunted, by my own initial eagerness more than by anything else, I did nothing more. The day went, and the night, in uneventful pursuits and ordinary sleep. And after that some further days and further nights.

Of course, he was so beautiful, and he was a man and I a woman – worse, he had unmasked me as a woman, casting away my literary shield. It was all very dangerous. I had come to value the calm sky-pool of my life.

And then it struck me, walking out one morning to the bright sunlight of spring, birds twittering on the roofs, and the women everywhere with their baskets of dew-beaded violets – it struck me that this was the last day of the week he had postulated for his life.

I stood amazed, the violets I had just bought glistening like coloured shards of glass in my hand.

Thissot, who was with me, laughed at my aberration. He pinned the flowers to my lapel. "What have you forgotten?"

"Somebody's death."

"Dear God. So serious?"

"Perhaps."

But I breakfasted with him before I set out. It would not do, I felt, to upbraid the liar on a sinking stomach.

Once, the ascent to the Observatory had been wooded parkland. Duels were fought there under the misty trees, and in a number of ruinous little cemeteries all about, lay the unknown bones of the stabbed and shot. But now the cemeteries were wedged between the high walls of tenements. And where the cannon had pounded at the end of the Years of Liberty, neat flats now stood one upon the head of another, with bell-flowers and papery gentians pouring through the loops and slots of iron balconies. De Jenier's street was tucked down between two others. Three or four largish houses dominated it, his being the third. On arrival, seeing its number, I learned the whole building belonged to, or was rented by, him. It was a very new house, I thought, not even ten years old. Nothing had been done to it to give it any character. It looked like those villas at the seaside, occupied for only a couple of months a year, kept up by workmen and gardeners, never properly lived in.

I went up the steps and rang the bell. I expected a servant, but when the door was suddenly opened, I saw the face of one I knew. It was the second, talkative man who had come to arrest de Jenier in the café.

It seemed he also remembered me.

"Ah – mademoiselle. Did you –? That is, I'm afraid I can't let you come in."

I was not in the least surprised. I felt only dull horror.

"But you must," I said.

"No, no. Louis – that is – no. It won't do. If you'll leave your card, mademoiselle, a telephone number if possible, where we may reach you –"

I did not want to say, Where is the corpse? Because that would be incriminating, perhaps. I said, "He told me to come here. Let me in, or shall I call the police at once?"

The man quailed. Oh indeed, so they had not yet resorted to the means of the law.

"All right," he snapped. "In, then."

He hustled me through the narrow opening which was all he would allow.

The hall was clean and empty of anything except for an equally empty umbrella-stand. Two closed doors, a passage leading away below, and an uncarpeted stair leading up.

We stood in this oasis. I said, "Upstairs?"

"All right."

He directed me to go ahead of him. The heels of my shoes clacked on the treads, and a strange light began to come down. I hesitated, to look up, but he fussed behind me. I went on without looking and reached the first landing to be told, "Go on. Go on, then."

On the top floor under the attics, a double door stood wide, and out of it came the densely-tinted light that had fallen into the stair-well. The room stood at the back of the house, of medium size, a sitting room perhaps, but it was entirely bare. In the polished wood of the floor, the marble fireplace, and on the plaster walls, reflected four cobalt pillars of light from four west windows blind with cobalt glass.

What a fancy. What an artifice. I thought of opium-smoking and other drugs, where the eyes are affected and require deep shade. The window-glass was like a drug in itself. You stifled, grew drunk, stumbled and lost the awareness of balance. It was like being hung up in a thunderous evening sky. No oxygen available. Blue above, beside, below. Nothing substantial anywhere.

I thought we should have to stop there, maybe until I was overcome and fainted or ran away. But now the second man moved before me, also weaving, holding his hands away from his sides slightly, a wire-walker. He took me through another door into a study.

It had a skylight, it was not drowning in blue. I could breathe again, and looked about. Sofas and chairs crouched under dustsheets. On a sheetless desk lay dramatic impedimenta – polished pens never used, a tidily stacked column of books, scholarly artifacts, such as a skull of quartz, and a leather diary and pencil. One chair stood away from the desk, also unsheeted. Its back had been broken, and some wood splinters scattered along the Persian rug.

On the wall beyond the desk, over the small fireplace, a convex mirror was flanked by two big photographs, both depicting women. One, to the left, wore period costume, perhaps of the Liberty Days, with a corseted, sashed waist and plumed hat, pearl bracelets, long, dark, curling hair. She was beautiful, and had been labelled in copperplate: *Anette*. To the right of the mirror, the other was a contemporary of my own, her figure freer, her face more obviously powdered and mascaraed; she was clad in a sequined evening gown, furs across her breast, her hair, also dark, pinned up with lilies. Her label read: *Lucine*. It was apparent both were the same person in a different role. Across the convex mirror in between them striped a colossal gash. Since glass can only be scratched by diamond, I supposed a ring had been used, but over and over. In fact, the marks were more like those made by a set of claws.

Of the dead body of de Jenier there was not one trace.

"Wait here," said the man who had brought me. He turned towards the blue room.

I did not want to wait. I did not like the feel of the room with the desk, and the blue chamber outside had unnerved me.

"Where is he?" I said. I reached out and caught the man by the sleeve.

"Let go. This is disgraceful."

"Yes it is. What's happened?"

He worked his lips. "*Something's* happened," he said, idiotically.

"I asked you what it was?"

"You're no one he knows. To invite you here was just his joke, Louis told me. You shouldn't have come."

"Let me see him then," I said boldly. "I'll go at once."

"You can't see him. He – he's not on the premises –"

"You carry on, monsieur, as if he is dead and you have hidden the body."

I was being rash, but my nerves now drove me. As for this man, he was more nervous than I was. We both trembled. Finally he said, "You must *wait*. *Please*. I'll return directly."

He scurried out. I stood a while and looked at the chair and the claw-marks on the mirror. Nothing else seemed to have been disturbed. I picked about, cautiously lifting a corner of a dustsheet, peering down at the splinters on the rug. I was partly afraid of finding something. But what?

That man was taking a devil of a time.

Suddenly I resorted to the desk, and picked up the leather diary. This was, probably, the written account de Jenier had referred to. It was unlocked. I opened it. The inside cover formed a pocket into which a number of documents and papers had been carefully compressed. The fly-leaf had pencilled untidy writing on it, his own. It said, "For you, Mademoiselle St Jean, to do with as you think fit."

St Jean was the literary pseudonym I used, after the wild poet who is said to have lived on my street and for whom my street is named, and who one day mysteriously disappeared for ever. Either Louis de Jenier did not know my true name, or he had kept this as a sort of password between us.

Whatever, he clearly meant the book for me.

I slipped it, with scarcely a qualm, into my purse, and walked quickly out of the study. It was now evident to me that the man who had let me in, having no answers to my annoying questions, did not intend to return. All the doors of the house, but for these two and that of the front entry, were doubtless locked. There were to be no clues. They only wanted me gone. It might anyway be unwise to remain.

As I started across that room dyed cobalt, something peculiar happened to me. I have said I disliked the room, and the study, though for varying reasons, neither quite deciphered. But in the blue room now a wave of dizziness and emotion came over me. I say emotion, but what was it? It was like a sort of smiling fury, a sort of sensuous silent *howling* – it was bestial and beastly. I began to run towards the doorway, and in that instant the double doors, with no one by them, swung in and closed with a bang. The room seemed to rock. The floor tilted, like the floor of a balloon up in the air, caught by lightning.

I was terrified. The hair bristled on my scalp and I moaned aloud. And something insisted to me that I turn, and look at the four windows, the windows of cobalt glass.

So, in the trap, I did turn, and I ran towards them, not knowing why.

I was about three metres away from the two central windows when abruptly one of these displayed a pattern all over itself, an intricate but abstract pattern drawn fine in black ink. I stared at the pattern, stopped in my running. Then I seemed to understand all the glass in that window had fissured. Next second it fell to bits. It exploded – not inward but outward, with a sound as if a huge tap had been turned on.

The glass of the window flared like a bomb of violets, violet and blue confetti, jettisoned into blue space beyond.

After half a minute, I went forward, and looked out of the vertical where the window had been.

The view was perfectly normal. Some house-backs and dormer lights, trees and walls, on the right hand the descent of the City to the river, gracious in the morning. Below, the glass lay glittering all across a small enclosed garden. Between the window and the sky, suspended in air, a rope that seemed to flicker and smoulder, coming down from above. A man's body hung from it, the dark head lying towards one shoulder.

I started to cry, from shock and grief. The blue room had now no feeling in it. Then something made me lean straight out and crane upwards, and I saw two men, the foremost the one who had let me in, and another, vague at his back, both looking down. We stared at each other, they and I, a few seconds.

Then I turned and ran from the room and down the stairs and out of the house. They did not seem to pursue me.

I got as far as the cafés along the embankment, where I had to go in and ask for cognac.

At first I was simply frightened. Pretending to have the spring influenza, I concealed myself in my flat, putting on a hoarse doubtful voice when Thissot called me by means of the telephone in my landlady's parlour.

Gradually I concluded the men at Louis' house could not have known who I was, or my whereabouts. They would not be able to run me to earth. I wondered if they were themselves the agents of his death, but did not really think so. I was haunted by a dull distress and sense of loss. My sleep was peaceful and free of the nightmares that filled my conscious hours. I had locked the diary and documents into a drawer of my bureau.

At last, one afternoon, the city veiled in rain, I lit the gas-lamps and the fire, then went firmly and unlocked the drawer, and extracted the diary.

Even so, I hesitated. I decided I would look at the papers to begin with. They were many. I took them forth and laid them out. Some I saw at a glance had to do with the rental of the house. Others I could make nothing of (or would not), but they were randomly numbered, and since the pages of the diary were also numbered, presumably they were notes or additions to these. Then again there were scribblings in another hand I could not read, except, here and there, for a large black letter T. One sheet in Louis' writing bore what seemed to be a line of poetry, which said only: *Kingdoms of the sky-blue universe.*

In fact, I was daunted, was afraid to delve. My visit to the house (blue room, breaking window, hanged man), that had been enough.

Then a small notice fell from among the rest. It had a business heading, the name of a shop in one of the by-ways of Sacrifice Hill. I skimmed that, for beneath was a typed message. It seemed the firm were pleased to inform Monsieur de Jenier that a picture was ready for his collection.

I looked at my clock. It was not yet five. If I went out I should be in plenty of time to reach the place before it shut.

Something had galvanised me. Perhaps only the excuse that by doing this, I was investigating the diary – while completely avoiding it.

On the streets the rain attacked a hurrying umbrella world of wet black tortoise-backs. I hailed a taxi-cab, which shortly deposited me high on the south bank, under the shadow of the Temple-Church. The shop lay in a narrow sloping passage leading up towards the Church, roofed by dirty glass on which the rain beat, and with a carpet of peels and papers. The shop itself was a photographic salon. I had not read the bill properly, and had been anticipating art. Art there possibly was, in the dusk portraiture of young women lurking under a shrubbery of ferns within the windows.

The bell jangled as I entered, and from behind a curtain a man glided out to look askance at me. I was not the usual clientele, plainly.

I handed him the chit at once. He gazed on it, on me, and said, reproachfully, "This has been ready for some while, m'mselle." I stared him out, but he next said, "I understood a gentleman was to collect the portrait."

"Monsieur de Jenier has entrusted that task to me."

"The work has been paid for," said the accusatory man. "The money was sent round."

Prepared to pay, this alerted me: Louis had bought the photograph but not taken possession of it. What could it be, this mystery? I recalled the phantom women on his study wall, Anette, Lucine.

"Just one moment," said the man.

He slid behind his curtain, and I heard a faint rumble of conversation, the words: "Most odd. Something funny here." And I was, in a manner of speaking, hand on sword-hilt preparing for battle, when back he came beaming, carrying in his arms an oblong item, already scrupulously wrapped. It was quite large, the "portrait."

A chill went over me. The garish electric light, with which the shop was gifted, seemed to darken.

"Will it not," he probed hopefully, "be awkward for you to carry, m'mselle?"

A premonition of police – death's revelation – "I live close," I lied, and named an area to fool them all.

Then I took the wrapped thing from him. My second of prescience was done and the package felt perfectly mundane, weight, paper, string.

By the time he had cancelled his chit, and bowed to me, and opened the door and let me out in the covered alley, the cab-driver was from his cab, leaning in an arch at the entrance, smoking.

He aided me and my parcel back inside the vehicle.

"That's got a bad name, that has," he said, "that place."

I wondered if he meant the shop only, or the alley entire. But I hardly wanted conversation and did not reply.

Returned home, I went directly upstairs. Again I lit the gas, and the oil-lamp on my desk, and stoked the fire. I propped the covered picture against an armchair.

Then, exactly as I had with his diary, I sat down and looked and looked at the hidden form, with terrific, immobile reluctance.

The clock chimed gently. It was midnight, I had fallen asleep. On my hearth the fire had perished, and the gas was bluely waning.

I got up in a dull trance, and tearing the wrapping off the photograph, revealed it.

She was not Anette, nor Lucine.

Her hair was modishly bleached, platinum blonde, but unfashionably cut in a kind of long, shining hood, that reached her shoulders, but framed forehead and cheeks with a high invert crescent of fringe. Her eyes had been inked in by kohl; that, and the gauffered sleeves of her dress, indicated it was all Garb-Egyptian, which had been something of a rage in Paradis, seven or eight years before. She wore a costume-jewellery collar, too, gilded and set with opaque gems. Strangely, only one earring, pendant from the right ear, a disc, with an odd design on it, perhaps a flower, having eight thin rays ...

No, she was not Anette, or Lucine. She did not smile or provoke, as they had done, there on Louis de Jenier's study wall. This creature looked filled by *darkness*. Her eyes, though they could have been any rich colour, were miles deep. Through the obligatory minute, as the photograph was taken, she had sat so still her soul might have gone from her body. Look into the eyes, and fall down the miles to nothing. To nothing but – nothing.

But she too had a label, a name. There on the photograph's edge. *Timonie*.

She was portrayed, however, by the same being as had modelled the others. The bone-structure of the face, the set of the eyes and heavy brows; even the figure as far as one saw it, the small shallow breasts and flaunting shoulders – this one too belonged to the group. The three were one. Yet ... Timonie – was so different.

The silver earring in the right ear had caught a weird high-light. Stared at, the dark flower seemed to wriggle on it, wanting to detach itself. A trick of tired vision. I recalled the large letter T on certain of the papers in the diary. The line of the poem, if it was, returned. *Kingdoms ... sky-blue universe.* It struck an uncomfortable chord, but nothing more.

"You're full of secrets, Timonie," I said aloud, but softly. "I won't like them, I think. I don't care for any of it, this game of yours."

And I turned her face to the wall before I made ready for bed. I would have to call Thissot, and it would have to wait now until tomorrow.

I did not sleep that night.

"It's curious, I mean that you were asking about him, and then this. I take it you haven't seen any of the journals yet?"

"No," I said to Thissot, cautiously, as my landlady buzzed about her morning parlour, tweaking at furnishings, ears pricked and elongating visibly to a rabbit's.

"He seems to have fallen down the staircase, and broken his neck. Not found for some days, I gather. This man, his agent, Rudolf Vlok – he discovered the body and ran out in hysterics on the street. Apparently it's not the first death in that house. Some mayfly of a girl was murdered there seven years ago."

"But the papers quote a profession?" I asked Thissot.

"Our own *Weathervane* does so. An entertainer, your de Jenier, sometime actor, acrobat, mime, mimic. Latterly much in demand at select nightclubs of the south. His speciality had come to be the impersonation of female beauties –" Thissot's voice assumed a self-protective archness and aversion. "He dressed as *women*. Starry actresses, singers, and so on. Later quaint ladies of his own quaint invention. *Very* successful. To my way of thinking, that's just –"

I heard what Thissot thought he thought, thanked him, and almost ended the conversation, when I decided to say, "One other thing – a quotation I came across that's been bothering me. I'm sure I know the source, but can't pin it down."

"What's that?"

"Kingdoms of the sky-blue universe."

"Ah –" he began. Then, "No, I'm not sure at all. I thought I knew it too, but differently, somehow. Now why am I thinking of alchemy? No, I'm quite eluded, I'm afraid."

Having placed my telephone coins in the landlady's box, I hurriedly got my coat and hat and rushed out to purchase an armful of journals for myself.

Returned, I spread them everywhere and raked them through. Most carried a mention, and some made much of the sinister aspect, that this was the second violent death in a building barely a decade in age.

Depending on the type of paper, so its bias went. But very swiftly, nevertheless, the facts sprang out.

Here was a smudgy photo-image of Rudolf Vlok, and so I could identify him as the second man in the café, my subsequent guide and deserter at the house. He had been implicit, then, in the fakery of accidental death, along with another, still nameless, and unpictured. And now I could read for myself brief details of a career, and the retreat to this City, of one Louis de Jenier, the colour of whose eyes they did not even mention. There he was, in that almost new house under the Observatory, among the litter of duellists' cemeteries. And next, I was reading of a wealthy young woman who, years earlier, had conducted orgies of grape and poppy and hemp in that house, until one sunrise found there in a bizarre upper room made blue-windowed for her pleasure. The body was "mutilated." It took another journal (although I rightly guessed which one it would be) to inform me in what manner. The murderer had cut away ears, eyes, breasts, her hands and her feet, even her teeth and tongue, and capriciously distributed them about house and garden. That time, apart from the blood, the house showed no other signs of savagery, and not a bank-note or a curio had been stolen. While of all her quantity of jewels just one small piece was missed, an antique spider of sapphire, possible to sell anonymously only if broken up into its one large and thirty tiny corundas.

There were no other leads, the murderer was never apprehended, and for some months fears of a European "ripper" ran wild. Such a crime was not repeated, however. The fears died. The journal which itemised so much, gave the dead girl her name, but also a second name by which she had come to be known. That was, of course, Timonie. She was what they call a platinum blonde, with very blue eyes. There was no photograph. By then, I had begun to feel I did not need to see one. (But maybe what I know has bled back across my knowledge of that day, time at its eternal trickery.)

In the City, the bells began to ring for noon, the other side of midnight.

There was nothing left now but to put the journals away and take up the diary.

I did so.

I read straight through, referring, where the text so indicated, to the documents that had been in the cover. He had commenced only when events thickened about him. But he was, obviously, used to and adept at writing things down. His script was for the most part legible, and where sometimes it failed to be, the empathic wave of horror which now gripped me, bore me on to perfect understanding.

Outside, brilliant sunlight set Paradis in crystal. But in my rooms, darkness came and blossomed.

To copy out the whole diary would not be wise for me, I believe. Third person then, at a remove, I must present its happenings, propped by all other evidence and occurrence as I knew it, or have come to know it, since. I invent nothing, for even the dialogue is as Louis noted it. No. I invent nothing.

He had escaped Vlok – "the jailor" as he tended to call him – on a train. It had been travelling north to the border, and stopped at a crossing, as a caravan of goats was driven over, to take on mail. De Jenier had happened to be in the corridor, smoking, while Vlok and his assistant sprawled asleep in their compartment. They were en route to another city, another round of private parties and public performances, and on impulse, Louis had suddenly opened the nearest door and jumped down into the plucked fields and vineyards, leaving his luggage and his jailors together for the steam-bannered train to bear away into the evening.

He was about nine and a half miles outside the suburbs of Paradis, through which the train had already passed. He started to walk back to them, got a lift in somebody's young, snorting car, and arrived before the dinner-hour.

It was not the first time Louis had behaved in this way. Life was not serious. The antics of a Vlok, always concerned with profit and decorum, amused and irritated him. Louis rarely obeyed any rules, and routines exasperated him.

Having plenty of money, he checked into a good hotel, then got to work on finding a house to live in. He had not lived in a house for years, not since, that was, his earliest childhood. Both his parents had been beauties, but paid for it. When Louis was five, the handsome actor father had been shot in the back by a jealous rival; the lovely actress mother promptly swallowed ratpoison. The only child of only children, now an orphan of orphans, he was kinless, and placed in an institution. Here he existed in bleak misery and mercurial grace for a further seven years, before a male patron ran off with him, used him, gave up on his uninterest, and left him on the bosom of a world that would be prepared always to rhapsodise and fall abjectly in love with him, but would never attempt to clarify his needs.

If Louis ever properly believed in the reality of others is doubtful. It was not that he was callous, rather he did try to be kind. But so seldom did anyone act in a reasonable fashion when he confronted them. He brought out the simpering fool, the liar, the viper, the cheat. It was the curse of his attractions.

The house had been standing empty a number of years. Though its history had been damped down, it kept an amorphous but nasty reputation. It was boarded up, the attic filled by dead birds.

Open, scoured, and slapped in the face with paint, it was soon ready for its tenant – gaped for him. About its rumours he did not give a damn. He had, in repose, a cheerful disposition, thoughtless and clear.

He furnished the house frugally and carelessly. He had not wanted a home. Meanwhile, Vlok would be naturally in pursuit, and those who noticed Louis' appearance accosted him wherever he went. The hollows of the house were privacy. They gave him what others seek in deserts and on mountain-tops.

He must, too, have made in it journeys and explorations. In the second week of occupancy, he found the silver and sapphire earring.

Of all the rooms he had furnished the room which pretended to be a study the most thoroughly. It may have evoked some memory, even that of a favourite stage-set, the desk with its romantic symbols – books, pens, skull. He had hunted for a realistic astrolabe, not found one that passed the test, for bones and shells, hour-glass, compasses, scales, a pestle and mortar. He did not utilise the desk in the beginning, but he looked at it from the sofas, walked round and round it, rearranging objects. (Contrastingly the bedroom across the way had a bed, with a decanter of mineral water standing on the floor beside it, and a clothes closet.) For the blue-windowed room he had some plans involving musical instruments, a slender violin he had seen, a cittern.

The blue windows were fixed and could not be opened. Through them, the City became an abstract.

He wondered if he might have time, before Vlok caught up with him, to experiment with other shades of blue glass, or with patterns of white glass.

Across from one of the windows, gleaming on the wooden floor in its reflection, lay a disc of ornamented silver.

Louis knelt down. He examined the disc. He thought it had not been there before. It looked as if it had come from the attic, for the dead birds who had nested there had also been something of collectors. The workmen must have missed the silver thing, somehow it had fallen through into the room below. It was an earring, or had been made into one, with a ring and silver hook to pierce the lobe.

Not until he took it through into the study, into ordinary light, did he see the spider, which was sunk into the disc, was composed of one large, and thirty tiny, sapphires.

The piece was fine, not necessarily beautiful. The metal of ring and hook did not match the metal of the disc, which had also been beaten in an odd way, much older. There were two small holes on either side the upper curve of the disc. A wire or ribbon would have passed through them. The earring had been hung on the ear, not from it, once, long ago.

Louis was quite pleased with the find. He left it on the desk beside the scales and skull. He felt no urge to have the jewellery valued or dated. He forgot about it.

During the night. Louis de Jenier woke. Something had woken him: a heavy sound of movement, and repeated soft high little cries, close by in the house.

His first thought was that someone, perhaps even Vlok, had broken in. But the noises were not like those of burglars or even agents.

Louis left the bed, and went out of the bedroom into the passage. The sounds came from the room with the coloured windows. Its doors were shut, although he had left them open. Everything was dark. Louis crossed the angle of the passage, the stairs yawning black to his left, below. It felt very cold there, as if winter waited in the stair-well. He put his hands on both door-knobs and turned them, but the doors to the room would not oblige him.

Inside, the noises went on. Something heavy was being dragged about, something throbbed, like a gramophone which had run down. Then the girl's voice, which had paused, began again to moan and whine, to hiss and cry out.

Then – silence. In the silence, a cold glow seeped out between and under the doors. It was blue, like daylight through the glass.

Louis had a premonition the doors were after all about to open, and stepped back. He had been correct, they did so and forcefully, banging against the wall to either side. A gale went by him. This was not cold, but burning hot.

The scene in the room was done in blues and whites and greys, lit, not by the windows, not by anything visible. There was a sofa, a sort of chaise-longue, not a possession of Louis' own, and on it lay a young woman. She wore only a silk robe, and that barely. From her position and her expression, you saw at once what she had been doing to elicit her outcry – not of pain, presumably, but pleasure. Her face, which was very beautiful, was also slack, and still wanton, the white-blonde hair falling all over it.

She stared directly at Louis, and though she was a psychic recording, what is termed a ghost, she seemed to see him.

And, "I know you're there," she said. "I know you are."

Louis, cynical enough to accept most things, was not alarmed, merely unnerved. But besides that, the physical aspect of the manifestation, those extremes of heat and cold that were now coming in waves out of the room, were making him ill. Nevertheless he did not retreat, thought he though it useless to go forward, let alone answer.

"I made you come here," she said. "I can do that, can't I? Did you like it, seeing me doing that? Better than with any of them, those toads. They can't give me that, not one of them." Then she moved her body, slim, firm and young, stroking it, its skin and hair. She said, "Why don't you come close to me? I know you can. I've *got* you." She shook her head, and through the pale strands, one silver earring flashed.

Then the other noises started up again all round her, the heavy dragging, the dull throb. The girl seemed to hear them for the first. She looked about, and as she did so, a last wave, of utter black, came boiling through the room. It poured over the girl and the light and they went out. The wave poured on, over Louis. It was almost palpable. It was an emotion, incredibly strong. Yet indecipherable. It seemed to go through him as well as over him, and then there was only night in the empty house. He was dizzy and leaned on the wall a moment before going back to bed. There he lay down and heard a distant car-horn in the streets, the bell from the Sacrifice, and later birds singing.

Drained, he slept. When he woke it was midday, the sun standing on the roof.

When he went back to the blue room, it was undisturbed, except that the sapphire spider-earring was lying, not where he had left it, but out again on the floor.

That afternoon Vlok, and his dark, pretty assistant, Curt, arrived at the house.

There was a furious drama, during which Louis remained quiet.

On this occasion, the tracking process had not been easy for the jailor. The jailor was in a rage, which increased on meeting no opposition.

Finally rage resolved into resolve. They would take him, the captive, to their grand hotel. Then, tomorrow, on. Some of the cancelled northern dates might yet be salvaged.

"No," the captive then said. "You don't understand. I intend to stay. I meet a girl here."

Volk volleyed out a string of profanities.

Physically-sexually, de Jenier was dormant, or non-existent. His sexual engagements had been with men, overtures received and complied with indifferently. Emotionally-sexually he responded to women, but as he had no wish to form a union, let alone consummate it, he had learned early on to limit his company, words, glances and caresses. At last, prompted by a promoter more seedy though no less ambitious than Vlok, Louis had discovered how to create all he wanted from himself. His minutes and hours as a woman, women, lightly padded to their shape, wigged and dressed and painted and gemmed for them, afforded him a transcendent excitement, not merely sensual, or if it was, then also a sensuality of the mind. He swam strongly in the sweetness of it. But it did not disturb him. That vital element, a sort of guilt or shame, had passed him by. The dictate of the light says: Know yourself and what you are. The dark replies, By all means, but then become afraid. By-standers, particularly those able to cash in on aberration, tend to encourage and expect the latter state.

"Girl? When did you want girls? My dear Louis. I'll forgive you your antics on the train, my money wasted and my time. Tomorrow, we shall go north together. My God, if you want to, bring the fancy bit with you. A boy, yes? Dressed up as you do it? I thought your taste was otherwise."

All these entirely inappropriate comments on Louis' sexual life, which he heard without a flicker, were prompted by ignorance, awareness that the guilt-shame should be present, and an undercurrent of resentment that it was not.

"How you bother me, Rudolf," said Louis. "I can't invite her with me. She's indigenous, I imagine. A ghost."

Vlok shrugged. Louis often cried wolf, or inventively lied from boredom.

"I'll send for the luggage from the hotel. If you won't move, we'll stay here with you."

"Oh please, don't."

"Introduce me to the ghost."

"Where shall I sign, Rudolf, and what?"

"What are you talking about?"

"To terminate our agreement."

An hour later, at the foot of the staircase, Vlok shouted: "You need me, and you know it quite well. Squander another week, then. But you'll be watched. If you take flight again, my bird, I'll be after you. Depend on it." The front door slammed.

In another hour, Curt, having received a secret signal, returned to the house. Louis entertained him with white wine in a downstairs room bare of anything but for bottles, a bowl of peeled almonds, and a pot of forced white camelias.

Curt was the slave of both, Vlok's in the matter of finances, and Louis' in the sense of feelings. He betrayed one to the other as need demanded. Now he accepted Louis' errand. It seemed no threat to business enterprise. Curt had also brought, in a small case, the framed photographs of Louis' two most admired animas: Anette, Lucine. Louis permitted Curt to put them up in the "study," either side of the mirror. Across the blue room Curt passed with scarcely a look. He had torn off a camelia for his buttonhole.

"Perhaps you'll let me sleep on a sofa one night. I've never seen a ghost. I'd die of terror."

"I couldn't allow you to die. No. I won't let you stay here."

When Louis returned alone from dining, about eleven-thirty, he felt at once, on opening the door, that the house was waiting for him. During the day it seemed to sleep, the way a night-animal must, for it had grown busy after dark.

The moment he closed the door, was shut in with it, its life began, as if, now, mechanical.

He heard from above a violin, that was the first sound.

Not a melody, but three or four quivering wails, then a spasm of tuneless plucked pizzicato. He had not yet bought the violin. He anticipated the unbought cittern next, but instead there came again that deep throbbing, the turntable of the imaginary gramophone let run down. Light started to billow slowly down the stairs, in a plume, like phosphorescent smoke. Nothing was adrift in the light-plume. There was time, if he wanted, to open the front door and get out.

Louis walked into the light, which had now spread all through the channel of the stair, and climbed upwards. He became aware of a faint smell, rather cloying, like a kind of joss-stick.

Nothing else happened, just the light and the throbbing noise, until he got up to the landing of the blue room. The doors were open, and the familiar wave of cold drove out and drank up all his body-warmth. The dead needed that, a live temperature drunk in, to make their show. But before, there had also been heat. And what was that for?

Then the girl was there, in the room.

Her hair was cut in a new way, and the earring glimmered from her right ear. She wore a long skirt of some pleated translucent stuff, held up by a type of silver braces. Her small breasts were bare and her long slender arms and ankles. It was that style known as Garb-Egyptian, taken to extremes, but she looked less oriental and classical than like some artist's model, a bijou waif … All but her eyes, of soaking, starving indigo. She started right at him. It was a terrible stare.

"Are you there?" she said. "Is anyone out there?" A reverse of what the still-mortal thing is supposed to say when questioning a presence.

Then the wave of heat came. It almost knocked the breath from his body. When it passed, or when he had accommodated it, he began to go forward, slowly, looking at her, wondering all the while, though he knew she could not, if she really did see him, and if it would be possible to touch her.

He had drunk, for him, a lot of wine at dinner, preparing for this. It was what Vlok would call a "loosener."

"Who," he said to her, "are you? *Were* you? – Is that more politic? Won't you tell me your name?"

But she was only a recording, a photograph on the room. Time had not somehow slipped. No, he could see it in her starving eyes. She and he were of a height, so the eyes fixed directly into his. They fixed in and on him, and *through* him, still looking for something. He had got very close to her now, wondering what he would feel. There was a slight disturbance in the air about her, even inside the spectral light. And a sort of clammy quality, the aura of fever.

"Why won't you?" she said. "You tease. You know you meant me to have the earring." And coaxingly, "Are we the same?"

Are we the same? How odd. There *was* a resemblance. Not only the eyes … He put out one hand, letting it alight on her breast, something he would never dare do with a woman of flesh and blood, who would then expect more. This one did not seem to register the caress, and he saw, as in all the supernatural clichés, that his hand, insisting, presently passed right through her.

For some reason it was that which turned his stomach.

He drew back.

"*Who* are you?" he said.

"Are you *there*?" she said.

And abruptly they both burst out laughing bitterly.

It was nothing shared, only a coincidence, caused by a fluke of their characters, a similarity of reactions.

"Go away then," he said.

He did not think such an exorcism could work and was dismayed when suddenly she disappeared from in front of him.

The light went out also, and the throbbing ceased, came back – and was only the jumble of his own pulses in his ears.

The violin had been the strangest part. But that did not mean she had read his mind. He did not know what it meant.

Near morning he wakened, and thought he heard her again, walking about nearby, on bare feet. He thought too he would have to be careful. There might sometime be a genuine break-in, and he, complacent, would assume it was only his pet ghost-girl. Then he wondered if, recorded thoughtless phantom or not, she would pursue him to the bedroom. He experienced then a sort of sexual stirring to which he was quite unaccustomed. He lay on his belly, floating in the sensation that was between dreamy anomia and dreamier lust, half awaiting her fingers on his neck, his spine – passing through *him*, and how would that feel?

Then he slept until Curt woke him about ten, rapping insistently on the front door below.

It was a blowing day, a febrile wind tore about the street, coated with rent blossoms. Wilted, one more broken stem, Curt was propped in the doorway.

He had brought, as required, scattered and scribbled through a notebook, "as much" as he could "reasonably get" on the previous tenant of the house. Curt had a knack of worming out information, of finding what was in hiding.

Curt followed Louis back upstairs.

"Did you see it again?"

"What, Curt?"

"*Her.*"

Louis would not reply, and finally Curt grew tired of watching him returned to and lying in bed, drinking mineral water and reading yesterday's papers. There seemed no chance of communication or breakfast. Even the notebook lay unviewed.

"Were you just telling lies again?" said Curt. "Rudolf says he's through with you. Every hour brings another tantrum. We're to go south, without you. He has plans to sue."

"He's actually planning to come over here again. Keep him away, Curt, please. And I'll buy you a present. What about that jacket you said you saw? Yes, *that* jacket. Now go to your hotel and pour laudanum and aspirin into Rudolf's coffee."

"Well, you'd better buy me the jacket." Curt smoothed his collar, thinking of collars to come. "You haven't bothered to read my notes, there. You should be contrite. It's a gruesome tale. I need soothing."

When Curt was gone, Louis opened the notebook. He kept these notes, in appalling shorthand, making a precis in the diary later.

Female, blonde, rich, she had been noted also for her unusually blue eyes. She had no family, and appeared in the City in the way of such beings, as if from thin air.

For a while she moved from apartment to hotel to apartment, incurring the wrath of each establishment by late and licentious celebrations, drunk guests, lovers of all sexes, drugs and loud music. She was also subject to crazes. A craze to paint the walls and ceiling of one apartment black, a craze of enormous plants. Later came a bicycling craze, during which she might be seen flying up and down the steeps of Paradis, generally attended by bicycling young men. On one occasion, one of these attendants escalated down Clock Hill into a hospital bed. Later yet, there was a monkey craze. That ended in a rescue by a zoological organisation. For, like the paint, plants, bicycles, young men, once a craze ebbed, its constituents were neglected.

At length, she had taken the house in the Observatory Quarter, and put in the cobalt stained glass. She was now in another epoch, where she had begun to call herself *Timonie*.

This ultimate craze (it was to be her last) seemed to commence with her purchase of an antique earring. A City museum had been forced to offer for auction certain treasures. In with a stash of Roman marbles and lamp-stands dug from the river mud came one jewel. The catalogue presumed it had been the property of the Egyptian mistress of a Roman commander then in charge of the river fort. She was remarkable for being of the Greek Alexandrian strain, blonde and blue-eyed, but skilled in the old temple arts.

The modern girl in her sleek day-gown, lace gloves, high-heels and flowered hat, bid for and claimed the antique earring of the sorceress-mistress, whose name the catalogue gave as Tiyamonet.

Garb-Egyptian was then coming into vogue, and Timonie entered the vogue by throwing "Egyptian" orgies at her new house. They drank thick beer, and burned fake *kuphi*, the temple incense of the Pharaohs. Timonie often appeared at these gatherings in dresses of transparent gauffered linen that sometimes left bare the breasts.

Then the orgies ended. The doors were closed. After some while, two cleaning women, unable to gain customary entry, called the police.

No one was amazed at Timonie's death, even at the manner of it (listed by Curt). As moths to candle-flames, so a Timonie to a ritual butchering.
"I performed a test then." (Louis, writing in the diary.) "I went into the room, where the earring was still lying under the window. It was easy enough to take it to the small garden at the back of the house. Here I buried it about a quarter of a metre down in the soil, and marked the place with a lump of stone. During that afternoon I wrote this, and I paste it in here:

Timonie. Self-obsessed. But unable to clarify, externalise, and so centre, as someone taught me to do. "Lovers of all sexes," says Curt. He even alludes here to the monkeys – and, wilder, the bicycles. Unlikely, not human. As I saw her it was love before a mirror or an invisible audience. Passion so strong it forms the print of an astral photograph on that room. Who is she inviting? She said – Tease. You meant me to have the earring. Are we the same? It must be the other, then, Tiy-Amonet. Waiting and coaxing an Egyptian sorceress. And so the earring becomes all-important and acts like the photographer's silver fixative. Now I've put the fix into the earth. What will happen tonight?

"And that night nothing happened, except a foolish telegram came from Rudolf. And in the restaurant I was taken up by yet another stranger, my bill paid, and I barely got away with a whole skin.

"But in the house complete silence and absence. Unable to sleep. I lay awake all night.

"Then the plan came, to steal her from herself. Timonie. A rape, the usual way. How to dress her, more decorously as I should have to, for the obvious reasons. And how the hair should be done. Planning it, I could see more and more a likeness between us, or how one could be created. I liked the sexlessness of her disembodiment. All look, no substance. I would have to catch that too."

Coming back from expeditions along Sacrifice Hill, in a booming dusk scraped by the flails of winds, Louis encountered Curt, bent and bowed at the corner of the street.

"Curt. Good news of your coat. Go for a fitting tomorrow."

But Curt curiously was not cheered.

"Horrible dreams, Louis. That girl. That house must be full of it. Don't stay there."

"She won't harm me. If it even happens."

"Perhaps it happens in your head."

Louis smiled, for he had considered that too, and did not find it threatening.

"Where have you been?" said Curt in a whine.

"You can tell Rudolf," said Louis, "that I'm creating a new character, very exotic. That's why I need the privacy."

"Her."

"The same."

"Don't," said Curt.

"Hush, Curt. You'll adore her. You'll rush me to a photographers,' again, to have her immortalised."

"I kept dreaming," said Curt, "pale blue flesh – the way she was – after –"

"She wouldn't like you to conjure her up that way. She seems to want to be seen all in one elegant piece. I don't think she remembers the murder. No, she's stopped her life before that point."

Curt abruptly extended a page of print. He had torn it from a book in the library of a museum. He explained this with a foolish pride, and how he had felt it needful to undertake this unasked extra of research.

"It tells you about the other one, the Egyptian."

"That was Timonie's interest. Not mine. My interest is only Timonie."

Curt stood in the stream of the wind, his eyes watering and teeth clenched. He said, "I don't like spiders. The jewel in the earring is a spider, and there's a thing about it there. When I was a kid, they used to drop on my face where I slept. I used to wake up screaming and my father beat me with his belt. If you pull off their legs, they grow another one. Eight legs. It's happening in your head, and it happened in her head. But it can get out of your head, it can get out." Curt whimpered. Then he straightened up and turned his back to the wind. "Don't tell Vlok what I said."

But Louis was not affected by any of this, Curt was subject to odd turns from time to time, and to a superstitious dread of his own beginnings. Louis did not comment, but he invited Curt kindly to dine with him, and was delighted when Curt refused.

Tucking the torn page inside the coat, Louis forgot it a while, as he had previously forgotten the earring.

For some nights, then, nothing took place. No manifestations of any sort, no manifested glimpses of the girl. It was a playful season with him, and he began to miss her, and he vowed to dig the earring up from its grave in the garden. He would soon want it himself in any case, for her costume. (He had sent Vlok a letter, mentioning this treat, and so partly appeased him.)

It was at this time that Louis began to keep the diary, putting in earlier events as a detailed preface. Nothing was now occurring, everything was dull and normal, and yet he mentions at once an atmosphere in the house, as if the building were a kettle on a low flame.

That week he bought the violin, and placed it in the blue room, ready to be fiddled at ghostly whim. He began to have the idea, when next she manifested, of appearing before her as herself, the earring hung from his ear by silver wire, in the correct way. He would be mirror to her mirror, if a mirror they were to each other.

"A couple of interesting dreams. I don't often dream, or if I do, remember. But, saw Timonie on her bicycle, her hair tied up in a scarf and great rolls and fetters of beads round her neck, looking like a fourteen-year-old from a convent in her divided skirt and black stockings. She whirled down Clock Hill, two or three young men in her wake. It was a dare, all of them hooting with mirth, and carts of fruit and flowers getting in the way, some swerves and abuse, and then a clear stretch past the florists and fashionable dress-shops on the west of the Hill, with just a disapproving face or two at windows. Last of all rattled along a fourth fellow. I saw at once he was dismayed, and as he came hurtling off the top of the Hill on his bicycle, he began to beat at the air, first with one hand, then with both. He beat, and smacked, and tried to push away something from behind him. There was nothing there. By now his face was white, frightened, and – something more. From how his hands went now, it was becoming obvious the invisible sprite riding pillion was intent on a seduction. All at once the eyes of the rider blurred. He leaned back, lying on the air, giving in to an irresistible ecstasy or hypnotism. The bicycle, left with no guide but the impetus of the Hill, went careering on and crashed into a pile of wooden crates and a lamp-post.

"The second dream, which came after this one, woke me. It had a quality of the *Arabian Nights*. If I were at all a serious writer, I'd be tempted. There was a vaulted sort of cavern, or hall, classical but obscure to me. The man – he might have been a merchant, some traveller – was well-dressed, in a long robe, but I can particularise nothing of his clothing. He walked up the cavern-hall with an air of unease and determination, for some – what do they call them – some jinn had promised to show him the face of the Devil.

"At the end of the cavern was a kind of curtain. It fell and rippled like water, or perhaps steam. The traveller stood before the curtain, and after a moment or so, it swirled and opened, and in the opening showed a stern pale face in middle life, bearded, with shrewd dark eyes. The traveller started back. He made some sign over himself, and then began to shout. He had some cause, for the face he had been shown in the mist was his own. His language baffled me, yet I know what he said. Then the jinn came. I didn't see it, but the traveller did. He spoke more guardedly, but no less angrily. One of those ethical legendary bargains had been dishonoured, he wanted recompense. And then the jinn – I heard its voice, rough and oddly pitched, like a boy's voice when it's on the point of breaking, the jinn said something to the man, which I understood to mean, Look again, and I will show you instead the face of God.

"At this, a proper altercation. Of course, to see the Devil was one thing, but surely God was not accessible, at the beck and call of lesser spirits. But the jinn persuaded the traveller. So the man looked again at the mist or steam, and it parted. I knew what was coming, and so maybe did he, for now he made no comment. It was the same face, shrewd and bearded, just out of its prime. God's face was the traveller's face, as the Devil's had been.

"I woke up in silence, madly overawed by the depths of my own theosophical sense. I never thought I had that side to me."

After this entry there is a gap of several lines. At the bottom of the page he wrote:

"In a kind of calm hysteria. Something is going on. I can't hear or see or smell it, it leaves me alone. Forces gathering? What forces could there be. Perhaps poor T is angry, I've stopped her expression by burying the focus. It seems I'm reluctant to go out and take away the stone in proper Christian manner, and dig up the prize. Yes, I am reluctant. I've so seldom been any more than nervous of anything. I don't know. Am I afraid? Is this fear?"

Turning the page, you saw he had written:

"I tried to find the place. Something, perhaps a neighbourhood cat, has moved the stone. I dug about where I thought it must be, found nothing. I'm distrait. I feel as if a cane has come down sharply on my fingers. Bad Louis. Bad negligent child."

In a dream, the mise-en-scène may simply exist. And so, a hot black night, starred with diamond brooches, moonless. A broad black river, without a bridge, the starlight plinking on it, and frogs faintly chorusing in the reeds. It might have been almost anywhere in a warm climate. On the dim banks shapeless shapes that gave no clue – mounds, huts – beyond, the rising of hills. And here and there, eastwards, a cresset on a wall-tower ... The fort too lay east, behind now, with the beacon burning in the great iron brazier on the roofwalk. Dis' light.

It was not that he walked inside the skin of the one who walked before. But he walked so close, he was her shadow, and invisible. The intimacy of it seemed normal in the dream. He knew himself separate, a witness. He knew himself involved, and not impartial.

There were trees now, heavy castaneas, a wood beside the water, and there an altar of stone against the post of the ferry ... He saw these things as she glanced at them, knew them by some trace that came from her. They did not interest her, these known things.

She was alone, not one of her slaves with her, and now there·were men standing up in the black of the trees. But they were obeising themselves. They were pulling something forward, showing her – the black and pale flickering among the foliage of the chestnut grove was confusing. Then he saw the face, the lolling tongue and half-moon eyes. It was a corpse they had brought. They laid it on the ground, and she made passes over it. She had put off the cloak. Her arms were smooth and rounded, strong but very female, braceleted wrist to armpit. And her hair was youngly-white.

He did not think, I am dreaming of Timonie by the Nile in Egypt. He knew it was not Egypt. And not Timonie, and not a dream.

Then she made a sign, and all the men slipped away out of the trees, all of course but the naked corpse. Another shape emerged between the cas-taneas, male and mantled. He spoke to her, and then she said something to him. Her voice was light but throaty. His, harsh, sounding angry, cowardly. They were speaking – not the classical Latin of the modern school-room – but the everyday speech of real life, tailored by a hundred foreign intrusions, and the colloquialisms of a military camp. The City had not been built yet, nor even the Roman town of occupation, just the walls, the towered fort, a storehouse or two. And over there were the bothies of the savages who had been here first. And underneath all, the silvermines for which they had opti-mistically named the station Par Dis.

He had told her, in a patrician's Roman slang, he did not care for it, now it was to happen. And she said, her accent not the same as his, Too late.

Then she made a kind of channel, in the mud among the tree-roots, all about herself and the corpse. At intervals in this channel she thrust in small sticks that seemed to be lying about on the ground. She lit them, it was not certain quite how. The light was bluish, unclear, like dying gas-glim. Yet as she moved, a single earring flamed and darkened from her right ear, and in the other ear, as it seemed to be, a part of an earring. There was a pectoral, over and between her small breasts bound in byssus. The Egyptian enamel and lapis was of eyes and hieroglyphs, but there hung from it a flat moon-disc spider, in silver, and there another and another was sewn on her skirt. She had placed some little images at points along the channel, the invisible watcher could see them now, though again, not exactly where they had come from. They were very small and appeared to have been formed of simple baked clay, and she was breathing on them, like a god giving life in a myth. Three he saw quite distinctly. A man sitting cross-legged, a great belly and a fat man's bosom on his lap, in either arm an urn, one up-ended to the earth, and one tilted skyward. Near him was a scales, empty and in balance. Now the woman sighed upon two little animals, like lambs or young goats, lying with their forefeet entwined. Having breathed on these, she straightened up. She stood a moment, slender and poised, and unhuman, like some wading bird, attentive to something other than the night.

It was the dark of the moon, and she was making magic, too black for the Roman's fort to hold it. For they were the children of reason. They built roads and armies, forts and baths and laws. Her kind built from shadows, different things.

Somehow the watcher-witness had been excluded from the spell, pushed back on its rim. He was looking at her then, from a slight distance, not seeing her quite clearly. In the peculiar light, her eyes might not have been blue after all, for all of her had a blue cast, jewels and clothing, skin and hair.

Then she turned to the corpse, and spoke to it shrilly, words that made no proper sense – like commands to an idiot or a beast. And the corpse sat up, and answered her in a whistling moan, not even in words.

There came a prolonged sequence after that, during which the dead thing rose and stood, showing that it glowed a little, and that in places it had indecently decomposed. At first it spoke only noises and gibberish, but the sorceress, she, Tiy-Amonet, she shrilled out again and again at it, she threatened it with its unburial, and some loss injurious to its soul-life. And finally it hung its head and began again to whisper, and the whispering formed words. And then she asked questions and the corpse replied. They were to do with a battle, and an enemy. It was for the commander of the fortress, her protector, that she asked. While he stood apart, his mantle held over his face, his eyes rolling with fear and nausea and a wish to be gone.

But it was impossible to tell anything from her eyes. Not even colour.

And as the corpse mumbled on, the watcher heard the frogs, unawed, chorusing, and then a deep explosion shook the world, a pane of light broke into a million pieces of rain.

The rain was not wet. It fell beyond a partition of glass and bricks. Louis de Jenier lay in the bed and watched the lightning of the storm crack again across his walls.

Then he sat up, aware that in just this way the corpse in the dream had got itself upright from the earth.

The night was full of noise, the breakages of heaven. A bolt seemed to pass right through the decanter of water at the bedside, and shatter it. On the pillow a fire-ball flashed and died. The silver earring was lying there, the spider at its centre. Louis put one hand to his face and found that, in sleeping, in the dream, he had lain with his cheek pressed against the earring. He left the bed and opened the wardrobe door and looked into the mirror there. In the next lightning flash, he saw the impression of the spider stamped into his flesh.

By ten o'clock the next morning, when he went to see about the costume, the spider mark had faded altogether, which was as well. He had arranged a photographic session to follow, to charm and stall Vlok with budding results.

That the earring had been returned was also – not a stroke of luck – but a stroke of some sort, perhaps of lightning.

By the time of the photography at the shop in the covered alley, Louis had recalled, excavated and read the page of print Curt had given him.

"A stranger, reading *this*, will assume I had seen the item previously, and so manufactured the dream on cue. Perhaps I had, because the name Tiy-Amonet seemed always resonant, in the way Timonie had done. The dream was correct in its details, even to the fact of being set on the north bank. Now even I begin to wonder, did I look at Curt's page before I went to sleep? Did I find the earring and put it ready on my pillow – sleep-walking, maybe. No, it isn't any of that. I'm caught in something now, can't stop, must go on. I dreamed *Timonie's* dream, her dream of her own alter-*icon*.

"At the photographer's, in my covert of screens, I donned the costume, exact to my design. Everything was perfect, and such gasps and purrs and *looks* from the camera fellow and his adjuncts, I might have been back in one of Vlok's carefully-chosen nightclubs. Even some muttered asides to me about a client or two of theirs, who would … etc., to match the other asides when I entered as a male.

"The mirrors in the screened back "room" were full of the image. I felt drunk, or rather full-flush as you do at the start of drinking, before the weight settles over the eyes and in the brain. A marvellous portrait, they assure me. The earring felt very cold. Then, when I removed it, burning blazing hot in my hand so it was nearly dropped. I keep it in my pocket now. Where might it go if, idly, I put it down. Back to the room with the windows, probably.

"Someone may be playing a joke, or I've gone mad.

"But – I'm addicted. *Too late* as the lady said in her wild Roman I forget but understood. Though we were never taught Latin, but for the religious niceties where I was raised. I can hardly wait for the darkness. My hand's shaking.

"I shan't dine tonight. I only want water from the decanter that lightning speared through. Bathe, put on those garments, the painted mask of cosmetics, the breasts and the hair, the jewel. Then take all of it, and myself, up *there*. Wait.

"If this is fear I'm feeling, it's more potent than a drug. I never felt anything like it before. The difficulty is if I think: what shall I do afterwards? So I don't think it.

"The sky through the windows is lapis-lazuli, and they're lighting the streets. The rain has stopped again. Clear heavens, not a cloud. Every window of the house now like coloured glass. Better start to get ready."

I looked at this point, in vain, among the documents in the diary pocket, for that torn sheet concerning the sorceress. Eventually I found it pasted in, as with some other of the entries, but at the end of the diary behind many blank pages. It scanned as follows:

Tiyamonet. Reputedly a healer, diviner and necromancer, as many of her race were reckoned automatically to be. Mentioned in several writings of the period, she was the mistress of that previously noted Roman commander, who controlled his part of the Empire's campaign here in the north with two legions, inaugurated the building of walls and fortifications, portions of which remain, and opened the silver-mines. These, actually mined out in fifty years, gave the area its original name, which soon came to be rendered in the records as Par Dis. Dis being Pluto, god of the Underworld, its mineral hoards, and incidentally, its kingdom of the dead. At the wish of her patron, Tiyamonet is supposed to have summoned up spirits and thus reanimated cadavers, then enjoining them to answer questions as to the outcome of impending battles, or the weaknesses of the commander's enemies. An old tavern, the *Imago* – the Apparition – which was destroyed after the Years of Liberty, was built it was said near the site of one such event. It stayed an inn of ill-repute ever after. The personal seal and sigil of Tiyamonet was the spider. The arachnid has always enjoyed connections with witchcraft, mostly due to the insect's abilities as a spinner – see also the Fates – and since it is able to build a trap out of an emanation of its own body – ectoplasm? – the thread and the web. A blue-eyed Alexandrian, Tiyamonet may have been feared in her own land, for in the East blue optics were, and sometimes continue to be taken, for the Evil Eye. When the luck of her patron changed, the commander being killed, as formerly stated, in a revolt of his own garrison, she committed suicide rather than submit to assault and torture. She is said to have employed for this purpose the bite of a poisonous spider, of the species – now extinct – shown in her seal and on the earring. Along with many magicians, Tiyamonet was rumoured to possess a particular secret, in her case to do with the ethereal powers of Air, Pliny the Other's *Regna Caerulea*, Galen's *Caerulei mundi regna*. As with most such secrets, for example, the Book of Gates, the precise formulae of the sorcery are unsure, but seem to have to do with a triumph over time and death. The method of the woman's entombment and rites, if any, go unrecalled. Her possessions were certainly stolen. The spider-earring of Tiyamonet, on view in this museum, came to light in another trove, of far later date, and may indeed be merely a Roman copy; its authenticity has never been verified.

(Nowhere else, in what is left of the diary, does Louis de Jenier make any reference to this information.)

The image into which Louis transformed himself that evening must be the same which is memorised by the photograph. Timonie's image, but modified. He did not, for fairly obvious reasons, bare his torso. He was not a woman in any physical sense. Instead, the pleated linen is very nearly opaque, and folds about him, with cape-winged upper sleeves, the lower sleeves bandaged down to the elbows, where bracelets take over. The ornate collar feminises the shallow breast. The face is exact, might be anything, *is* desperately beautiful. The hair of the wig owes too much to our idiom, Egypt seen through the lens of a vogue, but it will do. The eye-paint cannot be faulted. The earring is probably real.

When he had finished, the house seemed to have become timeless, nearly dimensionless, and he went across to the window-room in the dark, half-thinking the doors might open on a desert, the river of Par Dis, the past, space itself splattered with cracked stars.

But the room was only itself. He sat on the floor quietly, near to one of the central windows. (He had taken the diary in with him, though he could not properly see to write, as the sloping and overlapped letters give evidence.)

After a while the violin, which he had hung from pegs by the study door, began to make a noise. He could not see if anything played it, or even if the strings vibrated. This time there were definite melodics, harmonies and stopping, though all at variance with each other. Then, he heard the cittern, which he had *not* bought and which did not exist in the room save in his plan. After the cittern, there were a number of instruments. All had strings, and some bells. They seemed to be floating about in the air, passing and re-passing over his head, mischievously. The incense smell also came again, more strongly, the joss-stick *kuphi* lit at Timonie's drunken parties. There was a kind of lulling, rock-a-bye quality to all this. And then, something went out of tune. The cloy became a stench, and the combing of the strings began to tear and rip. Then the coldness came. He had been braced for it, but even so it nearly stunned him. It was like falling through ice into some win-ter glacier. And no sooner had it seemed to cut to his marrow than the awful heat blasted after it.

The room no longer cradle-rocked, it was in quake. The doors, which he had closed, crashed open, then crashed shut again. A high singing buzz sounded from the window-frames. He expected the plaster on the walls to snap off in chunks, and bricks to fly out.

And then the throbbing and heavy lugging noises started, and next the screaming began. They were ghastly screams, not human, like those of an animal in a snare. Agony and primeval terror, mindless, hopeless.

His euphoria had spired into an all-consuming horror. But Louis could not move.

He sat and listened to Timonie's murder, in the eyeless darkness. He vaguely thought, It's this, then. The murder was the fixative. That's usual. Do I somehow have to give her peace from it? And, trying to keep sane among the driving nails of the screaming, he thought of priests, and that some priest must come in to free her screaming soul –

And then the screaming itself ended, not dying out, not in a death-rattle or a groan, but as if the noise had been sliced off by a knife. All the sounds went together.

He thought, Get up, for God's sake. Light the lamps.

And then the lamps were lit. Not from the gas, surely, for he never heard its unmistakable hiss, the *spat* of a match, the ignition. Instead the gas-bulbs were full of some other light, the dying corpse-glow gas-glim of the spell in the riverside dream. Timonie's light, and by it – by it? No, nothing. She was not there, her mutilated body, the several bits of it. Yet on the floor, a pool of viscous liquid ran in a strange way, ran along and along the polished floor, gleaming black under glowing blue.

The black blood was running towards him. He got up. The forward motion ceased. There came a delicate movement at its edge, as if some tiny creature played there in the blood. Then, a gleaming mark appeared on the floor, and another; another and another. They circled away from the pool, returned to and skirted it: paused, resumed. The shape, each time, made in wet black, was of two narrow naked feet.

He stood and watched them. He could not take his eyes off them, these perambulating footprints. The steps of Timonie's dismembered feet. There was a stillness and a silence that enclosed the room. He realised, in these extreme moments, that he could hear nothing from the City. The sealed chamber had dropped through the basement of the universe.

It was searingly hot, even to breathe exhausted him, but he had begun to shift towards the doors. He was not convinced he would be able to open them, but before long he must lose consciousness. Then the footprints began to come towards him, to cut across his exit. Louis drew back to the wall.

Something struck the wall very suddenly, near to his face. Then again and again. He looked, and saw there some smeared, wet handprints.

"*Timonie.*"

He had decided he must speak aloud. Must try to reason with the reasonless unreasonable.

"Timonie, what do you want? Shall I take off the costume? Is it an affront? What do you want me to do?"

Then one of the invisible hands struck his face. It was freezing cold, wet with blood – he cried out in revulsion, and pulled the earring from his ear by its loop of silver wire, flinging it away across the room.

It was like throwing a pebble into water. The air of the room seemed to smash into fragments and whirl up at him.

He ran then, for the doors, directly through all of it. They would not move. He shook them, and pieces of wet stinging flesh slapped and clawed at him – he plunged away, and cast himself against the door of the study. To his amazement it gave. He had some notion of hurling something and smashing the skylight, and somehow climbing out on to the roof and so to the drainpipes. He had a distinct inspiration that he must get into the *air*, off the *earth* or anything that passed for it. Then he stumbled against the chair beside the desk, fell with it and broke its back, and finding himself down, *earthed* on the Persian rug, at once all the strength left him.

In that second, everything stopped.

He felt the house settle, as if dropping back a few inches from the sky. After that, there was nothing to be felt at all.

He wanted frantically to get up and escape the place, but had no energy. He lay on the floor and heard the Sacrifice ringing the four o'clock bell. And next some drunken boys or women singing, fifty streets away, the sound carrying on stillness like a leaf on the wind. And then he thought how cool it was, how warm, and that everything was over and he could sleep now, and so he slept there, lying face down on the carpet among the wood of the broken chair, and clothed rather like the dead girl but for the spider-earring he had thrown away.

Louis entered Vlok's hotel-suite the following afternoon. He was unshaven, his clothes thrown on, and Vlok, taking one look at him, exclaimed: "You're ill! What's the matter with you?"

"An acute attack of wanting to please you," said Louis amiably, dropping into a chair. "I'm finished with that house. Let's go north. Or wherever you like."

The next thing he was conscious of was of being in bed as it seemed in Vlok's room, but actually in an adjoining suite. A satisfied physician was asking him moustached questions to which he, the physician, already knew every answer, and so was sometimes helpful enough to prompt his patient.

"Nervous exhaustion."

"Then there's nothing –"

"Monsieur Vlok, the young man needs good food and rest. Get him out of the City as soon as you can. The coast, perhaps, or one of the pastoral areas."

Louis let go of them both and slept again. The sleep was beauteous, dreamless or amnesiac of dreams. Deep, reviving deaths.

He had brought nothing away from the house but the clothes he put on his body when he took off it the gown and hair and breasts and physical soul of Timonie.

Later, Vlok was murmuring to him nonsensically, anxiously, "The new costume has been damaged. But Curt will get that seen to. You told me there was a photograph taken?"

"It's been paid for."

"But the name of the shop."

"No."

"Louis, why must you be difficult."

"I'm ill." Louis, the sick child, played his part suddenly to its full. "Don't you want me to get better?"

"Louis."

"Then let me rest, as the whiskery doctor told you."

He had brought nothing away. But Curt, dispatched on Rudolf Vlok's orders, had scurried about the house, packed clothes and personal items, and included in his itinerary the Garb-Egyptian dress, wig and jewellery he had found lying on the study floor. Curt also tidily reinstated the broken-backed chair, and next had dust-sheets brought in and laid reverently over all the few furnishings, including the elaborate desk. Off this he had first taken the diary, but it was locked, and rather ingeniously, and in his inquisitive efforts to pry it open unobtrusively – which failed – Curt did not bother to clear any other matter from the desk. Also he forgot the two precious portraits by the mirror. Thus Anette and Lucine were left in residence, while the accoutrements of Timonie, even the violin, were borne away to Louis' rooms at the hotel.

Louis had not asked for this. If he had had a minute or so more to himself before he fainted, he might have thought to tell Vlok to leave everything in the house untouched. Vlok might have obeyed. Or he might not. The violin, for instance, was worth a very great many livres (it could be sold when Louis' craze for it wore off), and as for Louis' personal accumulation of cuff-links, tie-pins, and so forth, these too were worth a few pennies. Louis constantly abandoned one set of toys for another, and Vlok always sent Curt to pick up after him.

Curt himself had not liked being in the house, especially alone. He would have seen no marks on the walls or floors, or heard anything unusual. He was not psychic or even sensitive in that way, but had a morbid dread of morbidity which occasionally put him right.

"First of all, not a single engagement." Vlok was idyllic in his selfless devotion. "You see, someone has painted a watercolour for their brochure. A residence, yes? Comfort *and* finesse. Total quiet and nourishing food. A little Paradise. Cream and cheese and fresh eggs. Fruit straight off the trees and fish from the waters."

"But the place is in the north. Away from this City?"

"Miles away. No smoke, no noise, no river damps, no neurasthenic fancies. You'll be bored but you must stick to it. A week at least, the doctor says. And you can tell me there, about your new girl."

"Never, I'm afraid."

"Oh Louis, so temperamental."

"Your placatory tone is always your least successful, Rudolf."

"Now, Louis."

"And why were there furniture-removers in the other room? Or did I dream that?"

"Furniture-removers? Of course not."

"Someone bringing something in, dragging it across the floor. It sounded like a trunk."

"That might have been Curt, fetching up your things."

"Things."

"Everything you so carelessly and thoughtlessly discarded at the rented house."

A long silence. Noticeable pallor. Vlok grew nervous.

"What's wrong? Do you want more of those drops?"

"I want to kill you," said Louis, with a sweet, dazed smile. "Nevermind." Then, after the Vlokian storm had calmed, "What exactly did he fetch? I seem to remember, you talked about the new costume. You'd seen it, then."

"And it is being repaired after your maltreatment. Very interesting. I'm not sure this one will work. I'd have to see you, how you manage it. What will you make her do? Monologue? More of that throaty singing, I suppose, but they like it, don't they, your worshippers."

"What else, Rudolf, did Curt bring?"

"He forgot the photographs and won't go back alone. He's avidly been reading all the accounts of that girl's murder. I just hope she has no relatives concentrated somewhere. We don't want any lawsuits over this impersonation."

"The violin?"

"What about it? Oh yes. Naturally I had him get them to pack that and bring it here. Have you any conception of how much you paid for it –?"

"And the jewellery."

"All the jewellery. Including a battered silver earring on a loop of wire. I believe it's an earring?"

"Where is that?"

"You want it? Well, it was on a table in the outer room. Drink your champagne. I'll fetch it."

Louis did not drink his invalid's champagne. Vlok went into the sitting room of the suite, leaving the door ajar. In the stripe of the opening, as in an ultra-modern painting, Louis beheld the violin out of its case, leaning at a contrived angle, a plash of white muslin that had been part of Timonie's gown and, nearly preposterously, the blonde wig poised on a wig-stand, a faceless wooden head, only waiting for its features to be filled in.

Vlok was a long time.

"You can't find it," Louis muttered.

Then Vlok returned. "Here. The chambermaid must have moved it. It looks old so I suppose it is, but isn't it reckoned to be a fake, Curt said ... Something set in there, once, I'd have said."

Louis put out his hand and allowed the earring to be laid on the palm. It hardly mattered at last, contact.

"What's wrong now? Louis? *Louis!*"

"Nothing at all. Everything is perfection."

"No, I don't care for the sound of you now. You're up to something. You were warned, Louis. You must stay in bed for another day at the very least."

"Yes, Rudolf."

"And now, I'm going down to dine. Try to have a little more of what's on the tray there."

"So reminiscent," said Louis, turning the silver disc, strengthlessly, uninterestedly, in his fingers, "of the farmer with the pet goose. Eat just a little more corn, my dear. Just a grain. We must get you fit and fine, for on Sunday I shall drive a pin through your brain and kill you for the feast."

Vlok pranced out. He slammed the intervening door, and presently the outer one.

Louis reclined on his halted avalanche of pillows, in the constant light (the hotel was most contemporary and electric). Beyond the drapes, darkness lay on the City of Paradis like black bloom. There were the sounds of cars and carts and angry taxi-cabs, but the hotel's upper corridors had stilled, for it was both the hour of dining and theatre-going. And in the ballrooms they would be striking up the tango, the dance of sin, which, like so many things, creeds and treasures and marching empires, plagues and mysteries and magics, and even the sun and moon themselves, had originally come out of the East.

Of course, it might have been dislodged, when he cast it away across the blue room in panic. But not every gem, surely, not at once. Unless they were in some way moulded to each other. They had not seemed to be. The one stone, shaped and impressive in size – the body and head; the other smaller stones, thirty of them, the eight legs. All rested individually in the silver disc. Curt had never been shown the earring. He had simply picked it up off the floor. The indentation where the sapphire spider had been had not, it seemed, concerned Curt, though he had read the description of it earlier. Safety in inattention, non-avowal.

Louis seemed to understand it all, and there was undoubtedly nothing he could do. There had been a slight chance, now there was none.

He lay back and closed his eyes in the bright light. He could smell the perfumes of the clean hotel room, hygenic fabrics, soap, and polish, and sometimes, from the partly-opened window, the City's spring, gutters, soot and violets, and from a baker's shop across the street, poppy-seeds and gingerbread.

But the City's sounds seemed to be drawing away. He waited, for the other sounds to begin, that dragging, that leaden revolving *drum-drum*, like a turntable. Perhaps this would not be possible here, away from the house. Then again, it might be, for Timonie had had her say. It was the turn of the other, now, and *she* had travelled wherever her earring travelled.

It had fallen from his hand. He would not open his eyes to see where it was, or anything. He felt drowsy, ill again. The room was growing very warm, and he heard a pale dry little scratching. It was like the noise of a paper settling, stretching itself after it had been screwed up and thrown away.

Louis opened his eyes, Blurred, heavy … The room seemed in shadow, the light must be faulty. Something moved on the bed, like a trick of tired vision.

Yes, not Timonie, if ever it had been she. She was the recording shown to him, the moving picture. Because, of course, Timonie had summoned it, or attracted it, through the medium of the earring. In the end, it had killed her, and portioned her. There was some Egyptian occult rite, surely, to do with that – some method of revenge – so it had hated Timonie. And it should hate him, too. The sorceress Tiy-Amonet must now be hunting for Louis de Jenier, all out of time, across a landscape twenty centuries too late.

The trick of tired vision was affecting both eyes now. It was moving steadily up across the counterpane, it was on the edge of the sheet. The light smeared and blinked on a hard surface of sapphire blue.

The jewellery spider paused. It raised itself a fraction, the slightly shorter foremost legs, composed each of three gems, exploring the air. Then it lowered itself and walked quietly aside, the individual legs extending, overtaken by others, extending again. It crept quickly on to his right hand. And as it touched his flesh, it hesitated once more.

It felt very cool to him, but the room was boiling, his skin feverish, he thought. The spider was full of poison. There must be a hollow in the larger jewel. She – Tiy-Amonet – had known how to release the poison, in order to facilitate her suicide. Perhaps there was a sort of pincering motion, crab-like, with the front legs, like that which it was making now – He felt the needle-like little nip from far away. He heard himself give a faint gasp, yet he was not startled. The gasp sank in a sigh. He began to sleep. To sleep and wake as if dozing in a drifting boat. The river was black again, and it had a riper scent. It smelled of crocodiles, papyrus and inundation, like the Nile of his imaginings, and of elder ages, of a primal state.

He was lying flat, on a type of stretcher. His eyes were shut, but he saw upward through his lids with unimpeded clarity. Men were rowing the boat, two soldiers with dirty faces. Another, his helmet off and head wrapped in a bandage, crouched nearby. All three looked afraid. They must be the burial detail, or burning or drowning detail. The fighting was over and the witch was dead, so get rid of her, somewhere over there, outside the station and the wall of reason and law.

His – Tiy-Amonet's – hands were folded over her breasts. Yes, the swell of her small breasts was against his arms, which were also hers. There was no breathing, no heart-beat, no ability – or desire – to shift any of the limbs. Yet complete awareness. Was the throat useable? Suddenly he, or she, laughed. He heard and felt the laugh passing through the body, somehow without breath, to be emitted, an eerie warbling note, not laugh-like, but audible.

The three men heard it too. There were some seconds of fear and confusion. Then the bandaged man smote about him. "Keep rowing. It was over there. Sound carries. Only a fox." Reluctantly, they rowed on.

Tall reeds rose from the river, and next the boat passed around an islet. It seemed to Louis they were a great distance from the garrison-station of Par Dis.

The body was clothed in its grainy Egyptian linen, and wrapped in a long cloak. All the ornaments were gone, even the metal spiders from the skirt. Someone, less scared than these three, had taken the hoard of the sorceress.

Soon they would reach wherever it was they had been told to reach, and do whatever they had been told to do there, or not do it. It was immaterial. Even burning, in this instance, would not have mattered. The jewel mattered, and the jewel was secure. And the will mattered. But now the will must rest. How long would it continue, the waiting? Be indifferent to that. Sleep now. Rest now.

The river lapped against the boat and the oars spooned it over. There never seemed to be a moon in the past.

They slept together, he and she, a sleep of death.

Curt had brought the leather diary to the hotel and Vlok, in search of business clues, had also attempted to open it, fruitlessly. Louis must have the key concealed somewhere. This was true. Louis had placed the key inside the tube of one of the unused pens on the desk in the study at the house.

"What in God's name are you doing?"

"Getting dressed. As you can see, can't you?"

"Don't be such a fool, Louis."

But Louis went on tying his tie before the glass. He seemed relaxed and careless. He had breakfasted to a degree, been shaved and manicured.

"Do you want to be ill again?" raged Vlok.

"Hush now," said Louis, "sound carries. It was only a fox on the near bank, not anybody laughing."

"*What?* Oh stop talking in riddles. Where do you propose to go?"

"There's something I want at the house. Curt, naturally, left all the important, useful things behind."

"Then, if you *must*, I'll come with you."

Louis only put on his jacket.

On the street, after a sufficient number of blocks, Louis feigned faintness and pleaded for a taxi back to the hotel. Vlok in smug dismay lurched in pursuit of one. Returning with it, he found Louis had given him the slip.

Half an hour later, hammering at the door of the house in the Observatory Quarter, Vlok received no reply. Either Louis was ignoring him, or had postulated the venue of the house to throw Vlok off another, real, scent. Vlok inclined to the latter notion and stormed away.

The house, chandelier-lit by sunshine, was peaceful. Birds skittered over its roofs and sang in nearby trees. A milkcart passed, and from the boulevards below and above wafted the songs of day.

The diary unlocked, Louis wrote it up to date. Then added, "Timonie was murdered. I am permitted to live. That was Timonie's anger, but it didn't have the power to kill me. The other has no intention of killing me, though Timonie it killed. Indeed, I'm cajoled, invited, made party to private reveries of Tiy in her death hour. And I admit – she's snared me. In the web. Depending and waiting. For this is not a reprieve. Only that I misheard the sentence."

After that, Louis made a note concerning a journalist who wrote in "one or two of the better journals. She – I'm sure it is a woman – writes under the male pseudonym *St Jean*. The invaluable Curt is finding out for me where this being dwells, or at least where she frequents."

He wanted to put his affairs in order. He wanted to leave a legacy of truth with someone he reckoned reputable, honourable. Not he, nor his diary, say why he wanted this.

He was relaxed, as Vlok (and I myself) beheld him, in the condemned cell. Although he stipulates he has no idea what form the punishment may take, he was as accustomed to being under the sway of another persona as any actor. The supernatural wooed him; it had got endemically close to him as live human things never did. And in a way, too, he was playing, and I wonder if he even believed it, even at the last second, desperate as it was, entirely.

Louis intended to leave the house and return to the hotel for the night. The sorcery had fragmented and was everywhere – the blue windows, the very source, being in the house, the violin, the disc of earring, the costume, they were at the hotel. The portrait of Timonie was at the photographer's. The spider – that might be anywhere, even travelling in his clothing. Enwebbed, he was not intending to step outside the spell, only to move freely within it.

But the desert quality of the house, the privacy, after his fresh term with Vlok, seduced Louis. And then there came a sense of danger, and he could not resist it. He would stay.

He left the diary therefore unlocked on the unsheeted desk, ready to be found. He left Anette and Lucine, too, beside the convex mirror.

There is only one further entry in the diary. It is almost illegible, but by this point, familiarity with the script enables a reader to attempt it. I remember how he was at our first and only meeting. I wonder if I should be appalled at the interrupted abandoned narrative, or only at his lazy perversity. How much choice *was* there?

"Already" (he wrote) "it had happened. We see with our eyes, but cannot *see* our eyes, except in a mirror. In the mirror, looking, I scored it across with the small diamond in a ring – and was answered. The glass was scored again, back and forth – from *inside*. Magic. Symbol. There will be coherence in patches – A spider: female devouring male – and phases of speech like the moon. I must learn some lines for you, Mademoiselle St Jean. If I find you in time. No elbow-room allowed. To explain. Couldn't anyway. You must guess. Or – but it slips. Slips, down and down."

Under this was written in a strange spiky jumble, almost like the writing of another: *Caerulei mundi regna.* I had seen it printed previously, and so could decipher it, now.

That vanished poet, St Jean, who some schools of thought tell us died in a duel, mooted for his last words: "I have no last words." He also said, Fire is Will, Water is Grief, Earth is Thought, Air a Vision. And though I had never seen Pliny the Other's Latin, or read Galen through, I had once, in translation, come across a non-illuminating reference to *Caerulei mundi regna* (which Louis had managed to translate literally, as kingdoms of the sky-blue universe) – the Empires of Azure.

Now, shivering all over as if with the influenza I had pretended, I reached the end of Louis de Jenier's diary none the wiser. I was confused and unnerved (especially at being directly addressed!) and resentful, yes, very resentful. As if I had been reading, on another's recommendation, a rare detective novel, only to find the last pages – those with the solution – deliberately and *neatly* cut out.

He had approached me and coherently informed me of this material. Yet the material itself, implied to be completed before the approach, finished in nonsense. The mirror had been scratched by a diamond in his ring. And then itself had scratched back, unnaturally … These facts I would not dispute. I had been present when doors slammed and windows shattered of themselves. But what *else* had gone on?

It was the awareness of *un*finish that disturbed me more than anything. It made me jittery. As if I was being manipulated. I suppose I knew that a conclusion must be sought, or that it was seeking me.

By now it was early evening. I went downstairs, finding myself very nervous at emerging from my rooms, and assailed the landlady for her telephone. I called Thissot, but he did not answer, and then, in desperation, my editor at *The Weathervane*, but he too was absent. Quite what I wanted to say or ask I am unsure. A contact, a reassurance, is what I truly wanted. Both were unavailable.

So, out I went to my dinner in one of my three usual restaurants, trying to be jaunty and at ease. But I could not eat what I ordered, and the proprietor, who knew me, came over to enquire. "Oh, it's simply that I've had the influenza." He commiserated and sent complimentary brandy to my table. I wondered if I should confide in him, but the preamble of explanation daunted me and shut me up.

Nagging always at the back of my mind was the memory that Curt, who had a "knack for worming out … what was lost or in hiding" had been put on my trail in the first place by Louis. Would Curt abruptly arrive, and with Vlok? Would they attempt in some way to threaten or blackmail me, or even to silence me? I had seen a man hanging by the neck in an abyss of air, and Vlok at least positively looking down at him – the other in the background had been too vague to see, but must have been Curt himself. Should I go to the police? "Why, mademoiselle, have you waited so long to come to us with this business?"

I began to have the wish to abandon Paradis altogether. Louis' beauty had enmeshed me, but he was dead, and the rest of it a weird nightmare, lacking even a proper ending. Let me take flight.

I walked home under the watery street-lamps. Rain struck the pavement all about me, dancing. The sky arched over the City and the world. It held so much, that vault, winds, vapours, clouds, distance, and colour. No wonder ancient belief had peopled it with elementals and powers. From there, lightning struck, and the sun blazed, and weather and angels fell. I pictured a teeming universe unseen behind the shields of blue or black. Then the vision left me, I went into the house and my landlady came flouncing out from her parlour. "Oh mademoiselle, a gentleman has been telephoning you every quarter of an hour." I thought with enormous relief, Ah, Thissot. I'll have to tell him all of it and risk his scorn. And exactly then the bell whirred and she went to answer, saying to me, "That may be him again." Presently she waved me in and gave me the receiver. As usual, she began to busy herself about the room, listening.

Then a voice spoke in my ear, giving me my proper name. It was not the voice of Thissot.

"Who is that?" I demanded, but it was all I could do to stop my own voice from shaking.

"Rudolf Vlok, mademoiselle."

"I have nothing to say to you."

"Please, mademoiselle. I must – that is, it is essential that I see you. Tonight if possible."

"Don't be ridiculous. I have friends with me."

"Send them away." he said. "It must be alone."

"You must think me a fool," I said.

"I mean you no harm. But – there are things to be cleared up. You agree, don't you? You've read – that diary."

"Which diary?"

"Mademoiselle, I shall be at your apartment in ten minutes time."

"You'll find me gone," I said wildly.

(My landlady had run down into slow-motion, she was so intrigued.)

"Mademoiselle – it isn't – for myself. I have to say that if you refuse to see me now, there must be a meeting at another time. And that I'll do anything I can, and I have some influence, mademoiselle, to see to it."

"Why?"

"Only – only in order to settle things."

"You want the diary returned? I'll mail it to you at any address or office you wish."

"Mademoiselle –" His voice had been, all the while, different. It was earnest and determined, and yet placatory. He had said, this call was not for himself. And he did sound to me, now, so much an underling. Someone had primed him. He was anxious not to displease them. It must be some backer I had not been told of, fearful of a mention in the diary, perhaps. Suddenly I thought, Let him come, I want to know. Maybe this can give me the key. It was, after all, still a social hour. The house was full of people who knew me, the rooms and streets well-lit. It would be safer to face it here, whatever it was. I broke in on his rambling insistence. "Very well. In ten minutes, as you said. If that is all right, madame?" I added loudly to my landlady, making her jump in her lethargic fiddling, letting Vlok know the world anticipated his visit.

When I got up to my rooms, I lit the gas, the oil-lamp on my desk, took off my coat and hat and gloves, and put round my shoulders a shawl of my mother's, which comforts me. I was glad I had had the brandy.

Minutes ticked by on my clock. It struck for nine, and I heard a noise below, and then footsteps ascending.

When the knock came on my door I went slowly to open it, and in one hand I took my lethal little paper-knife.

As I paused, only the door between us, I heard that special thick quiet of presence, of awaiting, and remembered the children's game: *Who's there? Who's there? No one is there. Then ask Monsieur No One in.* At that the hair rose on my scalp and I grasped the door-knob and dashed open my door in a sort of rage.

"*Louis!*"

The lights of my room burned against his face as it poised there above mine. Then I saw the eyes. The circlets of indigo, the centres falling miles deep, filled by *darkness*. I saw the eyes before I saw any of the rest of it, and giving a stupid small cry, I stepped back, and back, until the bookcase stopped me.

It came into my room then, what had been Louis, gliding and silent, with the faint perfume about it of sands and sweet resin, and with the shadow of night.

And after it, Vlok, his polite hat in his hands.

The creature had gone towards the fireplace. It stood there and did not move. It seemed to value the heat. Egypt was a hot country, and here, the north had been far warmer, then.

"Be calm, mademoiselle," Vlok said. His face had a still, solid look to it. Yes, he had been primed. He was the servant of the fiend. How much had it devoured of him, to make him so obedient? Not so much. He was in all other ways himself. Only, the jailor had become – the slave.

"I'm quite calm," I said. I added mundanely, "I saw Monsieur de Jenier hanged on a rope from an attic window. And his death was reported in all the papers. How can it be he's here now, and so convincingly in one of his rôles?"

And I made myself look at the creature. It did not seem to be angered that I did so. But I must be careful of those eyes. They were so horrible, I had nearly died of terror … The rest, if one did not know, was only a fashionable woman, tall and slender. She affected a contemporary coat with fur at the collar, a flattering hat. Her hair was blonde as ice. She did not wear earrings.

"No, mademoiselle, I'm here to explain all that, what you – thought that you saw."

I had already noticed that the feet and hands of the woman with Louis' face, feet and hands which give away the man and which Louis would have been careful to camouflage, needed no camouflage. They were not large, not masculine. And the line of the breasts under the coat, a gentle, mellifluous swelling, nothing false to it. Even the bones of the face, very fine, and the brows plucked, and no sheerest shading on the upper lip, the skin nowhere roughened by a razor.

"You say, a hanged man, dangling from a rope, out of the attic window. I'm afraid," said Vlok, "it was poor Curt who died. He fell down the stairs in running away – he was so frightened. And his neck was broken. It was a convenience to discover him – later – and to identify and bury him as Louis. Louis was not so well-known here. Not that he couldn't have been – we hadn't come to that. And Curt was nobody. It will save trouble in the future."

"Who then," I said, "who then is this?" And trembled so much I sat down and heard the paper-knife plop on to the rug.

Then, out of the silence, it spoke to me.

"Tuamon," it said. The voice was like a boy's, high, feminine, yet intently male. "Tiy-Amonet," modifyingly amended the voice.

The eyes were turning on me. I looked away. There was no extreme of heat or cold, and despite the pale fragrance of what I must take to be *kuphi*, this was no ghost, it was real. An altered reality.

It said, to Vlok now: "You tell. Tell."

"As yet," Vlok said to me, fussily, with a curious pride, "she hasn't the grasp of our language. After he lost it – at first – but never mind that. I can see to that."

I thought, Why not let her talk herself, anyway? Let me hear what it sounded like, the tongue of the Ptolemies, the Greek Pharaohs, the land of Set. Or the Roman's Latin … But even from the thought I recoiled.

"I shall be ill if you stay here very long," I said, not looking at either of them. "If it's necessary –"

"Yes. I'll be quick then. But you must listen."

And the other voice repeated, "*Listen,*" as she stood against my fire, all the light and darkness of the room upon her, but vague as something covered by centuries of dust.

Tiy-Amonet, who had *been* dust two thousand years, here in the flesh. Or had it been so long? Might she not have played her trick, whatever it was, before? Timonie had enraged her, for Timonie had not been suitable – since she was herself a female? And Tiy-Amonet rebuked Timonie, and dismembered her body as in the sub-rites of Osirus, depriving the soul of continuity in the after-life, unless all the bits be gathered together. But then there entered Louis.

What had been done to Louis? For Louis was here but Louis was not.

Vlok had seated himself, his hat on one knee. There was something silly about this, and about the way he then began to give me a lecture on the facts. He spoke prosaically, not even making, any more, those apologetic pauses of his over the odder revelations. He looked, and behaved, like a cheap lawyer. How she – it – how the thing called Tiy-Amonet or Tuamon – had informed him, I did not know. Perhaps the residue of Louis had been employed to do it. Before any slightest iota of Louis as we knew him ceased to remain.

It was all quite straightforward. And quite unbelievable. And it happened. Not only was the proof before me, but the air quivered with it – the magic air which the sky let down like a net upon the earth. I never doubted a word. Not even the ultimate ones, demonstrably.

The framework, as I had mentally positioned it, was correct. *Then enter Louis*. And when this occurred, the corner stone was laid.

Timonie had certainly been useless to the essence, the leftover, the spirit and will of the thing once known as Tiy-Amonet. But Louis was nearly perfect. There was a facial resemblance, as with the girl, and the eyes, blue to madness and absurdity – but it was much more than that. It was the mind and the psyche which counted.

The essence, electrified, reached out at once, and began its spinning all about him. Louis thought himself lured by the after-image of Timonie, but it was the spider-witch who worked on him, who showed him pictures of the dead girl, easing him on in stages, until allowing him to feel the recorded horror and fury of her death. By then, and long before the sapphire walked up his bed, its poison had entered him and was infinitesimally active.

The being killed the girl out of pique, but it did not want, primarily, to kill, only to have, itself, life. Louis represented that. And yes, it had had life in this way before Louis, but that was long, long ago. So long, it had been irked at the waiting.

On that last night in the house, it must have shown him the truth. I was not told how, but there would be ways, I imagine. Then he scored the mirror in fear, or anger, or some other emotion. His feelings were in thrall. Yet, he must have been swept by pangs of every kind. Even of excitement. There are plenty of hints of that. Then Tiy-Amonet came down the web to devour him.

When he went back to Vlok the following morning – for he *did* go back – Louis was already losing contact with his previous life, his own personality. He forgot how to dress himself, and how to use utensils of eating. He could not read. The toothbrush and the modern razor baffled him, he achieved their service by other means. Then he would lose speech for hours, then for days. He spoke unintelligibly, gibberish, a compound of his native phonetics and those of some otherwhere, or just of the brain's abstraction. Sometimes he seemed to be blind, dumb and deaf. He lay on the bed in his hotel-suite looking up at the ceiling, unblinking. He did not lack control of any other bodily function, only of the functions of society. He did not demonstrate distress, and only once a torrent of ferocity seemed to take him. During that, he smashed things, and snatching the unused razor appeared to be about to cut someone's throat. But Vlok and Curt overpowered him. Until then, and even then, Vlok half-suspected Louis was playing one of his jokes on them. However, after the razor, the doctor was again summoned. When he arrived, suddenly Louis was better. He talked and acted normally, implying it was Vlok who was inclined to jokes and exaggerations, putting the doctor *en garde*. Louis himself was worn out and charming. The physician, bewildered, fooled, left the hotel, and next Louis left it, by another way. He seemed to have recovered himself, had got hold of Curt, and learned from him where the female journalist frequented.

Louis went across the City, sometimes getting lost – Paradis had not been this way in the times of Tiy-Amonet. When Louis at length found his quarry, he and Tiy-Amonet found it as one. For of course, Tiy-Amonet had no objection to Louis' finding and lucidly conversing with this woman – myself. Indeed, had wanted her found, and conversed with. So I had seen that day before me a creature that was already two creatures, but mostly the creature it had not been and did not appear to be. Soulless also, behind its blind-blue eyes. For what was left of his soul after she had been at it, and what was left of hers? I had seen what he had seen in the dream, the young man swooning back in ecstasy on the runaway bicycle –

Then Vlok pushed in and in a quavering act of normalcy bore *them* away. Which was permitted. I had been made heir to the written diary. It was done.

After that, Louis vanished. Not outwardly that was, but totally within. By the time they reached the hotel, the body was speechless, and almost catatonic. Up in the hotel lift they went, theatricals, covering, and made him a prisoner in his suite. Summoned, but *en garde*, the doctor would not return, and seemed to have alerted besides his colleagues.

There is another meaning for the word *Imago*, this being the thing which emerges from the chrysalis.

When I was told he would last a week, she had apparently judged how long the rest of the transition would take, whatever its outward shows. On the seventh day, Louis' voice had spoken to Vlok one last sentence, over and over. He wanted to go back to the house in the Observatory. He must, he must. Over and over. Until the harassed Vlok agreed and took him there, with Curt at their heels. Presently, I arrived.

During our interchange, Vlok's and mine, Curt had naturally been unable to restrain "Louis," who had gone up to the attic. Here he wandered about, Curt wandering after, all nerves. When Vlok rejoined them, leaving me in the study, "Louis" – or could it have been Louis – had sat down under one of the dirty attic windows, smiling, playing with the silver earring.

Below, I had taken the diary up. And this must have registered throughout the web – which now, it seemed, had meshed all the house, and half the City. A few moments later, Louis rose, opened the attic window, climbed the sill in one step, and tipped himself out.

It may have been, I had begun to think so, the last surge of his persona trying to prevent what was to come, had come, upon it. To baulk and escape, after all.

But, by throwing himself from the attic, he had placed himself for the fall, in the magic condition, the correct one. He was between heaven and earth. *In the air.*

Vlok's face now was like the moon, idiotic, pale, expressionless. He spoke of things that had nothing to do with Vlok the agent, the man of his time. He said flatly, "You thought you saw him hanging from a rope, mademoiselle, but didn't you see how the rope was, how it vibrated and smoked? Even as he was falling, suddenly one of the windows broke below – the blue windows – and as that happened, a substance started to pour back and upward, out of Louis' neck, about the top of the spine. It was that stuff they called ectoplasm. I admit, I had to look it up to find out. A kind of flesh that isn't flesh. He was Tuamon, by then, you see, and Tuamon can do that, make a fleshly cord out of his own body. And the ectoplasmic rope shot back into the attic, and attached itself everywhere, to the walls, the floor, and it stopped his fall – not dangerously suddenly, but resiliently, like the safety net in the circus. And then I saw you looking out at it too, mademoiselle. At the time, I didn't know any more than you did, what was going on." (A touch of amusement, at his unenlightenment of then.) "As for poor Curt, he was gibbering behind me like a monkey. And then you left the house, I believe, so you didn't see what took place. The rope of matter pulled Louis' body gently up, back into the attic, and presently he told me who he, or perhaps I should say, she, was. And at that Curt lost control of himself and ran away, and I've told you the rest of that."

There was a silence after this. Minutes passed again over the face of my clock, microcosm as it was, as all clocks are, of Time itself, that terrible enormous relentless thing we domesticate with porcelain and ormolu even while it preys upon us.

Eventually I said, with care only to Vlok, not to the other, "Why did you wait so long to come to me?"

"Till you had read the diary."

"You knew when I did?"

"Tuamon."

"Why is the name changed? Why not Tiy-Amonet?"

"Tuamon is the correct name. Tiy-Amonet was the name for the Roman's use. Of course, she'll want to be known by some other name now, of the City, the present day. For convenience."

"And a further question," I said. He waited as I swallowed more than once. "Why do I have to be told all this?"

"*To finish.*"

The voice terrified me. It terrified me every time now. But I had to say: "Finish – what?"

Another gap. Was it telepathy after all? Vlok said, as if instructed in the actual words, "He comes from Egypt. He was, and is, a sorcerer. You know about the hieroglyphs in their picture-writing? Well, mademoiselle, to an Egyptian sorcerer, writing is itself a magic, a sort of spell –"

"And old habits die hard," I said, "like mutilation for vengeance. Louis began to write about all this, and in all sorcery, every ritual must be completed for the safe-making of spell and mage."

"Exactly, mademoiselle."

"And so he – or she, you keep changing the gender now – wants me to complete the account. To write down what you've told me."

"Just so. Except it would be better if you begin at the beginning, that is, if you will re-write, or copy Louis' account. A broken sequence – it needs to be re-started, and then carried through as one. Also, you see, you are a professional at this – it is, if you will, *your* special branch of magic. You assume therefore the place of the sorcerer himself." He waited, then said, "And I am to inform you that it doesn't in the least matter if your view of Tuamon is – unsympathetic. You are naturally afraid and averse to Tuamon, and he expects nothing else. You must write as you feel and see. It will be irrelevant to the ritual, or to the person of the sorcerer Tuamon."

"Yes. Very well, I do all that. Then what?"

He gazed at me. He put on a look, of an agent whose client may possibly have been exposed to a swindle.

"What could there be, mademoiselle?"

"No, I'm not such a fool as to expect to be paid. I'm inquiring if I'm not to be killed when I've completed the *task*."

And then it – yes, *it* – it laughed.

This was so awful to me that I found myself on my feet, running towards the door – Vlok caught me. He must have caught Louis this way dozens of times, there was a distinct sense of practice.

"There's nothing to be alarmed at. *She doesn't need your death*."

"But if I refuse to obey the task, I'll be punished?"

Silence again.

In the end Vlok said, "There's one more thing that you have to be shown. Then you'll be left to yourself. You'll write everything down. Then publish, if you want to, or not. That isn't of any importance. Just the act of the writing. You can even burn the diary, and your manuscript, providing your own work is finished. Then nobody will trouble you, mademoiselle, ever again."

I might have asked him if he liked being its slave, or if he grieved over Louis, or Curt. Or a hundred things. But I did not, and did not care. I cared only to have it over with. I said so.

"Then I'll just step down into the street. Tuamon will show you. There's nothing to be *afraid* of. Good night, mademoiselle." And so saying he nodded and walked out, closing my door behind him. I heard his feet go down the stairs as I stood alone in the room in the gas-light with that thing, and waited for the concluding revelation.

I had wanted the key to the mystery, or it had made me want it.

Before Vlok's footsteps had died away, it moved. The dull fire shone around the edges of the body which had been Louis de Jenier's body. It was taking off the woman's coat, her hat and gloves, her dress –

It was undressing itself in front of me, with no sensitivity.

I said nothing, made no protest. I sank back into my chair, and gripped my hands together. I already knew.

Louis' frankness in his descriptions of the costuming of his rôles had told me anything I needed to know about his quite-ordinarily handsome male body. In these split seconds I became aware that this spider-witch, capable of producing from its own fleshly case a string of ectoplasmic gossamer, could thereby reshape and refashion as it chose. The smallness of the hands and feet, the truthful appearance of the breasts –

A silken camisole, silk stockings, suede shoes. Every stitch.

Yes. Now I understood. Presumably that would please, that I understood, so that I would write it accurately, here.

Physically, Louis was a male. Temperamentally, emotionally, a male. Ethically, a female. He was like one of a pair of twins, boy and girl, torn apart at birth. The female twin had been lost to him. He recaptured her – not through male lovers, who offended the maleness of his body – but by clothing himself to her various possible forms. And in that way he had remade himself into the whole double blossom, both sexes.

But Tuamon had always been that. His presence, now the woman's garments were lying on the ground, was assertively masculine. The pose and the poise of him were masculine. Yet the face under the gleaming hood of hair was a girl's face, with only a boy's arrogance to the brows and lips, and the neck, the boyish shoulders and the arms and the firm apple breasts – a girl's. There was strength in the limbs, in those rounded arms, and the long, muscled legs, the flat belly. And there was strength in the loins, which the room's warmth, or the stillness, or arrogance itself, had caused to flower, so I should have no doubts. And then he – for it was, for all and everything, *a man* – he positioned himself, with no coyness or display, to let me view that the strong loins had also their vulnerability. That this man might be possessed as a woman, too.

Tuamon, taking the feminine name Tiy-Amonet to smooth the sensibilities of a Roman commander attracted to otherness. Tuamon was hermaphrodite. Male and female, in all particulars. The face and breasts of a girl, the essence of a man. The loins of both.

Timonie had been solely and only a woman. Outside and under the skin. She was discarded, and punished. But Louis, under the skin, under the skin of the soul, was potentially dual. He had been worth the centuries.

The gas was turning blue, and that part of the room where Tuamon stood became a vast hollow drum. I thought I glimpsed – lotus pillars, the dune-shaped sarcophagae of Egypt – but then I saw instead an azure sphere, flashing and dazzling with movement and with integral life. In the heart of it, the fabulous monster basked, its eyes like port-holes on a sea of sky, through which passed colossal waves, tidal clouds, while the evening star hung on its forehead, the crescent moon and the full hung one from either ear. And on the disc of the full moon, a blue spider depended from a thread of pulsing ether.

And I did not want the vision to end.

I did not want the safe drab darkness to come back.

And I thought of Louis, closed inside, the food of this power, and I did not feel anything but hunger.

Then it too was done. Over and done.

Reality flooded back to me, and I was ashamed and petrified. And in this state I sat, hugging close my mother's shawl. I sat and the shadow-of-night gathered up itself, and masked itself again, and went by me like a burning whisper, and was gone.

And after it was gone I remade the fire and turned up the lamp, and sitting at my desk, wrote this.

THE BOOK OF THE BEAST

THE GREEN BOOK

eyes like emerald

PART ONE

The Scholar

She with apples you desired
From Paradise came long ago:
With you I feel that if required,
Such still within my garden grow.

Shelley

By the end of the first night, he knew that his lodging was haunted. From the night's first minute, he should have guessed.

A hag greeted him on the threshold.

"M'sire Raoulin?" squawked she in her old-fashioned way. And in the dusk she held high one quavering candle. He learned at once by that the interior would be ill-lit.

"I am Raoulin. My baggage and chest have arrived?"

"You are to follow me," she said, like a portress of the damned in Hell, who could not be expected to have luggage.

"To my host, your master?:"

She said, "There's no master here. There's no one here. M'sire No One is the lord in these parts."

She led him in across a black cavern of a hall, over a blacker courtyard, up an outer stair, in at an arch, along two or three corridors, and in the light-watered darkness opened for him a wooden door with her keys. When she had lit a pair of candles in his apartment, she told him she would bring his supper in an hour, or if he liked company he might partake below in the kitchen with herself and the groom. Plainly he was not royalty, and she intended him to see she knew it.

Out of malicious curiosity therefore he said he would dine below. She gave him directions he was sure he would forget.

"And mind out, on the stair," she said.

"Mind what?"

"For M'sire No One," she replied, and cackled.

She was a cheery eerie old soul.

217

Raoulin was a tall, well-made young man, good-looking in his ivory-ebony mode, for he was by stock a black-haired northerner. His father owned horses and cattle, vineyards, orchards and numberless fields, and in the long low house, while the other sons toiled at the land or galloped off wenching, there was Raoulin, constricted by tutors. They swelled his brain with Latin and fair Greek, they made inroads on his spirit with philosophy and hints alchemical.

Raoulin was to go to the City and study at the university of the Sachrist.

When the hour came, he was not sorry. He had been set apart from his family by increasing erudition. It had come to pass he could not sneeze without being accused of some sophistry or conundrum. For the City, he had heard it was packed with churches, libraries and brothels. It was the epitome of all desired wickedness: teases for the intellect, pots for the flesh.

The lodging was arranged via his father's steward, who told him only the place had been, a decade before, a great palace, the home of the noble house of d'Uscaret. They had fallen on hard times, through some political out-management, the steward believed. For the mighty families of the City had, even ten years before, been constantly engaged with one another, fighting their blood-feuds on the streets and cutting each other's throats besides in the Duke's council chamber.

Certain members of tribe d'Uscaret were still supposed to live in the mansion. It was said to be dilapidated but also sumptuous. A prestigious residence, a good address.

But no sooner had Raoulin ridden along the narrow twilight street and seen the towers of the manse arising behind their ruinously walled gardens, the ornate, unillumined facade, like that of some antique tomb, than he was sure of poverty, plagues of mice and lice, and that the steward of his father, altogether fonder of the other sons, had done him a bad turn.

Supper was not so bad, a large vegetable dish with rice, and a gooseberry gelatine, pancakes, and ale. Though money had been provided for his fare, Raoulin was not sure he would not be cheated. As it was, grandma tucked in heartily, and the bony groom, smacking lips and clacking their three or four teeth like castanets.

"Perhaps," said Raoulin, "you might get me some beef tomorrow."

"Maybe, if beef's to be had. And my poor legs aren't fit for running up and down to the meat market," replied grandma.

"Then send the girl," said Raoulin casually. "And by the by, I hope you'll see she's fed too."

A silence greeted this.

Raoulin poured himself more ale.

The groom sat watching him like a motheaten old wolf, dangerous for all his dearth of fangs. The hag peered fiercely from her mashed plate.

"We have no girl. He and I, is all."

"Then, she's the lady of the house. I beg her pardon."

In fact, he had not thought her a servant, not for one minute. It had been a test.

Now the hag said again, "Only us. And yourself."

"And M'sire No One. Yes, I recall. But in the corridors I passed this lady. A maiden, I believe."

Then the groom spoke. He said, "That can't be, for let me tell you, sieur, there's no other living soul in this house saving we and you."

"Oh, a ghost, then," said Raoulin.

His heart jumped, not unpleasantly. He did not believe in ghosts, therefore longed to have their being proved to him, like the existence of God.

He had of course lost himself on emerging from his apartment. There were no lights anywhere, only the worm-runs of windowless corridors on which the occasional door obtruded. Now and then, from perversity, he had tried these doors. Three gave access to barren chambers, empty of nearly anything. One had a shuttered window, another a candle-branch standing on the floor. (The branch was of iron, worth little. The candle-stubs had long ago been devoured by vermin.) A few other doors resisted his impulse. He fancied they were stuck rather than locked. Presently he reached an ascending stair he was certain he had not seen on entry with the hag. He paused in irritated perplexity, wondering if it would be worthwhile to climb. Just then a woman appeared and went across the stair-top, evidently negotiating the corridor which ran parallel to that below.

She did not carry a candle, and that he saw her at all was due to his own light, and the pallor of her hair and skin which caught it. Her gown was of some sombre stuff, high-waisted as was now not always the fashion, and she held her hands joined under her breast. A stiff silver net contained her hair; it glittered sharply once as she glided by. That was all. She was gone literally in that flash. Her face he did not really see, yet her slightness, something about her, made him think her girlish.

Anyone else, going over the unlit upper corridor, must have glanced downward at his light. Not she.

He had lacked the impertinence to pursue.

He waited all through supper to see if any reference would be made to the fair passager – he had decided she was attractive; she had to be, being mysterious.

"And if she is a ghost," he continued, "whose ghost?"

The groom and the old woman exchanged looks. Raoulin had seen such before. The camaraderie of age against youth, stupid cunning against stupid intelligence, the low against the better who was not better enough to get respect.

"There's no ghost here," said the old woman at length. "You were dreaming, your head full of scholar books."

"All right," said Raoulin, pleased by the heightening Stygian shade of deception, faithfully observed as in any romance. "Probably a trick of the candle."

Returning towards his rooms, he tried for the fork of the corridor where he had lost himself and found the stair.

He could not regain it.

Having gone up and down and round and about for quite an hour, having peered into further fruitless rooms of dust, mouse-cities, broken furniture, he only rediscovered his rightful corridor with difficulty. His heart, which had begun by beating excitedly, was now leaden with weariness. Reaching his bed, thank God aired with hot stones, he flung himself among the sheets and barely had space to blow out the candle before he was asleep.

Here, unconscious, he dreamed the door to his apartment was stealthily opened. A slim shadow drifted over the outer chamber. He sensed it examining as it went the closed travelling chest, the books he had already set out, a small reliquary his mother had pressed upon him. Then, entering the bedroom, all in black night, the shadow cast around. White fingers, that glimmered in the void, traced his doublet where he had thrown it down, a purse of coins – he heard them chink – his dagger – he longed to warn her to be careful, the edge was newly honed.

Then to the brink of his bed she stole, this immoderate phantom.

In utter black, through sleep and closed eyelids, yet he made her out.

A mask of Parsuan porcelain floated above him in a silver-grilled aureole-light of blondest hair. As he had known it must be, the face was lovely, and cool as snow. And the eyes – ! Never had Raoulin seen such eyes. Wide-set, carved a touch slantingly, fringed with pale lashes, and very clear. And oh, their colour. They were like the jewels he remembered from a bishop's mitre, two matching emeralds, green as two linden leaves against the sun.

Asleep, miles off, Raoulin attempted to order his body to speak to her. But the words could not be dredged up from the sea, his lips and tongue refused obedience.

Drowning, he could only gaze on her as she drew aside from him, swimming far away, over the horizon of night.

One day remained to Raoulin before he must present himself at the university. How he regretted its brevity. He had meant to use the time in exploration of the wicked City of Paradys, but now a morning sufficed for this. He visited the markets, and pried amongst the crannied shops, saw the shining coils of the river straddled by bridges, gazed on the great grey Temple-Church of the Sacrifice, where he must hear at least one Mass and report the fact to his mother.

By early afternoon he had strayed back south-west of the City, to gloomy House d'Uscaret.

In daylight, the upland streets – the mansion was on one of the many hills that composed Paradys – were not appetising. Nothing fell so low as the highmost. There were other large houses and imposing towers in the area, now gone to tenements, tiles off, stones crumbling, strung with torn washing. In the alleys was disgusting refuse. Every crevice seemed to hold debris or the bones of small deceased animals.

Having gained the house by a side entry, to which the hag had given him a key, Raoulin set himself to master the building.

He had determined to recover the ghost's corridor, and all through the hot post-noon he sought it, and, wide-awake, finally found it, too. The corridor seemed redolent yet of her ghostly fragrance. And shivering slightly, he started along in the direction she had chosen. Soon enough it gave on a further flight of ascending steps – perhaps the spectre had a lair ... But the solitary door above was disappointingly jammed – or secured – Raoulin could only concede that this kept up the best traditions of romance.

Then came another fall of stairs leading down, with, at their head, a slit of window covered by a 'grill'. Looking out, Raoulin realised himself to be in a tall tower of the house. He saw the pebbled slope of roofs, and, to his surprise, noticed the distant miniature of the Temple-Church adrift like a promontory in soft haze.

Taking the downward stair, he next arrived against a low door, which for an amazement opened.

There lay a garden, walled apart from the rest.

It had been made for a woman, he supposed; even through the riot of weeds and ivy, a map of vestal symmetry was apparent. A garden of more southern climes, modelled, maybe, on the classical courts of the Roman. Clipped ilex and conifer that had burst from shape, a tank of marble all green with lichen and with a green velvet scum upon it. The wrecks of arbours were visible, and a charming statue, a young girl in a graceful tunic, holding up an archaic oil-lamp which once it had been possible to kindle.

Raoulin trod down paths, breaking the skeins of creeper with his elegant shoes, the ivy trying to detain him by clutching at the points of his sleeves and hose.

No birds sang in that garden of emerald green. He knew it had been made for her – or that she had made it her own.

Therefore, he was not startled, reaching the end of an avenue, to confront the bank of yew in which gaped a black frontage: the arched portico of a mausoleum.

The tomb was not very big, nor very old, quite fresh. He read with ease the name on the arch in its bannering of stone. While, student-scholar that he was, he had no trouble either with the Latin underneath.

> *Helise d'Uscaret*
> *Brought a bride to this House*
> *Now at the court of Death below*

A huge lock maintained the entrance of the tomb. But, thought Raoulin, leaning on a tree, a ghost could pass straight through all walls, of wood, iron or granite.

Useless then to fasten up his own chamber. Even had he dreamed of doing so.

He wished to be served his supper that night in his rooms. He did not question the hag. He told her nothing. He did not even note she had put some morsels of beef into his stew, as requested.

During the evening, he glanced upon a few books, and partly turned his mind towards the morning. But the Sachrist had lost its stature.

In a strange condition he took himself early to bed, soon after the City bells had rung the Hesperus. (He would need to rise at Prima Hora.)

He lay on his back, besieged by sensuality, and lovely listless desires that had no need to exert themselves or to hold back. Lethargy stole slowly but certainly upon him, the harbinger. Sleep came in drifts, easily, totally, before the window had quite darkened.

But she, *she* did not come at all.

Though he had been trained to be something of a thinker, Raoulin was not properly a dreamer. Where he inclined to poetry, it was the cadence of the moment.

The ghost had failed to keep their assignation, and continued to fail.

Within a month, unsupplied by anything further uncanny, and by then thoroughly embroiled in the student life of the university, Raoulin had put the green-eyed haunt aside. It is true that he referred privately to the house as "bewitched" and even once in conversation with a fellow student had described his address as "d'Uscaret the ghost mansion." But the fellow student had only absently remarked that among the desuetudinous old houses of Ducal times, there were scarcely any that did not have either a phantom or a curse.

By day the university, which was run rather on the classical lines, worked its claws into his brain, and Raoulin caught a fever of learning only before intimated. By night he had now friends of the same feather, unlike his leery brothers, with whom to go debating and drinking. More often than not, as the first month enlarged to a plural, Raoulin did not bother to sup at his lodging, but dined in some cheap tavern with his comrades, went to a cock-fight, or to watch in their season the street players, who would set up their stages under the walls of the Sacrifice, or such commemorative plague churches as Our Lady of Ashes. His head was either burnished with wine or bright with ideas, the licence or strictures of Petronius, Petrarch, and Pliny the Other, the miracles of Galen. Raoulin was aware he was happy, but wisely, like a superstitious savage in some travelogue of the Caesars, did not name his state.

With the wine-shops and bookshops and passing shows, temporal or religious, he was soon familiar. Not so after all with the brothels. Some caution from home had stuck, concerning dread diseases, and heartless females intent only on robbery. Raoulin had been accustomed to the wholesome but difficult girls of the village, or to celibacy perforce.

The ghost had fired his blood, but that was only to be expected. Women were the Devil's, and if dead or damned, their power must be irresistible. You could not be blamed for fancying a ghost.

But the phantom came no more to tickle him in helpless sleep.

Instead it was Joseph who caught his arm and said, "Tomorrow is a Holy Day."

"Good. Let us be holy," replied Raoulin.

Joseph laughed, and the dark sunlight of evening glinted on his eye-glasses and the silver tags of his points – for Joseph was not poor.

"I had another notion in mind. Over the river is a tavern, by name the *Black Smith*. Behind lies a house which calls itself the *Sweet Cup*."

"Ah ha," said Raoulin cautiously.

"The girls are clean, you have my word," said Joseph. "I've been there."

"I have a treatise on the fifth humour –"

"First come and console the possibly non-existent other four. The world is for man's enjoyment."

On the board of the tavern was a mighty Nubian – the eponymous smith – who, swinging high his hammer, was about to crush the noddle of a fallen enemy sprawled across the anvil. Raoulin regarded this sign with interest, disfavour, and amusement. They drank no more than a token goblet, however, before going through a hind door and out across a yard. Here a ladder had been fixed, seeming to ascend into a hayloft. "What kind of pastoral cubby is this?" demanded Raoulin jollily: the one goblet had been of the strong kind. "Never fear, you shall see wonders," answered Joseph.

They managed the ladder and so got into the loft. It seemed bare, and they crossed in near blackness.

The far end of the loft gave them a shut door. Joseph knocked loudly in five spaced raps.

Presently a tiny aperture, like the spy-hole of a nunnery, was opened, and someone looked out at them invisibly. A woman's voice inquired: "Who is there?"

"Two men."

"Are you thirsty?" asked the voice.

"For a sweet cup," said Joseph.

Apparently all this was in the nature of a password. The door of the brothel came unbarred, and they were let through.

Raoulin stared. He was in a lobby, the plaster of whose walls was covered by paintings of a vivid and obscene nature.

There a shepherd disrobed a shepherdess by means of his crook, there a minstrel, his curvaceous viol put by, gently bowed the naked breasts of a lady instead – and there a priapic faun frolicked with two dryads in garlands of grapes and vine leaves. Swerving about from this, Raoulin encountered the door-keeper herself, who was startlingly clad in the draped garment of an antique Roman lady, a thing of such fine gauze that through it every contour, glint and shade of her otherwise nudity might be seen.

This nymph greeted them with an Eastern flourish.

"Will you drink of the bowl of joy?"

"We *will*," said Joseph.

The nymph ran her glance across Raoulin. Her eyes were edged with kohl and her cheeks powdered. Her face had on more clothing than her body.

"Do you know the custom of the house?"

Joseph nodded. Raoulin, his blood thundering in his ears, was prepared to learn it.

From a pedestal the nymph raised a large cup of white ceramic. She held it out before them.

Joseph reached in a hand, and plucked something forth.

"Take a counter," he said to Raoulin. "That's how you select your girl."

"What? Unseen? Suppose she's not to my taste –"

The nymph said to him smoothly, flirtatiously, "Every one of our damsels is beautiful."

"Whose word do I have?" (Joseph wriggled uneasily.) "What if," said Raoulin, primed still by the one strong goblet, "I prefer you?"

But just then he became aware of a man stirring in the shadow of a curtain beyond the paintings. Big and black he looked, like the smith off the tavern sign. So Raoulin shrugged, paid as Joseph did what he was asked, and took a small square counter like a die from the cup.

The nymph, while she had not responded to his sally, did not seem to dislike him for it. She said to Joseph, "You know the way, sieur. I'll guide your friend."

Then the curtain was drawn aside (the bully had effaced himself) and they entered a corridor. It appeared to run back a long way, and its sides were made mostly of high wooden screens which creaked mysteriously and emitted driblets of light. Although the screens were occlusive, weird shadows had been flung up on the low uneven ceiling, tangles of writhing knots, like serpents. And there were sounds too, perhaps like the noises in Hell, gasps and grunts, squeals and moans, and now and then a cry, a blasphemy, a prayer.

Raoulin was filled by apprehension as by lust. They had long since become, these two emotions, mutually conducive.

Suddenly Joseph slunk aside. He went through one of the screens and was consumed into the abyss.

The door-keeper had not looked at the counter Raoulin selected, perhaps it made no difference. She led him unerringly, and all at once the corridor was crossed by a pair of aisles. These were both of them in darkness. The nymph halted, and pointed to the left-hand way.

"Yes?" said Raoulin uncertainly.

"Yes, m'sieur," said the door-keeper. And reaching up, she kissed him on the lips with a little snake's flicker of the tongue. "The very last of the doors. It's marked with the same mark as on the counter. For you, something special."

Then she was gone, leaving him alight with the thirst of the house.

He went into the corridor and saw that it did indeed have doors rather than screens. The last of these, blundered on in the gloom, was marked with – what was it? A sort of mask ... He did not wait for more, but pushed at the barrier. It swung open with a lubricious croak.

Again, Raoulin had pause.

There was a pale-washed room with an Eastern carpet on one wall, the floor very clean, and lightly strewn with colourless flower-heads picked for their scent, as in a lady's chamber. One felt one had stumbled into the wrong house. Against another wall stood a couch, perhaps too wide for virginity; yet otherwise this was all the stuff of a well-to-do and pure girl's bedroom – even to the straightbacked chair and the little footstool. These, turned a fraction away from the door, were occupied.

Raoulin's heart, ready engorged like his loins, took a leap. Was it all some jest – some mischief – but how would Joseph have known –?

Raoulin closed the door with stealth, and began to walk silently forward, his heart noisy, and prepared for anything –

As he circled like a fox, the posed picture came visible, the chair and the girl seated in it, her blonde head slightly bent, her face dipped into shadow ...

She wore a black gown, but its lacing, at the bosom not the back, had been loosed, and under it there was no modest "breast-plate" of embroidered linen or silk, only the silken pressure of two breasts. Her feet were bare upon the stool, and nearly all one leg, the skirt of the gown caught up as if through negligence. Her left hand lay idly at her throat, just above the portion of white flesh that rose, swelled and tugged at the laces of the bosom, and sank down, leaving them slackened. The right hand rested upon an object which nestled at her belly. It was a skull.

Here was a maiden discovered alone and untrammelled, her hem carelessly raised, but in the most solemn act of contemplation advocated by the church: dwelling upon the martyrdom of the saints, and on the personal death. *To this shall you come.*

But her face – whose face was it?

At that instant, as if quietly wakening from a dream, she lifted her head.

Despite the blondness, and the skull, she was not Helise d'Uscaret.

Raoulin shuddered. He was dreadfully relieved and sorry.

It was a pretty face, too innocent, with a weak kissable mouth, and cool weasel eyes that knew everything.

She had seen him shudder, and she said in a whisper, "Thinking of death makes me remember life."

And she took his hands and put one upon the skull and the other upon her left breast.

So warm one, and beating itself with a heart, and the other as cold and hard as a stone.

"We're only mortal," said the girl. "How constricting are these laces –"

For a moment he could not unclamp his hands, from the icy apple of corruption, the hot fluttering apple of quickness.

But she released him and drew his fingers to her laces.

Then, the skull had rolled down into the flowers and he knelt between the bared limb and the covered one, his hands sliding on the treasures of Eve, and her hands, not those of a maiden, everywhere upon him, so he could hardly bear it.

She showed him how he might have her in the chair, if he wished, and he could not wait another second.

As he united with her, the whole room seemed to thunder. He had not had a girl for half a year.

She urged him on with wild cries that, in his tumult, he believed. As the spasm shook him, he kicked the damnable skull, and it rattled away across the floor.

"Have I pleased you?"
  "Oh, yes."

"Then … will you give me a little gift –?"

Raoulin frowned. He had paid at the door and reckoned this unsuitable. But then again, perhaps they robbed their girls here, and it had been very good. If he tipped her, she might let him have her again, although she had already gone behind a curtain to wash, and she came back with her laces tied, and he supposed his time with her was up.

He put a coin between her breasts, and leaned to kiss her. She allowed it. But then she said, "I regret. The Mother's strict."

"*Mother* – what, of your nunnery?"

The blonde whore lowered her eyes. But she removed his hands.

"Unkindness," he said. "No charity."

"It isn't my choice. In a minute I shall be wanted."

"And if I protest, that hulk of a door-fellow will throw me out."

She said nothing.

Raoulin straightened his clothes and did up his points with surly tardiness. "This is a churlish place. I won't come back. Even the old hag's more friendly at d'Uscaret."

No sooner had he uttered this than he was puzzled at having done so. To name his lodging to a chance harlot would not, even in the nicest circumstances, have seemed sensible to him. But there, too late, it was said.

He expected no response. Perhaps she would have the grace to be deaf.

But then she asked, in a peculiar tone, "How is it called?"

"What?"

"Your lodging is it? *There?*"

"Where?" And now he looked up with a merry smile – and met the eyes of a terrified animal in a trap. "Why – what's up with you?"

"D'Uscaret?" she said. "Is it *there?*"

"Possibly I may have –"

"You lodge *there?*"

She was so insistent she seemed to drive him.

"Very well, I do. But don't try to make anything of it –"

Before he had even finished, she began to scream.

He stood astounded, without a thought in his head. It seemed to be occurring in another room, this appalling outcry and madness – for while she screamed she ran about, threw herself at the walls, tore at herself with her nails in the most horrible way – dragged down the costly carpet from the plaster and writhed with it on the ground.

As had to happen next, the door burst open. Two roughs, one with drawn dagger, came shouldering through. The larger, unarmed, man seized Raoulin, while his companion laid the dagger under Raoulin's ear.

Raoulin kept quite still. He said firmly, "I did nothing to her that wasn't natural. We were talking after – and then this!" He had to raise his voice, for she went on shrieking, though now her vocal chords cracked. The doorway filled with clusters of frightened or curious male and female faces. A girl, clad only in a shift, pushed by and ran to the blonde harlot, tried to take hold of her and quieten her. It was beyond her powers. Two others hastened to join the struggle, calling the blonde pet names as they ripped her ripping hands from her hair and breasts –

Then the proprietress, the "Mother," was in the room, a pockmarked frump one would not turn to regard once on the street.

"Explain this hubbub."

Her presence bore such authority, even the demented creature on the floor grew abruptly mute, and then began to weep. The three other girls cradled her.

The Mother turned her unadorable gaze on Raoulin.

"Well?"

Raoulin thought quickly. Only the bizarre truth would do. He reluctantly rendered it. "– And when I told her d'Uscaret –"

"*D'Uscaret!*" exclaimed the woman. Her face had altered. She did not look afraid, but a wily sort of blankness was stealing over her, the appearance she would put on for the confessional.

Raoulin took heart. He said boldly, "This isn't what I called *here* for."

"No, no doubt not. There's some superstition, concerning that house. An old curse. I'm surprised my girl knows of it."

Abruptly the blonde harlot raised her raw voice in another spewing of screams.

"Be silent!" cried the Mother. And the screams went to weeping again.

"Let him be," she added to her roughs. And to Raoulin himself, with all the casualness of cunning unease, "And you, sieur, had best get off."

As the slabby hands released him, Raoulin caught in the doorway now the wink of Joseph's humiliated and resentful spectacles.

Crossing the bridge in the torchlight, between one dark bank and the other, Joseph lamented, "I can never go back there now."

"Do you want to? We find it's a hospital for lunatics not a bawdy," said Raoulin, obscurely embarrassed.

"Frightening a silly trollop with your foul story –"

"I *told* no story. I said that name – d'Uscaret – and all the hordes of Hell broke loose. I can tell you, any fun I had wasn't worth *that*."

They parted unaffectionately on the upper bank. Laude was ringing softly from Our Lady of Ashes. The river flexed its gleaming muscles. Raoulin was sorry to have lost Joseph's regard. Probably tomorrow, or in a few days, they would laugh about the affair.

Yet somewhere inside his head as he climbed the hills, the awful screams of the harlot rang on and on. One believed she might have seen and heard and done a thing or two. Whatever had made her afraid was something proportionally horrible.

Going under the Sacrifice, beneath the winged cliffs of its buttresses, he considered his lodging. He considered the ghost he might only have dreamed. Was it that?

Some late revellers from a tavern roiled by with lanterns. They seemed to have come from another world than the darkness in which he moved, through which he climbed, and to which he went.

And then, as he entered the twisting alley that led up to the back walls of the house, he saw the black tower-tops, and the one black turreted tower with a faint greenish firefly-light flickering in it.

Raoulin stopped as if he had met the Medusa's petrifying head. For a moment he could not breathe.

The tower was that which looked north, towards the Temple-Church – the tower into which he had penetrated the first day, trying its one door that would not open. The tower whose stair gave on the weedy garden and the tomb.

How ominous the light looked there, dim and shifting behind its pane of corrupt glass. Did someone move in the room, up and down?

Had he the spirit now to go in and seek the chamber, to push wide the door and maybe find there a young woman in a chair, her hand upon a skull ...

Raoulin broke into a chill sweat. To his dismay he realised he too was frightened. He remembered the porcelain face of his dream and the cat's-eyes of perfect emerald hovering above him – and marked himself with the sign of the cross. "The Lord is my keeper. The sun shall not smite me by day, nor the moon by night –" And, at the side door, unlocking it, whispered: "Be not afraid for the terror by night, nor for the arrow that flieth ..."

To the kitchen he went, and lit there two of the candles and stuck them on the spikes of a branch. This he carried before him. Somewhere the hag and the groom snored in aged sleep. They were not juicy enough for demons to chew –

He crowded such ideas from him, and crept like a scared child up through thick night to his apartment. And there he locked the door, and there, by the shine of many extravagant wicks, he opened the reliquary his pious mother had sent with him, and took out the bones and the nails of the saint, and kissed them.

And in bed he recalled that to go with a whore was a sin and if he died tonight, the Devil would get him.

So at length he slept and had nightmares, but nothing else of the quick or the dead approached.

In the morning came summer sunlight, and the now familiar sounds and stenches of the summer city. Birds chimed past the window. Raoulin lay in the warm brightness of the reborn earth and called himself a dunce.

Too timid to go to the tower by night. Well, he would go there presently and smash in the door if he must.

It was even a Holy Day, God watchful.

In the kitchen, where he broke his fast, the hag pottered about. An evil grey cat, thin as a string and kept for the mice, hissed at him from the hearth like an adder.

"Well, puss," said Raoulin to the cat, "I'm off to watch the priests and processions. Is it a fact, granny," he added for the hag's full benefit, "they carry a Christ out of the Sacrifice made all of alabaster and silver, with wounds of malachite?"

"Go see," said the hag.

He promised he would, but instead of course made straight for the yard stair and the rooms of the hinder house.

Again, he had difficulty locating the exact spot. Then on the proper steps, up in the correct passage, confronting the solitary door, in the dark, doubt wormed under his skin, his flesh *crawled*. Until, turning, he saw – as if he had reinvented it – the slit of window above the garden stair, and day and daytime Paradys (in which reverential bells were ringing, to encourage him). He went and drank in the vista, like a draught of medicine. Then returned up into the passageway. Here he tried the door again, courteously. As before, it was immovable. It was a formidable bastion, too, looked at with an eye to damage. The timbers were heavy, and thewed with iron.

Dunce again. He had brought no implement to help him.

But then there was the adjacent garden, some handy bough or up-levered stone would do the job.

He was on the garden stair, descending, past the window and into shadow, when he heard a noise above.

Raoulin clamped himself against the wall. His lips formed a prayer. He thrust it off angrily. This was broad day. No non-existent fiend had power now –

What he had heard was the sigh of a woman's skirt, sweeping along the corridor. Then his heart roared loudly enough he could scarcely hear anything else – until the rasp of a turning key somehow reached him.

The big obdurate door was being breached, and Raoulin could no longer cower there in ignorance. He went back up the stair, crouching like a toad, and peered above the top step.

The doorway gaped. It was a gap of paleness, not dark, a chamber lit by a window. That was, from this quirky vantage, all he could see.

And then, out of the door walked the hag.

Over one arm she bore some bed-linen, and in her other hand a platter on which there balanced a costly goblet of glass. There were some dregs of murky fluid in it, some brackish wine.

Not looking about, the hag proceeded along the corridor, and as she did this the door swung suddenly shut, and again he heard the note of a key turning in a lock.

Raoulin sat himself on the stair. He was grinning, bemused, disturbed, but no longer afraid. Did a ghost require wine and food and fresh linen? Did a ghost lock itself in by hand?

A voluntary prisoner lurked within the tower. The lady of d'Uscaret was a recluse. They had said no one lived here, to confound the lodger. But, by the Mass, it was his own father's coin went to feed her now. He had some say in her doings.

He half resolved at once to burst upon her. The hag must have a secret knock. He would have to batter in the door, explain the act as a notion of rescue in ignorance. After all, she could not have reported or complained of his previous attempts.

In a moment he thought better of this idiocy. There were other ways to come at her. Whoever she was, she was not Helise, the dead bride. He had only glimpsed her, for that dream, he saw now, was only a dream. Perhaps the reality was old, toothless and ugly. Be careful. He would spy, and woo her slowly, to see if she was worth the effort.

With an abrupt easing of the heart, Raoulin ran up the stair, along the corridor, and off through the house, which he left inside another half-hour. He went to join the throng of the City, the religious processions, the hucksters, players, taverns.

It was as if he had been reprieved from a severe sentence, but this did not occur to him.

There was a summer storm, the sky the colour of cinders, and the rain falling in remote leaden drops. In the tavern called the *Surprise*, Joseph tapped Raoulin's shoulder, and Raoulin, turning with some pleasure to pick up their friendship, was only surprised when Joseph said, straight out like a cough or swear word: "That girl's dead."

The sentence shocked in several ways. Raoulin could not sort them.

"Eh? Which girl?" he blurted.

"The little blonde harlot. Shall I say how?" Joseph's spectacles enlarged his eyes like two monstrous tears.

"How then?"

Joseph sighed. "She filled a bladder with some corrosive tincture and squirted it up inside herself."

There was a nothingness then, rather than a silence, between them, while the normal racket of the *Surprise* went on all about. At last Raoulin murmured, "How did she come by such a thing?"

"Oh, there is a physician for the girls. He practises with the alchemical arts and keeps a cupboard of ointments and mixtures. She visited him on a pretext, and stole the essence. It may be she didn't understand its strength ... They heard her cries but couldn't save her. A ghastly death."

Raoulin had turned deathly sick, as though he himself had been poisoned. His genitals burned. The room trembled as if under water. "And do you blame *me* for this?"

"No! Blame you? No. And yet."

To his absolute confusion, Raoulin felt the pressure of grief mounting up his senses into his eyes like a wave. He rose suddenly, pushing away from the bench, thrusting by Joseph as if he hated him – he did hate him and was sure the sentiment was shared – and got out into the alley by the wine-shop. Here, leaning on the masonry, he vomited his drink. Good. *Good.* He should suffer some penance. Where to run? Into a church? Oh *God* – what had she reckoned, that stupid little trull, with her sweet face and silly mouth, and eyes wise to everything except what she would work on herself.

He had not even now been able to vomit away the question – *Why?* — or the cause – *himself.*

It was a truth, he had been spared much distress. He was young, and lucky. Death and illness, misery and want, the ancient degree of panic itself, were matters apart from Raoulin. He had read of states and afflictions, in books. But until this hour the wing of night had not brushed him. Scratched by its metallic feathers, he quailed.

The lead sky leaned on Paradys. Her heights pressed up against it in luminescent stabs. Still the whole impact of the thunder and the rain was not released.

He beheld above him the cliffs of the Temple-Church. He had gone over much ground, had crossed the river, without seeing. A cruel olivine glare glittered on the holy windows. The processions were done. Christ had gone in again and left the world to sin and savagery, and to all the inexplicable shades.

Raoulin stood a minute on that runnel of path nicknamed, by some,

"Satan's Way," and did not know it.

Then continued his dreary ascent towards the house called d'Uscaret.

The storm broke loose on the City at midnight, and roused several thousand sleepers, of whom Raoulin was only one.

His last thoughts had been of a childish running away. He had wanted to leave it all, the City, the university, the fever of learning, to escape back into the dull safe farm where nothing bad had ever happened to him, or been told to him in any way he had to credit.

But waking at the blast of the thunder and the shattering rain flung through the windows, he knew at once what he must do instead.

There was after all one here in this house who could tell him what had made the name of d'Uscaret so vile it killed.

Raoulin got up and secured the shutters of his two rooms. He had slept in his clothes and now tidied himself, and drank the ale left with his untouched supper.

Then, with two candles lit on the branch, and his knife in his belt, he took himself from the chamber and went to seek the recluse in her tower. No longer in the spirit of romance or unchastity. But with a grim purpose; as a right.

On the stair to the upper corridor, something checked him. He had the thought to put out the candles. Thunder bellowed and the stone-work seemed to whine. What use two feeble flames? He quenched them. And then, entering the corridor there was candleshine enough soaking out from the hidden chamber, whose door was standing wide. A figure came from it, slender, high-waisted, *hers*.

The light she carried dipped, swooped up and formed an arch, a funnel. The dark centre of the light, she flowed away and seemed drawn down into the earth – she was descending the stair towards the garden.

With the stealth of a starving hunter, Raoulin followed.

From the stair-head he glimpsed her below, a spectral creature still, on the threshold of the garden and the tempest. Then with one blow the howling night quaffed her candle. A rushing filled the doorway – rain and noise. She was gone into the weather.

On the edge of night, his civilised self held him back half a moment. Then he too was plunged in wet and chaos.

The water gushed upon his head and shoulders. It beat him, and slapped his face over and over, and he could not see.

On all sides the trees of the garden groaned and foamed like rivers.

The quick-growing weeds which, if trodden down and broken, in a day or night of fecund summer would reweave themselves, had formerly concealed any other excursions through the garden. It had seemed unvisited for years. But perhaps she walked here often, under sun and moon, under downpour, in the winter snow –

He had continued forcing himself forward through the night, and now he glimpsed the great yew ahead, where the mausoleum gaped from the foliage, the little house of Helise the dead bride.

The rain all at once slackened, and was lifted up like a swag of heavy curtaining. He heard the fountain breath of the drenched trees, and the individual notes of oval glass beads falling from branch to branch. The moon struck suddenly from a cloud like a spear. In the entry of the tomb stood a woman in a black gown, with dead-white hands clasped upon a dead candle, a white stalk of throat and a white face in a powdery bloom of hair.

In those instants she was uncanny, the dead one risen from her grave.

Because of this, he could not make himself move or speak.

And then, the shadowy features of her face (like the smudged shadows on the face of the moon itself) realigned themselves. It was she who spoke to him.

"Who are you? What do you want?"

A fundamental inquiry, perhaps a fearful one, given the time and place, and since she was not a phantom.

Raoulin took some random steps nearer. There was no explanation he could offer that would in any way humanly excuse his action.

Thus he said, "And you, lady, why did you come here in the rain?"

She leaned out of the porch of the tomb at him, her face tilted upward. He saw it was the face of the dream and that, even in the moon's colourless ray, the discs of her eyes, lent only a hint of proper light, would flood with greenness, like the trees.

"Who are you?" she said again.

"My name is Raoulin," he said, wondering if she had been told of him. That must be so. For she had come seeking him that first night, and stared into his sleep when he dreamed. "And you, demoiselle?" he added, for it appeared she was young, after all the speculation, and yet, being moon-like, ageless and old, under her surfaces.

"I?" she said. "Who am I?" She lowered her lunar-emerald eyes. "You may read my name above me."

He looked irresistibly above her head, and there on the stone banner ran the letters, as he had seen before: *Helise d'Uscaret.*

"A namesake of the dead girl," he said.

"Oh no. This tomb is mine, which naturally is why I visit here. I'm long dead, Sieur Raoulin. And therefore why should a storm deter me?"

For all her reality, her body, her shadow going away from her on the path, again the skin crawled over his bones.

Harshly he said, "The rain wets your gown. You drink wine from a glass and need a candle in the dark."

"Do I? You mean to say I'm flesh and blood. Yes. But yet, I died. I died and was awarded this black box. I went down to the court of death as they so prettily describe it, or so I take the Latin to mean, and perhaps I decipher wrongly. You are the scholar, Sieur Raoulin. Do I have the message right?"

He said, "You questioned the old woman about me."

Then she smiled.

"It's been many years," she replied, "since there was any life in the house. And suddenly, a young man from the provinces. I confess the fault of curiosity."

"Do you confess, too, stealing into the room and watching me as I slept?"

"You are unchivalrous, sieur. Asking that I admit such a thing."

"The dead can't expect much courtesy," he answered boldly.

Her glancing conversation irked, but also flattered him. She was very beautiful. It was very strange.

"Perhaps," she said then, "perhaps I shall resolve this riddle for you. If you have the will and wish to listen."

"What else," he said.

Her eyes fixed upon his. Even in the darkness now he saw that they were green.

"You may not believe the story I tell you. It's incredible and utterly exact. I can't lie. That is my – atonement."

"I'm all impatience," he said.

"Then, I invite you to my chamber. With me, no codes of propriety remain, to be upheld or sullied. As you say, the dead can hope for slight courtesy."

"I won't harm you," he said.

She smiled again. "Don't trouble. It's understood."

She went before him through the garden, the skirts of her gown brushing off rain-opals from the bushes. Such jewels were strewn in her hair, grey gems in a white web, for she wore it quite loosely, carelessly.

He followed her back into the house and up the stair. His pulses beat, insisting on carnal matters; but his brain stayed wholly clear. It was not for a tryst he companioned this one.

The room that she led him into was unlike the rest of the house. Eight candles burned and lit a painted floor of squares, and showed the ceiling too was figured with scrolls and smouldery fruit. The posted bed stood partially away behind a curtain, and guarded by a chest of carved ebony. There was the window, to glow its marsh-light on the City. There, a broad fireplace bordered by columns, with a pale fire frisking in it. This, after the rain, was solacing. Two black chairs, with footstools, faced each other across the hearth, a table between with a book upon it, and also a silver pitcher and two glass goblets of the valuable kind he had seen before.

He could not fail to be aware this room had some resemblance to the make-believe bedroom at the brothel. Or that it too had been prepared for a guest. Madly it came to him that everything that had gone on, since his first entry to the City, was in the nature of a dance-measure, and none of it quite real, or what it seemed.

"Be seated," said Helise d'Uscaret, if so she was, and why should she not be so?

He obeyed her, taking the right-hand chair.

In the window-embrasure, another book lay, and a little casket. Here and there were scattered small tokens of life, of femininity – a hand-mirror of polished metal, a ribbon, a flaxen bud in a thimble of water. (Nowhere, that he could see, a skull.) Charmingly, from under the bed-curtain, a satin slipper peeped out.

And like the attitude of the table and two chairs, these items had an air of considered arrangement.

Into his glass she poured a dark wine.

He caught the scent of it, and of her, as she bent over him and drew away. Certainly, she was a living woman.

Beauty. Strangeness.

She seated herself in the opposing chair, and sipped from her own glass a vintage like ink. But now he could see the impossible colour of her gaze.

"Be at ease," she said.

"Your eyes," he said, as if he could not prevent himself, "never in the world – so *green*."

"Long ago," she said, "my eyes were not green at all. That is the badge of what befell me. The mark on me. My eyes are my scar, after the battle."

It seemed to Raoulin he would not move now, not even to raise the fine glass to his lips. This stasis did not distress him. His mind was alert, to be instructed. Nothing else was of importance.

PART TWO

The Bride

And what will ye wear for your wedding lace?
  One with another.
A heavy heart and a hidden face,
  Mother, my mother.

Swinburne

A girl is grown like a flower in the house of her kindred. She is nurtured for her hues and perfume. At the blossoming she will be plucked from her native soil and planted elsewhere. In other earth she will give fruit, fade, wither, and finish. This is all the usefulness of such a flower, the well-born girl among the great houses of Paradys.

Helise la Valle knew, as she had learnt her alphabet and orisons, that this was her destiny.

Indeed, she had looked forward to the event of her transplanting, once she became conscious of the future. Rather than be afraid, it seemed to her child-mind like the festival of Christmas or the New Year, a season of celebration, dressing-up, the giving and receiving of gifts. Late to these images came a dreamlike icon: the bridegroom.

It was not until her adolescence, actually her saint's day, in her twelfth year, that this procrastinate shape at last stepped forward to overwhelm, to *crush* all the others, and fill her with pervasive dread.

On that day it was that she heard his name for the first time. What is named, in the oldest rituals of witchcraft, takes power.

"Heros d'Uscaret," sang out the youngest cousin.

And at this, all the elder cousins fell entirely silent, passed over that robbed them of speech and motion.

"Who is he?" asked Helise.

She was a fey girl, whose quiet attentiveness led adults to She had never been discouraged in asking questions, for she

"You're to be wed to him," said one of the elder cousins, for propriety had been breached. "You are betrothed."

237

"Am I?" said Helise, merely interested.

But just then one of the most senior cousins came briskly into the room, clapping her hands and frowning.

The maidens were disbanded. Only the Name was left.

It was at the hour of candle-lighting that Helise approached her mother.

"I am to marry Heros – d'Usc – d'Uscaret?"

The mother started. She was seated in her chair before a glowing hearth (it was autumn, and the nights already were cold) idly combing the long hair of her little lap-dog. At its mistress' start, the tiny animal growled. Helise did not like the dog, for it had once bitten her with its sharp rat teeth. She blamed the dog for this, and not the sickly cosseting and ill-temper of her own mother, which had formed it.

"What did you say, Helise?"

"That I'm to marry – am betrothed –"

"Very well," said the mother. "You are. It's a distinguished match."

Helise stood between excitement and disarray. She had always known her life would alter, but here was sudden proof.

"Heros," she said again, "d'Uscar – et."

"Someone has been twittering," said the mother. Her sallow proud face was unkind. "Your cousins."

"But Mother, mustn't I know?"

"In good time. You mayn't wed tomorrow. It will be three good years before you are fit. Your father is strict."

"But shall I know nothing of it?"

"The suitor is young enough, twenty years when you are fifteen. Sound, not a cripple. Fair, I have heard. His house is of the best. They've the favour of the Duke."

Helise, at twelve, had already been in love, with a painting of Jehanus the Baptist on the Martyr Chapel wall of the Sacrifice. She understood that it was futile to love a saint in such a manner. But since her own sensuality was to herself undivulged, she did not perceive it for what it was, and had never realised she sinned in her wild thoughts. In her head she pictured to herself the court of Herod, where she saved the saint from death (thereby depriving him, of course, of his martyrdom, maybe of his sainthood) and the clutches of Herod, shameless Salomé, and the Romans. She accompanied Jehanus into the desert where, respected among his followers, she wove him garlands from the locust tree, tended him in sickness, swooned and revived in his miraculous embrace, and, in the river to her breasts, was baptised by the fiery water spilling from his hands. The face of Jehanus in the fresco, formed by an artist of genius, had often become the subject for some young girl's fantasy. The arched throat, mane of hair, and great upraised eyes, were tautly luminous with that agony of suffering or joy inherent in worldly pain. Or pleasure. Kept ignorant, the perceptive instincts of Helise had already been a trifle warped.

It was her whimsy perhaps that Heros d'Uscaret, described, should resemble her first love.

But the Lady la Valle would not describe Heros d'Uscaret.

It took a maid in the closeted bedroom to do that.

She was crying, this girl, only a year or so older than her mistress. Helise, having been well-educated in many alternative areas, beat her maid's hands with an ivory comb, to come at the cause.

"Oh madam – they've promised you to a monster!"

"What do you mean?" said Helise.

"There's a curse on that house."

The maid snivelled, and Helise raked her again with the comb.

"Madam – Satan claims all the men of their line – and the women. But the men are – shape-changers – they are *things under the skin*."

At this nonsensical, beastly phrase, Helise left off her interrogation. Her immature mind had now quite enough to play upon.

For five days she was in a fever and the physicians despaired of her life. Then she recovered, and they congratulated their own skills.

The talk of betrothal and terror seemed sloughed with illness. It was not referred to. Helise resumed her former habit, and never asked.

(The maid was gone. There was a new maid, a country girl who was not acquainted with the City.)

What one does not speak of need not be believed.

So Helise continued until her fifteenth year, near the end of which they informed her that, soon after her birthday, she was to wed a noble lord of the City, whose name had already been made known to her. By then she had all but forgotten the awful words, her fever dreams. Therefore the icy hand that gripped her heart seemed to have no source.

In the assembled months before her wedding-day, Helise was wan and languid. Her mother and aunts chided her. She would lose her good looks and demean her house. She must eat this and drink that, she must have these unctions applied to her skin and those pastes to her hair.

At fifteen, Helise had mostly dispensed with questions. Her native indifference to the outer world was augmented by realisation that what might be answered was invariably told without inquiry – and what would not be answered would not.

At night in her narrow virgin's bed, Helise offered vague prayers to a fate

that was unavoidable; she prayed as a man prays to be spared death. Perhaps
delay was possible.

But the months clambered over each other and the wedding-day came
hurrying nearer. The bride was not afforded a single glimpse of the groom.

A priest came to instruct Helise, a man elderly and superlatively uncomely,
as was thought correct in the case of a young girl.

One morning, as they sat in the la Valle vine court, Helise spoke to the
priest.

"My betrothed is Lord Heros, the heir of House d'Uscaret." It was not a
question, nor did the priest reply. Until now he had somehow managed not to
name the name of the bridegroom, though referring to him always deferen-
tially. "Spiritual father," said Helise, looking only at her knotted hands,
"when I was a child, I was frightened by tales of evil that had to do with –"

"This isn't the hour to dwell on such foolishness," said the priest. "You
must think only of your duties as a wife. Be wary, my daughter, that you don't
interpose such nasty and aimless chatter."

"But spiritual father, these tales concerned my husband."

The priest looked as steadily upon the vines as Helise upon her hands.
Neither met the other's eye.

"Put superstition from your mind, my daughter."

"But father – I'm afraid."

The priest inhaled and expelled a noisy breath laden with garlic and
kitchen wine. He said, "There have been stories told of d'Uscaret, by the
ignorant and stupid, notions instigated by enemies of that valiant house."
Then he paused, as if girding himself, and added, "What have you heard?"

Helise stammered that she could recall no details.

At that, the priest seemed happier.

"If you can remember no absolute, how can you fear?"

Helise attempted to confide that she did not know, yet fear persisted.

But the priest would have none of that. He rebuked her with sins of self-
attention and untrust. Would her loving parents give her over to any tainted
man? And did she not have faith in her God to protect her?

Helise sat quiescent under this garlicky lesson, until he left off and went
on with the others.

It appeared to her that all with whom she now had dealings, all that were
caught up in the train of the approaching marriage, adopted an odd manner.
Faces she had been familiar with now looked like masks, and voices did not
run along but went choppily, with words left unsaid. And how often she saw
the hands rising and falling upon the breasts, marking there a cross. Did the
maids stare nervously sideways at her, as if at one who may be infected with
plague? Did her aunt's singing bird go dumb in its cage at her passing?

The shadow is on me. Am I going to die?

She knew nothing of the real rites of marriage, nothing of sex beyond the untutored flarings of her own body, which she had obliquely discovered by then were dangerous, as they might lead her into unchastity. Connubiality was this: the husband lay beside his wife all night in the same bed. Sometimes (so certain cousins had assured her) he kissed his wife, even her nakedness, and some men, though surely they were depraved, set their hands on a woman's private places. Helise had never even seen cats mating. Though once she had beheld a cat in labour, and was appalled. Later on, hearing her brother's wife shrieking in childbirth, Helise had had some idea why. The angels of God brought the baby. It was God's will, and His will also that a woman suffer in travail, the female penance for the disobedience of Eve.

Could it be that Heros d'Uscaret would perpetrate on his bride some alarming foul act, something worse even than the embarrassing things that apparently quite normally went on, these lewd kissings and touchings already mentioned?

Ten nights before her wedding-night, Helise recalled precisely what her maid had said to her: "Satan claims them – shape-changers – *things under the skin.*"

She woke in a bath of sweat, and bit her hands with terror.

Paradys turned out to recognise the wedding processions of the houses la Valle and d'Uscaret, and to catch the sweetmeats and small money retainers might throw the rabble. They were able to watch besides many scores of men on fine horses, dazzling in brocade and gems, some quantities of damsels clothed like graces and strewing petals, musicians with lutes and shawms, and pages with banners.

The bride rode on a dappled palfrey with a headstall of pearls. The girl's dress was of cloth-of-silver, with undersleeves of cream silk stitched with brilliants. Her blonde hair fluttered loose but for a jewelled cap of silver daisies and sea-green peridots. Her face was white, but there was nothing uncommon in that.

The bridegroom's family cantered up, heavy with their colours of sable and viridian. The sigil of d'Uscaret was a cruel preying bird, perhaps a falcon. They were a wealthy house, and bullion clanked on everything, and in the jaunty hat of the young groom was a diamond said to have been dug from the forehead of a dragon in the Holy Land … Otherwise, the hat, the light, the shade, hid the young man's face, though he cut a brave enough figure. His locks were blonder even than those of the little white bride.

Helise found herself entering the Temple-Church, and acknowledged that the astonishing horror had arrived, was here, about to happen to her.

From the moment of her waking at dawn, through all the preparation of her person, somehow *she* had gone far off. They had bathed and anointed her and clad her in the silver gown – but she had been at a distance, hanging in the air.

As her body rode along the route on the demure palfrey, the wedding music in its ears, the finery flashing at its eyes like drawn knives, her soul was in a trance.

But now the wanderer had returned, was trapped and must participate. There was to be no escape.

The grey pillars of the Temple-Church rose like tree-trunks of a petrified forest. The roof was ribbed – the inner belly of some apocryphal beast which had swallowed the processions whole. Rays of daylight pierced through. From a massive window a bolt of sunshine streamed and smoked.

An angel of white marble shone out in the path, but did not save Helise. Beyond, the Angel Chapel was an underwater cave where she would drown in marriage.

And now she was at the rail, and now she was alone but for one who stood beside her.

It seemed to her that no one else at all was there.

No maids-of-honour, no gentlemen, no witnesses, not even the priest. Not even her parents, who had condemned her.

Only this other at her side.

Something – the priest's injunction – brought them to kneel.

Helise knelt, and her gown rustled and the small jewels clinked against the tessellated floor. And she heard the scuff of a shoe, the brushing of a viridian sleeve.

The blessing was being spoken, the magical water was being sprinkled. Could a devil endure that? Seemingly yes, for he had not sprung aside, his garments did not singe.

The responses of the Mass drew from her a whisper. At her side a male voice murmured low its clear Latin. A young male voice, younger than the voices of her father and brother.

Surely, a demon could not utter the responses of God's Mass?

The one beside her had a voice, and now a hand, resting upon the rail. The hand stayed Helise, for it was in shape the hand of a warrior-saint, made thin and strong for the hilt of battle, the clasp of prayer. And on the fourth finger, an onyx ring.

The priest, having changed the wafers to the flesh and the wine to the ichor of Christ, fed them at the rail like two hungry sparrows.

But could a demon take between its lips the body and blood of Heaven?

Now she must stand up again. She must make the correct replies to the questions of the priest. Like all questions, in her experience, the answers were preordained, unavoidable. Only questions that might be answered could ever be asked.

And so, in a few minutes more, she had been wedded, and had barely noticed, puzzling as she was over the paradox of the pale hand with the onyx, and the Host penetrating the intestines of one accursed.

Finally the pale hand itself took her own and on to her finger ran a coil of cold metal, to bind her, and the priest in turn bound her right hand to the pale hand. Tied, she must turn. Or, *they* turned her.

Handfast, Helise looked at her bridegroom, her husband. There before her, straight and slender, his face in a halo of uncoloured hair, was Jehanus, the beautiful, harrowed martyr from off the very wall. Only his eyes were altered. Their beauty had been brought to life with a green and stellar fire.

Bound fast hand-to-hand with her, he kissed her passionlessly with his cool mouth. It was a fearsome kiss, for it struck Helise in the breast and heart, into her womb even, down to the soles of her feet, like lightning. As in the Bible, a sword had gone through her. She had never known before what that phrase could mean.

Outside, the crowd shouted. She was put again on to the palfrey. They went up through the City, up to the mansion of d'Uscaret. And sometimes the thrown flowers smote Helise, and some wisps of paper, one of which lodged in her sleeve, and looking at it she saw it was a votive prayer for her safety. But now she did not mind. He rode at her side.

The viridian banners by the doors were garlanded with myrtle. This house was black, like a sarcophagus, and the great hall was black, with old charred flags like broken wings drooping from the rafters. But the candles burned and white damask clothed the tables and he led her to sit beside him.

Helise was happy. Her eyes sparkled and everything had become wonderful. They gave her white wine to drink, and on the gallery minstrels sang like angels.

They banqueted on fowl roasted with figs and cakes of flour and sugar, milk jellies, fish served in their armour, doves in their feathers. There were salads of spinach and beans made into gardens, and castles of rice and pine kernels, and almond puddings sweet as the promise of life everlasting.

A pageant was performed, displaying the prowess of d'Uscaret, her knights and lords, their deeds of valour.

Lilies fell from a canopy.

At the table sat the new father and mother of Helise. He was a dark and peevish man, fretful, who drank until huge drops spurred out on his forehead. The woman was like something cut from wood, having only two dimensions, angular in her tourmaline gown, her silver caul and steeple headdress from which black spiderspun floated.

What did they matter?

At the side of Helise sat Jehanus who was Heros, still and nearly silent, real as all things, given to her by God.

I am his wife, and he is –

He was beautiful as a young divinity. Had she suffered so only to be intoxicated by this ecstasy?

The masque in the hall was now of a girl and youth embraced upon an isle on wheels, while tame panthers frisked about – but they were all men inside the feline velvets. A dim cry floated on the sea of delight: *shape-changer.*

"Come, madam. Now, lady, come with us –"

D'Uscaret's maids of honour, the young girls of the house, were urging her bashfully, wantonly. She must get up and go with them, to the bridal chamber.

Helise rose and let them lead her out. Their butterfly mutters and touches, playful, childishly-naughty, swirling her through a door and up an inner stair where brands blazed in brackets. A vast heat was on the stair, bringing out the scents of flesh and unguents, and above in the curve of a shadow, the arch, the corridor, great doors carved with falcons, through which they slipped like thieves. And there the room, the room, and the tall wide bed, where tonight she would lie beside her lord.

Now she could reconcile herself with all of it. Yes, she could conjure endless darkness furled in ceaseless embrace. His mouth on hers, his arms about her. And if he should wish more – whatever he wished she would grant.

The girls of d'Uscaret, with sighings and nonsensical acid ribaldries – traditional things they probably did not, all of them, comprehend – disrobed Helise and clad her in a shift of samite, combed out her hair and wove lilies in it. She climbed into the high bed, and they arranged her there like a toy, leaning on the pillows.

At the hour of Matines, the wedding-party bounded up the stair with torches and candles, bells and lyres, bringing the husband to his wife.

The solid doors flew wide, and between them the uproar surged, the lights and sequins and the blowing of tin trumpets. The old men making sour old dirty jests, and the women laughing or compressing their faces. The Lady d'Uscaret was there, like a pillar of flint. Her perspectiveless face also contorted to smile or grimace, but it was like a disc of paper.

Before all the horde, the bridegroom. He made the rest into a dumbshow.

They brought him forward to the bed, and the men instructed him and the women looked away.

The eldest of the maids of honour bowed.

"Your bride is here awaiting you, m'sire. May you have joy of your night."

Then, hiding their faces coyly, the maids ren away, and the old men tried to catch them going down the stairs, so there were shrieks and a scattering of sugarplums.

With a susurrus of trains and mantles, the doorway sucked back the last of the crowd. The doors were shut.

Heros and Helise, alone now, in the bedchamber.

She sat in the bed, as if in a bank of snow. She knew she must be shy like the gentle female deer. Her heart drummed, and she watched him under her lids.

What would he do now? She did not care, so long as he would lie down with her. She was parched for his nearness, the pressure of his mouth and body. This was true lust she felt, and did not even know it.

But Heros went straight back to the doors, and in came one of his gentlemen. Behind a screen painted with a hunting or hawking scene, the bridegroom was undressed. He stepped out from the screen wrapped in a mantle, and the gentleman took himself away, and again the door was shut.

And now, now surely, Heros would come to her.

But, as if he were alone only with himself, Heros d'Uscaret wandered along the length and breadth of the chamber. He seemed deep in thought. Now and then he hesitated, picking up some article or other. Once he stood for several minutes reading at an open book on a stand.

Helise did not dare to call to him. To question.

Her suspense became firstly painful, and then sickening, as gradually her trembling warmth died into chill.

As though he perceived this, Heros circled once more and snuffed the candles.

A veil of blackness covered the chamber, edge-to-edge, shrinking it to the area of the bed, where one light remained burning on the chest at the bedfoot.

Heros now moved towards this final candle, it enamelled him upon the dark.

There and then, he looked at his wife.

Before she could control herself, she leaned from the pillows, as if to hold out her arms to him.

But Heros d'Uscaret, her husband, blew out the candle. And as she shivered there, he got in beside her, and reclined, with the space of a third person left between them. And he said, "Goodnight, Helise."

Perhaps only minutes later, lying beside and apart from him, she whispered, "Have I offended you, my lord?"

"No," said the darkness.

"But will you not then –" and here she faltered on her own unspeakable audacity.

After her anguish had gone on for some minutes more, Helise stretched herself out, and visualised that now they lay together as man and wife should. But her instinct knew perfectly well that this was not as it should be. Blindly, her instinct clawed at the night while she kept like a stone, but after a century had passed, she murmured, "But will you not – kiss me, my lord?"

This question was answered.

"No," darkness said again. "I won't do that."

And then there went by aeons of blackness and heartbeats like massing tides in the shell of the ear. After which Heros d'Uscaret said, "In the morning, Helise, you must take a pin and make your finger bleed. Stain the sheet with it, and your shift. That's for the showing, to prove your virginity is gone. Without that your life will be miserable here. More miserable than necessary. Do you understand?"

She did not, of course. Of course she said that she did.

There were a hundred things – she did not know how they must be expressed. She lay in black silence, until he added, "Go to sleep now." And then she lay awake all night until the dawn.

"Well, demoiselle. Do you please my son?"

Helise, a bride of eight days, gazed modestly on the ground. Eventually she found some words. "I try to, madam."

"Come, lift your head. I can tell a liar by his eyes."

Helise lifted her head, but not her gaze.

"Look up," said the implacable Lady d'Uscaret.

Helise looked up. Just like her other mother, this one in her inlaid chair, but having no lap-dog.

The eyes of the second mother were black. Her dark hair was imprisoned within a birdcage of silver-wire, with a band of nacre across her pallid forehead. Everything was hardness, even the folds of her gown seemed hacked from steel.

"You're afraid of me, Helise," pronounced d'Uscaret's lady. "But that's as it should be. Your family's rich, but has no history, in comparison with this house. Beside my own lineage, your name is a title written in sand." Helise might have been surprised; already, not interpreting, she had seen that the new mother despised her own husband. But the new mother continued. "I too am by birth a d'Uscaret. But of the elder line. *We* may trace our roots to the days of the emperors at Rome. My lord is of the lesser branch. My blood kin are dead. A plague ..." She paused, her eyes not softened but made adamant by memory or bitterness. "Perhaps you've heard legends of the d'Uscaret? These concern *my* kindred." (Helise could not ascertain if this boast concerned legends of might, or myths of – other things.) "I alone am left. And my son. My son is d'Uscaret. He has the sign on him. His fairness. His wonderful eyes. Once, my own eyes … Do you love my son?" said the Lady of d'Uscaret as if she spoke of dross.

Helise bowed her head again.

"Madam, yes."

"Naturally. How could it be otherwise. But to you he is indifferent. Am I correct?"

Helise wavered between shame and fright.

"Oh," said the hard woman, as she would flick a fly from her gown, "you are serviceable. You may entertain his nights and bear him a boy or two. But that's all. His brood-mare."

Helise stared at the flags as if at the gate of Hades.

"Poor little mite," said Lady d'Uscaret, without compassion. "At least you have the wit to know he is a god, and far above you. You won't annoy him, I believe. Never do that. It was a marriage of convenience. You brought cash, and we thank you, Helise. Remember your place here. You are a pretty beetle we keep to amuse us now and then." She leaned her snake's head thoughtfully upon her bone hand. "Go away."

And Helise gathered up her skirts and hastened from the room.

The world was as it always had been, incomprehensible, unyielding. She had her part. A lesser part perhaps, here. She had fundamentally as much sway over the house as had her brother's wife at la Valle. If she was dutiful, and did not thwart them, they would not chastise her.

The humble were the elect of God. Did not the priests teach so, in their gemmed, kingly robes, from their towering pulpits?

Helise spent her days in ladylike domestic forms. She embroidered, she pressed flowers. She had no talent for music, and reading soon tired her. At the proper times she heard Mass with the household in the family chapel. Food might have been a diversion but she had no appetite.

At dinner, sometimes she saw her husband.

Generally the great ancestral hall was not employed, d'Uscaret dined in a parlour of panelled walls, where were displayed some paintings on classical and religious subjects. Above the table, whose legs were in the shape of eagles, three silver herb-censers depended from the ceiling, with aromatics burning over charcoal, to perfume the air. All d'Uscaret that was present in the house assembled here, in this show-place, with their house dogs lying at their feet, and the tame monkey of the lord's brother eating candied cucumber or running about the length of its leash.

If he should be there, Heros was seated beside Helise. But sometimes he had gone hawking, beyond Paradys, or to some library, or cloister, or to another house. Sometimes father, uncle, and son were all of them absent, at the Duke's table.

She seldom saw her lord during the day in any case. As, by then, she saw him seldom at night.

The first month he did spend with her, prostrate every night at her side. She would lie sleepless most of the hours, tortured by nervous cramps, afraid to be restless. Hearing the level breathing of his sleep, the dim bells of Matines and Laude, sometimes the reborn bell of Prima Hora. If she ever fell asleep it would be towards the dawn, and waking when the sky was light, she would see he had already left her.

She had stained the sheet as he had told her to, that initial morning, with the blood of her finger. She had had to force herself to prick her skin with the point, for she was, that way, a coward. She did it to content Heros, ignorant as to why. Were they then supposed to have acted out together some rite of viciousness and tearing, to cause blood? Was she fortunate to have been spared?

After one month, he did not come to sleep by her often, maybe every eight or ten days. Foolishly, when he entered the room, and when his gentleman unclothed him behind the screen, Helise hoped – but did not know for what. For a kiss, an embrace?

He gave her nothing, no more than in the beginning. Usually he would bid her goodnight, as he would greet her when he met her at dinner. They exchanged few other words, and at night none at all.

In the third month of her life at d'Uscaret, an elderly woman of the house came to Helise in the small square chamber allocated her sitting-room, that lay off the blank bed-chamber.

The woman was bustling and beady-eyed. She seemed respected in the house, and sat at dinner with the family. Her position Helise had never been certain of, but had once or twice heard her referred to. "Consult Ysanne if you still have your cough." Or, "Hush, that's a matter for old Ysanne."

Now the old woman, who was fat, and wrapped her head in an Eastern turban of silk, sat across the fireless hearth and watched Helise, until the young girl turned hot and cold together.

"Have you noticed anything?" said old Ysanne at length, in a gossipy tone.

Helise could only look.

"Come, come," said Ysanne. "Speak out. Do you vomit in the morning, or at certain foods? Have your courses stopped or grown erratic?"

Helise suddenly became aware that sickness and the stoppage of blood implied a gift of pregnancy.

She shook her head. Here was another failing. And yet (she had randomly grasped enough) she suspected the fault was not all her own. There was something which occurred between the husband and the wife, in bed, some sorcerous communion or vow, which invoked children.

Ysanne now got up again, and said, "You know you must give your husband an heir?" Helise did not reply. What could she say? "Timid," said Ysanne. "The young wife must overcome her blushes and cherish her lord. You mustn't shrink from anything he wishes."

Helise felt faint. It was terrified lust, although she did not know it.

After a litter of more meaningless admonishments, old Ysanne went flat-footedly out.

Helise, as she had not done before, broke into sobs and tears. She even prayed, although she had long accepted God did not listen. Who else was there to talk to?

Then, in her abject wretchedness, when she could think of no shelter and no friend whose counsel she might seek, piercing her like the awl, her inner heart told her what she should do. She must run to *him*, to the one who never spoke to her, who never or rarely lay beside her, to he who was the cause of all her hurt, for he was also her love, the reason she had lived at all.

The decision of unthinking love was an insanity and it made her bold, perhaps for the first time in her existence.

She left her futile stitchery, and walked slowly, as if with an invited purpose, up through the house.

She had begun to learn its thoroughfares almost by default. She knew the situation of that other room, in which her lord slept, when not with his wife. She must go northerly, towards the most ancient portion of the building. She passed servants, but none challenged her. To them, she was a lady, a facet of d'Uscaret, however slight. Long corridors lit by windows, hung with tapestry, and quartered with carven benches, gave on thinner darker lanes, whose windows had no glass but only bars, whose occasional tapestries rotted. No longer did any servants appear. There was a dull silence. Yet she did not lose her way. For in the wilderness there was still some sign of habitation, or passage. Here and there a landmark of a great chest, even the mossy blackened hangings – for elsewhere the corridors were closed by grilles of spiderweb, the floors seas of dust – empty of anything human, limitlessly undisturbed.

So she found her way to a twisting stair she had once or twice heard described. It was the path into the tower-top, the Bird Tower they called it: doves had been kept there once. Now Heros dwelled in the apartment, as if upon a rock in that desert of wasted corridors and rooms.

The door was abruptly above her. On its timber, a falcon's mask in iron, and an iron ring.

As she put her hand on it she realised the door would be locked fast. She would have to sit down under the door-sill and await his return.

But the door gave at a pressure on the ring, without even a resistance.

That frightened her. She saw at once all her temerity in daring to invade the sanctum where no servant, no kindred, would enter unasked.

Yet it was too late, for the chamber opened before her, all its mystery, its spell, for it was his.

She stepped straight off the stair into the room.

It seemed to her the cell of a scholar. The bed was narrow and low, with a footstool by it, and a plain chest. No evidence of luxury was in these things. But across the floor, beneath a high, round, glassed window, that showed only air, was a table laid with a feast of objects and books, with measures and globes, the bones of hideous creatures mounted up as if they lived, weird instruments of alchemy and science.

There, on that board, his interest and his commitment were spread. She knew immediately, and with the jealous pang of a rival.

Between the table and the wall a three-paned triptych had been raised upon a stand.

Peering over the items on the table, careful to dislodge nothing, Helise did not pay the painting much attention. But then something in the angle of it, catching the window light against the shadow of the wall, caught her eye. It was his, of his choosing. She went to see.

How strange then, these images after all, strange as anything maybe in the room, or stranger ...

In the first painted panel was a fang-like mountainside parting a ravenous sky. A procession of men and women had ascended, with livid torches; they stood like mindless things, staring into the clouds. Something with black wings was carrying off a young girl in white. From her lolling limbs and head there streamed draperies and hair, and a wreath of flowers went tumbling earthwards. This ominous tableau was titled in gilt: *Nuptiae.*

In the second panel, the scene was a bedchamber by night, a vast couch where something lay asleep. In the foreground, holding back the curtains with one hand, and tilting in the other an antique, flaming lamp, a pale girl leaned forward, her slenderness rigid in lines of anxiety and expectation, endeavouring to see –

This picture was labelled: *Noli me spectare.*

Helise knew now what the triptych portrayed. It was the legend of Cupido and Psyche. The maiden had been left as a sacrifice for a demon, and was accordingly carried off. In a mountain mansion, cared for by invisible sprites, the girl was visited in deepest darkness by one who claimed to be her husband and lord. He was to her only the best of lovers, but warned her in the blindfold black: *Never attempt to look on me*.

(Hence the two titles – *Nuptiae*, an ironical "marriage," and the second, perhaps perversely mimicking the instruction of Christ: "*See me not*.")

But Psyche had been persuaded by desire and doubt to forget this ban. When he slept she lit a lamp, and so beheld her spouse. He was the god of love himself, handsome and perfect. And in her amazement, her shaking hand let drop a scorch of oil upon his shoulder. He woke, he disowned her, and into the unkind world she was cast out lamenting.

Helise glanced at the third picture. Yes, here was the banishment of Psyche following her transgression. And yet, it seemed to Helise that something in the vision was awry. What could it be?

The title exclaimed, once more with apparent irony, *Femina varium et mutabile semper*. Her Latin was restricted, but this was a quotation she had heard before. "Fickle woman is always changeable."

And indeed, Psyche had altered from carnal curiosity to frenzied terror.

She was depicted rushing down a winding granite stair, her arms flung out, her face ugly and contorted with screaming. All the rest of the small canvas conveyed pitchy nothingness – but for one curious whorling hint of motion, seeming to come on behind her, somewhat like a flock of birds –

The door of the tower room shut in a hollow clap.

"You are here with reason?"

Helise darted about, guilty as a robber, almost afraid as one.

"I came to ask of you –" But no, she had not come to ask.

He stood before the closed door. His doublet and hose were the colour ice, his hair nearly whiter. His face appalled her, it was so fair, so inhuman.

It occurred to her to throw herself on the floor at his feet. She did not do it. Etiquette, which had chained her to a life of slavish unhappiness, also prevented such servile extremes.

"Didn't they tell you, Helise, never to meddle with my possessions?"

"I've touched nothing – I was so careful –"

"Why are you here?"

She was too frightened even to cry. She loved him. But who? This god of ice and snow?

"My lord," she said, in a little voice. Then, "Oh help me! Everywhere they accuse me – I didn't know what I must do."

"Who accuses you? What are you talking of?"

"Your mother, the lady – that old woman. I see – I don't please you – but I'd suffer anything – only educate me, my Lord Heros –"

"Crucifixion of Christ," he said.

The partial blasphemy checked her. She bowed her head and now tears streamed from her eyes. Useless: he would not comfort her.

Presently he moved across the room and, going to the table, ran his hands recklessly, as she had not had licence to do, over all the compendium of scales and jars, parchments, mummies, vertebrae. It was even violent, this sweeping, for one of the wired skeletons gave way when his fingers encountered it. At that he took the horror up and threw it across the room. It smashed to powder on a wall.

But when he spoke, his voice had no edge or noise.

"I believe they must have asked you, Helise, if you're with child."

Something gave way within her.

"Yes, my lord."

"And naturally, you're not. Poor innocent," he said, rather as his mother had, lacking all pity. "You must learn fortitude. Now if I were a sodomite, or impotent, you might divorce me." (These syllables were like a sentence in a foreign tongue.) "If you had the will and the power, you could seek an annulment. But do you even comprehend, Helise, how I fail you?"

And she thought of kisses and his hands upon her waist. She burned, but it was ice. She could not say anything.

"I see you nearly do comprehend," he commented. "Well, madam. You'll go wanting. I could, but I will not. Understand this. Think me a monk. I'm sworn to chastity. Of a kind."

"What will become of me?" said Helise. She had made out one word in ten. To inquire of the Infinite was a ritual, like the *peccavi* before a priest, one's mind elsewhere.

Heros had proceeded to the room's hearth (empty), and there he leaned, looking down on the bruises of finished fires.

"There's a dream I have sometimes," said Heros d'Uscaret, conceivably to the hearth stone. For it was unlikely he would confide in the pathetic wife they had allotted him. "It began when sin began. I mean, impurity. The body's urge, Adam's rod, that makes him one with the beast, the reptile, the bird, and all the copulating, fornicating mass of lower creation. I remember the first dream. You see, I'd caught sight of a girl, washing herself in a river. The blood rushed to my head, and swelled my loins. I itched with my gluttony. It was manhood, and it was vice. Or, as they tell us, it was the natural order. All day, I could scarcely think of anything but that naiad in the water, laving herself, her round breasts with their eager tips, and the smoky hair in her armpits and under her belly."

(Helise, arrested, gazed dry-eyed. Her heart raced. But he, he might have been meditating on the digging of a grave.)

"Night fell, and I into the night, and into the dream. Because I was well-schooled by the priests, I had not thought to ease myself. But asleep, the Devil took gentle charge of me. What were my hands doing, there in the dark? How should a sleeper know. And up and up I rode upon that delirious wave that had begun like an itch and mounted to a storm. And there was a pressure in my brain, a green torch behind my eyes – and at the end there came a kind of fit in which I groaned aloud – and then, then, everything unravelled in me. I tell you, my sinews, my bones ran as if molten. And my skull was burst inside out. Where was I then? No longer in the throes of my pleasure. It was a place of mud, and I crouched there. Above were stars that blazed like pain. And beneath me was something that writhed only a very little, and I lowered my face and tore at it, and raw meat was in my mouth and hot salt gushed between my lips and up into my nostrils."

Heros drew in his breath and let it go.

"I woke in indescribable panic. Sin had changed me. I'd become – I did not know what I had become. But in the dark I found myself with my criminal hands, which had betrayed me to Satan in my sleep. God's benison. I was only myself. In all ways, a boy, a man. In those nights then," he said, "I'd have them tie my hands to the posts of the bed before I would sleep. But by my sixteenth year I'd trained myself to wake from the snare before the dream should go very far. Do I disquiet you, Helise? Of course. You should never have come into this room. This is where I look upon my soul. Stupid girl. You see in the picture what happens to the curious."

Helise, her palm pressed to her mouth, drum-beats shaking her body, turned to remove herself from the chamber.

"You must never come here again," he said. "You must forget what I've said to you. Tell no one. Swear it. On your saint."

In a crumb of a voice, she swore as he required.

He did not, with his emerald eyes, observe her creep away. He was staring once more into the hearth.

All down the stairs, and in the corridors, going south now back across the house of d'Uscaret, to her nuptial bedroom and the room of sitting which were her jail, she imagined him borne upwards on the inexplicable wave, twisting, arched like the Christ on a cross, and his face an agony like the face of Jehanus. And when at last she reached privacy she sank on the wide bed where they had lain side by side, sword by sheath. And she too twisted and turned and was arched on her scaffold, and upon her also came the fit, so her cry rang clear against the ceiling. It was like the call of a bodiless preying thing that flew about there.

She did forget the other element of which he had told her. The meat and wine among the mud and stars: that was gone.

She had only been able to learn one lesson from him.

It had killed her. She had exploded from her own skin, and lay stranded on the pillows. No longer was she an innocent.

She was defiled, she had entered the lists of the wrongdoers. She felt relief. If she was wicked, she need no longer rein herself in. She could admit her wants and where possible indulge them.

When she was in the d'Uscaret chapel now, her eyes on the prayerbook, she thought, This one never bothered with me. But Satan covets me. *He* will attend.

And then, frightened, she put away the idea.

But in the night, lying alone, recaptured it.

Would Heros ever return to her, to their bed? Surely yes. It was expected that a husband lie now and then with his wife. Such forms he honoured.

But she had learned what had been missed from their lying down. She had learned, by his voice and words, if not his embraces, the communion they might have shared.

Of course it was a fearful thing. Uncanny, astonishing. That escalation, that paroxysm –

She recalled now only that chastity had prevented him. His hands tied that he might not dream of lust.

Helise visualised that she came to him in the dark, and untied the bindings, and his hands fell instead upon her own body.

But although the bed had at last pleasures for her, he did not return to accompany her in them.

Ten nights went by, twelve, twenty.

Having confessed, would he never come back?

She saw him seldom, even at dinner. He was on some business of his father's, Lord d'Uscaret, the peeved man who drank and sweated and kicked at his dogs.

Yet one morning early, going into the Sculpture Garden, Helise beheld Heros walking with his mother slowly up and down.

The garden lay on the north-west side and had high barriers. It was supposed to be a retreat for the women of the house and Lady d'Uscaret would frequently avail herself of its shade in summer at midday. Helise therefore restricted her forays to dewy twilights, dawn or dusk.

She did not like this garden, either. It had none of the quaint simplicity of the courts of la Valle, where figs and vines grew up the walls and flowers lived in pots. The Sculpture Garden was ruled with straight paths, partitioned by yew and box, conifer and ilex, all coerced and sheared to the shapes of balls, cones, squares and other symbols, or if not that, let out into birds with beaks and stretching tails. Where arches crossed the way they were thick with foliage, mathematical hoops of solid green. In the marble water tank was a hairy water-lily, which ate flies, a curiosity: Helise had witnessed a gloating gardener feeding the plant. In the shrubs nested statues. Leaves and boughs strove to swallow the statues up as the lily gulped insects, but this was not allowed. At the end of the garden was a statue of Psyche, so Helise had come to apprehend. She carried a lamp, on her way to discovering her naked, handsome lover.

But one thing was certain, and that was the ease of hiding in such a garden.

A month before, Helise would have slipped away. Now she slipped into the cavern of a prodigious yew, and as he went to and fro with his steel mother, devoured Heros with her eyes.

After the two figures had patrolled in silence for some minutes, the lady spoke.

"You must know, if you take yourself away, I shall have nothing."

And Helise was amazed to hear the passionless metallic woman say such a thing in her remote voice.

"Mother – I hoped you'd excuse me this."

"Berating you? You know I won't rail at you, or weep. I shall be quiet. But if you leave this house, my light goes out."

"The Duke's commission –"

"Is needless. A ploy. For your escape."

Heros smiled faintly. Helise did not think she had ever seen that before. The lady's hand rested on his sleeve like a long bud of the motionless carnivorous lily. Then it twitched, as if it could not help itself, losing a fly.

"Madam-mother. You must let me go."

"When you were a child you had these notions. That the City choked you."

"Don't you prefer me at peace?"

"It's that wife he foisted on you that drives you away. A witless female spawn of la Valle, got by your father for her dowry, because he cannot leave the pots alone."

"It's true. Marriage doesn't suit me, Mother."

"I've noted your aversion to her. But what is she? Less than one of the bitches. You live your life as you wish, and leave her to hers. She's barren besides. In time, you can slough her for this."

And then, sick and trembling, Helise saw that he grinned, the beautiful saint's face split like that of some riotous drunk. Not laughter, but this bestial snarl of mirth, quite soundless, behind the woman's head, so she did not even know. And when he answered his voice was composed.

"Oh, let Helise alone. What might her replacement be?"

"But you will remain at d'Uscaret?"

"No, Mother. I'll be gone."

They had halted, there beneath the statue of Psyche with her lamp, forever frozen in her marble moment, never to reach revelation and despair.

"Heros," said Lady d'Uscaret, and then, after a second, "you should have been a priest. If I had had any say –"

"And I mine, Mother. It was the only chance for me."

"That drunkard I wed, that disgrace to our name, that clod. A fool in everything."

In the umbra of the statue they hung, neither looking at the other, not speaking.

Then she said quickly, "We must never fear shadows. It strengthens them. What are the nightmares of your childhood? What, you and I to credit a delusion?" But suddenly she seized hold of him. She clung to him, and her flat hardness was like petrification. And he, he bowed his head until it rested on her shoulder. One could not see his face. Yet they were like any mother and son in a scene of awful grief.

And then they drew apart, and this might never have happened.

"In a month," he said, "I'll be in another country."

"As you think fit," she said. "Yes. We're in accord."

When they had vacated the garden, Helise stayed rooted in the tree.

Her stomach heaved as if she were indeed pregnant. But all she had truly discovered was that Heros would soon leave her.

That night, the door of the bedchamber opened. Heros entered. Behind the screen with its running of white dogs and grey hawks, the gentleman undressed his master. Then the gentleman, as ever, discreetly left. Heros approached the bed in his silken robe. And Helise ceased to breathe or think.

"Sad little wife," said Heros, looking at her not in complacency, or pity, definitely without excitement or intent. "We did you an ill-turn. I'm sorry for it, Helise. Will you forgive me, and pray for me sometimes?"

"Yes," she murmured.

"Have they told you? In a few days, I'll be away on the Duke's errands."

Someone must have told her, superfluously after she had spied.

"Yes, my lord."

"You'll be glad to see me gone," he said. "Believe me, your disappointments weren't my aim."

Helise let out her breath in a shivering sigh. She did not look at him any more, and he went about the room as usual, dousing the candles, so the dark tide came sweeping from the stones, and followed him to the bed's foot, and there he blew out the last candle, and blackness filled the room and the bed alike. And he and she were alone inside that blackness, like two birds shut inside a cage.

Never before, not even on the first night, had she been so conscious of him, his proximity, as he joined her in the bed. The movement of his flesh and limbs against the sheet, the whisper of his hair over the pillow. She felt a warmth from him like the radiance of a cool flame.

He did not speak to her again. In a short space, his respiration assumed the levelness of sleep. Could he really render himself to oblivion so readily? It was some cantrip he knew, this knack for slumber.

But she must lie awake and think of him. Of his nearness. And if he slept, might she not approach him more closely? Would he wake and chide her?

Helise swam through the sheets and her hands encountered him, as the swimmer in sightless deep ocean encounters another living thing, with a galvanic shock.

He was naked. Like Cupido, like the god. With her palms she had contacted his flank, the architecture of ribs under its suit of skin.

He had not woken, no, he had not. Therefore might she discover him once again? Or, more crazily, lawlessly, why not, like Psyche, *look at him*?

No sooner had the fancy taken hold of her than it seemed she must do it. She could no longer control her need, or savagery.

She slid from the coverings and sought her way by touch along the bed, a mile of stuffs and ungiving framework, until she found the chest, the candle, and the tinder set by.

She struck the spark. She might say she had heard some noise, or – at long last – that she could not sleep.

But not a murmur of protest issued from the bed. And when the fire leapt up on the wax, shielding it with her own body, she glanced about. He had not moved.

Like Psyche, and with all her stealth, Helise stole back again, along the length of the couch, cupping the candle flame. The curtains of the bed were drawn back, she had no necessity, as Psyche had, to lift them away. It was the sheet, the covers of brocade, these she meant to pull aside.

She must kneel up on the bed. She did so. The candle palpitated and steadied, flickering only with her rapid pulse, as if illumination itself sprang from her heart.

She leaned over him, her left hand now on the coverlet.

His head was turned from her, the blond hair rayed upon the pillow. Bare, the shoulder presented itself to her for the scald of spilled burning matter. She must be wary.

And as she leaned there, her left hand getting its slow grip on the sheet, he stirred.

Helise started away. Instinctual precaution made her thrust the candle aside to the length of her arm. The flame bent, flattened, sputtered – and the room reeled. But he, after all, did not wake. He had merely pressed his face further into the pillow, away from a light unconsciously perceived.

The walls and ceiling settled, the candle-flame resumed its steady trembling. Helise looked down on the sleeping man, and saw the hair had been caught away now from the nape of his neck. A strange shadow emerged at this place, from the roots of the hair, coiling along the spine, to dissolve between his shoulder-blades.

With caution, she brought the candle close again. The shadow dimmed but did not move. Helise leant nearer. She inhaled the clean maleness of his flesh and longed to brush her lips against the flax of hair, and saw the shadow on him was a scar, a curious plating, a trail of tarnished studs – she could not make them out. Like a lizard's scales.

It was a birthmark. (Had not her own maid had a raised discoloured nubbin on her knee, the shape of a star?) Helise put out her hand to finger the mark, the sweet flaw in his beauty – stayed herself, reached again for the edge of the sheet.

She stripped the covers from him deftly, in a leisurely receding wave, inch by inch, her heart hammering in her breast.

Would he wake now? No, he would not. His sorcerous sleep was like a breathing death.

She had never seen a man's nakedness, save in a statue or a painting, there never fully. He had the appearance of both statue and painting as he stretched there in the light amid the shores of darkness, adrift in the bed, his skin more swarthy than the linen, the smooth musculature carved and scarcely troubled with breath. Not stone, perhaps, but some strong ashen wood, tinted faintly to the hues of life, in order to deceive, and equipped with quiescent manhood, something at which the young girl had guessed, dismaying to her more in its first-seen familiarity than by anything alien, the tempter, the serpent of sex.

Careless of the glimmering, burning tallow, Helise bowed over the body of her husband. Her kisses printed themselves along his arm, his side.

But the hot wax did not drop upon him, and her mouth, the helpless small noise she could not now keep herself from making – these did not break in the membrane of his slumber.

He was enchanted. And she dared do no more.

Helise quenched the candle, and removed herself from his vicinity.

He did not rouse even at that.

The chamber seemed distended and tinderous with her solitary sins.

It was because of his aversion to her that he made the opportunity to be gone. He did not want her. If she had been able to cause him desire, how could he have resisted? He would then have remained. He would have been her lover.

But it was a witchcraft on him.

Did a woman then have no skill in such magic? It was the most ancient sorcery, Eve's art, practised at the foot of the apple tree in Eden, that which brought down the race of mankind.

They said, at d'Uscaret, they muttered that Ysanne ... that Ysanne was clever in women's business.

"Cherish," had said fat old Ysanne, "she must overcome her blushes."

"I'm unsure what is meant. The lady should be plainer," said Ysanne. Her beady eyes were cunning.

Helise sat in her chair and her humiliation, clenching herself to endure.

"My Lord Heros is tired of me. Now he departs the City. How shall I provide an heir if – if –"

"If he doesn't assist you. Yes. A woman's lot is a rare fix." Ysanne had changed her tune. Now she and Helise were co-conspirators against the masculine order, conceivably the masculine God.

"They say –"

"And what do they say?"

"That you can make a potion that will – enhance –"

"That will make a girl too good to be left alone. That will swell the male member so it must get busy. I can do that. And several other things."

"I think – he won't visit me again."

"Ah, that's tricky. I'll give you a charm. It will call him. If he doesn't arrive directly, then you must find some excuse to bid him. The charm will render him pliable. Then something for his wine, and an unction I'll give you to rub in your skin, very fragrant. Leave it to me," said Ysanne. "I've always relished that little chain you wear, with the pearl."

Helise removed the chain. She held it out to Ysanne.

"No, no. Are you offering that to me? But lady, I serve the house. I'm your slave." Then seeing the chain flutter, knowing Helise inept, Ysanne quickly added, "You're too kind, madam. I thank you. It's always safer to seal a bargain. Naturally, this is a secret." And with the pearl in her bosom off she went, leaving Helise to pace about, between repentance and vaunting, dread and disbelief, praying with untame transgression for Heaven to grant her profane hope.

She wore the charm, a mouse's sack of herbs, under her shift. Not seeing Heros d'Uscaret by night, morning, afternoon, she sent him word. Through servants, she entreated he would speak to her before his journey. The servants said they had not found him. Further inquiry told her that her husband was dining at the house of this family and that. That her husband was dining at the palace with the Duke. That her husband was in his tower, where they did not venture to bother him except at the summons of his father, or his mother.

Days ebbed. She stitched them into her embroidery, and picked them out again, but still they were lost.

Ysanne's herbal charm did not work. Her other mixtures would be as useless, the unction, the drug for the wine. She would not address herself to Ysanne again.

Then, from a dry husk or two let fall by the voice of Lady d'Uscaret, Helise had made known to her that in three nights, Heros would leave the City. She did not even recall – perhaps they had never mentioned it to her – where he was bound. Whether by ship or overland route. The date of his return had not been coined.

There was a page who sometimes waited on Helise when the household gathered. She supposed he had been designated hers. On the stair she beckoned him.

"Where is my Lord Heros?"

"In House Lyrecourt, across the City."

"You will follow me now and I will give you a letter for my lord. Then go with it to the door of d'Uscaret and wait for him. Wait all night if you must."

"He'll be home at midnight," said the page, perkily privy to the doings of her husband as she was not.

"That's as may be. Only behave as I tell you."

In the bedchamber by the void hearth, the great chimney-piece with its falcons either side, she wrote: "Call upon me tonight, my lord, or, such is my misery, I shall kill myself and damn my soul for ever."

What fashioned these words, succinct and awful, she could not decide. The Devil? It could not be her own desperate mind. She was a fool, but Satan was wise.

But then, would Heros attend to her threat?

It seemed Satan ascertained he would.

She handed the letter to the page, folded in a scarf which she had smeared with Ysanne's unction.

Alone, she anointed her body, rubbing the spicy-smelling oil into her breasts, her thighs, her throat and belly. The friction maddened her. She sprinkled the powder into some wine. She wondered in alarm at all she did. But now, as if a bell had struck the hour, she knew that her prayers were heard in Hell.

She heard too, finally, the midnight Matines tolled from the Sacrifice, and not many minutes after, a dog barked under the wall. It seemed then she felt the reverberation of the shutting of a door.

Time passed, or else time was stilled. And in the midst of the candles' shining, as if in a slab of crystal, Helise waited.

Until the great door of the bedchamber was opened.

On a frame of dark, her pale husband stood looking at her.

"What is it, madam, that you want of me?"

Some feminine slyness had kept her in her gown, her hair bound in its metal caul. The same slyness stayed her on the spot, staring at the floor, her hands clasped under her breast.

"My letter to you," she said, "told everything."

"No, nothing. Are you so desperate?" he said coldly. "You seem in command of yourself."

"I die of sadness," she said. "But since you don't care for me, I strive to hide the hurt. What do I want? Only courtesy. Not to be the mock of the house. That you should say farewell before you leave me for ever."

Ah, Satan, her tutor.

Now Heros had closed the door and advanced into the room. Helise did not lift her eyes, although he was before her.

"It isn't to be helped," he said quietly. "But since you wish it, I'm here to say farewell. And for this talk of death ..."

"To kill myself? Why not? What should I live for?"

"You are God's. What worse insult can you offer the Creator than to fling back His present in His face? Do you think He would ever forgive you? Through the endless centuries until Doomsday, He would not."

He spoke as sternly as any friar. She recalled the conversation between himself and his mother in the garden. To be a priest, his only chance. He was wrong. *She* was his chance. Her love, so strong and vital that it seared, this would set him free.

"You must be my guide," she whispered.

"Then cancel every idea of self-destruction."

"I will remember your words. If you were here to guide me –"

"Helise, I can't remain. Sweet girl," he said, suddenly very tenderly, "you must guide yourself. Let your own angel instruct you. You're so young – not one iota of blame ..." And he ceased speaking, and she knew that his concentration was centred wholly on her. Either her vehemence, or Ysanne's ointment, possibly both together, had taken hold of him. She had come to life for Heros, with all that implied.

Saying nothing she turned from him and poured the wine into a glass. She offered it to him, meekly, still her eyes lowered, afraid he would glimpse the fires in them.

"The cup of parting," said Helise. She employed the phrases of courtly songs, these came with facility, now she needed them, or Satan sent them, for how could she have a vocabulary to manage this?

He accepted the wine slowly. He did not drink, but stood regarding her.

Then, at last, at last, he raised the cup.

She looked, and saw him swallow, once, twice.

"What wine is this?" he said absently. His eyes were fixed on her. At their intensity a wonderful terror submerged her. Never, in any of their dealings, had he studied her in this way. It was the gaze of desire, or so it seemed. He drank again, not taking his eyes from her. And then he frowned, and said, "There's something in the wine – did you mean to poison me?"

"Oh no!" she cried. Her heart seemed cloven by its hammering.

"But – what is it? What have you done to me?"

"A love potion," she said. The admission was safe now.

"Then, there's no choice."

He smiled, grinned with the deadly dead mirth she had witnessed once before, and tilting the glass he drained it, and let it go. It crashed in bits upon the floor.

"Perhaps, Helise," he said, "perhaps you haven't been sensible. Come here." And when she took a step, he took several more to meet her, and caught her between his hands. "Love potions," he said. "Did you think I didn't want you? For every night spent in bed with you, first a draught to make me sleep. So that I shouldn't be tempted. For you're adorable, my white wife. Better than any dream. But perhaps the dreams won't matter now –"

The earth gave way and the room broke off in shards. She clung to him and he kissed her, a kiss of serpents, his tongue in her mouth.

His hands were those of a saviour, supporting, rescuing her in tumult, but also the hands of one who would destroy her, finding purchase on her body, ripping at the laces of her gown –

She had unleashed desire, the carnal entity. His breath burned on her throat. He held her so tightly she herself could not breathe. He bore her backwards and the hard floor was harsh under her uncushioned slimness. His weight pushed her down. A sore sweetness shot through the core of her breasts as he drew on them with his lips. Almost delicious but partly horrible – almost a torment – and then a tickling and probing between her thighs so her instinct was to evade – but he would not allow her now to evade him, and then came a terrible pressure, like that of a thunderbolt trying to cleave her, and she felt she would be burst, but there was only a shrill tearing, like a broken string.

She saw his face as he invaded her. She did not know him. He bore upon her, his skin engorged with lust and his eyes opaque and perhaps unseeing. There seemed no longer any contours to his face. He did not behold her and was unrecognisable. His hair tossed about him, shaggy as the mane of a beast, lank and dark with sweat as if with blood –

The thrusting of his body within hers was a punishment, a horror that was nearly an ecstasy, and far worse for that.

Helise heard herself moaning and pleading in pain. The fire-making action of his loins scorched her. She struggled, and the ghostly ecstasy surged in her again, and she no longer cared what had mounted on her, what killed her there on the ungiving ground. It was not Heros. It was some hideous thing, some creature of the Devil, torturing her in Hell for all her sins –

She heard terrible sounds rising in her throat, and then the spasm hurled her apart. She was screaming. It would never end. In animal fear she let go her clutch upon the excruciating peak, and fell away.

Only then was she revolted, finding herself on the floor, ground into the tiles under the weight of him, a hard mass of flesh that still moved upon her, still thrust mercilessly inside her.

He was lifting himself up, his head thrown back –

On the arch of his throat, the weltered light caught a dull sequin that all at once flashed, and then another, and another –

Helise lay pinned under his racking body. She stared at the altering skin of his throat. It was coming out in tiny jewellery slates, which ran together. His neck was scaled now. It was all a perfect tesselation.

Something scraped along her breast. Her head rolled and she saw a black claw retracting from her behind a thread of blood.

She could not scream. Her screams had been spent. At that instant, the quake of his crisis rocked through her, and it was he that cried out. It was not the cry of a man.

A whirling clotted the air, a fume of candles shaken by a gale.

The sword of flesh unsheathed from her. She was filled only by pain.

Something rose up, many miles high against the ceiling.

She did not want to see. Her eyes refused to close.

The shape of a man, but the face, the head …

It must be a mask, a visor – it was a bird. A bird's head, formed from a streaming mosaic of scales, but for the blackish carved beak, the thin black worm of the tongue … the eyes were green bulbs. There was no intelligence in them, yet there was *being*. They *lived*.

Helise lay on the floor. She had no breath, no reason. Her heart had stopped, her blood was frozen cold. Yet she *saw*.

The thing moved from her, left her. It lurched across the room. It came upon the fireplace and there it squatted, and then suddenly leapt. *It was away up the chimney*. It was gone.

PART THREE

The Jew

I looked to Heaven, and tried to pray;
But or ever a prayer had gusht,
A wicked whisper came, and made
My heart as dry as dust.

Coleridge

The Jew had laboured into the night, poring over the antique scrolls, the tablets of wood, the books bound in vellum or horn. Haninuh the Scholar, so they called him. The Jew's House they called his dwelling near the corn market. There was no ghetto in Paradys. No Jewish area even. Those Hebrews who inhabited the City were of the travelled kind, accustomed to a gentile world. Some had committed themselves to the Christian faith, some had given over God entirely in their intellectual venturings. The Jew Haninuh was not precisely of these orders. Then, too, other than the Jewish *mezuzah*, his door was guarded by a Grecian head of Hermes. Called "Scholar," Haninuh was reckoned to be versed in mysteries.

It was not rare with him, to spend the hours of darkness in study. Tonight, however, he had felt restless, and was unable to keep his mind on his reading. The cause of this unease was not personal. Rather it was that kind of nervousness particular to certain animals before a storm.

Haninuh neither sought to quell his discomfort nor explain it away.

About two in the morning, he left his books, and went up through his house to a pavilion he had had built on the roof.

Here he found, kneeling on a bench before one of the pavilion's open shutters, a small girl-child of no more than eight years, arrayed in an embroidered shift and quantities of curling black hair.

"Now, Ruquel," said the Jew, "what are you doing there?"

But Ruquel, who was his daughter by a slave woman long since laid asleep in the earth, only answered, "What a bad night it is. What shadows there are."

With these statements Haninuh could not argue. He had been aware for some while that his child seemed to have inherited a sensitivity to occult

265

things; he had already, for her protection, in simple ways begun to prepare and train her.

"Yes, my Ruquel," he agreed therefore. "It is a night of some meaning. But perhaps you'll trust me to keep watch in your stead?"

At that the child nodded, and getting down from the bench yawning, kissed her father, and returned to her bed.

Haninuh then took up his vigil in the dark, going slowly from one window to another of the six-sided pavilion. All the shutters hung wide on the close black night, and from this high vantage, at this unlit hour, one saw clearly the brightest stars caustic above Paradys. Below to the northeast wandered the river, coils of which, leadenly glimmering like a dragon, were partly visible between the roofs. Southwards on the heights stood the ghost of the great Church.

What could there be in this dark like so many others, which set the hairs electrically upright along the body?

Haninuh tensed, and leaned slightly forward, his hands upon the uprights of the window. Keen-eyed, he had seen something moving, away along the south-west scallops of the City roofs. This in itself was not bizarre. A cat might be hunting there, or a robber. And yet something in the manner of the movement did not suggest either feline or man.

Haninuh the observer saw again a curious flapping lunge, like the wing-beat of some huge raptorial bird. Of too large a size –

And whatever went about there in the night was capable, it seemed, of running up stonework, folding itself over housetops, and sliding to the street below like water flowing from a jar.

Haninuh was abruptly very glad he had sent the child to her bed.

Half-unconsciously he murmured, "From the visions of the night, when deep sleep sinks on men, fear came on me which made my bones to shake, and then a spirit passed before me and the hair of my flesh stood up –"

Haninuh fell silent. The apparition had poured suddenly from view.

There was then a long second of the sort in which, as they said, death might pass over; the space between two breaths.

But then, from the black hollows of the City there tore a frightful wail, a wavering shriek so truly appalling that for a moment the Jew doubted his ears.

The night seemed splintered, and dropped back in pieces. An abysmal quiet staunched the wound of the single cry.

Every nerve a quill, Haninuh poised to see a hundred windows lighted, a hundred people dash out on the streets.

Nothing occurred.

Like a thrown flint, the grisly screech had gone without a trace into the swamp of night.

If any others marked it they did not act.

Only far off a dog or two howled, nearby a rat scuttled. Presently the notes of Laude drifted from a convent by the quays. The stars swung noiseless overhead.

Some drunkard has been throttled in an alley, or some old score settled with a knife. One had witnessed nothing.

The Jew turned from his watch, listening intently now to be sure his own house stayed peaceful. It did. One must be grateful for that. For the rest, it was the world's way.

The vice which tuned and strummed the night had not let go, but only slackened somewhat. Yet Haninuh was weary. Spared a revelation, he could descend now and sleep, as a soldier slept between his watches.

"Blessed be the Lord at our lying down and blessed be He at our rising. Into Thy hand I commend me, my redeemer, O God."

Next morning, Haninuh awakened with a feeling of oppression. This did not surprise him, nor was it due to lack of sleep. He spoke a prayer of thanks giving for the new day; in the house above he heard the beaded laughter of his child.

Having some business near the upper markets, Haninuh went in that direction, southwesterly. The route shortly took him into a square with a public fountain. A crowd was gathering here, jostling and exclaiming, and it was impossible to proceed.

"What is the matter?" Haninuh asked of a man in the crowd that he knew, a cobbler by trade.

The cobbler turned to him hotly and said, "Something happened during the night. A murder in the gate of the tanners' yard. An apprentice found the body not an hour ago."

"There are frequent murders in the City," remarked the Jew.

"Just exactly. But not like this."

"Why, what is its novelty? Murder is murder."

The cobbler was about to speak when a party of the Duke's soldiers rode into the square and breached the crowd.

Unable to go by, or to get closer, Haninuh waited impassively.

A stillness was settling. The soldiers had grouped at the tanners' gate. Suddenly a woman cried out wildly: "Oh! Oh sweet Jesus!" And there was a small commotion as if perhaps she had fainted.

Rumour ran like a current back through the crowd. Men mouthed it in each other's faces. It came to the cobbler and to the Jew. "The throat and eyes all gone."

"That's what I heard," said the cobbler, complacently afraid.

"What does it mean?" said Haninuh.

"Some animal with the madness must have done it," said the cobbler, "ripped out the lad's eyes and his throat – and the whole body's in ribbons, and the entrails expressed. He was a poor weaver's assistant coming late from his work."

"Did nobody hear his cries?"

"No. None at all. A street woman said she thought she heard a yell, between the second and third hour. But one cry can mean anything, even enjoyment, begging your pardon, sir Jew. Then supposedly if it had him by the throat, he couldn't cry again."

Another man close by, in the apron of the tannery, morosely said, "They'll want to push the blame on us. We've a feud with the weavers' guild."

Yet another man said, "Only a monster could make such injuries, a unicorn, or a tiger."

Soon the body had been covered and removed. The Duke's soldiers grimly warned the crowd to disperse.

Able to continue on his way, the Jew noticed, under the tanners" gate (the place at which, last night, he had watched the bird-like thing pour down the wall) a black slur on the cobbles, and trampled in it, one pointed, broken shoe.

Violent death, as Haninuh had remarked, was not unusual in the City. Many mornings carried a small cargo of corpses along the river; the alleys of the lower bank were often paved with cold flesh.

Even so, this other death, which thereafter began to be a feature of the nights of Paradys, though frequently unreported, undiscovered until its unique signs had been obliterated – this death was a different death. It was a rending, *debauched* death. It bore an older mark.

While locks and bars were checked on and enhanced in many a house, the house of the Jew acquired (they said, those that spoke of him) less obvious safeguards. For example, from the street had been noted some bunches of herbs hanging in the narrow lower windows. For the Hermes at the door, it was freshly cleansed, and had been anointed, too, in a pagan way.

The City, where it knew, discussed these matters.

Otherwise Paradys went about its business, as it had always done. As do all cities, like ancient beasts, which, on a strong soiled hide, only idly scratch the little embers of disease.

A month had moved over the calendar and was gone. The Jew walked up into the Scholars' Quarter of the City, along the canals of aged libraries, and by the new university. He went to visit an elderly rabbi, a black-robed old lion, who dwelled near the river.

They sat together in a low-ceilinged room that smelled of books.

"And you tell me you watch every night, Haninuh, from your roof?"

"Every night without fail. Sometimes I detect some disturbance. Never the relevant one. I've seen nothing since the first night. And on that night I do believe I saw a thing, a thing I can barely describe, let alone envisage."

"Is it not," inquired the other, "dangerous for you to watch in this manner? Do you have, I think, a child in the house, a daughter of your handmaid who is dead?"

"My Ruquel is well-protected. I've seen to that above all else, by forms you know I can command."

"Ah, then. But for yourself?"

"This is strange," said Haninuh. "There is that in my blood which recognises this thing as a natural foe. The memory of our forefathers in me contains some glimpse of it, so I reckon now. And have been attempting, from scrolls and parchments I possess, to learn the source."

"Now I will relate," said the old rabbi, "a story of a recent death among the gentiles here. Perhaps you will not have heard of it, for the affair is smothered."

He then regaled Haninuh with this:

A young girl of good family, closely kept, had let slip to her maid that a gallant lover had begun to court her. He must have seen her on her way to Mass, for this was one of the few times she was allowed from the house. He approached near midnight and somehow climbed up the wall, perhaps by means of the ivy which grew there. Then he attracted her attention by scratching on the shutter. Naturally, the damsel did not go to the window, but, having an imagination, she had already decided on the cause of the nocturnal visitation. Sure enough next morning she found, on opening the shutter, a scrap of paper fixed there with a thorn. Some ill-scrawled words of love (they were later seen by others) and a line of poor poetry, confirmed her in her triumph.

The maid, another silly girl, resolved to help her mistress in the interesting adventure. She spied from a lower window the next night. Sure enough, the ardent lover again climbed to the upper window, and getting no reply, except maybe a stifled giggle, left again a slip of paper with a couplet. The maid for her part was able to attest the suitor was most agile, though rather odd in his mode of ascent. For the rest, she had made out the slim figure of a young man in a cloak who, for his protection, seemed to be wearing some kind of eccentric mask. Later too, in the hideous aftermath when she was called to account, the maid detailed this mask more fully as that of a peculiar bird.

For several nights more, the fun and games went on. Until at last, moved beyond reason, the damsel dared to open the shutters, hoping for a look at her love.

Ghastly shrieks and a noise like blows brought the entire household to her chamber door. Unfortunately it had been bolted from inside.

The girl's two brothers and an uncle put their shoulders to the obstacle, urged on by the most terrible sounds from within. To their shouts, the girl seemed unable to respond. She screamed ceaselessly, as the uncle subsequently averred, like a woman he had once beheld racked for witchcraft. Until abruptly all noises finished.

The door gave in a rush, and the men of the house burst forward into the room.

The window stood wide and empty. Nothing was there, save that there were some black stains and scratches on the wood of the frame. Below and about nothing was visible in the night, except for three of the City watch who had come running at the outcry, yet not in time.

At the chamber's centre lay a fearful sight. The girl had paid dearly for her foolishness.

The wounds were unbelievable, though of the usual type now known, in the subfusc of Paradys, as relating to the rending, debauched death at work there. Her throat was torn out, her eyes ... there were great incisions in her belly, although interruption had prevented a disembowelling. Quantities of her hair had also been ripped from her head, and were strewn about. Scratches, like those on the wooden window-frame, scored her white throat and breasts. It was presently discovered that, amidst this carnage, an attempt too had been made to violate the girl. But being a virgin, she had proved difficult, and her assailant had not had space to complete the rape.

Now all this in itself was bad enough (though not so much worse than some twenty other like murders current in the City). But the stricken family was next advised by agents of the Duke, that they should not make public either their loss or their quest for vengeance. It was to be given out the girl died of a fever. In return for this favours might be anticipated.

The important houses, though apt to feud with each other, were united in aristocratic respect of Ducal prerogatives. The family, that of Lyrecourt, did as bidden.

It was further believed that the girl's body was burnt rather than buried, a priest counselling cremation. The corpse, which seemed to have been attacked by a giant bird, was accordingly rendered into ashes.

"It is thought, too," added the old man, "that the corpses of all females assaulted and slain by the creature, have also been incinerated."

Haninuh sat brooding. At length he replied:

"There is more to be feared of it than death only?"

"So it seems." The rabbi laid his hands upon a little book of black leather, with a lock of damascine steel. "Myself, I have been searching for this demon. Though I lack the courage to look for it in the dark, there are other darknesses. After some trouble, I found this volume, which is a fragment of a larger work sometimes called *The Book of the Night*." And saying this, he pushed the book across the table to Haninuh.

On the black cover was embossed in silver the Solomonic Seal, and in one corner, a *menorah*, also in silver.

"Here is the key, Haninuh. Take it away with you, and read the passage I have marked. But no other. I can trust you in that."

Haninuh assured the rabbi that he might.

Soon they parted, and with the black book fastened into his sleeve, Haninuh went back across the City to his house.

It was in a small chamber set off from his cubicle of study that Haninuh unlocked the book. The door was shut on him. There was no window, and the space was illumined by a single candle of honey-wax.

When he had cleaved the book, with much care, at the place where a flat wand of bone divided it, a faint light seemed exuded from the vellum, and then to suspend itself upon the page.

The text was on the left side Hebraic, and on the right in Latin. Haninuh read, comparing each text with the other as he did so.

"There was a man in the fort at Par Dis, at about the time the seven-hilled city of the Romans, and all their empire, fell. He was a soldier, a centurion, having charge of a cohort, and from Roman lands. And at his death, he left his arms and honours in the temple of Mars here, marked for him *Re Va*, which temple being excavated, has preserved them in the City with many others.

"Now this soldier, after some misfortune, had recourse to an amulet said to have been fashioned in Khem." ("Aegyptus" said the Latin.) "However, the amulet had its origin in the country of the Assyrians, possibly at the City Calah, in the days before David was King in Israel.

"Now the Assyrians worshipped all manner of idols, and were beset by all the races of the demons. The amulet took its power from just such a being, an *utuk*. Its shape was graven on the jewel of the amulet, and was that of a man, but having claws upon the feet and fingers, and the head and beak of a bird of prey.

"At first the Roman found that the amulet was helpful to him. But then, it seemed to draw away his strength, while the demon began to haunt him. At last he assayed riddance of the article, but through this very means was enslaved by it for ever. Thereafter his line was polluted by the demon, which was wont to manifest itself among his descendants here in Paradys. Its method was this, that it was carried in the semen of the male and the blood of the female, in the way of some poisons or diseases. And as with disease, a proportion would prove to have a natural resistance to the effects of the pest. Therefore, generations might pass without any sign, though all were tainted, until one would be born who was vulnerable, in whom the *utuk* could get a hold. For the *utuk* was given its life through metamorphosis and shape-changing. The woman who was susceptible would birth a son or daughter infected by this evil, most often the former. That man was then, once grown, capable both of transmuting into the form of the *utuk*, and, through his seed, causing other women to conceive a similar miscreation. In this case, tainted kin, or not, all women were impressible. It has been recorded, there are further permutations to this generative transfer at the injection of seed, but no document had been discovered regarding them.

"The *utuk* is in itself a terrible thing, a ravening thing, which craves human life in its form, and more sensually in a robbery of blood and flesh. It is an Eater, a Devourer.

"Though magical safeguards are of protective use, the *utuk* itself, while possessed of a human host, is impervious. For the carrier may be killed through any normal means, at which the demon makes its escape by whatever route is to hand, into another host, for an example in his infection by the spilled blood. Where no transference is likely, that aspect of the demon may be considered extinct, providing the body of the carrier is burned and the ashes laid. However, though every individual manifestation of the demon be destroyed, in its poisonous disease-like form, it remains inherent in that kindred it has afflicted. Who are by name the *Vuscarii*.

"For the amulet itself, it is lost. The hue of it is said to have changed, as do particular jewels when heated, or exposed to wear. This tint, the shade of the jewel as it was or has become, is believed to offer warning through a colour of the eyes of those contaminated."

Haninuh, having gained the end of the text, replaced the bone marker, shut up the book, and locked it.

As he did this, the candle flickered wildly and would have gone out, but the Jew spoke at it a Word, and the Word stayed the candle flame, which burned up straight and still once more.

It was night, and there was no moon.

Haninuh paused at the threshold of his daughter's apartment. She had been washed in a little bath of lettuce enamel, and, her prayers said, got into her bed with her wooden doll and her striped cat. There all three were, staring at him clear-eyed, doll, cat and child.

"And are you ready for sleep, Ruquel?"

"Yes, father," she answered, and put her doll into the sheets with its tow head on the pillow, while the cat purred and kneaded the covers.

"Have the bad dreams stopped, little girl?"

"Oh yes, since you put the water dishes out to catch them."

"You must tell me if you dream anything bad again."

Ruquel smiled. "I say to her," she nodded at the cat, "we're safe. You won't let anything hurt us. Though she was frightened when we had the dream. But not now."

When he had kissed all three goodnight, as was obligatory, wood lips, soft lips, fur cheek, Haninuh climbed up the house to the roof pavilion.

Blackness hung over Paradys, the book of night open randomly at the darkest page.

As usual Haninuh performed three rituals, and uttered some prayers which, upon white deserts and obsidian mountains, had long ago invoked the benign forces of fierce angels.

In just such centuries, the Jews had kept vigil against the hordes of Assyria. They had fought with them sword-to-sword under skies of flying arrows. The wolf-like Assyrians, whose cities were lilies of a river bank, had riven Israel. And Israel had brought down upon them the bolts of the one true terrible limitless God. Until the people angered Him, and He turned from them, and then the Assyrians leapt at the throat of Israel ... it was all to do again.

From those times Haninuh's soul remembered the demon. The *utuk*.

Night lay motionless on Paradys, yet it moved towards the east. Haninuh heard the bells ring for the offices of Christendom, the hymn of drunks from an alley, smelled the corn market, and flowers on the house vine, saw, heard, smelled nothing from the ordinary.

About two hours after Laude had sung from the convent near the quays, deep weariness overcame the Jew. A longing for sleep weighed on him. Soon it would be dawn. Though hidden senses told him grim events had gone on somewhere, he had been vouchsafed no clue.

He rose from the bench and made his way towards the pavilion's door. His hand was on the latch when he heard a muffled scraping and rustling from nearby, on the wall.

Sleep dropped from him like a mantle. A chord of sparks shot across his body. Something was coming through the vine, up the side of the house.

Haninuh turned to confront the six unshuttered windows of the pavilion, his back to the closed door. He did not have long to wait.

A black lump of darkness came sliding over the roof's edge and slewed across two windows, enlarging itself into the third.

Haninuh, back to the door, the third window before him, whispered, "I believe with perfect faith that the Creator, blessed be He, is the maker of all things created ... I believe with perfect faith that all the words of the prophets are true ... I believe that the Creator ... knows every deed of the children of men, gives heed to all their acts – for my salvation I hope, O Lord! I hope, O Lord, for my salvation! O Lord, for my salvation I hope!"

Blackness, and from the black a sort of twisting into form, like a man's, but the hands were talons and clacked against the pavilion wall – and out of the black leaned something. It was the head of a bird composed of the green sequins of scales, and a beak black with dried blood, and two eyes like emerald.

There was no intelligence in these eyes – and yet they *were*, they *lived*, they *knew*.

"In the presence of my enemies," said Haninuh, "You are with me. Even in the valley of the Shadow, You are there."

The beak of the *utuk* cracked apart, and a snake tongue whipped outward and in again. The eyes were smoky now, as if drowsy. It came and pressed on the open window – and started off again. It had struck the invisible lines of power that barred every aperture of the Jew's house. And it did not like them; perhaps they stung.

At that instant the Jew woke into movement. Casting before him a cabbalistic incantation that smashed the etheric lattice of the window, and seemed to carry him with it, out of the pavilion he sprang, snatching up as he hurtled through a sword of honed steel from the bench.

In that moment, in his blaze of fear and rage, the magus Haninuh touched terror with his body, came knee to knee with the unearthly, deathly thing, and with a moan of dread raised the sword, on which the names of angels, the script of most arcane talismans, were scored –

But the horror shuffled off from him, like the nightmare. It evaded the stroke, flounced on a flightless wing-beat away, and over the rooftop, smearing and roiling itself in, getting like an ape down the wall. The fragile vine was ripped now, and fell with it into the street. There in the pure black the beast of night disappeared.

Haninuh stood and trembled.

He had been too slow, yet too strong for it – or else, by flight it mocked him. For it was drawn to him as he had sensed it might be. A traditional foe. Doubly in danger now. Worse, he had let it escape to continue its mayhem. For this hour he had planned, but he was found wanting.

The Jew bowed his head before his own failure, consenting, bitter.

PART FOUR

The Scapegoat

Remember me – Oh! Pass not thou my grave
  Without one thought whose relics there recline:
The only pang my bosom dare not brave
  Must be to find forgetfulness in thine.

Byron

For thirty-nine days she was their prisoner. On the fortieth she was their victim. It was her punishment. She knew that she was guilty. She had looked for no kindness, and her first actions were prompted by the habit of human commerce, not fantasies of pity.

The truth had come to her gradually, as if she returned to consciousness: nothing had happened to alert the house.

Even her screams had been those of pleasure, and doubtless, if anyone had overheard them, they were correctly interpreted.

The metamorphosis occurred in silence.

It had been visible only to herself.

At the recollection – the *full* absorption of what had taken place in front of her – Helise wrested herself to her feet and swayed there in her ripped gown, her hair raining round her shoulders. She felt herself dirtied, bloody. But the only wound, of course, was one which would be acceptable, despite the fact that it was out of date.

Nevertheless, her helpless need was to seek others, to raise her voice to a new pitch, and tell what she had been the witness of. That this was not believable did not cross her mind. She had watched. She had no choice *but* to believe.

Some while it took her to recall how a door was to be opened. That achieved, she went out into the corridors of d'Uscaret, almost wandering, and coming to a lighted spot, she did raise her voice, and began to scream. Once begun, this expression was not easy to leave off.

People came. She did not know who they were. Shadows jostled on torchlight and the eyes of candles blinked at her.

What she screamed, if there were words, Helise did not afterwards know.

Presently someone struck her in the face. She fell down, and looking up from the stones, beheld Lord d'Uscaret. One of his rings had cut her eyebrow. She felt the numb hurt of it and putting up her finger, caught a bud of wetness.

She was now quiet and they dragged her to a room. Here the kindred gathered and glared on her. The servants were shut out.

Lord d'Uscaret paced about. His wife sat in a chair and gnawed her lip. For a long while they did not ask. At length, this question: What did Helise mean by her noise?

Helise said, with the clarity of an honest child, "When he lay on me, his face and head became the head of a bird."

As Helise said this, Lady d'Uscaret let out a single sharp cry, as if she had driven an awl into her hand. Then she rose and left the chamber. Her face was awful, as though its bones had collapsed and no blood was anywhere under her skin. One of the men followed to support her.

D'Uscaret came back to loom above Helise, and he was sweating as he did at his evening drinking.

"Who told you, you witch, to say such a thing?"

Helise was confused and did not answer.

Then d'Uscaret slapped her again, and though now the rings did not cut her face, she darted away, and fell once more, and crouching on the floor she said, "He never would, my husband Heros. But tonight I made him, and he lay on me, and when the thing happened to him which happens, he altered. His flesh broke out in metal spangles, and I saw he had a bird's face, and the beak, and a demon's eyes, like a hawk's eyes, but green. It ran away up the chimney."

D'Uscaret turned from her. "Go search the bedchamber."

Pale as their lady, two of the men went out. The few left behind looked half-mad. D'Uscaret sweated. Not one of them had declared these events must be impossible.

Helise saw that her statement seemed obtuse, which was mostly due to a lack of carnal vocabulary. Feeling no reticence, she tried to put this right. "I mean," she said, "that when he was being a husband to me, when the fit comes, then he was changed."   Suddenly a wild lament swept down on her. Tears gushed. She sprawled on the floor.

Shortly after this, everyone went out, and locked her into the room.

Helise wept until all awareness was wrung from her body. Perhaps she slept then.

She wakened to torchlight. A steward of the house, and a woman who waited on Lady d'Uscaret, pulled Helise upright.

"You will make no sound," said the waiting-woman.

They took her through the mansion, along passages, up stairs, rather as she had taken herself earlier, searching for the secret apartment of her beloved.

Finally there was another room, with sparse furnishings, a window of lactescent glass. A ghostly servant had arrived before them, and was putting out a ewer and cup, a covered basket. One candle burned.

The servant, the woman, the torch-bearing steward, drew off from Helise, until she was alone in the middle of the gloom.

She said, stupidly, and for no real reason, "What am I to do here?"

"Stay, at my lady's will," rapped the woman.

Then they went, and closed the door, and locked it on her as the other door had been locked.

Helise crept to the neglected, ill-prepared bed. She felt nothing, no fear, and no alarm, no longer the agony of sorrow. She slept again, and only realised, reviving to sickly awareness at the entry of light through the vitreous window, that she had been imprisoned for her crime.

They brought her food and water and a small amount of wine, her tiring table and embroidery, fresh linen. The room was cold, was summer waning? Although she sometimes asked the servant, they sent no logs for her fireplace, and only allowed her one candle at a time.

There were no writing materials, and if there had been any, who would have agreed to be her messenger? Besides, to whom should she apply? Her family of la Valle had loved her only in as much as she had been wanted by d'Uscaret. Now d'Uscaret hated her.

I prayed to the Devil. He granted my desire and now collects his fee.

She slept a great deal, and dreamed of Heros. Nearly always he was breaking in to rescue her. But overcome with lust, they fell at once to coupling on the floor or bed. In the midst of this she would try to push him away, shrieking. Also she would dream she lay down and the pillow slowly changed into a staring, decaying eagle's head. And once, that her aunt's pet bird flew out of its cage and went for her eyes.

She would wake in fear, or crying.

They gave her no news. One morning, in desperation, she had muttered to the dull unkindly servant who brought the food, "What do they say of Lord Heros?"

The servant sent her a glance.

"Nothing, madam. He's away on his journey for the Duke."

Helise was bemused. Later she began to see that d'Uscaret had used the proposed excursion Heros had intended, on Ducal business, as the excuse for his vanishment. He had merely set out a day or so in advance. The City, and half d'Uscaret's own household, were handed this tale, and would accept it. Probably it was put about that he hurried to escape the difficult young wife, who now turned hysterical at her lord's absence, hence her confinement to a remoter region of the manse. Had even the Duke himself been deceived?

But meanwhile – where was it that Heros had gone to, or that thing had gone to he had become? Thinking of that all her nerve deserted her. She had a vision which seemed almost palpable. She imagined the creature on the roofs of the City, at upper windows, perhaps availing itself of chimneys. It flickered in and out of her inner sight. What it did she could not be sure. But they were deeds of darkness, hunger – and in the end it would hide itself. She did not know where.

However, she had one other dream, and only once. She saw the thing (*her husband*) seated in his chamber in the very house, at that table under the round window and the triptych of Psyche. Among the paraphernalia of former studies he had paper, pen and ink, and was writing … she saw what he – it – wrote. Even in the dream … incongruous. For they were rhymes of love. She had not wanted to approach, had been afraid, but the creature did not see her, for in the dream she was incorporeal. Besides, its head lolled, the eyes were dull, and the tongue ran from its beak. The hands wrote busily, alertly, the claws scratching the paper. Some human facet of Heros, some memory from his man's brain, plainly supplied the task, at which the bird's head moronically attended.

Close by on the desk, among the apparatuses of silver and glass, the balances and skeletons, lay some strands of hair, caked with blood at one end. There were also several teeth in a pewter dish, fresh and white but for the old blood on them.

After this dream, Helise did not cry out or sob. She got up as if tranced and went to her tiring table, where the mirror was, and stared in at her own young, shrunken face.

She had never before realised that her eyes were of this shade. Definitely, if looked upon closely, there was a greenish cast to them.

On the thirty-eighth day of her captivity, Helise was visited by her second mother, Lady d'Uscaret.

The woman entered the room and had the door shut behind her. She wore the black and viridian of the house like mourning. All her hair was covered. Her collapse, which seemed to have maintained itself, had not softened or fleshed out any part of her.

"You may stay in your bed," she told Helise. "What else are you good for? I came to look at you. To see this insect which destroyed my son."

Helise lay with the covers up to her chin, and endured the looking-at.

"Merciless Heaven," said Lady d'Uscaret. "Is it a fact, you made the old fool Ysanne give you aphrodisiacs of Alexandria? Don't bother to speak. She was beaten, and confessed. A meddling wretch. But I am to blame. I judged the tales were lies, or advised myself they were. Who could live otherwise? Sometimes, one would say I was green-eyed. I should have guessed from that. My mirror reassured me. But the mirror was old and cloudy ... And my son, that beautiful boy from such a loveless match – there are such eyes in other houses, other lands. Why attend to a legend, a story to frighten children with at the hearth in winter?"

She spoke in a composed, indifferent way.

"And you. I reckoned *you* harmless. He had his night, so I thought. There is proof, I thought. He took pleasure with her, and no uncommon thing occurred. He had always feared it. Unspoken. I would never listen. Until we walked in the garden, not long ago. "I must be away," he said to me. Then I knew. He'd left you untouched, was virgin still. The curse was in our blood. He dared not."

D'Uscaret's Lady looked on with her eyes not green, nor black.

"But you forced him to it."

Helise was nailed on her pillow. She could not move or reply.

"Make no mistake," said her second mother, "I'll have you killed. Expect it. Some bane in your drink, a cushion pressed to your face. Or a strong man will come and hang you."

In her coffin of a bed, Helise could not even feel terror.

Lady d'Uscaret opened the door and went out of it, and it was locked again.

That, and its after-taste, were the thirty-eighth day.

On the thirty-ninth day, women filled the chamber.

They pulled her from the bed, washed her and dressed her, combed out her hair. There was a spurious air of the preparation for the bridal. No one said anything to her, nonetheless. They did not even address her as "lady" or "madam."

When the women had gone, without explanation, Helise sipped the watery wine of her confinement, wondering if it had been doctored. She seemed to have a burning sensation in her throat, but then it passed.

In the afternoon, men of the house entered, without preamble or apology. The steward said to her, "You must get up, and come with us."

"Where?" she said listlessly.

"That you'll learn."

Where she was not an article of barter, or a sexual pawn, she had never been treated as an adult, only ever as a baby, save some of the cruelty might have been restrained in a baby's case.

She went with them, and they took her away along the corridors and stairs, and she noticed the rotted tapestries, the lost chests mice had chewed. She did not pay much attention. She had no say in the world to be interested in it.

Finally she did know where they carried her. She began to scent their fear, and then her heart stumbled and in their grip she almost sank down, but they hauled her on, up the twisting stair into the Bird Tower. The door was in front of her with its ring and falcon's mask. A hand flung it wide, and straight off the step she was lifted, into that chamber, that cell of the scholar, which had belonged to Heros d'Uscaret.

At the hour they gave her no reasons. She was nothing to them, useful only for her femaleness and expendability. It was later that, by small sproutings of gossip, by a letter or two uncovered from forgotten cabinets, such things, that the brain of Helise evolved and ordered a theory of events.

Her dream of him, as he wrote the uncouth verses, had verity. She was spiritually linked to him, she, the author of his damnation. In the moment of union, two becoming one …

No sooner did she enter the room with d'Uscaret's men, that thirty-ninth day, than she glimpsed the strands of hair, the teeth in the dish, ink spilled on paper, on the floor. He had left other marks in that room, once so esoteric and cleanly. (The painting on the triptych had at last been overturned. Perhaps this was some vestige of human anger, or only the upsetting of flight.)

The Duke had sustained d'Uscaret, and one other great house had reluctantly held its vengeful arm. But there had been atrocities in the City. Not only a daughter of Lyrecourt was won to a couch of blood, not only the rich and mighty howled for an end. The Duke had said, it seemed, he would leave d'Uscaret to its own affairs, whatever their nature, providing d'Uscaret would see to them.

It did not always come to shelter by day in the Tower of the Birds. No, only seven or eight times did they detect it had entered there, going over the roof and in at that round window inaccessible to any other. It would possess scattered eyries. The vaults of chapels, wild land about the old City wall; it had been seen climbing the turret of a ruined church, by a man who took it for a monkey – but some, hearing the rumour, knew otherwise. Elsewhere, near the markets, two fornicators were scared in a corn-bin by a beast they swore was a giant beaked lizard that had on man's clothing.

Yet the human memory, some urge, brought it now and then to d'Uscaret, and most often by night.

It could be slain. No legend had ever prohibited that. How, was less sure. And they were afraid, sickened, loathing. Something must be put between them and the actuality.

A drinker and feeder, it had another proclivity. The horrid reports had made this obvious.

Lord d'Uscaret stood before the narrow monk's bed, and pointed to Helise, his daughter by marriage.

"Put her there. Tie her. The cord round her waist, with enough slack. Let her go about the room if she wants. He'll smell her the sooner and come in."

Like a bitch-dog then, they leashed her by a rope-girdle and a long tether. Nowhere in the room was anything that she might employ to hack herself free. She would not even have thought of it. The inevitability of their plan, of which she was so strategic a part, of which she had at that time scant grasp, gave her over for their use.

They did not assure her men would be waiting, with drawn swords, with javelins and clubs, below in the lobby under the twisting stair. They were not, anyway, there for her protection.

A watch would be kept on adjacent heights of the building. She would not even need to scream. She was the bait inside the trap, the distraction, the scapegoat for all their sins.

Like Psyche, sacrificed on the mountain to save the rest.

"He may not come tonight, or tomorrow," said d'Uscaret. "We may have to wait."

A priest in black said solemnly, "We must go down and pray."

They were glad to leave the chamber, with its strange tang, faint, like that of a hawk's mews. Glad to leave the scapegoat. The priest, whom she had not seen till he spoke, did not offer her word or look.

She roamed a while on her leash, up and down. She could not quite get far enough to right the triptych, or to finger the elements on the table.

For her sustenance had been left white bread in a napkin, fish and mushrooms, cheese and grapes, milk and wine, and sweets.

She ate with appetite. She was not frightened. She sang softly to herself, for company, as she had done in childhood.

When the dark began to come, she spread herself on the low bed. He had slept here, her husband.

She lay and thought of him, and suddenly her body was alive with desire. She longed to feel his weight lowering itself upon her, his caressing ravishments, the thrust of him against her womb.

She remembered a tale at least as antique as the dooms of d'Uscaret, of the monster transformed to human beauty through love's kiss.

Was it a miracle she might accomplish, she who had sent him into Hell, to bring him forth again into the light?

She lay in the blackness, and her body moved with the rhythms of fire. She slept, and dreamed his weight crushed her, his strength pierced her. She was opened out, stretched to her limits, her brain shattered in stars.

But nothing but dark and dawn entered the chamber, the thirty-ninth night, the fortieth day.

The window was a bowl of jade, translucent twilight.

Helise gazed at it, surprised to have slept so long.

On the floor the panier and plate were empty. The food had not been replenished. A mouthful of wine was left. Shadows curtained the room, and silence had spun her web there. Helise shifted again on the bed, and sang a phrase of song, to hear the web quiver, then regather on the frame of the dusk.

The rope had begun to chafe her ribs where it had ridden up over her gown.

She lay and watched the window ebbing from green jade to marzipan grey. She might sleep again. Sleeping was benign. She had dreamed of loveliness, though she could not recall it now.

Drifting, she heard a mild scrape-scrape at the window as if far away. A leaf or branch, unsettled by some evening wind. Or a bird against the panes. She was not inclined to look, to try to make it out.

She drifted on, borne by a smooth river, the room a dark forest that rustled gently, and blew upon her an open breath of sky, until she bumped against the wharf of awareness, and her eyelids raised themselves.

Where is this place? Not a forest, but a chamber, its one green eye now black. The aroma of a mews was stronger.

Then she heard. A crisping of garments, a step on the floor. She heard, there in the darkness, unseen, a *breathing*.

"Is it you, my lord?" she called softly. "My Lord Heros?"

And the breathing was arrested, began again, and drew nearer.

Somewhere deep-buried by forty days in a wilderness, Helise d'Uscaret knew that she should, at this second, be whimpering or shrieking, weak with horror, tearing at her fetters, crying to God. But all she felt was a slight curiosity, a glimmering want, to see again what she had shaped him to. And even in that, lust moved, lust murmured like a tide within her. She was under a spell. She was the Devil's dupe. She was damned as he was.

"Is it you, my lord?" she said again, and held out her arms.

The reek of a preying bird was thicker, musky, and there was too another darker flavour, like the scum of a marsh. The stink did not repel Helise. It intrigued her. Even the butcher's whiff of blood did not offend.

"Heros," she said.

She felt more than saw a blacker blackness between her and the window, beside the bed. Then the eyes, catching some flake of light from the sky, flashed, and turned on her their soulless motes. The eyes of Satan, pendant there in nothingness, this they might have been. But she was not afraid.

Then, from the bedfoot, the heat of a body came crawling up on her, the weight of the body covered her, and two hands slipped across her, her breast and throat, and there the talons scratched her, but it was glancing and inadvertent.

In the dark, she put up her own hands and touched the roughness of the scales, and the emerald eyes floated, watching her, seeing her as she could not see, in the dark.

He had not harmed her before. She had not been told what had been done, out in the City. Her images of those things were nebulous.

Something swung across her face. It was the wicked beak, but she did not realise. Instead the questing, ugly, (invisible) tongue extruded, and sipped at the skin of her neck, strayed across her breastbone. Sinuous and serpentine, it described the mound of one breast.

Lying on her, the monster from the myth made love to her in the blind dark, as in the blind dark the Unseen had made love to Psyche.

Helise, who should have doubted, should have lit the lamp of her ordinary virtue and cancelled love with howls and screams, clung to darkness, which had the arms, the muscled back, the thin pelvis of a man, and which filled her with the organ of a man.

She must not cry aloud, even in ecstasy –

Just at that moment, as she twined him with her limbs, on the crazy threshold of abandonment – just then, Psyche after all kindled her lamp.

Beneath his body, some black filaments of clothes, her eyes dazzled – she was conscious the door had been pushed wide, and the torch glare streamed into the chamber.

Her silence, as maybe her screaming would have done, had betrayed them.

Helise attempted to speak. To rouse her lover, to ward off the spurl of fires and men, the glint of weapons that came pouring down on them.

But the lover of Helise, he knew. He knew, and did not leave her. As his loins thrust on, frantically, against her and within, the head of the monstrous bird was turned, to look sidelong into the crowd of assassins.

A look. It stopped them. The men fell back. The weapons were folding over like blades of grass before a scythe.

A sound came out of it, the thing that rode upon her, and turning again, it buried its fearful head among the pillows.

Helise clutched at the shuddering muscles, cloth, silk, flesh, scales – the crowd in the room had no meaning. Enormous beats began to echo through the core of her, and in the insanity of delight, she beheld a woman like a long opaque shadow push by the wilted kindred, the strengthless swords. In the carnivorous hands of Lady d'Uscaret was a soldier's spear. Her eyes were all the face she had. Her eyes were no longer black, but blazing green.

The shock of the javelin, rammed into the body of her son by this woman, who thrust with death as he himself thrust with the weapon of life, rocked both lovers like the quake itself. And Helise felt the point of the spear, tearing through his heart, prick out to graze her breast.

She gaped her mouth to scream after all. And on a backcloth of lights and shadows, where the woman seemed to topple away (like a flat figure in a church window), there was a spurt of blood, a falling, a throe, of generation and of terminus.

Helise, between all the many gates of Hell, was thrown into the Hell of ecstasy.

She shrieked and writhed and a spear seemed to enter her also.

In this state she was, flailing and lurching on the bed like a broken snake, until they dragged the dead thing out of her and off her, on to the floor.

Then, only then, the delirium guttered and extinguished. And she was left behind.

She lay, covered in his blood, soaked by that, by tears and sweat, and the waiting-woman of the mother of Heros leaned over her and said, "Drink this."

Helise drank. She had no choice, for they held her.

Long after, she became convinced that all the people had gone away.

When she sat up, it was so. The chamber was black and shut, as earlier.

When she stumbled from the bed and pulled herself on hands and knees across the floor, she encountered a bloody spear, but nothing else.

They had taken their dead away. They had left her here with their poison in her to die in her turn.

Already she could taste death, and in her arms and legs it stole like cool water. There was no pain.

Sitting by the hearth, she attempted to perform a contrition. Would God hear? God had never heard her.

Eventually she was in the fireplace. Still, she was not afraid. Her body was cold, but for her heart, and then her heart was cold too.

She felt it cease, she felt herself die. It seemed irrelevant, pointless.

What happened was this:

The Lady of d'Uscaret went to her own chamber, and there she hanged herself. She was buried in state in a family mausoleum near the Temple-

Church. It was explained she perished of sadness, learning her son had been killed by robbers on his journey. His body had been lost in foreign lands.

For the bride of Heros, who took her life at news of his death, there could be no holy ground. But out of compassion they made her a bed in the walled garden.

Not much after that, a feud sprang up between the houses of d'Uscaret and Lyrecourt. Its foundation was obscure, some insult or obtainment. Despite the stern jurisdiction of the Duke, the flower of d'Uscaret's young men were soon mown down, and the lord himself was slaughtered like a pig on his way from Mass. At least, his soul went well-prepared to Heaven.

Inside a year, all the candles of d'Uscaret were put out. A few of the kindred, obscure relatives, old women and men, lingered in the mansion with their elderly servants.

A decade, and d'Uscaret had become little better than a lodging house.

Though there were yet some who, passing it at dead of night on the street, would cross themselves under its walls, not knowing why.

PART FIVE

The Widow

Be a god and hold me
With a charm!
Be a man and fold me
With thine arm!

Browning

As if from the tomb, sleepily, he rose up from her narrative. (Which might be apposite enough.) She had anyway bewitched him. He had seen what she said, in vivid pictures, masterful paintings come to life.

Raoulin stirred, and stretched himself, as he would not have done so freely in the presence of a lady. He took care not to look at her directly, but into the pallid glow of the fire, which had either been fed while he sat entranced, or which magically never went out.

"But Demoiselle Helise," said Raoulin, sportive with the supernatural for there seemed nothing else to be, "if you died, here you are, and you haven't yet given me the alchemical formula for that. Besides – am I to take you for twenty-five or twenty-six years? Not more than eighteen, surely?"

"Time for me has made a stop," she said. Her liquid voice thrilled him. The voice of a sorceress. One could not be blamed for anything under the same roof as a witch.

At his own thought Raoulin struggled briefly. He reached back after the dead prostitute, the anguish that had brought him here. But a balm had been salved over them. They did not hurt any more.

"Shall I," she said, "conclude my story at once?"

Then he had to look at her. Into her eyes like emerald. He nodded. She said, "That part's swiftly told. The poison my husband's mother had administered was insufficient. I did not die, but lay inert, flexible and wholesome, and with a slight breathing that some doctor ascertained. They did not have the heart for more murder, to finish off the bitch's work. The feud was out with Lyrecourt, the Duke's frowns glowering. And there was Heros to be seen to. His corpse had rotted in one night, with a fearful stink, all bits, human and avian. So they made my tomb, and named it for me, and laid the box of his bones there under a proud drape. For me, I was hidden again in this room, and sometimes tended. After many months, it seems I began to revive. I recall nothing of that period, not for three or four years, rather as the infant does not. Then I became myself, and remembered what I had been and what they had done to me. I was content to be hidden, and to hide. I heard tidings of their various deaths from servants. One evening I was told how Lord d'Uscaret, my second father, had been bled on Satan's Way, under the Temple-Church. I laughed and had to pretend it was weeping, because I was still nervous of my jailors." Helise put up her hand and rested it on her delicate chin. "You see, Sieur Raoulin, it had driven me mad. You can't anticipate from me any fine feelings. I cackle at corpses. I burst into tears at the newborn baby's cry."

Raoulin shivered. It was not her words, only some latent truth inherent in them for all mankind.

"When most of d'Uscaret had gone, I began to win out of my prison. I was let go about. I caused no trouble with my walking of the corridors, my occasional peeking into cupboards. I learned a little, but did not take up arms. Like the old ones dying here, I was only and all acceptance. Now they think of me as a part of the masonry. I do as I wish. The two servants feed me and serve me when necessary. Of course, I'm spoken of as one deceased. They recall that much, it must never be admitted, my resurrection."

When she said this, Raoulin was not moved to horror or distress for her. She seemed only reciting the part of a character in a drama, and not even very well. Her passions were dead even if her heart went on beating. But she startled him next.

Her voice had an avidity when she said, "Yet, I've waited."

Raoulin found himself, bewitched or not, on guard.

"For what, lady?"

"Why," she said, "I think, for you."

"For me? I can't assist you – or, if you've some petition I could go to the courts with it – my father has some influence, but not in the City – and do you think – the tale, being or seeming, improbable –"

"No, m'sieur. Be at ease. I want nothing like that."

Raoulin was ashamed of his reluctance, yet now, as reality came back to him, uncomfortable as blood returning to a numbed foot, he began to yearn to be done with this. In the eldritch room he had formerly deemed coy and feminine, the miasma of her history shimmered. What hour was it? Surely Laude had struck –

"I might have roamed the City, but that wasn't in me to do. My early training was as a daughter of a noble house. You'll understand, Sieur Raoulin, only aged men have recently entered d'Uscaret."

Raoulin found himself staring at her again, into the jewel eyes.

"Women also may burn," she said. "I've been chaste as the nun for all these years of my widowhood. The last violation, the monstrous intrusion – never, since then."

While she had recounted those things, though they seemed enacted before him, they had not aroused. But now, abruptly, with an extreme pressure, lust possessed him. He got to his feet, not meaning to, and clumsily jarred the table where the wine cup stood – and he thought of the wine, Ysanne's drugs of Alexandria. And through the murk two ideas struck clear, like rocks in a flood. That despite everything, she was a woman of a line older than the City, higher than he could ascend with safety, and, of course, that though his flesh throbbed for her, he did not want to lie down with her, even in a falsehood, the resurrected girl who had pleasured a demon.

But there in the firelight of the sorcerous hearth, Helise d'Uscaret was combing her blonde hair with her fingers, she was shaking her tresses so they flew about her like white foam from the sea. She was putting up her hands to the nape of her neck, the lacing of the gown. "Come here," she said, "and help me."

And he discovered he was there behind her, eagerly fumbling at the undoing of her dress. And as it slipped from her shoulders, she drew his hands around her body, over the shift, to her breasts and belly. The fire shone through the linen as through the strands of her hair. The scent of her drenched his lungs, his mind.

"There's a pact between us," she said. "This must be."

"Amen," he muttered, and pulled her around to have her mouth.

Indeed, could you credit her story? Yes, she was insane a little. The prologue to an enticement, all that rigmarole, with the old hag of the kitchen an accomplice.

Somewhere in his brain, like a bell distantly tolling, some tocsin of unease kept on. But he forgot it as he brought her by the carved posts of the bed, and she threw off the shift and lay down before him like a nymph of pearl.

She gave a low laugh when he entered her. It deterred him half a second. Then she had flung up against him, and he could do nothing but begin with her that dance of death called procreation, the invention of the fiends.

Her cries came like those of one under torture. He lifted himself, and saw her, her face contorted with ravening agony or joy, her whole body pulsing as if rivers broke beneath her bones, as if she must dissolve. One look and he too was set off, like cannon by tinder. He leaned on her groaning and an exquisite needle seemed to pierce through the centre of his loins, into his spine, so he also shook and struggled to be impaled or to get release.

And at the height of it, somehow he began to see her again, to see what clasped him and gave him this, and even in the instants of orgasm, some quarter of his brain started to rip at him, to tear him back into his senses. That quarter howled. Then sight and thought smote him together like blows.

Raoulin shouted out – not in pleasure, not now. He tried to spring backwards, and fell heavily against a post of the bed. There, he lay. He lay looking at Helise. At what Helise had become. *Became*.

The fever-image had been correct. For she was, it was a fact, dissolving. Her flesh was slopping off, the skeins of muscles showing, melting in their turn, pouring over the bones like heated wax. And the bones themselves were sere. As they came poking up through the deliquescent body, it was revealed they were old bones, meant to be naked a decade at least.

She – no longer *she* – was a sludge, silt or mud, upon the sheet. And the bones rattled slightly, settling in their improper bed. About the skull, the brittle flax of hair, going every minute more to mould and dust. And in the death's-head, all stained with the passage of sudden decay, two green gelatines were fixed, the eyes of what she had become, of what had allowed her corpse to live, *in waiting*, all these hungry years.

THE PURPLE BOOK

FROM THE AMETHYST

PART ONE

The Roman

Easy is the descent to Hell
Black Dis gates stand open night and day.

Virgil

The Roman stood under the wall of the Insula Juna, listening to his wife crying in the room above.

The apartment was on the first floor of the block; in the street, it was but too easy to hear her lament, through the hot noisy afternoon air. Perhaps she cried more loudly only to be heard by him, her heartless husband. Once she detected the sound of his horse's hoofs she might leave off.

Better get on then. Better allow her the chance.

He beckoned briskly, and the boy came from under the platanus tree with his cavalry mare. Vusca tipped him a silver denarius, that was the sort of times they were. The boy ran off, and the soldier mounted up and started the mare moving.

Lavinia's threnody unravelled along the walls.

As he rode through the shadier back lanes around the temple of Venus, and out on to the broad East–West Road, he thought of Lavinia as she had been, the girl he married. He first saw her in an orchard, just west of the town. He had gone out for the hunting, and come back chastened by unsuccess. The sun was low behind him, the dusty road fringed with dark trees that glowed after the day as if they kept the heat. On a curve of land that looked down to the cemetery and the town's west gate was a villa one always passed going this way. It was a modest building, by now in need of some repair. Like all Par Dis, it had seen kinder days. Then, over a low wall, appeared the orchard, and by the plum trees in the mellowed light, this girl. Her skin was luminous, succulent. Her dark hair, drawn back into a simple knot, had mostly come unbound. He fancied her at once, and hoped she was some nicely-dressed slave. But although she looked admiringly at him in his leather tunic, the casual-wear of the Fort, and as recognisable as full parade armour and cloak of Tyrian purple, she did not answer his polite greeting, and next ran away. She was fourteen. She was not a slave, either, as he presently managed also

293

to find out. When he started to find excuses to go back along that road, when he started to gossip with the stray servants, or beg a drink of milk at the villa farm, when he saw her very often and realised that she herself found excuses to be there at such times as a passing officer might happen by, then he learned she was the ward of the house.

She was a Christian, as well. That he liked even less. He was himself a Mithrian, and had the mark between his brows. He sensibly worshipped Mars, too, the Warrior, for his profession, and gave seasonal respects to Jupiter the Father. The odd mysteries of Jusa Christos put him off, what he knew of them. It sounded like Greek Dionysos, without enough wine.

He began to frequent the house, though, and became friendly with her uncle, the guardian. He was allowed to talk to her, then, and here and there they sneaked off and furtively fondled. He saw he would only get what he wanted by marrying her and that there were advantages in that – for though rough, the villa had some money in it. Then he wondered if they would insist he become a Christian. But that was not their formula. Apparently he might do as he wished, providing he let her practise her own religion.

He saw later, once he had wedded and bedded Lavinia, had had her, and installed her in married quarters at the Insula Juna, that the whole point of this understanding was that she should then attempt to convert him, day and night long. Those were the first arguments.

He did not mind it too much. He was a Centurian Velitis. His bed was in the Fort.

She next withheld her favours, to punish him for not wanting some priest to push him in the river, half drown him, tell him all his sins were washed out, and now he must love his enemies.

"You forget, Vinia," he said. "I'm a soldier. *My* enemies I kill."

"The armies of the Emperor are upheld by Christian legionaries," she said promptly. Obviously someone had told her what to say. It was probably true, and if it was, accounted maybe for the great running cracks that were dismantling the Empire. There were certainly no legions left by now in this hole of Par Dis where, like a fool, seven years before their meeting, he had got himself sent. Someone had said the best means to promotion were the difficult and savage postings. And Par Dis, with its town of baths and basilica and circus, was not even so bad. It had originated from some silver mines, hence the name (for Pluto-Dis, god of the Underworld and its riches). But the silver ran out after a few decades. The Empire had been ever-stretching in those days, however, and saw no harm in making a frontier station on the site. There were already roads, a fort, a native settlement. The walls and town were added. The river was useful in the trading way, and sometimes provided fine oysters.

The oysters were all gone now, like the silver and the two legions. Only men of the Auxilia, native companies under Roman officers, held the line in this flung forth province.

He had had his promotion. He had reached centurion, with a command of skirmish cavalry. There he stuck.

It was a curious idea: when he was travelling the miles here from Rome, to begin all this, Lavinia had been seven years old. For seven more she grew up, lying in ambush for him on the west road, coming out with the plums at the fatal moment.

When she would not have him, he went with the amiable whores at the *She-Wolf.* One evening the drunk uncle stormed to the Fort, and made a fool of himself (and of Vusca) over it. How could he (Vusca) be such a barbarian, wasting his strength on these women, neglecting his wife, when all she longed for was to bear him a son.

This turned out to be a fact. Lavinia had now decided to pine not only for a Christian husband, but for a baby.

She went and lived in the villa a while. When she returned to the married quarters, they were reconciled. She had become thin, scrawny with dis-satisfaction, or sadness. Her mouth turned down and there were two cut lines either side of it. He did his best. But he did not seem able to please her now, even in bed. They tried for her baby in grim sweaty grindings.

One day she was pregnant. He, less interested than she, made the correct offerings. He supposed she merely praised her ghastly slaves' god, who refused presents with typical petulance.

It was a bad winter. There were wolves at the gates. Uncle went wolf-hunting and was mauled. He died a week later and when Lavinia heard she miscarried in the fourth month.

After this, she did not conceive again. They eventually left off the dutiful grindings. He went back to his whores and she went off to her Christ. When Lavinia met her husband, she would cry. She greeted him in tears as if after an absence of months. Then they would talk, attempting to be rational. But soon her niggling would commence, her whining. She could not seem to control it, like foul breath. At last he shouted, or he was cold, or he mocked her. Finally all he was able to do was leave her, and hear her crying again, from the street below. He tried to enact this repetitive scene as seldom as he might. He had only come here today because she sent him a wild message. He had got the impression she was ill.

But she only said she had had some dream. Her god had told her something or other. And that Vusca and she must return to full relations.

She was using her god now to drag in the erring spouse. If he had been a

Christian, it might have worked. He could not think why she wanted him. As lovers they had nothing, and as two people, nothing.

She stood there, fragilely brittle and dry as a dead leaf somehow preserved. One tap, and she would be in pieces. His annoyance would not resist that. They might separate, he said. She was not, after all, by blood more than somewhat Roman, and had relatives in the north. Surely she would prefer to go to them. And perhaps, if there were a divorce, she might (he grimaced, who would want to?) remarry, more happily.

To a Christian, divorce was unacceptable.

She had not married a Christian, he reminded her.

He, she said, had undergone a Christian marriage.

To please her, he said.

He had loved her then, she said.

He apologised, which was cruel.

She cried. On his cue, he left her.

The East–West Road ran straight through the town, straight through the forum, with its market, law-courts, temples, straight on to the East Gate and the Fort. The plan of the town was still pure, whatever else crumbled, whatever slums accrued, the two highways unswerving as ruled lines, the original buildings symmetrical. Above the town, to the south, west, east and north, were the endless ups and downs of the hills that held the river valley. The route east, the view of the hills, even the bustle of the forum – when going in *this* direction – cheered Vusca up. The sight of the Fort itself, though it was the cradle of his disappointments (his life had had little besides), had a look of home which the Insula Juna never did.

Vusca was a man who preferred to be among men. He distrusted women, did not understand them. The life of the legions suited him, with its fellowship of the march, camp or barracks, the orderly routines marked out by trumpets. Though he had yearned in his youth for more active service, now even that had stopped its gnawing. The practice skirmishes of his corps of Velites ably substituted. He realised it was a kind of make-believe. They all indulged in it: the code – that they were ready to repel the hordes, and could do so; the symbol – of Rome astride the world for ever. Rome was not going to last. She was tearing her own heart out. For the hordes, they were those same smiling tribesmen who had their hutment the other side of the river, who bartered with the Fort and in the market, sent stray daughters to train in the brothel, or crossed the water entirely to take up Roman ways, like Lavinia's grandfather. One knew the horde was still there, of course, behind the friendly obligement, the tunic or *dalmatic*. It could turn into a snarl, that smile. And then what? The other bet was, Rome would pull the Auxilia in as she had pulled in her legions already, leaving the frontiers bare, letting go. Then you must decide on marching home to the Mother you could scarcely remember. Or deserting.

No, Vusca did not delude himself. He simply, along with the other centurions, and doubtless the Pilum Commander, lived in the moment.

One thing, if the Auxilia was recalled, he could go to Rome and leave Lavinia here.

He was thinking of this in the forum, and its wryness amused him, when he saw a woman coming down the steps of the Temple of the Father and Mother.

There was nothing in that, everyone but the Christians – and sometimes even some of those – went to make offerings to Jupiter or Juna Anga. But she was not dressed like a Roman. Her garments looked more Eastern, and her face was covered by a wisp of veiling. There was an element in her walk, provocative, liberated, that suggested the hetaera rather than the she-wolf. A Greek prostitute's freedom. No doubt she was a whore, for she had that other look, too.

Something about her aroused him, even as he sat on the horse fresh from Lavinia's howling. Desire did not come so readily now. He wondered what it was about this one that stirred it. He was not even close enough to catch her perfume.

Behind her trotted a slave, hurrying with a parasol like a huge pansy-flower to shade her mistress. They went away towards the Julian Baths.

Vusca rode on towards the Fort.

"There's a new woman. She's set up house behind the Julian Baths. The chief Lupa's roaring. Reckons this one will put her girls out of business."

Dianus laughed, and the dark sunlight of evening glinted on his eyes and on the silver of his service bracelets.

"Ah?" said Vusca cautiously.

"An Eastern bit, or so they say. I've not been there. Yet. Her name's some foreign thing, Lilu, Lillit – so they call her Lililla."

"If she's an Easterner, she'll be a Christian."

"The Christians can't be whores, their thighs are done up," said Dianus. "This one worships properly."

"I maybe saw her," said Vusca.

"You maybe did. Come and see her again. Or do you want to go back to your wife?"

It was dusk, and up on the roof-walk of the Light Tower the men were igniting the brazier. As they walked away from the Fort, the flame fountained behind them, Dis Light, for a guide to the river traffic, for a warning to any dreamer on the hills: *Rome is here, and Rome is still awake.*

The evening was thundery, close and hot. Fireflies blinked in the bushes of a garden. Dianus swaggered. He was not a man Vusca had ever liked, but yet, like a brother he had grown up with, he was accustomed to him, prepared to be loyal.

A trumpet sounded *gates* from the Fort rampart, now several streets behind. The whole town took its timing from there, rising with the sun at *cockcrow*, securing its door at *gates*. All but the wine-shops and eating houses which were blooming out on the dark like the fireflies.

They did not go by way of the forum, but cut around to the south. Beyond the Julian Baths was a maze of side lanes. Here Dianus located a modest house that had once belonged to a minor official of the basilica. A baker's that took up the front was closed, but over the house door hung a shining lamp of expensive Aegyptian alabaster.

Dianus rapped on the door.

After a pause, a male voice spoke up. "Who's there?"

"I," said Dianus flirtatiously, "and a friend."

"Which house are you seeking?" obtusely demanded the porter through the door.

"The house of Lililla."

"This is that house. Is my mistress known to you?"

"Soon she will be," said Dianus. And losing patience, battered on the door.

A growl answered from within, not human but canine. Dianus stepped off.

"By the Victory! I think there's a real wolf in there."

"Take yourself away," advised the porter, over the growling. "My mistress receives no one without invitation. There are men and dogs here."

"So I can tell," bawled Dianus. "Keep her then, your bloody mistress. But she'd have done better not to fall out with the Fort." He waited, listening to see if this did any good. It did not. With a volley of oaths Dianus strode off. Vusca kept pace. He was more tickled than anything. Whores came three to the denarius, but this one, as he had suspected, traded by the Greek mode.

He considered the woman Lililla slowly. This was not the hot haste of his passages along the west hill after Lavinia. Lililla was available for an honest price. The dealings of harlotry, if not of women, he grasped.

Eight mornings later, when the drills, and a store inspection, were over, Retullus Vusca went up to the forum and searched among the stalls and shops. He ended up in the cave of discreet Barbarus (a blond hill tribesman, now more civilised-Latinised than half the town, and capable of speaking

Greek more honed than the Pilum Commander's, though this latter was not difficult). Here was found a suitable article. A painted vase of Aegyptian *nard* – a most generous, but not effusive, down-payment. It was dispatched to the house of Lililla by one of Barbarus' own sons. The papyrus read: "This from your admirer Centurion Velitis Re. Vusca. If he calls upon you this evening, may he hope not to be refused?"

A smaller papyrus reached him before sunset at the Fort.

It answered: "Lord, I touch your gift to my heart. Come."

This time the door was opened and the porter bowed.

Lamplight, and a pleasant foreign smell of other oils and incenses filled the lobby. The atrium was the old way – it was an old house – partly unroofed, with a tank of water, but it had been made attractive with Greek lamps and the paint redone on the walls. At the shadow's edge stood a man with two wolfhounds on leash, just visible, a tactful reminder.

In the central room Rome ceased, and Par Dis too. It became an Eastern pavilion. Silk ropes, draperies, images of ivory. On glowing charcoal burned sticks of something that the Pharaohs might have favoured.

Vusca found himself suddenly excited and nervous, like some boy.

He planted himself firmly, and as the slave went out, looked round and saw the woman, Lililla.

She reclined on a couch, in a fringed robe that gleamed like water even as she breathed. Her lips were nacred and her eyes all kohl. She got up without hurry, and came towards Vusca. When she reached him, she kneeled down with the liquid boneless movement of a snake. She brushed his foot with her fingers and got up again, and looked into his face.

"The centurion honours me," she said. Her voice was low.

He discovered he had no words. He had meant to play her game with her, all courtesy and fakes. But everything about her was sex. Though she was not to be tumbled like the she-wolves, heated and quick, every line of her said *Take me*.

He would have to leave it all to her.

Perhaps that was the idea.

She conducted him to the couch, and gave him a wine bowl of silver. Lovers performed acts thereon that, when he caught glimpses, startled him. The wine was black and spicy. Something in it?

Soon, she made him lie back upon the couch. She undid his clothes with damning competence. She began to do things to his body, with her hands, with a fan of feathers she took up, with smooth strigils of enamel. He need do nothing. She worked on him like a complacently smiling physician. She removed her own garment only when he had showed himself ready, as if to reward him. She was small, with round breasts, round heavy hips, an indented waist, strong thighs. Her feet and ankles, like her hands and wrists, her face, were delicately shaped. She was fleshy but firm, like a satiny fruit. Her lips were the same. When she absorbed his penis into her mouth he was half alarmed. She seemed to have no teeth. When she drew on him, he almost could not check himself. He held back with some trouble, wanting to possess her. She seemed to read this from his eyes, let him go and mounted him, and took him in again at the second mouth, the mouth he wanted most.

She performed all the labour, she also controlled him with a wicked, subservient mastery, not permitting him to ejaculate at first, reining him by a strange pressure at the base of the column. When his seed did spurt, it came in a convulsion. He had seldom if ever known a climax so intense. He found, astonished when she removed herself from him, that she had also penetrated him.

She went away briefly, while he lay there, and returned freshly robed, carrying the wine-cup, which she offered on her knees.

Unlike the other whores, she had made no pretence of her own pleasure. Neither had she shown a whore's aversion, any impatience or indifference. She had been created for his use. It was as natural as that.

When he had drunk the wine and sat up, she said, "It grieves me that my lord must leave me so soon. But I too have some tiresome business that must be completed this evening. I shall number the days, until my lord's return."

Vusca was better able to take up the game, now. He said, "I'd meant to buy you a present, Lililla, but found nothing worthy of you. If I left this purse, perhaps you may know of some small thing that might divert you a moment?" He reached among his clothes and handed her the purse, open just enough she could see he had been generous again.

"My lord's kindness will enhance any gift a thousand times," said she.

Vusca was aware his kindness would go straight into the coffer.

When he left he was untired, for she had done all the work, and the extreme ejaculation seemed to have robbed him of nothing. He felt fit and jaunty, and congratulated himself on having found her. Though she was rather costly, he could afford a luxury now and then. He had no others.

He began to visit Lililla quite regularly every third or fourth week. He did not know who her other clients were (certainly not Dianus). They were reticent, and so was he.

He and she never talked, beyond short beginning and concluding euphemisms. She wanted no conversation. She wanted, though never appeared interested in, only money. On several occasions, if he was willing, they did things he had never before heard of, let alone experienced. These things were never strenuous on his part, and she seemed a creature with wax for bones. She always welcomed him smiling, and with an obeisance. Her face was not loving, or liking, bored or sly. It simply *was*, without pretence. She was perfect.

Until, near the summer's end, Retullus Vusca went to the house of Lililla and everything altered.

That was a rainy twilight, with a lilac tinge to the hills and sky. Even the stones and plaster, the tiled roofs, had a mauve, wet, lizardskin sheen.

He knocked, the porter admitted him. In the lobby he smelled that the aroma of the place was wrong. The gums burning were swarthier, more cloying. In the tank of the atrium the rain plopped. They walked around under the covered area, and the man with the dogs was absent.

The central room was in a mist, a sort of damson gloaming like the streets outside.

The slave shut the doors. Vusca saw where the smoke came from. A large skull, perhaps of a bear, sat on one of the inlaid tables, and resins were fuming out of it.

She was on the far side, dim through the smitch.

He said harshly, "By the Bull, can't you get rid of that thing."

Then she stood up, and he saw, with a peculiar clutch somewhere in his loins, that she was clad like some kind of priestess. One breast was bare, and her body bound in a tight garment crossed diagonally by white fringes. On her head was a wig of mulberry black, in ringlets with silver discs on them. Her arms were gripped by bangles of slick black lacquer.

Was this some new sexual gambit? He did not care for it if it was.

"Lililla –" he said.

She said, "Lord, I have had omens. When this happens, I am not my own. Come here, you must attend."

He was disgusted. Very nearly frightened. And there was the same slithering in his veins he had felt at the initiation to the Rites of Mithras, when he was only seventeen.

He had a veneration for the gods. After a minute, he went to her, and when she told him to sit, did so, gazing at her through the choking smut from the skull.

Presently she started to croon, to sway like a serpent. He thought of the sybils, inhaling volcanic vapours, prophesying, reading riddles. He did not want this to occur. He did not want any of this. He decided, sourly, if she was prone to this, he would not come here again. It was a shame, but he might have known there would be a flaw.

She stopped crooning and swaying.

The smoke was thick in his nostrils, his mouth seemed coated by it. Through the pillar she abruptly said, "You have never had any luck, centurion. Should you relish some?"

It was so unlike her way of speaking to him. Even the timbre of her voice was higher and slightly shrill.

He said, "Don't be impertinent. I don't come to you for this. I respect your gods, but my business is my own."

"I spoke of luck. Is it not true? All you hanker for you miss. Your days with the legions left you here. Your promotion you did not have. Your wife is barren and not fair. If you go to hunt, you kill nothing. If you dice, you take the Dog."

"You've been asking questions about me," he said. He added, measured, "You bitch, don't forget who I am. Rome is the power here. Insult me, you insult Rome."

"Rome is far off. You are not Rome. You are a man who stinks of his disappointments. All your days are marked with blots. I say again, should you wish to change it?"

He swore at her. (How different from the rest, this ultimate dialogue they had managed!) His mind said clearly, She speaks only the fact. Whether she has gossiped or is wise, she does not lie. I am who she says. Change it? Yes, I could wish that.

Just then the smoke in the bear's skull flattened in a most striking way, as if some vortex sucked it down.

He could see her directly now, before him. Her face was white, her eyes like pebbles. This did not seem to be Lililla. Something had taken possession of her for sure. Some god. Some thing.

"If," she said, or the god said, through her, "you accept what is offered to you, reach into the skull. Remove what is there."

Vusca found it hard to look away from her. He made himself do so, looked at the fuming skull instead. The smoke was almost laid now. It clotted in the cavities of the skull-eyes, foamed at the rim. Still he could not see past it, into the hollow case.

"If you accept," the woman repeated, "reach in. Remove what is there. It will be yours."

Suddenly, like a boy who is dared, he could not put it off. He thrust his hand, or as much of it as he could, into the baked smoke. And felt something on the hot crusts of the gums. He brought it out. It was warm, glassy, black with the smoke as his hand now was. He brought forward a piece of his damp cloak and rubbed, and the mauve rain-light of sky and hills was shining there on his palm.

It was a small oblong of amethyst, an amulet, presumably, for it was incised with the figure of some protective deity – Vusca scrutinised this, uncertain of its form.

Lililla said, "You have taken it now."

"Yes, I've taken it. But it's precious, this stone."

"You gave me gifts, lord," she said. "I render to you a gift." It was the other Lililla, the perfect harlot. He looked, and saw she had returned, and was kneeling there beyond the table, with blood behind her skin and sight in her eyes. Even the wig and the costume looked only garish now. It was the smiling face of mere being. "The amulet is from Aegyptus," she said, "the wine-stone."

"That is Thot, then," he said, "cut into the surface."

The image had a man's body, a bird's head. Thot, the Mercurius of the Aegyptians, was bird-headed.

Lililla did not reply. She went away as Vusca sat there staring at the jewel, turning it in his hand. That she should give him something of high price seemed odd. Perhaps her gods truly had made her.

The stone was no longer hot. It had assumed the temperature of his palm. It seemed made of his own flesh, only harder, and more smooth.

The woman came back with her hair loose and her silks, carrying the lewd silver cup.

Vusca stood.

"No," he said.

She stood in her turn, looking at him. She continued only to smile and only to be.

"I've left the money on the table," he said. "This jewel's worth more." He said, to test her, "Do you want it back after all?" And made a movement, as if to hand it to her.

At that she gave ground. She stepped off three or four steps, quickly. The smile stayed. She shook her head, smiling.

"No, lord. My omens told me. Yours."

"I never heard of a woman of your sort," he said, "giving the client a payment."

If she had fallen on him with all her most cunning caresses and amazing tricks, he could not have had her, not then. She had spoilt all that.

As for the jewel, probably it was some stained crystal. If it would be lucky – well, he was due a little luck.

It was dry dark outside. Dogs were baying a rising moon.

He walked down to the north wall, had a drink with the sentry captain at the river gate. Below, the water spread to catch the moonlight, and on the other side were the thatched huts of the native Par Disans.

Rome was far away. Perhaps this very hour, she was burning again, broken. They would be the last to know.

A day later Dianus, meeting him by the quartermaster's cubicle, informed Retullus Vusca the lily whore had decamped. She and all her trappings had vanished away in a night. The house was empty. Hopefuls, who went in to

rummage, found nothing worthwhile. Someone said the Lupa at the *She-Wolf*
had paid her off.

On his hard bed in the officers' block, Vusca asleep was walking through a
long narrow corridor whose ceiling almost brushed his head. The walls were
whitewashed, but took no light until the way opened into a courtyard. In the
dream, Vusca glanced about ironically, responding as he tended to, to foreign
things. The walls of the court, like the corridor, were whitewashed and
painted over, with lions and chariots. The other end of the court gave on a
flight of white steps going down to dark water under a tight drum-skin of
heat-drained sky. Palms grew against the steps, and in the water pale cupped
lilies and purple-coloured lotuses.

An overblown altar stood in the court near the water-steps and a man was
making an offering there. He was naked but for a kilt of dressed skins. His
body glimmered like metal from sweat or from oil; his hair and beard were
curled. The incense steamed on the altar, it had an overpowering smell,
almost kitcheny, like something cooked or fried, like offal, and like musky
sweet things, too.

The altar was carved with creatures that had male bodies, wings, the
heads of lions, rams, birds.

Sun hammered out the river. The man's flesh and hair shone. The stream-
er of incense rose.

Nothing else happened.

When Vusca woke, the trumpets were sounding the third watch. Here, it
was night. Known, every angle and shadow of the cell, its two chests, the
lamp, the chair which had once been uncle's at the villa, the weapons on the
wall and the bearskin he had bought from Barbarus one bitter winter. Beyond
the door, left open, the mathematical Roman yard, with a ray of light playing
down from the torch on the Praetorium wall.

Vusca heard the trumpets out. Then turning on his side, returned into
sleep, and did not dream again.

On the evening of the Wall Walk, the Commander elected to lead the
squadron. Formerly, there had been a manned sentry-post for every half mile
of town wall. In the lax climate that now prevailed, only ten posts were kept
up, besides the south, west and river gates.

Every month, at the Calends Moon, one of the ranking centurions took the
Walk, a tour of the entire wall, which lasted upwards of four hours. The Fort
mason was supposed to accompany the presiding centurion, but normally
contented himself with a question or two the following day. Otherwise, the
Walker was supported by his adjutant and a block of ten of his men who

would have been happier in the Fort. For the Pilum Commander, he seldom if ever took the Walk, as he seldom bothered now with the Night Inspection, delegating this also to his Centurion Secundo or whatever officer was most handy.

Vusca had overseen Nights more times than he could count, and the Wall Walk nearly as often. He learned that he was not to escape on this occasion either. The Old Man wanted both the mason and Vusca for escort, with ten Velites (who as usual would fret and feel insulted, since for the Walk even the cavalry went on foot. In the old days a skirmisher division would never had been put on such a duty. But then.)

Dianus spoke scathingly of the Commander. "What's stirred him up? Afraid the Emperor's watching from afar?"

Vusca shrugged. He despised the Pilum Commander, who liked wine too much and spoke Greek like a pimp and Latin like the fishmongers' descendant he was. Long ago, Vusca had partly hated the man. Yet even in those days Vusca served him impeccably. A soldier must honour the command, if not the dross which might fill it. One did not tarnish one's own vow because of a fool, a stroke of rotten luck. Nor did one, like Dianus, yap about his faults. It was part of the great pretence that every commander be sufficient.

They started out just after *gates*. There was still a flush of light in the west, mauvish (like that other night). It was autumn weather now, and the remainder of the sky swagged low with cloud. They would probably get a wetting before the Walk was done, which made it stranger still their comfort-loving Pilum had decided on it.

He strutted ahead, like a barrel on legs, in that dress armour of his with the inlay of silver, iron cap plumed with its white coxcomb, and the Tyrian cloak swaggering, full of wind. He was jovial too, and cracked the odd joke with the mason. Centurion Velitis Vusca kept the proper number of paces to the rear, his Velites marching with a dull clink and clash behind him. At the manned posts, the Commander received the salute with theatrical earnestness. He spoke to the handful of sentries, encouraging them in the wind and light spat of rain that was beginning, as if enormous enemy battalions lay below on the garnering night. A couple of times, he called Vusca up. The second time it was: "That man to be disciplined. Sloppy. Probably drunk." Vusca accepted the criticism on the man's behalf. His name was Quintus. He had bad teeth and sometimes dosed himself with poppy. It was irregular but understandable. And was the drug more distracting than constant pain? The Commander, of course, knew nothing of any of this.

They got down to the river gate inside the first hour, the tour had gone briskly thus far.

The Pilum paused for a drink with the sentry captain, complained about Quintus, had another cup against the dank evening.

Out on the wall again, behind the Commander's cocksure, rolling advance, Vusca heard one of his men mutter, "He thinks he's going to his Triumph."

Vusca, for once, saw fit to be deaf.

In the second hour, marching over against the north-west hills, the rain began to come from Jupiter's slingers. It lashed the right cheek, whistled into the right ear, blinkered the right eye. They tramped on, shimmering iron men with seaweed cloaks. That clown, with his damned plumes, carved through the rain, wine-insured against the weather.

They reached the west gate. This time Vusca was invited to join the drinking. He touched the flagon with his lips.

The core of the storm came when they were on the western stretch, with the rain striking their backs.

For some reason, Vusca thought of a minor engagement in hill country, all of thirteen years ago. The downpour had started in the hour before battle, slanting on the ranks, and up had gone the shields, to make a tortoise against the rain. He was reminded of the sound of it now, a barrage like nails, hitting those hundred or so crossed lightnings, torches, the Medusa faces and snake hair washed and slapped. They had fought in the rain too, skidding and sinking in the mud, while the sky flickered with levin-bolts. They won, that went without saying. When the tempest lessened, the barbarians lay everywhere, while the rain gently cleansed their wounds. His infantry shield remained with him to this day. It had a hole through one of the Medusa eyes where someone had almost finished his unpromising career.

A white crack suddenly wrecked the sky. Everything leapt out stark and dead, a place with no dimensions, colours or shadows. Lightning was here, too.

Then came the boom and shock of heavenly ballistas.

One of the Velites shook himself as he marched, with a rattle. Water down the neck.

Not alone in that, thought Vusca. He watched the Commander rolling on ahead, impervious it seemed. Even the mason had dropped back. The next manned sentry-post was visible, ten minutes away, and below, the town, wild on this side, bothies and brothels, though along the slope the ruined circus stood up like a raised scar.

Vusca turned his head and saw, across the streaming night, the dim glows of the easterly town, the spark of Dis Light on the Light Tower. He felt together a dismal sense of futility and a raw pride. He had come to care for it, this outcast place. Perhaps, when Rome was only a pile of rubble, Par Dis in exile might survive.

More rain went down his neck like a cold lesson. *Remember you are mortal.*

So much for the whore's amulet. Even now, like a dolt, he had it in a pouch round his neck. It surely failed to keep him dry.

And then the world blew up.

There was just a dot of white and then a drench like fire. As he flew, turning, falling, he thought, quite distinctly, he had known something like it before, but he did not know where or when – an earthquake maybe, or a nightmare.

He landed hard, bruised on the metal of his armour. He lay and thought about this, and then he found a heap of armoured men tumbling over him like clanking puppies.

He pulled himself out and to his knees, and saw the mason running in a circle screaming. He was naked, and his body smoked.

"By the bowels of the Bull," said Vusca, standing up.

He seemed to be lightheaded. Drunk after all? He fought the urge to laugh. He lifted his hands. They were scalded. He put up these scalded hands, and touched his singed hair and brows.

The mason fell down.

Beyond, three sentries were pelting up the wall towards them.

The terrible rumbling was only thunder.

Something was on fire.

Something was burning there, just past the mason, between him and the running soldiers.

It was all that was left of the Pilum Commander.

"Jupiter, Father Jupiter," moaned one of the Velites.

Vusca had the urge to laugh again. He held it down.

"It will be yours," said the Centurion Secundo. "Not a man here doubts it."

Vusca did not want to seem like some blushing virgin. But he was afraid too of what had always happened in the past.

"It may be you," he said.

"You've seen more service than I. I'm content."

The authority would not come from Rome. There was, at the moment, power enough in Gallia to settle this. A few more days, and he would know.

The Velites carried on as if they already did know. How not, when Father Jupiter himself had made the choice? He had struck down the Pilum with his own divine thunderbolt, and left Retullus Vusca and his men unscathed but for a memento of crisped hair. (The mason, though he lived, did not count.)

The authority came at the end of the month, slipshod as things always were now, all language. But the seal was the correct one.

Vusca went out to look at his troops.

They cheered their new Pilum with willing lungs.

He was surprised. He had never thought himself popular, had been sure he was not.

His heart was in his mouth. That moment, perhaps, was the apex of his life.

Lavinia wrote him a letter, and for days he put off reading it, for she seemed only able to say, think, accomplish one thing: misery, complaints, and tears on paper were little improvement on the personal hand-to-hand variety.

Eventually he did read the letter. It was very simple.

She had been a poor wife to him. She regretted this. She wanted to go and live in the villa. If he preferred to divorce her, she acceded. On his advancement she praised him. It was only as he deserved.

He had come to realise there would be monetary complications if they divorced. Besides, he had no plan to remarry. He doubted that Lavinia had. She did not mention it.

He pondered his answer. At last, he preferred not to put anything into writing. He would go to visit her instead, at the Insula Juna. If she really was contrite, she might be quiet. Perhaps she would not cry. He could tell her she could live at the villa, he made no demands. He was sorry for her, and did not want her always on his conscience. He had not seen her for months.

In the dream, he recognised the bearded man, his kilt and oiled muscular body. They walked as if physically together along a white platform, under the leaning wall of a white building. The sky was the drum-skin sky Vusca had seen before, but smooring into darkness. Stars came out. The white glazing caught the starlight, and Vusca saw three shadows falling before them. He was astonished to cast a shadow himself, more curious as to the third. He turned to see who made the third shadow, which was of an odd shape.

No one was there.

She had done something different to the room. It looked brighter, even in that dull daylight. A bowl of purple grapes had white flowers wreathed among them; a local shawl he had never seen before was draped prettily across a couch.

Lavinia came to greet him. For a minute, he did not know her.

"How well you're looking," he said lamely, staring.

She had gained weight. Her skin was fresh, her forearms, her throat, were rounded as they had not been since she was sixteen. The linear cuts in her face had filled out and were gone. She wore her hair a new way, not Roman, more Greek, with a ribbon across her forehead. She was not old, ten years his junior. Suddenly he remembered.

She waited on him as she had been used to do when they were first together, sending the slave away. She was very soft. She said very little. She left it
all to him.

In the end he was lost for words.

Then she said, "Do you think I've changed?"

He looked. He said, "Yes."

She told him why.

"I'm not a Christian any more."

She said she had failed all the Christian precepts, although she had tried so
hard. She went around with her heart withering, blaming him, blaming God.
Then, on the forum, she saw a procession from the Isis Temple. That afternoon
she went there. It was not, she assured him, a hive of orgiastic rites. The religion had altered. It had to do with Woman. Lavinia had found herself at the
cool feet of the statue. She said that suddenly the terrible gnawing, which had
been feeding on her for years, was lifted out of her. She made an offering and
joined the prayers. After this, she went regularly to the temple. She had not
forgotten the Christos, she said, but it was a religion she was too weak to follow. Isis, who understood, had redeemed her. She could be at peace, now.

She could let him go, now.

Vusca hesitated. Then he said, "It isn't necessary. A divorce."

"But Retullus," she said, "you have an important command. You'll want
to marry again. Get children. Your name can become illustrious."

"Who should I marry here?" he said. "Some native girl, or a harlot?"
Lavinia lowered her eyes. "Let's leave things as they are," he said. "We need-
n't bother each other."

"My dear," she said, "I'll always love you. But let me go to the villa. Then
I won't be in your way."

He was embarrassed, but not displeased.

"Of course," he said, "except – why not keep here until spring? The winter's nearly on us, snow, wolves – you'll winter better in the town."

"If you wish," she said. She smiled. "Whatever you say."

Her eyes were limpid. He longed suddenly to embrace her, kiss her lips.
She was the girl he had seen in the orchard, or the woman that girl had never
before become.

But he did not kiss or embrace Lavinia. He stayed only as long as courtesy
required. When he left, she did not cry.

The winter truly was a harsh one. The snows came sweeping down; the river
froze. All night the wolves howled in the voices of lost souls that could not
find the way back to Avernus.

Added to the normal duties of the Fort were the tasks of winter. The roads were kept clear, the surrounding stations open in case horses might be needed. Even during the blizzards, Dis Light unlidded its nocturnal eye.

In the Commander's quarters above the Praetorium, Vusca relentlessly attended to the business of the outpost Empire. There was no time to think of anything much beyond work.

Only once or twice he took the amethyst out of the pouch around his neck, and set it down in the brazier light, to study.

Had it changed his fortune?

Had it invited the Thunderer to strike? Had it whispered to the musing powers in Gallia until it brought him the staff of office? And had it borne Lavinia to the feet of Isis?

One twilit day, going over the bridge near the Fort gate, back from a successful winter hunt, Vusca's horse slid on the ice. He should have gone off, into the iron water, maybe under the panes of the ice itself, from which probably he would never have surfaced. But somehow neither he nor the mare fell.

He played dice now and then, with his centurions, to see. He got a reputation for winning. Perhaps they only let him.

Sometimes there were the strange dreams. He had become used to the platforms and corridors, the court above the lotus water. To the bearded man, a Semite of some variety, conceivably a priest or prince, for Vusca had seen him now both naked, and decorated in silver and jewels, a kilt with fringes, a diadem. He performed rituals at the altar in the court, or in an underground space where something towered away, dark into darkness, and only the offering fire gave any clue. Nothing spectacular or significant ever occurred.

When he dreamed of the man, the priest-prince or magician, or of the places he inhabited, Vusca went armed with memory. He knew, even asleep, he had been there before.

The dreams did not worry him, at first. Then only the recurrence disturbed him. As soon as time allowed, he meant to seek a diviner at the temple of the Father and Mother. But that winter there was not much time, except for sleep.

He did pay a few visits to his wife. His intention was to ensure she had not suffered by staying in the town, that she lacked for nothing. Sometimes he lingered. He got into the way of dining with her, of spending an evening with her. Their conversations were neutral. He spoke of the Fort and its management, or they discussed aspects of the town. He found these interludes to be comfortable, pleasing. She did her best for him. She had learned how to be gracious. They never slept together, as if such things did not exist. He preferred that. It was sex that seemed to have upset the equilibrium before, along with Christianity. Now she had Isis, and for him there were always the she-wolves. But he did not want a woman very often; he supposed that even Lililla would have palled, she had been only a novelty.

As the year turned over towards spring, and the tall clepsydra in the Praetorium began once again to drip and to tell time, Vusca, who had been feeling a little done in, was laid up a day and a night with mild fever. He put the amethyst under his bolster, to keep it out of the way, for the Fort physician was a busy old boy.

Near morning, Vusca thought he dreamed how the amulet was made.

It was not the underground place, though it seemed the priest-prince had come from there. He was walking in the starlight back across the platform, white as the snow of Par Dis in that boiling Eastern night, that had the whiff both of marsh and desert. Together, they entered the low door, passed through the fox-run of the corridor, and came into the court of painted walls.

Going down the stair to the river, the native of the dream took Vusca with him, and gave him a first – and as it transpired, final – glimpse, through the palms, over the water, to the distant bank. Other buildings arose there, raised on platforms as was this, and one ascending in a series of terraces, a pyramid of seven steps. Huge clumps of reeds grew beneath the further bank, and something swam there, some colossal snake it looked, but the priest paid it no heed.

Leaning down, he drew up from the water a sort of basket, and in the basket lay a fish. It had been dead some while, and at a touch, its belly parted to disgorge a lilac-tinted counter.

The purpose of the fish, if it had been made to ingest the jewel, or miraculously had been caught with it already swallowed, Vusca did not ascertain.

The priest plucked the amethyst and carried it to the altar with the creatures carved around.

There the jewel was anointed with oils, beer, milk, and other liquids, and words spoken above it (a sluggish murmuring and chanting Vusca had heard the man give vent to previously). At last the priest moved away, right against the wall, as if to become one with the paintings on it.

The jewel lay on the altar.

It lay there a long while. Then it began to glow. It was like a lilac flame, balanced on the altar stone. One flame – then three. Just above, two other lights had kindled.

In the dream, Vusca, pressed back to the wall with the priest, experienced a gust of fear. It was the correct terror of holy and profane things he had no right to witness. But he was trapped and had no choice.

What burned above the jewel were the eyes of one of the beasts carved in the altar. He could not see which it was, and did not need to. The shape was on the amulet.

The jewel blazed and the eyes of the bird-thing blazed, and there was otherwise a deepening darkness and a terrific silence that seemed to shriek.

Presently the three lights faded. As starshine returned into the court, Vusca thought he saw, for a moment, a shadow cast up against the wall, thrown by a third figure that was not there.

The fever had broken in a sweat. When he could, he shifted the amulet away from him. It felt hot from contact with him, even through the pouch.

That was the beginning of his unease.

When he came into his quarters on the third occasion and felt that someone else had recently been there, he went to the door and called the sentry in.

"Who's been here in my absence?"

The sentry looked surprised.

"No one, sir."

Vusca's soldier's instinct, the same that had made him able once or twice to sense ambush or treachery, told him flatly that, though the sentry did not lie, neither did the ambience of the rooms. The smell was even wrong. Not of men and a man's belongings, leather, metal, papers, the charcoal and logs in the brazier. Something – almost female.

"Concentrate," said Vusca to the sentry. "Now."

The sentry began to roll his eyes.

"Yes, sir. *Something*'s been in."

Vusca crossed to the window. The glazed pane was in place and below the drop ran down sheer thirteen feet to the yard. A sentry on the adjacent tower stood alert and unmoved.

There was no explanation, and being inexplicable, it was put aside. Nothing had been damaged, there was no theft. The sense of a presence evaporated quickly.

Thereafter it would happen, or not, apparently as it chose. Once the guard on the door himself reported he had caught a noise inside, during the Commander's absence. He went to see, and investigated the two rooms, finding them vacant. He admitted that it might have been a rat or mouse. It was a kind of soft scratching he had heard, as if something clawed stole over the floor.

Vusca was tired. He awoke tired, and at night, lying down exhausted, could not sleep, hearing the trumpets through the hours till it was nearly dawn. Something nagged at him. He did not know what it was. It was as if he had forgotten some vital task. He would get up and light the lamp, and check his itinerary at the table. It was nothing to do with the Fort, this forgotten matter.

It oppressed him. It never went away. If he slept he even dreamed of it (the other dreams seemed to have come to an end). He dreamed of worrying at forgetting, of trying to remember. He roused agitated, still trying. There was nothing *to* remember. He had seen to it all.

He hoped spring would lift the malaise. Spring did not. He could not consult the Fort physician, since then word would be round the barracks in half a morning, that he was sick. He visited a healer on the town's west side, who prescribed an oily draught. It made him sleep. He could scarcely wake up at all. And the nagging, the non-existent forgotten thing, went on nibbling away at him.

Something had made him take off the amethyst. He stored it in a box of bits and pieces, wrapped in its pouch.

One pale evening, as the days began perceptibly to lengthen, his Centurion Secundo, coming in to make some report, was obviously curious at finding Vusca alone. When pressed, the centurion said he had seen, so he thought, two figures at the window above the Praetorium, and meeting no one on the stair – "Oh," said Vusca, "I had the soldier in from the door a moment."

A month later, he saw it for himself. He had been waiting, in his heart of hearts, aware he was haunted. He had seen the form before. He was not startled, only afraid.

He had taken a mouthful of the healer's draught, and slept, and woke suddenly, as if at a loud cry.

But there was no noise. The room was pitch black, but for the thinner darkness of the window. And across the window passed the creature from the amulet.

It was visible for less than a second, yet it left an imprint on his sight, as on the jewel. A tall, provisionally masculine outline, but winged, clawed, and with the hook-beak head of a bird.

Vusca heaved himself up and lighted the lamp. He shook so much that he could not manage it at first. But nothing came near him, and when the light poured out the room seemed empty. *He knew it was not.* Like a child, he left the lamp to burn all night, sitting bolt upright on the bed.

And that was the beginning of his terror.

That spring Lavinia had joined the circle of initiates at her temple. This, he had to admit, as well as his position, assisted Vusca. Isis was not his goddess, but he had adequate reverence for her, which he demonstrated with a showy offering at the altar. She was depicted in decent Roman matron's garb, a crown of corn on her head, and a moon in her hand from which shivered drops of crystal "tears." After the offering, he was taken to a cell where a priest of the upper tier received him. The man was shaven, jaw and skull, in the Aegyptian way, nothing like the priest of the dream.

Vusca did not prevaricate. He told the truth. A harlot had given him an amulet, quite precious, and he had found it benign. But latterly it had brought on some illness that deprived him of energy, though physicians pronounced him fit. Also, an entity was expelling itself from the stone, a ghost, that was sometimes to be viewed, and which seemed to become stronger as he, Vusca, weakened. The priest, Vusca concluded, must say nothing of this to anyone. The Commander's respect for the goddess would not prevent his punishing an abuse of trust.

The bald priest, face like an egg, regarded him gravely.

"You may trust me."

Then Vusca got out the amulet and put it before the priest.

"Here. She said it was Aegyptian."

"No," said the priest, looking at it, not touching it. "She misled you."

"I thought that was the case." Vusca spoke, less decidedly of the dreams. He had to fumble after them now. They had no coherence. The priest, however, listened carefully.

When Vusca finished, the priest said, "I must consult another, more widely-versed than I in these things. Do you allow me to tell him what you've said?"

"If you must."

"Yes."

"When shall I return?"

"Tomorrow night, before the third watch." (Even this temple told time by the Fort.) "I've seen it, now take it away with you."

Vusca went, dissatisfied and nervous. He had not told Lavinia the truth, only that he wished the services of a diviner, and would like to favour her own chosen temple. He thought she guessed there was some other problem.

After he had done the Night Inspection and retired to his rooms, he sat by the lamp and accepted that the presence prowled about him. Now and then, something caused the lamp to flicker, although it was a windless night. A faint aroma, like musk and blood mixed, was barely detectable. The shadow appeared plainly once, twice, against the plastered wall, where his legionary's sword was hanging, the old infantry shield, the knives, the dented breast-plate with the gouge of the axe-man's dying anger –

The shadow was, and then it was not.

The thing he found the hardest to bear was that it should be here that he was attacked, in this place which represented for him security, totality, reason – *here* –

He fell into deathly sleep at last, over the table.

The creature from the amethyst had sucked up his bad luck, and now it sucked his life. He dreamed he was with Lililla. She too sucked upon him, in that way she had taught him. He felt no pleasure but he knew he would spend his seed and she would swallow it. Her eyes were a weird dull mauve, and had no mind or soul inside them.

Three of the priests were in the chamber where he was led the second night. Lamps burned; other than a small statue of the goddess, nothing and no one else was there.

"You told me one other priest," Vusca said.

"For this, three are necessary."

It was pointless to practise hauteur and the Might of Rome now. He was as much at their mercy as under the surgeon's saw.

"Very well. What will be done?"

The fattest of the priests, who had a blond skin (a barbarian in Isis' order), approached him and said, in the beautiful Greek so many of them mastered: "Commander, the amulet the woman gave you is like this: it is, as you found, benign, but then it turns. Before the first symptom, one who knew its secret would pass on the gem to another, who must accept it willingly. That is how to be free of it, to escape the turning of the energy back upon you. The woman did this. You did not know to do it. Now the time for such passage is over. We must try another course."

"Yes." Vusca frowned. His hands were wet and his belly griped. "What course?"

"A casting out. A returning."

He did not understand, but he followed their instructions. They made marks on the floor, and anointed them. One stood outside the marks, by the goddess. In an alabaster bowl he made fire. It was this priest, the one who had never addressed Vusca, who had been given the amulet.

They began to chant. Vusca did not know the words. The sounds they made, keening harmonics, droned up into the roof like mosquitoes, and set his teeth on edge.

He realised he was now more than terrified.

It was very hot in the room.

The priest who had the amulet had never touched it save through a cloth. It lay on the cloth now, before him. He spoke to it, and Vusca caught the names of Isis, and of Thot, and of Osiris. The priest sprinkled water on the cloth with the amethyst, and powders, and salt.

The ritual seemed to go on and on. All the while, Vusca felt his strength bleeding away. His head swam. It was tedious, it was horrible. He realised he had grasped already that it could not work.

Finally, bellowing something, the priest beyond the marks raised the amulet in the cloth and cast it into the fire. The other two broke from their pen and hurled things into the basin after it. An unsuitable smell of cookery rose – they had thrown in onion, and some kind of fruit.

Vusca staggered. He went down on one knee, wiping the sweat from his face. He wanted it to be over. It was useless. He would have to think of another remedy.

When the fire died in the bowl, the amulet lay there. The heat had done something to it, meddled with its colour in some way.

He must take it, they said. Go to the Fort. They tied a knot of little cords on his arm, above the elbow. They invoked the protection of Isis.

He put a sum of money by the statue. They did not acknowledge this, aware themselves that they had achieved nothing.

The Roman commander lay down on his bed, the lamp alight, the sentry at his door.

He could not keep his eyes open. He drifted.

Vusca gripped the sword he had brought to lie beside him. The creature was not corporeal, yet maybe he could smite at it. Besides, there was a power in the sword. The power of what a soldier was. His last companion, the only one who could know everything, and would not betray –

The light fluttered and went out.

At first it was so gradual, he was not sure. It was like a constriction of the breath after too much food and wine. Only like that. But the pressure grew. It became heavier, sentient. In appalling horror he lay there, and felt the weight of the demon, crouching as the woman had done, on his loins and breast. The weight grew ever more sonorous, danker, seeping through him. He could not move. He was rigid with panic fear. And then there came the glow of two eyes, like meltings from the amethyst, hanging over him, watching him, as it sucked his life from every pore and vein and hair.

Vusca howled. By a galvanic effort, seemingly irresistible as the action of birth or death, he flung himself upward, dislodging the half-existent thing upon his chest. And as it dropped away, with the sword he cleaved it through and through, *felt* the blade go into it. But with no likeness to muscle or flesh, and not the jarring of a single bone.

When the sword ceased to penetrate anything at all, he stood panting in the darkness.

The sentry had not rushed in on him. It appeared Vusca had not even cried out as he thought he had. That was strange. Strange …

He held the sword, hugging it to him. Here was the last solution, after all. One way to cheat.

He sat down by the table, in the dark, with his only ally. He propped the hilt against the table's edge, the tip against his abdomen, the crucial spot, under the ribs and heart. He leaned, fractionally, on the sword's sharpness, and felt its bite like sweet consolation. "If you're there," he said aloud into the dark, "I have my friend here. My friend will take me from you, if you come close tonight. Then you lose. Be warned."

He fainted, propped there over the blade.

Barbarus came to the Fort with some display, two of his sons, and three servants.

In the room above the Praetorium, Vusca said to him, "You had no need to be anxious. Did you think I meant to admonish you for something?"

Barbarus said smoothly, "It is the Commander's privilege."

"Why, have you been doing something wrong?"

Barbarus said, "Never knowingly, Commander."

Vusca forced a chuckle. As he had forced the coy opening gambit. Then he said, "What have you been hearing about me in the town?"

Barbarus raised his brows. His horse-boned Gallic face was bland, moving on oiled hinges worthy of a Greek.

"Nothing?" prompted Vusca.

"Merely that we prosper under your hand."

"And how do I look to you?"

Barbarus considered, and decided on a fact.

"Not well, Commander. There's been a lot of fever this spring."

"It isn't fever."

"No, Commander?"

"Do you recall, Barbarus, last summer there was a woman in the town. She had a house behind the Julian Baths."

Barbarus paused, to let the Commander see he had forgotten all that, could only remember if reminded.

Vusca reminded him.

"I thought nothing of it, when she left," he continued, rather archly he felt, but could not summon the requisite irritation. "But the amulet she gave me – it's begun to work me ill."

Barbarus had now altered. He looked like a man listening for a distant, expected shout.

Vusca added details, as many as he thought were needful. When he stopped, Barbarus, with great deference, asked a couple of questions. Vusca replied.

Barbarus said slowly, "The Commander knows I am his slave."

"Barbarus knows, I'm never ungrateful."

"This is so. What may I do?"

"Is there anyone I can see who can – rid me – of this – thing –"

To his horror, Vusca found his voice was shaking, cracking like a boy's.

Barbarus ignored the cracking voice. It had not happened. He said, "There's a man in the hills. About a day's journey in good weather –"

"He must come to me, here."

"That may be more difficult."

"The problem is," said Vusca humbly, "I find I haven't the strength, any more, to ride. Even to walk across this room is – a test."

It was impossible to tell what Barbarus thought. You never knew. Doubtless, at any stumble they rejoiced. But they must still pretend to be sorry, try to assist, for as long as the idea of Rome remained.

"On the table," said Vusca, "that box. Count the coins if you like." Barbarus bowed, tapped the box with his fingers, did not count, since Rome was also perfect. "Pay the man – this healer, magician, whatever he is – pay him as you think fit. For you, I promise you now, if – if I survive, a talent of silver. There's a letter in with the coins to that effect, having my seal."

Barbarus lifted the box.

"I shall naturally destroy the letter, Commander. The Commander's word is all that I require."

Somehow, he lived, and did not go mad, for three more days, two more nights. By day he oversaw the machinery of the Fort, the drills, a parade under a burning white sun, carried out to it in a chair. He did such sedentary work as he could, even went through an interminable itemisation of stores with the quartermaster. Elsewhere he delegated via his capable Centurion Secundo and various other officers. (Was the dead Pilum sneering at him?) The men put up with it all cheerily, and the rank and file even asked after him, it seemed, their Old Man, laid up with the bloody fever, too bad, and it was nice hunting weather, too.

Sometimes in the afternoons he slept. The steady diurnal rhythms of the Fort seemed to protect him then.

The nights he was alone, alone but in company. The three of them, himself, the demon, and the sword.

The sounds of the trumpets marking the watches were his sanity. They were the voice of human strength and human reason.

But he realised he did not have far to go. Barbarus' man from the hills was the final throw of his dice. Then it would be the sword. By the Light, he almost longed for it, now.

At sunset, on the third evening, they were sounding *gates* and he was writing a letter to Lavinia, telling her a crippling sickness had taken him, that he preferred the cleaner exit. It was awkward, this letter. He had wanted to put in some friendly, perhaps loving thing, to reward her for changing. But he did not like the written word other than in an itinerary or report, emotionless and exact. And the letter read just like a report, of course. He put it aside, and then they brought in the man.

He had been awarded a pass, through Barbarus, and would be taken for some roving spy in the pay of the Fort. There were genuine examples of such beings, several as tattered and matted as this one, few with such crazy and wilful eyes. Vusca thought: *When they leave him with me, he may fly at my throat. Let him. Only another way out.*

But, when the sentry left, the man did nothing, except to stand looking at Vusca.

It was unthinkable this ruffian could achieve anything. The final throw had got the Dog.

Vusca was suffused by a cold and awful relief. It was settled. He could die now.

Then the hill-man spoke, in uncouth Latin, in a scraping voice like a flint.

"See it in he. Seeing shadow. Bird thing. All the air, *smelling* bird thing."

A bolt of quickening went through Vusca. It brought him back. He took hold of the table and said, "Did Barbarus tell you –"

"Tell. Now see. Amulet." And more impatiently, as if with a stupid pupil, "Amulet! Amulet!"

Vusca took the amulet from the casket and its wrapping, and laid it on the table in front of the hill-man. The hill-man glanced at it. Then, he poked it with a black fingernail, and gave off an idiot's squealing laugh. He was not afraid to make contact, the only one who was not.

The wild eyes came back to Vusca.

"Eats you," said the hill-man. "*Eats* you."

Vusca shivered.

"Yes."

The hill-man grinned.

Vusca said, "How can I stop it – this *eating*?"

The hill-man pranced about. He said phrases in the native jargon. Vusca caught the word for eating again. He said tiredly, "Do you know?"

"Knowing," said the hill-man, coming to a capering standstill. "Eats you. You eat."

Vusca flinched. Some part of him understood, yet he did not.

"What are you saying?"

The hill-man ignored him. He began to remove an assortment of implements, iron sticks, pincers, little bowls made of bone or shell. They all came out of his clothes.

Vusca watched as these tools of a trade were laid on the floor. In one of the dishes the man lit a flame. Then, as if it were a bit of bread, he scooped the amulet off the table. He sat down with it on the floor as though in his hut. He put the gem into a kind of clamp, and started to work on it, holding it sometimes across the little flame.

Presently mauve dusts veered off into the shell dish.

The shadows were coming down on the rooms. Night had the window, only the torches from the Praetorium to alleviate it. On the floor, the solitary flame lit the wild man's polecat face as he filed and ground away at the amethyst.

There was no sense of menace. The room seemed empty of anything that was not mortal. Was this feasible? Did the wild man have some wonderful power that held the demon in check even as he destroyed its totem?

Vusca had full understanding now. The jewel was to be powdered. Then, he would "eat" it, swallow the crystals. He had heard of physicians prescribing powdered stones, as for his grandfather's rheumatism. Even Lavinia, when pregnant, had taken some resin in molasses.

The demon had eaten Vusca's trouble, and his trouble *was* Vusca. Bad luck had made him into the man he was. The demon devoured that, and then it could go on, devouring him, down to the marrow of his spirit. Yes, he saw it now.

He was drowsy. Should he make the arrangement with the sword? No, unnecessary yet, besides, he did not want the wild man to see it –

He heard the trumpets of the first watch. He opened his eyes and the polecat was sidling towards him out of the shadows in its draggled fitch, with a cup in its paws.

The wild man stank, much worse than any polecat. Something had screened off the smell before. Vusca basked in the new odour, of reality. One of the paw hands clutched his head, tilted his skull backward. The cup met Vusca's lip. "*Eat*," said the wild man.

Vusca *ate*. He gulped the wine, greedily, and in the liquid he felt the crystals pass over his throat, gritty, sandy, some larger and smoother, like tasteless pills of salt.

The wild man took the cup away, and peered into it. He was satisfied and made a smacking noise with his own lips.

Vusca became marvellously, swimmingly drunk. There was nothing to be afraid of. He had consumed the consuming one. Father Jupiter! What had he done – could this be the proper trick?

He went over to the bed and lay on it.

The wine had formed a glorious warmth inside him. His entire body seemed to be feeding from it. He felt a content, an assurance he had not experienced since childhood.

The polecat came and stooped over him, and laughed filthy breath into his face. Vusca relished it. He knew, as if the gods spoke in his ear, that he had been saved. He fumbled to find money for the hill-man. The hill-man had skulked away, was going without recompense. Barbarus would see to it. Someone … would see to it.

The lovely night, populated only by natural things, smelling of leather, horse-hide, flowers, gently closed the Roman's eyes.

He thought: *I forgot. The sword is over there.*

He thought: *I shan't need the sword.*

Then his mind was a river of amethyst light and he went down into it to drink it up and be filled.

"But so many gifts," she said. Her eyes were sparkling, she almost clapped her hands like a girl.

"I used to send you things."

"Yes, but that was –" Lavinia flushed and turned her head, shy of him.

She was beautiful tonight.

But then everything had a gloss and gleam upon it. Every dawn was a miracle. Dusk a blessing. Two weeks now since he had been cured. Until today he had been too cautious to be happy, with all the brightness of life summoning him. Today he had gone ten rounds, buckler and short sword, with his Secundo, in the yard. Vusca had the victory. But the Secundo, a man nine years his junior, was no faker.

And Vusca had made the offerings today. He even went down to the Greek Hercules on the forum, and gave him something. Strength for strength. The blood in him was like a young man's. Everything was better than it had been – his sight, his reach, his nerve, his brain. The accretions of the middle years were all washed off. He could begin again.

When she saw him, there in her house, she had blushed then, too. She had thought him fine. It was like the first look she ever gave him.

The orchards did not seem irremediable, overgrown and in need of pruning, but that could be done. She said she liked to be in the villa, now the summer was coming. It was really rather dreadfully run down. The window in the long atrium was broken and had been patched up with honey and wax. The heating did not work properly. There were swallows in the bath-house.

Somehow all that made it funnier, more likeable. The villa needed them. They could do things for it.

And to come out to her here, tonight, feeling as he did, free and young, that was well-omened.

When they had walked about a little, in the lavender afterglow, on which the fierce hills lay docile, like sleeping swans, they went in to the supper Lucia had set. It was a very familiar feast, the fried sausage and garlic, the basted chicken, black olives and sauce of mushrooms, the round white cheese with raisins, new bread, old purple wine from the home vineyard, and the dish of candied plums. He might have been here only a week ago, not years.

They talked about the villa and the farm. Later he went with her to the small shrine in the garden court. (The shape of the Christians' fish was gone from it.) After the offering, they sat under the colonnade, in the dark, and watched fireflies. It was what they had been used to do, in the days before their marriage. Now and then, a slave would go across the lawn on some errand. That had happened then. They had had to be furtive, then.

He began to want her, his wife, as he had wanted her long ago.

"Vinia," he said, "couldn't we ..." like the young fool he had been.

But this time there was no need to dissemble or to say no.

The cries of her joy were strangers to him. Whores never raised this paean, even in pretence. He gloried in what he could do to her, and in the vigour of his own body. His seed burst from him with an overwhelming pang. He had forgotten that, too, the edge a woman's love could give to it.

They coupled twice more in the night, like hungry wolves.

In the early morning, just before sunrise, her eyes seemed vivid, flower-like, more savage ... husband and wife parted like lovers.

Weeks after, he said to her, "Were your eyes always this colour?"

And she laughed at him.

It was high summer when she told him her news.

"The physician says I'll bear to term. The auspices are good. Nothing can go wrong."

He stood with her on the hill among the plum trees. Below the road went down to Par Dis, the cemetery, the walls.

"Isis will help me," she said.

The curve of her belly was barely visible. In there, the life was, the son perhaps he had made. His immortality.

The other thing ... was just a dream. (Now and then he had a slight pain, under his ribs, it was nothing, no worse than momentary indigestion. As the weeks went by, it lessened, never quite going away.)

As he rode back to the town, he kept thinking of her eyes. They had changed, as she had changed. But when he mentioned it, she told him that his eyes too had come to be another colour. And this amused them both. In the dull metal mirror he saw no alteration. Only sometimes, in the faces of men he knew well, a sudden uncertainty, a second glance –

She had a long labour, it was rough on her. But the child was flawless, and a boy.

His eyes, in the first hour he opened them, were the colour of the amethyst, might have been made from the amethyst.

Retullus Vusca, cold as death, held the life of his son in his arms. What should he do? And the impulse came to run to a high place, and there throw back this tiny breathing thing to the gods. But he only held the child, and Lavinia whispered, "You see now, he has his father's eyes."

It was the scar of a past battle. Let it be that. The cicatrice of a healed wound, that could no longer kill.

PART TWO

The Suicide

The prime retribution on the guilty
Is that no one can acquit himself of his own judgement.

Juvenal

Ten columns, dyed with Tyrian, marched down the cella of the temple, to the obsidian plinth, figured with shields. There stood the god: Mars Pater, in his armour, bearded and helmed, night-underlit by the votive lamp. The sprays of fig, oak and laurel from the spring festival were still aromatic and sappy. In his small house by the shrine, the elderly, tame wolf, sacred to the god, lay quietly, muzzle on long paws. He was a pet of the priests, more often than not his chain was off. He would eat from your hand, had forgotten he was ever a wolf at all.

The man who had entered, grizzled and muscular, perhaps in his fiftieth year, offered the wolf a titbit, watched him eat, nodded, and walked back into the central aisle before the statue.

The man carried a bundle, which he now unwrapped and put down on the altar. He bowed his head, and seemed to pray.

A priest came into the cella.

The man who prayed broke off, looked up; he appeared glad that the priest was an old man, someone he had known for years.

"Commander," said the old priest, then smiled. "I always forget."

"You forget, to please me," said the man. "A young puppy rules the Fort of Par Dis. I'm a retired pensioner of the Empire. I tend my farm. My business is goats and vines and fruit trees." He stopped, and said, "And the lies I tell myself."

The priest looked at the things which had been placed on the altar. There were three legionary javelins, three swords, some knives, the breast-plate of a cavalry skirmisher, service bracelets, bracelets for valour, the badge of command, a Medusa shield.

"The things that matter," the man said, "that the god values."

"The arms of the warrior," said the priest. "They should hang proudly in your house. Why?"

"Because my house is ruined. There's a disease – something due to me – do you remember, I told you once –?"

The priest's face closed like a fist. Not against the man, against the fate. "But that was finished."

"No. When the boy was born – I knew then. I *knew.*"

"You did nothing."

"Nothing. I should have killed him."

"You must speak to no one else in this fashion," said the priest. "There were only twenty at the Spring Rite. The priesthood outnumbers the worshippers now. These Christians have the town, as they have the Empire. The Christians are powerful, and understand nothing of this sort. Be careful, Vusca. I warn you as a friend."

"The time for carefulness is done. Don't you see why I came here, with the offering?"

The old priest reached out and took the hand of Retullus Vusca.

"Yes, Commander. Is that all you want? Isn't there some way in which –?"

"No, Flamen. No way but this."

"Then, it can be arranged for you." The priest touched the pattern of laurel on his breast, and let go the hand of the man, which was cold as winter marble. "Your family?"

"I have – left provision, all the correct documents. But my family's cursed, Flamen. I should have seen to it. I can't. It isn't in me. A weakness. I make this sacrifice to Mars in the hope that he –"

"Hush," said the priest, gently. "Only the god can decide that."

"The caterwauling of the Christos dulls all their ears," said Vusca.

"Hush," the priest said again. "Come now. There's the purification. They'll make ready for you."

"The room under the altar."

"Yes. Come now."

Lies and weakness. The deception of self. More than eighteen years of that, aided by them all.

The boy was handsome, his son. Everyone cherished him. He was his mother's. The women's. Vusca did not go too near. That much, at least, that distance … a sop to the truth. So his son grew up pampered by women, by Lavinia, and Lucia, and all the slaves. He liked the villa farm, had no hankering after a military career. At seven, Vusca had been dreaming night and day of the legions. But not Vusca's son. And Lavinia, so afraid: if he becomes a soldier he'll be sent far away. Sent away … something in that. Eighteen and a commission – it might be anywhere, now. It might be Rome. Vusca might send – *that* – to Rome. (Unnamed, unthought of, somewhere in his brain or heart, it stayed him.) Let the boy be a farmer, then. He was good with the land. That too was under the favour of Mars, and of Lavinia's Isis, if it came to that.

Vusca watched the boy grow up, as if from a nearby hill.

Petrus, they had called him. She had wanted the name. It had been the uncle's, popular among Christians. Vusca might have argued, but it did not seem to matter. He had no pride in this handsome son. He would say to himself that that was because Petrus did not take after him, would not be a soldier. That made it easy.

The boy of course knew his father did not really care for him. He seemed to accept it was for the logical reason, the reason of the army. Once he had apologised to Vusca, quietly, on his fourteenth birthday. Vusca had taken the boy to the Fort, shown it to him, since that would somehow be expected. There was no doubt Petrus showed an interest. And the men took to him, the way everyone did. A father might have been able to persuade such an interested and likeable son to a taste for the soldier's life. Vusca did not attempt it. And Petrus, feeling the lack, assuming it was his fault, his omission, said that he was sorry.

When others looked at Petrus, they saw the Roman virtues. He was a beauty, but not effeminate, not soft. He was modest, friendly, reserved without coolness, dignified but ready for a laugh. The farmer's life built his shoulders and legs, he could handle a five-horse chariot with skill before he was fifteen.

When others looked at Petrus, they saw all that.

When Vusca looked at him, he saw the peculiar eyes, which others found so attractive, grey-lilac, Lavinia's. And Vusca also saw an odd birthmark, the quarter ring of tiny dark blotches around his son's collar-bone. Isis' necklace of love – that was what Lavinia called it when he was a child, kissing the marks. Women who saw them always seemed fascinated. The villa slaves had said it was something holy. Even Drusus at the Fort, who had taught Petrus chariots, had been heard to say that the broken ring was the memory of a war-scar of some forebear, carried in the blood. When Vusca looked at the marks they turned him queasy.

He had never liked to touch his son. He found it difficult to pick him up as a child. Later, if their hands brushed over some dish at table, Vusca felt a surge of revulsion, to which he never gave its actual name, and which he refused to acknowledge.

Rome still stood, like a shadow. The power of the shadow took effect. Retullus Vusca quit his command at the ordained time and went to the villa to be another farmer.

He did his best with it, the portion left to him. He had got accustomed again, quite quickly, to disappointment, to sourness. There had been that shining space, less than a year, in the centre of his life. It died down like a fire and left him with the used-up charcoal, which crumbled and had no heat.

There were no other children. He did not sleep with Lavinia after the boy was born. Latterly he did not want women.

Then there was the day in the orchard.

It was the start of harvest, the fields full of men, and the pickers busy with the fruit. At noon, activity fell off. He sat polishing one of the swords by the trough, with the dog at his feet – and then the dog growled very low, and got up and went away, and his son came through the sunlight and the trees. It was curious that, the way the dog never took to Petrus. Vusca's dog, perhaps it had caught Vusca's allergy. Vusca thought of a recent incident with the horses hired by Petrus for the chariot, some trouble – then Petrus was in front of him. The sun was behind his head, giving him a sun god's halo, dampening down the shade of his eyes.

"Father –"

"Yes?" The false jovial voice came out pat, the tone which held Petrus firmly off.

"Father, can I speak to you?"

"Why not?"

His son – he was sixteen, a young man now – uninvited did not sit. He said, as if searching in a barrel for the words: "Mother's going to talk to you. She's been going on about it. A marriage."

Bored (and under the boredom the aversion rising in him like sickness). "Well, if you want," said Vusca.

"I don't, sir. I don't want to marry."

"You've heard the girl's ugly."

"No. I think she's supposed to be all right."

"Too old?"

"Only twelve."

"That's nothing then. She's young enough to train. Oh, I know who your mother has in mind. A decent family, with Roman blood. You might as well. Out here, choices are limited."

"I don't want to marry, sir."

"Wait," said Vusca. "What are you saying?"

"Never," said Petrus.

"Some vow?" Vusca scowled. He wanted to feel an ordinary emotion. It was coming, if he tried. Normal annoyance. A son who would not breed. "Or do you have the Greek ailment? You like your own gender best? You'll grow out of it. Have you never had a woman?"

Under this ballista strike, Petrus went very white. The pallor threw up the colour of the eyes. Suddenly they were brilliantly in evidence.

"Not – not what you said. And I've never had a woman, no. Father – I'm afraid to do that."

Vusca laughed. He looked away from the eyes, down the orchard. "Yes, you're not the first coward there. Believe me, it's not any punishment. You'll like it. Only virgins can be tiresome. You'd better get in some practice first. Go to the *She-Wolf.* The other places aren't worth –"

"*No,* Father. I don't mean any of that. I *can't.*"

Vusca was exacerbated, embarrassed. (Something in him said, Don't let him speak. Don't hear him out.)

"What about your friend Drusus? Hasn't he –"

"Father, I've never even – once, it started – and I couldn't – I knew if I did – something horrible – it was like falling out of my body, swallowing and choking –" Petrus was no longer rational. His voice was high and hysterical, like a girl's.

Vusca stood up. He pushed his son away from him.

"You spend too much time with your mother. Go to a harlot and tell *her* all this. Let her put you right."

He walked away and left Petrus by the trough.

What should I have done then? Heard it, and *known* it. I should have held him in my arms and told him, because I could have reasoned it, could have seen through the flimsy veil. I should have loved him like my son, that he was, and had the courage, with the enemy at our gate, to speak the truth and run him through. By the Light, he knew, he *knew*. Not knowing, and knowing it all. He only came to me for the answer. He would have made the sacrifice. *He was my son.*

Vusca knelt in the cell under the altar.

The purification was over. They were bringing him the wine, now. He needed the wine. He was so cold.

He could not weep, his whole life had taught him steel, not water.

The marriage came two years later. The same girl, fourteen by then. The family had waited, for Vusca's name was reckoned on. The girl brought a small house with her dowry. It was in the town, near the Baths of Mercurius, a poor area going generally to hovels. There seemed to be a reverse of the arrangement between Vusca and his wife: Petrus installed his bride in her town house, and kept to the farm. He only brought her there when for propriety he must.

She was a pretty girl, a blonde with dark Roman eyes, and all the Roman ways studiously ingrained in her. Though she was a Christian, she also worshipped the other gods at their festivals.

At first she seemed merely nervous. Eventually it was obvious she was unhappy. At some point, about a year after the wedding, she confided to Lavinia that Petrus had never slept with her. She was still a virgin. She thought it was her fault, that she smelled, or that he despised her barbarian blood. (Vusca only heard of all this later.) Lavinia reassured the girl, and took her to the Isis temple, where they procured some draught or other, an aphrodisiac.

Whatever the plan, it was carried out while the girl was still staying at the farm. She wanted Lavinia's approval and support, and perhaps to boast of success.

Vusca was off with a couple of the men, hunting. The woods to the north were full of boar that season, though they did not have any luck. They were away five days.

They returned one late afternoon, coming along the west road with the sun behind them. The villa looked as usual, the fields ripening, smoke going up from the bath-house. Then, getting closer, Vusca saw no one was out in the fields or the orchard, that the smoke was not from the bath-house vent, but from a burning strip on the slope beyond. He sent two men running to deal with that and rode fast for the villa.

The slaves and field-workers were clustered in the outer compound. They parted before him and could not seem to find any voices when he shouted at them. Then a mad screaming started in the house. It sounded like a woman in labour. The slaves made signs against evil.

Vusca ran into the building. His actions were horribly prepared. He was not amazed, or alarmed, there was only depression, a sense of futility and defeat.

Lavinia dashed into his arms. She said that in the night Petrus' wife had gone mad. She had begun to shriek, and done so intermittently ever since. She had also torn herself with her nails. They had had to tie her to her bed. Petrus, who had been with her, had vanished. A window was shattered and there were marks on the wall. Lavinia believed a murderer had got in and killed her son, carrying off the body. This was what had driven the girl insane. Far-fetched as it was, what other explanation could be possible? (She did not admit to the story of her son's sexual reticence, the aphrodisiac, until three days after.)

Vusca went to see the wife of Petrus.

Lucia watched over her, in apparent terror. The girl was trussed. Her body, partly bare, showed deep bleeding scratches, but her nails had never been long, these were more like the scoring of a bone pin. She screamed and tossed, then fell slack until another fit of screaming and tossing came over her. She had forgotten speech. The window had been covered now, for it seemed the sounds of pigeons flying by made her worse.

There was a faint odour in the room, something like poultry.

Vusca found that he had gone near the bed, and was staring into the eyes of his son's wife. They had a curious glaze on them. Then she screamed and screamed and her tongue poked out like a lizard's.

Retullus Vusca had the wine now, in the room under the altar of Mars Pater. He drank it slowly, longing for the warmth, which did not come.

He thought dimly of the time which followed his son's disappearance. Was it only now that it seemed to have such a preordained progression?

How they had searched, and not found. How the screams had flickered out in the shuttered room, and the girl who was Petrus' wife became silent and heavy and pliant like a piece of dough. The day when they knew she was with child. When he first saw the new colour of her eyes, like lotuses in a marsh.

How he heard of a demon in the woods. How a native man was killed and a native girl was raped by something among the trees. How *her* eyes looked, and *her* belly began to swell.

How Retullus Vusca began to go hunting, and when he went away in the twilight of the dawn, not after boar any longer, he saw the lotus eyes of Lavinia watching him from a window.

And when he slept in the woods, he saw the eyes in his sleep, all those eyes made from the amethyst, and waking and lifting his hunting knife he looked and saw the same eyes there, reflecting in the blade.

How he hunted over the hills, above the native hutments, in the woods, going always further and further from the town, the shadow of Rome, and reason.

He wondered if he would discover the polecat man from the hills, who had done this. He did not think he would. Barbarus had died years back of a stomach sickness. But Vusca too kept the small pain under his ribs, the scar of the battle he had not, after all, won –

The woman from the hutment gave birth before term, to a monster. Evidently they killed the baby, which was scaled. The mother died, or they helped her die. Then Petrus' wife started her labour.

As Vusca was in the atrium collecting his spears and knives for hunting, Lavinia entered. Her hair and robe were loose in the early morning. She smiled and said, "Don't go." She had not smiled since Petrus' "murder." Now she took Vusca's hand from the knife and put it on her breast. A flare of lust

went through him. For years he had not gone with any woman. Now he
engorged, and in her starving smiling purple eyes he saw the reason.

"Get away from me," he said. "It isn't you, you bitch, don't you know that
yet? How we are – what's in us, with our blood?"

She shook her head, she rubbed herself against him. He went past her, and
out of the villa. His dog, which had been running up to him, turned suddenly
back with a whine.

"*Good*, Remus," said Vusca. "Good dog, brave lion. Yes, that's right. Stay
away." And the dog wagged its tail, trembling.

Vusca leaned on the wall until nausea and darkness subsided.

Then he went towards the hill country.

He realised, almost too late, his error. Or perhaps the god – Mars the Warrior,
Mithras, Bringer of Light – perhaps the god told him.

He turned back, got on the road, and reached the town gate before sunset.

Only the whores of the west town now went to the Baths of Mercurius;
the deity was their patron, they had some claim. Behind, a plethora of huts
had gone up, among mud alleys where once a garden grew. There had been
some talk, in a wine-shop, some killings, orgiastic and bloody, the fanatic
work of some fresh sect … the women went out in pairs.

The house of Petrus' wife stood by a ruined shrine, and a great castanea
shaded the doorway, while it wormed roots like levers under the wall.

The decrepit slave who kept the door knew Vusca, and let him in. The
slave had forgotten, or else did not know, asking after the young master and
his wife. Vusca grunted some falsehood. He inquired if the house stayed
quiet. The slave said it did, but he was deaf and almost blind. The other slaves
had been taken over to the villa or reclaimed by the girl's family.

The ancient slave brought candles, and bread and wine for Vusca's repast,
then crept off to his quarters on the upper floor.

Vusca ate, and inspected his hunting weapons. Then he doused the
light.

Even here, over the quiet night, he could make out the trumpets from the
Fort. He had not heard them for a long while. *Gates*, and the first and second
watches. Then there was some clatter from a nearby brothel that cut other
sounds off from him. He resented that. He visualised the drunken party, the
men topped up with lechery and the whores loud with beer, the bad
musicians, all the stuff of a paltry world that he had looked down on and
which now he nearly envied.

The party guttered and went still at last. An owl cried over the roofs of the
town. The dining room, where the slave had taken him, looked on the garden
court (weeds and a cracked urn) and he saw the stars, and the opposite roof

over the colonnade and vaguely the stars darkened and the tiled roofs, the pillars, the urn, came clear. An hour to *cockcrow*, dawn. And something was moving on the tiles there, *something* –

Vusca sat in his shadow like stone. What was on the roof? He thought of the owl, the wide wings, a dart of a head – then it was gone.

In the stillness, sharp as a needle, Vusca heard the noise of something inside an upper room across the court.

It was not the slave. The slave slept at the other end of the house. It did not sound like the slave, either. It lightly shuffled, and hopped.

Vusca gripped one of the spears. The knife was in his right hand.

He went to the place where the stair was, and climbed up sightless, silent, to the second storey. He heard the noise again at once, behind a door, a bird's noise, scuttering and pecking about.

He felt nothing now. His heart raged, but he was numb, as if from poison.

He opened the door, and pushed it, and went through.

It was a room without furnishing, save for some old sacks. A window showed grey sky, and the other way in.

Under the window something was feeding. It glanced up, and a coil of black tissue trailed from its mouth back to the torn-out human heart that lay before it. The mouth was not a mouth, but the beak of a gigantic bird. The eyes shone, two mauve stars came in with it at the window.

Vusca knew it. He knew it for the demon on the amulet, and also he knew it for his only son. Then he plunged forward, kicked it down, crashed upon it, and drove the knife through its left eye into the mindless brain beneath.

The hands and arms held him in a desperate embrace as it died. It was the only time Vusca had been held in the arms of his son. When they let go, the creature was stretched under him, the beak open and the remaining eye glaring.

Vusca stood up. He felt neither triumph nor grief, only an awful freezing coldness. For a time he stayed there, aimless, and the sun started to come and *cockcrow* sounded miles away. The dreadful thing, the worse thing was, he did not know what to do.

It was broad day when he thought of something. He could detect the slave creeping about below by then, and sparrows twittered in the garden court.

Vusca rolled the body of Petrus into a corner, among the sacks. Then he struck fire, and gave the room to it.

When he was sure the flames had hold, he went down and collected the slave, explaining to him that the house was burning. The slave sobbed as they went into the street. Soon a crowd collected, and watchmen came running to tackle the blaze. Vusca got away easily in the confusion. Probably they would save most of the house, but not the upper room. Petrus had had his funeral pyre. He had even had tears, though they were the tears of a slave, and shed in ignorance.

He did not go back to the villa. He sent a man, discovered in a tavern, a former legionary who had served under him, and was known to Lavinia, to fetch the shield and breast-plate and swords. The man was an habitual drunkard, but could be trusted in the morning, if offered money. That was what the *Auxilia*, the legions, had become. He told the man to ask after his son's wife.

When the fellow returned he had had a drink or two, but carried all the gear in an untidy bundle. He grumbled, not bothering as to why it was wanted, said he had had nuisance with Vusca's slaves who seemed to think thievery was afoot. There had been another murder, in the native slum over the river – the heart of the victim was missing. And there had been a fire at Vusca's son's house on the west side, did Vusca know? Vusca said he had heard.

"And my daughter-in-law?"

"Ah that," said the soldier, "*two* of 'em. A fine boy, and a little girl. Now maybe you think that calls for a cup of wine?"

Vusca paid him and gave him his wine, and left him in the tavern.

Vusca went out carrying his nondescript bundle, wrapped in the old army cloak.

He had prayed she would die, and the progeny would die too.

Now he should go to the villa after all, go with the knife, see to it. Simple, to kill a child with amethyst eyes. But he knew he could not.

He sat on a stone bench in the street, near to a baker's. All the town passed him, the carters and loafers, the powdered girls with their attendants, a Christian priest, a sweating bricklayer who asked him to move his feet and said, when he did, "Thanks, dad."

Vusca sat all day on the bench. No one knew him. He was some old worn-out dad to this town where he had lived his manhood and commanded the Fort and walked the arrogance of Rome into the streets.

When it was dark, the whores began to call from their lamplit doors.

He shouldered his life and his soul, and went to the temple of Mars.

He had finished the priests' wine.

Only death could warm him now.

Retullus Vusca, purified for the act by an elder priesthood, took up the sword. He drove it in through the abdomen, upward, leaning into the agony to meet the point, until it bit into his heart. Then he rested. The stroke had been exact. He need do nothing more. He was not afraid. He did not mind the pain, which was already flowing out from him. A tender warmth blossomed where the pain had been, on the blade in his heart.

It was then he discovered the final task still to do. By the miracle of the sword cut, a warning had been left to him, under his hand, to give – somehow he must achieve it.

The Roman crawled over his blood to the spot where the Medusa shield leaned on the wall. Through the nothingness of death, he struggled to see and feel her wounded face.

He prayed for an impossible strength. The god heard him.

As he fell back on the floor of the cell, Vusca dragged the shield with him. It covered him against the cold and dark. He could sleep now.

THE GREEN BOOK

eyes like emerald

PART SIX

The Madman

My apprehensions come in crowds;
I dread the rustling of the grass;
The very shadows of the clouds
Have power to shake me as they pass.

Wordsworth

Because it was obvious he was mad, the crowds in the market made way for him. Only when he seemed likely to prove difficult did they shove at him, though once or twice urchins, and others nearly as or more unfortunate than he, pelted him with clods of dung and small sharp pebbles off the ground. Formerly, he might have been well-dressed, fashionably got up. Now the doublet was unlaced, half the points ripped out, the shirt filthy and torn, and he had lost a shoe. His hair was matted. Some said he had been come on sleeping or swooned among the pig-pens, like a regular prodigal. Even those that attacked him were wary, however, for he was young, and strong in his body. He might have been handsome, but for the affliction, and a curious film across his dark eyes.

Near the area where the pig market gave on the Dyers Street, a commotion ensued. A bird-seller was coming down with his wares in their cages strapped on all over him, and met the madman with twenty paces between them. Instantly every bird in its cage went wild, fluttering and cheeping, dashing itself on the wicker bars. The bird-seller tried vainly to quiet his charges. Seeing the madman, too, he nervously pressed back and invited him to pass. The lunatic, though, appeared smitten with weird fright. He fell against a wall, and beat his fists on his head. Then, with a shout, he ran straight at the bird-seller and felled him. The man went down hard at the impact and some of his cages were splintered and the panic-struck birds sprayed up into the sky. The madman meanwhile ran roaring up Dyers Street, where a few came out and pursued him, thinking he was a robber making off with something.

He was lost again in the alleys on the west side of the markets.

Raoulin, said a voice in his head, *you must go at once to the university.*

No, he answered. *No.*

339

In the courtyard of the Sachrist, the grave tutor led them in a discussion in the Platonic mode, but a girl stood under the colonnade, with a skull in her hands. Blood dripped from her skirt. The master indicated her. "Here we view the progress of corruption." And her flesh slid from her bones. Only a skeleton at last, holding in its latticed hands the second skull.

The madman sprang up from his bed of refuse under the ruined wall, and ran away.

Images hunted him through the alleys of Paradys like dogs. He would race until he went down, and then they were on him.

Even as he ran, he heard their belling behind him.

Raoulin, said the voice. *Raoulin*.

Yes, he said. But he did not know who Raoulin was.

Find a priest, said the voice.

He had sinned, and would die unshrived.

For some priests had already passed him, going up to the cliff of the colossal Church. They told their beads and murmured as they walked, unaware of anything beyond them in the world. Only one, younger than the rest, glimpsing the madman, quickly crossed himself and looked away.

What could he say to a priest?

I, a poor sinner … I lay with the dead. My fault, my great fault.

In the night, he travelled aimlessly, an escaped beast that takes the City for the jungle, and so cannot comprehend it. Down along the quays he rambled. The rats watched him as he drank from the dirty river. Under the water he saw a corpse go by, her hands clasped at her bosom, her hair brushing his drinking lips.

Near where some ships were moored with swags of sails across their broad arms, a fire was alight on the stones. Men sat dicing and he slunk closer, attracted to some forgotten code of fellowship.

Presently the men were aware of a presence.

"Something's out there."

"A dog. Can smell our dinner broiling." (This could have been true, for Raoulin had noticed that meat and spices cooked over the fire in a pot.)

"Doesn't the scripture say, as you do even to the least of my brothers?" asked another man, and digging in the pot with his knife, he took out a bit of meat, and threw it away into the dark where Raoulin was.

The other men cursed him. The benefactor cursed them louder.

Raoulin gnawed the meat down to the bone. But when he reached that bone, his gorge rose, he flung the bone from him and ran away from it, into the jungle tangle of the night.

In the hour before the summer dawn, two women went by the broken shed he had found to lie in, sweating and tossing and dozing, and they heard his sounds, and glanced as they crossed the doorless door. They were two harlots from the quays, who plied there dusk to dusk.

"Well," said the taller girl, "there's one won't be wanting our comfort."

And they laughed in the way of women who have nothing on earth to find amusing, and can therefore be amused by anything.

When they were gone up the shadowy path, Raoulin shuffled to the shed's opening. He had an idea, a want, to go after. No sooner did he feel this, and act on it, than his mind was wonderfully swept clean. No images or thoughts or voices started up to appal him. With a blissful singleness of purpose, he climbed behind the two women.

In a brief while he saw them before him again, outlined in the black by some vagary of night-sight that had come to him.

They did not converse, and walked sluggishly, doggedly. Then one hesitated, and turned to look back with a gleam of her pale face.

"Something is behind us." The tone was not amusement but dread, now.

"Oh you and your night fancies. Three years you've worked the bank with me, and you still see ghosts."

"I saw its eyes. Green, like a cat's. But up in the air."

The other turned then. She stared at Raoulin, and did not apparently make him out at all.

"There's nothing. If there was, they'll want the same as the others. Charge twice for a ghost."

They went on, and Raoulin continued after them, though hanging back rather more. Instead of the roiling abyss within him, now he knew a dim excitement. It was not hunger or thirst, nor lust, yet it was something, a need that was undeniable, though nameless.

In an impoverished street whose tops bowed together, the harlots parted. The scared girl flitted away under an arch. The other pushed open a door and went into the night hole beyond.

There was no bolt or lock to the door. It was simple to steal upon it, to peer in at the crack.

The girl had lit a candle, which made a huge light in the nothingness. Raoulin saw her like a cameo, white on umber. There was another, too. A man unbeautifully asleep on a pallet, who at the light sat up and snarled, "Is that you? What have you got?"

The harlot took out a few coins from her sleeve and let them fall into his hand.

"Is this all? You're not keeping anything back, slut-face? I'll –"

"I know what you do if I try to cheat you. And it's harder, my work, with bruises."

"Well and good. Now take a penny and go out and get me a pot of ale."

"Sweet Jesus. At this hour? It's almost morning and haven't I been out all night –"

The man rose up and slapped her glancingly across the head.

"Stop your nagging. Do as you're bid."

The girl palmed the penny and came suddenly back to the door.

No one was there as she stepped outside, but as she began her trudge towards the tavern, something did appear, like a greater shadow thrown up at her back, with, near the apex, two narrow green incandescences.

Eastward, over the heights and scoops of the City, the sky was draining of its black. The creatures of Hell, which preferred darkness, would be seeping down into the ground.

Years ago, when she was only a brat of five, there had been atrocities committed in the dark. Her own mother, a whore before her, had sat whispering over the cooking fire with her cronies, all telling each other of the woman by the fish market who had had all her parts torn out. And the body was burned, for they said a devil had done it and evil's infection might be there on the rags of the corpse. That thing, certainly, had toiled by night at its ripping, as she and her sisterhood toiled against posts, trees, and walls, or flat in some leaky boat under the wharf.

These were the thoughts in the trudging girl's head. She put them aside briskly and promised herself a swig of the stink-pig's ale.

As she was turning aside into Goat's Alley, the harlot realised that a man was behind her. She could smell him, and feel his heat, and next moment he caught her round the body.

"Hey, hey," said the girl, who was used to rough embraces, and she turned herself to look.

Her first impression frightened her, for the alley was still all of the night, and what she seemed to find had hold of her was a black shape, maned, and with teeth drawn, luminous-eyed, uncanny.

But she sloughed the notion, and stared, and saw instead the sick beggar from the shed-shelter.

He was shaking with a fever, hot with fires, and his eyes, if they were not demoniac, had a rabid glare she knew to be careful of.

"Now what can you be wanting, sieur?"

His teeth glittered as he panted. He seemed to try to force her to the wall.

"Not now," she said, "my old man's waiting. And you're not fit for it."

To Raoulin her voice was barely audible, and she herself seemed a great way off down a tunnel of mists and lights. It seemed he must have her, carnally. His loins had readied themselves, and so after all this had been the want which drove him to hunt her down. And yet, the want was not solely lust, as he had known it was not, in its parched starvation, a hunger or thirst. His entire body strained towards a sort of stretching and yawning, and the picture in his mind now was of a snake yawning off over its head its entire skin.

But the girl resisted, playful and determined.

She seemed scared now, too, like the other one.

"If I call," she said, "Jenot will hear me at the inn. He's a big man. He'll come and see to you. Now leave off."

She thrust at him and Raoulin slammed her into the wall. At that she did scream, and the cry brimmed through his brain. He saw himself, as if from the air above. He saw himself – and another.

A corpse-light was over him. It was in his eyes. It altered him. This one could throw the girl back and rape her. At the crisis, the stem of flame would mount through him, as he had seemed to feel it before, from phallus to sacrum, through the vertebrae, into the skull. And then –

And then the demon which possessed him, which he had conceived at his union with the dead girl – the demon would yawn off his skin and make him, as it had made Heros d'Uscaret, into the mindless, feeding unlife which was *itself*.

Raoulin, by an effort of flesh and will, wrenched himself from the terrified whore. He seemed, as he did so, torn apart. Nausea boiled in his guts, he went blind with pain and illness, and staggering away, left her. She ceased yelling at once, and let him go. No man came rushing to her aid, either. The alley was empty. And the next. Not that he saw.

He tried to pray to God. No words would come. He had mislaid all the orisons, all the entreaties.

But what he had almost done, to her, to himself –

It came to him he had been hearing her thoughts, those memories that concurred with Helise's tale, and that might be the prelude to the latest tale, the rebirth of the demon.

In the nightmare he had no compass points. There was nowhere he might return, no sanctuary to be had. Friends, family, the swamps of raptures, the pinnacles of debate and learning – nowhere could he perceive salvation.

And he recalled how an elderly stern sour priest had warned him of the loose women of Paradys, of some dire disease he might catch. But he had caught the contagion of the Devil.

The sky was bright now, over his left shoulder, where Satan stood in the stories.

Then the last alley broke into a slender street that passed under some tall houses. One had a vine growing up its timbers. He gazed at it, as if at a creeper from Atlantis. Then his legs gave way. He fell in the street. He lay there, and heard the world start to be industrious all about, the notes of brooms and pans, a donkey's complaint, a young girl singing. The Prima Hora was sounding from a score of churches.

Raoulin scrabbled in his belt, obscenely, as he would have brought forth the blade of procreation and death. This blade was better. Strange he had not recollected, until now, the break of day, his knife.

As he found the place between his ribs, and poised the steel there, an insane whirling and denying dashed through his blood. Suicide was the ultimate sin. (Did he think God would ever forgive him? Through the endless centuries until Doomsday, Heros had said, He would not.)

"It's you," said Raoulin, "foul thing, tempter. You can't dissuade me."

Raoulin did not credit God, besides. The Devil had won. But in this one game he should not.

Raoulin jammed the knife between two ribs, for the heart.

The pain was incredible. Bile and blood came into his mouth. He wept, and pushed the blade in further.

His heart seemed to break, like a pane of glass.

A woman was coming down the street with a pitcher, for some well. She was like an apparition. He saw her halting to consider him.

Before he saw what she would do next, night dropped back on him. Down into Hell he rolled head over heels.

PART SEVEN

The Demon

So runs my dream: but what am I?
An infant crying in the night:
An infant crying for the light:
And with no language but a cry.

Tennyson

They were respectful to her, in the City streets, when they saw her now and
then going to and fro with her nurse or her maid. They said, she had been
educated like a boy, could read many languages, was fluent in Latin, had
knowledge of music and ritual dance old as time … which was charming, and
of alchemy … which was unsuitable. They did not suggest she was a sorceress, as they never plainly referred to her father as a magician. But they did
call her, in general parlance, the Beautiful Jewess.

She had risen very early, and gone to pluck herbs in the house's inner
courtyard; these seen to, she sat reading a treatise of Galen's, there in her
bedroom which caught the morning sun. Her black hair hung about her like
clusters of black grapes, and covered only by a little black velvet cap. The
striped cat, now a matron of the establishment, lay playing with a sunbeam
on the bed. Even the doll remained, seated in a corner on a wooden chest, a
toy no longer, but venerable.

There came a noise from the street. The Beautiful Jewess raised her head,
and the cat paused, open-mouthed.

The noise was not especially usual. It seemed to be that of a dropped pot,
which shattered.

The very next instant, someone knocked on the street door.

Ruquel's window looked east, into the court. Even the sound had reached
her by a sideways trick, vision was not possible.

Yet something caused her to get up, touching the cat upon the forehead as
she went by (rather as the *mezuzah* was touched at the doorway) and out of
the room and down the stair.

In the hall below, Liva the porter had already unfastened the door. He was

345

almost seven feet tall, mild as a lamb, but evidently capable of killing with his bare hands. He had come to the household several years since.

The nurse was also at the door, and outside a throng of women and a few men had gathered. There had been exclamations. Now a silence. Into this, Ruquel descended.

The nurse, seeing her, made a motion she should not approach.

"Why not? What is it?"

The nurse put her hand over her own eyes. Though she was protective, she knew Ruquel had not been trained to docility, or ignorance. "An awful sight. A young man has slain himself at our door."

Ruquel stopped a moment, very pale and straight, then she came down the last of the stair and crossed the hall. Liva too gave way to her in the door.

He lay, the suicide, with no doubt across the very threshold, as if the angel of death, in a passover, had thrown him there. His black hair streamed on the cobbles, his face had been calmed by the darkness of his sleep, all but the eyes. Closed, they had about them a strange tension, as if he had been weeping. One seemly thread of blood ran from the corner of his mouth. His hand rested quite gracefully and couthly on the hilt of the knife, which otherwise was sunk into his breast.

Ruquel regarded him. The watchers observed the Beautiful Jewess went whiter than her own whiteness. Then she knelt down, and put her fingers to the temple, the throat, of the cadaver. Then she set her hand in the air over his lips, and brought it away.

After a minute, she lifted her long-lashed eyes and announced: "Liva, you must bring him into my father's house. He isn't dead."

Someone in the street protested. Ruquel did not take notice, but as Liva was leaning forward, Ruquel touched his arm, and said quietly, "Take care as I did to have no contact with the blood." Without a question Liva nodded. He leaned and gripped his burden, the weight of a full-grown man, like that of a child.

Ruquel rose. "You know that my father has tutored me," she said to the street. "The muscle in the young man's chest is very hard, and he, it seems, very weak. He could not complete the blow."

When the door was shut, the nurse said, "If he lives, they'll say your father, or you, raised him from the dead."

"So be it," said Ruquel, with an abstracted smile.

Haninuh, when he returned from an excursion into the City that twilight, was met by his daughter at the door. Though the house was always well lit, it was the hour of lamp-lighting, and Ruquel presented to her father a poetic oriental image as she stood before him, limned by the ivory candle-lamp she bore, in her silver earrings and little velvet cap, and barefoot as about the house she always was. The striped feline sounded its timbrels at her side.

"Welcome, my father."

The rite of homecoming was performed swiftly but warmly.

"You have a guest," she said then. "We housed him in the Cedar Chamber."

"Oh, does he have a liking for trees?" (The chamber was painted over one wall to the ceiling with a cedar tree; some guests had declared they heard all the owls and doves of Lebanon mewing in its branches.)

"He likes nothing, being nearly dead."

Haninuh frowned. "He's a man of the City?" This was a Jew who never spoke of "gentiles."

"I have not seen him before. If my father has seen him, how can I say."

But she revealed, as they climbed the stair, the morning's astonishment, passing on to the afternoon's labour. In an interpolation, she stressed the care she had felt prompted to take with regard to bodily fluids, the protections she had formed. She was very skilled herself in medicines, for the Jew himself had taught her, and in other elements more mysterious.

"Will he live?" asked Haninuh therefore, in the corridor.

"It's for my father to say. I trust he will." Ruquel turned her candle from a draught, and her face was veiled in shadow. "But, he longs to die."

"Why so, I wonder? You name him a young man, and sound but for the wound."

They reached the door of the Cedar Chamber. Inside, a lovely lamp of Eastern filigree hung from a stand and dusted the air with frankincense. The great tree spread over the plaster, and the nurse kept watch in its shade. In his bed, bathed and made clean, the suicide lay on his pillows, like a saint of wax.

The Jew went to a basin and washed his hands. He spoke inaudible words. Then he proceeded to examine the unconscious man thoroughly. At length, he straightened up and replaced the covers.

"He gives little enough sign of life. But life persists. Rarely have I seen such a wound seal itself so rapidly. I know your cleverness as a doctor, Ruquel, but from what you tell me, this is not so much your wisdom as some connivance in the flesh. Spirit and body are at odds."

Later, when they took their supper together, the father questioned the daughter over again, and they discussed their visitor broodingly.

"How is it, finding him thus, you thought he might survive?"

"I hoped for it," said Ruquel simply. "At first I could find no tremor of the heart. But at my touch it came as if to meet me. And then seemed to grow stronger."

"I cannot think he and I have been familiar with each other," said the Jew, "yet there's about him something I know or imperfectly remember. Well. Until he wakes, speculation bears no fruit. Before you sleep," he added, "if you're willing, go to the room and make music on your harp."

"Your will is mine," she said.

"And am I to think," he said, "you do it only to please me?"

The harp which Ruquel brought to the Cedar Chamber was a model of the little *kinnor*, a crescent of bow-horn which she leaned to her shoulder, from which crescent ten horsehair strings stretched to a horizontal bar of ereb willow. Beneath, the unstretched tails of the strings provided a fringe that, occasionally, the striped cat was wont to bite.

The nurse nodded in her chair. Liva was soon due to take his watch.

Ruquel sat where she could see the mosaic of the filigree lamp upon the sick man's face.

She plucked chords of a twanging fluidity from the harp, and, as the music found its way, sang very low a melody without words, old as the Jordan, perhaps.

She had serenaded him for less than three minutes when a sigh, more a convulsion, rushed in and out of him. His eyelids fluttered and one arm sought from the covers. (The nurse slept on.)

Ruquel did not stop her music, but now her eyes were fixed only on him.

The wordless song flowed and twined among the reedy pangs of the harp.

Another three or four minutes elapsed.

Abruptly, with no further prologue, the eyes of the young man opened wide.

Ruquel ceased playing and singing.

She was intensely unnerved, as if fire had been thrust into her face.

She had known that his eyes would be dark as her own. But the eyes looked at her now. Focused on her with feral acuity. They were brilliantly, violently and unhumanly green. Emeralds set in optic sockets.

Mastering herself, Ruquel said, "Sieur, you're with friends. Lie quietly. I shall fetch my father."

But the young man said, "It hears the music. It knows your song."

"Who?" said Ruquel, holding back her terror with a rein of steel.

Then he sagged into the pillows, and he only said, "My God, my God. Didn't I die? It's all to do over. If you're kind, fetch your father, someone, to brain me with a mace. Then burn – then burn the body."

Raoulin slept the slumber of opiates. In that deep sea, he lost himself, and coming back to shore learned a month of days had been sunk there too. He did not protest. In sleep he had been incapable of harming another, or of facilitating – *that*, which was now his constant companion, the unborn child of death and destruction caged in the male womb of his loins.

Somewhere in the sleep there had been dreams. He recalled none of them, and was glad of that. Sometimes, also, he believed Haninuh the Jew had questioned him, and he had answered. And perhaps *it*, too, had done so. And he seemed to have heard the soft jangle of the *kinnor*, then, across dark reedy waters under a lion moon.

There came an evening, when Raoulin had returned from the places of drugged sleep, and he was shown his body, a little emaciated, but with the wound healed to a plaited line. If he should move suddenly, then the muscle quirked and pained him, that was all.

The strong man came and lifted him, and the woman washed him and he was fed. There were some days of that, and some nights of shallow dozing, for sleep had been too long with him and now proved elusive.

He was afraid they would let the beautiful daughter in to tend on him. He was afraid of what the demon would make him do. And of the aftermath.

But the daughter did not come near him now.

There began to be days of letting him out to walk in a small enclosed court with fruit trees in pots, and herbs and flowers and a little sunken well. One day, as he marched aimlessly about there, to toughen himself – because they had said he must – he beheld a striped cat, which arched its back and hissed at him, then jumped up a series of perches to a window above, where it vanished. This furred angel was *her* messenger, he thought, the room must be that of Ruquel. And he longed to see her there, for an instant, for she was safe enough at that distance from him, he was not vital enough as yet to go after her. She had been very beautiful, very gentle.

He must not try to reason where her room lay inside the house. In any case, there was the giant, thank God, to protect her. And the Jew ... surely the Jew was a magician.

As he patrolled the courtyard, Raoulin kept thinking of Ruquel, as of something precious he could never hope to see or touch, some prize once within his grasp, and now lost for ever, like the hope of Heaven. And added to this forfeiture there came to be the remembrance of his family, his friends, the university, the City, time, youth, and the world.

Then he sat down on the plot of grass beside the well, and he cried, and he was so weak his body was rocked and racked with it, this grief. But all the while, even as he wept these scalding tears, he sensed the other, waiting, *waiting there*, within him, for the hour he would belong to it and exist only to achieve its will.

"Sieur, you've been my saviour. I thank you for my life. But I don't see why you let me keep it. For I believe you know why I shouldn't be let live."

These were the first conscious sentences he rendered the Jew.

They met in a parlour above the hall, about lamp-lighting, and the scent of flowers came in from the house vine, and olibanum from the antique lamp. There were a great many books, and some scrolls and ornate cases of leather. The two men sat facing each other over a table where there was wine to drink neither had touched.

"In honesty, Raoulin, I do know, for you spoke of it asleep, and I took the liberty to interrogate you."

"And that – *it* – did it answer you also?"

"Not in words. It has no use for those. But it was aware, I think, in its primordial way, of our dialogue. Consider, it has no intelligence, only an instinct and an appetite. Even so, it may employ such knowledge as you yourself possess, to gain its ends. This is a power of desire more pliant and enduring than any of the desires of a man. It is a demon."

"A demon. Yes."

"I know its race, even. Out of Assyria, an *utuk*, having as its own form the body of a man, the head of a bird, but a bird of the beginnings, scaled not feathered, from the fifth day of the earth."

Raoulin shuddered.

"Did I tell you all *her* story, too?"

"I have pieced it together. All your story and all the story of Helise d'Uscaret, who died and left her body for the demon to inhabit. For the matter of that, I sent Liva as a spy to the d'Uscaret mansion. He says the old kitchen woman and the groom go on about their doings as if nothing's amiss. I conjecture that what you left upon that bed crumbled entirely, even to the bones. If they think anything, there, perhaps it's that you and she have gone off together, in the way of heedless lovers."

Raoulin said, "That must come. Where else can I go but after her, into the grave and down to perdition."

The Jew replied, "God made all things. Even the creatures of his servant, the Devil. We are instructed to note the lesson their existence teaches. He never says we must offer them our throats."

"Do you suppose I might prevent it – by abstaining? Heros made himself a priest, but the Devil won. My blood's hotter than the blood of Heros. And when it works in me like yeast –"

"There now," said the Jew. And he poured out the crystal wine, and gave it to Raoulin, as if it were medicine. "This is a clever enemy. It adapts itself as any beast will do. The ways of it are various. It can erupt inward, changing the victim to the semblance of itself, thereafter enacting by that body all it wishes. Or it passes into the body of a woman at intercourse, and her child, when it comes forth, will be the shell of the demon. It can do both, or either.

It can lie down dormant too, even as with Helise, where it waited inside the womb, that terrible ambush ten years old. Only the key is constant, the procreative spasm. All the pure line of d'Uscaret were susceptible to it, but it can casually infect anywhere. Now that whole house has perished, only you are left to it. How can it let you die? It resisted the death of Helise until its transference was accomplished. The stabbing you gave yourself was sewn up in a day. I partly believe you might burn yourself alive, Raoulin, and this creature would find some means to build you up again. Death's no answer." The Jew sipped his wine. "Neither abstinence from the carnal act. The *utuk* provokes and seduces others to provoke. As you say, you're not proof against it."

The dark was in the windows now. Hesperus rang from a nearby convent. The nights were lengthening and drawing near.

"How can there be any escape?"

Haninuh looked at him steadily.

"You will have decided, perhaps, I'm versed in certain arts."

"A magician."

"If you will call it so."

"Then – can you cast this out of me?"

"Once before," said Haninuh, "it came, this thing, to mock me. I was unready then, knowing not enough. But after that failure, I studied in the school of demons, gathered together books, and artifacts from the Roman time here, when this began. Strange to say, I felt that the *utuk* would return to duel again with me. We're ancient foes. Its primal memory and mine contain rank seeds of all those battles. The cities of the desert, the chariots, and the chains. Yes, I suppose I can cast it out of you."

Raoulin started up. The Jew stayed him.

"This isn't without great danger."

"I'm ready to die," said Raoulin. "You know as much."

"Also you must give yourself into my charge. What must be done is in itself unholy. There will be for you shame, rank sweetness, confusion, and agony. You may die indeed, you may lose your mind for ever. But this I do promise, *not* your soul."

Raoulin stood before him, white-faced, arrogant with fear and courage. In the dusky lamplight, his eyes were only black.

"Sieur magus, do what you must. I'm your slave. When will it be?"

"In seven days, that is the new moon, God's remaking. Then."

The Beautiful Jewess, eighteen years of age, sat playing with her cat on the floor of the bedroom. The cat's play was more sedate than it had been, still adept.

Haninuh, having been admitted, stood gazing at them.

He saw the child clearly, as the kitten was still visible in the cat. But both were mature, and changed. Ruquel was a woman. He must acknowledge that.

Presently she looked up, and her smile faded into a serene strictness. It was his own habitual look, given back to him like a mirror.

"I've read the book, as you instructed, my father."

"That's good."

"You've spoken to the young man?" He was touched at her way of referring to Raoulin, as if she were by far the elder. In some ways she was. Raoulin had not been wise, but he had, in the end, striven to be virtuous, prepared to sacrifice himself for the sins of other men.

"We've spoken. It shall be done."

"And I?" she said. He was thankful for her quickness.

"As it's set down in the book."

She lowered her eyes. Her face shadowed with the self-consciousness of the girl she was. Then the woman governed the girl, she looked up again and said, "Yes, I'm willing. And I have the skills."

"I know what's asked of you," he said. "Such a dance, though part of your secret training as in the days of Salomé, is a hidden thing. If you refused, I should have had to find some other, a paid dancer, and perhaps she doesn't exist in this City. Those that tutored you know of none."

"Besides, the paid one could command no magic."

He had always allowed her that word, though it was not exactly accurate; it seemed to step appealingly from her tongue. She had from the first recognised she must be careful of its use with strangers.

"That's true, she could not. But let me say this, too. I'd never have petitioned you, my own daughter, except" — he hesitated, wanting to spare her, yet sure that there must be no lies, — "except, Ruquel, that I noticed at once you love this man, love him as your bridegroom, and your husband."

She waited, and then she said, "You'll think me foolish. It happened the moment I saw him there. Perhaps even before, hearing the jar break on the street. He was at my door."

"How should I think you foolish, Ruquel? You are a sybil. Your awareness has always been profound, even as a child. This love you have recognised, but not invented."

"I honour you. I'd do nothing against my father's wishes."

"I know. It is your father instead requests of you a dishonourable task, which only your love for Raoulin can redeem. You understand, despite everything, he may die?"

"Yes."

"You understand, though I can protect you by the powers I command, in this arena nothing is certain? We are bound to it by our gifts and his plight. There's peril for all."

"Yes."

"You understand, my daughter, you are my star?"

"Yes," she said, smiling again, "I understand."

Raoulin fasted on honey and curds and water, then on water only. The irritating hunger dissipated to a comfortable lack of all thought of food. Then he was cleansed with a potent cathartic herb. On the sixth day, the water was brought in a water-like goblet of glass. There was a drug mixed in it. His senses became abnormally clarified. His body was light, nearly weightless. He could smell the scent of flowering things and decaying things from streets away. He felt he could have reached up and clasped the vault of the sky.

That night, he supposed he would not be able to sleep at all, for everything had become so fascinating and had such nuances, even the creak of the mattress under him. But sleep discovered him and took him away up among the stars. He saw the City far below, he saw *stars* beneath him. When he woke at sunrise, he believed his soul had flown close to Heaven, and God had not flung him down.

Late in the seventh day, the woman brought him a bittersweet resinous drink. When he had consumed it, every doubt or fear he had had abandoned him. It was like strong wine, but without wine's blurring or analgesic properties, without wine's stupidity.

When Liva entered and asked that Raoulin go with him, Raoulin got up and did so, in a wild, still peace that was better than hope.

Nevertheless, Raoulin did not seem to take in the route they went by. Perhaps it only appeared irrelevant at that intrinsic moment.

Liva had brought him to a heavy double door of black wood, not ebony, something more essential, some tree that had altered into coal.

In the door were two handles of cold translucent onyx.

Liva had gone away. Raoulin gripped the door handles and turned them, one to the left and one to the right, or rather they seemed to turn themselves this way at the pressure of his hands.

Within, was midnight, without a star. But the Jew had already impressed upon him that he would come to the chamber and must go in. In he walked, and thrust the doors shut at his back.

Then there was nothing. Only the void.

There was only formlessness and darkness, but then the moon and the sun rose, and divided the day from the night.

After the great lights, came the fish and fowl like patterns, and the beasts and cattle, and there were mountains and valleys and enormous seas, and clouds and winds and stars, but in the end, men and women travelled across the plains, and he saw them though they had no names.

After this, he was aware he lay upon a mountain's top. A million miles high, gleamed the crescent moon, like the bow of a *kinnor*.

On all sides, granite, obsidian, salt, the mountain slid to a wilderness.

He knew the loneliness of a single being upon the huge plate of the universe, who can only reach out to God.

His soul seemed to yearn upward. A vast silent finger brushed his forehead. Maybe it was only the wind in that place.

For hours he lay and marvelled, free of anything, and nearly free of self, lying there upon the stone of the mountain, with all night above.

Until, miles off, he heard the murmur of a drum.

He knew it, had heard it often. He tried to guess what it might be or mean. Then he realised that it came always nearer, that the beat intensified, and rumbled in the rock below him, and so strummed upward through his body and his bones.

He became aware of his body. Not any one portion of it, but every inch of flesh, each tier of the recumbent skeleton. The soles of his feet, his legs and thighs, the torso, neck and ears, the arms, the fingertips, the face, the scalp, even the hair, the teeth and nails, even the inner canals, links, crevices, membranes and nerves, each had a sentience, was possessed of a complete conscious concentrating awareness, yet it had life only through him.

The drum he identified now as a heartbeat. Every particle of his body, so autonomous yet so involved with *him*, responded to its rhythm.

The feeling was of a wonderful totality, and self-knowledge.

It was only then that he began to discern the chamber which contained the mountain top.

It was itself night-black. Its ceiling was enamelled with constellations, and figures of the zodiac, set out in all their stars, and through this the upper heaven glowed, and the new moon, resting upon Aquarius.

No walls upheld this ceiling.

The ground of the mountain was figured over on its blackness. Done in silver, like the sky, a five-pointed star seemed extending to infinity. And within it, a seven-pointed star had been fitted, and within that again, a star of three points, a triangle.

At the three points of the triangle, to each of which somehow he could see, was a smoking silver brazier formed as an animal. All were unnatural. To the north, at the apex, stood a winged bull with a lion's head, from this the smoke rose white; to the west was a silver calf with the sun on its forehead, it had the tongue of a snake, the smoulder from this was nacreous; east was a scorpion or scarab-thing, with the head of a man horned and bearded like a goat's, the steam from this one was transparent, remarkable only by a scintillant tremor in the air.

Within the triangle lay Raoulin, with his arms stretched up above his head towards the west and east points, his feet together pointing to the northern tip.

From the braziers came a mingling aroma, of balsam and hypericum, myrrh and orris.

In his ears he heard the rush of the perfumed smoke, and over and beneath, the drumbeat.

He felt no curiosity. He had no thoughts. He was utterly aware, cognizant, content.

A silver-white ewe came picking daintily over the rocks, some way beyond the stars which contained him, up on a peak in the sky. On her brow was a shining ray. She went around the wall of darkness, and was gone.

Then he heard two heartbeats, two drums. Another being, another life, was with him on the mountain.

Something uncurled, stretched itself within him. It was pleasant, had no urgency. He lay inside the triangle, his arms to the east and west, his feet pointing north, attentive.

There was a sudden sensation, like a kiss, on his breast above the heart. It did not startle him, he seemed almost to have expected it. After a moment, it came again, alighting over his ribcage, winging away. The touch was delightful and provocative, he longed for it to be repeated. For a while, nothing, and then, the kiss fell once more, more lingeringly, at his throat, and even as his skin tingled from it, again, over the nipple of his right side, so a string of fire was plucked there. After this, like a fine rain, the kissing came down glittering all across him. In a moment his whole body had become a lyre, sinuously strummed and vibrating – the rain of unseen sprites, to whom clothing was no barrier, fastened on him, their lips and fingers testing every atom of flesh and muscle, the framework of bone, for its potential pleasure. Even beneath him the rock itself seemed to give rise to these quivering entities.

Under the onslaught, he found he was unable to move, like one chained, at the mercy of the incorporeal delicious torture.

Dizzily his eyes remained fixed upon the rock in the sky, from which the second heartbeat seemed to have arisen. He could not apparently keep closed his eyes, though waves of sensation continually drove him to do so.

No, he could not close his eyes, and now upon the rock peak he saw a moon with a woman's face, which hung there and regarded him, shameless, helpless as he lay. And as the moon stared, the beings which fastened on him stripped him naked, as if for her cajolement, as if to bare him to her light.

But the moon … had black hair, and a head-dress of silver discs which she shook with a sound that matched the sinful rain that kissed him.

The moon had a black cloak. She had white hands that stole out as the hands stole upon him, that made little motions like the circling and flittering of those that played upon his body.

He could not look away from her. (And yet, just then, at a distance, the ends of the earth, he saw a male figure was standing, with his back turned to the moon in her cloak, his head averted both from this and from the naked man bound inside three stars. The figure perhaps had folded its arms across its chest, a wand in either hand, and before him was a kind of shallow basin upturned, or hollow mirror –)

But the moon had a cloak, and she cast it from her. She was all a woman, clad in a garment of silver scallops that covered her from the neck to the wrists and the ankles.

And then, on her arched bare feet, to the rhythm of the drumbeats, one faster, one slower and in counterpoint, she commenced a dance.

It was the dance of a snake. A swaying liquid coiling and uncoiling, like that of a river let along the ground. The arms followed the torso to and fro, the feet scarcely moved. It was not a spectacular or frenzied dance. It was immensely lambent, deeply suggestive and descriptive of the body of a woman, immeasurably cunning. It was the dance of Salomé before the king, which had hypnotised and driven him mad, and brought her, on a salver, the severed head of Jehanus. It was the dance of a snake.

As the languid pulses wove, the silver scallops began to drip away. Under them was a garment of thin stuff, perhaps byssus.

The shoulders of the dancer, her arms, rose from the silver like those of a maiden ascending from water.

Over the shoulders of the bound man, the unseen hands curved back and forth, to the pits of the arms, the line of the ribs, the flared points of the breast, and along the abdomen and the belly, like streams into the restless pounding groin.

As the silver rained off from the girl who was the snake, the rain poured on Raoulin, the torrent of hands and mouths. They stroked him, they teased and tickled him, they ran like threads of moltenness across his skin, over and beneath him. They had woken the root of life. He ached with lust and became lust, played, tautened, tuned, caressed by waters and airs and fire – and the drumbeat galloped, galloped, and the scales quickened like leaves and guttered from the girl's body wrapped in its second byssus skin. But the byssus too worked gradually away from her, unfurling like the calyx of a flower, slipping from her breasts that were the cups of flowers, that now hid themselves again, that now were again and utterly unveiled, flowers starred with flowers, while the kisses of invisible lips visited like moths and tongues probed like trickles of silk, and hands feathered and persuaded and the girl was naked to her loins dancing upon the silver leaves of her dress, and the byssus unseamed like snakeskin and slid away like water from the moon belly with its tiny drop of shadow, the goblet of black hair, the stemmed thighs smooth like alabaster –

In this instant Raoulin, who had forgotten his own name, felt a terrible resistance, some clutch upon the choking pump of desire, which strangled –

Unable to move, his lust thrashed, trying to burst from the swollen blazing rod –

(And the figure he had not properly seen, and had also forgotten, the figure which did not look at the dancer or the naked man, this figure now stretched out the wands in his hands and touched the metal surface before him. He spoke. The words made no sound. Instead they shouted out in the air above the triple stars of five and seven and three points.)

> *Evil One show thyself and come forth!*
> *O dweller among ruins and maker of ruins*
> *Get thee up to where thy ruins are;*
> *For the Lord God has sent me*
> *He has elected me his priest in this,*
> *He has given into my hands the Seven Powers*
> *According to the word of the sixth Day.*
> *Evil One, Foul One, show thyself and come forth!*

And the snake dancer rippled her hands along her silver body and tore it in two pieces, flinging both aside, to reveal, under the third veil, the nude skeleton.

The stifled death-throe of ecstasy was pierced by a white and screeking pin. It came from inside the young man's loins. It rent its way through him, through the pelvis, spermary, and phallus. It was a birth. It thrust in surges similar to the birth-pangs of a woman. It seemed to rip his genitals like the beak of a vulture.

He cried, every prayer and blasphemy, every obscenity and childish plea he had ever known. Then he only screamed.

Strand by strand the rope of agony was pulled out of him.

It began as a jet of sheer semen, opalescent in the uncanny light. But the fountain rose and did not slacken or end. The moonstone gush travelled upward, spilling with a fearful elasticity, forming into a springing plume.

Until in its turn the plume, of a substance now composed not of any mortal sexual fluid, but of some astral plasmic material, coalesced, ran inward, began to construct another shape.

The chamber of night had gone all to blackness again. It was once more the void. But in the void, terror was made manifest.

Recreated without flesh, it was colourless, and dully shining. It had the limbs and torso of a man, yet lacking the procreative organ. It was winged. The head was the head of a bird of prey. As it was now, there were no eyes, only two sumps of cloudy darkness. It had no brain, this dark was not that.

Alone upon its stage it stirred, the bird head looked about with the un-eyes. It was seeking for what had been delivered of it, and for what had brought it forth.

Out of the black the figure of the magician Haninuh again grew visible. The two wands were gone from his hands, splintered at the impact of egression. But before him still there lay on the air the hollow length of metal. It was a shield of highly polished hide, iron-bound and gilded, with the lightnings and burning staff, from which stared a Medusa: a Roman relic of Par Dis.

In the left eye of the Medusa glimmered a bit of quartz, or flawed corunda. It, like the demon, had no longer any colour.

Haninuh straightened himself. He stood in the void and showed the shield before the demon.

"Come *thou*," said Haninuh, "for here thou art."

Then the demon spat and sizzled and swirled towards the shield of Retullus Vusca, and into the Medusa's eye – which like itself had waited, waited: cut by the stroke of suicide from the entrails where, undissolved, this one piece had nestled like a child, washed out by blood under the hand of the dying Roman, thrust by him into the broken socket of the Medusa, his warning, all he could give, a jewel that was an eye – the *utuk* fell crackling, and met the shield, the eye, the gem, roared – like wind or fire – and was gone.

The Jew bent a little, leaning on the shield after his battle, to see where the jewel-fragment lay, erupted from its setting of eleven centuries. The shield seemed battered at last, brittle, like clinker. And for the jewel itself, it was like a cinder rendered up from the common hearth.

Haninuh spoke a Word over that cinder. Then he spoke a Word to the chamber and the blackness. To God he could not speak. For this, there were no words.

The embers of a morning lay in the green tines of the cedar tree. It seemed a dove was murmuring there.

"Oh that you were my brother that nursed at my mother's breast. When I should find you I might kiss you, it would be no shame. I would bring you into the house and there feed you on fruit and quench your thirst with wine. His left hand under my head, his right hand caressing me, he will teach me love."

Raoulin's lids lifted. Beauty sat by the bed and looked at him with gentle sombre eyes. In colour, no blacker than his own.

"Who is this," she said, "coming out of the desert, leaning upon her love? Under the tree I woke you; let it be as the place where you were born."

He was so weak he could not move, could not even speak to her. But he had never thought to see her again. He attempted, and failed, to find some means to offer her his voice.

She shook her head, and touched his lips with her fingers.

Upon the bed itself a striped cat stared at him, pitiless, guileless, angelic, and kneaded his feet.

He slept once more, comforted under their gaze.

Folded in a parchment, corded with seven charms, the amulet, or what remained of it, was buried in a clod of earth the size of a boy's hand. This then was packed into a box of horn, and that box into another of iron. Between the two boxes was a space, where an alchemical substance, being intruded, began of itself to burn. The iron box was closed, and put into a tablet of lead.

The whole was then carried to the midnight bank of the river, half a mile below Our Lady of Ashes, and thrown far out by the mighty arm of Liva. The tablet sank.

It sank, perhaps, to the mulch of the river's bottom, to wait once more, now for the deterioration of its containers, horn and iron and lead, earth, air, fire, and water. To wait out the river too, maybe, until that vast elder Leviathan of Paradys should shrink to a few puddles under some future sun. By then, the life of the amulet might also be eroded. If not, in that unpredictable to-come, some wandering one in the dry river-bottom would stoop and take up a lustreless stone, curious, and find the Devil still kept his court in the world. But possibly that day would never be.

For Raoulin, he was a very long time ill in the house of Haninuh. But being excellently, and cleverly and lovingly, tended, recovered before winter sealed the City in its orb of ice.

In the spring letters went from Raoulin to his kindred at the northern farm. But then the happiness turned like cream. For Raoulin had set himself to become a Jew by faith, conceivably more orthodox than his mentor. The reasons that he gave were unhelpful, for the actual spur had risen in him as fiercely and insatiably as young blood. (Perhaps too he remembered a

Christian priest under the Sacrifice, who had turned from him in his hour of horrible need.)

But his family cast off Raoulin. That was that.

Among the scholars of Haninuh's fraternity, this scholar found more than enough to study, and took to these new tutors, these new arcane formulae, with greed. For themselves, the Jews were kind to him. Even in Paradys, in their hearts, they reckoned their way was the only one, and had grown used to the insults and cruelties this knack provoked. For the gentile who approached them from the night, innocent, quietly asking, they could not but feel some wondering affection. As he grew in stature among them, they came to speak of their foundling with pride.

By then, of course, he had wed Ruquel, Haninuh's exquisite daughter, under the canopy.

These two knew together more happiness than most, less pain than many. They seldom spoke of death. Like the draining of the river, such things were the concern of God.

THE BOOK OF THE DEAD

LE LIVRE BLANC ET NOIR

Paradys too has its cemeteries, its little graveyards tucked out of sight, its greater yards of death that hug the churches, the cathedral that is called a Temple. It has its places of graves, between the houses in sudden alleys. Between the paving stones, here and there you may look down and see a name that paves the way, a date of beginning and the other of surcease. Even under the house floors now and then they will raise a carpet and a board and point you a grave: *Sylvie* sleeps here, or *Marcelin*. Paradys is a city of the dead as she is a city of the live, the half-live, the undead, and perhaps the deathless.

And here, on this hill, shrouded by the pretty park they have made where once the scholars bored out their eyes (but shells have burst there since), overlooking the coils of the river, is a great necropolis of Paradys.

And here I have brought you, on this windy, colorless gravegray afternoon. To walk about, to look and see. If you wish.

We have come at an opportune moment, too. For over there, where you note that line of carriages going up, the funeral is taking place of Baubon the clown.

Baubon was immensely popular. To him of an evening, after their fancy suppers, went the women in spangles and pointed heels and the men in their capes, and white shirt fronts, like cats.

The hearse is huge, scrolled like an urn and hung with black drapes. The black horses labor beneath the black plumes and blacker tassels. No motor cars spoil the effect. Even the mourners have had to hire chariots.

Surprisingly, there are very few mourners (and no crowds rim the ground, held off by policemen). The chief mourner is a thin and white-haired man with the face of an elderly imp, enough like the mask of Baubon, publicly always seen in garish paint, to imply a brother or close cousin.

The black coffin, ebony with silver handles, is unloaded – an enormous wreath of flowers balances white upon it – and the service begins.

Everyone stands in silence as the priest speaks over the black (blacker even than the horses) hole in the ground. He has a pompous theatrical look,

and the boy swinging the censer so adroitly, why he might even be that
favorite of Baubon's among the acrobats.

A few women weep a few crystal tears. They are the ones able to cry
without help in the theater. The men stand solemn. There are three
eulogies spoken perfectly over the hole. We are not near enough to catch
all the words – Genius, Unique, Mourned, Never-to-Be-Emulated. Then
the coffin is lowered into the space. Earth and flowers rain down. A white
rose ...

The celebrants shift from the grave in an exact ring, like circling black
moths.

The chief mourner shakes the priest by the hand.

"Bravo, Jacques. It couldn't have been bettered. No, not at *The Tragedy*
herself."

And the old imp strokes the censer boy.

A woman laughs.

"Take off the lid, then," says the brother of Baubon the clown.

Two men scramble carelessly into the grave and haul off the coffin top,
flinging away the exquisite floral tributes.

In the coffin lies Baubon, in his patchwork and all his paint. As so many
have seen him, laughing then, or crying, turning enormous cartwheels, falling
from high towers.

"Lid back on," cries the brother of Baubon gaily. "That's enough. No
respect."

And there is much amusement, back goes the lid, and the flowers are
slung on any how.

Two gravediggers approach, and start to shovel in the black, moist soil.

"Are you satisfied, Baubon?"

"*Quite* satisfied."

"When we do it in reality, will you be watching then, Baubon?"

"Who knows? That's why I had my funeral now, to be sure."

Baubon *is* the imp. The priest an actor from the Comedy Theatre. The boy
is ... the boy.

Staged, the funeral. And now the grave almost filled in. The black chariots
roister away to some great restaurant where they will hold the wake of
Baubon the clown and chief mourner.

In five years, or ten, or more (or less), they will come again to do this
thing. Then the crowds *will* press at the fences and the policemen hold them
off. Then perhaps some of the tears will be real, and the single white rose, if
it falls, will not give its life for nothing, only a game. Or is it a game? Is the
real funeral *not* to be a game?

And *will* Baubon watch then, as today?

Perhaps the dead are always watching, and we should tread carefully and speak low.

There will be no skulls in the grass. Though the recent storm shifted a tomb or two from its moorings, the staff of the necropolis came out like beetles in the rain and tidied everything. Even the shell that burst here was tidied. The necropolis has stood some while, two or three centuries. Always neat, even during the days of Liberty and Revolution.

(The last carriages career down into the park. There an old gentleman and his lady are shocked to behold the hearse go by filled with laughing actresses.)

In places there are great houses of death, you see. And in other places tiny markers half hidden in the grass and ivy, commemorative plaques for those who have gone down elsewhere into the dark that lies below, if not exactly beneath, everything.

Are they truly there, under our feet? Walk softly, talk quietly.

I will show you their shadows.

Here is a grave, now. ...

The Weasel Bride

In the long echoing street the laughing dancers throng,
The bride is carried to the bridegroom's chamber through
    torchlight and tumultuous song;
I celebrate the silent kiss that ends short life or long.

– Yeats

There are stories in the country told today as though they happened only a
week ago. In many ways customs have not altered very much, and every
village is its own empire. It is possible to imagine such things still occur, in
lonely woods, under the stare of a silver moon.

A young trapper, walking home one evening across the water
meadows, stopped in startlement, seeing a girl dancing on a hill in the
moonlight. She was very beautiful, with long pale hair, but as she danced
she wept and lamented. Pausing to watch, he also overheard her
complaint. "Alas," said she, "that I may only keep this human form in the
full ray of the moon. No sooner does she set, than I must return to my
loathsome other shape, from which only the true love of a man can rescue
me, although that forever. But what hope is there of it, seeing he must
court and wed me in my other form, before his kin, and in the church. I
am lost." Fascinated, the young man continued to spy on this strange
maiden until at length the moon began to go down. The sky lightened,
then grew black. The stars stung bright as the lunar orb sank under the
hill. It was gone. At that moment, the maiden disappeared like the moon,
as if into the ground. The young man ran up the hill and searched about,
and as he did so he glimpsed something that flashed away into the bushes.
It was a white weasel.

Now the trapper had made up his mind that he would be the one to have
this girl, no matter what the cost. Therefore he laid his most cunning trap, and
baited it, and went down to his village. Here he started hasty arrangements
for a wedding, telling all sorts of lies, and bribing the priest and the mayor to

367

obtain consent. The following night, which happened to be a night of no moon, he hurried to the spot where he had left his trap. And sure enough, what should he find in it but the white weasel, caught fast and crying piteously. "Fear nothing," said the suitor, "I shall befriend you, poor creature. Come, be my sweetheart, love me a little, and I shall wed you, before my kin and in the church, tomorrow morning."

Then he carried the weasel in a cage down to the village, ignoring her cheeps and struggles, which he guessed to be a part of the spell on her.

In his father's house, he had his mother and sisters put on the weasel a veil made from a lace handkerchief, and a garland made from a baby's pearl bracelet. He was the head of his own household, his father being dead, and the three women were obliged to obey him, but they did so in terror, thinking he had gone mad. The weasel, however, was most gentle now, and bore with everything that was done. Only at her lover did she hiss and bare her sharp teeth.

At sunrise, out they went, the trapper, his mother and sisters, and the bridal weasel in her cage. The whole village was about and crowding to the church, and the priest was there in his habit, with his prayerbook, waiting. But when they all saw what went on, there was a great to-do.

"Holy father," said the trapper, "you must humor me in this. For I insist this creature shall be my wife, and nobody will gainsay me. Remember," he added in a low voice to the priest, "my father's coins which I have given you."

"God moves in His own way," said the priest, and brought the young man and the weasel into the church and up to the altar. There, in the sight of the village and of the trapper's sobbing womenfolk, the priest wed the young man to the weasel.

Thereafter they repaired home for the wedding breakfast, and about noon, the young man took his bride away to the nuptial chamber, above.

The husband removed his wife from her cage and placed her on the pillows. "Dear wife," said he, "I will be patient." And there he sat quietly, as the daylight streamed in at the casement and the weasel ran about the bed and climbed the curtains, and below the wedding guests, in fear and amazement, grew drunk on his father's wine.

At length, the afternoon waned, the dusk came, and at long last, the moon rose in the east and pointed her white finger straight through the window.

"Now let us see," said the young man, and he put his hand on the weasel and stroked her snowy back. But as soon as the moon's ray touched her, she turned and bit him, under the base of the thumb, so his blood poured.

No sooner was this done than her coat of fur peeled off her, she sprang upright on the bed, and there before him in the moonlight was the lovely girl from the hill, clad only in her long, pale hair.

"You have freed me," she exclaimed.

"But at great cost," he answered.

And this was so, for despite her tender care of him, and the equally tender care of his astounded mother and sisters, the young man sickened of the bite. Within seven days he was dead and put to rest in the churchyard. And as for the weasel widow, she slunk away in the sunrise, and none saw her again, in any shape, although in those parts it was the tradition ever after to kill any weasel that they came on, if it should be a female.

The two families, the Covilles and the Desbouchamps, had ruled together over their great sprawling village for a pair of hundred years. And as each century turned, the village grew larger, fair set on being a town. The Covilles' tailored house at least had business connections with the City. Theirs was the trade of wool. The Desbouchamps' low-beamed manor, its milk churns and dove-cotes, stables and wild orchards, drowsed comfortably in the meadows. The Days of Liberty had not yet swept through Paradys, changing all the world. There seemed no need to hurry, or to provision for any future that did not resemble the past.

It was to be a country wedding then, between Roland Coville and Marie-Mai Desbouchamps. It started at sunup, with the banging of lucky pots and pans down the village streets, and went on with the girls and their autumn roses taken to the manor, and the silver coin given to each as she bore her flowers into the cavern of the kitchen.

Then out came the lint-haired bride, crowned with the roses, in the embroidered bodice her grandmother had worn, and the little pearly shoes that just fitted her. She was piped and drummed to the church and met her bridegroom in the gate, a dark northern youth, and who did not know or could not see how eager he was? For it was not only a marriage arranged but a marriage arranged from desires. They had played together as children, Roland and Marie. He had pretended to wed her in the pear orchard when she was ten and he thirteen years of age. Seven years had passed. He had been sent to school in the City, and was no longer pure; he had known philosophy, mathematics, Latin, and three harlots. But unscathed he still was. And the girl, she was like a ripe, sweet fruit misleading in its paleness: She was quite ready.

And how he loved her. It was obvious to all. Not only lust, as was proper, but veneration. *He will treat her too well*, they said, *she will get the upper hand*. But she was docile, was she not, Marie-Mai? Never had anyone heard of anything but her tractability, her gentleness. *She will make a good wife*.

For Roland himself, it might be said that he had always known she must be his. At first she had reminded him of the Virgin, so fresh and white, so *clean*. But then the stirrings of adult want had found in her the other virgin, the goddess of the pastoral earth that was his in the holidays, the smooth curving forms of hills and breasts, shining of pools and eyes, after the chapped walls and hands, the hard brisk hearts of Paradys. She allowed him little lapses. To kiss her fingers, then her lips, to touch fleetingly the swansdown upper swell above her bodice. When he said to his father, "I will have Marie-Mai," his father smiled and said, "Of course. We'll drink to it." So easy. And why not, why must all love be fraught and tragic, gurning and yearning, unfulfilled or snatched on the wing of the storm?

And for Marie-Mai, what could be said for her? She had answered correctly all the searching lover's questions. Her responses were perfect, and if she offered nothing unasked, that was surely her modesty, her womanly decorum. Could anyone say they knew her? Of course. They all did. She was biddable, and loving in mild, undisturbing ways. She was not complex or rebellious. There was nothing to know. Who probes the flawless lily? It is the blighted bloom that gets attention.

A country wedding, then, and in the church Roland thought his bride like an angel, except he would not have planned for an angel what he planned to do to her. And the church over, outside in the viny afternoon, they had their feast on the square, under the sky. These were the days once sacred to the wine god. The girls had wreathed the clay jugs with myrtle; the great sunny roses crowded the tables like the guests. And when the humped western clouds banked up, and the faint daylight moon appeared in a dimming glow, they bore the bride and groom to the smart stone house behind the wall and the iron gate decorated with peacocks. They let them in with laughter and rough sorties. They let them go to the laundered bedroom whose windows were shuttered, whose candles were lit. They closed the doors and shouted a word or two, and left the lovers alone for their night. And in the square a band played and Madame Coville danced with Monsieur Desbouchamps, and Madame Desbouchamps was too shy to do more than flirt with Monsieur Coville. The moon rose high, and owls called from the woods. The roses bloomed in the dark over the old walls, as if winter would never come.

In the morning, an autumn country morning that began about half past six, Roland's manservant knocked on the bedroom door, and the maid waited behind him with the pot of chocolate. In the old days – not twenty years before – the elderly women of the house would have arrived, to strip the bed and view the blood of the maidenhead. This was no longer done in such sophisticated villages. When the first knock went unanswered, the manservant knocked again, and grinned at the maid, and called out, "Shall I return a little later, "sieur Roland?"

Then, and what follows now comes directly from the evidence given later in the courtrooms of Paradys, the voice of Roland was raised clearly behind the door. It was not an embarrassed or pleasured voice. It cried in terrible despair: "*Oh God, what shall I do?*" And then, very loudly and without any expression, "Come in and see. But leave the girl outside."

The young manservant raised his brows. More sympathetic than he, the maid was already trembling and biting her lip. The man opened to door and went into his master's bedroom. There he beheld at once, as he said, some vestiges of a slight tussle, but perhaps these might not be unnatural. Then he saw that the bride lay half out of the bed, in her ribboned nightgown. There were bruises on her throat, her face was engorged and nearly black, and her eyes had extruded from their sockets. She had been strangled, had been dead some while. The manservant exclaimed something like, "My God, who has done this?" To which the young husband replied quietly, "I did it. I killed her." And at this point it was noticed how two of the fingers of his right hand were very savagely bitten, doubtless by the dying girl in her struggle for life.

The subsequent commotion that next boiled through the house is easily imagined. It passed into every chamber, every cranny, like a noxious odor. There was screaming, and every sort of human outcry, male and female. Roland was led down into the lower rooms, where an interrogation took place, his mother on her knees, his aunts fainting, his father bellowing in tears. And all this was soon augmented by the frenzied arrival of the family Desbouchamps.

To each kind and type of entreaty or demand, Roland Coville would say substantially the same thing, as various testimony later showed. What he said was this: "I killed Marie. I strangled her. She's dead."

But to the eternally repeated question *Why?* he would answer, white-faced and wooden, "I have nothing to say on that."

In those parts, the unchastity of a bride might have furnished a reason. There were historic tales, to be sure, of girls slain on the wedding night, having been discovered unvirgin. The father challenged his son, but Roland shook his head. He even gave a grim and white-faced smile. No, he replied, she was intact. "What, then – what? Did she slight you?" No, he had not been slighted. Marie was a virgin and she had not insulted him. She had given no provocation. She had encouraged his advances.

"Why, then, in the name of God –"

"I won't say, Father. Nothing on this earth will induce me to do so."

It was the father of Marie, of course, who impugned the manhood of Roland. The husband had been unable to fulfill his duties, and had strangled the innocent maiden for fear she would betray him. There were a couple of girls in the city who could give the lie to this. Nevertheless, the fathers ended fighting in the cobbled yard of the Coville house, under the peacocks.

In their turn, the police came. They had little to add but the uniform and threat of the law.

The village had fallen apart like a broken garden. Stones rattled by night on the shutters of the Coville house, on the embrasures of the village jail to which Roland had been removed. They wanted his death.

He was taken to the City in the dead of night, unpublicized, in a covered carriage, like an escape. The Coville house was locked up like a box. They had gone too into the darkness, to the City. Like all cities, it reeked of Hell. This had a rightness then, the flight toward Paradys, as, not too many years in the future, others would flee away from the drums and blades of Revolution, into the outer night of the world.

The trial of Roland Coville caused no stir in Paradys, City of Damnations. It was not unusual enough. A man had killed a girl, his lover and wife. So what? It happened twice a day. That the case had been explosive enough it was removed from village to City was nothing. A cough out of season was a wonder in the provinces.

The young man stood bravely, deadly, and composed before his judges. He was courteous and exact, and he refused them nothing except what he refused all others, the motive for the murder. He was defended with great difficulty.

"It is plain to me, and to those who sit in judgment on you, that you are no murderer. Let alone of a defenseless girl at your mercy in the dark, your young wife, looking to you for love and protection, receiving death at your hands. Clearly, monsieur, there is a momentous reason. *Tell us*."

"No," said Roland Coville. "I can tell you nothing at all."

"But it may save your life, monsieur."

Roland shook his head. He looked only sad and very young.

"But *monsieur*, for God's sake. This will end in your hanging. Don't you prefer to live?"

Roland looked surprised, as if he were unsure. "Perhaps not."

"His face," said the lawyer after, considerably shaken, "was like, I think, that of a woman I once heard of. She had been shown the mechanism of the human body, its heart, viscera, intestines, all the tubes and organs that support life. And having seen, she was so disgusted at the method whereby she lived that, when she got home, she cut her wrists and died. To be rid of it all. Just so, he looked, my Roland Coville. He isn't reluctant to die."

Once, during the examination at Paradys, Roland was asked about the lacerations on the fingers of his right hand. He answered that his wife, Marie, had indeed bitten him.

"And this was during her final moments, as she fought for her life?"

"No. It happened earlier."

"Then your wife behaved violently toward you?"

"No," said Roland.

"But you say that she bit you without any act on your part that would have invited her so to do."

"No, I did not say this."

"Monsieur Coville, we must be precise. When was it that these bites occurred?"

Roland hesitated. "When I touched the lips of Marie."

"But this, then, was an extreme and unloving response."

"Perhaps."

"Did you kill her because of this? Because of her attack on you?"

Roland Coville thought for a moment, and then said, "Would it be deemed a suitable defense, to kill a woman because she had bitten me?"

"No, monsieur, of course it would not."

"I did not," said Roland, "kill Marie because of the bite."

"*Why*, then? You are bound to speak. The weight of this assembly, and of the law itself, insist."

"I can and will say nothing," said Roland Coville. "It is beyond me to say it." And then in a sudden and conclusive passion he screamed, so the room echoed and dinned, the spectators and the judges recoiled, "It would be as if you tore out my heart, to say it. It would be as if you cut out my tongue. Nothing. Nothing! I will say nothing."

And so he was judged a murderer. He was condemned. In a small gray yard at sunrise he would be hanged.

But in the cell, before that, he must confront the confessor, the priest who was to hear his final statements, and who must, of them all, get the truth from him.

"I can't tell you," said Roland Coville to the priest who angrily confronted him.

"You have forfeited your life," said the priest. "Is this not enough? You have spat upon the robe of God, and upon the gift he gave you."

"No, father," said Roland. "God knows, and understands, what I have done. And why."

And his face was then so pitifully pared, trusting, and desperate, so positive of the pity of God after all, that the angry priest was softened.

"Come, then," he said, "make what confession you can. I will absolve you, and God must do the rest."

Roland then knelt down, and unburdened himself of all his crimes, which were none of them terrible, but for that one. And then he spoke of that too, quietly and stilly. "I strangled my young wife, she was only seventeen, and I loved her. It was on her wedding night, in our bed. She was a virgin and died so. I killed her with no compunction, and would do it again." And then, head bowed under the hands of the priest, he added softly, "For my reasons, I believe such things can't be spoken of. This would be like showing the face of the Devil. How can I be responsible for that?"

The priest was in the end very sorry for him. He was a handsome and a good young man, guilty of nothing but the one appalling and senseless act. The priest absolved Roland Coville, and went away to watch all through the night before the execution, in the little church on a slanting street of the City. And when through the narrow window a nail of light pierced in and fell on the crucifix and the white flowers, the priest knew the rope in the gray yard had performed its office, and one more benighted soul had struggled forth into the Infinite, toward long anguish or the life eternal, or toward oblivion, for he was a wise priest, faithful and doubting, a man like men.

Two days after the execution of Roland Coville, the priest was brought a letter. It was on the paper obtained in the prison, and came from the dead man, written in the last hour of his life. As such it had extraordinary weight. But on opening it anxiously, the priest read these words: "I cannot after all go into the night without passing on this burden that has consumed me. Forgive me, father, that I turn to you. Who else can I rely on? Who else can bear it?"

And after that the priest read on, and the scales fell from his eyes, the dark glass was clear before him. He did not believe, then he believed. And he locked the letter from Roland Coville away in a place where none could come at it, not even he himself. And there it stayed for seven years, burning slowly through the wall of the safe and of his mind.

One spring, when the roads were muddy, a priest came to the village by means of the coach that stopped there once a month, and he inquired for the domicile of the family Desbouchamps. On being directed, he took himself off toward the manor house in the meadows. The lanes were spare and washed with rain, the tall poplars swept the sky. The manor had lost its roselike abundance and seemed now decaying, the shutters half off, the lofts rotting. No doves flew from the cotes. A dog barked only sullenly in the courtyard.

To his inquiry at the kitchen door, the housekeeper shook her head. "Mistress sees no one." The priest indicated his habit. "What does she want with another priest? She's had enough of you, burying the master."

But he won through, because he had set his mind to it. He stood with his habit and his bag and would not go. Finally a thin old woman of no more than forty years came down to the cold parlor, where drapes were on the furnishings, and she made no pretense at removing them or lighting the fire.

The hearth gaped black, and cold whistled down the chimney. She leaned to it and rubbed her hands.

"We are unfortunate," said Madame Desbouchamps. "In a year, everything must be sold. Those men, those men in their holy day coats!" (She presumably meant the lawyers.)

"I'm very sorry to hear it."

"It's been a great loss. Ever since monsieur died. It was the tragedy killed him. He always loved her so." And over her worn and discarded face there crossed a slinking jealousy, out in the open now, having no need any more to hide. Marie-Mai was dead, and her loving father was as dead as she, why dissemble?

"Your daughter, do you mean?" asked the priest with some care. "But she was very young to die."

"Murdered," said madame, "in her bridal bed."

The priest said what was inevitable.

"You will have heard," said Madame Desbouchamps. "It was the talk of the City. They made up songs about it, the filthy wretches."

The priest had never heard one, and was glad. He said, "I believe I caught a rumor of the case. The bridegroom had no motive for his action. The girl was innocent and chaste."

Madame Desbouchamps compressed her lips like withered leaves. She sat a long while in utter silence, and he intuitively allowed this. At length, the blossom came.

"She was a sly girl," said the mother. "She hid things, was secretive. She was no daughter to me. I knew no better then. But it was never affection she gave me. She saved that for her father, a clever pass. I remember, her courses came early. She wasn't nine years, she was crying and there was blood, and I said, Let me see, Marie, what's the matter with you? But she ran away. And the blood stopped, and then there was no more till the proper time. She was eleven years then. She wasn't fearful when it happened, only asked me for a napkin."

The priest might have been astonished and shocked at being awarded such information. Even in country people madame's reminiscence was forthright. But in fact he was not thinking of this. He had gone very pale. And she, she had a crafty look, as if she had meant to tell him something, and saw that she had.

"Poor young girl," said the priest after a few moments. "What a loss to you, the daughter, then the husband. Where are they buried?"

"And the house," interjected the woman brutishly. Then she said, "On the land. The Desbouchamps bury their dead close. Now what shall I do? The land's no longer mine."

"Their graves must be moved, madame," said the priest.

"I'll show you," she said. And again there was the flash of malign conspiracy. As if she knew what he was at, *liked* it, although that could hardly be.

It was a little mausoleum, like a Roman tomb, not unusual among wealthy country families. Through the grille he glimpsed the shape of coffins. He would need a pick to smash the lock, but the place was up the hill, hidden by trees and deserted. They chained the three last dogs by night, and there were only a pair of old men now on the estate.

So, at two in the morning, he duly returned, with his pickax and his lantern.

The incongruity of what he did had ceased to irk him. He was beyond that. The letter burning through the safe had gradually seared out his ethics. He struck the lock and broke it with four blows, each of which echoed away along the valley, but no light fluttered up in the manor house, no one rushed from the buildings, not even the owls hooted.

The stench and awfulness of the mausoleum did not check him either, for he had been expecting them, and once or twice he had stood over an opened grave, the stink of it worse than excrement or sewers in its omen of mortality.

Her box, the coffin of Marie-Mai, he located without difficulty, knowing what to look for. He dredged up the cobwebs and saw the tracks of a squirrel over the lid – it must have come in at the broken grille. What had attracted it to this one case alone? For it had ignored the others. Shuddering, the priest levered up the planks. He saw what he had reckoned to see, the bones of a young girl whose young girl's skin had gone to mummy and fallen away, some strands and traces of hair, the crumbled wedding garments in which she had been buried, the marriage ring rattling on the thinnest of thin fingers.

"God strengthen me. God forgive me," said the priest. And then he tore down the powdery bridal clothes. And so he saw, without any shadow of doubt, for indeed he held the lamp over the coffin, he spared himself nothing. Roland Coville had not lied.

Then, going outside, the priest threw up, tried to throw up it seemed his heart and soul. And when he was done, trembling, he went back in and shut up the coffin fast with a hammer and nails, closed it more tightly than before. This work finished, he left the place and went down the hill, and back to the village inn, where they were too respectful of a City priest to ask any questions.

The priest paced the length of three weeks, in his church on the slanting street, in his rooms, under the architraves of Paradys. There was no help for Roland, who by now was as near to dust as the thing he had killed and died for. What, then, to do with the truth, that terrible naked sword? At length, the priest made his decision, and it resembled Roland's own, for neither would he, the priest of God, tamper with the revealed face of the Devil.

He sat with papers and ink and candles, and through the night he wrote, and rewrote, what he had been privy to. And in the end, near dawn, he burned his experiments, and had it down alone on paper in a manner that at least was not hysterical, nor crude, nor yet of course entirely believable, but how could he help that? He added to it a line of Latin, by way of protection, and folded up the paper, and sealed it, and stored it, together with the letter of Roland Coville, in a new deposit that should not be opened until his death.

That, then, was how the priest dealt with what he had learned and seen. And so truth lay in the dark for another sixty years.

During that time, everything changed. The great Revolution came and went, the Days of Liberty, the Years of Blood. The paper lay in its vault, and Marie-Mai in her coffin, undisturbed, like shells of a lost sea deep in the soil, that all the turning wheels and veering scythes of the world cannot dislodge. Only the hand that knows their places, only that can find them out. Or some wild accident.

"There is a rat," said the landowner. "I tell you, I hear it, you fool."

"No rats, sir. I keep them away."

"Damn you, I tell you I hear them. I walk by this horrible spot, and I hear them, gnawing and gnashing in the vault. Look at this thing! A gargoyle of a tomb. Pull it down, I say. Scatter the bones. What were they, that family of no-goods? Rich men feeding off the poor of this region. I fought on the barricades against their sort."

He had not actually fought, he had been a clerk, but scum generally rises to the top. Now he had his farm here, and did well from it. His memories altered to fit present circumstances, and he despised the dead Desbouchamps whose land he had acquired, bloodsuckers, with their silly, half-aristocratic name –

"I watched all night. Saw not one rat."

"But did you hear the sound of their rat jaws biting together?"

"No, sir."

"Don't call me sir. You're not a serf any more. Address me as *brother*. And stop arguing with me. I gave you an order."

"Yes, brother?"

"We'll have this rotting tomb pulled down. We'll turn them *out*."

The mausoleum of the Desbouchamps was duly ripped apart, its Roman columns flung over, its piteous insides rolled forth into the blistering sunlight of that summer when the rain would fail and the crops die, and new plagues of want stalk the land, as if mere blood had not been enough. But he did not know that yet, the clerk from Paradys. Nor did he know anything of the priest's paper, which, that very year, too, had been read by a few august eyes, which had escaped the battery. A few clever eyes, that would take the paper and the letter for a symbol of the monstrous times, like the bleeding of a loaf or a frog with a tail, a portent, immaterial as to truth or lie.

The risen clerk from Paradys kicked the Desbouchamps coffins. A couple burst open and the inhabitants sprawled on the grass. He laughed at those.

"Here's one nicely nailed. More solid. Something to hide. Perhaps there are jewels in here." And thrusting off his brother workmen, to whom, to his wife, he referred as walking rubbish, the clerk prized up the lid and threw it off. "*Pough!* What an effluvia!" (He liked occasional long words.) He held his nose and attempted not to retch. Then he called one of the fellows to rummage in the bones.

There were no gems, no earrings, necklaces, only an old tarnished ring, perhaps silver, which he had away from the workman at once.

It must have been a woman. Her long hair had fallen off, her dress had been torn.

He peered at her to be sure he had missed nothing.

Then the workman gave a hoarse cry.

"What is it, you damned fool?"

The man drew away, potently terrified. He ran to one of his mates, clasped him, gabbled, and rushed off between the trees.

"Well, *he'll* be whipped."

The clerk laughed again, then he looked. And at long last he saw.

The woman was all bones, discolored as if charred, and in her skull the teeth, once young and white, had loosened and dropped out. But lower, where the dress was torn wide, he could see in at the tilted bones of her pelvis, and there, between her legs, she had another set, and these were perfect, still white and very sharp. They lay in the nest of her skeleton like a little wreath of snowy flowers. In life they would not have been visible, for plainly they had been tucked neatly away behind the smooth lips and taut maidenhead, secure in the second mouth of her vagina. There they had waited, as if any man had dared. What a bite they could have given him!

The clerk leaned back and laughed heartily. Then he got up, gray and shaking, and told his men to close the coffin. He did not want a sideshow on his property. It must go to the City. Perhaps a grave could be found for it there, in some corner of the overflowing cemeteries of Paradys.

It was about this time, that day or another, that the august and clever eyes of the priesthood also turned from the paper they had been reading. And it was then, while the one decided on a sideshow, a joke, that the others decided on a portent, the apocalypse.

Dominus illuminatio mea, et salus mea, quem timebo? said the Latin, put there on his paper by the priest.

While the clerk was telling his drunken cronies, and his drunken wife, at dinner, what he had seen, and the rafters of the old Desbouchamps manor rocked with the laughter of the jest, the wise men who had also looked on the face of the Devil crept to their hiding places, courageously repeating their affirmation, *The Lord is my light and my safety, whom shall I fear?*

So the years of Revolution swept over Paradys and her landscape, in a primordial sea.

The mysterious poet André St. Jean, who saw their beginning, apparently barely mentions anything of them, being taken up with his own affairs of the heart.

Enough is known of the bloodshed. The graveyard here bears its witness.

One anecdote is perhaps worth repeating, the curious tale of Monsieur Raccoon.

He escaped from the zoological gardens before the hungry and threatening mob could make a meal of him, and thereafter devoted himself to the rescue of forlorn innocents from the gallows. The flaunting banner of his striped tail was a fearful sight to the executioner and his assistants. From the rope he whisked away countless numbers, swooning pale maidens and paler gentlemen, in his capable paws. At length, Monsieur Raccoon was captured, and imprisoned in one of the most notorious of the prisons. But here he charmed them all so well that eventually he made his own escape, leaping high above the heads of the jailers and vanishing, swinging through the beams, with a whisk of his cream-and-charcoal tail.

He was whispered of among the forests of the gallows, among the stone cages of the prisons, for months after. The aristocrat upon the scaffold had only to mention, "Ah, for the Raccoon," to cause his assailant to blanch. In the zoo you will see a commemorative plaque concerning him. But here in the long grass where an angel's broken hand has fallen, here there is another marker.

This too owes its dead-life to the Revolution, although in a roundabout way. The name reveals perhaps a sidelong descendant of André St. Jean, or perhaps not, for the name is not uncommon in Paradys. The fate, more so …

The story was told me one evening in a café by the river, near to the ruined bridge. The dusk was blurred by fog, and somewhere below, where the bank ended and the water began, the vague torched eyes of barges were creeping up and down, slow and fearful, with now and then the mournful warning of a gong. In the café, the fog had entered too, and, with the primal oil lamps and the smoke of cigarettes, gave us the atmosphere of Venus. An old man was brought over suddenly under the ominous announcement, "Here is a fellow can tell you a few histories."

They sat him before me and there he was, creaking in his overcoat. I filled him a glass, and idly invited him to begin. He started to talk of the Revolution. He looked ancient enough to have known the participants, when a boy. Not until he was well into his third glass, did he squint at me slyly and say, "But the strangest stories come after the Revolution ended. When they washed the City clean of blood, and put the axes away. It was then."

After which he launched into a narrative that had something in it of a Shakespearian drama, and something of the nature of a myth. I did not know if I, or he, believed it. Punctuated by the eerie flickers from the river, dispersed through the lamplit fog, it clung inside my head. False or real, it had its own truth. I set it down; now you must judge for yourself.

The Nightmare's Tale

The Devil beats his drum,
Casting out his spell,
Dragging all his own
Down into Hell.

– David Sylvian

1

Of the many thousands who had died in the murderous blood tides of Revolutionary times, there had been a young poet and his innocent wife. Their names and lives may be found elsewhere, he a dark and clamorous man, she pale as a swan, following her husband to the scaffold in the white dress of a bride. They left behind a child, then only two years old. This off-spring was brought up by a surviving sister of the mother's – although in those days, it was not unusual, when one member of the family was confis-cated for the gallows, for the rest soon enough to be dragged in tow.

The woman, who shall be called Andromede, raised the little boy in the best fashion she could, and at the proper age saw to it that he was educated to the highest and nicest degree she could afford. Along with the nourishment of his body, clothing of his person, and tutoring of his mind, she also saw to it that her sister's son was fed, garbed, and schooled in most incredible amounts of pure bitterness. It may have been that she herself was once in love with Jean de St. Jean's father, the poet, or that she had loved her sister exces-sively. Or it may have been simply the fact of the terrible shock she had undergone when all her familial world was swept away in the space of two or three horrible months: Something made of Andromede a powerful and insidious instructor in the lessons of enduring hate.

How she did it can only be guessed. One half imagines that instead of grace before a meal, some other words were spoken, rather in the way of the antique toast "Death to my enemies." Or that over the beds were hung samplers that read "You shall seek out the wicked and destroy them." And "An eye for an eye."

Probably, when she knelt down like gray marble in the church at the end of the street, and the child asked what she prayed, Andromede may well have replied, "For *justice!*" And probably also she indoctrinated the little Jean with anecdotes of his parents, their vivid talents and virtues, their fairy-tale love, and their death.

For eighteen years, until the age of twenty, Jean de St. Jean grew to manhood in that shadowy City of aftermath, the wreckage of a revolution, going about between a grim stony school with turrets and cobbled yards, reeking stoves, mealy books, and a maze of crooked, crowded, dirty streets that led up into an apartment with windows that peered across a joiners' court at a high wall, three rooms that were thick with dust in summer and wet with cold in winter, and whose stove smoldered and reeked worse, and if there was generally sufficient to eat, it came at the cost of something, some gnawing, obscure pride to do with a state pension, a recompense for the unspeakable that could never be enough. And as he grew up, then, forcing his way toward the light like a plant in flinty ground, Jean de St. Jean, the poet's son, breathed up, with the damp and dust and the church bells from the street's end and the invisible samplers of hatred, an exquisite yearning for he knew not what. But it was not ambition or carnality or fame or happiness. And one day, one morning, by accident, he discovered its being and what it was. It was revenge. And like a luscious berry, God had put it in his hand.

He rushed home to the mean apartment of his aunt, along the knotted streets, his heart in his mouth, bounded up the stairs, and flung wide the door.

"Anny!" he exclaimed, which was his pet name for Andromede the hateress. "Anny, you won't credit –"

Andromede came through from her bedroom, where she had been pinning up her hair tightly. For the first time in eighteen years she felt the full spasm of fear. She stared into her nephew's face and saw him for what he was, as if, until this moment, he had been partly hidden from her. He was a man, with the hair of her sister in a sun-caught cloud around his face, and his eyes dark and clamoring.

"Whatever –" she began.

He held up his hand to silence her.

"I have seen," said Jean, in a wild cold voice awful to hear, "a *thing*, a *monster*, walking in the garden of the Martyr Church."

"I don't understand you, Jean," said Andromede. She did. She shook from head to foot and her bowels had turned to water, exactly as had happened eighteen years ago on the night the Citizen Police hammered at the door.

"It was Dargue," said Jean. "*Dargue*," he repeated.

Then he fell silent and stood looking at her. It would have been difficult to say which of them had gone the whiter.

Dargue was the man who had been directly responsible for the execution of the poet and his wife. It was he who denounced them, and later, by adding his signature to the warrant, he that ensured there would be no escape. He had supposedly been drinking wine as he wrote his name, and a spot of the drink fell beside it like a drop of thin blood. The document had since been displayed, with others of its kind, and perhaps Jean had even seen it. Of course he knew the six letters that composed the monster D.A.R.G.U.E. And, too, he knew the man by inner sight, having had his appearance and mannerisms described uncountable times over. That Dargue had, as Jean, aged eighteen years, did not prove a deterrent. He had been away all this while, like a fiend in Hell, reveling in the illicit riches the Revolution had given over to him when, in the last days of its madness, he fled.

"He has been living in the Colonies," said Jean, referring to these far-flung possessions of the City as to another planet. "An island ... Black Haïssa. He has a house there. They jokingly say he has three wives. Negré women."

"*I don't want to hear!*" screamed Andromede abruptly, clasping her hands over her ears.

"You must, you must," pleaded Jean. And going to her, he put his arms around her and held on to her just as he had when a child. For her various reasons, Andromede had never been a caressive or physical woman. Her returns to an embrace, especially an importunate one, were awkward and labored. Now she did nothing at all, but stood there in her gray marble mode, waiting perhaps for all this to end. "Anny," said Jean, "listen carefully. I'm not a boy now. You know, I'm well educated thanks to you, but have no prospects in this rotten, corrupt City. I've had it said to me already, my best chance ... would be to try my luck – in the Colonies." He paused, and when she did not respond, hurried on with, "There are fortunes to be made in the islands."

"Yes," she said stupidly, sounding almost asleep. Her hands had fallen back to rest on his arms as he held her.

"There's the money you put by for me. Let me have it, Anny."

"So you can take yourself to the Colonies?"

She stole a glance at him. Her eyes were stunned rather than bleak. Was he going to leave her?"

"Yes, so I can go there. Don't you see. Where *he* is."

"Why?" said Andromede.

It was astonishing, after all her work upon him. After eighteen years of a single lesson perfectly repeated and learned by heart. Now, when he replied, solving the mathematical formula in its preordained and only way, now she could not make head or tail of it.

"To kill him," said Jean de St. Jean. "What else?"

Andromede had the correctness of soul at least to bow her head and not to protest again.

"He's to return to the Island shortly. Out there," said Jean, "in that *lawlessness*, it will be easy."

"Yes, it's easy to kill."

"Anny, it's what we wanted in our dreams, and here's my chance."

"Yes."

"You'll let me have the money, then?"

"Very well. I saved it for you, Jean."

"For *us*. For *them* – my father. *Her*."

"Yes."

"You mustn't grieve. In a year I could be home. We might be rich. You'll have a carriage, and beautiful clothes – velvet for church."

"Silly," she said, brokenly.

She tried to smile. Maybe she even tried to take on again her serpent's craning, the foremovement of its venomous strike, the attitude of her insatiable hunger for justice, retribution, the getting of eyes for eyes. If so, she failed in that too. The smile was meaningless and unconvincing, but she pressed it on her face from that morning to the dawn, ten days later, when Jean caught the boat from the old Quay of the Angel, and was borne out limblessly toward the jaws of the sea.

Andromede, standing on the quayside, amid the plumes of hats and tears of others come to wave someone away, was dry and upright, like a thin blasted tree. It was her pride not to weep until she was at home, alone there amid the dust and cold and shadows, listening helplessly for the sound of his footsteps on the stair, for the snatch of a song he might now and then sing, the dropped book, the rustle of his coat, his *Anny, here I am*, his *Goodnight, God bless you, Anny*. She told herself she would never see him again, and in this she was quite right.

The journey was a lifetime. It passed across seasons, geographical barriers, climates, and spatial zones. Months were consumed by it. You could not embark on such a journey, and complete it, unaltered. And yet, with all its doings and happenings, its events of seasickness, storm, calm, boredom, the visitations that were foreign ports (and progressively more and more foreign as one advanced, moving tableaux that swam up from the depths of the ocean and slid away again behind like the white wake of the moon by night), the fishes that leapt, the stars that revolved, and the whole reasonless, rocking environ of the sea itself – such things eventually classified themselves into mere living, ordinary existence. For Jean experienced them and survived them all, and to some extent they were lost on him in any case, for he was already in pursuit. His hunt had begun at the Angel Quay indeed, when he learned which boat, and which ship, were to carry Dargue a week before him.

It was, however, as though the entire passage comprised and was framed within an afterimage: that of sailing through a sort of bottle of pale skies and water holding rain, and coming gradually out of the bottleneck into a violent sunset burning in heaven like stained glass.

Although the conflagration died as quickly as it blew up, going down beneath a curious cloud.

"There," said Jean de St. Jean to one of the less disreputable of the crew, "what is that?"

"Haısa," the man replied. He added that they had anchored eight miles out, and would not be going in until sunrise.

Jean was left to observe the cloud darken in a sheet of drained fire, and then to darken and harden on, blacker than the star-sprayed sky.

There were mountains on Haıssa. Haıssa was, in fact, it seemed, made of mountains. There was something in the Island he had not expected, the young man intent upon his quest and his vengeance. The Island itself had importance. It possessed some kind of sentience, dimly discernible across the rhine-stone rollers, the reefs, and the night.

As he stood at the ship's rail, Jean became aware of another being on the deck.

It is almost impossible to describe the way in which the awareness stole over him, especially in view of what will follow. The sensation grew rather in the manner in which a man may come to feel he has some illness, amorphous at first, the faintest disinclination, ebb of the spirits. Yet presently depression is reinforced by a score of other slight intrusive signals. At last he must acknowledge the onset of the fever that will lay him low.

Jean bore the feeling, which was not exactly of being watched, more of being waited upon, for a count of five or six minutes. They would have seemed interminable, except that all the while he was trying to argue himself from his certainty. Frankly, he did not for a moment think anything human or explicable was with him on the deck. He knew, from the evening's previous sounds, and a by now general familiarity with the noises of the vessel, crew, and passengers, the position of all men and objects. Even the ship's dog had become detectable to him during the voyage, as it lightly padded its rounds. *This* presence was of one who had not, until that hour, inhabited the ship.

Finally, Jean turned, and scanned the area about him. The moon was rising, the heavy lush moon of these regions, which on its nights of waxing seems full of sweet juice. The deck glowed and was laid bare, the masts and bundled sails, the cabins and hatches, the station of the great wheel. No one was there in all that stretched instant of moonlight. The vessel was like a floating coffin on the ocean. Only Jean remained at the rail. And nearby, somewhere, invisible and untenable and nonexistent – the other.

Jean crossed himself. It was an involuntary action, a reflex of boyhood. But when he did it, he thought he heard a soft, long, low laugh go pulsing around the deck. This laugh, if it even occurred, was suddenly in all places at once, and gone as suddenly and utterly. Jean had grown very cold, but he was not afraid. He said, under his breath, "I know you. What have you come to tell me?" But that too was only his instinct, for he did not know, either what was there with him, or what he had said to it.

Nevertheless, there came a swift flash, like a star falling or a light quenched somewhere between himself and the next item of solid material, which happened to be one of the masts. What it was he did not see, although it seemed afterward that it might have been the reflection of a face, glimpsed as if in a mirror. It was a peculiar face, too, more a mask, that was at one and the same time black and white, but whether the black was laid over the white or the white on the black, Jean could not make out.

And then he found he could move, the air had soaked back to its usual tepid warmth, and he started to hear real sounds from the ship, and to behold some sailors over by one of the hatches smoking their pipes, and the watch motionless aloft. The other thing was gone.

The young man went down to the saloon to take his supper, trying to put off a vague sense of shame, which apparently naturally replaced the super-natural sensation that preceded it. Below, he drank more than he was used to with his meal, and went to bed amused at himself and engorged by notions of his arrival at the Island in the morning, where his search would commence at once for Dargue.

The ship entered port an hour after dawn. For whatever other reason, it was likely Haïssa had earned the epithet "Black" in one way from her looks. Behind the harbor the Town straddled a vast swooping slope that expended itself abruptly, miles off, against enormous uplands cumbered in jungles or forests that showed jet-black against the vibrancy of the sky. Beyond these nearer heights yet more gigantic cliffs scaled up, thick with vegetation and trees, until distance reduced the panorama to transparency. In two or three spots a solitary waterfall shone like a straight white smoke. The Town itself was by contrast pastel and tawdry, the ripe smell of it drifting out across the harbor with the stink of fish and fruit. Parrots, in cages on peeling balconies that overhung the water, screamed. Although he had seen black men as he neared the Island, Jean had never gazed on such a quantity. Their species was so different he could not fit them into any comfortable niche. It was easier to detail them as some form of higher and less tractable animal. The brilliance of their teeth shocked him, and their women, walking barefoot on the sharp stones and broken shards above the shipping, with metal necklets and colored scarves circling their waists and brows. The women of Jean's landscape had figures made of laced bone and hair like raveled silk. These had pelt or fleece upon their heads. Their breasts swayed with the rhythm of their steps as they walked like cats.

Had he not been embued by his purpose, the young man, alone and mostly penniless in this alien world, might have given way to preliminary panic. But he was armored, was Jean. And in his armor he went ashore, and carrying his bag himself, went up the first curving street from the port, between the balconies and birdcages, across a square of big-limbed trees pendulous with gourds, under the stucco and the palms and over the steps, clung with orchids, that led to the upper Town of Black Haïssa.

And the cat-women passed him in their skins of velure, and higher up he saw the ones who were half cat and half human, swarthy near-white, driving in their carriages with fans of feathers in their carved, ringed hands. And he saw the gentlemen too, lounging by the barbers and the hotels, in striped waistcoats, and some of these were black and some not quite black. But the whites had gone to the very surface-top of the Town like froth to the top of coffee, and there were to be noticed, like pieces of mosaic among the plantains and palm trees, their froth-white mansions with faded names, and colossal gardens gone to seed, passionflowers and flowers that ate flies, snakes in the dry fountains, and giant spiders hung among vines, weaving with their legs.

But the visor of his armor was down across the eyes of Jean de St. Jean the poet's son. He knew the word "Dargue." That was what he had come for. He climbed up because that was the way the streets and steps led him, and the hanging parks of Haïssa Town. Dargue was a man of substance in this place, and should be simple to find.

And Jean knew an aching urge to see him again. It was nearly poignant. As if, in looking at this man, he could perceive, lifted miraculously out of time and decay, his two parents, whose faces he knew only from some little paintings kept in Andromede's apartment.

Jean had of course conceived a plan, partly conceived it in his home City in the days after sighting Dargue. Aboard ship, during the ocean months, he shaped the plan or was shaped by it, perhaps. The fuss that some of his fellow passengers made of him – as a young hopeful setting forth to try his fortune (naturally the true purpose was not revealed to them) – and the general talk of the way of getting on in the islands, molded the plan further. It became outrageous and possible. It appealed to Jean by its audacity, its very terribleness. For what he eventually proposed to do was to approach Dargue directly, rendering him the false identity which he, Jean, had already adopted for the voyage out – it was one of the few provisions the poet's son had taken to protect himself. And having so engaged his enemy, Jean would stand before him and beg for an occupation, flaunting the good City education, making of himself a charming and valuable prospect. That Dargue should take him on, employ him, as a secretary or assistant of some sort, was so balefully ironic, Jean did not believe it could not come to be.

Installed in Dargue's very household, privy to his secrets, which rumor suggested were often dark, debauched, dangerous, Jean foresaw a hundred opportunities both to ruin and, ultimately, to commit murder.

How the murder was to be accomplished – this he did not know, and had never truly visualized. It was a shadow act performed in dream. *That valid.* He trusted that the hour and the means would be given him.

Jean made his inquiries at Haıssa Town after Dargue in the manner of the young hopeful off the ship, a fellow citizen, speaking a common tongue, clever, and prepared to be industrious. Quite quickly he had his directions to a mansion out along Oleander Road. It was a two-hour ride, which to Jean, on foot and with his bag in hand, would furnish an afternoon's walk.

Oleander Road was not a road in any sense of a city street. It was a broad avenue of earth that rambled out of the edges of the Town and curled itself away for miles through the hills. It was barricaded by banana trees, and continually encroached upon by the forest, a swollen, lubricious wall of leaves and trunks that bulged inward with incredible potency, alight with sun, with bird noises, and the quiver of insects. The air was warm, it seemed to run down in rivulets, so that everything to be seen wavered. Along Oleander Road, at considerable distances from one another, the old houses lay off the track, behind spilled paths, rough-haired lawns, and plantings of cocoa and tobacco. In one place there was even a milestone, but it indicated the leagues back to Haıssa Town.

Shade was thrown all over the road, and shots of sun. The shambling route went always higher and higher, and began at length to show, through windowpane openings, sky and sea below.

Drenched in sweat, Jean walked the road. His bag came to weigh like the weight of the sins of the one he sought.

There was nothing else he could do. It was out of the question to turn back, and he never debated that he should. He went on, sometimes turning his head to catch the weird bird cries of the forest, or slapping at some blood-sucking thing that had bitten him. It was a type of hell, this walk. He had not foretold the punishment, but neither did he resist its infliction.

The shade pool on the road deepened, and spread, and a breeze started that shook the huge hammered-iron leaves of the plantains. It was evening, and abruptly, on his left hand, Jean saw the notice that indicated the estate of Monsieur Dargue.

He felt a start of the pulses, as though he had encountered a lover unexpectedly.

The garden of Dargue's house was positively enormous and dense with the coming of darkness. The overhanging shrubs and trees seemed hung with heavy coils of snakes. A scent began of strange pale-colored flowers. The stars were piercing the sky like drops of silver sweat or blood bursting out upon a thin black skin.

Jean wandered through this tangle of night, and behind the little fires of flowers the house had suddenly appeared, two stories of masonry in a cage of verandas, lighted by oil lamps that hung on it like ripe fruit.

A dog commenced to bark and howl drearily. Jean stood beside a foun-tain and saw the mansion of his enemy before him, and everything became for a moment unreal. It was as if he did not even know who he himself was, or his own name. As if he had forgotten the name of his father, and why he had come here. And the word "Dargue" was meaningless.

The moment was frightful to Jean. It actually frightened him, but more than that, it caused him to struggle with some faceless adversary, and to win.

After that the house was Dargue's house, and he must get to it at once.

Perhaps he became aware as he drew nearer that there was a hush on the building. The dog had left off its dirge and the crickets were very loud. One lighted window burned in the second story, nothing else. The lanterns around the veranda seemed to grin. Beyond the house stretched the fields of the estate, but no lamp moved there – it might have been a primeval swamp.

Jean rang the bell, which was quite ordinary. He had to wait some while, and was reaching out again for the bellpull when he heard a kind of dragging step coming toward him through the house.

Jean was conscious then that something had gone wrong.

The door opened. An elderly black man was craning out, peering up at him. He had the face of a beautiful marmoset, which themselves resemble the princes of another world. But he was so old and bent, and maybe had had to bend his inner self also; he looked at Jean with a timorous indifference, saying nothing.

"Dargue. I am here – to see Monsieur Dargue," said Jean stridently, his voice too noisy, like something that escaped him.

The old man continued peering up at him.

"I've come a long way," said Jean, and suddenly realized that he had. He trembled.

"Monsieur Dargue," said the black man, softly.

"Yes. Tell him –"

"No, monsieur," said the black man, "I can't tell him. Monsieur Dargue is dead."

The whole night caved in upon Jean, shadows, trees, darkness, stars, all came rushing down, pouring in through the top of his skull. He dropped his bag somewhere in the maelstrom. Then found himself leaning against the wall.

The servant man still watched him, still indifferent, but saying now in a craven way, "He take ill on the day he come back. He take to his bed. Then the doctor come. Then the priest come. Then Monsieur Dargue, he dies. He dies last night."

In the silence that followed the servant's recital, Jean heard himself say, equally softly, "But I've come such a long way. I came to find him."

"He dead, monsieur."

Jean said, "Yes."

And then the servant seemed to try to reward him for his compliance.

"He is lying out on the bed. You want come in, monsieur, have look at him?"

A rush of nausea. "No," Jean said. "In God's name –"

When he recovered a little, the servant had closed the door, and was audibly making his dragging progress off again through the house.

For a few seconds Jean leaned on the wall and wept. It was the ghastly disappointment of the passionate child, whose desired gift has been snatched away at the last instant, literally out of his hand.

Worst of all, he did not know in the least what to do next. He had been almost four months tending to this, more, his entire life had in some sort latched on it. But the dream act was already performed. Even as he had stood on the ship's deck, scenting the odor of Haïssa across the night, even then. Death himself had preempted the frail revenge of Jean de St. Jean. Face to face with his own mortal inconsequence, the young man turned from the house of his enemy, a shell as meaningless as if gutted by fire. He trudged away, not quite knowing what he did, through the serpentine garden.

2

On Oleander Road, near midnight, Jean beheld a strange procession.

He supposed he had sat down at the road's edge, as he might have done in some country lane of the north, above his City. Here there were snakes and poisonous toads, hairy lianas, vampire insects – but he was past considering them. He did not sleep but sank into a stupor, in which he was aware of moisture, the dew of old rains dripping down, and things that hastened over his hands. The moon crossed the road, and when it was gone, through the dark a throbbing seemed to come, like the pulse of blood along an artery.

Jean gazed with dull eyes. Presently the curtains of night were parted, and from some obscure avenue among the trees of the forest, a troop of men and women emerged onto the road. They looked themselves black as the night, and would not have been easy to see but for the fact many of them wore light-colored garments that shone in a skull-faced flicker of lanterns. Jean noticed that several of the women carried bunches of some plant. It was not unfamiliar, perhaps he had seen it growing wild here and there, an ugly shrub, stringy, like an uncombed horse's tail.

The leader of these people was a tall man dressed in white. He stalked ahead as if alone, staring directly before him. He held a whip with a bone handle. There was also a girl who lugged in a wicker cage two or three black birds that jumped and flapped, but their outcry was lost in the drums and a deep, ceaseless murmuring that went with them up the road.

Jean was aware, incoherently, that he looked on something that maybe it would have been better he had not seen. There was an overt secrecy to the procession, which seemed to make no attempt to hide itself simply because, by an inexorable law, it must not be witnessed.

When the vision had disappeared into the tunnel of the road going in the direction perhaps of Dargue's estate, Jean stayed motionless, listening after the fading drumbeat, until it mingled with the beating of his own heart in his ears.

When he moved again, it was with a stupefied caution. He was not afraid, but he suspected he should be.

He stumbled on, and with no further encounter, came eventually back to the brink of the Town. Here, earlier, he had found a possible lodging. Having climbed the wall, he slept in the garden of this place, for he would not rouse them at that hour, the prohibitions of his upbringing forbade such a thing. It was almost dawn in any case. The sky's membrane palpitated. Beneath a mango tree with savage leaves he fell, and using his bag for a pillow, began to tell himself mindlessly over and over what he must do. That all there *was* to do now was to seek labor, as a clerk, or even at a meaner occupation, earning his return passage to the City. What else could he attempt? For he was like a somnambulist roughly wakened. The dream had misled, he had lost his way.

Although he could not sleep, every now and then the image of the procession on Oleander Road went swaying through his thoughts, scattering them.

Had the procession been going to the house of Dargue? But they had told him on the ship, the black race of the islands hated the white race. The last wave of the Revolution, breaking there, had freed the slaves of Haïssa, but made of them instead mostly serfs. And those that had become black masters, in their turn, hated too, in a more perilous, educated manner, anything that was pale, even where darkness ran just visibly under the skin.

This was a land of nightmares, this country he had woken up in. He must get home. Anything else was futile. He was broken.

It is probable Jean went mad that night. Of course he had been tinged by insanity for years, for all his life. But like a deadly flower it burst open in him then, in the hours on the road, going back, cheated. Beneath the mango in the garden of the lodging house.

That is not to say his madness was incurable.

When day arrived, he heard persons stirring in the house and went and claimed his room there. Next, having washed himself and shaved, he went into the Town to look for employment. He did all this very correctly, and like a man with no soul. There is a name for this condition in the islands, and he was to hear it quite soon.

In the afternoon, when a bruised light hung over the Town, the outrider of the storm that usually occurred daily at that season, Jean de St. Jean was sitting in the dusty little office of someone who might be willing to give him some work. He had been waiting an interminable time, which was in reality only a few minutes, and his nerves were urging him sluggishly but repeatedly to get up and leave, for this could be no use to him. Then the door opened, and a black man entered.

He was dressed as a laborer, and his personal scent was strong, like the musk of the panther. He looked directly at Jean and, without a word, jerked his feline head toward the street.

Jean saw this, and said, "What do you want?"

He had not achieved the proper purblind arrogance of the white in Haïssa, or the proper uneasiness either. He reacted as he would have done to something unreal yet fundamentally inimical. To a threatening and *superior* thing.

The man did not answer him, but poised there, plainly expecting Jean to get up and go out with him.

Jean was so exhausted, so demoralized and unhinged, that in a moment this was exactly what he did.

When they were on the street, Jean said, "But –"

That was all.

They went down and down, through a kind of corkscrew of streets, where vines and palms poured over walls, and the houses came to be built of planks and tin. Finally there was a space, and a rickety hut with a tin roof, and the black man pointed at its door.

"Who are you?" said Jean.

The black man laughed. He looked like a god when he did so, lawless and all-wise. Then he spat on the ground and walked off another way, and Jean was left there, at the bottom of the corkscrew, with only the door in front of him. So he pushed the door wide.

Inside was the dusk again, redolent with such stuff as cooked rice, blood, spice, tobacco, washing, and rum. He could make out no furniture, but some black beings were seated on the earth floor in an open circle, and before them was a scatter of objects lit by one window. Jean saw dried beans and cards, a shawl, a fruit, and the bones of a dog brightly painted.

"Shut our door," said a voice.

Jean drew the door in against him, and the shack became more solid and less visible, and the bones glowed, and the white eyes in the faces like ebony, like beautiful alien masks, and like nothing human.

"Sit down with us," someone said. And someone else gave a cruel laugh.

Jean remained in the shut door. They were figments of a new dream.

Finally, a man said from the circle, "M'sir Dargue is dead. Are you sorry he dead?"

Jean choked back a confused reply. He felt compelled to respond, unbearably excited, could not speak.

"Why you would want him alive?" said the voice.

There was a great attention then. They focused it upon Jean. He did not know how many of them there were, but the eyes fastened on him like claws.

"Alive – so I –" said Jean.

"He not loved, Monsieur Dargue," said the voice. The others purred in the dark. "No one is sorry."

Jean covered his face with one hand. He longed, as though to vomit, to evict the cry: *My father's murderer!* It would not come.

"You not sorry," said the voice, soothingly.

The illness flooded from Jean, the words released him. He said hoarsely, "Yes, I came to kill him. Too late."

"Not so. We give him you, for killing."

And the others purred.

They were smiling at him. In every night of a face a sickle moon.

But Dargue was dead.

"We invite you to come our God-Place," said the first voice. A black hand reached out and took up one of the bones from the ground. The bone moved as if still alive, and animal. "We invite M'sir Dargue. We fetch him. You be surprised. But we give you have M'sir Dargue, because you want him so."

Jean thought they must have pursued him back along Oleander Road on the previous night, and read his mind. They were sorcerers, so much was apparent. He had always half believed in sorcery.

But what were they saying? That Dargue was not dead, but in some way their prisoner?"

"You pay the price," said the voice.

Jean said, "I haven't any money –"

They purred again. The shack reverberated. Jean thought, Not money. It isn't that. Something they want and I want, but I must pay and then they need not.

He thought, very clearly: What am I doing? Where am I? What is happening to me? And someone else said, *"This is the Religion of the Night."*

Then he was sitting close by them on the earth floor, cooking hot as if above a volcano, with his back to the wall and the tin ceiling above, from which feathers and paper blossoms and bells hung on threads. A mirror floated in space, like a tear, a small lizard clinging to its cracked, uneven rim. A black woman was giving him drink out of a calabash gourd. It was rum with something sweet. Jean drank, and thanked the woman, and she laughed, and touched his brow with her finger. Her touch was like a star, it burned.

Rain was drilling on the tin roof. They had given him a direction, where he must go tonight, not too late....

"No," said Jean.

"Good day."

Jean returned to his lodging and dozed feverishly on the bed. He dreamed his Aunt Andromede was standing over him, wringing her hands, saying, "Let me advise you, Jean, you mustn't go anywhere with such people." But there were feathers pinned into her tight hair.

The storm flew toward the sea, and the evening descended clear, as stars rose up through it.

He went out and moved toward a market at a crossroads known as Horse Tail. He had already asked the way. He received solemn looks and vague replies, until a wizened black woman had shown him the route, drawing a diagram in the dust. Still, he meant to be late. He did not guess why he was going. They might set on him, though there was surely no motive. He was destitute; he had done nothing to annoy them, except that being alive might be enough. He concluded they meant to play some trick. But he was drawn as if by a magnet. It allowed him to dawdle, but not to resist.

It was dark when he reached the crossroads. There were some carts and awnings, and fires burning on the ground, and candles in gourds strung up. Commerce of a desultory type was in progress, scrawny chickens changing hands, some barter over beans and pots of jelly.

The market ignored Jean, as if he were invisible. Then a man came walking straight between the carts, the refuse, and the market seemed to make way for him. He wore a black robe, black on black, but in his hand was a whip with a white bone handle.

When he reached Jean, there were all at once five or six other men at this man's back.

The man said to Jean, "Come, now. We invite you."

And turning away, he strode off again, toward the forest and the hills. The other men went with him and, pulled as though by tough cord, Jean walked after them.

The God-Place crouched in a somber clearing. Water ran close by, snarled in the roots of an enormous tree, making a weird tearing sound. The roof of the temple was thatched, with an open court beneath, enclosing the sanctum, and full of the night people of Haïssa. As the man with the whip had ascended the forest path among his guard, and Jean followed, he heard the subterranean notes of conch shells blowing in the woods above. When the temple came in sight, and they approached it, these shells were blown again, a dubious, threatening greeting.

The man with the whip strode to a boundary of the court, which was marked by some small heaps of meal, petals, and paper. He used the whip's bone handle to point with. "You will stand there. You say nothing. If you fear and run away, you not get what you come for." He did not look at Jean, had never really looked into Jean's face or eyes.

Jean did not protest. He went to the indicated spot at the perimeter of the court. Five women who had been grouped inside the boundary, near where he must stand, ebbed away, turning their shadow masks from him.

The man with the whip passed into the temple. They had brought a chair and set it by the entry to the inner shrine. The chair had an abnormally high and upright back resembling a coffin. The whip man seated himself, and the crowd in the court deferred to him. Evidently he was their priest, and their magician.

The skull lamps of the calabash gourds burned from the thatch, and here and there glimmered wicks in cups of oil. The light only made one with the darkness. And the smell of the God-Place was intense and disturbing.

A girl in white came flaunting over the court. She carried a lighted candle and a jar of clear rum, from which she poured a libation under the central post of the thatch roof. Another white-clad girl came after her, an echo, a smoke-ghost. She poured flour or meal on to the ground in a pattern. A third girl came with a snake's rattle in each hand, and she whirled like a top until her white and her black merged into a vortex, out of which all three girls seemed to vanish away.

Then the three drums of the spirits began, and Jean saw the Dance of the Religion of the Night, a forbidden thing, both prayer and invocation, during which power descends, along the temple's very spine, and rays out among those who call themselves the Night Beasts, the black lynxes of the hills, whose true hills are older yet and whose rites began in cities of stone and bone when white men only whimpered at their cave mouths, afraid of all things and the dark especially, with some continuing cause.

Jean saw how the people formed into a black serpent of flesh, a body of many parts linked by a communal soul. And they passed about the spine post of the temple in the ancient benign positive right-to-right motion known in the Craft of Europe as God's Flowing, and commemorated by artisans in the action of clocks and watches. The steps of the Dance were a rapid stamping and tossing, and the drums formed these steps out of the muscle and skeleton of every dancer, lifting them, setting them down. The names of the three drums, which were later told to Jean, were the little cat's drum, and the drum of the second, and the mother Drum, which roars like a she-bull under the ground, the earthquake birth, the summoner.

As he watched, Jean felt his own body beginning to move with the rhythm of the Dance, although, too, he was rooted to the spot. A crazy exhilaration rose with the sweat and perfume of the God-Place. Naturally, educated and refined as he had been, Jean was instinctively resistant to it. He could not and would not give himself to the surge of power. He stayed outside, his breathing rapid and shallow and his eyes on fire, steeled, aroused, dismayed, in chains.

After a while, out of the dancing serpent, a young woman broke away. She raised her arms and screamed aloud. The dancers gave her room. She was the mare-horse, and one would come to ride her.

She was the mare among the Night Beasts and the horseman would possess her, riding in her skin, a god mounting her, and she would lose herself, gaining him.

The woman who was possessed was now in an open space against the central post. Her eyes were like blind windows, yet something flashed behind them. A girl in a pale robe came to the woman and handed her a black hen.

Its terrible fluttering exploded in blood and feathers as the possessed tore off its head and wings with her teeth.

The woman flung the hen down, and drawing a pin from her dress, she thrust it through her arm, once, twice, three, four, five times. Jean beheld the bright point going in and coming out of her, but there was no blood now, no pain. She danced on the carcass of the dead bird, twirling and shouting.

The magician-priest had risen from his coffin-chair. He pointed at the woman, and all at once the blood-beat of the drumming fell away, leaving behind an extraordinary absence, as though part of the very ground had dropped into space. He spoke in the patois, which Jean did not truly understand. It was evidently a welcome.

The possessed ceased her whirling. She stood before the priest, laughing with tiger's teeth. Then she cried out in a deep man's voice; Jean caught the idea that she was now a lord and would be obeyed.

The priest nodded and bowed. Clearly he said, "Lead us."

And then the woman, or whatever she had become, went springing out of the court, and bounded away through the clearing, and the dancers broke and raced after her.

Jean stood still, not knowing what to do, until fingers brushed on his arm and someone said to him, "We go to the graveyard now."

He did not see who spoke, and the hand was gone from him like the flick of a paw.

He turned and half staggered into the rear of the swirling wave. It accepted him and rolled with him away across the clearing and up into the matted forest darkness sprinkled with wild stars.

Afterward – that is, one month later – Jean conjectured that some drug might have been pressed on him. Though he ate and drank nothing throughout the ceremony of the Night, yet there were certain poisons he had heard the Night Beasts used, and these, rubbed into the skin, worked very swiftly on the blood and brain.

As he ran through the forest, Jean had only the sensation of forward motion, and that his eyes were strangely enlarged, like those of some nocturnal animal. It occurred to him he saw, in glimpses, creatures that normally a man does not easily see – birds upon branches, lizards and frogs, etched in fine silver.... There were other things, too, of which only the vaguest impression was left – of a huge man, naked but for a cloak, of a species of demon that grew in the trees like leaves, of a woman anointing herself in a glade. None of them were real, yet he saw, and acknowledged, each of them, as he ran by.

The graveyard must have been some way up behind Oleander Road. It was presumably respectable, but to the Beasts of Night, open as a door. They made an invocation at the gate, and again it seemed something went prancing along the wall, but it was gone before Jean could identify it.

His next formed impression – which was abnormally apparent, in fact – was of a woman he took for a priestess standing out before the others at a place where the ground was freshly dug. All around were Christian crosses and ornate monuments on which the lianas fed in a still gray moonlight. There was a headstone, too, naked and unfinished, and here the woman's snakelike shadow fell. She wore white, like the others, but it was a gown that might have come from Jean's City, ivory satin, sashed, and sewn with brilliants, leaving her shoulders bare as smooth black lacquer. She wore a plumed hat also, and a white domino with scintillants stitched about the eyes. He did not know where she had come from. He thought she carried a fan, then he saw it was a bunch of the ugly horsetail plants. She smiled as she stood over the new grave. Jean could make out no name on the headstone, but there was no need.

The priestess straddled the grave in her satin gown. She frisked the horsetail in the air and shook her head of plumes. From everywhere there came then the clacking together of rocks and stones.

Jean held his breath, could not catch it, had surrendered. He believed in anything at this moment, and accordingly, liberated night did not fail him.

"Monsieur Dargue!" cried the night, in all its voices, over and over again.

Jean found that he had called out, too.

And the stones clacked.

And something pranced along the wall, and there went the possessed woman whirling with a burning branch in her hands, and a man's face, and the black masks all turned one way and the moon that was like a quartered fruit –

And the earth on the grave shook. It shook and shattered and a piece of wood shot up out of it, and the satin priestess screamed down into the grave, "Come out, come out, come out!" And then half a wooden coffin lid burst up and stood on end and a colorless white man's hand came creeping out of the soil like a blind crab.

The priestess stayed as she was. She never moved. The strength that seared from her was hot and palpable as the smell of living bodies and decay.

Then the ground fissured, and Dargue came up out of it.

Instantly the noise of the rocks and the shouting ended in a dense ringing silence.

Dargue stood in the bell glass of it, or what had been Dargue, a sort of man, clad in a nightshirt, and a crucifix on his breast pushed sideways. His nails were torn and dirty where he had used them to thrust off the coffin, a feat of great strength, which, alive, he might have been incapable of. His face was a dead man's face. He had lost his good angel, they said, *soul-gone*.

The dead eyes did not look around, the head did not turn, having got up from his bed he did not stir.

"*Ha!*" said the priestess. And she spat a stream of something that glowed into his face; it might only have been the white rum. Then she moved aside.

Some men ran forward. They carried the horsetails in their hands, and with these they slashed Dargue across the head and body. The spiky plants made wounds in his flesh, but Dargue did not bleed. He did not attempt to protect himself, and when, quite suddenly, he fell to his knees, the gesture evoked neither pity nor satisfaction, it was plainly only that the tendons of his legs had relaxed.

Jean stared at what he was witnessing, and now he tried desperately hard to feel something in response. Perhaps he did not even know that this was what he did. He was not afraid, no longer exhilarated. If anything, he felt very tired, for he had not slept properly or eaten much, and everything was alien, and therefore somehow all strangeness had abruptly become mundane.

What he tried most to feel was his anger, hatred of Dargue. It was there within him, but he could not get hold of it. It had faded to a memory.

The priestess moved up in front of Jean. She looked as thought she were laughing at him, her wonderful dreadful teeth glittering. Her hands were gloved as if for the opera, and she was balancing on them, before him, a sword.

She nodded, and the plumes in the hat fluttered, while the sword was motionless.

"What do you want me to do?" said Jean. He used the stupidity as an amulet, but of course it was ineffectual.

"Take the sword," said the black priestess. And she put it gently into his hands, which had somehow risen to grasp it.

The Beasts of the Night waited, and the moon waited, and the graveyard, and the Island, and Dargue who was dead, he waited too.

Jean went across the silent ground, toward Dargue, who kneeled there with his head sunk on his breast.

In all his least lawful, most incoherent dreams, Jean had never deployed his vengeance in this fashion.

He used both hands and all his strength to swing the sword backward and forward again, ramming it in through the wall of Dargue's chest, through the linen, and through the flesh, which crumbled like biscuit. A trickle of murky stuff oozed out. A rib snapped and came pointing from the cavity. The body of Dargue crumpled over and took the sword with it out of Jean's grip.

Jean stood there like a fool, feeling nothing except a faint disgust, until someone should tell him what to do now.

Shortly someone did come up, and murmured – was it courteously? – that he might go, his portion was finished, out of the gate, and follow the path, and he would soon come to the edges of the Town, with the moon to watch over him.

So he stepped off the grave and walked away.

He kept repeating to himself as he went, *My father's murderer*.

This did not help.

Then, when the graveyard had been left behind and he was on a rambling track through the forest, with the moon glimpsing out like a girl's face among the balconies of the trees, he saw what he had done, that he had cheated death in an odd, insulting manner, and this was why he had been allowed to perform the act with the sword, since death was probably venerated here, and to cheat him was such a bit of cheek it must require payment.

But all Jean wanted, actually, by this stage, was to find his lodging and go to sleep. He no longer cared about anything else. He shook everything off him as he went on, like dust from his coat. And like dust, some of it was already in his system, he had swallowed it, it was a part of him.

When he reached the lodging house he no longer had scruples about waking them up. He knocked and banged on the shutters. When they let him in, he crawled through the house and dropped on the mattress in his clothes, with the dust of night in his belly, mind, and spirit. And without a single dream that he knew of he slept, like the dead.

3

As it happened, at any rate as it was told, the story of Jean de St. Jean has here a break or interval. Real life, and its experiences, are seldom completely serial. Yet the space of a year may be recounted quickly, the method indeed of my informant.

Jean's recovery – or lapse – from the hour of his murder of a dead man seems to have been immediate. His impulse was to ignore what had happened, then boldly to question it. Though he kept his reasons private, by asking casually here and there in knowledgeable, biased circles, for facts concerning Haïssa's Religion of the Night – that is, among the skeptical white community – Jean learned to behold himself as a victim of drug or fantasy. Perhaps the shock of Dargue's death had unhinged him temporarily, perhaps he had the voyager's malaise, a kind of earth-sickness, induced by stepping ashore after months on the ocean. Whatever it had been, any slight fears he may have had that some further pursuit might be made of him, threats or pleas offered, based upon his participation in the ceremony, were allayed by the passage of time. No one approached him to accuse or mock or coerce. He even grew used to the black beings of the Island, and came to think of them as inferior men, or sometimes as men, so that they lost for him their appearances of shadows and panthers, lynxes, and night personified. He was even briefly tempted by their women, but some moral code he had always tried to obey precluded such adventures. He had been brought up on a diet not solely of hate but ironically of an ideal of true love.

The previous votive of working to obtain his passage home he quickly sought and achieved. His City education and person assisted Jean, and he gained the secretary's job formerly mooted. Presently, along with the accumulation of bank notes, he was absorbed into the social context of white Haïssa. Class was held, since the Revolution, to be immaterial, but was still insidiously observed. Jean's manners were of sufficient quality, however, and his looks of enough attraction, that insidiously observed class did not much hinder him. He rose, and he bloomed, and even as conditions bore the harvest of money to return him across the sea, they drew in about his roots and began to secure him to the Island earth.

It must be wondered, in this time, if he wrote at all to his Aunt Andromede, and if so, what he told her. His reports could, soon enough, be of the nicest, full of good prospects and nostalgias. How he put it to her that Dargue had perished is conjecture. He could not have made of it the grim joke it was, nor, certainly, even in the most unsolid terms, could he have hinted at the scene in the graveyard. Letters took so long, in any case, going back and forth. It is possible that they were mislaid, or unsent. One senses she did not receive any, but that may be false. One knows at least she never heard the facts in their naked form.

Presently, along with the rest, Jean became accustomed to the climate. He came to look for the seasonal afternoon rains, the thunder, the moon-drenched nights in which, by then, he would stroll or ride without glancing over his shoulder. He liked the friends he had made. Though assiduously he saved his fare, it had turned into a sham.

He did not exactly know this until one morning, going to his office along a street above the bay, a carriage slowly passed him. Looking into it inadvertently, he saw a young woman in a dove-colored frock and pearl earrings. Her name was Gentilissa Ferrier – he identified her from the carriage, which he had seen about before. Monsieur Ferrier was a little known to Jean, and had mentioned that his daughter was to come home from one of the other islands, where family connections had for months concealed her. The sight of the girl startled Jean. For some minutes, when the carriage had gone on, he did not know why. Then he recalled the features of a Madonna from a painting he had seen as a boy. The Venus of Haïssa was also a Madonna, both carnal and immaculate, having two aspects, a flower virgin and a black virgin. Jean had in his researches heard the name of this goddess, who is wedded to all men and to none. He did not, naturally, for a second associate her with Gentilissa Ferrier, but by the time he had reached his office, Jean sensed an immanence. His father and mother had fallen in love at sight. In his efforts to recreate them, possibly Jean had yearned to do the same. Now the opportunity was before him. He took it.

Once he had convinced himself of what had happened to him there came about one of those coincidences that, to a person obsessed, indicate the hand of Destiny. Jean found he had been invited to a dinner party at the Ferrier house. This had already happened twice. There had been no reason not to invite him again; he had behaved very charmingly before.

It is curious, maybe, through this sliding frame of a year, to see Jean now, earlier an incarnation of Hamlet, currently Romeo. But the passion is constant, merely the object has been changed.

With the same headlong zeal that sent him aboard the ship, that goaded him along Oleander Road toward the estate of Dargue, in just that way he prepared himself for his first meeting with the girl Gentilissa. His eyes blazed, he was excited, fiercely determined. He had been disappointed then, by those appalling words: *He is dead.* But he put all that behind him, and could not credit a disappointment now. Gentilissa was there to be won. A year of success proved that he was able to win things. He had a half vision of her in the City on his arm, when his fortune had been made. Or they were driving through the forest roads above Haïssa Town in a taper of brief dusk, and she leaned her head upon his shoulder.

The Ferrier family was quite wealthy. This pleased Jean only because it meant Gentilissa would have been elegantly reared, though she would not, he understood, be as sophisticated as a girl of his City. What impediment could there be? He had prospects, and it was up to him to make her love him. If only he could do that.

He said a prayer to the Virgin. It was not the Virgin of the two faces, but the albino Madonna in the church. But he had already noted, if he had thought of it, that the shacks of Night Beasts often had their crosses, their icons of Christ. The gods had many names and were everywhere.

When he rode up to the house, it had a certain look of some houses in the Island. He knew it, anyway. Set off the road among large mango trees, ferns, and thickets of bamboo, constructed of apparently crumbling sugar, with orchids, and a tame parrot in a cage on the veranda, that called out in the tongue of the City: *"Who goes there?"*

A black servant ran to see to Jean's horse. Jean climbed the steps and went up into the big dining room, lit like the church with candles. Once the sun set, the moths would come in droves to die, and the sun was setting now. The guests were for going down to the classical pavilion, to see it.

Jean, with his glass of white wine in his hand, was lightheaded and anxious. He had not found her yet among the women. He wondered if he had been mistaken in her, if she would look the same.

Below the veranda on the other side, screened by a towering plantain, the kitchen fumed and two black women were poised there to be ignored as Jean had learned to ignore them.

The pavilion stood against a break in the trees, and beyond, far down, the sea was lying, with the sun going into it like a bubble into glass.

Jean wandered off a short way. He had seen the sun set before. He was instinctively searching for Gentilissa. And suddenly there she was.

It was perfect. Against a dusky, mossy wall, she was sitting on a bench, in her party gown, which was white and left bare her throat and shoulders. Her dark hair was done in ringlets, with a rose.

This he observed, and that she was lovely. But he noticed too she cast a shadow, and the shadow was a house woman, who sat with her on the bench. And by the bench there was a plant growing that Jean remembered.

It was true, he had seen it since about the forest tracks and the cemeteries of the Town. He had even garnered its title: the Queen-Mare's Tail. They said it flourished where there had been a death. A graveyard bloom. He had never quite come to like it, or be comfortable in its vicinity – that was the residue of the night he had once spent in the hills.

Now the sight of it struck him a glancing blow, that it should be growing there, against Gentilissa's skirt. And all at once the shadow figure beside her assumed an unnamed identity. For a moment Jean even thought he knew her. But she was only an old black woman, a house servant.

Just then Gentilissa got to her feet, and looking up she saw Jean gazing at her. She must have taken his apprehension for interest, for she lowered her lashes, and hid her face behind a little fan she carried, in the coquettish mann-erism of young white women of the islands. It was a silly gesture, and it reassured him.

He followed her with his eyes as she went away behind the wall, the black woman slipping after.

The sun had gone down and night smoldered in the Ferrier garden and on the veranda the parrot called. There was nothing to discompose. The family and guests and Jean went in to dinner.

Gentilissa Ferrier was beautiful and adorable; she flamed like the candles, she was serene as a nun. Her moods were variable but not hectic. Jean was fascinated. She was all he had surmised. And in addition she had the power of speech, and thoughts, she could play the piano, had a thin sweet voice that sang. When they asked her about books she had read some, and she had a dream of going to the City.

When Jean attended her, she did not seem to mind it. As he turned the pages of her music, once or twice her eyes rested upon him.

When the dinner came to its end, he was sure, and going up to her candidly, with the mantle of the City she dreamed of nonchalantly over his shoulders, he asked if he might have the rose from her hair.

She was prettily flustered. For what could he want it?

"It has been close to you, Mademoiselle Ferrier," said Jean. He was a poet's son. He had the taint if not the gift.

His final sight of her that night was upon the veranda, the whole sugar house caught in a splash of stars. The lamp that twinkled upon her put the stars at her ears and in her eyes to the very last twist of the path. The black woman was her childhood companion, a sort of nurse resembling Juliet's. She dressed neatly and had a bracelet. Jean had been polite to her on the veranda, and the woman bowed. They called her Tibelle.

In the weeks that followed, Jean often found occasion to be passing the Ferrier house. They were never unwelcoming. Monsieur spoke of the City, and of business, Madame was earnest to have cards. Then Gentilissa would come and serve juices in crystal jugs. She would take Jean away to show him birds and butterflies in the garden, and Tibelle would be their chaperone, gliding some distance behind them. And sometimes they would sit in an arbor while Gentilissa coaxed tunes from a mandolin, and Tibelle would sit far off, a black shape still as the iron owl on the gate. The woman had a pipe and now and then would smoke it, and the smoke moved in rising, but not Tibelle. The jewelry birds darted through the foliage. Jean began to court Gentilissa.

It was pleasant, there was no hurry. Everything acquiesced. Time seemed to stretch forever. If he was impatient, it was only through physical desire. He had not kissed her. These things, this temperance, were inborn. The climate, which could incite, could also calm with its false assurance, Go slowly. Lazily, a man and woman drew together. No one denied.

Then one evening, as Tibelle the black volcano sat smoking on the horizon, Gentilissa leaned to Jean and brushed his cheek with her warm lips.

It was as if a barrier fell down. He turned upon her and pulled her to him, but before his hunger found any expression, she moved away.

"No, Jean," said Gentilissa, as sweetly as she sang and out of her nun's face. "You mustn't."

"But why?"

"Because Papa would be horribly angry."

Jean was reckless at last. "But he'll have to be told. I shall ask him for you. You know I will."

"No," said Gentilissa. She looked neither sad nor unnerved. She was entirely at peace.

"You feel nothing for me," said Jean. It was a boastful demand. Despite her look, he was certain by now that she loved him.

"Oh Jean," she said.

"Then I'll ask him tonight."

"He will refuse you."

Jean hesitated. He had not made his intentions obvious, but neither had they been opaque. Would Gentilissa's father not have sounded some warning previously, if he were vehemently opposed?

"Allow me the attempt," said Jean.

"I can't. How can I? Papa has no objection to my holding court ... that I should have admirers. But he expects me to marry a man of substance. Already there is someone in view."

"That's barbarous."

"It's how it is done here."

"Nonsense. I –"

"Jean, you will grieve me."

It was so shocking, this development, he could not credit it. He sought to take her hand. Gentilissa would not permit this.

"I love you," he said. "I think you care for me."

"I may not answer."

"Your eyes answer." This was a lie. Her eyes were blank. She said nothing, either. But he had all the evidence of several weeks, when every sigh and tremor and sideways look had concocted meaning. "Gentilissa, in a year or so I might be a rich man. It's been said to me, promised."

"Dearest Jean," said Gentilissa. Her breast rose with delirious softness as she drew in her breath. "I can't go against Papa. He means me to marry a man from another island. There's nothing I can do. I never guessed the strength of your feeling. I thought you amused yourself with me."

Jean swore by God. Gentilissa averted her head. She said, very low, "You must leave me now. We must never see each other again, until after I am married."

Jean sprang to his feet, but already Gentilissa was moving lightly away, like a piece of white cotton down. And summoned uncannily without a cry, the servant woman, Tibelle, was slinking toward them.

In a rage of powerlessness and disbelief, Jean stood in the Ferrier garden until the black woman and the white had disappeared together beyond the mango trees.

There is another name for the Religion of the Night among the islands. They term it Nightmare Magic. Once you have ever been touched by it, there is no getting free. To the devotee that is no problem. To the outsider, whom the gods, however obliquely and remotely, have ridden, the Religion is fever. It may lie dormant ten years. But it is not to be escaped from, in the end. They tell you, have nothing to do with it. But sometimes wanting is enough to bring it down, like a cloud from the mountain. No sooner did Jean run into the apartment of his aunt with the branch of their hate in blossom, no sooner did he set sail, than he called the Devil, and the Devil started forth. Before he left the ship, the first night, the entity had shown itself. It was too late. Death brought Jean de St. Jean to the Island, and cheated him and bargained with him and claimed him. There is not a boulder or a leaf there without some life in it, or something of death in it. It was not only the forests or the human skin of Haıssa that earned it the adjective *Black*.

For a month, Jean dwelled in a condition of misery and fury that was almost lunatic. Initially, he did his best to go about his affairs of business and existence otherwise as before. But that was impossible. His heart had been cut out. He was in constant agony and barely alive. Sometimes he would lose himself in awful daydreams, riding to the house and confronting Monsieur Ferrier, bursting in upon her wedding and shooting down the groom. At other, worse times, he visualized his own life stretching to infinity bereft of Gentilissa. It seemed to him his pain would never cease. If he got drunk it might abate for half an hour, only to return with redoubled ferocity. Sober, he was like a man beneath a ton weight, he could hardly raise his head.

He was thought to be ill. He was treated with sympathy, next with concern, ultimately with impatience. This was not the obliging, efficient Jean they knew.

At night he would sit in his rooms and look at his money saved for the homeward voyage. It was like the coinage of oblivion. To go away was out of the question. To remain was not to be endured.

That he also thought of killing himself is conceivable, but it was a symptom rather than an intent.

Then one afternoon there came to his office, where he was sitting in rapt dejection, a letter. He knew at once that it was from her. Tearing it open he read: *I can bear our separation no longer. If you still love me and will dare the consequences, be this evening just after sunset by the statue of the slave. Tibelle will bring you to me.*

The effect upon Jean, after his unhappiness, was galvanic, almost injurious. He shook, went white, laughed aloud once or twice, and generally furthered the prevailing opinion among his colleagues that he was not long to be among them.

The letter he did not let go of, and leaving his post early, he rushed to his rooms to prepare himself for this clandestine and romantic assignation. He had not a single qualm, although he did think her a trifle foolish, and very endearing, to trust him so much. Surely she loved him, and through the blessing of that, everything else could be made to come right.

The statue of the slave, a rough and ready work attempted in the classical mode, stood near a crossroad and a market. They were unfamiliar to Jean, although he found the statue easily enough. He had arrived before time, and watched the sun go down behind the towers of a pair of churches, and then the darkness came, and he beheld the fires burning in the market, and the ragged awnings, and the chicken corpses along the carts, and smelled the overripeness of the gourds, and heard the chattering of the black men and women who idled there. An unpleasant memory wakened in Jean. Before he had satisfactorily thrust it off, he saw the woman Tibelle coming across the street. Her hair was tied up in a cream kerchief as always, and on her ebony stick of wrist the bracelet dripped like water. She walked right up to him, and scrutinized his face. *To be sure of me, for her mistress' sake*, Jean thought to himself, but he was not easy with her look for all that.

"Now you come with Tibelle."

"Where?"

"Tibelle take you."

"Where are we going?"

"You come, you see."

Jean shrugged. He no longer felt as he had done, elated, slightly drunk, a little afraid. Now there was something heavy again, something pressing down on him. As he went after the servant woman, his entrails were cold and his heart beat in hard leaden strokes. His father might have told him, these are the sensations of a man en route to the gallows.

Up behind the market the streets rose and then there began to be the wide avenues where the fine old houses had been built, the houses of broken sugar under the poured molasses of the vines.

And then they were on a stretch that could have been Oleander Road, or Mango Tree Ride, or one of those other flowery, fruiting tracks that led into the forest and the hills. And then they came over a stony slope showing the sea in a net of trees, and there was a cemetery before them, a graveyard.

Jean stopped, and in front of him his guide halted and turned to look at him again.

"Where you think she can meet with you," said Tibelle contemptuously, "in the hotel?"

"But here –"

"Here is safe," said Tibelle. "What you got to worry?"

And she went on again, in at the gate with a sort of stumble that might have been an obeisance, and between the graves.

Jean followed her. There was perhaps no going back. The night was all around, and the hills of Haïssa. It was too late to fly.

He noticed as he got down the ridged path behind her that things were hanging out on many of the headstones, like curious washing. There were bunches of feathers, and beads, and garlands of paper flowers, with here and there a rosary, a mask on a string with staring eyeless eyes, bones and bells that clinked and rang sometimes as the night breeze twisted at them. There was a feeling of immensity and congestion, everything too close and the night outside vast as all space where hung the bells and bones and stars inaudibly clinking and fluttering in the breath of the gods.

Jean began to cough a little, something that had not happened since he was a child, it was a sign of nerves.

Tibelle said, "Hush, hush, here you are."

And there was a shack or hut before them under a stunted palm, in the middle of the death-place.

Tibelle went aside, as she had been used to before, as if to smoke her pipe, and Jean was left by the hut in the darkness. He knew quite well that all there was to do was to push the door. He knew, and it no longer mattered. The interval of a year had evaporated, and its pleasures and agonies with it. Therefore, without hesitation finally, he opened the door and walked into the hut.

He was half surprised. For Gentilissa was sitting there before him, on a small chair, with her hands folded in her lap.

"Jean," she said.

Her eyes were large and luminous. He had always been struck by some quality in them, an effect he had taken for purity or innocence. But it was a sort of vacuity really, he could see as much now, a sort of vacancy, and when she had been with him and seemed to shine, it was because her eyes reflected him, he filled up the emptiness. It had made her attractive, like a flattering mirror.

"Jean?" she said again, now in a questioning tone.

She was wearing black. That was arresting, for Tibelle the black woman had worn white. Gentilissa in black was changed. her face was like a moon, a mask.

"Oh, Jean," she said.

And outside, the drums started, as he had heard them countless times from the hills, throbbing and rattling, for some festivity or dance. the little drum and the drum of the second and the mother Drum who roared in the earth.

Gentilissa came to her feet. She stamped lightly and tossed her head and her hair flew out, the heavy ringlets. Her eyes were flat as windowpanes. Then he began to see that something moved behind them.

Gentilissa laughed and gave herself. Her face slackened and became an idiot's. Her eyes rolled. She seemed about to fall. But something caught her and held her. Her head turned on her neck and moved around again to confront him. Behind the mask of her face, another was there, that Jean recalled. It was at the same time black and white. Whether the black lay under the white or the black was fleshed out upon the white he could not be sure. But in the eyes there was no mistaking it, the night being, the lord who had come to ride his mare, and to claim the bargain price.

Gentilissa's mouth gaped open. Out of it boomed the note of a deep bass bell. "I *here*. You *know* me," she said, in the voice of a giant man taller than the treetops, older than the Island, with the sea for blood and the bones of all the Island's dead in a necklace at his throat. "Know *me*," said Death. And Jean knew him, knew him. Knew *him*.

They said he died of a fever in Haïssa Town, having been sick for some while. The Island is noted for its seasonal fevers. They said it was a shame he died so young, the same age as his father, indeed, and far from home. You may come across the grave in a shady corner of the Christian Cemetery near Oleander Road. There is no inscription beyond his name, *Jean de St. Jean*. Though sometimes flowers may be left there, by girls in colored scarves who walk like cats and smile, blackened by the sun to the darkness of night, Negré girls, who cannot, probably, have known him.

This grave is modest, here in the cemetery of Paradys. Easy to overlook it, but we shall not.

Weeds grow, unpruned, there are no floral tributes.

The name: Julie d'Is.

Beautiful Lady

Sugar and spice
And all things nice.

– Traditional

Chorgeh said, leaning a little over the balustrade, "How does she merit the name? I wouldn't think her even somewhat stylish. Her hair scraped back under that worm of a hat, her gloves darned. Her figure is all right; her face is nothing, only sallow. Her eyes – Well, they seem a little unusual, tilted, like an Oriental's. Is that the clue?"

"Not at all," said Chorgeh's informant. The two men (Chorgeh young and dangerous-looking in his fashionable coat, the elder conservative and restrained, yet tapping a new-fangled cigarette on a silver box) stared a moment over the gallery at the woman passing underneath along the arcade. "No, it's nothing about her appearance. Put it in the Roman tongue. Have you never heard of deadly nightshade?"

"*Poison,*" said Chorgeh, abruptly smiling, pleased and satisfied. "I *see.*"

Below, the woman had paused to glance into one of the tiny, dainty shops. It was true, she looked poor, shabby, and neglected, by others and herself. Close to, her face would be unpowdered, her nails too short, her hair carelessly combed and stuffed into a small bun, unbecoming and resentful.

"Other than *Bella Donna*, her name is Julie d'Is."

"You know this for a fact."

"Oh, I know all about her. I make it my business to know such things."

"You romancer," said Chorgeh. The man was his uncle, inasmuch as he had once been Chorgeh's mother's lover, and remained her friend. The man was also a writer of some eminence. His stories were always interesting, and sometimes real, but Chorgeh felt free to insult him, since he was one of the few persons Chorgeh genuinely respected. The "uncle" smoked his cigarette, and Julie d'Is, the Beautiful Lady, gazed in at delicate eggs of enamel and

415

wonderful chocolates in the shape of flowers. Her face was like a snake's now, without expression. Clearly, she regarded such items as having nothing to do with her, she only watched their strangeness, perhaps to see if they would provide prey.

"She does look," said Chorgeh, "a remarkably horrible woman."

"Be well advised. Keep far away from her. No, I'm not joking. A distance of ten feet was reckoned barely sufficient."

"Then she *is* a poisoner."

"Aside from Bella Donna, she was called the Angel of Pestilence."

"But not any longer?"

"Now she's avoided. She lives in a tiny apartment near the Temple-Church. No one visits. She calls upon no one."

"Look, she's moving on. Shall we follow her?"

"If you like," said Chorgeh's "uncle." "But I warn you, if she turns, we retreat."

They descended from the gallery, and moved after their quarry through a light, pushing, frivolous crowd. It was a bright winter day. There was hard sparkle on everything, and now and then the wind attacked from corners, the columns below libraries, and wolflike down long steps, mutter-howling under its breath. The sunshine insisted that they be pleased by it, but it blinded them at every white wall and pane of glass. The people on the street, not knowing about the story, brushed by Julie d'Is, almost collided with her.

"There she goes," said Chorgeh, "into a pastry shop after all. Does she eat pastry?"

"I expect so," said the "uncle." He lit another cigarette, the case a plaque of cold fire. "There were times when she was invited to dinners. She ate and drank like everyone else. Rather greedily in fact."

"Were you ever present?"

"Thankfully, no. There was only one occasion … I had been warned, and so declined. That was when I heard the story first, four years ago. When you, dear boy, were only thirteen."

"The worst years of my life. Tell me about Julie d'Is."

The "uncle" began his tale in a manner quite unlike his means employed when writing. Chorgeh knew that the story, if it had been or were to be translated into printable prose, would gain ornament, elongation, and proper suspense. But as a raconteur, the writer was quite brisk, almost abbreviated. Mentally Chorgeh was not above adding a brushstroke here and there.

The parents of Julie d'Is had come from the colonies of the East, some place of fans and ivories, rice, camels, bazaars, and flying carpets. They had been disgraced, the family, or simply the father, in some gambling or speculating of a nature that was kept obscure in the City – the odd codes and loyalties of the returned colonists, who would cut Monsieur d'Is, yet not betray him to outsiders. The d'Is child was female, and two years old, a weak infant mewling and puking in the tradition of weakly infants. The climate had seen to her as foolish villainy had her father; both were undone. Yet she continued, weakly, to persist, like a wan plant that straggles on, refusing to die and give up its pot to a nicer specimen. And certainly there were no other children. Shortly there began to be an exotic rumor, which was that the family had fallen afoul of a sorcerer in the Eastern lands. That just so the father lost his work and his name, and so the mother produced, from the huge burden of her womb, only the one ailing weed. Since no one spoke to the family d'Is, however, no one could verify the rumor.

Monsieur d'Is toiled as a clerk in a seedy business near the docks. Madame did her best. And the miserable daughter went on with a grisly graceless tenaciousness redolent not of courage or hope but of a dripping tap.

It was when the child, Julie, was six years old, that the tide turned for them all. They were, if not forgiven, at least forgotten. That is to say, suddenly people came upon them, exclaiming that they were the persons d'Is, and what were they doing now and how did they go on? Such reversals of attitude were not uncommon in the bored City. It was less an act of charity than a desire to see, squirming and doing tricks under the microscope, suitable microbes.

Madame d'Is began to appear in sewing circles, at afternoon teas, her husband and she played cards and dined at this house and that once or twice in a pair of months. They were hardly overwhelmed, but no longer were they excluded. Presently the child, too, perhaps perforce and in a moment of aberration, was absorbed into a children's party.

She was not, after all, such a horrid creature. She did not cringe or seek to intimidate, often the failings of the weak. No, she went along with the little-girl games, was a modest pleased recipient of favor or victory, good at losing, quiet, but with a spark. "That child," they said, "might look almost pretty, if her mother would wash her hair in softer soap, and dress her more like a child than a parcel."

Julie began to be a social success superior to her parents. She did not fawn as they did, yet was plainly genuinely impressed and grateful as they were not. She was not without animation. She could exercise tact, unusual in a child: She was not one of those to pass raw comments on a hostess's hat or wallpaper. "Poor mite. I expect she gets little enough chance to shine at home, with *those* two." "The mother keeps her like a little slave. She heaps the child with chores. Her schooling is being carried on by the father. Not right, I am sure."

"Mama," said Sandrine, the daughter of the house, "Mama, please will you not ask Julie d'Is to my party."

"*Not?* Why ever is that? Don't you want poor Julie to see your dear new doll?"

Sandrine began to cry. She was not generally a tearful girl.

After some coaxing, it was got from her.

"I don't want Scamper to die!"

Leaves of silence, oddly flavored by mystery and darkness, fell in the room. The ladies looked at each other.

"Well, you know," said one at last, "it's a very curious thing."

"Yes," said Sandrine's aunt, "I remarked on it myself to Madame Claude only the other day."

"Of course, a coincidence –"

"Or do you think the d'Is child –?"

They stared at one another now.

During the past year, Julie had attended seven parties. Thereafter two cats sickened in a week, the Claude dog had succumbed to a malady and been put down. A parrot was found dead in its cage before the guests had even left.

"Scamper," said Sandrine, the name of the kitten. "*She'll* put a spell on him like the others."

"Good heavens, is that what the child says she does?"

Sandrine looked blank. Julie had said nothing. Her peers did not question her, for fear.

It was borne in on the ladies of that circle, and all those other circles with which it connected, that while the mothers had not been badly disposed to Julie, their children did not like her. Overnight, as it were, Julie ceased to be a social success.

"But," said Chorgeh's "uncle," "regardless of that, soon enough the child was obliged to go to school."

"My God," said Chorgeh, encouragingly.

"It was thought to be an epidemic," said the "uncle." "A fever, in some instances accompanied by vomiting and a rash. There was only one death. But somehow, again generally unspoken, the unthinkable was mooted. The child was removed from the school. It was because, they said, she herself was too unsturdy to be exposed to childish ailments. She was then tutored at home, and only ventured out on errands with her mother –"

"Whereat the drawing rooms and byways were littered with sickening small animals and babies."

"Exactly," said the "uncle," unperturbed.

Julie d'Is emerged from the pastry shop before them.

"She's been in that shop a long while," said Chorgeh. "Do you think she's assaulted anyone?"

"Very likely," said the "uncle." "But if so, the assault will have gone unseen. In all the instances of those who fell ill, nothing was reported, nothing was witnessed. Rarely did Julie make contact – she was not a tactile child. She did not fondly clasp her playmates and class-fellows to her, did not strike them, pinch, or tap their hands. They had soon got in the habit of making very sure she never came near their food or drink."

"Now where is she going?" said Chorgeh. Their object had turned into a long sliding street, a funnel for the wind.

"Toward the Church, I believe, homeward."

"She looks more interesting now," said Chorgeh. "Quite attractive in fact, as should every female poisoner. Her hair, let down, would make her seem fascinating with those slanted eyes. A veritable Medea."

Years retracted. Madame d'Is had come into an unexpected fortune, sole beneficiary of an obscure relative. With the malice of the microbes they had been, monsieur and madame began to intrude themselves everywhere, riding to horse races and galas, attending balls, financing things, overbearing all before them. Julie too appeared again out of her cupboard. Her childhood aura was dismissed or suppressed. She was found to dance well, to speak little and with some wit, to listen attentively. If not a jewel, still she shone slightly, and her hair was washed in soft soap and padded becomingly, her gowns were not parcel wrapping save in the most acceptable sense.

"Who died?" asked Chorgeh, as they strolled along the sliding street, the crowd lessened, and above them the façade of the cathedral suddenly loomed masklike in the sky. They had begun to climb hills, aware unconsciously of the backbones of Paradys beneath the streets. It was appropriate that the story should shadow, even if there was less breath for it. The brightness too had clouded over; there was a flutter of rain.

"Several died, of course. At first it wasn't associated with Julie d'Is. She was a young girl with her hair dressed low, and sometimes loose as you have recommended. Not a Medea, an Ariadne. A piquance, an intelligence, a softness suggesting pliancy."

There was a particular supper. Twelve people were there, and Julie d'Is – the magical number of thirteen. The next day two of the younger girls fell ill, quite seriously.

"Like the two cats," said Chorgeh. He noticed that despite himself, his "uncle" was elaborating quite naturally now.

"The table being stocked with an uneven number, three girls had sat adjacently. One opposite Julie, and beside her the daughter of Madame Claude."

"Must the veterinarian put her away?"

"She died by herself on the fourth night, raging with fever and calling aloud."

"Perfect," said Chorgeh.

"I never cease to enjoy," said his "uncle," "the beastliness of youth."

Julie d'Is, with her small bag of cake, was now far ahead of them. She went lightly up the hill, and vanished at a turning.

"She's getting away."

"We must allow that. It is her own street."

Chorgeh said, "You're very disappointing. Is this the end?"

"To some extent," said the "uncle." "There's only this to add. The occurrences of severe illness and occasional deaths, mysterious and unsolved, attendant on Julie at various functions, led the old suspicions of her out again. She was called the Peste Virgin, the Angel of Plague, and so on. At best, she was a harbinger of extreme unluck. Of course, no one could pin a crime to her. She came to be watched very closely, and those placed next to her at table, female or male, would find all manner of amusing excuses to absent themselves. Not every episode resulted in a fatality, or even a sickness, however. At one memorable dinner twenty-one people sat down with Julie d'Is, and afterward her neighbors exchanged bets on who would expire and when. But all stayed healthy. Eventually both her parents, neither of whom had ever been seriously ill, died in the mundane way. Julie inherited their dwindling wealth, and lived on it. She was left scrupulously alone."

The "uncle" extracted another cigarette. The two men stood beneath a plane tree, as the sky tried to attract their attention.

"I must be getting on, I have to meet Vincent at my club," said the "uncle."

"But you can't leave me like this – finish the story, you devil!"

"How can I? Only life can do that. And life has just gone around a corner with her pastry."

"But – how is it done? How does she poison them?"

"Who knows? Plenty have tried to learn. Some have even resorted to inquiry of the lady, holding her the while at bay the length of a cane or umbrella. She looks amazed, it seems, insulted, normal. They can obtain nothing."

"The police –"

"The police have generally not been involved, though it's true they observed Julie d'Is for a year, after an especially tiresome death, that of a minor minister who shared a carriage with her. No evidence was found. No motive, as there had never been apparent motive. She has shown in her career neither passions nor attachments, nor jealousies, in love, or otherwise. How unusual. We all give ourselves away. You yourself, my little foreigner, have your wild and untamable streak, by which we know you."

"Indeed."

"And you are young, which gives besides a great deal away at once. Julie d'Is was also young for three decades. And gave away nothing. Since she seems to pollute and kill, that must be her only vice, and her only hobby."

A raven-wing cloud scuffed through the plane. Rain dashed down. "The club," said Chorgeh's "uncle" with decision.

"No, I'm not coming with you," said Chorgeh.

"For God's sake, don't go knocking on the door of Julie d'Is."

"I shan't," said Chorgeh. "That much I do credit, that she's unfriendly. Inimical."

"Do please believe it."

Chorgeh stood and watched his "uncle" hurry off downhill through the rain. The road was a tide of blackness. Something hung heavy, not thunder, but the bottomless story. It must be concluded, somehow.

The bell of the pastry shop gave a brittle sugary tinkle as he went in. On all sides were terraces of sweetness, layers and marblings, bubbles, cords, plaits, and flutes, that made the eyes if not the stomach hungry. In the middle of it all, unmoved through long acquaintance, a plump, pretty, curly girl lifted her head like a deer at a water hole.

"Can I help you, monsieur?"

"Yes. Give me some of those, please, and a couple of those," and Chorgeh, thinking of his mother, who disliked sweet things of any type, food or human, and pictured her astoundment, when he should get home. Into the masculine study, which once Chorgeh's father had occupied, kept now as a cross between a shrine and a lumber room, Chorgeh might take himself and eat each refused cake, remembering the cake shop girl, for she was very charming.

Yet, as she reached for the second batch of cakes, she looked puzzled, this charming girl. She stepped away, and turned to Chorgeh as if to ask him something, and as she stood there, seemingly at a loss, Chorgeh instead asked something of her. "Do you recall a woman who came in here, about half an hour ago?"

"I – don't know, monsieur," said the girl, looking more puzzled than before, frowning and gazing at the ground, as if she had glimpsed a mouse, perhaps.

"A drab, nasty woman. Obviously scheming. With holes in her gloves."

"I – don't know, monsieur," repeated the girl. And then she looked at, and straight through him, as if to some other place that had suddenly grown visible in the doorway. Next moment she dropped on the floor. She lay there in a compact little puddle of skirts and curls, her eyes shut, her face icing white.

Chorgeh banged on the counter and shouted, and by magic the shop was full of women.

A minute later, the girl had been lifted up and was murmuring that she was quite well, quite well, but so cold.

"There, Olizette," said the women. And one ran out to the pharmacist's along the street.

"That gentleman," said Olizette, "is waiting for his cakes. I was serving him when I was taken queer."

"Good Lord, don't worry about that," said Chorgeh, flustered for an instant. It seemed likely the women would reckon him in some way responsible for the girl's faint. Metaphysically, was he not?

Then the pharmacist came, and after a cursory examination of the girl, declared she was feverish and must go home at once.

Chorgeh stood there with his heart beating violently, in the presence of the insanely wicked and bizarre. Evil was a palpable entity in the shop, bending to the women, its tattered wings and skull face glaring intently and specifically above Olizette. It was as if Chorgeh had invoked it, by his arrival, his quest, his query concerning Julie d'Is, Angel of Pestilence.

"Oh, how am I to get to my room?" said Olizette, made childish by her weakness. "Oh dear, oh dear, what shall I do?"

And Chorgeh rushed out to fetch a cab, into which he and a woman of the shop next bore Olizette, who was now touchingly crying from embarrassment and feebleness.

Every bump of the wheels and hoofs on the journey caused the poor girl to gasp and moan.

"There, there, Olizette," reiterated the useless woman. "She's *never* ill," she added to Chorgeh over the dark, drooping, flowerlike head. "A country girl. Two years, and never a sniffle, never once a migraine or a fainting fit. And I myself, well I'm a martyr to them, monsieur."

They reached Olizette's room (set predictably in a conglomeration of chimney and flowerpots, rambling steps, skylights, and lopsided balconies, near the old corn market). Chorgeh paid off the cab. He then went to summon a doctor, taking all responsibility on himself. It was his fault.

"I don't like the look of this," the doctor said to Chorgeh, on the landing. "You are the young woman's protector?"

"If you like," said Chorgeh, disdaining the explanatory truth.

"Then someone must be got in to look after her, a nurse. She must have fresh fruit, broth; cream and eggs as she improves."

Thus it was not cakes that Chorgeh presented to his mother. It was a plea for an increment upon his allowance.

"If you must know, I have a girl. I must give her a present, mustn't I, now and then?"

"I'm not interested in the silly details. Is she clean? Does she love you? I trust that you do *not* love *her*? Very well."

During the month of Olizette's illness, Chorgeh visited her once a day, in the afternoon. He brought flowers, fruit, and later boxes of confectionery – she did not like cakes. Her plumpness had melted from her, and the paleness and

slightness of her debility made her ethereal. Although he did not in the smallest degree "love" her, Chorgeh was very taken with her, had become fond of
her, as one may with a docile and pleasing invalid one has chosen. Their
words were affectionate, and soon familiar, but quite decorous, and the nurse
was always in the room with her tatting, or just along the way making soup.

Chorgeh's mornings were spent on quite another woman. It was not that
he made any contact with Julie d'Is, of course, only that he had begun to spy
on her movements, and to question, in a carefully blatant style, her neighbors,
of whom she had several, all at a distance.

Both activities, the caring visits to the pastry seller, the observation of a
poisoness, were united, being two halves of a whole.

He learned a great deal more of Julie than of Olizette. Olizette told him
everything he wanted to know, and her entire simple life was soon before
him, lacking all complexity. But Julie's life was if anything more simple,
there was no information to be had solely because nothing happened to her.
From the comments of those in her vicinity, who seldom any way saw or
noted her, and from his own scrupulous view of her doings in the quiet and
normally deserted street, Chorgeh was quickly privy to her existence. She
ventured out, this viper, about twice a week, to purchase groceries and feminine articles (he followed her where he could). Sometimes after these excursions she also took a turn in a park nearby. Her face was always blank as a
stone. She must surely be frustrated, maddened by this solitary limbo, her
lack of volition, yet quite inarticulately and hopelessly, for she seemed to
want to do nothing more than she did. She did not, when indoors, ever appear
at her window. (He had soon located her address, her room – which had no
flowerpot, no lamp, and which on the few evenings he had overseen it at
dusk, turned to dusk also, and lit no light – did not alter. Even once at midnight he had passed, and there it was, a black oblong, empty. It was as though,
on entering her domain, Julie d'Is ceased to be alive or actual. And perhaps
this was so.)

As the "uncle" had said, to poison must represent her only passion. All
she lived for, dreamed of. And yet, visiting those same places where she
made her purchases quite regularly, Chorgeh found no such startling evidence of her malignity as he had in Olizette's pastry shop. Evidently Olizette
had been unlucky, perhaps because she had been alone with Julie for several
minutes. Possibly too the murderess did not strike on her own territory, but
always outside it.

Meanwhile long leading conversations with the latest victim gave no clue
as to *how* Julie had managed her work: Olizette herself was ignorant of having
been practiced on, and Chorgeh naturally did not enlighten her. He was
legitimately afraid of how such knowledge might affect Olizette, for even
while she improved, on some afternoons there were lapses; he would find her

very white, trembling, saying that she ached from head to toe, or that the mild winter light troubled her eyes. The doctor had already ceased calling, *he* was sanguine, but Chorgeh treated the girl with caution. For the doctor had not understood the case at all. In answer to Chorgeh's probing, the doctor had remarked on the foolishness of young country girls in the City, infected by its fumes, living on cakes, neglecting their well-being in favor of unsuitable romances.

Chorgeh had one image. He nurtured it. It involved the stone-faced serpent Julie d'Is leaning slightly forward to take her pastry, and scratching the fingers of Olizette with the underside of a thin silver ring. By now Chorgeh had glimpsed such a ring on Julie's finger. (Had not the Borgias used a similar device to cart off whole table-loads of enemies?) By the time he had noticed the ring, however, he could find no cut or scrape on the smooth hands of Olizette, though he examined them meticulously, telling her he would read her fortune. Obviously, so slight a wound would have healed by now. He had been lax, too late. Another black mark.

"Good gracious, Chorgeh! It isn't suitable. After all these years! Mother will think you've come to court me."

"Your mother is far too sensible, Sandrine, ever to think that."

Like a butterfly, Sandrine hovered over the ornate and overdressed drawing room, in a tense powdery light. He had not seen her, it was true, save at a remote distance – across salons, at the end of fashionable avenues – for five years. She had improved visually, but not necessarily in any other way.

"Well, sit down. You shouldn't be here. Mother will be out for hours."

"During which time we can get up to the most scandalous activities." Sandrine giggled. Encouraged, Chorgeh said, "Tell me everything you know about Julie d'Is."

"Who is Julie d'Is?" asked Sandrine, in such a voice that he knew she recalled perfectly.

"A dear little girl," he said, "with whom you used, once, to play. Now a woman, looking I'm afraid a great deal older than you or her years. In rather impoverished circumstances. Retiring."

"I remember ..." said Sandrine. "... Julie d'Is." She went slowly very pale. Chorgeh watched, interested. "I haven't seen her since I was ten."

"But your playmate."

"*Never*," said Sandrine vehemently. She shuddered. "Even now, at the very thought." She got up, paced over the room, and back again, and standing there before him said dramatically, "That child was a beast, a hobgoblin. Ugh! We were all terrified of her. She could make you die. She's done it. She never said so. She never said anything. To the adults it was all *May I* and

Thank you. When she was with us, she would just sit there. She *was* older. Her eyes were down. She had horrible eyes, small and sharp, cold and colorless. And long lashes, not beautiful, but like a sort of fence, as if to stop anything getting by. Then her mother would call for her, such a poor silly woman. We had a rhyme – how did it go? I can't think – but it was about Julie d'Is whisking you down to Hell if you didn't watch out."

"How did you know she was a hobgoblin? Apart, of course, from her eyes."

"Because the kittens died. And then Alyse, and Lucie. Surely you've heard?"

"But why a hobgoblin? Wasn't she just a poisoner?"

"A *child* who poisons?"

"Why not?" said Chorgeh. As a child, he had once or twice considered the method.

"There was a story," said Sandrine, at the fireplace where the dried flowers still stood petrified, stiff on their stalks as she now was on her stalk of dress. "Julie d'Is was a *changeling*."

"Ah," said Chorgeh.

"You can laugh" (he had not) "but when they were in the East, the silly mother offended a sorcerer. He was an old man who came to the kitchen door in rags, and she had the servants chase him off. But he was powerful, it was all a test or prank. If she'd been nice to him he would have blessed her, but she wasn't, so he exuded a curse. Madame d'Is was carrying two babies, twins. But when she gave birth, one baby vanished. And the baby that was left was changed. It stopped being wholesome and like a baby. It became this awful cold-eyed stony little toad. It became Julie."

"Yes," said Chorgeh. "But what about the other twin?"

"I suppose Julie killed it," said Sandrine flatly, "and they wrapped it in a shawl and the nurse took it and threw it in a reedy swamp. They couldn't tell anyone. It was too disgusting."

"Yes," Chorgeh said again. He imagined the two little girls lying in their cradle under the mosquito net on some veranda, the one child in the stasis of death, the other in the static condition of concentrated being that Julie d'Is so oddly evidenced. And then from Sandrine's facile and foolish words he contrived the exact perfect image, the nurse-woman with eyes of slanting slate, bearing the dead bundle, casting it in like a failed Moses, for the gurgling mud to have, and the frogs chirruping and the strange orient pearl of the moon watching from the trees. Through its curiosity this last picture was made to seem true. He believed it, even though knowing how and why he was convinced.

"How is it you suppose she manages her crimes?" he said to Sandrine.

"Oh," she said, simply, "it's Julie herself, isn't it. She's poisonous. Like certain substances – if you're near them, they can kill you. Julie is like *that*."

They had little cakes, and he thought of Olizette, and that he would be late to see her today, but never mind, he would stay with her until dinnertime. He had seen some bright flowers for sale, to his townsman's eye fresh from the country, and he would take her those, and perhaps some wine. He was growing faintly bored with Olizette, in the most gentle and patient of ways. After all, she was almost well, and had yielded no clues, and what could they talk about?

When he was sufficiently bored with Sandrine, which happened fairly soon after the cakes, Chorgeh made charming excuses and left. Sandrine seemed disappointed, and he realized with surprise that she had really not believed in his mission at all, she imagined Julie d'Is to have been only an impulsive ploy to visit.

With Julie d'Is he was not bored at all. He felt for her a wild sheer loathing quite novel to him, quite energizing.

When he reached the apartment house of Olizette, among the pots and steps, the sun was on the edge of the City, hesitating for a moment. The shape-changer light of dusk already flooded the street. Chorgeh saw the doctor's carriage there in it, like a stone in a river. Somehow Chorgeh was not startled by this. He felt a sinking in his belly, but it was neither alarm nor regret.

He went up, and met the doctor again on the landing. The doctor regarded him with dislike, resentful of an added burden. "You must prepare yourself, monsieur, for very bad news indeed."

"She's dead," said Chorgeh.

"A sudden relapse. The woman called for me as soon as she saw what went on."

"Did the girl have a priest?" Chorgeh asked anxiously, for he had learned enough of Olizette to realize she would have wanted one.

"Yes. He is there now."

Chorgeh went into the room, and when the priest glanced up Chorgeh said directly, "Please understand, Father, that the young lady was befriended by me, nothing more," for now getting the facts of her chastity straight seemed imperative for her sake.

She looked shrunken and elderly as she lay in the bed. Worse, she looked like nothing at all, like discarded washing, an old dress.

Chorgeh stared at her with heartbreaking sympathy.

The priest began to try to comfort him, and Chorgeh, perturbed, went away at once. It seemed there was a brother-in-law who had been summoned, and all the arrangements now were in hand. Even the priest had known

Olizette, her character and means – there had not needed to be, after all, any embarrassing explanations.

On reaching home, Chorgeh found his mother had filled the house with guests. They were everywhere, like a plague of well-dressed mice, squeaking and waving their paws. Of the writer "uncle" there was no sign, however, and Chorgeh was consumed by the detestation of a man whose last bolt hole had been soiled and overturned.

"Good evening, dear. Do change your clothes and join us."

He wanted to seize his mother by the throat, shouting in her face that she had ruined him, how dare she – But she had all the rights, and he none.

"I've a terrible headache," said Chorgeh. "I must lie down. If I'm better, I'll make my entrance later."

He went to his room and locked the door from the outside, to mislead anyone who came to seek him. Then he removed to his father's study and shut himself in there.

There was a faint odor of leather, tobacco from a sacred jar. The room was protective of Chorgeh, securing him. In a closed drawer, skillfully negotiated, Chorgeh found what he was looking for. Prior to dying, the father had initiated the son into a number of the male mysteries. If he had lived, possibly they would not have got on at all, but death had flung a glamorous veil over their parting and their relationship. Everything that Chorgeh's father had ever said to him or taught him, Chorgeh remembered vividly.

When he had completed his transaction, he went back to his room and locked himself *inside*. Beyond, the noises of the guests ebbed and flowed. He visualized Julie d'Is arriving, floating among them in a pale gown and padded hair, some of it loose on her white snake's neck. Here she touched and here she breathed, and once or twice she merely looked, and the mark of death was on them. Chorgeh patted his pillow, beneath which lay something hard and cold now. Smiling, he slipped into sleep, and dreamed of Olizette's burial at a tiny church in the fields, a grave with a willow, mourning doves. He did not feel sad for her, asleep. He threw the flowers on her mound, and drank the wine from the bottle cheerfully, and bought a cake from a tree.

The next day Chorgeh rose early and went out. His hours were often premature, for his business in the City was that of a sightseer, flighty and opportune. No one had remarked anything unusual.

When he reached the street of Julie d'Is, Chorgeh positioned himself as he had grown accustomed to do, almost opposite the apartment building where she lived. There was a portico there, into which he could conveniently slip and be hidden. It was a morning when, generally, she would go out, attend to her minuscule amounts of shopping, and then perambulate the park. No one was about, the day was lowering and rainy, and now and then a sharp report of thunder came. It was made for him, this day, and he only feared it would put *her* off; perhaps she dreaded storms. But no, the door opened, and out stepped the creature of the legend, the serpent, clad in her squalid coat and coiled, unbecoming hat, with an umbrella to ward off the scimitars of heaven.

Chorgeh followed her, without undue caution, just as before. No one had ever noted him; she herself, the demoness, had never turned on him, never even looked over her shoulder. She went into a draper's shop, into a shop that sold cold meats and cheeses. Did she eat these things? *What* did she do? He had never fathomed, no one had ever said, he had never seen her, crouched in her room, the spider in her web, grooming herself and preening, smacking her lips over her kills. He was inclined to think she went into a cupboard in her apartment, and stayed there, like a lead soldier in its box. Whatever it was, he would never know.

In the park, which he had thought she might avoid but which she entered as ever, the black trees dripped and hissed, the paths were wet. Everything was noise, flashes and rushes and the crack of the thunder. When Chorgeh shot Julie d'Is with his father's pistol, the thunder obligingly roared and the lightning sparkled. The reek of powder was crushed in rain. He had been fifteen feet from her back and the bullet had gone in under her hat. There was a painterly wash of blood on the path, but it flushed away. Her purchases lay scattered, sodden in their paper wrappings. She was a pathetic heap of old clothes, as Olizette had seemed, a scarecrow. Chorgeh did not approach, but kept to his plan. He knew she was quite dead, for presumably she could be slaughtered in the normal fashion, and the bullet must have entered her brain. He hurried away, feeling nothing, only a little bit sick, but then he had taken no breakfast, it was probably only that.

Rain fell steadily for a week, then on the first clear day, the writer came to call on Chorgeh's mother. She was taken aback, not having seen him for months. After a while, almost surreptitiously, the writer climbed the house, and knocked on the door of the study-shrine of Chorgeh's father.

"Yes, you may come in," said Chorgeh.

He sat in the leather armchair, while the writer tactfully passed about the room, examining items with the cunning reserve of a man in a museum. Presently the writer sat down also. The fire was lit. They stretched their legs to it.

"Had you heard?" said the writer.

"That the Beautiful Lady had been killed? Yes. There was a small passage in some of the journals. I was only waiting for you to come and ask."

"What did the journals say?"

"Couldn't you read them?"

"I never read them. Nasty things. I have my knowledge from another source."

"Naturally. Likely you know much more than the rest of us. All that the journals said was that a Mademoiselle Julie d'Is had been bizarrely shot in a garden near the Temple-Church. That there were no witnesses. That nothing at all was known. They did add, a pair of them, that unpleasing speculation had surrounded Mademoiselle d'Is in her youth. But that nothing had been said against her latterly, she seemed to have neither relatives nor friends, no one in fact with a reason or wish to slay her."

"We may always rely on our relatives and friends for *that*," said the writer.

"Tell me all the rest of it, then," said Chorgeh, apparently intrigued.

Under cover of his porcelain exterior he held himself tight. He knew perfectly well the "uncle" was here in his literary capacity only. He supposed that it was Chorgeh who had murdered Julie d'Is, maybe he had no doubts. Although such pistols as Chorgeh's father's were common, although Chorgeh, even Olizette, had no glaring link to Julie d'Is, and although the writer indeed knew nothing at all of the ultimate involvement of the pastry shop, yet he had deduced the obvious. Though the police would never attach Chorgeh to the killing, the writer did, and the writer was here solely as that, to observe him, to see how Chorgeh went on. And it was possible, if Chorgeh gave himself away to the writer, that the "uncle" might take over from the writer, and feel obliged to give Chorgeh up to the authorities. Chorgeh had known this moment would come, and he had prepared for it. He was a practiced deceiver, and his youngness was on his side, for with the widespread fault of the middle-aged, the writer coupled youngness with inexperience.

"I know very slightly more," said the writer to Chorgeh. "I know there was, of course, a post-mortem. I know the result of this was the news that Julie d'Is died because of the entry of a bullet into her brain, which was evident from the first. I know that a few of her erstwhile familiars were questioned. But none of them had seen her for years. It seemed to me," said the writer, uncrossing his legs, and lighting, without permission, a cigarette, "it seemed to me that you and I, say, were worthier of an interrogation. We'd been watching the woman and discussing her fairly recently."

"Oh, not so recently as all that," said Chorgeh. "I say, I'm very sorry, but you mustn't smoke in here. Mother would fly into a fit. It's awful isn't it?"

The writer cast his cigarette into the fire and smiled. Chorgeh had revealed an arch-cleverness. The writer could not last for more than ten minutes longer without a cigarette. He would have to go out, and why should Chorgeh, plainly intent on his father's books, go with him?

"You haven't, then," said the writer, "been following Julie d'Is?"

"Why would I do that?"

"Because she fascinated you."

"That's true. Then I found someone else who fascinated me even more. You recollect how skittish I can be."

"What do you think of it, though?" said the writer.

"Of what?"

"Of her death."

"I think it's ideal," said Chorgeh. "I think it's inevitable."

"Since she had no life?"

Chorgeh did not fall into the trap.

"Well, she may have done," he said, "for all we know."

When the writer "uncle" withdrew, tapping his cigarette case, seemingly quite delighted with Chorgeh's acting or innocence, not entirely sure now either way, Chorgeh relapsed, looking at the fire, himself overseeing what he had said. He had made no slip, yet he had been truthful in his pronouncement. The death of such a beast was both ideal and inevitable. He felt himself no hero, and no villain, for seeing to it. It was a shame the post-mortem had shown nothing of significance, but perhaps it had and the "uncle" merely had not learned in his prying what it was. Some things would be hushed up. Chorgeh constructed for himself something more fanciful than the spike in the ring. He saw one of Julie's bony fingers, and out from under the nail a sort of talon extruded. It pricked the plump hand of Olizette, finer than a needle. But the bullet had not been fine, it had been harsh and shattering. He had taken no chances, aiming for the head. Her hat was so unalluring, it really served her right. For he would have found her more difficult to kill if she had been lovely and dressed with taste. He would not have wanted to spoil her appearance, and perhaps must have risked going close with a stiletto. She had fallen straight over, directly down, and her soul went deeper yet, diving into Hell. Chorgeh considered the twin of Julie d'Is, the sister she was supposed to have had, and to have killed in babyhood. He saw the cradle again under the netting, and the nurse-woman throwing out the bundle into the mud. Was that what had decided him, or was it only Olizette?

Chorgeh sat back in the chair and composed himself for a nap. He would be sensible to avoid the writer for a month or so – until any ideas or fresh rumors ceased after the postmortem and the burial. The firelight glittered, and went from under Chorgeh's eyelids, and he heard his mother's operatic laugh rill through the house. Everything was well.

God and men pass over the battleground, prizing great gems and silver bullets from the helms of the fallen. Then the rats come in gray, smooth coats and find the secrets of the labyrinth.

There was nothing ratlike to the appearance or manner of Monsieur Tritte, who was tall and plump, with the large and capable hands of a country doctor. He had a baritone voice, a balding head, a face at once handsome and benign. The watchman of the morgue, he was the exact antithesis of what such a man was reckoned to be and frequently was. Tritte was abstemious and sober, without perversity or cruelness. He pitied his charges, with a dignity that became him, yet he found them on occasion interesting. He was himself capable of scientific investigation, having studied at the elbows of eminent practitioners, unflinching, and uncareless, as they sometimes were not.

It had happened that the men laboring at the morgue had known the name *Julie d'Is*. They had therefore had great pains over her. Though the corpse had lain on its slab for a day and a half before any work commenced, precautions were taken. Not an inch of skin, other than that of the face, was presented to the cadaver, which was then gone over minutely for a hidden armament. None was found. Weighed, pierced, portionally dissected, the poor dead thing offered no answers. To Tritte this was only what he would have expected. Her method of inflicting fatality, whatever it was, had lost its potence in the moment of her death. He had no doubt, as did not the scientists in the chamber, that Julie d'Is had been executed by one she had wronged with the sickness or demise of a lover or family member. That the police had failed to curtail her had after all given the public some rights in this matter. It was only surprising the sentence had been so long in its enactment. The killer might be discovered through a mistake, or a confession, but there were so many potential assassins, among them even victims who had recovered, that apprehension on evidence alone would seem to be hopeless.

Solely one man of the three had scoffed at the stories of the Pestilent Angel. He was an old fellow who thought he had learned all there was to know, a casual butcher of the slab who made jokes over the severed organs and the cups of brains.

When they were all gone, and the corpse lay at peace in her white cold meat, Tritte watched through the night in his room, where many books, and a microscope worthy of the morgue's visitors, gave notice of his serious inner nature.

In the morning the City was to bury Julie d'Is, arbitrarily, shoveling her off. Tritte felt no dismay at his last, second, night alone with her, but he felt a strong sense of her nevertheless, more so now she had been cut and over-hauled, as if her silent flesh cried out – not for justice or remission, not even to be heard – it was more like the low, exhausted crying Tritte's mother had once made nightly, from toothache and worry. Though he had grown, and res-cued his mother, and now she did not cry, Tritte *felt* the sound. There had never before been such a weeping in his morgue.

Thus, when he went on his rounds, he left the remains of Julie d'Is for the end, and then, peeling off her gauzy mantle, he stood and looked on her under the ray of his lamp, not seeing her nudity, her thinness, the remnant of thin soft hair, but gazing slowly and thoroughly after whatever it could be to make her cry.

Her face appeared, under the debris of her brow (from which the bullet had ejected), like a carved stone. The undamaged eye was closed, and the lips also. Her ears and nostrils were exquisitely shaped, the mark of beauty showing up, as so often, at an unpublicized part. Her breasts too were lovely, and he was profoundly sorry, the watchman of the morgue, that she had lost herself. She was not old, not lined or wizened. What had it been, her wickedness, and what did it mean?

It was as he was viewing her that something flickered at the rim of his eye. He glanced aside, and there on the inner curve of her arm, he saw a speck. Tritte's vision was keen, but the lamp smoked somewhat. The speck, whatever it was, had not moved but only seemed to. Then, it moved once more, the length of one of his fingernails, and so stopped and was still.

He watched it, the watchman, for several minutes, and then, when there was no further movement, he bent down and stared. But all he could see was the speck he had seen at the first, like a grain of tea, there on her arm.

Tritte went away, back to his room, and here he loitered for perhaps half an hour. And then, taking up the lamp, he returned, through the shrouded marble and the dark, to the place of Julie d'Is, and held the light over her.

The speck was still there, where he had last seen it. Suddenly Tritte, from faraway memory, knew what it was. It was a flea.

An abrupt and searing shock ran through him. A lesser man would have dropped the lamp. His emotion was made up of astonishment and horror and a violent influx of realization. Here, *here*, was the method of the murderess, the poisoner. It was a *flea*. A tiny drinker of blood, for some reason so venomous itself that when it feasted on another (for surely normally it had sustained itself by the blood of Julie herself), it was liable to cause illness, and even death. Some were immune, as happened in all cases of infection, others recovered, several perished. Julie obviously was among the initial category, and doubtless her parents, and long associates, often bitten, also. To a stranger, the flea might be always inimical. It leapt upon them – a second of vampire action – then leapt back again to the host. The bite was so minute they either did not feel it or did not know *what* they had felt.

Everything fitted to the hypothesis. Everything combined with it to form a piece of evidence as ludicrous as it was horrifying. *A flea.*

Now, it too seemed dead. Or it was very sluggish; if not dead then dying from lack of food, the ruin of the host. He must be careful ... or did it lack the will now to feed from another? Of those who had discovered and subsequently handled the body of Julie d'Is none, so far as he understood, had fallen sick.

After he had stood over the cadaver fifteen or twenty minutes, Tritte made a decision. Fetching an instrument, Tritte separated a wafer of the white skin from the arm. The vessels came forth, like veins in marble itself. There was, naturally, no blood. The flea, secured pathetically to the surface of the skin, did not shift itself. It clung on in its death or near-death, like a desperate child to the dead arm of its mother.

A further ten minutes, and Tritte had arranged his valuable microscope, had set the inch of skin and the flea upon a slide.

In the core of night, alone, in pity and amazement, Tritte put his eye to the magical telescope of life, to see what death had been doing.

After he had looked a long while, the man drew back. He wiped his forehead and going to the cupboard, poured for himself a measure of brandy. Only then did he look again through the microscope.

The image was as before.

There was no alteration.

Death had come, and still the miniature thing clung to the skin. Its crying, too high for the human ear to hear, too loud for the human heart not to, had ended. Under the magnifying lens, it was a woman, the flea. Almost a human woman, beautiful and perfectly formed, with short luxuriantly curling hair, and deep dark eyes set fast in oblivion. The lips were parted, and there were the usual even teeth of the human female; the infinitesimal hands had no claws. There were flowerlike breasts. But the body stopped at the pelvis. There it became a tube, scaled like a scorpion, finished in a thin coiled whip, some sort of sting or sucker. It was so ugly, this finish, so unlike the rest. You saw at once how the creature had flung herself, daring space and danger, to cling onto her prey, striking like a wasp, turning then maybe to apply the perfect mouth to the wound, and springing off again, back to the safety of the sibling. For it was clearly to be seen also, a likeness to Julie. They were of an age, only one plain, and the other beautiful: sisters.

Monsieur Tritte put on his gloves. He spoke to the woman on the lens. "Forgive me."

And then he crushed her, between his nails.

The sepulcher of ornate granite that stands on the hillside, overlooking the river, has the apt, odd name of Morcara's Room. Those that know the name do not necessarily know the name's reason. Behind a door of leaden metal the bones lie properly in a box; the lintel above the door has only the name: *Morcara Venka*, and two dates – which show that the occupant of the tomb died young, at the age of about twenty-five years. The date of the tomb itself, however, which is also to be found, cut into one of the mossy pillars, reveals that it came into being more than a century after the death of its tenant. Inquiries may reveal that Morcara Venka's descendants erected the mausoleum and ordered her remains taken to it from another place. There may also be mention of some ill fortune, even a curse, that once had connection to this woman, so that even now a faint smolder rests, as you will sense, on the hill, some hint of smoke without which there is no fire. And it has been said that to enter the tomb, even on the most legitimate business, would be unwise.

The truth, perhaps more peculiar still, is as follows.

Morcara's Room

The secret of passing away,
The cost of the change of the moon,
None knows it with ear or with eye,
But all will soon.

– Swinburne

One evening a young man, who shall be called Rendart, was walking in the country above the City. It had been a hot close day, and the mellow air had now a tint of thunder. Rendart had grown tired of walking, of climbing over boulders and peering into defiles where tiny rivulets flashed and shone as in oil paintings, of the forest's edges that, so invitingly redolent of becoming forever lost, would only lead him back onto some path that ended at a farm. There were no longer wolves in the woods, or Rendart might have been tempted to stay out all night. Instead he was now looking for some house where he might foist himself. His trick was, wherever possible, to avoid the convenient inn or hotel. This was not because he lacked funds (rather the reverse, his means were private and helpful) but because of a compulsion to view the interiors of the homes of other persons. To this end he had once regularly pretended to a wish to buy property, and agents and owners had conducted him over varieties of premises, singing the praises of much and revealing almost everything but the bad points. It was their reticence here which had discouraged him eventually from the practice, since bad points are frequently so interesting. That and, maybe, the annoyance of certain agents who finally doubted Rendart's desire actually to purchase anything.

As the sky deepened and the shadow of weather bloomed along its perimeter, Rendart came on a wide, straight track, leading between poplars in the direction of a house – indeed, a mansion. The walls of the building were very tall, and the roofs that rose above them, dilapidated and picturesque.

Highest of all rose a round dark tower with a cap the color of the approaching storm.

Even as he gazed, a few spaced drops of rain plumped on the track, the poplars quivered, a darkness bubbled up in the east.

Rendart ran gleefully for the mansion.

Of course, he ruminated as the echoes rang away from a clanging bell upon the gate, it was possible they would turn him off, conceivable also that the fascinating house could be empty – then, might he not break in? Almost in disappointment he saw a shuffling movement in the rank bushes that crowded the gate. An elderly man emerged, dressed in the clothes and skin of earlier decades.

"Yes, monsieur?"

The heavens obligingly opened. Thunder pealed, a curtain of rain descended.

Rendart gasped his plight. Alone, friendless, and shelterless in the wild hills and the storm.

The servant (Rendart had classed him, and was presently proved correct) stared a while, as if listening to a foreigner speaking in an unknown tongue.

Then, through the rain, from the concealed house, came a querulous call. "What is it, Pierre?" Pierre began to answer, when out of the bushes scampered a precipitate woman in a pale dress and with an umbrella extended over her head. Seeing Rendart she beckoned frantically. "Let him in. Of course you must shelter with us, monsieur. This dreadful thunder – it may strike –" Rendart kindly did not allude to the tip of her umbrella, which might attract the very catastrophe she feared. Probably Jove would aim first at the dark tower above.

The gate was breached, and the trio hastened between the bushes, into a mad garden run to seed, where everything and every metamorphosis of a thing fought for existence under the charcoal sky.

Rendart was rushed to the house so fast he barely saw it. His hostess he had already noted, sadly, was neither young nor lovely, but she might be mysterious with luck.

It did not really seem she would be.

"Pierre, go at once and fetch some dry clothes of my brother's. You can change in the smoking room, monsieur. Poor monsieur is soaked. Then you must come directly to the salon, we always have a fire – we feel the cold, Monsieur de Venne and I."

Within half an hour, while the tempest still cascaded on the jungle outside (from which statues protruded here and there like leprous teeth), Rendart was seated in a hot and avid salon, while Monsieur and Mademoiselle de Venne regarded him. They had lapped up his advent so gladly, he half wondered if they meant him some harm. More likely they were starved of visitors. Monsieur de Venne was indicated as being rather younger than mademoiselle, which apparently set him at about ninety.

"You'll stay to dine with us, Monsieur Rendart?" said she. "What a pleasure, a young man of education. We so seldom – yet our nephew –"

"Our nephew never calls on us," interrupted the brother testily. "Except to borrow our money. Money – does he think we have it? Where do we keep it? Would we live in this lachrymose pile if we had any?" And having recourse to the brandy tumbler at his elbow he added: "How frequently I've thought to myself, send that fellow to the *room*."

"Cesar!" cried mademoiselle.

A silence thundered in the salon, to be broken in turn by the deaf clangor of the elements.

Mademoiselle was very white under her rouge. Rendart envied her, for the fire was overpowering. Getting up on the pretext of helping her to more tea (she fluttered; her brother stuck ferociously to his brandy), Rendart managed a quick half tour of the salon, which was neither boring nor intriguing. He longed for a chance to go through the mansion, the commencement of whose enormous carven stairway he had already glimpsed.

"Rooms are a problem," said Rendart, idly. "There's one in my house by the coast. Simply uninhabitable."

"Yes, there you've got it. *Uninhabitable*," snarled the pickled brother.

Mademoiselle thanked Rendart so profusely for the tea that it was an obvious signal she did not want *rooms* discussed.

Rendart ate the petit fours and bided his time, for it appeared there would be plenty. Already mademoiselle had mentally transferred him past the dining table to the white bedroom. She had given guest-conscious orders to the doddering Pierre, and a brisk stoat-faced maid of two hundred.

It was a very good dinner of five courses, two of which were cold, and Rendart was delighted to suspect things had been "laid on" for his sole benefit. Monsieur de Venne progressed from the brandy through three differing bottles of pleasing wine, two-thirds of which he drank personally, before returning to the brandy with all the snug comfort of an occasional rake returning to wife, pipe, and slippers. Mademoiselle fussed and flighted about with her hands and her conversation, and now and then let slip, as if unavoidably, a reference to the absent nephew. Monsieur said no more upon this matter, merely cleared his throat in a horrible way. As for *rooms*, the only room mentioned was the white bedroom Rendart was to occupy, and the bathroom along the passage from it. Rendart formulated a dream of tiptoeing about the mansion in the night in order to see it, as evidently he was not to get a guided tour. It would not do, however, for if they apprehended him they would be sure to think him a robber after their few and rather chipped and rusty valuables. He could not bear to tell them they had nothing he fancied thieving.

Pierre and the maid served the dinner in the salon, and after it was cleared and Monsieur de Venne had re-ensconced himself with the brandy, everyone ran out of things to say. This did not deter mademoiselle, though, who merely whirled on in a repetition of all she had said before. From her catalogue Rendart had almost instantly learned that, on inheriting the house, her mama and papa had been hard put to it to manage, that soon the gardeners had left them ("And Mama declared anyway she had never known such terrible soil, everything that grew there was poisonous"), while the servants absconded with the heirlooms ("A great clock that Papa saw at auction two years later, the very same, and could not afford to repossess"). Meantime the young versions of monsieur and mademoiselle grew up, were deprived, stunted, jilted, wilted, done out of this and that expectation, to arrive at last in near penury and the latter years, amazed at both, unequal to them.

Rendart said, as he had more or less said before, "But this excellent house. It must be a consolation."

"Upkeep," snorted Monsieur de Venne. "We don't use more than three or four of the apartments. To hear her talk about this white bedroom! Damp and cobwebs. You'll think yourself lucky to get out with pneumonia. Then there are the rats –"

"Oh hush, Cesar!"

"Eating away at the foundations, nibble and gnaw, squeak and gibber. It's the room. The room does it."

"Yes," interposed Rendart – mademoiselle had been protesting again – "rooms *are* a *problem* –"

"Want to know what it is, I daresay," gargled Monsieur de Venne through his brandy glass.

"To know what is what?" inquired Rendart.

"Cesar, I must beg you. Think of poor Mama, think of poor, poor Grisvold."

"Grisvold may be damned." ("Cesar!") "He got no more than justice. His own fault. There was the warning, did he heed? No."

Silence fell again, and Rendart realized uneasily that the rain had ceased to fall as darkness fell in its place. The night was calm, and still.

"Grisvold was an innocent, poor sickly boy," cried mademoiselle. She turned to Rendart and implored him, "Who could command a poor sickly simpleton, Run to the Devil – the *Devil* – and expect the poor creature to have the wit to abstain? It was *your* fault, Cesar, and you'll carry the blame to your Maker."

"Grisvold be damned," said the brandy glass.

Mademoiselle turned to Rendart, mute with outrage.

"Something happened to Grisvold?" he asked.

Mademoiselle buried her cheeks in an inch of lace that was unable to cope with them.

"Confounded curiosity," said Monsieur de Venne. A glow burned brightly in his eyes. He wanted and yearned to speak his confession. She also, in her way. They were a haunted pair.

Rendart gazed on them with pleasure. "Is there some strange story?"

"The tower," whispered mademoiselle. "Did you notice it, to the west of the house?"

"I did," said Rendart.

"*There*," said mademoiselle.

"I'll tell him," said monsieur. He put down the brandy glass.

In the great stillness that was the night, a change had come upon the salon. The fire burned, and the candles, for the house did not seem to run to any modernity of lights. Either side the fire the two elderly people sat, like waxworks or mummies in their old quaint clothes and sewn faces and papier-mâché hands. Once they had been elastic and fresh, had played as children, wept as lovers, screamed and sung their rage and joy. Now they piped and rasped and stamped their feet, which might so easily be shattered were the carpet too hard. Rendart liked them very much, for the wonderfully weird evening they had almost given, and might now be proposing to give, him. He liked them with a capacity he had for liking strangers as he liked their houses. And now he longed to know the worst, as he had always wanted to see the unsafe stair and the blocked drains they tried to hide.

"In the tower," said Monsieur de Venne, "the steps lead up to a single round chamber. It's locked tight, my father locked it. It was locked before that, over a century ago, and not opened. Out of fear."

"Out of terror," whispered mademoiselle.

They glanced at Rendart, to be sure he was attending, which he was. Then they continued.

Morcara Venka was strong and beautiful and rich, and, from the age of five, an orphan. Her guardians were on the timorous side; they had been chosen out of her father's dying wisdom to be precisely so. He had benefitted from the horror writers of his day, and knew that a clever and powerful guardian will either seduce, dupe, or murder his female ward. Morcara's guardians were straw, and before her burgeoning vitality and arrogance, they bent, snapped, and were flattened. Nothing stayed her. She grew and flowered, and no man stood against her, and so this was the lesson she learned: That no one

could. Her hair was black, but the type of black that is black still when the
sun shines on it. She did as she wished. She rode astride, as a man did, which
then was thought very shocking. Indeed, she dressed as a man when it suited
her, and memories were left over of how Morcara looked flaming white with
some enthusiasm or rage, in her male britches, her waistcoat, the ruffled linen
at her wrists, the black tide of hair down her back. And there were images too
of Morcara in silver silk and diamonds, dancing. But once she picked a live
coal off the fire and threw it in the lap of a woman who (she thought) had
insulted her, and once she challenged a man to a duel, and when he did not
go to it because, he said, he would not fight a woman, she visited him and cut
him across the forehead with her rapier.

Like a rushing river, Morcara had only her own banks to check her, her
own uneven moods to rein her in, and she was at all other times ungovernable.

She took lovers. She cast them off. Who was strong enough to charm her
became weak at her eyes, under the lash of her words, became weak simply
by wanting her in return.

Morcara desired only what she did not have, and lost desire for it when she
had sampled it. Her dining room, they said, here at the mansion, surrounded
then by her fields and forests – her dining room was littered by just-tasted
dishes, plums bitten once and thrown away.

Some believed she was in league with the Devil, had the Evil Eye.
Perhaps she had not grown jaded with that.

When she was twenty-four years of age, scandalous Morcara met a man
two years her junior, at a house in the City she had charmed by visiting. He
was the son of a banker, permitted in society but not lauded there, and he had,
perhaps because of his situation, an extraordinary offhand and controlled
arrogance that matched the flamboyant, careless arrogance of Morcara
Venka. He too was rich, partly an outcast, and, incidentally, he was handsome;
a portrait remains to establish this, although there are none of Morcara.

Morcara saw the young banker's son, whose name was, curiously,
Angelstein. She was too accustomed to her effect to make much of an
advance to him. She merely, as was later reported, touched his gloved wrist
with one feather of her fan, remarking, "Well, here we are, and where tomorrow?" But her eyes met his, she looked and so did he. In the minds and
mouths of others he was, by the next day's sunrise, her conquest and her
lover. But in fact this did not happen. No, not at all.

During the following week, Morcara took care to be at those functions,
those dinners and balls wherein Angelstein had been patronizingly allowed a
part. *She* had only to enter to be admitted, such was her power, financial and
otherwise.

She dined beside him at tables where swordfish lay in castles of ice and champagne jetted in fountains. She danced with him in her silver silk, with diamonds in her hair that was black as black under the candles. Angelstein was polite, but nothing more. At last, in an arbor very early in the morning, just before the dawn came, when the grass was drenched with dew, she propositioned him. She is supposed to have said something along the lines that if he were the woman and she the man he would long since have felt her weight. No one was certain, of course, for no one had chanced near enough properly to overhear. But some did see Angelstein, courteous as ever, disengage her snowy glove from his breast, her lips from his own. Saw the curt bow he gave her, heard the *tone* of his voice, a hint amused now, some regret at parting.

As he walked across the lawn, Morcara called after him, "You will come to me. I'll make you. I shall wait."

"No, mademoiselle," he said dismissively. That was all, not even looking back. *No, mademoiselle.*

Then the sun came up, and Morcara Venka vanished, like the demon spirit she was said to be.

At home in her mansion amid the fields and forests, she waited for him one whole month. She had everything made beautiful for him. She was restless, always pacing, looking from the high windows to see him coming, riding a horse maybe, or in a carriage, but always coming toward her out of the distance. She climbed at last up into the highest part of the house to keep her vigils, the round chamber in the tower that once had been her father's study, and by then was a store room only, with chests about the curving walls and an old nest under a beam, for the casement had broken in a storm and the glass had not been replaced. She preferred it that way, the round room. There was no emanation of her father, she had barely known him.

But when the month was over, and Angelstein had not ridden or driven to the house, Morcara Venka sent to him one letter. Its contents are unknown – he had the prudence, being prudent in all things, to destroy it.

Seven more days she awaited a reply. When there was no reply, she came down from the tower. She went into the house, next into the gardens, and she walked about for a while, looking at things, picking them up and examining them, a book, a little vase, a leaf, a stone.

Her servants, who were afraid of Morcara with complete justification, did not feel any pity or anxiety at her state of mind. One of the maids is supposed to have said, "She'll go to the Devil now. She'll do something that'll bring the house down around our ears."

But all Morcara did was to call the men to clear the chests from the chamber in the tower and to put into it instead a high-backed chair from her own apartment. When this was done she went to her bureau and, sitting down quietly, wrote something on a piece of paper. Again, one of the servants had a premonition at this that Morcara was invoking or bespelling something or someone.

But all Morcara did was light a candle in the settling dusk, put on her silver dress and comb out her hair, and go with the candle and the paper up into the tower.

There they left her well alone, and through the early portion of the night one or two beheld the wan flicker of the candle, but later it was out.

The new day began, and Morcara was not in her bed, and nowhere to be found in the house.

Then they decided she had better be sought, for after all she could only send them away again, but for lack of diligence she could chastise them. They were used to her angers and her sparkle, not to her absence.

When they came up the steps of the tower to the round room at the top, the door was shut fast, and to it was pinned a sheet of paper, with Morcara's writing on it in black ink.

Not all the men on the stair could read, but one of them could and they brought him forward. He looked, read, and went white. "She's put a curse on this room,' he said. "Go back." And he started down the steps. Just at that moment the steward came in and caught the fellow below, and asked him what had been discovered. The man blurted out then, loud enough they all heard, what was written on the paper. It said: *All you who dare to enter here will die.*

After that the men scattered, and what with Morcara's half unearthly reputation, the steward could do nothing with them, and although he tried the door himself and knocked loudly, the way was secured and no one answered.

Four days later a priest was brought from the City, along with some lawyers and other officials. They approached the tower with trepidation. It was a hot and thundery afternoon, and reaching the steps, they hesitated. One of the lawyers turned faint there, and announced that he could smell, as he put it, death. Three men went up at last, the priest with them, and the strongest – since the men of the house still refused to touch the door – put his shoulder to it. After a great deal of hammering and heaving the inner lock burst, and carried by the momentum, this man stumbled a foot or so inside the room.

A most grisly sight met all their eyes, and his firstly. There in her chair sat Morcara Venka, in her silver dress and her long black hair, with diamonds at her throat and flowers in her hand, but she was a corpse, which because of the hot summer, had already begun to rot. The stench came fast on the heels of the vision of her crumbling flesh and its fish eyes and the white bone that jutted out at her cheek and brow, and the others in her fingers like the tines of a fan. The men fell back in horror, and the first one, who had stumbled into the room, he turned in mindless fright and dashed by them, and fell the length of the stair so his neck was dislocated and he died on the bottom step.

The others who witnessed Morcara's finish survived it, but then, of course, they had not "dared" to enter Morcara's room.

Old Monsieur de Venne, Morcara's remote relative and indirect inheritor, stabbed at the fire with a poker. Sparks showered up and the wood sank, letting show two glaring hellish hearts.

"The room was locked and sealed, and the door of the tower itself was boarded up. The corpse they left to rot in the tomb it had chosen. That Morcara was the initial sacrifice to her own curse had doubtless been her design. The poor wretch who went in there by accident was its initial victim. There shouldn't be any more. No one should enter. No one."

"*All you who dare to enter here will die*," repeated Mademoiselle de Venne, with shrinking relish; she clasped her agitated hands as if they might fly away.

Rendart sat looking at the fire with his hosts. He was savoring what he had been told, but not quite yet sprinkled with the condiment of belief. Finally he said, "But do you mean, monsieur, mademoiselle, that the remains of Morcara Venka are still up there, in the tower?"

"Just so," said monsieur to the wickedness of the fire. "*Just so*."

"It is," said Rendart, carefully, "a marvelous and awful story. But surely by now, someone –" He paused, to choose his words with more tact. "Surely someone must have been drawn to take the risk, at *least* to undo the door and verify the tale from outside the threshold?"

"One did," said monsieur, with a grim satisfaction that Rendart, then, found extremely convincing. "But only one."

"Cesar," murmured mademoiselle, "you mustn't –"

"'Mustn't' be fiddled," said monsieur, and had another abrupt swipe of the brandy. As he raised the glass the fire caught it and his eyes and isolated teeth. He appeared wolfish, satanic. "Piddle," he said, "on 'mustn't.'"

Rendart braced himself.

"You referred earlier to a certain Grisvold...."

"Yes. So I did. Bloody Grisvold – Oh, stop your noise, you senile old hen. Am I to confess to the priest? Where is he? Hasn't been near us in a twelve-month. I could die tonight. Go up the stairs and open her door and enter into the room –"

"No, no, Cesar," implored mademoiselle.

Rendart perceived it was a rite between them, that possibly they often acted it out, if infrequently with the benefit of an audience. These two, so adjacent and yet so hedged against death, she with her provisions for lightning and wet clothes, he with his preserving brandy. Unsatisfied, sere lives burned almost down, clawing at the wicks.

"Poor Grisvold," said Rendart, temptingly.

"Poor Grisvold, yes," said Monsieur de Venne.

Grisvold had been the son of their father's cook. A wonderful cook she was too, and partially for that reason she had stayed with the family despite the birth of a child, who was not merely a bastard but an idiot as well. The illegitimacy was hushed up, and the cook equipped with a husband off at some war who was presently suitably killed during the enemy advance. The idiocy of the boy, conversely, was exaggerated, for he was retarded rather then moronic, and could tackle, despite bouts of illness, feverish and unidentified, a number of perfectly useful tasks, such as blacking boots, helping with the horses, of which at first there had been several, and so on.

In age Grisvold was six or seven years the senior of the nine-year-old Cesar de Venne, but mentally Grisvold was a year or two his junior. On this Cesar, a cruel and experimental boy, had played. Cesar had been, in his own case, very unhappy at the time. He was about to be sent away to school, far from his mama, whom he loved, and his elder sister, who irritated but admired him. Cesar had realized from the treatment his papa now and then gave out, to make of him a "man," what was to be expected more regularly at the school. Nor was Cesar overjoyed at the prospects of study, which he disliked, or the ultimate goal which would be to create him a lawyer, an occupation for which he would have neither aptitude nor eagerness (and at being which he would eventually resoundingly fail).

Grisvold Cesar had always hated, but in a casual way. Cesar did not like mess, or messy things, and Grisvold's mental messiness, as Cesar saw it, abraded. So Cesar would make Grisvold commit stupid and time-wasting actions, for which sometimes Grisvold would gain a beating – and that made the worse beating Cesar might then receive bearable.

One day, Cesar managed, fairly easily, to convince Grisvold that there was a monster, a beast of some sort, in the well from which the kitchen water was drawn. Up until this hour, Grisvold had always happily obtained water there when told to. Now he flatly and hysterically refused. A row presently ensued, and gazing over the kitchen roof from the fig tree that grew behind it, Cesar was enabled to observe Grisvold dragged screaming and wetting himself in terror to the well, there to be shown no monster existed – by the expedient of lowering and withdrawing the bucket, of leaning into the well, and of Grisvold's being made to lean into the well, after which Grisvold puked, just barely not into the well, and was beaten

on the bare buttocks with a switch. Soon after, however, the row progressed into the main areas of the house, and Cesar was hauled before his
father, who, after a lecture, administered a beating the like of which his son
had not yet undergone.

Sobbing in agony on his bed, Cesar de Venne plotted a revenge upon all
mankind, but first and foremost upon the only one of its numbers he could
hope to reach, hapless Grisvold.

To this end Cesar had sworn his sister to secrecy and collusion, for he was
determined now that Grisvold should suffer and he, Cesar, go unscathed –
although in Cesar's opinion, "If he beat me like that again, I'd die, I'd die in
front of him, and serve him right."

Cesar's sister had not entreated Cesar to reconsider what he meant to do.
She was flattered to have been included in the villainy, which would involve
her saying that she and her brother had been together during a particular time.
She did not like the idiot either, and did not, naïve as she was, truly grasp
what they were about.

Neither of them knew, indeed, exactly the nature of Morcara's room in the
old tower. All the firm information they had ever gleaned was that the tower
was unsafe and full of rats, therefore to be avoided. But too there was a sort
of rumoring among the servants, which everyone had somehow garnered,
including Cesar, and including Grisvold, that a female ancestor had slain herself there and haunted it.

"I'll make him go up," said Cesar, "into the tower. Perhaps he'll meet the
ghost. That'll show him."

Given some supernatural choice, Cesar would doubtless have preferred to
send his father to this shock and horror, but only Grisvold was available.

"You've always wanted to know what these words say," said Cesar to
Grisvold the following morning, when they met in the garden behind the
kitchen. The words in question were engraved in the wall, and related to the
shrubs and vegetables grown beneath, their order being strictly adhered to,
since various poisonous items also willfully came up there. Grisvold had a
strange kind of lust for reading, limited to things suddenly come on or seen
rather than to the mystery of books. "Well, I'll tell you. I'll tell you slowly,
so you learn, and then you can go in and say them to your mother, and won't
she like that, won't she be proud?" Grisvold, who had been fooled this way
on another occasion into saying something obscene before his mother, for
which he was beaten, had already charitably forgotten that. He stared at the
words in the wall. He was still pale and sweaty from his latest thrashing. He
said, gently, "Tell me."

"Not yet. You've got to do something first. Something so I'll know you're
brave. Because you weren't brave about the well, were you?"

"Mam says thee lied, there ain't no monster down in it," said Grisvold, doubtfully.

"Of course there is," snapped Cesar, "and she's impertinent to say I lie. Don't you know you make a monster strong by being afraid of it? We all go to the well as if it's nothing to fear, and then the monster can't do anything. But *you –*"

Grisvold was abashed. He did not protest that Cesar had not explained before this salient point.

"Now," went on Cesar, "I'll let you prove you're not a coward another way."

"How's that?" said Grisvold.

Cesar told him.

"But there's a hant in the tower, thee knows it," said Grisvold. "And the door's boarded, and the top door's locked."

"The boards are all loose on the bottom door," said Cesar; they were. "And I know where the key's to be got." He did. Prolonged observation of his father, his father's routines and concealments, a study made like the other before him at school, perforce (know your enemy) had led Cesar one day to notice an enormous key that seemed constructed from stone, which hung in the west wine cellar. As it was not the key to the cellar itself, Cesar had pondered on it and decided at last it had to do with the west tower. He might have been wrong, but he was not wrong, and therefore once Grisvold had been got to take the key, peel off the rotted boards, and enter the tower, with Cesar, someone was in a position to undo the door of Morcara's room.

Cesar's plan was to remain the far side of it, and to bolt at once, so adding to Grisvold's terror. He would then return secretly into the house, and to his sister's company, where, if questioned, they would both declare their unity in a project to do with the pressing of plants, and encyclopedias.

As for Grisvold, anything might befall him.

The chosen hour was dusk, when the area of the west tower was unfrequented, Cesar supposed at his preparatory work, and the servants busy with their supper.

That Grisvold might disobey Cesar's orders crossed no one's mind. Least of all Grisvold's.

He stole the key and had it in his grasp when Cesar approached him in the twilight under the tower.

Most of the boards had already worked away from the door. Grisvold's inopportune brawn had soon removed their vestiges. The warped outer door also gave before it.

In the gathering of the dark, as bats flitted over the yard, they stared together, these bad companions, up the stony corkscrew of the stair.

"It'll be pitch-black, it will," said Grisvold.

"No, I've brought a candle."

They went in by the base of the steps, and Cesar lit the candle with a vivid splutter from the big match.

A bleak and grim place it was, the vein of the tower, all fissures and rats' nests, the steps dank and pocked with ancient stinking rains that had come through and collected there. They went up, Grisvold first as he had been told to do. The candle flung great wheeling arcs that seemed to topple the stair, so they clung to the unsafe railing. Cesar was already unnerved and had a want to fly constantly. But Grisvold's chittering fear sustained Cesar. Helpless in his own world, Cesar wished, godlike, to see to what depths his subject's fear might go down.

At the top of the spiral was the vast timbered door, girded by iron, and with the great iron lock that had been established some two hundred years before.

"Try the key," said Cesar firmly.

Grisvold hesitated, shaking and muttering, and in that instant Cesar beheld that some message had been scratched in the wood above the lock. "Wait," said Cesar, and shone his candle there.

"What do it say," gabbled Grisvold, sweating violently and shivering all over. "Thee tell me."

And Cesar, without properly thinking, read aloud the words some admonisher had inscribed there, that the warning not be lost (who that was was never learned; everyone currently in the household disclaimed it).

All you who dare to enter here will die.

Grisvold tried to turn, and Cesar struck him lightly and correctively, another lesson learned from Papa.

"*No.* Do you want everyone to think you a ninny and a coward? Open the door. Open the door and prove you're a man."

Grisvold bleated in abject terror. But he turned back to the door, got the key into it, and by dint of his strong hand and wrist, forced the door to give and so swing wide.

Cesar too had waited on this. He was half petrified, and yet his reason had not deserted him. The warning cut in the door concerned entry to the room. As for *looking*, he would allow Grisvold to do that. Cesar crept, stiff with fright, back down two or three steps, and so he never saw, never chose to see, what the room contained. Obviously, bones, for the dead woman who had laid the curse had prevented anyone's ever shifting her to hallowed ground. There she must have sat, propped in her chair, in the desiccated ruins of her gown, and with the eternal diamonds still cold and bright upon her. Worse than a ghost, very likely, the actuality of mortal death.

Above him, where the candle held high in Cesar's hand could reach, and where the dusk faintly came through the chamber's broken window, Grisvold stood quaking, and noiseless now, staring at something which was undoubtedly Morcara's skeleton. And the Devil, who but the Devil, made Cesar whisper loudly, through nausea and panic, "*Go in*, Grisvold. I dare you to. *Go into the room.*"

And Grisvold, like a stage magician's doll, took some unflexing cloddish steps, and went into the room, into the room of Morcara's curse, and was there perhaps the half of one minute, before coming out again. And standing on the top step, the doorway of the room behind him, Grisvold looked down on Cesar his tormentor, and said to him, "It's death to go in. It says so. And thee made me. Thee killed me."

Then he dropped flat with a thud that seemed to disturb the foundations of the tower, and did not move, and Cesar fled, throwing away the candle as he did so.

There was, as the brother and sister described it, a deal of fuss. For Grisvold's mother went to look for him, and then some of the grooms went, and they found him halfway down the stair of the tower, where, somewhat recovering, he had crawled. He was carried to his mother's room, and there on her bed he raved and burned, so the doctor was called from the village. But by morning Grisvold was dead.

Then all the old truths of Morcara's room were brought out shamelessly, and Cesar's father went up alone, shut the door, and locked it. And coming out, gray himself as the stone, he set about ordering bricks and cement to seal the tower's lower door forever. A fortnight later this was done.

As for Cesar, when questioned he and his sister adhered to their pretense. They were not believed, but neither was it feasible to disbelieve them, for that must be to accept that two children, below the age of twelve years and of good birth, had perpetrated something evil.

Presently Cesar was sent away to school, where he was subjected to all he had dreaded, and worse, and might have felt, if he had thought there any need, to have expiated his sin. Mademoiselle de Venne paid in other ways for a crime she soon shifted totally to her brother. The copious diaries of her girlhood contain only one reference to Grisvold's death, as follows: *Cesar once did, in childish ignorance, a very wicked thing, and made me lie for his sake. I have no luck, nothing goes right for me. Have I too been doomed by Morcara's curse?*

When they had finished their story, the two mummified objects at the fire fixed on Rendart their glassy eyes. After a few moments, the young man sighed. That was hardly response enough.

"What do you say to it, eh?" demanded Monsieur de Venne. And reaching out almost absently, he rang the bell for the stoat-faced maid, since his brandy decanter was empty.

Rendart sat considering. He had rather astonished himself by being deeply offended. Not only at the appalling viciousness of their childhood personas – which still in some form persisted, flutter about *poor Grisvold* as mademoiselle had, and make intimate confession as had monsieur. But also at the insane stupidity that had preserved the pair of them, to this very night, in the crediting of Morcara's curse.

It was true, Rendart would have liked to punish them, but sternly he had put this idea behind him. Then he was only left with the much harder puzzle of how to bring them to their senses in a tactful and open-ended way.

At length, after several quite harsh or insistent promptings from monsieur and mademoiselle, and after the brandy had been refilled by Pierre, Rendart spoke.

"I take it, the lower door of the tower is still bricked up?"

"What else?" flared Monsieur de Venne.

"I have to tell you," said Rendart, "it could be unbricked tomorrow, and the remains of Morcara Venka removed for burial. That might allow her peace. Perhaps you might feel easier."

"God have mercy!" cried Mademoiselle de Venne. "How could it be possible?" she said. "No one can enter that room and live."

"I've heard the words of the curse on the room," agreed Rendart. "But I wouldn't put any faith in their effectiveness."

"Haven't you had proof enough?" grated monsieur, recharged with brandy fire. "Morcara herself. The man who broke in the door. And bloody Grisvold."

"Yes, I've heard what you've said," murmured Rendart, "but it seems to me the first man who rushed into the chamber by accident rushed out again in horror, missed his footing, and fell quite naturally, if unfortunately, to his death. Poor Grisvold, from what you say, was subject to undiagnosed fevers, which may have been linked to an inflammation of the brain. He had also been recently and savagely beaten in a manner, dare I say, the awful beatings given monsieur perhaps did not approach. Add to that a superstitious and overwhelming terror, and I must suppose his latent disease erupted and carried him off. As for Morcara," added Rendart determinedly, as alcoholic waves and pale flappings threatened from the fire, "I rather think she took her own life. From what's been said of her she would brook no denials. To live her life without a man she genuinely had come to desire would have seemed to her dramatic spirit an imposition. Neither man nor God should tell her what to do. So she shut herself up and concluded her existence with poison."

"Ridiculous!" roared monsieur.

"Not at all," said Rendart. "Mademoiselle has herself assured me the garden abounded in dangerous and venomous plants; I myself spotted three or four. You picture Morcara in her ball gown, with flowers in her hand. Probably they were one of the deadlier species, and she ate them to effect a swift dispatch."

A space of wordlessness followed this statement, during which the fire and some clocks ticked away the minutes. Seeming to understand what they did, it was Mademoiselle de Venne who quickly if hoarsely broke the silence.

"But remember the words, Monsieur Rendart. They are scratched to this day on the door."

"I do indeed remember them, perfectly. *All you who dare to enter here will die.*" Rendart paused, and let his pity for them both, even his pity of their nastiness, their evil, come back to him. He would spare them, he must. "Suffice it to say, mademoiselle, if you wish me to undertake the commission, I'll see to it the tower is unbricked, the upper room entered, and the bones removed to holy ground. For myself and those I hire for the work, I haven't any fears. I guarantee their safety – and their wages – and if you like, I'll furnish proof of their survival for, say, a year after the reburial. I'll even go so far," said Rendart, with a sudden smile, "as to set up a tomb for Morcara Venka, at my own expense. Out of respect for her romance."

They sat dumbfounded, glaring at him. They loathed his interference and yes, they would like him to perish of the curse of Morcara's room; they would give their permission.

Rendart regretted his smile all night as he lay dozing in the fearful dank white bedroom. He was sorry he had lapsed, for it had been the smile of a torturer if not the executioner: He had punished them by making a gift to the dead, rather than to themselves, the living – that state and title to which they so obstinately clung.

A month later, as the heat of summer baked into a fruiting jamlike autumn, the tower of the mansion was opened, the stair ascended, the door undone, and the heap of bones placed in a box and borne away.

Rendart for his part contracted with the workmen, and the priest who had spiritually cleansed the room of any impressed miseries, that they should monthly submit to the de Vennes, for one year after the enterprise, continued proof of their life and health, which was accordingly done. All those who entered Morcara's room, including Rendart himself, are still hale and going about their deeds in the world.

For of course, as Rendart had seen, having the youth, the scope for it, it was no curse at all Morcara Venka had laid upon her room in the tower. For she told no more than the truth, the truth which the old monsieur and mademoiselle must not be made to face so bitterly, the truth at which she, Morcara, in anticipating, had thumbed her nose. Pure self-deception caused others to dance thereafter to Morcara's tune. (As she surely knew, adding a cunning flick of the wrist to her phrase.) It was only necessary to open the eye of the mind as well as the door of the chamber, in order to go in there without terror. Or at least without any terror that was not already inherent and inevitable, and that each of us must dwell with for every year we are on the earth. *All you who dare to enter here will die.* It was a fact. All who dared the room would die. What else? For death is the destiny of all, and unavoidable, be it now, tomorrow, or eight decades hence. But how often do we like to be told, how often do we not convince ourselves we are *immortal*?

You can tell the graves of the bourgeois, always so ornate and yet so cautious, as if even here they were afraid to try too far above their stations, lest they be smitten. Sometimes you see how the living attempt to make reparation. Here the neglectful parent has strewn stony flowers above his child, but none of the real sort. The story associated with this grave is very horrible and very strange. Hearsay.

The Marble Web

Daisy, Daisy, give me your answer, do!
I'm half crazy, all for the love of you!

— *Harry Dacre*

From the glycerine water they pulled her up, first hauling on the sodden shreds of her robe, but these gave way, finally getting purchase on the bones of her corset which had not rotted. Her hair streamed back into the water, like weed, and in the pre-dawn nothing-light, she was no longer pretty, or easily to be recognized.

There were many who got their trade out of the river, that Styx of Paradys. By night suicides came down to the edge like parched deer. Others, murdered, were thrust out into the depths, surfacing days or weeks later, by this or that bridge or muddy bar, to render up, to the scavengers of the river, a pearl locket, a silver watch, or a jet in a ring of mourning.

But Jausande Marguerite, she was not quite of the usual order, for they had heard of her, perhaps been looking out, and for that reason, wrapped in an oilskin, her body was taken presently to one of the judiciary buildings behind the Scholars' Quarter. Here, under the dreadful probing of the new electric lamps, she was identified, she was given back her name, which was no longer any use to her.

And soon after that the hunt was on, but the hunt found not a thing. Thereafter all this was sensational for a brief month, then passed into the mythology of the City, that makes itself from the ragbag of everything.

"Lower the lights," said the young man in the loud coat. "He'll perform a miracle."

"What nonsense," they said generally. And then, another: "It isn't necessary to lower the gas. He'll do it without."

Across the salon, the man with whom they were spicing their conversation glanced at them, and the group fell silent.

457

"What eyes," said one of the women feebly, once the man had turned away.

"Oh? I thought them surprisingly poor, considering he's supposed to use them in order to entrance, and hypnotize."

"Probably uses his ring for that," said another.

The loud coat admired the ring, someone else remarked pointedly that it was very vulgar. But others had not at all observed a ring, and looked for it in vain.

Then the group began to discuss a different topic. Their flylike minds were unable to remain for long in any one spot.

The man they had spoken of, however, was now and then commented upon by all sides. His nickname was The Conjuror, for it was said of him that he had made some money in a vaudeville act to the north. He represented therefore to the bourgeois evening salons of Paradys all that was ludicrous, contemptible, quaint; a butt for jokes, and perhaps needful in a dry social season.

In appearance, certainly, The Conjuror was recognizable by his very ordinariness. Not short, decidedly not tall, thinly built, and neither well nor badly dressed, his hair was combed back and his face shaven, leaving – washed up there, as it were – two normal eyes, without exceptional luster, and actually apt to turn as dull as misted spectacle lenses.

His notoriety was founded on a collection of odd stories, the facts of which came always in an altered version.

Meanwhile, he had not said, written, done, or vowed to do anything at all celebrated. There was a rumor the walls of his narrow flat near the Observatory were plastered by bills and photographs depicting him as an archmagician, raising the dead from the floorboards of a stage. But who had been to the flat to see? He was unmarried, had no servant. He went out only to those functions to which some frustrated hostess had, on a whim, summoned him. With the perversity of the City, however, his utter dreariness – he had neither wit nor charm about him – soon lifted him to a bizarre pinnacle, that of the Anticipated. There he stayed, or nearly stayed, by now fading a little, for even if lighted by others, a candle must have wax enough to burn of itself.

"My dear," said the hostess of the evening salon, as she led her niece into the room, "I should have been lost without you."

"Why?" said her niece, who dreaded finding the salon tedious, and longed to escape.

"Your youth and prettiness," said the flattering aunt, "your poise. That dress which is – oh, perfection."

Jausande Marguerite smiled. She was one of those girls who had somehow always managed to draw genuine praise from both sexes. She was attractive enough to please but not beautiful enough to pose a threat, she was kind enough to be gentle, cruel enough to amuse, and young enough to be forgiven.

"Look there, what a fearful coat," said Jausande, and avoided the eye of the loud young man swiftly, with a delicate, apparently spontaneous vagueness.

"Yes, his father has been a great help to your uncle. Vile people, but money … there we are …"

Jausande sighed, and cleverly concealed her sigh as she had learned to conceal a yawn at the opera.

Beyond the salon windows the evening, through which she had been driven, still had on it a light blush of promise. Jausande had caught the terrible sweet illness, often recurrent as malaria, and most unbearable in youth and middle age, the longing for that nameless thing given so many names – excitement, adventure, romance, love. Every dawn, each afternoon, all sunsets, aggravated the fever.

But through the promising dusk she had come, to this. Already her eyes had instinctively swept the room over, and found all the usual elements both inanimate and physical. There was nothing here for Jausande Marguerite. But she must pretend that there was.

Her aunt led the girl about, introducing her like a flower. Everyone liked Jausande at once, it was one of her gifts, and she perpetuated it by being nice to everyone, but not so nice that they felt under an obligation. Of course, Jausande's aunt did *not* introduce her to any but the most deserving. And beyond the pale, no doubt, was The Conjuror, that awful little man. No, he did not meet Jausande in the formal way.

The gas lamps were already lit, and burned up steadily as the windows went out. The long room in which the gathering mingled grew close. White wine was being drunk, and small unsatisfying foods eaten. In half an hour, the evening party would break up, unless something should happen.

"Now what about" – shouted the young man in the loud coat – "a game of some sort? Some charade –" He winked at Jausande across the crowd, and she did not notice. He added, to a ripple of encouragement, "What if we have some magical tricks?"

"Now, now," said Jausande's aunt, "Philippe, we mustn't turn my drawing room into a bear garden."

"The idea," said loud Philippe. "But surely there's someone here can give us a show?"

At that, some of the heads turned, looking for the drab figure of The Conjuror. There he was, between the windows, a shadow with a glass of wine in its bony hand, and something repellent to him, like a smell – but he smelled of nothing at all.

To become abruptly the center of the room's gaze did not seem to trouble him. Nor did he bloom. He did nothing.

"Monsieur," said Jausande's aunt, who had forgotten his name into the bargain, "you must forgive Monsieur Philippe Labonne."

It was very strange. It was as if (as with a spell) this silly outburst, drawing attention to the supposed origins of The Conjuror, which in fact had never even been verified, were all hearsay, called up some power. The creature himself was not imbued by anything apparent. He did not change, in looks or manner (which were rather those of a funeral assistant caught out at the wake). And yet the salon, so boring a moment earlier, took on a dangerous quality, like the air during a bitter quarrel when any terrible truth may be said.

"Madame," said The Conjuror, quietly, and there was nothing of note either in his voice or his accent, accept that the latter had a slight tinge of the streets. And he gave a nasty graceless little bow.

"There now," said the aunt of Jausande. "But perhaps *you*, darling, will play for us on the piano?"

Jausande did not wilt or beam. She played the piano as she did all things – nicely, effectively, not brilliantly. It gave her sometimes a quiet pleasure to play in private, none in public, nor any qualms. She would do what she must.

But it was as she took a step toward the piano that she saw The Conjuror looking at her. She saw, and she could not help but see and show that she had seen. And a flush, of a sort of ghastly shame, spread over her face and neck. There was something so awful in The Conjuror's look, for it said everything that must, by such as he, never be said, and so very openly, and so very intently. *I love you*, said the look. *I love you at first sight.*

"Whatever –?" began Jausande's aunt.

"I'm very warm," said Jausande. "Will you excuse me if I don't play for a moment?"

She had averted her eyes, but still, still, she felt the eyes of *him* clinging on to her. Here and there in the recent past indecorous outpourings had been made to her. *Never* in *that* way.

And now other people in the room became aware of it, both the intensity of The Conjuror, and its object, and tiny, barely audible sounds were breaking across the audience, the whispers of sneers and laughs.

Perhaps what made it so appalling was its mediocrity. Here, in this unimportant drawing room, the birth of an obsession. And if he had been grotesque, and she amazingly beautiful, there would have been to it the dignity of tragedy. But she was only rather pretty, and he – He was nothing on earth.

And then he spoke again. They all heard him.

"If you like, madame, I can offer my poor skills, a few of them. If the ladies won't be alarmed."

"Why – monsieur –" and Jausande's aunt actually stammered, so instinctively startled she was. Every line of her corseted form revealed she wanted to deny him. But it was absurd – why not? In hopes of something like this she had asked him here. It would be a coup. Nowhere else, that she knew of, had he "entertained."

Besides, the mechanism was already in motion. As if at a signal, her guests were drawing back, leaving a broad space at the room's far end into which The Conjuror propelled himself. He had discarded his wineglass. His hands were empty. He lifted them slightly. They were horribly bare, as if peeled.

"Look – nothing up his sleeve," loudly said the loud Philippe.

And one of the others called, "Lower the gas!"

"No," said The Conjuror, and from his position at their front, he had now taken some authority. "That won't be necessary."

And then the extraordinary did happen. He snapped his fingers (as the aunt of Jausande said afterward, for all the world like a grocer's clerk) and each of the six gas fitments in the room was reduced to a smoky sublume. Contrastingly, the light in the area of The Conjuror was heightened. Its source was invisible.

Some of the ladies shrieked. Then there was chastened laughter.

Philippe said, "Been at the lamps – planted a helper in the basement –"

"Monsieur," said The Conjuror, "please do yourself the kindness of becoming silent."

This was nearly as dramatic as the trick of the lamps. It was so audacious, so frankly rude. It carried such weight. The stance of The Conjuror had changed, his voice had done so. This must be his stage presence, and as such, it was a good one.

"Now," said The Conjuror. "Mesdames, messieurs. I must ask you all to remain as still as possible. Not to move about. To restrain your outcry. If you will do that, I can show you something, although very little. We are surrounded by wonders, kept from us only by a veil. You must understand," he said, and now there was not a sound otherwise, "that I know how to twitch aside that veil, a fraction. To reveal more would be to endanger your sanity. You must trust me in this. You must trust me utterly. From this moment, your lives and hearts hang from my grip. I will not let you go. But your obedience is essential. How else can I protect you?"

The room was quiet as death. He had frightened and awed them. They would complain after they did not know how. But he was clever, give him that, he had done it. That common and unmusical voice had become an instrument by which he gained dominion over them. And the lamps burned low.

Then his pale hands darted out and seemed to lie there, suspended as if upon the surface of a pool.

A girl appeared. She appeared out of nothing, or the brocade wall, half transparent, ghostly, and then she grew quite solid, and was entirely there before them. She was no one they knew.

The girl was dressed in a long draped tunic with a diagonal pattern. Her hair was done up in a knot, with combs. She stretched to light a metal cup that apparently floated in the atmosphere. It blossomed out like a flower, and dimly at her back they saw the columns and cistern of a Roman atrium. Then she had turned, and the atrium was gone, rolled up with her into nothingness again.

The room was as it had been. Someone dared to speak, not Philippe Labonne. "Shadow play," the man said, "images thrown up by a small projector."

"Monsieur," said The Conjuror, moving to look at him, but holding his arms still upward, the hands suspended, a position that should have been ridiculous, but was not, as if, now, he grasped gently by ropes two opposing forces, two great dogs, perhaps. "Monsieur, you must do as I asked. Or I can't be responsible."

"Devil take you," said the guest.

"No, it is you he will take, monsieur. Be quiet, be quiet at once, or leave immediately."

Jausande's aunt said, rather tremulously, "Yes, do let's all be obedient. This is so interesting."

And somehow there was silence again, awkward and unwilling for a moment, and more fraught and nearly frightened than ever.

A man walked up out of the floor. (A woman screamed and her scream was choked down.) The man, solid as the Roman girl, solid as anyone present, wore hose and tunic, and the rounded, color-slashed sleeves of an alchemic century. He climbed an unseen stair out of the floor, up across the room, and through the air, and vanished into the ceiling.

The Conjuror spoke to them. "What I show you here are only the pictures of the past, the things that have been, on this spot. But there are other things that coexist with us, in past ages as now."

He spread his arms a little wider, as if allowing the two great dogs to pull forward and away.

There in the middle of the cleared space, where the light had been, was a globe of night. Stars shone over a garden made to the formal measure of three hundred years before, and a woman in a high-waisted gown and cap of silver

wire moved among the statues and the sculpted trees. She spoke words from
a book, but though the watching salon heard a murmur of her voice, her
words, the accent, were so alien, they could not make them out.

Perhaps it was ventriloquism, for The Conjuror too moved his lips, but
not it seemed in the same rhythm as the woman.

The woman stopped, facing out into the salon and not seeing it. She
closed the book together on a jeweled finger and her cold eyes glared.
Then the ground cracked at her feet. It opened into a chasm. And the
woman looked into it, not stepping back, nor seemingly dismayed. And
something shouldered up from the chasm, pitch dark as the night, putting
out all the stars. It had no proper form, yet it was there. And leaning to the
woman it made a thin, sweet sound, like distant music. But she answered
angrily in wild, ornamented words, what might have been a name. Then
the creature from the pit flowed and lowered and compressed itself. It
made itself over. And on the grass it alighted, and with a ratlike shake, it
assumed the form of the woman, even to her dress and her silver cap, and
to the book in her hand. Then she gave a cry of laughter or terror – it was
impossible to tell which – a sort of sneezing derision or panic, and whirled
into a hundred bits like a shattered vase, and these fell down into the crack,
which then healed over. And the monster that had taken human form
walked away between the statues.

There was something so horrible in this scene that the silence The
Conjuror had induced was now augmented by a second silence, far deeper
and less negotiable.

But the garden and the night went out. And The Conjuror pointed upward,
and they looked, and saw a great glowing cloud hanging in the ceiling. It lay
over the whole of the drawing room, sending down soft rays of light, and a
sudden mild rain, which fell among them, moist and fragrant. There came a
muted exclamation, another, and these were stifled at once. But the cloud
brought a feeling of hope, of possibility. There was nothing fearful to it, until
there began to be glimpsed in it an exquisite angelic face with pitiless eyes,
looking at them as the other apparitions or demons had not.

And it was as if they thought, *I hate this, it is too beautiful, it asks too
much.*

And Jausande Marguerite thought quite clearly, *These things shouldn't be
shown. Make it go away.*

At which, as if The Conjuror read her mind, it did. It dissolved like a
warm ember.

A third change had come on the salon of Jausande's aunt. There was a
restlessness, an anger that had nothing to do with the petty anger of before.
Throats began to clear themselves, women's dresses rustled. There were faint

muffled inquiries. And Jausande's aunt, the hapless hostess, said, "Do you think, monsieur –?"

Then through the brocade wallpaper something burst like a bomb.

It was black, racing, lunging, roaring – there were cries and shouts – it was a carriage with six horses going full tilt. It tore into the room, into the crowd of evening guests, who fell and tumbled in front of it.

Jausande glimpsed the savage gaping mouths of horses pulled wide on reins, felt the wind of passage graze her and saw a man flung sideways from the impact. The stink of animal sweat and fear, heat and thunder. Hoofs like iron and wheels from which white sparks sprayed off. The carriage rushed headlong through the room and out, into some tunnel of the dimensions, and the walls were whole behind it.

The guests had scattered with the furniture, where they had thrown themselves or, as it seemed, been thrown. Women sobbed and men with sick faces ranted. Two of them had seized The Conjuror, that ineffectual little man.

"You must let go," he said. "Do it, before I make you."

And they let go of him, stepping back, offering him verbal violence instead. But he only shrugged.

Jausande's aunt whispered, "Someone make him leave quickly, for heaven's sake," and pressed her handkerchief to her mouth.

It seemed to Jausande she stood on an island in the jumbled, tumbled room, she was quite alone, as if deserted by midnight in a waste. And to her, over the elaborate carpet that was the sea of sand and rock, he moved. He stood about three feet from her and said, quietly, "You will come to me."

Jausande was unnerved but not afraid. She said, "How dare you? You don't know what you're saying."

But she realized that no one else had heard, and that though there were men enough to throw him out of a window, not one would lay a finger on his dingy sleeve. She looked, and saw his insignificance. She imagined his fusty, pointless life, cramped in his little rooms by the Observatory, an area fallen into disfavor, a place she would never visit.

"But you'll come to me," he said again, "when I'm ready. Then."

"You're mad," she said. She could not see his eyes. It was as if he had none. As if he had no physical shape at all.

And then he was gone, and in the distance over the desert her aunt was entreating her for sympathy, while round about, under the lonely mysterious howls of hyenas, ladies swooned and gentlemen swore vengeance.

At first from an embarrassment, presently from the reassembly of common sense, Jausande told no one what The Conjuror had said to her. Half an hour after his departure from the salon and her life, she had returned to earth and dismissed him as what he was, a fool and charlatan with a cunning line in tricks. It was his essential inferiority that drove him to attempt to distress the gathering. She was merely another intended victim. Some abrupt thought she had had of repairing to her father with the story was soon forgotten. The father of Jausande was elderly and bookish, and her mother long dead. Her uncle, meanwhile, was away on business in foreign climes.

Long after the curious and unpleasant evening, however, Jausande remained glad that no one had heard the invitation – the order – that The Conjuror had issued to her.

She did not believe in ghosts and demons. Her image even of God was that of a just, stern magistrate.

If she had turned a hair, then she plucked it out.

The year passed with a great chrysanthemum of summer, an autumnal pause, a snowy winter of festivals and feasts.

By the coming of spring, the flowers piercing the parks with their needles, the snowdrops, the showers that turned the building of the avenues to amazing edifices of wet newsprint, by then no rumors of The Conjuror were any longer heard. He had gone down again into his mouse hole under the boards of the City. Spring was not the time for him. It was as if he had been papered over, and the flowers grew out where he had stood.

And by then, anyway, she had truly forgotten.

Jausande Marguerite sat down before a window. It was late in the afternoon; the slanting champagne light looked sensational, as if new, as if the sun had never shone in this way, although it had in fact, since the dawning afternoon of time.... Jausande glanced at the light, where it invaded the stout trees of the Labonne garden. She felt middle-aged, the young girl, because she had seen through the wiles of sunfall. She had found it out: It promised nothing, neither adventure nor romance. In token, she was betrothed, to – of all people – the elder brother of Philippe Labonne. She had resigned herself to life.

For here was what life was, such long, quite pleasant, tiring, and tiresome mornings and evenings; the luncheon, the game of cards, the prospect of dinner, of more cards, of the male discussion of finance and politics.

Her fiancé was a good-looking and smart young man, who worked in his wealthy father's business. It was Jausande's aunt who had introduced them. Paul was "superior" to the rest of his family. But no, his family were in themselves perfectly delightful. It had come to be said more and more often. And Jausande had told it to herself over and over. Madame Labonne was *not* irritating, ignorant and saccharine. She was a good woman, full of kindness. And Philippe ... well, Philippe might improve as he grew older. But Paul was elegantly mannered, and had impressed that upon Jausande from the start: his manners, financial expectations, and his looks, of which last he was a little secretly vain, but you could not tease him about it, for then he became stiff, reproachful. Jausande's future would be, as her past had always been, a method of pleasing others, which she did so easily and so well. She would make an excellent wife. She would be weightless and charming, serious when required, firm with her children, fanciful prettily and properly within the fences of decorum and finesse. She had liked Paul at first, had almost been glad, almost excited at the first prospects of their meetings. But then she could not deceive herself quite so much. Paul, provided he was never openly crossed, always subtly praised, pampered, and respected, could make the ideal husband. "And Paul likes his books laid out just so, one must never touch. You must be sure the servant burnished the glasses. How he abhors a dusty goblet!" Such helpful hints Paul's mother gave her. "Oh, he's a stickler. What a boy!" Sometimes Jausande played the piano, at Madame Labonne's request. Then Madame Labonne would doze, and minuscule snores would issue from her. Waking, she would say, as she said now, "Such a lovely piece. Such cleverness!" Today she added, "Paul should be here quite soon. And his father, I hope, but the hours that man works, why, a general on a battlefield couldn't work harder."

Jausande imagined for an idle moment saying to this woman, soon enough to be a form of mother to her, "What do you think of dreams?"

Jausande was sure that Madame Labonne had many notions on dreams, and would launch into a recital of them.

Herself, Jausande had no yardstick at all. She was one of those people who do not recall their dreams. It seemed to her all her nights had been dreamless, even in childhood. Never had she roused weeping, or crying out at a nightmare. Never had she known the extraordinary and fantastic happiness, the marvels of the slumbering consciousness, that pursues what we will not.

Last night, Jausande had dreamed. The dream had been long and complex. On waking it lay on her like a fine mist, and as she rose and went about her habitual day, the dream was remembered, grew clearer and closer, as if focused by reality.

And with the recollection there grew also the need to speak, like a pressure on heart, mind, and tongue. But speak to whom? Never this one, surely. Nor the correct, smug young man who was to marry her. Not her father, even, who only wanted her happiness, and had been relieved she came on it so modestly. There were many friends, but no confidantes. They could not understand. It would be as if she said to them, "Last night I flew to the moon."

The fussy clock ticked on the mantel. All at once Madame Labonne, refreshed by her piano snooze, went trotting off to bully her cook. Jausande found that she reached out and drew toward herself some sheets of paper.

She had meant to write letters. She dipped her pen into the ink and pressed its blackness on the paper. *I had a strange dream.* Jausande gazed at this sentence, looked up guiltily. The room was empty and the westered wild light streamed over it. She would have at least half an hour, for Madame Labonne would want to taste every dish in the kitchen. Jausande wrote: *I never had a dream in all my life. But this is what I dreamed, in case I should forget, and never again –*

And then she raised her head and murmured aloud, "I may never have another dream, as long as I live." And something struck her in that, with its intimation of mortality. So she scored through the words she had written and put down, *My Dream*, like a child with an exercise.

It had been so vivid, so real, something that awed her, for she was of course unused to the persuasiveness of dreams.

She had woken from sleep into silence. It was the silence, in the dream, that woke her. She went to the window, to see.

There was a moon, in the dream. It was very large, low, white. She knew, in the dream, she had never seen a moon of such size, and yet it did not frighten her. She thought perhaps it had drawn nearer to the earth, and that this must change everything, but in what ways she did not consider. Beyond her window a flight of steps that never before existed ran down to the garden, and over the wall was the City of Paradys. She had a curious sense as she looked at it, in the dream, of the thousands who, as she did, must have regarded it by night through all the ages of its sentience. She saw towers and hills, the loops of the river, and yet it seemed to her that its architecture was not as she had remembered, some buildings more ruinous or in better repair than she had seen them, and some not in the places that she recalled, even to the mass of the cathedral-church, which, rather than dominating the heights of the City, had drawn down into a valley of the river, as if it went there to regard itself in the water. Nowhere were there any lights, the moon had canceled them.

And then she stepped out of the window and onto the stair. She descended, and went across the little garden, which suddenly in the dream was full of palm trees, the giants of an African shore, ages old, their pineapple stems firmly fixed amid the borders of wallflowers.

Outside the garden wall, the street she had known since childhood glided into the City. Jausande walked up the street. It was very wide. On either hand, the buildings, with their peaked roofs and striped railings, seemed half a mile off. The road was paved with huge white blocks. The buildings too were extremely white in the moon, and where there were shadows they made a sort of network of black.

Jausande walked up the street she had known since childhood, which

went on for much longer than she remembered, between the moonlit white
buildings fretted with shadow. She thought of two lines of a poem; she could
not recollect who had written them. They moved in her head, again and again,
as if they were a password for traveling the City by night.

> *The spider moon she spun with her glow*
> *A marble web on the earth below*

A password to travel was perhaps necessary, for there was no one else out
on the street, nor when it ended and she turned in to another, was there anyone there. No windows were lit. There was no sound at all. She wondered if
she could hear her own footsteps, and then she listened, and heard them very
faintly, for her feet were bare, and she had on only her nightgown and dressing robe. She realized that none of the street lamps was burning. Or perhaps
there were no street lamps anyway. Astride the second street was an arch of
white stone, skeletal and strange, with slender shining tines that rayed against
the moon's disk.

> *A marble web on the earth below*

Under the moon, the City had become marble, had become another city
altogether, with bone-white towers, with terraces like ice.

She passed beneath the arch, and entered a park. Tall trees of a kind she
did not know clustered across the smooth gray lawns, and things moved
among them, grazing, but she could not tell what they were and did not want
to see them distinctly. Above the park rose a rounded hill, and on its top was
an eye of crystal. This did not startle her by now, not even when it moved,
scanning over the sky. The eye was beautiful, like a great clear jewel. *I am
almost there now*, she thought. *But where?*

Behind the park, rising up the hill where the observing eye tilted and
quested on its axis, was a dark wood. She went into its nocturnal velvet and
fragrance. And in the wood, deep inside, was a light that was not the moon.
And even in the dream, she pictured to herself a shape, a kind of being, there
in the light. She could not be certain of anything about it, save that its hair
moved and was alive, and that it was winged.

Jausande felt then the feeling that had come to her since adolescence, at
dawn, or with the westering sunfall. She felt that beckoning enticement. It
was now so fierce, so heady, poignant to the edge of pain. For here the promise, whatever it was, was terrifyingly at hand, here the wish could come true.

I shall have to leave everything behind, she thought, and left her robe
behind her on the bushes. And in an agony of excitement and abandon, a radiance of hungry fear, she began to run toward the burning center of the wood.

And woke. *Woke.* The shock – had been horrible. Like a fall, a faint. But
she fainted into consciousness. She was in her bed. And that – had been a

dream. Which in a few moments more was nothing but a mist upon her, vague, not urgent, until now. Now, in the Labonne house, when it had returned with such power.

Jausande got up and looked about at the few books teetering on the Labonne shelves. Would the library of her father furnish her the poem from the dream? *The spider moon –*

Outside the window, the light ravished, darker and more lush, more blatant than before. The spider moon would not rise until eleven o'clock....

The door opened, and Madame Labonne bustled through.

"My dear, how pale you are!"

"I'm unwell," said Jausande Marguerite. "I must go home."

"But Paul –" exclaimed Madame Labonne.

And being a fool, amiably misinterpreted the violent toss Jausande gave with her head, like that of a starving lioness distracted a moment from her kill.

Because she had always been amenable, Jausande had her way. She was sent home in the carriage, and Paul, arriving ten minutes later, was vexed. He hoped aloud Jausande would not turn out after all to be one of those women given to "vapours." She would not. He would never see her again. None of them would.

Those that did see her the last, they were an assorted crew.

Her own father was the first of them. He found her in his library, and was mildly surprised, thinking she had been going to dine with her fiancé. All about Jausande on the table were her father's precious books of poetry. She glanced up at him, like a stranger. And that was usual enough, for they would meet in the house rather than dwell there together.

"Papa," she said, "I can't find my poem about the moon."

"There are so many," he said. He smiled, and quoted parts of them. Jausande interrupted him. She spoke the lines from her dream. He frowned, at the interruption – which was unlike her – and at the words. "Now, let me see. No, Jausande, it isn't a poem. What you have is a peculiar doggerel ... from Pliny, I believe, the other Pliny. *Aranea luna plena* ... As I recall: *The full moon, like a spider, lets down her light that covers the earth, as with a web, and there we mortals helplessly struggle, we flies of fate, until the night devours each one of us –*" His daughter rose. He said, with mild disapproval, "A very poor translation. Where can you have discovered it?"

"I forget," she said. Then she bade him good night and went away.

And this was the last *he* saw of her, the pretty, unimportant girl who lodged in his home.

In the dead of the dark, that was not dark at all, for the high round moon stood over Paradys at one in the morning, Jausande had let herself from the house. None of the servants witnessed this, but on the fashionable street outside, a flower seller wandering homeward from her post by the theater beheld a young woman with her hair undone, clad in a satin robe, and under this nothing, it would seem, but her petticoats and corset. The flower seller had, in her time, been shown many things. Jausande Marguerite in her robe was not the most amazing of these. Yet, she was odd, and the flower seller did not like her looks, and hurried away toward her burrow.

The City was not empty, nor especially quiet, even at that hour. In three more the sun would rise again, and the turmoil of the markets would begin; even now wagons were passing in from the country, while at the taverns and less salubrious hotels an all-night noise went on and the lights roared.

Near the Revolutionary Monument, two whores saw Jausande Marguerite and almost took her for one of their own. But as she went by, they thought otherwise. "Why, she's had some fright," said one. They stole up after her and asked what had happened to the lady, could they help her. But Jausande apparently did not hear or see them, and they fell back.

Perhaps through sheer accident, no police of the City happened on Jausande. Or maybe she directed herself away from the areas they frequented.

In a small park, near the Observatory, once a graveyard and still stuck here and there with an awkward blackened slab, a thief, resting from his night's ingenuities, jumped up as Jausande moved by him. He assessed her fine robe and the sparkle of a gem on her finger. A somnambulist, he reckoned her, for so she looked to him. No one was near. He caught her up and walked at her side.

"Sleeping, are you?" he said. "You shouldn't be out alone in the dark. You need Pierre to see you safe. Now, where is it you"re going? You can tell me," he wheedled after a moment. His knowledge of those tranced was limited to an act he had once seen performed in the street, when a fellow hypnotized a girl from the crowd, whereat she would answer all types of lewd questions with a fascinating honesty. The sleepwalker, though, did not reply. Pierre the thief dogged her. She seemed about to go up into the cluttered streets above the park, where all manner of ruffians might be lurking. "Now, now, lovely," said Pierre, "you'd be better off with me. Perhaps someone's lost you? Perhaps they'd like to give me something nice for bringing you home?" And then he took her hand gently, to see if he could ease off the ring. It obliged him most kindly. It was new, a betrothal gift, and had not adhered to her flesh. Pierre slipped it in his pocket, and at that moment they had come out of the park of graves, into a winding alley.

Pierre later told his tale to his cronies. He was not ashamed, and did not believe he had imagined what he saw. No one taunted him. The places of the night they trod were filigreed with weirdness. Each had some anecdote of a haunt, of jewelry with a curse on it, for, moving outside the law, they were exposed to lawlessness of many conditions.

The walls of the alley, which were the sides and backs of decaying houses, were hung with weeds. The girl moved between them, with her sleep-walker's eyes still fixed inward. And Pierre loitered after. And then it was as if a curtain, which all this while had hung across the alley and the sky, shivered and twitched aside. And for two or three seconds, only two or three, Pierre saw the girl was walking in a forest of gigantic trees. It was like, he said, the world of a million years before, for he had seen paintings of such scenes in a museum. A primeval landscape, great ferns that swung into the upper air, and the stars there glaring and flaming, and the moon too big, too low. And maybe there was a suggestion of buildings, also, but not any that he had ever seen, either in Paradys or in any painting. He did not care for them, or the forest. But that was only for one or two seconds. In the final second, Pierre saw a sort of bubbling and glowing up ahead.

"God knows," said Pierre, "what that was."

The girl ran toward it. And Pierre ran the other way. He ran, and somewhere he threw the ring he had stolen over his shoulder.

"It was as if there was a second curtain behind the first. The first was lifted up for me to see, but the second was being *melted* away. I had my choice, to run or to stay and look and turn into a pillar of salt."

Pierre, then, was almost the last to see Jausande Marguerite on her journey.

Her ultimate witness was a sleepless small boy in the window of a poor apartment near the Observatory. He saw a lady with loose hair mount a flight of stairs toward a narrow door along the avenue. As she approached the door it turned molten, it blazed and gaped – and the child hid his eyes but knew better than to cry, for his drunkard father would beat him, any excuse. And in the morning, the door was only a door, as it had always been.

The disappearance of Jausande made far less motion in the pond of the City than her re-emergence, later, from its river. There was no hushing that up. And the police, who had formerly tried here, there, and everywhere, gathered themselves to the narrow flat of The Conjuror. It seemed certain persons had once overheard a whispered threat offered by this man to Jausande Marguerite. He had told her that he could make her do whatever he wanted. She, and they, had laughed at this. But suppose –?

The flat was vacant. Nothing was in it but for the rats in the walls. The windows had not been ventilated for years. Clouds of dust billowed about.

The search extended itself, spreading like a ripple from Observatory Hill, beyond the rim of Paradys, out and away into the far bays of other cities. And like a ripple, growing less and less. Who had heard of him, The Conjuror? The very world seemed vacant of him, the rats busy in its walls, its shutters fastened, its dusts blowing. The curtain that encircled it closed *tight*.

There was one who searched about this graveyard, as we are doing, but more intently. He was looking for his lost love, who perished almost as a child. They had loved as children, uncarnally but surely, and she had been taken from him first by her parents, next by death. He did not know where she lay, save it was over some other's grave, for she had been buried in secret during an epidemic of typhus. So he confused the authorities with tales of a buried treasure, a jewel, dropped in some grave, and uprooted all those of which he had a suspicion.

The jewel was really in his own possession. At length he pretended to find it and gave it over. A small price.... It was a black diamond, or some white pearl of unusual size.

By then he had unearthed his dead love. She was gone, she was bones, but he raised the skeleton and kissed the toothy lipless smile of the skull. To him she was beautiful still, fresh and childish, unwithered, let alone rotten.

Perhaps she had stayed for him, and dreamed that he could free her with a kiss, his forgiveness of her dying. Perhaps then she was able to sleep in peace.

But this is another marker, the memory of one lost in a far-off clime. He too searched out a sort of skull, and was in love with it. We all have our dreams. May we find them, and God have mercy on us when we do.

Lost in the World

Magnanimous Despair alone
  Could show me so divine a thing,
Where feeble hope could ne'er have flown
  But vainly flapt its tinsel wing.

– Marvell

1

On the last day of every month, at the same hour, the same visitor would mount the steps of the narrow house on the west edge of Clock Tower Hill. In summer it would be sunset, and all the normal phantasmagoria of dragons, galleons, and burning towers would be on display in the sky. In winter the dark was well set, the stars above the hill dimmer than the street lamps, perhaps a light snow falling. In autumn, there was the magical dusk as now, when Monsieur Mercile, immaculate and apparently stern, would stand on the top step and ring the bell. And it would be evident that the dusk's magic was quite lost on Monsieur Mercile, that he felt no pang, just as he rarely noted the stars, the dragons, and towers, of winter and summer. This was custom, his visit to the narrow house, not unmixed with duty. He was a man of the world, understood its rules, had kept them, and prospered. But the one he visited, he was different.

In answer to the bell, a servant woman came, compact and elderly, a being from an earlier era, where she had completely stayed in all but body.

Monsieur Mercile acknowledged her, and passed into the house.

The rooms of the visit were on the floor above. The first was a sort of pleasant alcove, lined with books, a kind of library, having padded easy chairs by the fire, and on a highly polished stand a globe in ebony. Through the open doors of the alcove was a dining room, an oval table perched with candles, and a sideboard of sparkling decanters; here too a fire burned gently, cheerfully.

The comfortable rooms showed nothing of a woman's touch: Beyond the meticulous servant and one careful girl, no woman ever had access to them.

475

They were graced with bachelor things, and Monsieur Mercile might have felt happiness and security in them, but he was never quite able to do so, here; here there was always a demand on him. The demand was implicit in his friend, Oberand, who now stood up before the library fire.

The two men greeted each other as if they had not met for a year, and yet with the sort of offhand sidelong glances of the eye that evidence usualness. They asked each other how they went on and mentioned the weather, and a certain cognac was produced, which they both settled to like pigeons to a familiar roof.

Oberand, like Mercile, was slim and upright, and in his fifties, but where Mercile's waist had slightly thickened, Oberand was only a little stooped at the shoulders. Oberand's hair receded, where Mercile's had retreated altogether. Oberand's eyes were larger, brighter, lacking glasses, and fraught with thin lines of pain, perhaps physical, but perhaps of something older, deeper, more difficult to bear. Mercile had no mark like this. His hands had stiffened with a trace of rheumatism, but his heart was light. What of Oberand's heart?

After their brandy, and their introductory conversation, they went into the dining room, and here soon appeared an extremely tasty, ordinary dinner. There were too a trio of excellent wines. It was all very good, orderly, and pleasing, redolent of the male satisfactions and luxuries often used in literature as the preface to a ghost story.

And Monsieur Mercile warmed like wax, lost a certain hardness of contour he had had, seemed to be thinking, *Now this isn't so bad. You see, there's nothing to dread.*

Then they took their cigarettes and wine to the fire in the library, and Oberand paused to lay one finger on the ebony globe.

Here it comes! thought Mercile, and braced himself.

The stroking of the globe was an omen as constant and unfortuitous as a comet.

"I took out the small map again," said Oberand softly, as if they were conspirators, as if they had waited only for this moment to begin – and probably this was true of Oberand; Mercile thought so. "I mean Eshlo's map. I sat up over it until three this morning. After a time, I began to seem to connect a particular ridge with a description in the geographia. I took out the two other maps of Klein's. There is one distinct formation, to the south. Eshlo marks this as the Mountains of the White Moon – I love that name, so evocative, so unhelpful, and yet. … so alluring."

"Yes," said Mercile, "it is a marvelous name."

"It's possible to pinpoint this geography. The first of Klein's maps relates it to the Charda region, as you know. But then, I wonder with Klein if there isn't some game involved, if some of his assertions aren't meant to be misleading."

"That might be likely."

"And does he offer any reward for struggle? But my struggling attention seems to bear fruit."

Mercile could not quite bring himself to answer, but naturally Oberand did not take this gap for disapproval. Oberand trusted Mercile, had done so for more than ten years. It was incumbent upon Mercile, now, to be trusted.

As always happened, every month, the floodgate of Oberand's obsession had opened as it did before no other one, since no other *could* be trusted save only Mercile. The waters roared and poured forth, as vehement and strong as they had been a decade ago, stronger probably. And Mercile listened, as he always did, every month, with a great patience blunted even as it had been honed, threadbare even as it was perfected. Every visit to Oberand concluded in this way, in two or three hours of Oberand's obsession (until Mercile escaped) – Oberand's maps, his notions, discoveries, dismissals, the throbbing violence, only just held in, of what he believed and *knew* and could not prove, and for which he had been mocked and laughed from eminence, squashed into the gutter, discarded by everyone.

For Oberand had been reckoned a genius, at the start. He was not merely a literary figure of reckoned worth, a bright star elevated at an age supposed precociously early, but also a scholar. Among the countries of manuscript he was thought an explorer. For Oberand had translated screeds previously declared inaccessible, he had unearthed, paying terrifying prices for them, obscure treatises and scripts – of the Romans, from Egypt, and further back and farther off. He had dealt in a murky underworld of the esoteric as other men had trafficked in bodies. And by that he made of himself a creature fabulous, permitted only in the glaring light of its own cleverness. And then it happened that Oberand, thirty-eight years of age and corruscating brightly, came on the work of Eshlo, an explorer out of the countries of landscape. And, too (doubtless), a liar and romancer.

But Oberand believed the words of Eshlo; they caught his fancy and fascinated him.

There had never been in the life of Oberand anything but his work, the pen and the page. He had never, except perhaps briefly in adolescence, felt anything special for a woman, he had not itched, let alone ached through love. The pursuit, the conquest, the culmination were intellectual, and he knew them regularly.

Now, as with a mighty philanderer, for whom love had been always too easy, there must come an elusive quarry, one that did not consent, succumb. In a space of weeks Oberand left everything he had in hand to search after that which Eshlo proffered, to hunt down the clues and keys of which there were hundreds, spurious though they might be, *ridiculous* though they might be. In doing this, Oberand uncovered Klein, a scholar so obscure he was almost invisible, but Oberand lifted him up on high, to the very pedestal where he had placed Eshlo, and lit before them a flaming torch for all to see. From the hilltop Oberand bellowed. He had been given an unlicensed and uncensored voice, he had been made a darling of that most dangerous fraternity, the mature, wise, cunning, erudite, and cruel. They will worship heroes, then at a stumble tear them to pieces in their teeth. And Oberand had stumbled. What a distance he had to fall.

Eshlo had traveled widely, in the Indies, and in Africa. His accounts were exotic, combining the information of facts with flights of elaboration having a logical wildness resembling the development of inspired symphonies. Was it the logic that had misled Oberand? If so, only at a single juncture. Many of Eshlo's claims he had amusedly sloughed. But one story, the very wildest, he had defended as if he had been present at its inception.

For Eshlo claimed to have come upon a pocket of incredible land, a freak valley locked inside a mountain wall unscalable, and penetrated by him via a secret entry that, even in his documents, he had omitted to describe, referring to it only as the Hidden Door, and marking it only in this way on his maps. The valley, when reached, was of an appalling beauty. It was a land from the prehistoric dawn, a place of giant plants, carbon swamps, and a sea like sweat, and inhabited by monsters, huge beasts, and flying things that stormed and raged and *were*, in defiance of time.

Like an echo, Klein backed up this wonder, claiming himself not to have witnessed such a place but from innumerable sources to have heard legends of it. The natives of that area, which Klein posited with imaginative flirtatiousness, avoided the mountain slopes for fear accidentally of being precipitated to their doom in the valley of monsters. (Eshlo, who had refused the secret of his entry, also denied readers the means of his exit.) Several of the indigenous populace of hutments and villages had been lost in this manner, Klein avowed, stipulating a cave or hole through which they descended. A god was propitiated in the region, a god said to be white, and of abnormal size, a giant like the plants and beasts of the valley. Klein quoted many passages, both in their original language and in adequate translation, but the oddity of sections of syntax pretranslated instantly led a critic to deduce that Klein had himself invented these paragraphs of Latin, Greek, Graeco-Persian, and the Egyptian hieroglyphs with which his essays on the subject were scattered – for the Egyptians also had heard of the monsters of the valley, which they had at first named in terms of a coffin of the day's fall, a land of shadow through which Ra the sun must pass each night, overcoming what rampaged there in order to return into the world.

The maps of Klein's related to Africa as he had known it from travelers' tales and the official reports of colonial officers. Everything was second or third hand, but he too, though never having met with Eshlo, never having himself gone farther than the hills above the City of Paradys, had caught the fantasy that Eshlo exhaled, had been poisoned by it. As, in turn, was Oberand.

To make matters worse (perhaps), both Eshlo and Klein were long dead by the hour of Oberand's first discovery of the Valley of God, as Eshlo, next Klein, had called it. Oberand could not, no one could, question the perpetrators of this nightmare-dream. Alone, he impaled himself on the hook, and presently was nailed up, crucified, by those who until then had sung his paean and encouraged him in everything.

Possibly his eccentricity alone would not have alienated them. If he had kept a measure of lightness, and so of light. If he could have chuckled, smiled at his own enthrallment, if he could have said: *Well, I may be wrong.* But Oberand was accustomed by then to be right. And such was his passion that he shouted, argued, insulted, twice came to blows.

No one would believe in his belief. His brilliance and innocence went bitter and rotted on the boughs of his mind.

Inside three years he had shut himself away. He reformed his life to an insistent search, a scientific chiseling and scalpeling, of the truth as he had found it. He amassed further material, he dissected and quantified that material he had.

Sometimes he wrote a little. But always, in some however subtle way, it was tainted with his obsession. He was published as a curiosity, and then he was not published. The lecture halls and palaces of books did not any more clamor for him. He was cut. He was forgotten. It was as if a solid figure of iron had faded into mist.

And yet, this stooped man, fifty-two years of age, seared with a hot-cold life, a dreadful fire that could not be put out. And it was this Mercile confronted, this intolerable and pointless, relentlessly gouging fire, howling on inside the unobliterated shell. Confronted tonight again, also, for the thousandth time, or maybe the thousandth-and-tenth. For Oberand could not keep it down. Mercile was the only one left to him, the only one who had never scorned, never ridiculed, always apparently tacitly accepting the veracity of Eshlo's valley, listening to the facts of it over and over, never quibbling, offering only sympathetic assent, the occasional partial challenge by which Oberand might fuel himself further for his burning. Mercile had never let him down, not once, not in fourteen years.

And to Oberand this had been because Mercile credited the truth of the Valley of God. But it was not that. It was only the valiant loyalty of friendship. Something as deep, and as shallow – as useless – as that.

An hour passed. Mercile knew this for he had begun to glance surreptitiously at the clock on the mantelpiece. It was terrible, the slow passage of time now, for decently he could not yet absent himself. Calm and unequivocal, Mercile felt building within him, as always, an unspecified urge to flight, or worse, to choke Oberand to silence.

The maps were now spread on the table, the geographia had been brought. Animated, like a boy, Oberand went about the display. He discoursed on the potential of Klein's frivolity, of Eshlo's secretiveness. "No one is meant to find this place. Yet we are invited to it. Irresistibly we are seduced."

He dreamed of the valley. Mercile knew this, for Oberand had told him, now and then. Oberand already had gone there, had wandered the jungle forests, stared into the pools of salt, and heard the trampling of the vast feet of things that elsewhere had left only bones under the rocks of centuries.

"I feel the moment has come to collate these disparate works, to publish my own conclusions," said Oberand suddenly. The clock ticked. Oberand said, "Don't you agree, some reorganization of the treatise is in order?"

"But," said Mercile, slowly, "your publishers –"

"No, I must approach others. Perhaps I'll need to put up the money myself. I realize perfectly the low esteem in which I'm held, as if by tongs."

"But," said Mercile, "further efforts with this work – What else can be said of it?"

"Very much," said Oberand. "I can speak volumes."

"You should not," said Mercile.

"Oh, my friend, don't worry on my behalf. What else can they do to me or say of me?"

Mercile felt the knife rise in him, its handle toward his hand. He had never understood it was a knife that had been forged by the years of patience and listening, the *boredom*. He tried to evade. He said, "But why expose yourself to more of the vicious attacks that –"

"Why?" Oberand cried, his eyes giving off a flash from the flames of the hearth and the spirit. "Because the truth must be spoken at whatever cost."

"You must face it," said Mercile abruptly, "this truth is doubtful. For God's sake, give it up."

And now the clock ticked more loudly, and the fire cracked like gunshot. Little sounds in the street, a whisper of wind, a distant song, came up and filled the room, thickening its air until it was nearly unbreathable.

"But I thought," said Oberand, "that you, of all of them –" He stopped, and Mercile hung his head. Inside him was an awesome sadness, as if Oberand had just told him he, Oberand, was near death.

"Pardon me," said Mercile humbly, at last. "I've tried very hard."

"No, I don't pardon you," said Oberand. "You should not have tried. Or you should have tried much harder. Did you only wait all these years to make a fool out of me tonight?"

"Oberand, my faith in you is unimpaired. Only I believe that your trust in this thing – is preposterous, ill-founded. I should have said so long before."

"You must leave my house," said Oberand. "You must go at once. There's nothing to say."

Mercile was shocked, yet not surprised. The knife had glittered in his hand, he had used it. What did he expect now? With an exhausted relief strongly enhanced by automatic regret, he rose, shaking his head in an effort at normalcy.

"Then I shall leave, at once. I'm very sorry."

Oberand said nothing. His face was blank, wiped of everything. He had been stabbed in the back, of course, what else?

Mercile went down, donned his greatcoat, stepped into the street. Below, he glanced at the house, wondering if he would enter it again, aware he would not, then turned into the night of lamps and leaves. He felt a satisfaction. It was terrible. He nearly laughed as he walked homeward; certainly he could not keep back a smile.

2

The great mountain range filled the sky, and was the sky. Pitted and scarred, fissured and cracked, it was not white but dark. It had earned Eshlo's name for it not through its tints, but because it seemed to belong to the surface of a dead satellite circling the earth. Anything might lie inside the wall of it. It was impenetrable.

The man who sat in the camp half a mile from the mountains' foot was tall, thinned, and sunburnt by the lion orb of summer. He was thirty-eight. So much he knew, feeling these things sit on him, the frame within which his soul balanced. He looked from his own clear eyes, scanning the dusty plain and the first clawed slopes that pushed out of it. In the etheric sky a pair of vultures dawdled. They had been there about an hour, interested by something on the middle heights, something not yet dead enough to warrant their descent. He had noticed, no bird ever flew toward the summit of the mountains. Nothing came up over them, except rounded drifts of cloud toward sunset, like steam.

He had been here, at the foot, a month, thirty-one days. Before that was the journey, a period not of time but of time's dissolution, an unraveling of dates and seasons, flowing sidelong, nearly backward. There had been sea, a crust of land, a wide river with a belching steamer, at length the long sinuous tributary of the Charda, with its curtains of banks dropped to the water, the masks of its reflected islands. Lions passed, or lay in the sky. A herd of zebra galloped, an alligator raised its artifact of head – such images pinned themselves upon his brain. The man thought he should and must remember such things distinctly. But then he saw that visually they did not matter, that he might let them go from him if they wished; thus they stayed.

At first he had been fearful. So much so that seasickness and mal de terre had almost disabled him. Then, as he began to accept that he was quite adrift, lost and companionless, without hope of assistance, he relaxed, grew stronger, left behind the stomach cramps and blinding migraines, and emerged from his five decades into the newer younger body, which had wasted no years, which had sprung here immediately after Eshlo's song and Klein's echo. Somewhere on the river of the Charda, while the two black men rowed and the black white stared about, his rifle ready, Oberand caught up his younger self, who all that while had been there ahead of him, waiting.

They moved through the land as Eshlo had, as if nothing had altered, save in the villages they could now barter for cigarettes. It was all quite familiar to him, the people colored like coal and the beasts of the plain, and the towering sky and the river, and the mountains finally rising into view. Eshlo had been here, and told him. More, he had himself been here, often.

They made the camp under the Mountains of the White Moon. None of them had before approached the place, apart from Oberand. The man who cooked was superstitious; he had heard something of the region. He made a shrine by his improvised cook house and sank into it a collection of bones and teeth, for the god, the giant. Oberand had tried to question this man. The man then became heated, hysterical. Sweat flew off him and he gesticulated, refusing to look at the mountains or to say anything that was of use. Froth sprayed out of his mouth and André, the black white, touched Oberand's arm, glancing at him from his odd eyes, one black and one pale gray. "He knows nothing. Best to leave him, monsieur." Oberand obeyed, and André ordered the cook back to his rice with sharp staccato words.

Oberand explored the base of the mountains with André. They climbed a little, André the guide and adviser. He would never fully meet the eyes of the white man, he had been taught not to.

They found caves, and chasms where smoldering chains of water fell, they found the carcasses of things, one with hyenas feasting on it, the nests of birds abandoned, a defile with old painting on a wall, but these symbols gave no revelation. Every cave had a back. Each access ended against the gut wall of the rock. From boulders they looked down at the tiny camp, and saw the blacks lazing or quarreling over a game, and the river far away like a varnished seam in the ground.

"There is no way through," said André.

"Yes," said Oberand, "of course. There is."

André was the first man Oberand had had any prolonged conversation with since Mercile. For this reason Oberand did not trust André. André was not like Mercile. He was young, and could have been a prince if his blood had not been mixed. His white drunkard of a father had taught him books, mathematics, and two languages. André had grown up aware he had been ruined for everything, accepting, wise, and mostly silent. Of the Valley of God he had heard, distantly, now and then. It was one of the dim wandering wisps of myth that go about any continent. It was a white man's myth of the darkness, and as such he gave it a defined and cordoned pen. The white portion of André's mind suggested to him that only white men would evolve a legend of black men worshiping a white god. But the giantism was not alien. There were stone cities of the jungles, and the size of these cities did not belong with the six-foot men of present days but, like certain temples of Egypt, suggested bigger beings nearer to the sun.

Eshlo's maps, and Klein's maps, brought into the realm of the actual, were a travesty. Though the mountains had been recognizable, they were also altered by reality. Small vital geological clues, essential in locating Eshlo's Hidden Door, were changed or unrevealed, or else had only existed in the imagination of the writer.

It was the splitting off from Mercile, the betrayal by Mercile, which had brought Oberand to the Mountains of the White Moon, more than Eshlo or Klein, more than fourteen years of waste, and fermenting humiliation.

Oberand did not miss Mercile. At first there had been no time, for within a week of their dinner, Oberand had been making arrangements to travel out from Paradys into the wide world. Presently, looking back, there was only a slight disgust that such a man as Mercile had been permitted to deceive him. At last, and very soon, Mercile was a shadow. Beneath the Mountains of the White Moon, however, it was Eshlo that Oberand began to miss, and Klein, although Klein less painfully and clearly.

The sun was setting on the rim of the plain, and the mountains flared up, then turned suddenly to ash, lit only at their tips. There came a curious half-heard whirring note, perhaps the sunset wind passing through some hole or crevice higher up, sound carrying in the glassy air. Transparently the night came to Africa, without subterfuge, bearing the bone moon from which the mountains had been transposed. If the sun was a lion, the moon was a white-faced buck. It peered, vulnerable and savage, above the plain, lighting it as bright as day. The mountains glowed. The fire of the cook house became the center of the earth, marking, like a cross on Eshlo's map, their place in things.

"I am here," Oberand said aloud. "*Here*." But that was not enough. Yet the excitement stirred in him, properly, the first occasion. It had taken so long, for he had been so long coming to it, he had kept it waiting, like his younger self.

André stood smoking, looking at the mountains, thin and still in his European clothes. The blacks squatted at the fire, where the pot hung, full of God knew what jumble.

Speak to André, Oberand thought. Why was that important? André knew nothing, less than the cook, who feared.

Oberand watched the camp from his tent, the pale dust and the moonlight, patches of sand between the mountains' claws, shining. The strange sound had died out from the mountains, and the reflection from their tops. Miles off a lion roared. The stars were liquid, like mercury, in the bulb of sky.

Here I am.

"My father taught me that men have no souls," said André, "that this life is all we can expect, and that it will probably be unpleasant."

The moon had set; it was darker, and somewhere hyenas were busy. The night was not the same, and André had begun to talk at the fire. He had started by saying he thought the two blacks might run away tonight. He said they were not so much afraid as anxious, a kind of anxiety attack that, because they did not see it as nervous in origin, they attributed to bad spirits of the plain and mountains. Oberand said that if this happened, it must be accepted, but would the two men steal very much? Only enough, said André, to support them on their journey back down river. Let them go, then, said Oberand, they would manage, but what of André? André had said he would remain. He was not afraid, since he did not believe that anything lay over the mountains, even if a way to it were to be found. A dry crater perhaps, an extinct volcano, poisonous and dead. Oberand was not offended by André's pragmatism. His truthfulness, coming in a straight line after Mercile's years of deception, was nearly appealing. Because he had wanted to, Oberand indulged himself, beginning to attempt the drawing out of André, whom he had judged as clever, and almost in his way as educated as anyone met with in the vanished metropolis. André had alarming potential that, since he was black, could never be realized – André was not strong enough, evidently, to evolve solely for himself, as so many were not.

In the background the hyenas had commenced, and then the two blacks initiated a vague annoying chanting from a stand of trees a hundred feet off. André opened a little like a crumpled paper. He spoke of the ancient cities of giants, the legends of white gods. He explained he could not believe in anything like that, although its metaphysic intrigued him.

"But why, André, is it necessary for men to have souls, in order that there be gods? Can't this be something of a different order?"

"Man tries," said André, "to find something greater than himself, promising himself he will one day become such a thing. Is that not the basis of the religion of Christ?"

"I think that the religion of Christ offers a chance that we are already such a thing, and have only lost the way."

"Without a soul," said André, "where is the need for a god?"

"But this is a god with a valley like the Garden of Eden, the Garden before the Fall. This is a god so large that he could cover the bodies of thirty men with his palm, and crush them. What are men to such a god?"

André did not reply. He smoked his cigarette. Then he said, "What would you give to find this secret valley?"

"Everything," said Oberand. He said, "Already, I've given most of it. From the first, the idea possessed me. I sacrificed all I had, and followed it."

"Be wary, perhaps something listens."

"But," said Oberand, "what could that be, if there are no gods?"

"I don't know, monsieur. But I sense it. The way a man whose hand has been cut off will feel the hand at the end of his arm, itching him. Like that. It isn't real, but it affects him. What listens may not be real either, yet it may hear."

Oberand felt a sudden emotional liking for André. Why in God's name had this man not been given him to argue with, to wrestle with, this black angel in the night, over the body of Eshlo, on the ladder of light? But it was too late now.

"Let it hear me," said Oberand, "please God."

After a while longer, André put his cigarette into the fire.

"If we go to sleep, monsieur, the men will have their chance to run away. I will take the sugar and hide it, or they may have that too, for barter."

Oberand got up, half tranced. His muscles ached as if a heavy wine were swirling through his system. He held out his hand. André shook it solemnly. They parted without further words, the black man to his shelter, Oberand to his tent.

He lay on his back for half an hour, and the chanting ceased. The night was silent as an open bowl of space upturned upon the land.

In the night's middle darkness, sound awakened Oberand. It was as if he had been expecting it, had been prepared by a lesser sound of the evening, the huge silence that had domed in the plain as he slept.

What he heard was a sort of low rumbling, and at first he took it for lion in the distance, then for the movement of a herd of animals, shaking the plain. Then, thinking of some tremor of the earth, he sat up suddenly, but although there was the faint sense of vibration, it was not that of an earthquake. Nothing moved, rattled, or fell. After a moment, Oberand got up and went out of the tent, to see what André made of this.

Outside, the night was incredible. It had changed itself yet again, the way no night of the north ever did, or so it seemed to him. The clarity of the darkness was wonderful, like crystal, the sky miles high, drawn back like a blind to reveal the world. On the horizon something vaguely shifted about, probably deer feeding. The other way, the wall of the mountains, lunar, frozen.

Nothing stirred in the camp. Perhaps the runaways were already off. But neither had André emerged. And the sound – it was real and definite – could not be ignored.

Oberand took a step, meaning to wake André, then instantly checked.

André had not woken, or had not come out. The sound was not a summons to André, who did not believe. And the men who were afraid had already run away.

Oberand's heart gave a great leap, catching him like a spear in the breast.

He ducked back into the tent, and picked up the knife and the pistol he had not yet used, some ammunition, water. It was not a careful readying for any vast expedition, it was a token. The token of the traveler. It was ritual, as if before an altar of the night.

When Oberand emerged again, he stood, staring up at the Mountains of the White Moon. They were charcoal gray now, with pale frills of silver from the stars. To climb without ropes would be impossible. Even roped, with the expert advice of André, to reach the crest had been thought out of the question.

The rumble of sound went on, becoming part of hearing. It emanated from within the mountains, borne upward on a column of stillness, opened like an umbrella into the bowl of the sky.

Oberand walked away from the camp, crossing through the shrub and boulders, to the foot of the rock. He came among the patches of sand. He began to climb diagonally, going along the base of the wall, moving south to north, circling. He did not investigate the upright slopes of the wall, as he had been doing, he climbed up and over, and down, and up again. The starlight sliced out swaths of rock, and made pits of luminous blackness between them. He got down into these, and each time, without words he thought, *It will be this one*, but it was not. He did not know what he anticipated, some crack in the rock, something so evident as an avenue with pillars of stone.... The camp disappeared around the curve of the mountains.

As he was climbing down, the sound stopped. He felt a moment of deafness, almost disorientation. As if the sign had been taken from him, the promise. He hesitated, and after a moment, the sand on which he stood tipped and settled, lurched and lay flat again. And then gave way completely.

There was no time for Oberand to think. He was falling as the earth caved in. He knew what this was. It was a quicksand. It sucked him under and he caught at the land, but it slipped sideways and nothing would stay put or firm, nothing would hold him. He knew instantly reasonless mad terror and cried out, but his cries hit the void of space, and the gleaming stars swallowed them. Terror and despair, without thoughts. Screaming, he was sucked into turmoil. The sand filled his nostrils and mouth, and he struggled, choked, his eyes were put out, his ears were full of miasma, and panic began to recede into a ringing emptiness. But something struck his heels a blow like a mace. His whole spasming, suffocating body was jolted and spun. In a rush of mass he seemed catapulted down into the stars. He saw them, burning and mocking him. This was death. He lay in the belly of death and vomited out the sand, and as he did so, the grains of other sand sprayed down on him in the dark. He could breathe, he heard the noise he made, but the thing which had smote his heels struck him across the skull. He slid with the darkness closing. Thought had not yet returned. He thought nothing, and nothing. Nothing.

3

"Like a pearl, softly the morning was, and rained ..." He could not remember the line. He saw the soft pearl light and tried to recall, "... and rained ... like ..." But this did not matter. The poem was not important now. It was the light that was relevant to him. The light – Oberand pushed up from the cloud and discovered himself, bruised and sore – headed in the tunnel of darkness with the fresh light, so pearly, raining at the tunnel's end a long way off. He should go that way. And he must go on his knees for there was not the room in this cave to stand up. He was in the mountain, in the wall. He had fallen in there through a place of sand, and somehow under it was the cave and the air; he had lived, and there the light was, he had only to crawl. In the light he could see the plain. He crawled, hurting and breathing, forward. After five minutes the outline of the cave mouth grew concrete and exact, and beyond it a dripping pre-dawn mist, and out of the mist a fern cast its tendrils like a dagger, a fern so large it surprised him. But he crawled on, and drew level with it, and from there he beheld the place outside the cave, which was not the plain.

First, perfect stasis, dim reflection of water polished under smoke, tricklings and susurrous unseen, and the nets of things flung over, and the pylon of a tree where flowers clung that were the size of flowers in a dream. Next, motion: Birds lifted from the shallows, while their pale shadows sank away from them like ghosts. They were very big, with the heads of anvils, and the leather slap of their wings tore water drops from the air. Then through the mist the creature came, quite slowly, gracefully, like a vehicle of armor, wet like silk. It was a giant lizard. Reaching the water, it glided through the colossal reeds, which bent from it in the action of courtiers. It dipped its slender and enormous head, and drank. It was beautiful as a thing fashioned, with the life blown into it by magic, and at its delicate step, the ground had moved.

Oberand watched the lizard drinking. It armor made towers upon its back. He did not know its name. Its eye was like a jewel. Ripples spread in a muscular glittering from the firm licking of its tongue that was the length of his body.

He had reached the Valley of God.

There was no exit from the valley. Inside four weeks he knew this. He had become, again, a new and different man; he did not care, he had resigned himself to death or madness, and to life. He had met Eshlo in the dark, and the *true* truth of Eshlo. Which was romancer and liar. For somehow Eshlo had guessed the existence of the valley, perhaps even found the clues to the valley, but he had never entered it. For if he had, demonstrably, he could never have come back to write his account. The genius of perceptive imagination was Eshlo's gift, what he had handed over to Klein, and to Oberand. No more.

Oberand had searched systematically along the inner rim of the mountains. He was more thorough and more experimental than in his outer searching of a way in. There was nothing, of course. There was no route from Eden, save God made it, and ushered out there with a flaming sword.

Once this problem of escape had been dealt it, all vestige of rules or ethics was sloughed from Oberand, and he was free.

Perhaps because Eshlo's dream adventure had been charted, Oberand had ceased to calendar events. On the journey to the mountains, and in the camp, he had kept a journal. But that had been left behind. He made and attended to no device for the recording of time. The season did not alter, and he had no constant but for the recurrence of day and night. Dawn was not as he had ever seen it, neither sunset. The dream had been made leaf and flesh and feather.

He lived (the mere necessity) through lessons already learned. He set traps in which small rats and lizards, once or twice a tiny type of pig, enmeshed themselves, and these he killed with the pistol, as at other times he shot things that ran before him. He rationed these meals, knowing that with the end of his ammunition he must resort to other more brutal methods. He did not like to kill, but hunger made him able. And at last he would have to do it with a stone. Among the plethora of growing stuff he found roots and pods and berries, which he ate. He had no means of judging them, and some caused him violent sickness. One species laid him up for two days with a fever. He considered if he might die, yet did not believe it. And always he recovered. The fruit of the garden was mostly to be eaten, he had not yet come on the Forbidden Tree.

At first he sheltered in the cave tunnel from which he had first emerged. Nothing troubled him there save for inquisitive rodents (food) and once a fly with wings of jewelry gauze, larger than he from shoulder to shoulder. It startled him, but did not haunt him long.

During his search around the inner base of the mountains, the valley was hidden from him by the fern forest, which began between ten and twenty feet from the rockside, with here and there a break or glade such as that where he had seen the great lizard. Swampy places and dips of silver water lined these glades, but nothing else came to drink there that he saw, except for infrequent, peculiar birds. Others he beheld in the air, birds like a sort of enormous swan, and again arrowings of the bat-winged anvil-heads, which seemed to emanate from a distant smooth height that emerged only in the clearness of midday far above the cycad forest. His search of the mountains for an exit point was instinctive and foolish and actually alien to the person he had become. While it took his days and his thoughts, he understood it was futile, unimportant. Although he saw no further lizards or mammals of the valley at that time, apart from those little ones that supplied his traps, he heard them. Their voices were various, thin and sweet, or trumpeting and terrible. They could not be compared with anything. He sensed there would be huge beasts that fluted and sang, and smaller more fearful things that roared, ate organs and muscle, and drank blood.

When he gave up the search and his freedom came, Oberand took the few items he had constructed, the pillow of rolled dried fern and the best traps, and went down into the forest. So far he had come across several shoots of pure and drinkable water splashing from the rocks, although the pools were consistently full of salts and slimes.

Initially the cycads detained and distracted him. He must cut a way with the knife. He moved by a chain of pools where the giant spangled insects were swarming. He did not know what they were at, perhaps mating like dragonflies above a fountain in a park of Paradys.

The cycads harbored groves of magnolia and laurel. Conifer trees rose in dark pagodas. The scent of these mingled through the heavy, curious air. The sunlight began to stream in shifting smoky shafts, between embroidered eyelets in the canopy.

Oberand watched in wonder. This world was imbuing him, its smells, the lens of its mist where sunrise and sunset dissolved their fires, from which mountains came and went like ships lost at sea.

Oak trees appeared, around which lianas roped and spiraled, and flowers like faces looked at him. Water droplets, the warm dews of the forest, sprinkled from bough to bough, so the atmosphere was filled always by this sound and sense of gentle rain.

He went slowly, and found in the mud the footprint of a mighty creature, perfect as if sculpted for him, although already the moss was growing in it.

Then the forest parted. He saw across the valley.

It was rimmed by mist, was a lake of mist, from which its shapes rose, a map of jungle forest, and silken troughs of open land. The great mountain cone ascended from it, and today a twisted skein of white extended from a vent. It was a volcano, sinisterly sleeping. Even as he stared, a flight of birds went upward. Beyond, a steel-shining water. And on the curve of the misty skyline were twenty waterfalls (he counted), descending in pristine lines like frayed thread.

A bird passed overhead and its shadow enveloped him. It was enormous. He felt no fear in the presence of something so extraordinary. He was in the country of the god. And did the god live on the volcano-mountain? A new goal now. Oberand had reached the unreachable, was here in the unreality he had always known to exist. The god, then, also existed. Did he walk through the Garden in the cool of the day? Which of the cries of the valley heralded his passage?

He had been alone for years. He had learned that each man is alone, even in company. He missed nothing of civilization in the valley, not even books, for his books had all *been* the valley, had something of the valley, and here the valley had become his book at last, open and to be read. He did not mind the random and ill-cooked food, it interested him. His body, which had hardened and improved on his journey, had now reached a peak of fitness and energy that delighted him. His eyes were never tired, his eyesight had sharpened. Noises he had sometimes heard in his head had vanished in the constant natural sound of the valley. Everything was better.

It took almost a week of angling descent for Oberand to reach the valley floor. There, he had only the volcanic cone for his guide. A herd of cattle, huge and black with devilish horns, burst out of the mist and over his path on the morning he came down. They were the size of elephant, and filled him with joy. One hour later he saw three lizards, upright and grazing on the trees, with long serpentine necks, tiled with plates like burnished iron. Their bodies moved very little, their heads were busy with the leafage. Once one of them spoke. Its voice was of the sweet bell-like sort he had heard from above.

That night, in his shelter of reeds and steams, Oberand dreamed of the god walking through the valley. The great lizards lifted their heads to see him pass, and he rested his hand briefly upon them in blessing. To him they were tiny, like squirrels in a shrubbery. The earth did not quiver at the footsteps of God, it was his constant movement that caused a ceaseless, now unnoticeable tremor, which turned the world.

Oberand worked toward the cone of the volcano. Cycads grew again on its slopes. The water beyond he judged for the inner land-locked sea of Eshlo's descriptions. For Eshlo, who had never entered the valley, had yet somehow been here, so much remained obvious.

Oberand was by now mad. It was a fact. Much of his freedom came from it. It was sanity that had caused unhappiness, as so often it does.

Time, then, in the valley, unspecified. The beauty of the days of traveling toward the mountain cone, the sights and wonders, the giant snakes, the feeding vegetarian towers of lizards, a fish in a lake like a fearsome sword, the snows of the birds, the cattle that roamed the valley like soft thunder. The sun coming up in tempest, going down in such colors the sky was another country, with other mountain ranges, other seas, other airs. And the nights of stars.

He missed André just a little. He would have liked André to have seen certain of the wonders. André would have respected them, André who had not believed, would have accepted the magic instantly. But André had not fallen through the sand into the mountain wall, André was not there.

Oberand had begun to see something white, dully gleaming on the lower slope of the volcano, where the cycads grew.

The way up the volcano was a zigzag of lush and grassy tracts. Among the cycads, it had absurdly the charm of a wild orchard, and miniature reptiles darted from the path like rabbits. The sea lay beyond the body of the mountain, a sheet of light at the edges of vision. Oberand climbed, eating the fruit of the vines, which he recognized from below. And in a dusky grove he found a headlong pillar. It was gigantic, and broken in many pieces lying with gaps only of a foot or so between them, ribbed and veined, yet freshly white. He guessed the length of the pillar covered half a mile, and not far behind, between the cycads and the vines, were four others.

Standing at a break in the trees, Oberand saw other evidence stretching away, parallel to the places through which he had climbed. A tier or sloping plateau of the mountain cone ran out, with a white line on it like the base of a toppled barricade, and further below was something similar, hidden until now in the patches of forest. Above, as he moved onward, a vast gate reared up, parting the sky. Oberand did not stop, he went to the gate, and under it, and trod across a fissured bridge that in places raised him perhaps twenty feet from the ground, and came into a hall. Nothing remained of it but the arched struts which once had held its masonry. Their whiteness burned and turned the sky between to darkness. The height was limitless. That was of no consequence. He knew what he had found. It was a temple, of colossal bigness, erected to the god of the valley. He sat down on the grassy floor, and gazed at the arches of pure whiteness, where the moss grew and the lianas festooned themselves. Again, he wished that André had seen this. Presently Oberand lay on his back and watched the darkened sky between the arching ribs.

The temple had collapsed, and the forest moved over it like a slowly turning wheel. Everything was eaten away but for this marvelous fretwork, its bones.

Oberand felt emotions that had no name.

After an interval, the light altered, and the sun was setting. He made a fire there in the grass on a flat white scale of the temple. He ate some of the meat he had cooked the night before, and drank water from the bottle.

"I have found a temple to the white god of the legends. I do not pace it out in cubits or miles. It is of exceptional size and surely that is all one needs to know. Besides, I have no one to show it to, no means of sketching it, no means even to write of it. And so I simply write this in my mind. And perhaps, by going over these phrases again and again, as doubtless I shall come to do, I will memorize them.

"There is the remains of a walled avenue leading to the temple, and about two-thirds of the way along it I found the fallen pillars. Probably other pillars have weathered or been absorbed entirely by the forest, for surely others there must have been. Everywhere are great plates and chippings, everything so white, and oddly crenellated, and often split by the ravenous plants of the region. The gateway and the bridge puzzle me. I can find no steps, and only a crumbling of the material of which the temple is made – I do not know what that is – enables me to get up and down. The hall is awe-inspiring and staggering, like a glimpse into outer space. Even if it could be measured exactly, its circumference could only baffle, it is so huge, and yet so perfectly constructed. What walls hung from those alabaster struts? What windows pierced them? And what creatures moved about here, to worship?

"Beyond the arch-vaulted hall is a white mass at some distance, over a ravine in the mountain. Here, too, there must have been a linking bridge ... smoke from the volcano sometimes rises in the ravine. I cannot so far reach the farther building, which is very overgrown. I think it must be a shrine, some holy of holies. This is frustrating. But possibly, approaching from another direction of the cone, I may find a route over.

"I am very excited. I do not begin to grasp what may happen now. Sometimes the mountain rumbles faintly. Perhaps it will erupt. I feel so well, so fulfilled and gratified, so optimistic, I do not believe it can go on. But my traps continue to feed me, although now I have resorted to the method of the stone – my bullets are all gone. There is water from a rill just above the temple hall.

"When I remember the City I do not credit it. It does not exist for me any more. The world has gone and there is only this.

"Tomorrow I will go down to the lower slopes again and try to find a way across the ravine, to reach the shrine."

As the sun was rising, Oberand was woken by a disturbance from the forest. Something too large had entered one of the traps, and was destroying it.

Oberand went out of the temple hall and beheld a tusked pig wrenching itself out from the trap in a shower of wood and broken vines. It rolled hot eyes at him, then bolted away, the creepers unweaving over its back.

At that moment an ink black shadow fell on Oberand, covered him and all the ground, cold and depthless as sudden water.

He looked up – and saw a whirlwind.

Out of the whirlwind flashed a wing beat, the writhing and whipping of a snakelike tail, also eyes like fire, a scimitar beak open to reveal the little pointed endless teeth, and claws of steel that gripped. They had him. The pain of them was numbing and unrealistic, and even as he tried to pry himself away, to fight this demon of the upper air, it soared and bore him with it, up between the railings of the cycads, into a vortex of sky.

Oberand heard himself shouting. He flailed and beat at the demon. It was a bird from the volcanic cone, massive, and feathered as if with wire. Its talons held him more tightly than any trap. It peered at him with its soulless mechanical eyes, seeing only his meat, not caring that he fought it.

Already he was fifty feet above the earth. It was hopeless. Oberand ceased to shout. He found he had voided himself in utter terror. Tears of pain and fear ran down his face. The bird dived upward, obliterating gravity, bearing him to some nest high on the cone, where it would kill and feed on him.

The calm of death smothered Oberand. It was as if every sensation and every thought were extinguished together.

He looked down and saw the shape of the world of the valley under him. From the claws of the bird he was granted a vision of the mountain, laid sideways and flat, combered with its forest, wreathed by its smokes and steams, and there the sidelong plateau where the temple stretched downward against the sea. And Oberand, in the claws of murder, saw what the temple was. It was the skeleton of an enormous man, a giant to whom the giant beasts of the valley were small things, like fowl and squirrels. A giant fallen, the tibias and fibulas of the legs an approaching avenue, the pelvis a mighty gate, and the smashed metacarpals of one hand, five toppled pillars. The rib cage made the hall of arches, and over the smouldering ravine was the detached head of the shrine, its two eyes forever wide, its teeth choked by the reclaiming vines. The god lay on the mountain, the god of white bone. Held high in the air in the claws of murder Oberand looked and saw, and an irresistible smiling lifted his face against its bones. Carried toward his horrible death, he could not keep back a terrifying laughter.

What a tomb this one is. Visible for a mile around, from the right positions, towering between the graves. It was designed by a well-known artist, also responsible for a quite remarkable portrait of the dead actress who lies here. It is called the Tomb of the Angel – as you see, for obvious reasons. The angel is beautiful, and bears some resemblance to the actress herself. With spread wings, she offers a mirror to the sky. The glass in the mirror is real, but unfortunately fissured by the elements.

The Glass Dagger

Out flew the web and floated wide;
The mirror crack'd from side to side.

– Tennyson

"But," he said, smiling a little, "I believe, in reality, you don't love me."

"Of course," she said, "I hate you very much."

He stood out on the balcony that overhung the canal. The afternoon lay in a broad sheet across the water which, once the sun moved below the western buildings, would grow sober, equally impenetrable. It was not a surface ever to be seen through, it must be taken on trust. And so too perhaps the somber cool young woman who lay in the rumple of sheets and pillows, their bed of love, looking at him sidelong as did men of his acquaintance with whom he gambled.

"No, not hate. Nothing so intent. You like me, you enjoy me, somewhat."

"And you, Michael, take me much too seriously."

She rose from the wave of sheets, shaking back her black hair that was neither luxuriant nor very long. The warm sunlight described her as she would have described a subject in one of her own illustrations. A slim body, quite strong, of course not ugly, but hardly luscious, or perfect. Her face might have passed unremarked a million times, and had done so. Her eyes were oddly shaped, very dark, but often lacking luster when she had worked too hard at her paintings or been locked up too long in the dusts of her sculpted stones. Her hands were graceful, but rough and calloused; they passed over his pampered athlete's body like sandpaper.

He was a fundamentalist; he had never fussily asked of himself why, from the instant he beheld her, in blank, unmagical daylight outside the Temple-Church, he had wanted the artist Valmé: her. He was handsome and rich, an aristocrat, a foreigner, much pursued. He had had many women. He *could* have, within temporal reason, almost anything he desired. And in this way, desiring her, he had got Valmé also.

She had arrived calmly, in cotton gloves and a washerwoman's dress, with a straw hat on her head. She entered their liaison without demur, willingly but not eagerly. Her work she continued and he would never have dreamed of attempting to prevent that. Though he did not understand it, or even especially value its results, her talent was obvious – besides, others too thought so. She was independent, and perhaps this was part of her allure. Though probably not. It seemed to Michael Zwarian that if he had found her begging in a market, able to do nothing but whore, he would yet have had to have her.

As it was she came to him a virgin. An accomplished practiced lover, and in all his physical beauty, he rode into the kingdom of her body sure that through this alone he could make her love him. He had expected her love, for love had always been given him, usually unasked. But though he was innocent of complexity he was not a fool, and by now he knew. It was established between them. And his sad joking on her balcony was not an appeal or a test of her. It was if anything to show her that she need not pretend. And she in turn was too courteous either to protest or to confirm. In her bed (hers, like this room – she had refused to leave them) he might give her pleasure, if she were patient enough to allow it.

Today she had wanted to return to her folio of work, seven ink drawings for a volume of poetry. She had been glad to please *him*, as if he deserved it for his niceness to her, his good heart. And she herself had said, "Forgive me, I haven't the energy. I'm content. Bless you," and kissed him. And now she had begun to dress, wanting him to go away, but not to hurt or offend him. So he said, "Well, I regret I must be off. Tomorrow evening, you'll dine with me?" And she, rewarding his tact, replied that she would happily be present, she anticipated it, she might relax then, her labor completed.

Outside with him he carried away the image of her ordinary body captured in the vast tilted mirror beyond the bed. This held too the perpetual exact image of the canal, the far western bank, the sky. So he had seen her, in the glass. Had he looked at her in the flesh in that last moment?

Zwarian's carriage trundled down a cobbled alley, following the canal to its source, the river. One day soon, discounting tradition and having no one to answer to, he would want Valmé not as mistress but as wife. Would she refuse, or would her avowal be as benignly unimpassioned as her mistressdom? It was not that she used him (he would never forget the first trinkets given back, apologetically, sternly). She did her best. She had never loved anyone else – except once or twice creatures on paper or in marble. He went to supper in a tall house near the Angel, where pretty women stared at him in astonishment, blushing and fretting.

Valmé's room was L-shaped; beyond the crook of its arm, and behind a screen, lay her studio. Two or three figures always stood in it, silent attendants on all her doings – they were larger unfinished works, one of which would occasionally be completed, only to be replaced by another. At present the god Dionysos dominated the chamber, draped in a sheet as if the City sun would never be divinely warm enough. The walls were covered in sketches, and a few paintings of which Valmé was fond. A stove, now cold, and a huge worktable holding a convention of paints, brushes, pencils, papers, rags, and implements, apparently of torture, occupied the remainder of the space. There was no window, but in the ceiling a round vent brought down the light to make a blazing hole as though into another dimension.

Valmé, dressed now for her trade, did not at once go to the seventh illustration propped up on its board. Instead she moved about the studio, silently realigning herself with its inner structure, as if she had been several months away. On these returns, there were always certain objects that she touched – the Dionysos now, inevitably, a particular ink drawing of towers, an ivory elephant ... things that held an intimate reminder. She was very private, Valmé, and even her few acquaintances, even her lover Zwarian, who had sometimes looked on the studio, knew the personal significance of scarcely anything. One item, though, which was seldom on display, Valmé had recently begun to remove from its box, holding it up into the well of daylight. This she did now. In her hand it was a shard of burning nothingness, a sort of hard-edged flame. To glimpse it in this way was to be entirely puzzled as to what it might be. And when she lowered the thing, it gave off a flash like lightning, striking the walls in a flaming cartwheel, before going out. What was this apparition? Was it some magic trick learned from her wretched beginnings in the slums of Paradys?

Her father had been a priest. That is to say, was suspected of being one. Her mother's husband, a bookseller, had caused them to exist in a strange, dim gray artery of a street, where he crouched over his wares, and drank heavily, selling virtually nothing. Into this grim life, somewhere in the intervals of boiling turnip soup from half rotted vegetables gleaned off the market floor, and applying ointment to the bruises he gave her, Valmé's mother absorbed a child. The only man she might have been said to spend time with (including her husband) was the priest. His church stood minutes away from the apartment above the bookshop in the artery. He was old, but very strong, and things had been said of him, once or twice. Valmé's mother's husband suspected some discrepancy, and unoriginally struck her, but she too was strong, and he weak. That his wife carried the bastard of another man, probably a religious one, fueled the drunken bookseller's self-pity. He was enabled to become for himself a character in one of the books upon which he crouched like a gargoyle on architecture. "You know what she has done to me," he would say to fellow drinkers in the tavern. Meanwhile the woman had instinctively gathered about herself the impoverished and tangible wives of the district, who, as they assisted her over her pregnancy, became a fortress of chignons, skirts, and aprons. Giving birth amid a thorn hedge of women, she had nothing to fear but the dangers of parturition, and these her tough body refused.

The child, Valmé, emerged then into this world where women were reality, and men soulless creatures, monsters, myths.

Of course, the drunkard hated the child that was not his, but some indefinable moral sense kept him off her in the first six months. By the moment, therefore, when, at her baby's fractious crying, he turned on her, his arm upraised, the woman had reached a momentum. "Touch her, I'll kill you," she said, and in her hand was the knife from the turnips. As he moved, however, she did not after all stab him to death, which would have sent her elsewhere, and so deprived her child, she caught him instead a blow with the side of her fist on his nose. It bled, he fell. And lying on the floor, he vowed to see to her. But Valmé's mother answered, "No, we'll have an end to that. I've had enough. What are you, you sniveling bottle? What have you ever done for us that gives you the right of violence over me, or her?" "Not given *her* to you, surely," he said, through the blood. At that she laughed. "No, squeeze *you* and only cognac would come out. Think what you like," she said, "touch her and you'll never touch another thing in your life. They'll have you out in a box." She was strong, he weak, and this, at that time, enough.

It would come about, in later years, that the drunkard, by then reduced to total sponge, would fawn on his wife in company and out of it, praising her, saying she was his rock, saying he would be dead but for her, and perhaps all this might be said to be true. He never again raised his hand to her, or the child. He ceased to curse her quickly too, for that alone did not satisfy. He dropped easily into the role of the pathetic, guilty, and useless, surviving on the kindness of his wife. For her part, she went on feeding him and securing his clothes, she took in sewing and even began to sell cheap novels in the shop (from such works he hid in fear), thereby making an income for them all to live on.

Valmé had the little schooling that the nuns could give her. She showed an interest at six or seven in the Virgin. She began to draw the Virgin, taking strange, lovely, unblasphemous liberties with her garments and symbols. The drawings were remarkable, said the proud nuns and the proud mother, in the way partial teachers and parents always do. But it happened that, in the case of Valmé, they were correct.

At twelve years, the scrimping and saving of her mother put Valmé into a school of art across the river in the old Scholars' Quarter. Among the quantity of pupils, only five were females. On this distinction, most of them rose and sank, but Valmé paid no attention to anything that did not have to do with her work. Her reading improved, that she might read books on her subject, while to her tabulated species of the male was added one other, the Tutor. Those whose tuition she found valuable became nearly real, for Valmé. The others, like the pupils, she dismissed. None of that made her popular. But in the end this did not matter. For once, the best was also the most influential. These powers protected her and, at the age of fifteen, she emerged from the cocoon with remunerative and creative work already before her.

Five years after this she was able to buy for her mother a modest house in the hills above the City. Here the dregs of the father swiftly flowed away, mopped up finally by the healthful air, the pure food, the gentle lowing of cows and white meandering of sheep. For herself, Valmé acquired her apartment at the canal, her reputation as an artist, her consolidated and pleasing life. For pleasant it was. She liked to be alone, for her solitude was never unpopulated by anything except the human race. The aspirations she had observed in other women – to be fêted, to be adored, to mate and to produce small toy replicas of themselves – Valmé lacked. She did not even deposit in her room a cat, to act as surrogate for these things, although she was fond of cats, spoke to them on the streets, and fed such strays as occasionally haunted the bank of the canal.

One morning she had gone to church, as she did three or four times a year, to absorb the embers of windows, the music, the genuine excellence and truth of the teachings of Christ – which did not affect her in any way but the intellectual, as a perfect mathematic would the mathematician. Coming out of the Temple-Church, she was met by a tall and handsome young man in exquisite clothing. He delighted her eye. She stopped and allowed him to speak to her. Economically, he apologized for his approach, expressed a desire to walk with her, and being permitted this, gradually, another desire to take her to dine. Valmé had been propositioned by one or two others, though possibly by more than she had noticed. She had fobbed them all off. Now it seemed to her that perhaps an affair might be of value to her, extending her perceptions. To his riches she was, and remained, impervious. She saw no want of them, she had what she needed. As for his looks, although they had arrested her, as a masterful painting would have done, they evoked no fleshly response: She could only, if she had to, place Michael Zwarian in the category of the Mythical Man. She did not think he would like her for long, and was surprised when he neither tired of her nor imposed upon her. For his tact in every area of their relationship she came to value him somewhat. But only for himself. If he had left her, she would not have mourned. He did not enhance her life, merely added to it elements she felt she did not properly require, and sometimes, momentarily, he cluttered her. But he deserved only good of her, like her mother, and to both she was dutiful, the one because she was real, and the other because he tried to be.

She had been – the accepted term – Zwarian's "mistress" for two years when they were strolling one day together through the long traceries of shops below the cathedral. It was his intent to buy her a present, hers to frustrate him. Already there was a basket of dark grapes, but on this they feasted together. At the bangles, silks, even at the books, she stared as if such items were incongruous. "You'd let me think you live in a cave," he said. "So I do," she said. He was subtly persuading her toward a place where artistic materials were sold. Here she might give in. He did not want to buy for her such stuff, but would consent if she would. Then, under an awning, there was a pheomenon, a glass window full of glass. It was so odd, it caught her eye, Next, the colors, clear, smoky, chemical, and ethereal at once. "Something here?" he asked her gently. "No," she said, even more gently, for he made her impatient. "But to paint such a thing."

So they stood gazing at goblets and vases sucked out of the sky and the river, from various drinks and ichors, some mingled.

It was not allowed, to go into the shop. She would be off if he suggested it.

Finally, she said, "Michael, what is that? Isn't it a knife made of glass?"

"Yes," he said.

"But what use could it be?"

"A glass dagger," he said. "I imagine one would be able to kill an enemy with it."

The dagger of glass lay on a cushion of black plush. Where the other objects of the display were made of colored, perhaps liquid, emissions, this one thing had been cut from sheer air. It was hard, not fluid. Yet, colorless, it was hardly there. She could not see any ordinariness in it, for first of all she had assessed its parable, though not to understand the meaning.

"This you'd like," said Zwarian softly. "Let me –"

"No, of course not. You're already too generous. *No*. But tell me about it."

"I don't know anything. Shall I find out?"

"I'm so thirsty," she said, and turned from the window.

So he must buy her crushed fruits in a common glass, not the paradox. That once, he went against her. Part of his tact maybe, to judge where he could overstep the mark, or rather what might be essential enough she must accept.... Luckily no price had been displayed on the dagger. It was costly. Probably she would guess, but had not seen.

His note, which accompanied his gift, relayed this:

"The proprietor was vocal on the dagger. A century ago they were, he said, in vogue at Rome and Venice, the weapons of assassins. The blade kills, much as a shard of bottle glass can. The top and hilt can then be smashed with a stick, leaving slight evidence to the undiscerning. At least two hundred skeletons, according to my informant, lie in Italianate mausoleums, with such glass blades wedged between the ribs, and lacking a handle. Dearest, be careful of the point, which really is quite sharp."

It was this, then, this dagger made of harsh and tactile air, which Valmé had taken from its box and lifted up into the light, flashing and dying, like a flame.

Why should that be so? She had never attempted to paint the dagger. She kept it close. Had it become for her a cipher of what her lover should have been? Not necessarily noble, handsome, or wealthy, but an enigma, transparent and merciless, blazing and incalculable, the instrument of sudden death, and mystery?

"You'll come to the theater?"

"Perhaps," he said, because they hemmed him in. He did not want to go. A walk along the river alone in the dull lamplight would have agreed with him better.

"Yshtar is singing in the comedy."

He had heard of Yshtar (who, as was the fashion now among artists and performers, went by one name only).

"Very pretty, I believe."

"Oh, a sensation. Not a hoyden. A woman of class. A lovely voice, and the whitest arms, palest hair. They say she's parted from Dauvin. Naturally, how could that grocer keep her?"

At the *Goddess of Comedy* they watched two acts of a play with songs. Michael Zwarian was bored and restless, but his good manners kept him by his companions. In the intervals, they drank champagne. In the third act, Yshtar appeared. She portrayed a Roman priestess in a charming, inaccurate costume, whose main function was to bare her arms, feet, ankles, and half her breasts. She was indeed beautiful, an amazement, and with a delightful voice. Zwarian was impressed by her, as most of the City had been since her advent half a year before. He had never seen her, as it were, alive, although he had read of her in the journals, most especially the flighty *Weathervane*, whose proprietor was said to be one of her patrons.

"We'll go backstage before the last act," said Delorette. He knew Yshtar, at least had met her. She was, he said, yet more wonderful when seen close to.

If Zwarian felt anything at this moment, as he was towed behind the towering bulwarks of the sets into the warren of the hinder stage, it was curiosity. He was not considering the actress Yshtar as a woman, or even a female creature. She was a marvelous waxwork that lived.

Her dressing room was cramped and shabby, crowded with stained mirrors and fly-blown, candle-spotted velvet, but freshened by torrents of flowers sent up that very evening by admirers.

The maid admitted them, reminding Zwarian of the brothels of which he had heard but to which he had never had recourse. It amused him, and also he felt sorry for the singer. She was like a poor lily put out for insects to crawl over and try to feed on.

Then she emerged from behind a partition.

She was clad in a satin dressing gown that fulfilled the rules of decorum as the costume had not. Her hair was still pinned up in the Roman mode, and her face was garishly plastered with the cosmetics demanded by her role. Through this mask the gorgeous, flawless sculpture of her face and neck, her lips and eyes, looked out like unsullied swans from a thicket.

"Gentlemen," she said. She appeared neither pleased nor offended, in fact immune, but kind, mild. She would not hurt them if they observed the boundaries.

It was easy to be taken with the actress Yshtar. She favored none of them especially, was gracious to all. She declined to have supper with Delorette, although he was so insistent. (She allowed Gissot to joke about writing a play for her.) Only as they were leaving, just before the last act, giving her merely five minutes to don her concluding costume – she did not, either, try the trick of putting it on behind the partition in their presence – only then did she offer Zwarian the faintest and most insubstantial smile.

He stayed for the last act. As he watched her on the stage, he wondered if it would be possible to strike a bargain with her. She was, he thought, primarily a woman of business. She had no heart, only some dainty, strong silver clockwork that ticked away in its place. Her own talents would gain her whatever it was she desired. But she would presumably like money, provided it were coated with delicacy, offered via a placid etiquette, to match her own.

He grasped exactly the spirit of Valmé's past from the very little she had told him. She had had to work for everything she found valuable. She had never had to work for the attentions of Michael Zwarian.

The affair of Yshtar with Michael Zwarian was somewhat talked of, as was inevitable. (Valmé's attachment to him had scarcely been noticed.) Meanwhile, he did not see Valmé, although he sent her a very courteous letter, explaining that although he would not be intruding on her time, he was, should she want his assistance, always her servant and her friend. With the letter he sent no form of money or expensive present, which she would have disliked, only a basket of fruit and flowers. This the artist painted. In reply she sent him a letter even more courteous than his own. If he had tried to frighten her with the loud whiff of desertion, she seemed not to mind it. She thought of him most warmly, she said, and with gratitude for his many generosities. She did not think she would need to call upon his assistance, but as a friend she would always remember him, and wished him well as such.

Zwarian was not yet daunted. He had expected nothing else. Nevertheless, even expecting nothing else, perhaps he had *hoped* for something else. Would Valmé, hearing of his attentions to the actress, fastidiously brush him off the cuff of her life? He did not actually enjoy the sense of manipulating her. He became impatient, and sequentially, a few hours after, the lover of Yshtar.

There was a summer storm of great force. The sky cracked and roared and pieces of it seemed to fall dazzling in the canal. Seen through the casement wavered by the downpour, the water boiled in the rain, while on the skylight of the artist's studio a herd of crystal beasts galloped ceaselessly by.

She had lit the lamps, it grew so dark. And yet the energy of the tempest, penetrating like a germ, sizzled in the air. Restlessly she paced from the fluttering dimness of the studio to the angle of the bedroom, longing perhaps to run out into the cauldron of wet and galvanism. But some veneer of decorum did not let her now, when three years before, probably, she would have had no scruple.

How strange. Surely she had avoided convention. What had changed her? Could it be her short time with Zwarian had done this? Insidious, then, maybe to be feared. It was as well he had, after all, grown tired of her and taken up with his actress.

The rain stabbed down. It wounded the canal over and over.

Valmé conceded that she was becoming absorbed by the idea of the woman called Yshtar. She found she thought of her often, and never having seen her, formulated idle pictures, both mental and on paper, of her appearance from description. There was, it seemed to Valmé, a momentary intimacy between them. For Zwarian had known the flesh of Valmé, and now embraced the flesh of Yshtar, and this provided an infallible, if curious, link, as though indeed the two women had lain together face to face and breast to breast, naked on a bed. There was to this nothing either sensual or homosexual. Yet it was immediate, and constant. How can a man take the impress of a lover and not carry away some of it, like the mark a shell will leave in sand, which the new consort must sense stroke against her, as they couple?

Perhaps she should visit the theater, and watch Yshtar at her trade. That would be difficult, however, without an escort – and of course now she had none. Besides the vapid sugar of the plays in which Yshtar practiced did not appeal to Valmé.

The rain continued through the night. It washed the heat from Paradys, down her towers, along her roofs and walls, and through her gutters, Unseasonably cool, the morning.

Five weeks after Zwarian had left her, held in that season of cool and filmy weather, another letter was brought to Valmé. It was not vulgar, not scented, and yet a reflex in the handwriting gave it away. Before she opened it, the artist knew she had hold of something of Yshtar's.

"Mademoiselle, it has been suggested to me that it would be useful to my career at this time to have painted a portrait of myself. Your name in turn was recommended, the freshness of your work, its faithful yet unflattering likenesses, which I have myself seen and been moved by. Your fee is yours to state. My agent will attend to that. I hope most sincerely that you will be able to undertake the commission, and trust that you will not find it inconvenient if I call on you tomorrow at the hour of eleven in the morning. I am, mademoiselle, very truly yours. *Yshtar*."

There was no question or offer of evasion. Like an empress, the actress presented herself, inescapable, and sensitively tactful as only such authority demanded.

Then again, Valmé had no wish to evade. To her slight surprise, her pulse had quickened. She was to meet, here in her "cave," her lover's lover. She was to see her, hear her voice, was to be given indeed the ultimate power over her, that of painting her picture.

Could it be Yshtar knew nothing of her connection to Valmé? Or had she too been drawn to see the ghost of the shell?

Rain was falling, and the City was a wet slate where nothing could be written, when Yshtar's carriage entered the yard below the apartment. Shielded by a manservant's white umbrella, Yshtar entered the building. Five minutes later she stood in the L-shaped room.

"It's very kind that you should allow me to call."

"You gave me little choice," said Valmé quietly.

"My God, is that how it struck you? I'm sorry. If you prefer, I'll return another day." Yshtar too was quiet and composed. Naturally, she said without a word, I must remain.

"Naturally, you must remain," said Valmé. "Do sit down. Will you take coffee or tea?"

"A small glass of kirschvasser, if you have it."

"I do," said Valmé. She kept the liqueur on her sideboard in the corner opposite the bed. Had Zwarian told?

Yshtar wore a pale-gray dress, white gloves, a hat with a smoke of feathers. In her ears were silver chains of pearls. That was all. Her skin and hair, her garments, were in accordance with the weather. *How does she garb her-self in the heat of summer? In winter?*

After they had sat in silence a long while, the actress sipping her drink, Valmé coiled in her chair, studying her, Yshtar finally spoke. "Will you be able to grant my request?"

"Probably. I must discuss the fee with your agent."

"I have his card here with me." The white glove laid the small card on a table, where it might be picked up or not as the artist chose.

"Why," said Valmé, ignoring the card, "are you disposed to favor me? My name's scarcely well known."

"Perhaps," said Yshtar, with total un-bad taste, "I can make your name for you."

"Yes, that's a chance. You're very beautiful and your bones would be a challenge to anyone, and your pallor. One of the oldest exercises, mademoi-selle, is to paint a still-life, lilies, and clear glass on a plain table napkin. White on white. Who," said Valmé, "is the portrait for?"

"For myself. But obviously the theatrical management is interested in it. A classical play, something in the Greek mode. Will that be possible?"

"You would make," said Valmé, as if hypnotized, "a sensational Antigone. But could there be songs in such a play?" she added to insult.

"They would be written especially," said Yshtar, implacable. "But you must be a reader of minds, mademoiselle. That's the very part."

Valmé said, "You'll hang at the end."

"Off stage," said Yshtar.

Valmé thought her a worthy opponent. She gestured to the bottle of kirschvasser, the bowl of almonds. Disappointing her, Yshtar shook her head. She said, like a princess, "I may come to you, then?"

Valmé felt a deep masculine surge. Again, it was not sexual, but it caught her, was not deniable.

"I'll look forward to it, mademoiselle. Whenever you wish."

"Tomorrow," said Yshtar.

"Tomorrow."

She sat for her portrait for two hours almost every day, between noon and two o'clock. If she was unable to attend the studio, a message was brought around at about ten. Valmé became apprehensive until this hour was passed. Then she would begin her preparations. At twelve, Yshtar would manifest in the doorway. Her clothes were never the same, but for the sitting she would put on, behind the ebony screen (while Valmé prepared coffee), the Antigone cos-tume, with its clusters of unreal but creamy pearls, its darted pleats. Her flax hair was already in the Grecian mode.

They spoke very occasionally throughout the sessions. Yshtar might eat a candied fruit, sip coffee or water – never again the social kirschvasser.

Valmé wore always the same dark smock, striped with tines of chalk, clay, oils.

They never mentioned Zwarian.

The painting, beginning like a scatter of pastel seeds, the faint outlines of the map of a garden, gradually blossomed out in tones and contours, colors and form.

Valmé was excited by the canvas. It seemed to her the finest thing she had fashioned. She would not let her sitter see the work; Yshtar obeyed this stricture without a hint of unease. When the actress was gone, punctually always at two, Valmé would labor on at the picture, perfecting, exacting from memory every iota she had missed in present time. In the night, wakened by rain upon the skylight, she would get up, light a lamp, prowl about the picture, the brush in her hand.

She has known all along that he and I were lovers. Didn't she place before me the clue of the liqueur? And how else had she heard of me?

At three in the morning, under her lamplit parasol of roof and rain, Valmé stood considering the portrait she made of Yshtar. Soon – four more sittings? – it would be done. The task would be over. And what then?

As the artist worked, the actress sat, each woman had maintained her trance, with only those occasional movements, words. Now and then, Valmé had crossed the room to rearrange a pleat of the Antigone dress, to draw a highlight onto a coil of hair or jewel. The body of the actress she never touched. She was not afraid of the firm muscles and damask effect of Yshtar's skin. But it was as if she knew Yshtar through. It was as if Yshtar were her own self, a reflection: altered, new, the same. And Michael Zwarian the pane of glass that separated yet made each one accessible to the other.

Shall I confront her? What shall I ask?

How beautiful she was, there was no need to be beautiful oneself if such stars rose from the mass of humanity.

Valmé studied the lines of the painting. As she had studied the face. As if in a magical spell. Surely, surely she had captured the soul of Yshtar.

Standing before the conjuration of her own sorcery, Valmé felt start up in her a winding wave, emotion, thought, part unidentifiable. She had never felt it, its like, before. She clenched her fists, and in the right of these the sturdy paintbrush, pointed forward like a weapon, snapped and splintered. Valmé gazed after it, amazed.

Jealousy. It had come to her at last. The eternal beast, the creature of the shade by the glim of whose eyes all things are made freshly visible. Could it be?

Why ask her anything? I have her here.

Valmé remembered a story she had illustrated, in which a cheated lover, a great portraitist, had thrust into the painting of his mistress the knife for grating colors.

The women of Valmé's world were real. Through the truth of Yshtar, Valmé had found the way, by night, onto the shining terrible path of actual feeling.

Suddenly she let out a cry. Through the mirror of Yshtar, she saw what she had lost. The tears ran down her face, as the natural rain poured in the water of the canal.

Four, five further sittings arrived, were. And had ended.

"And may I see my painting now, mademoiselle?"

"No ... Not yet. If you'll be patient just a little longer. Some further details that are best worked on alone. And then," said Valmé.

"But, mademoiselle," said Yshtar, the first time that Valmé had known her arch – perhaps a method kept for inferior opponents – "I shall start to wonder what you're hiding."

Valmé said, with pain, "You're too beautiful, mademoiselle, to have any qualms. The only danger would be that I'd paint only your beauty and not yourself. But I don't think I've failed you there. You'll be able to judge quite soon. Let me get all as perfect as I can before you look. If you'd be kind enough to return tomorrow, say –"

"Alas, not feasible. Rehearsals begin for the new play. You will have to send the portrait to the theater. Tomorrow? My agent can arrange the means. What hour would be suitable?"

"But then," said Valmé, "I shan't know if you're pleased with what I've done –"

"You're too modest. I have no doubts," said Yshtar, dusting off the weeks of their duality so it scattered in tiny motes about the room.

Valmé must say, "Four o'clock would suit me."

A minute more and the actress was gone. Her carriage was gone. The rain filled up the spaces.

Valmé knew a feverish tension. The last vestige of Michael had been drawn out like a thread from a needle. She had let it go, could not have held on to it. For Yshtar had long since become Michael. She had brought him to the studio tinted on her fresh skin, smoothly tangled in her hair and breath. Yshtar's lips had caressed him. Her arms had held him. Now everything was gone.

What shall I do?

Valmé stared at the painting, which needed no further work – to work further upon it would be to mar, to unmake.

Taking up paper and a crayon, she began to draw the face of Michael

Zwarian, to sketch with now unsure lines his body. She blushed as she did so.

What would follow? Enormities of time, and she adrift in them. There were two commercial commissions. She glanced at them in a sort of scorn, for what could they be to her now?

Days not like any others, and nights without sleep. She saw them waiting. The vista was like that of a cathedral, a place of anguish.

She did not even doze until dawn. At midday she started up from a pit of nothingness. Remembered: Yshtar – Michael – would not be with her anymore.

At four o'clock three strong men appeared in the doorway where Yshtar had gone in and out as a nymph of rain.

They took away the portrait. They were like warders, jailors.

Valmé tore the sheet from the Dionysos and began to polish its cold dead limbs. She knew the great madness that this god was able to inflict – drunkenness, hate, religious mania, or love.

There would be omens. There began to be. (She had longed for them.) A sudden shaft of sunlight through the forward window, over the canal, so clearly wrought twice, outside and in the tilted mirror. A boat passing down to the river with a shadow sail at twilight, in the glass a barque upon the Styx. And a crack in the skylight through which the rain had commenced to infiltrate, a single tear dropped over and over on the worktable. *He will be mine again. No, he never will be mine.*

Days not like any others. And nights without sleep. But the days grew slumberous, as if impregnated by opium – easy to sleep then, deathlike, and to go back in dreams. To see him. At night there were the confines of her marvelous prison cell which she might not leave, and where she could summon up no wish to labor. Waking dreams, hallucinations, omens, in every corner. He had said this to her, and that. She was full of hunger, the greed for pain, and *almost* knew it. She rubbed herself against the razor's edge. She reveled in her wounds. She had loved him. She loved him now. It was always to be so. She drew his face over and over. She depicted him as a knight, a priest, a king, as one who had died. She sketched the lines of his body, blushing.

When she must go out, how sharp as broken glass the intervals of sun. The knives of the rain entered the mirror of the canal a million times over. On the street, returning with her meager provisions, she would weep. (She had wept before the laundress, who had not known what to make of it, had asked if she was bereaved. And Valmé recalled her mother like a stranger.)

Yshtar had all of him now.

Valmé dreamed of Yshtar. She sailed on a mirror of water, dressed in white, the white sail of the boat above her and copied out below, a swan. In the dream Valmé yearned and became Yshtar. Yshtar-Valmé raised her white arms and Michael Zwarian lay down in them.

Waking, she wept her rain into the pillow.

Her clothes were all too big for her. She was growing thin, and in the darkness of her hair had come all at once a strand of white, Yshtar's hair brought on by grief.

Valmé went one night to the *Goddess of Tragedy*, where Yshtar's latest play had been put on. To her astonishment, in the foyer, an exquisite painting was displayed, Yshtar as Antigone. Valmé's portrait. *(He will have seen it, he will have understood that I painted it. He will recognize how I have captured her, a butterfly on a pin. But no, of course he will see her quite differently, imagining I have fashioned wrongly.)* The fee for the portrait had long since been sent to Valmé, who had scrupulously placed the money where it would do most good, old teachings of her thrifty mother – but without being quite aware of what she did. Yshtar's small note of praise and gratitude she had had too. She had kept the note. The hand that penned it traced the flesh of their lover.

At the theater, a woman alone, she was somewhat insulted. She watched Yshtar from a great way off. Could Yshtar, after all, act? It seemed so. She had something of the quality of a vacuum, elements and passions, powers and perhaps angels flowed in, and filled her. Her stasis expressed more than the ranting of the best of her accomplices upon the stage.

Valmé remained through the several acts of the play – in which no songs occurred. At the end, a standing ovation bore up Yshtar like a lily.

Valmé pictured Zwarian among the audience, alight with applause. Now he would go behind the scenery, up into the cliff behind the proscenium. Aloft, he would take her to him.

The artist walked through the night, twice accosted, on the northern bank, as a whore. In the gutters peelings and papers. In windows miles high the sweet dull lamps of love.

Never in her life had she known such hurt. Nor lived so, from the gut of the heart.

Those very few who had believed themselves to be intimates of Valmé discussed her briefly. She had become thin and peculiarly graceful. She had the qualities of an actress immersed in a serious and probably classical role. It must end in her death, whatever it was: She walked in the rain, ate nothing, drank too much wine or that odd liqueur of hers. She would fall prey to a consumption. She would be consumed. A pretty, a fearful death. Who would have thought her legitimate for it? She had always been so practical. And her work suffered. But there, she had *become* her work. She had become one of her own pictures, an exquisite witch bereft and languishing after some deed of terror. She was almost lovely, now.

Those who had known of Zwarian did not guess that he might be the cause. No, this was some other swift affair that had sunk its teeth in her.

And some of them mentioned the glass dagger they had located in her studio. It had recently been hidden behind a pile of books – they glimpsed the locked box. Had she not said, despite the information given her on its uses, that she still asked herself its proper purpose – for there was more to a dagger of glass than mere butchery, mere murder.

It was as if the glass dagger chiseled away at her, as her own implements had down at the stone, finding out the thing within. Whittled, pared, polished fine by an agony of crystal. Down, down, to the bone of the soul's soul.

Michael Zwarian had been away on business in the north. It was winter when he returned to the City, everything set in a pre-frost waiting whiteness. He had had letters every fifth or seventh day from Yshtar, during the weeks of his absence. She was clever, the actress. He was intrigued by the network of spies she had amalgamated – what a criminal she would have made. He had never fathomed her fully, or maybe it was only that he had not felt the driving need to sound her depths. Or again, probably she was quite straightforward, by her own lights simple nearly in her dealings, her cunning only learned through the rule of survival, put to his service with the selfless, careless largesse he had formerly associated only with saints.

The building, the stair, were adorable to Zwarian. He could not stop himself running up the steps like a boy. He was anxious too, and behind him the man was already toiling with the hamper and the wine. "Wait a moment," said Zwarian. The man halted thankfully a flight below. Zwarian knocked. His circulation was sparkling in him. He was conscious of not wanting to shock, and of wanting to shock, that she might scream or shout, slam the door at once, drop in a faint, and he would be ready to catch her. He was remorseful. He was half frightened by what he had achieved – or what Yshtar and he had achieved between them. He longed for this to be over. He desired these moments stretched to infinity. Like Valmé, although he did not consider it, he had found true feeling, its colossal rush like wild horses, winds, chariots, blood.

The door opened. The artist stood at the entry of her cave, the irritating and beloved L-shaped room. He did not see it. He saw her, haggard, demented, and voiceless before him, her eyes glazed, her hair lank and unwashed, her lips colorless and dry. Love churned in him. He was the master magician who had produced this awful wreck. He gloried in her ruin, for he could repair it. Yet he was stunned, despite all that Yshtar, through her own observation, her web of gossips, had relayed to him. Valmé was his, could not exist entire without him. It was so cruel what he had done, what he had allowed Yshtar, clever Yshtar, who had thought of the scheme of the portrait, to do. And he loathed Yshtar at that second, and himself, naturally.

"Don't speak," he said softly. "Let me come in."

"Why?" Valmé said. She was like a dumb thing given the ability to talk by accident.

"What you've thought of me – you were mistaken. I love you, Valmé. Always and only you. Let me come in."

"No," she said, but vaguely. "This is some joke."

"Don't make me offer my confession here, on the landing."

"What confession?"

"Valmé," he said, and laughed at her and guided her gently into the room, and closed the door to shut them inside. They were before the mirror. He noticed how they reflected in it, upon the misty gleam of the canal and the passing boats, the boatmen and their passengers visible, these irrelevancies superimposed backward upon the reality of the chamber and its two lovers.

There, innocently enough, he told her, he confessed what he had arranged, and why. The trap to take her. And if he did not confess that he had once possessed Yshtar, that was kindness, not cowardice. Valmé need never suffer that sting. He could now atone for it for the rest of their lives together.

"But you're saying to me," she eventually murmured, after he had repeated, in various forms, the truth of the bargain and the charade, over and over, conceivably twenty ways, "that you and she are nothing to each other?"

"I owe her my happiness, if she's brought you to a revelation of need for me. I'll be in debt to her forever. But nothing else. It was all for you. A wicked game, concocted in desperation. My darling, how I've hurt you. Can you forgive me?"

"Oh," she said, "yes."

He held her then before the mirror. He took joy in her thinness, her sad hair. He knew that he was their balm; an infallible healer, his touch could cure all.

When she pushed at him a little he let her go, and led her to a chair. She sat down and said, "This is a surprise to me," as if nothing much had happened. Truly a shock, how terribly he had shocked her – he saw it like a physician.

"Allow me," he said.

"Please," she said, so muffled it was inaudible, he thought he read her lips, "I must be alone. I must – will you go now, Michael?"

He did not know for a moment what he should do. Then he saw, beneath the flimsy wrack of wires and tatters she had become, the vestige of her strength, which he had loved and respected, and which had so discommoded him, returning. And he was glad, for now he had brought it on, was its fount, and need be averse to it no longer. Alone – yes. She would want to enhance herself as best she could for him. She would need time for her recovery, for the lessening smart of happiness burning like a warm fire after snow.

"Then, I'll leave you. Allow my man to put in some things I brought – a few savories, some good wine. I'll come back at six."

"Yes," she said. "At six."

He went down the stairs, only slightly put out. He had expected something else, but given the circumstances, anything had been likely. In seven hours he would be with her again. He was a villain. He deserved to be kept waiting.

If startled by an apparition, Yshtar did not show it. Valmé had gained access to the actress's dressing room during the late-morning rehearsal. There they had placed a chair for her – the room itself was locked in the maid's absence. Now she sat on the chair, a figment of darkness, and stared at Yshtar in a detached yet feverish way. "Did you suspect the porter is susceptible to bribery?" asked Valmé. "You'd better know he is."

"But he would understand," said Yshtar, "that you painted my portrait, and might therefore be permitted to seek me. How can I be of service, mademoiselle?"

Valmé rose. There in the corridor, at the ends of which other doors were now opening and shutting, young women darting to and fro, Valmé blurted, "He came to me with a lie. He assured me that you and he are no longer anything to each other. What do you say?"

"One moment," said Yshtar mildly. She unlocked her door, and beckoned Valmé inside. A huge vase dominated the room, bursting with flowers. Amid the paraphernalia of drama there had begun to be the symbols of wealth.

"Michael Zwarian," said Valmé.

"Yes," said Yshtar. "Do please sit down again. I'll tell you without delay. As he will doubtless have stressed, Monsieur Zwarian and I have only been allies. He was kind enough to extend to me some patronage. Our arrangement was of a business nature. In regard to you, mademoiselle, I'm afraid he was so determined to acquire you, he played the oldest trick. He made you jealous. And I was the accomplice, a piece of acting I performed for a good friend."

"I don't believe you," said Valmé.

"Of course not. You love him, mademoiselle, and suppose all women must do the same. This is the common mistake of the lover. But I'm a businesswoman, mademoiselle. I daren't let my heart rule my head. It was a naughty game. But if it's brought you to your senses – then excellent! I apologize most sincerely for any pain or anger I had to cause you. But Monsieur Zwarian is charming, virtuous, and estimable. You've been very fortunate in winning the regard of such a man. One who would go to such lengths to have you."

Valmé stood on the floor of the dressing room like a lost child.

"No," she said, "it's absurd."

"I can," said Yshtar, "offer you proof that I've no connection in the romantic way to monsieur."

Valmé looked at her. Valmé's eyelids fluttered convulsively as if she might faint or be overcome by nausea. She said thickly, "What proof?"

"Tomorrow afternoon I shall be in the company of Monsieur de Villendorf. You've heard of him, I expect, a great patron of the arts. He's at his City house for the winter. He and I ... I needn't, I think, offer particulars."

"So you've taken another lover."

"No, mademoiselle. He and I have been intimate some while. And tomorrow there's an excursion in the delightful boat he has had built, in the classical mode, and frivolously called *Antigone*. We'll pass your very window, mademoiselle. You may see for yourself."

Valmé said, "You never loved Michael Zwarian."

"Never. And for him – though he was never so indecorous or unkind as to speak to me at length on your peerlessness, you alone are of interest to him." Yshtar smiled. "You were liberal enough to call me beautiful. But there are many other qualities that inspire passion. He has his own beauty, and doesn't need mine."

Valmé cast at her a strange, long look. It was of a hatred so deep, so static – as to be unhuman. Yshtar did not seem to recognize it.

"Thank you," said Valmé.

"If I've set your mind at rest, I'm truly pleased, mademoiselle. Some small token for the wonderful painting. Some slight recompense for any wrong I did you."

On the stairs as she went down, passed by two girls of the theater sisterhood, Valmé was noticed. They grimaced and thought her an ill sign, some unlucky fortune teller or sick prostitute come as a last resort to beg money from a relative.

In the half-light they held hands, the lovers. They had drunk a glass or two of wine. It was he, as formerly, who had been vociferous. She sat passively. She had only told him one specific thing.

"But I must go with you."

"No, no. That would fuss her. I'll go alone."

He had agreed reluctantly, seeing the sense in some of what she said, only nonsense in her refusal of his carriage, his servant to attend her on the journey. Her mother's house in the hills was easy to reach. Her mother, so unwell, must have utter quiet, no novel thing to alarm, until she had recovered.

"But you'll send for me if you've any need?"

She promised that she would.

It was with the news of her mother's illness, her own necessary departure to nurse and tend her, that Valmé had put him off from the second scene of love he had determinedly planned. His restraint, his consideration now were – as always – faultless. He did not carp or agitate. He wanted only to help. He even mentioned cash, boldly, if it should be required. For herself Valmé would accept nothing, but on behalf of her mother, no foolish qualms must interfere. Valmé vowed that if matters came to it, she would also apply to him for funds.

And so the bed lay pristine as the windless canal under the moist hushed onset of evening. And so tomorrow and for an unstipulated number of days and nights, he could not be with her. Thus, through the falsehood of her mother's malady, a kind of dreadful tempting of fate, she had kept him off, could continue to do so, for a while.

"But you'll write to me, Valmé." At first she might be too tired. He must bear with her. "Yes, how selfish I am. Then I'll write to you, my darling."

He had thanked God that he and she were reunited before this latest blow fell. He had been forestalled in mentioning marriage. She knew she had forestalled him. His eyes, his mouth, his manicured hands were brimmed by what he might have said and done.

She managed even to get rid of him before the stroke of ten sounded from the river churches.

Then, in the dark, she sat alone and drank the wine.

She was like the victim of a disaster, a hurricane or earthquake. She could not feel. All feeling had left her. She had been robbed of it.

For she believed in the plot they had laid, Zwarian and the actress. Their flamy flight had been a masque. Now she had been shown, the character of each made it plain. Yshtar had not enchanted him, he had not loved Yshtar. Tomorrow her proof would be on the canal, the curious boat, the party of perfect figures of which Michael was not one, disporting themselves in a crisp winter radiance.

All the agony was past. It need never have existed. Valmé was reprieved.

She stood under the scaffold like an orphan, knowing as only her kind could know, that the despairing moments of her ride toward death had been the climax of her experience, her triumph. For then she had *lived. She had lived.* Not cerebrally, not emphatically through the pen, the brush, the aching insensate stone and blind canvas. Not in her mind but in her body. She had been real. She had been one with all the generations of those, the billions, who had loved and suffered, that vast entity, that unison of exquisite, comprehending grief.

And none of it was left. No tumult of yearning, no unscalable mountain of desire. Zwarian loved Valmé, as usual. Everything was as it had been, in the days of unwoken boredom and unneed. He would marry her now. He would snatch her up – how could she refuse? And all her days would be dust.

Sunlight rained in the L-shaped room, finding every perch. It was the cold sun of winter that has no mass, a spirit. On the canal outside a few curious papers floated like swans, moving behind Valmé as she stared into the mirror.

She was waiting, stupidly, for the last act of her drama, for the passing of the silly boat named *Antigone*.

She could not have said why, or only that through this she beheld a completion, however pointless and nullified. As if, once it were done, she might retire from her stage, and cease to be.

On the bed, different from everything, lay the glass dagger.

She had taken it out of its box during the night. She had turned it in her hands. She had wanted something, some cipher for her predicament, but the dagger was not that. The sun described it as it had in the shop window, air cut sharp and bright and hard. The dagger was all she had. It resembled a memory – but of what?

Midday, and the glacial sun went over the skylight, and then the skylight faded somewhat, and the sun had slipped beyond the roof.

Valmé watched the mirror. She was there inside, and the canal, the farther bank, its buildings, bits of sky that hung between: The stage.

But Yshtar did not come, the boat did not appear, sailing out beneath the mirror's proscenium arch.

And a wild and groundless hope stirred in Valmé – that she had been deceived. And miles down, the glory of her pain, which being life to her she had loved, that stirred. And faded. For it was all so trivial. Whatever happened or did not, the facts had been established.

And it seemed to her for a moment that there never had been any great love. They were all deceptions, of the self or another. It was only this, to live, day to day, and the forcing of illusions by eye or hand, the pretense to enormities of which no mortal thing was capable.

She turned from the mirror and went to look at them, the actual unmagical world, the truth of the water, the bank, and the sky.

On the balcony, she glanced about, bitter as a soldier whose city has surrendered. And saw, drifting toward her along the canal, all that humanity was liable to, the idiotic representation of the dream. It was the boat, modeled after some ancient dictum misunderstood and made suitable for present-day purposes only by technical jugglery. It had a type of Grecian style, a curving sickle of sail. Oars moved in the water, but they were little and out of proportion, not rowed by fairies but through some mechanical device.

At windows here and there on the farther bank people had affixed themselves, amused by the boat. The canal had just sufficient depth to bob it up.

The boat was a parody, and as such completely apt. It said everything.

As the craft wallowed nearer, Valmé made out the ten or so persons on the deck, the glitter of wine goblets, heard a chamber-music trio of musicians playing a song in spurious classical mode.

And Yshtar. The flash of white like the glass.

Seen from this slight distance drawing close, in the crowd of ordinariness and insipidity, Yshtar shone like a pearl.

Valmé remembered. The face she had portrayed. The being. Of all things, Yshtar was the reality of the dream. There she was now, encircled by the arm of a big man in furs, her de Villendorf. That was the proof she extended, but of course the proof was of another order. For Yshtar demonstrated what was possible.

So beautiful. No, Valmé had not forgotten. But she had lost her faith. Here was the miracle to open her eyes.

The actress's furs were white for the man's sable, he set her off as black plush had set off the gleaming crystal. The sun lit her hair into a cloud.

The artist saw and judged as only an artist could. If Yshtar's beauty had loved Michael Zwarian, if *it* had determined to have and possess and keep him, whatever his plan, he could not have strayed. Not from the beauty of Yshtar. But Yshtar had let him go, not exerting herself. She was a sorceress with the power of demons and other dimensions in her grasp – but she did not bother with them. She might take up a wand of fire, instead she plied a purse.

Valmé slunk back into her cave.

The warmthless sun was bright; to any who passed, her room would be a hole of darkness, a cave indeed, with the balcony hung from it like a basket.

In the dark after the bright, the artist stood beside her ashy bed, and gazed back at the mirror on the wall.

She waited, and the confectionery boat slid into it prow first. In the mirror now she watched the dummies of the extras, the unimportant, self-important rich man, and then the beauty of the dream, the reality of the magical woman.

Yshtar was drawn slowly over the surface of the water and over the pane of the mirror. Her reflection floated behind Valmé, coming out from her side like the birth of the moon.

For moments only, the mirror would contain her. There, she slipped toward the further edge –

Valmé sprang, her hand to the bed, and up into the air. Something dazzled like a lightning. She saw what she did, and what occurred, for one split and splitting second – a shard of light, a point like clear ice entering a frozen lake – and then the tilted tear of the mirror shattered. It cracked into a hundred distortions, and triangles and orbs of glass flew off into the room.

Outside, beyond the window, there were shouts. The music ruptured and ended.

Valmé turned her head a fraction. She had an impression on the tail of her eye, as the boat drew itself from the window frame, of confusion and rushing, and she heard the high voices of women crying out. She did not go to see, although all along the opposite bank the watchers were craning forth, gesturing and squeaking. Valmé did not need to verify. The first glimpse had been enough. It had turned to vitreous in her mind. That second when the propulsion of the glass dagger she had flung had pierced through the mirror, penetrating to the hilt the reflected left breast of the whiteness of Yshtar. And the ethereal face caught forever in a faint incredulity, stopped like the heart. And the ripple that spread from the dagger's plummeting, the breast, the cessation, and smashed the mirror into bits.

Every one of the journals reported the death of the actress Yshtar. It was a sensation painted black. The sudden and inexplicable destruction of the young and beautiful: the sacrifice to the gods of a matchless thing.

Perhaps it was the extreme cold of the day that had killed her, and the drinking of the chilled wine, an unforeseen flaw in blood or brain – the word apoplexy could not be used in conjunction with such a woman.

"She was standing one moment on the deck of the boat, laughing with her friends and admirers, the next, without a premonition, she fell."

"The actress made no sound," reported the judicious *Weathervane*. "Her companions said she gave no evidence of feeling unwell. She looked, as ever, and as this bereft City has so often seen her, unrivaled in charm and wholesomeness. The stage has lost in her perhaps a budding genius, all else aside, certainly one of its loveliest and best."

A lesser journal, of slight circulation, reported that two or three of her fellows on the boat had noted, at the instant she was struck down, a muffled sound of breaking glass, which seemed to happen in midair.

There was not a mark upon her. Nothing had been spoiled.

Not one journal remarked upon the inevitable postmortem dissolution of the human body, the breaking of its flesh so unlike the shattering of glass or an image in a mirror. Not sudden, nor clean, not sparkling bright and of a cutting edge, having no noise but a dim murmur like the swamp, the blunt crack of a bone, the shifting down to dust.

urio shops are wonderful things. Who would think they lead to graves?
Of course they do, like everything else.

One night an astronomer was searching the skies, so high and far beyond
Paradys as to bear no relation to the City, when he saw something, beheld
something, out in space itself. Naturally, he had been looking for things, for
planets, nebulae, after the machines of war had passed, for the machines of
war had made the night sky full of other stuff, fire and flesh falling, and metal
arrows of death unlike stars.

It was a quiet time, the peace. It was a convalescence. And staring through
his extraordinary lenses, the astronomer saw on the tapestry of space a silver
man, walking through eternal night.

The immediate reaction of the astronomer, once the initial shock subsided, was to think someone had played a joke on him. Someone had, somehow, interfered with the immaculate telescope, forcing it to produce this
sight, some superimposition on the fields of space.

But then he looked again, intrigued, and watched the silver man walk, and
the stars show through him, or the nearer ones show *before* him. And a cold
clear conviction stole over the astronomer that what he saw was actual, was
real. And it meant something, but in God's name, what?

Curiously, he did not think he looked upon God Himself. A god, perhaps.
An angel. A giant, who could move about the airless, gaseous regions alight
among beautiful poisons, at home stepping across the distant worlds, too
large to be seen except like this, suddenly, freakishly, and by accident.

The astronomer stayed at his lens until the great figure finally went from
view, vanishing away as if over a hill of galaxies.

The silver man had been only that. He had had nothing very peculiar
about him, except that, unclothed, he had neither any hair nor any organs, yet
was so manlike he could be nothing but a male. His face was not handsome,
but it was perfect. He had no expression. He shone, and the light of suns
gleamed upon him like lamps.

After he had gone, the astronomer did not bother to investigate his telescope (although in after days he dismantled it, had other experts in to try it, rebuilt it, and later searched the skies again for his first sighting of the silver man, which was ever repeated). He merely sat that night, in his chair, the vague hum and glow of the City beneath him, the cool air of his hilly garden on his face through the open roof.

What he had seen had no significance. It was too monumental to carry any import.

He told no one, making only a brief note in his diary. *I saw tonight a silver man who walked across space* – something like that.

In later years once or twice he referred to the phenomenon in company, without explaining, as if it were a common thing many had witnessed. Perhaps they had.

Once, but once only, he dreamed that as he lay on his bed, the silver man walked through the room and through his, the astronomer's, body. There was no discomfort, not even a warmth or coldness, the feeling of a breeze in the blood. The vast limbs went by like columns, and were gone. Waking, the astronomer felt annoyed, as if he had missed something, but what was the use? He slept again, and in the morning made no note of any sort.

It is a poor little plot, this one. Who is lying there sleeping and dead? Bend down, part the uncut grass, and see.

The Moon Is a Mask

I danced over water, I danced over sea,
And all the birds in the air couldn't catch me.

– Traditional

The mask seemed to have alighted on a stand, in the window of a small shop of crooked masonry, wedged between two alleyways – a thoroughfare seldom used by anyone. It was as if the mask, flighting by in darkness, had been drawn to rest there, like a bird at sea that notices the mast of a benighted ship. Somehow it had melted through the glass. The rest of the window was full of secondhand or thirdhand articles, unlikely to draw much attention, a plant pot, a set of fire irons, a rickety table with the feet of a boar. The mask was not like these things. It was a jet and liquid black, black feathers tipped and rimmed by silver sequins in such an aquiline way that it resembled, even alone and eyeless, the visage of a sooty hawk or a black owl.

Although almost no one frequented the alleyways, a very few people did pass there. Sometimes others came to the shop purposely, to sell, and, rarely, to buy.

Twice every seven days Elsa Garba trod up the south alley and turned into the east alley, on her way to clean the house of a rich doctor on the street Mignonette. On other days Elsa Garba took other routes to her other drudgeries about the City, and did not pass the shop at all.

The morning that she walked by, the mask seemed to see her. She stopped, transfixed.

After a moment, she went up the step and pushed at the shop door. It opened, and a bell rankled loudly. From a strange gloom that comprised boxes, chests, stacks of books, the shopkeeper emerged like a shark from some rock shelf under the sea. He was not surprised to confront Elsa Garba, although he had never seen her before, not even noticed her on her twice-weekly treks back and forth outside his shop. She looked twenty, and was perhaps younger, little and thin and gray. Her hair was scraped into a scarf and her coat tightly belted at a bone of a waist. She was like so very many others. She was nothing.

"I must tell you," said the proprietor at once, in a fruity jovial tone, "that business isn't good. I can't promise you very much, whatever it is you have to offer."

"I don't want to sell," said Elsa Garba. "How much is the mask?"

"The mask? Which mask is that?"

"The mask of black feathers and silver."

"*That* mask? Oh dear me. *That* one." The shark fluttered its fins lugubriously. "I'm afraid I hesitate to tell you. A very beautifully made article, from a festival I believe, worn by royalty –"

"How much?"

The shopkeeper closed his eyes and told her with a look of terrible pain. It was laughable, absurd, that such a creature as this one should even dare to ask.

Elsa Garba said,"Keep the mask for me until this evening. I'll bring you the full amount in cash."

"Oh, my dear young woman. Really."

"I don't suppose," said Elsa Garba, "you'll have many takers. At such a price. But I won't quibble. I expect you to have the mask ready, wrapped and waiting, at seven o'clock this evening."

"I close at seven."

"Then I won't be late."

And so saying, the gray little thing went from the shop, leaving him between annoyance and amusement, definitely unsettled.

That day Elsa Garba stole from the house of the street Mignonette. She had now and then done so in the past, as she had done so from other houses of her various employers. They were all oblivious, having far too much and not keeping proper track of it. In this case it was a bottle, one of many dozens, from the doctor's cellar – she had long ago learned how to pick the lock. She sold it in Barrel Lane, near the church of Our Lady of Sighs. No questions asked. It was a fine brandy. It gave her just enough.

At seven o'clock she returned to the shop at the joint of the two alleys. The proprietor had shut up early, perhaps to spite her, or only to ward her off. Elsa Garba rang the bell on and on, on and on, until a light appeared and next the proprietor. She showed him the money through the window. Then he had to let her in and wrap up the mask – naturally, he had not done so before – and Elsa Garba took her prize away into the night from which it had come.

Elsa Garba had been a drudge all her short life; she was actually sixteen. Her mother had been a prostitute and her father a lout who soon vanished from the stage. At first Elsa had carried the slops, scrubbed the floors, dusted, polished, mopped up vomit and other juices, at the brothel. Then, when her mother perished of overuse, absinthe, and gin, Elsa had been offered work of another sort. She had not wanted it, and besides was thought too poor a specimen to earn much in that line. The madam, however, affronted at Elsa's aversion to the trade, kicked her out. Elsa bore her skills, such as they were, into the wide world of the City.

She could read a little, she was self-taught, and she could write a few words, and add a few numbers together if she must. In this way she was not often shortchanged. She worked in a laundry until she saw how the vapors killed off the laundresses. Then she took herself away and hired herself to anyone who wanted a maid of all rough work. So effective was she at her profession that employers thought her a perfect treasure, and although drab and lifeless she was also clean in her person. She never thieved anything obvious, such as food, and so they loaded her with discarded dainties. Elsa Garba often feasted on the tail ends of salmon, on stale caviar, and exquisite cakes whose cream had ever so slightly turned. Drink of the alcoholic type she disliked, having been given forced sips by her mother and the madam in her formative years.

Soon Elsa had acquired an attic room at the top of a gaunt old house near the clockmakers'.

No one was ever admitted to this room.

Elsa had no friends.

At night, when her long day's employments were done, she would climb up the stairs of the old house and come to her door, which she would unlock with two complicated keys in a motion known only to herself. And then she would leave the earth behind, and step into her chamber.

The room was not large, with a ceiling that sloped sharply down to one side, having set in it a skylight. By day, the skylight showed only the skies above the City, their washes and clouds, their dawns and sunsets, and after dark, the skylight showed the stars and the passing of the moon. In itself, therefore, it was valid and beautiful. But additionally around the edges of the light had been fixed on some pieces of stained glass, like a mosaic, which by day threw strange rich colors upon the room. The walls of the room had been covered in an expensive wallpaper of ruched silk, and where here or there a patch of damp or a particularly virulent crack had defaced the paper, some object stood before the blemish, hiding it. In one place was a great urn from which grew a gigantic jungle plant, whose glossy black leaves reached to the skylight and spread across the ceiling. There were pendant paper lamps with tassels and prismed lamps upon stands of silver gilt. The great bed that filled up the higher half of the room had a headboard of ebony and carved posts – how it had been got up the stairs and in the door was a wonder. Embroidered pillows, lace, a feather mattress and quilts covered the bed. In one angle of the room was a tall pier glass. And in the other a gramophone with an orchid of a horn. Upon a silvered rail hung four or five dresses of incredible luster, and from an ivory box left purposely open, spilled jewels which, though made of glass, were nevertheless reminiscent of some trove of the Arabian Nights.

Once Elsa Garba had entered and locked herself in, she put a record on her gramophone. It was a symphony of the composer Cassarnet. Then Elsa stripped off her work clothes and her scarf, and put them neatly away in a chest. She next washed herself from head to toe as, on every third night, she washed also her hair. Revealed, her hair was fine, silken, and inclined to blonde. Next she dressed herself in a dress of sealike satin hung with beads, and delicately powdered and rouged her face, darkened her lashes. Then she sat down at a tiny table to her supper, which tonight was only some sausage, cheese, and grapes from the market, and a crystal goblet of water from the tap in the communal downstairs kitchen.

When she had finished her meal, Elsa rose and went to look at herself in the brightly polished pier glass. Her exotic room was as spotless as any of those to which she attended. Over her shoulder she saw reflected the white china head of a beautiful woman, life size, which she had bought years before and which she called Mélie. By sleight of eye, Elsa was able to transpose upon her own features the exquisite ones of Mélie. And presently, instead of tying it on herself, Elsa took the mask of black feathers from its wrapping and presented it to Mélie. Then she went to the gramophone and rewound it.

Elsa did not speak to herself, or to any object in the room. She had no need for this solace, which presupposes the desire for a listener, confidante, or bosom friend. Nevertheless, one word did escape the lips of Elsa, as she tied the mask upon Mélie's face by its black satin ribbons. "Oh," said Elsa. It was not a cry of alarm or pleasure, merely a little sound, a little acknowledgment. For the mask, fastened upon Mélie's pure white features, altered her. She became grave, full of flight, *hollow-boned.*

The hour now grew late for music, for like herself the other occupants of the house near the clockmaker's were prone to rise at dawn or earlier. Elsa let the music fade and went to her bed. She always slept fully clothed in one of her beautiful dresses, and such was her instinctive care that she moved very little in sleep, never harming or crushing them. She slept also in her paint and powder, which she would wash off at sunrise.

Elsa Garba slept, with her hair spread upon the tinsel pillows. And Mélie watched, with the eyes now of an owl.

All was quiet. In the City from far away came once a sound of riot, a smashing of bottles and a drunken scream, but these things woke no one, being not uncommon.

The stars moved over the pane, and dimmed, and the sky began to glow with another light.

Elsa woke as a brushwork of this light fell on her neck.

She rose and washed her face, put off her dress and donned her drudge's rags, bound up her hair, and drank a portion of weak, gray coffee from a china cup.

Then she descended the house, having locked her door upon her chamber, and upon Mélie in the mask.

There were four apartments to clean this next day, and Elsa Garba did not arrive at her attic again until after nine o'clock; she had heard the bell striking from the Clocktower.

The moment that she had opened her door and closed it behind her, she felt an alteration in the air of her chamber. So she did not turn on her electric light but lit instead her candles in their pewter stands. And by this light, then, she came to see Mélie was quite changed. She had become a harpy. The china skin was corruscated by china feathers, from her head her hair rayed out, tiny claws seemed to grip the cabinet beneath her. The candles gave to her eyes within the mask a feral gleam.

Elsa Garba washed and dressed herself in a deep new silence. She did not bother with the gâteau someone had given to her. She drank some water, lifted the mask in her hands before the mirror. Would it be conceivable to risk such a thing?

Mélie sank back into the candle shadow. The tiny claws vanished from beneath her and her skin was smooth.

Elsa placed the black mask over her own eyes and brow, and the upper part of her nose, and slowly tied the ribbons.

She felt a tingling. She looked into the mirror. She saw a young woman, slender as a pencil, in a dress of water drops and cobweb, and her fair hair flowed down like rain. But she had the face of a bird, a sort of black-feathered owl, and her eyes were the eyes of an owl.

"How light I feel," said Elsa, *aloud*. "I feel I would float."

And she lifted her arms. And she rose two or three inches, but only two or three, from the carpeted floor.

"What shall I do?" Elsa asked. She looked at the skylight. Then, mundanely climbing on a chair, she opened it a little way. She went to her bed and lay there. Elsa slept in the mask.

In the morning, Elsa took off the mask and washed her face free of feathers, and her eyes became human again.

She locked her chamber, leaving the mask lying on her pillows, where her head had rested.

It took a week of such nights before Elsa Garba turned into a bird. The metamorphosis was gradual, strange, and sensual. Elsa's sensuality had until now been all to do with *things*, but through the mask she graduated via an object – the mask itself – into the world of living matter.

At first only her head was altered. She came to see upon her features not a mask but an integral inky feathered skin, from which the rest of the face of the owl, its *actual* mask, evolved. Her eyes, rather than being contained behind the mask, were set into the mask. It was a curious owl, unlike any she had ever heard tell of, or seen in any book of pictures her various employers might have owned.

The feathers spread down her neck, over her shoulders, down her arms, little by little, with a delightful tickling. Then a vast new strength came into her thin strong worker's arms. Her hands, that only makeup and powder could whiten, turned to exquisite claws like diamond. She had grown smaller, and compact. Her body bloomed like a bud. Her tiny breasts were feathered and the beaded dress, now enormous, fell away. Her feet too grew claws. She raised her arms and, like the spreading of a peacock's fan, she found herself winged. Armed and armored, weaponed and flighted.

And so at long last she rose up through her skylight as the bell from the Clocktower smote for one o'clock in the morning.

The moon was slender and going down, Elsa, or Owlsa, had now an impulse to soar over it, leaping it like a bow. But instead she circled the old Clocktower, staring down on the roofs and pylons of the City, mystic in starlight, weirdly canted, wet-lit, like some painting of an insane yet talented artist.

Here and there in the country of rooftops, she beheld a faint late light burning. Electricity, even at this hour and from this height, and behind the proper drapes, had its romance.

Owlsa dropped. She dropped to stare in with her great masked eyes at the scene of a drunkard sitting over his brandy. She spurned him, giving off a faint derisive screech, maybe like the cry of a hunting owl. It startled him; he spilled his drink and staggered to the window, pale and fearful. Something is always watching us, especially as we sin against ourselves.

At another window, Owlsa saw the sick, dying, and the priest bending low, and the incense was so sweet it reminded her again of the upper air, and she spun away.

She spun like a dart from the City, out over the suburbs, which the river divided in a cruel and wanton way, its bridges like hoops, and the lamps upon the banks so wan and treacherous, who could cross by night without their hearts in their mouths? But there were people abroad. They moved about.

Far off too, she saw a train, a gust of fire upon the darkness, springing on its meaningless journey somewhere, clamped to the earth, without flight.

At last there was a window with an oil lamp, one whose electricity had failed or been taken from it. The window was ajar on the night as if to beg a visitor.

This was also an attic room, but dusty and dirty. Tumbled clothes and books lay about, used plates and glasses.

On a bed too narrow for them lay a young couple. In sleep they had separated as much as they were able. She wore a grubby slip, and he nothing at all, and in the liquid lake-light of the stars, he was naked to the ankles, naked enough that nothing was hidden, but his feet.

Owlsa came on to the windowsill, where by day the girl fed sparrows.

Owlsa looked upon her prey.

She lifted like a ghost and settled like one on the young man's naked breast. Daintily she stepped across him on her diamond claws. She bent her beak to his arched throat, and rent him. He did not struggle, could not wake. He writhed a little, and Owlsa beheld and felt as she stood upon him the mighty thumping of his heart. The blood poured out black, and Owlsa put her beak into his blood. It was good. It was the freshest food and drink she had ever known. She sucked it up, and he trembled and groaned faintly, his smooth body surging under her claws, and she stroked him with her wings to soothe him, until she was done. (His partner did not wake at all.)

Then Owlsa left the lamplit room and soared out again into the night.

She felt filled by lights, by sparks or stars. But she was not satisfied.

She flew away, inward again on the City, and heard the clocks and bells tolling for three o'clock in the morning.

There was a window without a light. It was a window whose frame seemed stuck with platinum and cold, faceted stones. It was not. But it was the window of a rich woman who lived high over the City in a tall tower, in an apartment lined with white furs. And her window stood open, for she thought this healthful.

The rich young woman lay face down in her pillows, having herself drunk a little too much champagne. Over her neck and shoulders streamed long black tresses, heavily curled and shiny from attention.

Owlsa sat upon the young woman's creamy back, above the guipure lace of her night robe. Owlsa parted the long hair with her beak, and fanned softly with her wings: A lullaby. Lulled too by her champagne and her capsules for sleep, the rich young woman did not know Owlsa sucked out her blood from the nape of her neck.

Then Owlsa tore out strands of the young woman's wonderful hair, plucked great clumps, to line her owl's nest. It would be enough to leave the victim partly bald for the rest of her life. With the sheaf of black curls in her beak, Owlsa lifted from the window and flew away. She was satisfied. For now.

Below her the City wheeled. A faint blush was on the edge of the sky. The stars set.

For a moment Owlsa did not know where she should go. Did she not have some nest, high in some ruined belfry of the City? No. It was an attic room near the clockmaker's.

She hurried to outfly the dawn.

As Elsa Garba trudged to and from her work, she saw peculiar tidings on the stands of newspaper sellers. A young woman of great wealth had been set on during the night, wounded, and a third of her hair torn out at the roots. Some gangland vendetta – the money her father had left her being unwholesome – was mooted. Elsewhere, a young man had been taken ill with an injury to his throat, but he was a nobody, and only the smallest paragraph about him worked its way into the journals several days later, following a spate of such attacks.

A plague of bats was suspected. The citizens were warned to keep closed their windows by night.

By night.

How she flew about. She was just. From the poor she drank the life blood, as has always been done. From the rich she took other things. Their glossy hair, their manicured fingernails, small jewels of unbelievable value, silly items they loved and which were worthless. From one, a banker, she took an eye. It was only glass, but what terror it caused, and what headlines.

In Elsa's room Owlsa left her trophies. They were cleaned where necessary of blood, and laid out upon velvet pin cushions, the hair wound around silver pins. An eccentric display. Sometimes a name or place she had heard murmured was written down for Owlsa by Elsa. Armand, Cirie, The Steps, The Angel, Klein, Hiboulle.

She did not attack her employers. She discarded them contemptuously. Owlsa did not remember them.

It was a dark wonder in the City, the bat plague. Windows were closed, but always there were some that were not.

There was a tenement that craned toward the moon. Everything below was sordid and unprepossessing. The streets mean, the alleys sinks and quags of filth. Refuse and miserable lives made dustbins of the rooms. But above the skyline of the City, and especially of the tenement, up there, always, something was beautiful. The sky was a source, if not of hope, at least of cleansing. Even the smokes that trailed across it became gracious. The shapes of cloud were wonderful as statuary, the evenings and mornings, the stars and planets. And the moon, which on this night was full.

Alain was a mender of things, and he had been mending some old iron pans, a flowerpot, a doll with a head that had come off, and other articles, for people who could not afford to buy new. By day he worked too, in a grave-yard, where he cut the grass with a great scythe, like the Grim Reaper him-self, but apart from the scythe Alain did not resemble the Grim Reaper. He was fair-skinned and handsome and his dark curling hair had turned the heads of ladies at funerals.

Alain's room was a cluttered place, of no special attractions. Cracks ran up all the walls, and the lopsided bed would have crippled one unused to it. Everywhere lay the items of his mending, so that it was also like an odd sort of curiosity shop. And in one corner, on a pile of old newspapers, sat a birdcage.

The cage was wonderful. It had belonged to an old lady who had fallen into penury, and once had contained three parrots. It was very large, and its bars were silvered. In shape it was like a great dome with two lesser domes, one at either side. Alain had been mending the bird cage, in which the old lady had perhaps wanted to keep a pair of sparrows, when she had died. Sometimes he thought of selling the cage. But the difficulty of persuading anyone to buy it, or give him what it was worth, daunted Alain. Money of any worthwhile amount was forever out of his reach; to chase smaller coins seemed pointless.

When he had finished his mending of things, Alain would sit long into the night at his narrow window, gazing at the sky. He had become insomniac gradually, although he was so young and worked so hard. He was unhappy with a sadness that can be borne, that does not starve out pleasure, but that never goes nor ever can go away.

And this night, as Alain watched the sky above the tenement, he saw a great black owl fly by, out of a window half a mile off and up over the disk of the full moon.

At once a spark of wild excitement pierced Alain in the side. For he knew (at once) that what he saw was neither natural nor perhaps real. It was as if he had yearned for hallucinations.

Moreover, the owl, as though it knew of his inclination, did not fly away. It circled over and over, and then suddenly came down upon a neighboring ledge only an arm's length from the window.

Alain stared, and quickly saw what was so strange about the owl. Its head was far greater than its body, and was like a beautiful black mask of feathers set with glowing eyes. The owl too had little breasts buried in its feathers, and its claws, of which it had also a pair, batlike, at the ends of its wide wings, were like diamanté.

Alain opened his window, quietly, not to startle the night owl. "Beautiful thing," he called, "beautiful thing." And he poured for it a saucer of some cheap but nourishing wine he had supped on, and put it out onto the sill.

The owl hesitated awhile, but then it came. It landed daintily, and folded its wings. It looked into the saucer and he saw its glowing eyes mirrored there. Then it turned suddenly and flew into his breast. Even as he felt the soft firm feathered warmth of it and his hands went out to hold it to him, there came the needle thrust of its beak as it tore into the side of his neck.

"A vampire," said Alain. "You're a vampire, my love."

And he held the owl gently, supporting it while it drank the wine of him.

The most odd and sensual feelings flowed through Alain, perhaps because he expected them to. As the drinking creature went on, he drew dreamily nearer and nearer to a floating and dissociated orgasm, unfelt since the innocence of childhood. Wild images of a naked woman clad in black feathers, with fair silken hair, pressed to his body, her teeth in his throat, her soft claws milking him another way, tipped him suddenly into ecstasy, and he cried aloud.

The owl, startled after all, went to spring back. Alain seized it strongly. He held it to him, and as the shuddering left his body, he held it still. The diamanté claws – they were hard as diamond – scratched at his breast. But now he was the cruel one. He bore the black-feathered thing to the birdcage on the newspapers and thrust it in. He shut the door on it. "Come live with me and be my love," said Alain, who had shifted back the slabs of storm-tilted stinking graves, and mended toy soldiers. "I shall feed you as you like to be fed. But stay with me. Stay."

In the great cage the owl padded up and down. It found it could spread its wings, and spread them, but there was no room to fly.

"When you're used to me," said Alain, "I will let you go. You'll fly over the City and come back to me."

Then he placed wine and water and some crumbs of bread in the feeding dishes of the cage. The owl tried to peck him with its silver beak. He laughed. The wound in his neck had ceased bleeding. He would wear a scarf tomorrow.

He hung the cage in the window, where his bird might watch the sky, and watched it in turn from his bed until, near dawn, sleep claimed him.

Those who were used to Elsa Garba's punctuality were surprised. "She must be ill," they said. But none of them knew where she had her room, or cared enough about her to inquire. "If this goes on," they said, after the second or third omission of her visit, "we'll have to look elsewhere."

Elsa Garba knew, inside the feathered shell, the mask of Owlsa, that she had another life, but it grew dim and vague as she lived in the cage of Alain.

At first she longed only for freedom. At night, when (the window closed) he let her from her confinement, she beat about the room. She scratched him over the eyes and he laughed at her and slapped her away, and caught her and brought her to his throat. And there Owlsa drank like a child at the breast. Her bad temper faded. When she had been fed, she would allow him to pet her and stroke her feathers. His groans and cries of delight had only the meaning for her of given responses to her own obsessive cue. He was not rich, and so blood was all she asked of him. Soon, when he let her out, she would fly more softly around the room, alighting only to look at things – an unrepaired toy caravan, a pot of dead camellias – then she would spring to his neck and he would receive her. They would lie on the lopsided bed. He would tell her she was a maiden from a dark forest. If he pulled one feather from her wing, she would assume her true shape and he could bind her forever. But he never did this. Perhaps he was afraid her true shape might disappoint him.

Weeks passed, and this was their ritual. But Alain did not yet allow Owlsa free to fly about the City, for fear she would not return to him.

He grew very pale but was not listless. If anything he was stronger than ever, and worked at heaving up the great stones that a winter's storms had toppled. As he scythed the graveyard grass, the young women turned their heads, sometimes even through tears, and saw him.

Alain brought gifts for Owlsa.

He wound the cage bars with bright beads and put mirrors of silver-gilded frames into it. He placed a pot of living camellias in the corner of the cage for Owlsa's convenience, and also to give her a screen, a garden wherein todisport herself. Her cage grew beautiful, as the room was not.

Then came again a night of the full moon, and Alain opened the window, and opened the door of the cage.

"There's the night. Here am I. You must come back to me or I shall pine to death."

Owlsa left her cage slowly. She flew slowly to the windowsill and looked out into the night.

The sky was clear, a lily pond of stars, and the great white face of the moon like a drowned girl floating in hair.

Below lay the City, its slanted roofs, its towers and pinnacles. Here and there a chimney gave a cloud of lighted smoke.

"Remember," said Alain, smoothing her back, her folded wings, "if you leave me I shall die."

But Owlsa lifted up into the sky, up and up, higher and higher until the light of the moon seemed to burn her out.

"Faithless. Lost," said Alain. And he slammed the door of the cage angrily shut upon its riches.

Owlsa flew.

She flew across the tops of churches like palaces and churches like temples. She saw the colored windows and heard the singing to God, which to her was like the sound of cattle lowing in the market, or the rush of the river beneath a boat. The river she saw also, its shining loops and flimsy bridges. It was as if she had forgotten everything. She flew above graveyards and parks. She saw revelry on the streets, where tables crowded the pavements and cold electric lamps were lit, for she was out very early.

She even flew about the Clocktower, and over the gaunt old house where Elsa Garba had had her room. But Owlsa had forgotten Elsa, and Elsa's room was long since raped, the door smashed in, pin cushions thrown out in marveling disgust. A prostitute lived there now, as if in mockery, and her faint complaints could be heard to the music of the gramophone, which now played not Cassarnet but a tune with syncopation and a saxophone.

Owlsa flew and flew. She joyed in her freedom. The night was her tapestry, which she stitched with her wings. The hours were cast off her needles.

The moon turned thinner and gray, as if it might melt and reveal some shadow shape behind it, but it did not. Then toward morning there were only stars.

Owlsa flew toward the tenement that now contained her chamber of bars and beads, mirrors and flowers.

She came to the window of Alain.

She stood upon the sill.

The window was shut.

On the lopsided bed lay Alain in the arms of a young girl like a wilted chrysanthemum. They twined and groaned, and the girl sobbed, and Alain cried out in the way he had cried when Owlsa fed from him. Just the same.

In the cage, the camellias were dying.

Owlsa flew off from the sill like a cinder from a fire. She flew up into the sky, searching for the moon. She felt a frantic need to find the moon again, to follow it down to where it went under the world, and so she rushed with a rapid heartbeating of wings into the deathly west.

And the air tore by her, and the belfries and towers of the pitiless City that cared not even for itself. And as the wind rushed at her, she felt a peculiar loosening, at her face. It was as if a skin came painlessly away, and suddenly winged off from her. She saw it. It was black and feathered, tipped and rimmed with silver. It was the mask. The mask had flown from Elsa, in the sky.

And already and at once she felt herself changing. Her feathers were scoured away and she was only skin and bone. Her slender arms flapped meaninglessly, and her pale small hands. Her legs and feet weighed her to the earth. She fell.

And as she fell, she saw the mask fly on over the hill of heaven into the west, following the sunken moon.

Then she struck the ground. It was stone, and killed her outright.

She lay on a grave, on her back, all smashed. But her face was not damaged, and her face was the face of a beautiful owl-woman, with shining eyes yet open wide, and the long streams of her shining hair running off from her with her blood into the scythe-cut grass.

Those that came on her in the sunrise were amazed. They hid her quickly underground, knowing such things must not be thought of very much, for it was obvious she had fallen from the air.

But in our secret hearts we know: The moon is a mask; it conceals something that hides behind it, passing over the sky and watching us. What can it be?

THE BOOK OF THE MAD

Tired moons ask higher tides.

– Zelda Fitzgerald

LE LIVRE ORANGE

Paradise

The sun shall not smite thee by day,
nor the moon by night.

Psalms

It was early afternoon, but as ever the daytime City was enveloped in gray mist. The sun had been invisible for years. The architecture of the City itself – decayed, ruinous, romantic, and depressing by turns – was visible in shifting patches, or regularly to a distance of seven meters. So that, as Felion climbed the long stair of a hundred steps, his world sank away into a sea of fog from which a few ghostly towers poked. And above, the Terrace of Birds began to form around a single dot of light – which would be Smara's lamp. That is, he doubted anyone else would have climbed up here. The unhinged citizens of Paradise were also sluggish and indifferent, obsessed with rituals and trivia.

Felion stepped off onto the terrace. Through the mist, the strange dim stone figures of bird-headed things perched on the balustrade, their long beaks moistly shining. In their midst, the amber lamp floated obediently in the air. Smara stood beneath it. Slim and blond as Felion, and wrapped in a sleek, pale dress, she stared at him with essential recognition. They were twins.

"I haven't seen you for a week," he said. "How are you?"

"Sane," said Smara. "And you?"

Felion laughed. "We two," he said.

He went over to her, took her hand, and laid it against his face. He loved her, but in the wrong way. Brother and sister, they were expected by their society to be incestuous, it was the custom. But then the customs of Paradise were wild and sometimes uncouth. The polluted chemical saturation of the atmosphere, which produced the eternal mists of Paradise and eroded the buildings, had influenced the minds that lived there. For some reason, Felion and Smara were not mad, at least not in the accepted manner. They had therefore no friends, no lovers. They had had an uncle, but he was gone.

Nevertheless, he was their reason for meeting at this place, for climbing up the hundred steps to his tilted mansion on the City tops.

"Do you remember when he brought us here?" asked Felion of Smara. "These bird statues frightened you."

"That was your fault," said Smara, "and you made it worse."

"So I did. But you were the only one I had power over. We were just children."

"I know why you wanted to come here," she said. "But I'm not really willing. Don't you think, after all, it would be an act of madness?"

"Perhaps. Isn't that good?"

Smara looked away, down across the City. From the denser lower levels of the fog, the decayed towers of the cathedral rose. "Today it's quite easy to see, the Temple-Church."

"Yes. But tomorrow it may be hidden."

"Don't you think," she said, "our uncle might have lied? We were children, as you said. I barely recollect what we saw."

"I've never forgotten. I've dreamed of it for years. That wall of smoking *whiteness* –"

"No," she said. "No, don't."

"You must help me," he said.

"Why? If it *is* a labyrinth, it's simple. One hand always on the left side wall, and it will bring you to the center. And the right side wall to return."

"Then you don't want to come with me to see – "

"Maybe it goes nowhere. Why should it go anywhere? He was mad, too."

Felion gazed up at the bird things. He said slowly, "He named us as his heirs. That was straightforward enough. So we inherit this pile of stone, and we inherit the labyrinth, if it exists – and it does. And then there's that rambling letter he wrote to us. The *rest* of the inheritance."

"Suppose," she said, "you and I are insane, like all of them. But we haven't realized."

He shrugged. She did not look alarmed – even, possibly, hopeful.

"We've done our best to act out madness," he said. "What else can we do?" He took her hand again. "Let's go in. Let's see what the house is like, at least."

They went over the terrace to the big door, and Felion spoke to it the numbers written in their uncle's parting letter. The door opened, and a long dark hall stretched out, lined with marble abstracts, ending in a broad stair. High up, a round window let in the sinister light. Mist hung on the air.

They walked in, and for two hours they went over the mansion their uncle had willed to them. It was like everywhere else, no better, no worse, one with the other grand and rotting buildings of the City, bulging with furniture, art objects, defaced books, and technological gadgets, which, usually, had ceased to function.

Finally they came down into the basement, and there they found the narrow door that neither of them, in fact, had forgotten.

"Shall we see if it's still there? Perhaps it's vanished."

He told off the other set of numbers to the door, and when it swung away, he moved down the sloping floor beyond. After a moment, Smara followed him.

At the bottom, in blackness but for the glow of Smara's floating lamp, was the odd little railway track and the carriage that ran along it. But the car refused to work. So then they walked along the track, between the blank walls, and so out into a kind of cavern, which must lie somewhere inside the hill, behind the hundred steps, and under the foundations of deserted houses.

At the far end of the cavern rose a white gleaming wetness.

It was another wall, but it seemed made, of all things, from ice. An arched entry led into it. Inside, only more of the whiteness was to be seen.

"Of course," he said, "it would have scared you. You were afraid of winter, even though there never is a winter anymore."

"It was the picture you showed me on that screen. The snowfields, and the frozen water."

"But this," he said, "how can it be ice?"

"It could be anything," she said quietly. "*He* made it."

Their gnarled uncle had claimed to be a scientist, a physicist and mathematician. That one day in childhood when he had brought them to his house, he had explained to them so many things that they had understood nothing at all. And then he showed them this.

It was a labyrinth, he said, built by him, that formed a connection between two worlds: the world of Paradise and the world of another city, similar but also different. In this other city the atmosphere was clear, a sun and a moon and stars shone down. Technologically, its society was not so advanced, but neither had it atrophied. And while an aspect of madness prevailed there, it was not the rooted insanity of Paradise.

"I believe," said Felion, "that he did what he said. He reached the second city and he lived there. And as he approached death, he decided to offer us, too, the chance of freedom."

"How spiteful of him," she said, "to make us wait so long."

"But time is changeable in the labyrinth, didn't he say so? We could penetrate this world at any point in time, past, future – I don't grasp the ethic of it. It must be random, uncontrollable."

"Or a lie," she said again.

"But he was gone for years," said Felion. "Where did he go?"

"Oh, he concealed himself."

The white wall remained there before them, empty, menacing; unavoidable?

Smara moved away, and began to return along the track in the floor. Presently Felion went after her.

They negotiated the slope and emerged from the door, which shut, back into the basement.

"Did you," she said, "kill this week?"

"Oh, twice," he said. "An old woman on the river bank, and a painter near the cathedral. I saved you his brushes."

"I haven't killed," she said. "So I must. I'll do it tonight."

"Shall I come with you?" he asked, solicitously, gently.

"I prefer to work alone when I can. But thank you. Shall we meet at the bar beside the third broken bridge? I'll kill someone with rings, and bring you one, Felion."

ONE

Paradis

There was a little girl
Who had a little curl
Right in the middle of her forehead;
And when she was good
She was very, very good,
And when she was bad she was horrid.

– Longfellow

After the storm the wrecked ship lay on the beach, against the bright broken gray of the sea. From the ship's side spilled her cargo of smashed glass and oranges, like blood from a wound. Her sail hung, a snapped wing. In the sky, great white clouds massed.

Leocadia stepped back from the painting and put down her brush. She rubbed her hands on a rag.

Was the picture finished? Yes. Surely. And yet …

Perhaps there should be a figure, hanged, depending from the ruined mast, with long black curling hair.

If she painted that into the picture, it would help them, would it not? Of course, they would say, because she is insane, she paints herself hanged from the ship's mast.

Leocadia shook back her long black curling hair, which fell almost to her waist. Her features were sharply clear as porcelain, and out of her feline face looked two black eyes. She had been admired before, and she had lost count of her lovers, of both sexes, only recalling a few with nostalgia or irritation.

There had always been enough money to do as she wished. To drink and fornicate and paint. She had never envisaged anything else, except perhaps one day a novel she would write, a lover who might truly pleasure or pain her, the possibility that alcohol might undo her. But not yet. She was thirty. Her parents, who had died when she was five, in a car accident on one of the vast new City highways, would normally have lived long. Life expectancy was quite high, and her family, especially its women, survived. There had been the two grandmothers – thin, healthy, wicked old women, vaguely

545

resembling each other – one with hair that, at a hundred and three, was still thick with jet black waves. But the grandmothers were gone now, and the uncle, her guardian, had died in the winter (no one was invited to the funeral) at ninety years of age. He was incredibly, frightfully, frighteningly rich. That had never mattered. Then it turned out that it did.

Leocadia went into the little alcove, and opened the refrigerator. She took out a bottle of white transparent wine and uncorked it. The cold box was full of the things she liked, salads and cheeses, smoked fish, drink. She wanted for nothing. (They saw to that – was it their guilt?) Nothing but that amorphous element, her freedom.

"Imprisoned, poor thing." Leocadia spoke to the wine in the bottle. "Let me set you at liberty."

Her cousin, Nanice, had arrived at ten, on that morning in the past. She had not been alone. The man might have been taken for an escort, a boyfriend. Nanice was ugly, but she too had money. And anyway, the man was ugly also. They stood, uglily, on the steps below the old house which had, nevertheless, been fitted with an automatic door. The door relayed their images to the bedroom, where Leocadia was lying in the sheets with Asra.

Leocadia slept with women more from a wish for power than from lust. She loved their lips and breasts, but mostly she liked their helpless pleasure, and that they would tend to defer to her. Asra, though, was pert.

"Good God, who are those awful creatures?" said Asra.

"I don't know." And Leocadia had touched the intercom. "Who are you?" she asked.

"I am your cousin, Nanice le Vey. And this is Monsieur Saume. May we come in?"

"Lock the doors, load the cannon!" cried Asra.

"It's a little early," said Leocadia. She had felt nothing but mildly annoyed. No premonition.

"It's after ten," Nanice had said with strange smugness. "And we've come such a long way."

"Why?" said Leocadia.

"Do you mean to be uncivil?"

"Probably."

"If we must, we'll wait elsewhere, and return later."

"I repeat, why?"

Nanice preened herself, the redundant gesture of a well-but-ill-dressed, unattractive person.

"It's about Uncle Michelot."

"He's dead."

Nanice frowned. "Yes, I know the poor old gentleman is deceased."

The images from the door were incoming only, and Leocadia rose naked from her bed. Yet Nanice seemed to sense this, and she frowned more heavily.

"I will let you in," said Leocadia. "Wait in the salon downstairs. The service will bring you anything you want."

It came to Leocadia that the salon, which was often quite tidy, dusted by the house service, and the floor polished, accented by fresh flowers, was on that day disheveled. The previous evening she had allowed Asra to have a sort of party, and the service had not yet been summoned to clear up the mess. The ashtrays overflowed with the stubs of cigarishis, the pictures were crooked, bottles and books lay everywhere, the light was still on, and someone, probably Robert, had been sick in a vase.

Leocadia laughed. She visualized the stiff visitors in the midst of chaos as she went to the shower. Asra lay in bed, complaining: She hated people, they had had enough of people the night before. Leocadia, who had been stupid enough to have relatives, must make them go away.

Leocadia went down half an hour later to the salon. She wore a cream silk housedress, her hair was wet, and she was barefoot. In one hand she bore a tangerine, which she was eating, flesh and peel and pips together, and in the other a tall glass of white vodka.

The visitors were perched in the midst of chaos, as anticipated. Monsieur Saume stood, his hat in his hand, and Nanice teetered on a chair as if afraid it must be dirtying her skirt.

The room smelled thickly of smoke and drugs and perfume, thankfully not of vomit.

Leocadia pressed a button and the windows opened.

Outside, the spring day was warm yet brisk, and the gray streets of old Paradis curved and climbed among the ancient plane trees.

"So," said Nanice, "this is how you live."

She looked happy, and quickly smoothed her expression back to one of discomfiture.

Leocadia curled her toes about a black bottle lying on the rug, and picked up the glass with her foot.

"Yes, luckily you came at a quiet time."

"Quiet! My dear Leocadia – what are you doing to yourself!" exclaimed Nanice. Her protestation was so insincere, that even Monsieur Saume seemed embarrassed.

"I am," said Leocadia, "existing."

"And there is," said Nanice to Monsieur Saume, "a young woman in the bedroom, as you heard. And in that glass – don't *think* it's water."

"Would you like a vodka?" asked Leocadia. "I suppose you'd prefer something less pure; tea or coffee, I expect."

"No, nothing, thank you," said Nanice.

"Then perhaps you'd tell me, at last, why you are here."

Nanice lowered her eyes.

Her falseness was so utter, so unflawed, that Leocadia was fascinated.

"You have no guardian, now Uncle Michelot has died. I know," said Nanice, "you haven't seen him, been near him, for years –"

"No one has," said Leocadia. "He was a recluse. He disliked intrusion. One wonders why."

"Oh, I tried to see him," said Nanice. "One *could* try. Cousin Brand and I were constantly making approaches. But as you say, either he was a very private man, or else ..." Nanice looked momentarily laughably cunning, as if she could hardly credit how clever she was being. "Or else someone put him against us. Against all of us."

Leocadia shrugged. From her uncle and former guardian she had received adequate funds, and once a year, on her name day, she had been sent some gift, always simple, never very expensive, but infallibly strange. The news of his death had jarred Leocadia. She had scanned the letter bordered in black, slightly puzzled by its wording, which seemed to say, euphemistically, that he had gone to better things. The letter told her, too, that Michelot had made provision for her, and she was glad of that. She had never known him, beyond a glimpse or two in childhood. He had chuckled, apparently, when she was expelled from her school, and provided her with private tuition. He seemed to understand her well enough, and did not insult her with feigned affection.

Nanice, of course, would have wanted much more. Family gatherings of hugs and kisses, rich presents, and now, obviously, some remuneration that was, presumably, absent?

"He left you out of his will?" asked Leocadia, pouring more vodka and ice into her glass from the entering service tray, and from a silver pot a cup of delicate, slaty tea.

"His – oh, Leocadia. You know quite well that he left out all of us. This wasn't what I came here to discuss, but if you insist. All twenty-three of his nearest and dearest were discounted. His kindred. All but you, and – well, this is very odd – two other cousins no one has heard of and who cannot be traced. They are mentioned as *your* inheritators. But frankly, we think he *made them up*."

"Oh dear," said Leocadia. "Is that why Monsieur Saume is with you? In case I've been invented too?"

Nanice looked abruptly flustered.

"Monsieur Saume is – my companion."

"And he has no tongue," said Leocadia. "What a shame. A man's tongue has so many wonderful uses."

Nanice stared. Then she colored. Monsieur Saume did not alter. He had not moved at all, like a skillful lizard on a rock when predators are nearby.

Leocadia took a sip of tea, then a sip of vodka, and let the bottle drop from her toes.

"I still don't see what you want from me. Are you asking me to make you some sort of bequest? I will if you like, but your own lawyers must see to it. Such matters are very boring. I have things I like to do instead."

"Paint horrible nightmarish pictures and sleep with lesbians!" cried Nanice in an explosion of true venom. "And drink your brains to slop. Oh, I know. We've been watching you –"

"Mademoiselle le Vey," said Monsieur Saume.

Leocadia was surprised. At the final response of the silent Saume. And at the idea that someone had been watching her. It was true, Leocadia was used to being stared at: She was both striking and eccentric and did not much care what she did before others. But to be the object of a spy?

"Why have you watched me?"

Nanice compressed her little mouth into a littler line, like a zip.

It was Monsieur Saume who said, "There has been some concern, mademoiselle."

Leocadia raised her eyebrows.

"Well, it can stop now. As you see. Here I am."

"It can hardly stop," said Nanice. The zip wriggled vindictively. Again, Nanice seemed happy.

"But I," said Leocadia, "say it *must* stop."

And as others had done, confronted by Leocadia's anger, Nanice looked alarmed.

"Monsieur Saume," she cried, "you see she's quite unstable, like her paintings we showed you –"

There had been a recent exhibition of Leocadia's work at the First Gallery on Clock Tower Hill. Some pieces had been sold for quite extravagant amounts of cash. Did Nanice resent this, too?

Refilling her glass of white wine now, in the alcove of the refrigerator, Leocadia understood quite well that Nanice had wanted Monsieur Saume and others like him to note the content of the pictures, not their cost. The centaurs with the heads of swordfish, the horses in ballgowns, the women in the arms of women, men in the arms of men, winged cats and burning mansions.

But then, that day in the salon of the old house near the antique City wall, Leocadia had lost patience, and so rendered Nanice invaluable assistance.

"I'm afraid," said Leocadia, "you must get out. You're wasting my time. If I lay eyes on you again, Nanice le Vey, I'll have you thrown, down, off something, into the river. Do I make myself clear?"

Nanice sprang up. And her look now was of real terror mixed with great satisfaction. As she moved toward the door she knocked into the vase Robert had used, which broke on the floor, splattering her with sick and dead ferns.

Monsieur Saume, hat in hand, bowed to Leocadia before he effected his leave. She might have guessed from that, and maybe she partly did, that he had taken an interest in her.

The doctors came at five o'clock (seventeen hours, by the old, unfashionable time scale). Sometimes there were two, sometimes three or four doctors. There were no women among them, and Leocadia had long suspected that this was due to some notion that she would be able to seduce and subvert a woman more easily than a man. Or perhaps because all the men were hideous.

Sometimes even Saume came to see her.

They never stayed long, nor did they arrive every day. She never knew when they would come. Possibly this was meant to disorient, but it only irritated her.

Frequently, she took no notice of them, but now and again they played tricks.

One brought a cat, which Leocadia saw was clockwork. Even so she had liked it, and when they were all, apparently, sure of that, they bore it away and never brought it back. She was not allowed animals. She might "hurt" them. Leocadia explained that it was human things she disliked.

Another time a doctor had left her an orange. When she experimentally peeled it, it bled.

So now she kept an eye on the doctors when they appeared in her apartment.

"Mademoiselle. How are you today?"

"Anxious to leave."

"Ah," playfully, "*mademoiselle*."

They – there were now two of them, Saume and Van Orles – advanced on her painting.

"It's finished." They stared at the wrecked ship.

"Perhaps," she said.

"And what does this represent?"

"What do you think?" said Leocadia.

"A broken heart?" inquired Doctor Van Orles lubriciously, leering at her.

"No," said Leocadia. "Have you considered glasses or lenses for your eyes?"

Van Orles laughed. "Now, now, Leocadia."

"A ship," said Saume.

"Well done," said Leocadia. "A ship run aground."

"Oranges?" asked Van Orles. "Why is that?"

"Why not?" said Leocadia.

"There has been a storm," Van Orles explained to her carefully. "And the cargo has been lost."

"As I have lost my mind? I'm not," said Leocadia, "full of oranges."

"But of broken glass?" asked Saume.

"You're rather ignorant," said Leocadia. "The ancient ships carried smashed glass for recycling."

"Are there monkeys?" pressed Van Orles. "Perhaps the captain kept some." He seemed excited by the painting.

"Give me a model," said Leocadia, "a monkey to pose. I'll add a couple."

"And how much have you drunk today, Leocadia?" asked Van Orles.

Leocadia looked at him. "I don't count."

"But you *should* count, Leocadia. This is so bad for your health."

"All the better, I'd have thought. Maybe I'll die, and then the cousins won't have to pay for my place here. One less annoying little expense."

She had wondered, at first, if they might poison her, and of course they did, but only in subtle ways that would not be disallowed. Beams of light that penetrated the brain, and sounds she could not, or could barely, hear. Some nights, all through the dark, a slender bell chimed far away.

The walls of the room were a pale, soft dove color, restful, but against them, when her eyes were tired, she saw things in the fluid of her sight, disturbing and worrying, which, against a jumble of objects, textures, and colors, would not have been visible.

They destroyed her, inch by inch. Meter by meter. But she would not be destroyed. She must rebuild what was chipped away.

"There are no figures at all in your painting," said Van Orles.

"Alas," said Leocadia.

"Should you care for visitors?"

"Visitors put me here."

"Surely there's someone you would like to see?"

"I'd tell them how you torture me."

"Now, Mademoiselle. You're thinking of terrible crimes of the past. The *old* asylum. You mustn't dwell on that."

"There are drugs in my food. Unseen lights and unheard noises crisscross this room. I'm kept so docile."

"*You?* Mademoiselle, you? *Docile?*"

"You sedate me," said Leocadia, offhand. "How else is it I don't fly at you with my palette knife, my fork, the file for my nails?"

"Because you are civilized," said Saume, "and you don't wish to sully your art, your food, or your person by an artifact used in murder against, merely, us."

She regarded him. He was sometimes quaint and caught her attention.

"I shall need another canvas," said Leocadia.

"Oh, yes," said Van Orles. "It will be arranged. Everything for your happiness."

"Then let me out."

"Oh. Dear mademoiselle."

A week after the advent of Nanice at the house, Leocadia had forgotten her.

Asra, in an effort to energize Leocadia, had taken up with another woman, and Leocadia was quite pleased, getting her house to herself without the effort of making a scene. She intended to remove Asra's code from the automatic door, but she gradually forgot this, too.

One afternoon, Saume called. She would not have let him in, but she had been out walking in the park under the Roman wall, staring at the remains of gravestones left standing in the grass, and the sides of demolished houses up which ivy had been trained. She found Saume on her steps.

"Yes?"

"I am here to see you, mademoiselle."

"I'm afraid you're mistaken."

"I beg your pardon."

"I am going to go in, and you are not."

Saume only smiled – he had dreadful teeth, like something medieval, for generally teeth now were universally excellent.

He held out a slender book.

"You wish me to sign it?" asked Leocadia, for it was her collection, the only one, of short stories.

"I am simply intrigued by the content. Girls who turn into vampire owls. Raccoons who romantically subdue their jailers in prison and tickle ladies with their stripy tails. Where does your inspiration come from?"

"The City," said Leocadia. "These are old stories of Paradis."

"Indeed? I haven't come across them."

"Goodbye," said Leocadia.

She went in and shut the door in his face. He did not attempt to intrude further. Just then.

Summer came, and Leocadia lay under a white sunshade in her overgrown garden, which she had planted to a kind of jungle. Sometimes Asra called her, but Leocadia was noncommittal. She was in a phase when she was more than content to be alone, not realizing that soon this was to become a permanent arrangement.

Her house was supposed to be haunted. Robert said he had seen someone walk out of a wall. Many of the houses near the old wall were reckoned to have a psychic persuasion.

Leocadia painted a ghost standing on a rooftop, looking lost and slightly belligerent.

But when she had finished a painting, generally Leocadia grew a little restless. She had finished one. Now it was a landscape with dancing figures, lit by far high hills in sunset, pumpkin-colored, radiating heat and menace.

Leocadia dressed in a long, pale beaded frock, preparing to go out and dine in the City. And as if on cue, Pir called her. He asked, begged her to come to a dinner at the Surprise Restaurant. "So many people," said Pir. "Lots of champagne."

Leocadia decided she would go, because sometimes, at a painting's end, she liked to move among crowds, experiencing to the full her total difference from them.

Pir was eager and came to collect her in his long car, which moved slowly, as was the City habit now, save on the dangerous fast highways.

The Surprise lay on the lower bank, a block of bright buildings, perhaps (or not) erected on the site of an old tavern. The river glimmered down below, and above the hills lifted from the City with their crowns of new and ancient architecture. The Temple-Church was floodlit, and owls nested in its upper galleries. No bells rang from it now – they had lost their voices – yet sometimes in sleep, Leocadia heard them.

The people of the crowd in the restaurant were stupid and drunken, already stuffing themselves with dishes of quail in jelly and black caviar. On the tables of the private room where the party went on were tall cones of treated meltless ice containing flowers.

Pir led Leocadia to a table. She sat down and drank a champagne which had too much head, like stomach salts.

"All the world says 'never,'" said Leocadia.

"What?" asked Pir.

"An old song. Everybody says 'never,' always 'never.'"

"I don't understand."

"None of them have anything to say, and all of them want to say it."

Pir grimaced.

"You're too clever for me. What will you eat, you beaded monster?"

Leocadia selected a dish from the menu.

Gradually people flooded around her. She found herself the center of an odd type of attention, bantering and fulsome, with undercurrents of insult.

Asra was not there, and presently Jacqueline Degot remarked on it. "She says she's afraid to be where you are, Leocadia. She says you terrify and intimidate her."

"Not noticeably," said Leocadia, who was finding the food rather bland.

"But yes." Jacqueline was insistent. She was clad as a huge blond nymph. "Asra says you have frightened her so much she can't go anywhere near you."

"And yet," added Pir, "one can see she *longs* to do exactly that. Can't you relent, Leocadia?"

Leocadia found this incomprehensible and did not bother to reply. An idea for a short poem was beginning to come into her head. She realized the dinner was ghastly. Inebriated women already lay over the tables, with tiddly men nibbling grapes from their cleavages, and elsewhere. The waiters came and went like well-behaved penguins. Which was foolish, for surely no penguin would ever be so idiotic.

Leocadia considered penguins. She must visit the zoological gardens of Paradis.

"And Asra complains," added Claude Ful, "that you've treated her roughly. That you struck her."

Leocadia took no notice of this either. For some reason the image of penguins had taken hold of her, or rather of one especial penguin, a nun of feathers, upright and perfect on a raft of ice....

She rose to her feet.

"No, no," cried Pir, "you mustn't leave yet."

"But I must."

"Stay – at least until midnight."

"Certainly not."

Pir pushed against Leocadia, trying to refill her glass and grab her arm.

Normally people had learned not to treat her in this way. She thrust him back and he stumbled against a cavorting couple. "Oh! Oh! Don't be so violent, Leocadia."

"Then don't make me so violent."

Pir slipped aside, but others formed a garland around her. She went through them, and their gloved hands broke away, the sliding doors of their bodies slid.

"Stop her!" exclaimed Jacqueline, as if Leocadia were a thief who had snatched something.

Leocadia had never, since childhood – when she had vanquished it – felt fear. But now there was an unease that, in another, might have amounted to fear.

The dinner guests were swarming at her like a herd.

She plucked a silver knife from a table and held it up.

And the wall of flesh crumpled back with tiny sounds of disapproval and drunken laughter. "What's the matter with her? She acts as if we're the enemy."

At the door, three penguins (or waiters) let Leocadia pass without trouble. And she descended the noisy, lighted restaurant and went out.

She was on the street, the river flowing somewhere and the pure lamps of Paradis, which now never failed, shining upon her.

She walked idly, toward a bridge.

But something was happening. What was it? The new and the old areas of the City, rubbing their unliking flanks together; she had seen and moved through this before. Occasionally difficult persons might extrude themselves and attempt a woman on her own, but rarely, for the watching TV eyes of police surveillance were scattered about, and besides, Leocadia did not look a natural victim. Once when she was fifteen a mugger had come at her in an antique lane. She had punched him on the point of the jaw with her slim, steely hand, bruising the joints of her fingers but knocking him out. And now she had forgetfully kept the knife from the restaurant. Doubtless it would be best to throw that in the river, for a woman wandering Paradis by night with a table knife might also be suspect.

She was coming down toward the river, pausing to gaze at the ghost image of the owl-like floodlit Temple-Church aloft. It seemed balanced on a mound of darkness, and the river coiled below, a snake.

The night was warm and clean. Scents of vacuumed rooms and automatically swept squares. And the antiseptic water.

Parked across the road was a large truck, permitted the pavement, as it was in the process of delivery. Some other club or restaurant, for which vast blocks of treated ice were being brought, imbued with flowers.

Leocadia became aware of a noise behind her. It had been cloaked until now in the humming murmurs and squeals of the City.

She looked back.

Leocadia widened her eyes in contemptuous astonishment.

Pir had followed her through the narrow byways, and Jacqueline the obese nymph, and a tirade of others, all squashed and teetering in their polished or satin shoes, tight pants, and fishtail skirts. They bore their glasses of antacid champagne and laughed and called to her.

"Come back, my Leocadia!" howled Pir.

The two men unloading the truck stared at Leocadia. Between them they tilted a block of ice filled with a glowing fan of marigolds.

Leocadia came to the men and hauled the ice, burning, *burning*, from their gloved hands.

"Pardon me."

She flung the heavy chunk across the exit from the thin street, into the shoes and ankles of the approaching herd.

The ice shattered and smoked, and white sparks burst up from the chemicals of the ice treatment, causing Leocadia's pursuers to leap backward, some squawking and falling down.

The delivery men did not protest, they guffawed.

Leocadia saw marigolds, frozen flawless, the flowers of the eternal deathless soul, glittering in heaps and shoals like flamy fish, and splinters of ice, one of which had torn the fat knee of Jacqueline Dagot so she roared.

And then Leocadia lifted her skirt in her hand and she ran. For the bridge, the upper bank, over the river, into the night, toward the house and her sanctuary. Not knowing why, and not even particularly stung or startled. Instinct. Hunted. But so far, arrogant.

As she entered her street close by the Roman wall, Leocadia saw the darkness of the houses under the flare of the lamps that never failed. Rituals of decorum had come back to the City, and its fashionable quarters rose and bedded early. The manners of a century before, as with clothing, furnishing, but not always thought.

Yet on the street of dark houses, one light burned. It was in the attic room that Leocadia had made her studio.

She did not think for a moment she had left it on. She had shut the studio door upon the finished painting (removed from the easel) at four – sixteen hours by the abandoned scale. Then the daylight had still been rich and full.

Was the light another challenge?

She walked up the steps and put her finger to the required panel. Recognizing her, her door let her in.

The hall was in blackness, and only her touch on the proper switch woke up the hall lamps.

She paused. There was nothing in the air to alert her, only perhaps a faint scent of ozone. And she recalled another tale of Paradis, where shells from the ocean had been found at the doors of the Temple-Church, some manifestation of the primeval days when the City had been covered still by a hot and saline sea – or else a practical joke.

Leocadia climbed the stairs softly. Her hands were empty but flexed.

On the third landing she sought the smaller, crooked stair that went to the attic.

There was a faint electricity there, as if something had passed swiftly, voltage rather than presence.

Leocadia turned a fashionable enamel doorknob.

Her studio opened before her, a cave covered now by a black glass roof without even the moon. But the work lights shone down pitilessly, casting out shadow.

Leocadia's eyes went intuitively to her easel, a big bulky frame of metal that would support her largest canvases.

There was a new canvas there.

It hung by the crooks of its elbows, a sort of parody of a crucifixion. The head was thrown back and the neck arched. The breasts jutted erotically, but …

The nipples of the breasts were a blaring raw orange, and between the hapless female knees, emanating from the secret zone of sex and life, a curl of orange bled with a menstrual suddenness.

There were orange patterns, too, on the white flesh. Abstractions, looking like a map of unknown islands.

Leocadia experienced the sharp sour champagne, partially digested, creeping back into her mouth. She swallowed it, and walked around the canvas to its back.

There, tilted over, was the head and hair of Asra, known as Leocadia had known the naked form.

Something horrible had happened with Asra's head. Its eyes bulged and showed white. Between the lips was wedged a tube of brilliant orange paint, it had been squeezed to poison and to choke. Orange dribbled from the nostrils and the ears out into the silky fleece of hair.

Leocadia bent double and fire burst from her belly.

Far away, as this happened, she heard a tremendous crash, the roots of the house exploding.

As she stood up, wiping her mouth, and fell again and got up again, holding to the wall, a renewal of the sound of pursuit – the herd – drove up to the house, snorting and thundering on all the stairs.

The attic door bounced open.

It was like a party trick. For there they all were. Pir and Jacqueline and Claude Ful, and behind them Nanice and the peculiar Monsieur Saume. And then four men in white, who moved forward into the room.

Jacqueline began to shriek, as if she had been paid to do so.

Leocadia ignored her. The men in the white coats came right up to Leocadia.

"Now, now," said one fawningly.

"Poor Asra, it's what she feared," said Claude.

And Nanice exclaimed, "I warned you all – she's mad."

They had broken in the door below, and somewhere was the note of a police siren, rushing to contend with the door alarm.

"Oh, no police," said Nanice. "Our family name –"

Leocadia discerned a stinging in her arm, like the pincers of an angry beetle. She looked and saw the needle drawing away. The room wheeled and flew up into the dark.

After Van Orles and Saume had gone, sunset bloomed on the walls of Leocadia's room, deepening the colors of the broken ship that spilled glass and fruit.

On impulse Leocadia had painted a few shells into one corner of the picture, an insulting gesture, as if to overinform the watcher that this was the *sea*.

The room of pale gray was very plain, the furniture comfortable but modern, therefore unsumptuous, a large couch, small tables, a bed with a fearful plastic underlay. In the bathroom the fixtures were white and functional, and the floor was laid with stark black and white tiles, which leapt like rats at her blurred morning eyes.

Leocadia went to the door of the room, which opened. Past eight o'clock, or whenever presumably darkness came, the door did not open.

In the corridor was a hygienic nothingness.

Leocadia stepped to the elevator, which bore her seamlessly down to the garden.

The garden was a long slope of lawn, the grass seared by summer. A birdbath without water mocked the sky. At the bottom of the lawn stood a summerhouse, with curious windows of the shades of cinnamon and milk. Beyond, trees marked a boundary. A gravel walk led away, toward the crumbling biscuit buildings of the old asylum, as unlike the Residence as was possible. Black windows stared from those tall blocks, and copper pipes protruded from the shortbread walls. Between these monoliths and the modern site, an ancient hothouse, broken, held the corpse of an enormous grapevine, the black and withered grapes mummified upon it.

Huge outer barricades secured the entire complex. Within the labyrinth, you might wander as you wished, unable, ultimately, to get out.

Leocadia walked down to the summerhouse in the brazen glow. On a bench sat Mademoiselle Varc, a madwoman, who always mistook Leocadia for someone from her past.

"Have you brought my fan?" demanded Mademoiselle Varc.

"I'm sorry. It's been mislaid."

"Tssk," said Mademoiselle Varc. She had wispy white hair piled unsuccessfully upon her head, a white shawl. She was a White Queen, and twice as crazy.

"There goes the sun," said Leocadia.

"Goodbye!" cried Mademoiselle Varc, waving.

The sun eased behind the walls of the mo.dern block.

"You're late," said Mademoiselle Varc.

"I'm sorry."

"Soon the police will be here."

As dusk came, wardens stole through the garden, shepherding inmates back to their rooms. Everyone went quietly, for they were always fairly demure. No need for needles, or truncheons.

"The police – yes."

"I miss the sunset," said Mademoiselle Varc. "It used to be so lovely. But now it takes only a moment or two, as in India, you know."

The sun vanished. A bat flew over the compound, exquisite wild thing, ignorant of barriers.

Then a uniformed man came walking up the gravel way. He raised his hand to the two women.

"Time to go in, ladies."

"You know what it is," said Mademoiselle Varc, taking Leocadia's arm and hurrying her back up the lawn.

"No."

"It's that the trees come alive after dark. They stump about the garden and catch anyone who's abroad. They tear them limb from limb, and eat them."

"How terrible," said Leocadia.

"Yes, it is."

She had woken in that bed, that sanitary bed with the plastic underlay, which creaked as she moved, making her think for a moment she lay in a hammock. The room rocked, certainly, but this was the aftereffect of the drug they had injected into her. And as she remembered that, she remembered it all.

A couple of minutes later the door opened, and a friendly dark-clad young woman entered with a tray of breakfast. Rolls and conserves, fruit, coffee, and a little pot of tea.

"I take vodka with my breakfast," said Leocadia, from the bed.

"I'll fetch you some from your refrigerator, mademoiselle."

And sure enough, she went into an alcove and returned with a bottle and a tall glass. "It's nice and cold, mademoiselle. The way you like it. Anything you want can be ordered and kept there. And there's a heater, besides, for making hot drinks."

"This isn't a hotel," said Leocadia. The girl smiled nicely.

Leocadia got out of bed, and the room gradually righted itself. There was the bathroom, black and white and clean as disinfectant.

When she emerged, the attendant was gone.

As she ate a roll and drank her vodka, Leocadia explored the confine. She did not try the door, which she assumed would be locked. (It was not.)

On one wall was a shelf of books, which in turn, at the press of a switch, gave on an alcove also lined with books. These were her own, it seemed, or most of them. She saw at once there were new titles, volumes on art and design, current novels, treatises on animal and human behavior.

At the other end of the room, beyond the bed and the sitting area, was a broad space. An easel leaned against the wall, and three canvases, unprepared, beside it. Leocadia's worktable stood by, loaded with paints and accessory impedimenta. The light was excellent, windows on both sides of the room, and a light source above the painting space, nearly as good as the attic.

Leocadia went to both the windows.

The one beyond the bed looked out across the slope of garden to the summerhouse. Behind that were the trees, and then the vague shapes in sunshine of colossal block buildings, utterly square in form, indefinably blind, like a deserted factory – or a prison.

The window at the other end of the room showed only a high wall, but it was grown with blackish ivies, not unpleasant.

She tried the windows. Each gave easily, admitting light and air and the song of crickets and birds.

The distance to the ground was three stories. Too far to jump.

She knew at once that Nanice had had her restricted in some institution, but she was not aware exactly of what kind.

She considered dead Asra. Could Leocadia even be sure that she had seen such a thing? Was it some obscene jest, or the result of some tablet slipped into the poor champagne?

No. It must be real. What other excuse for her confinement here?

She thought of the dead Asra with a combination of revulsion and rage.

Leocadia was supposed to have killed Asra.

But what had happened, in fact? Who had done it?

Asra had been able to enter the house as she wished, since Leocadia had not blanked out her recognition on the door. But thereafter Asra must have let in whoever it was that attacked her. Was it some other lover, or only some maniac?

The police had obviously been fobbed, or bought off. There would have been enough money for that.

Perhaps because of the drug that had been given her, or other more insidious medicines administered in food or sleep, through the medium of light and sound, Leocadia did not at this point decipher that Asra had been specifically murdered in order to cast blame upon Leocadia.

Presently, an envelope of plastic paper came through a slit in the door. She impatiently opened it.

A small printed slip fell into her hand. Someone hoped she had spent a restful night and enjoyed her breakfast. The music panel beside her bed, which would bring her whatever music she selected, would also inform her of the time. At fourteen, some of her doctors would be coming to see her.

This friendly note was not signed.

Leocadia dialed the time on the panel. Thirteen – one o'clock.

In a closet off the bathroom she found some of her own clothes – a selection, but nothing dressy for the evening or dinner.

When she was dressed, had brushed her hair, and had used her makeup – located in a drawer of the dressing table near the window – Leocadia sat on the couch to wait.

Probably, they were punctual.

There were four of them.

They wore smart urbane suits, nothing clinical, and Dr. Van Orles sported a pastal cravat, Dr. Leibiche had a monocle. Dr. Duval wore his hair rather long, with a mustache. Dr. Saume, unfortunately for him, was as she remembered.

They were all ugly, squat men, not obese but having the look of partially inflated balloons. As they dressed in the fashionable pre-century style, just so they had kept old-fashioned unsightlinesses, of teeth in the case of Saume, warts and pimples in the case of Leibiche.

They sat in a semicircle on the three low chairs, with Dr. Duval draped on the other end of the couch.

Then, in a dreadfully personal, insolent gesture, Saume leaned forward and felt Leocadia's pulse.

She allowed this, but when he leaned nearer with some sort of glass to stare into her eyes, she pushed him back.

"Now mademoiselle, we only want to see how you are."

"Angry," said Leocadia. "What else would you expect?"

Perhaps they had expected fright?

"Oh, but there's nothing to be concerned at," said Duval, his hair sliding and slipping about like spilled unguent. "Indeed, you *shouldn't* concern yourself. You must try to be as quiet as you can."

"I was drugged and abducted. Why should I be quiet?"

Saume cleared his throat. He announced, with the gentle gravity of a father who must be stern with a child for its own sake: "Mademoiselle, a fearful thing has been done. A murder has been committed." And then, a phenomenon occurred, a hellish glare seemed to spring up around Saume, a sort of spotlight. A sign of impending ills.... "You must understand," he snarled, "only the intervention of your cousins has permitted your enclosure here, at the Residence. Otherwise it would have been the *jail*. Your sentence would have been severe. But under the circumstances, and with the proper evidence we have been able to gather on your critical state of mind, we are able to shelter you here. And here, of course, we may hope to cure you. One day, you may go free."

Leocadia had conquered fear in childhood. But it is a fact with fear that it tends to return in other guises and must be fought off again and again. Eventually, through dint of effort, it may find some means to throw you down into the abyss.

She clenched her hands, but then undid them, seeing all the beady eyes, and the extra eye of the monocle, glinting on her.

They had told her they were doctors, and that she was "sheltered" in the Residence. She had dimly heard of it. A building that rose above Paradis, in the hills, safely out of the environs of the City. The lunatic asylum.

The glare still shone about them. Was it some trick of the sun, or some trick of theirs? Or a warning from her own mind?

She was in the Madhouse, but now it was not even a hospital, but a professed *House*.

She said, "So I killed Asra?"

"You will have blanked the act from your brain, mademoiselle," said Leibiche. "This is common."

"It may be a hopeful sign," added Van Orles. "Indicating that you feel remorse for the deed."

Leocadia, used to saying what she thought, stayed herself. "You said I killed Asra. How did I do it, when I was with so many people at the Surprise?"

The glare fastened on Van Orles and blazed.

"But it was before you left for the restaurant, Leocadia."

"Oh, I see. How sensible."

Leocadia beheld then all the counters of the game lying before her, but it would be a while longer before she set them into their true positions. Before she drew the obvious conclusion.

Hungry for all the spoils of Uncle Michelot's death, Nanice and the cousins, perhaps even those two reckoned to have been made up, had had to prove Leocadia incapable of inheriting. And Asra – stupid, petty, pretty, *living* Asra – had died for their convenience, the stepping stone to topple Leocadia down. They had killed her, had her killed. Orange paint, and cold blood.

Confronted by the four doctors, Leocadia saw at last that she was sunk into deep water. The light glare faded.

She glanced at the easel, the waiting canvases, and said with a deadly compunction, "What am I supposed to do here?"

"Everything you wish, mademoiselle. Don't imagine there are any harsh measures. The old techniques were often crude, but they are long gone." Saume nodded.

"We shall," said Duval kindly, "simply take care of you."

"Talk to you," added Van Orles, "observe your progress."

"You've lived a life that has placed upon you," said Leibiche, "terrible unconscious strains. Once these are eliminated, we shall make headway." His monocle and all his warts and spots flashed like sequins in a smile.

"How dangerous am I reckoned to be?" asked Leocadia. "Since you think me a murderess."

"Ah!" Saume blinked as if startled. Why? "Come now," he said firmly. "With correct supervision, you'll grow calm."

"Things in the food," said Leocadia.

"The most harmless, naturally produced and nourishing –"

"But I'm given a knife for my butter," said Leocadia, "and over there is my palette knife. Also my nail file."

"We trust you," said Doctor Duval.

It flashed upon her, like the fireworks of the warts, that perhaps she was to be left potential weapons in order that she turn them on herself. For this she did know at once, she would never be free.

There would be no "cure." Since she was not ill, not mad, not a murderess, or anything else they said.

All they would want to do, rather than make her better, was to change her into the Leocadia of their invention. Nanice's Leocadia, who killed and was insane.

TWO

Paradys

A trick that everyone abhors
In little girls is slamming doors.

Belloc

Hilde.

Although they had just put her into corsets and long frocks, she was fifteen, and still a child. Pale and perfect. Skin milk white, hair a shining wonderful ginger, now piled up upon her head with tortoiseshell combs.

She did what little girls were meant to do. She was obedient and loving but not importunate. She had a doll who sat on her bed of frills and flounces. She read fine books of which her mother was the guardian. Her father, Monsieur Koster, was a wealthy man, descendant of a merchant family. Now high enough in society, he took care to comport himself with great dignity. Sometimes he chose also a book for Little Hilde to read (she was to them "Little Hilde"). She embroidered too. Her mother had begun to train her in the rituals of wifeship, seeing that the house of polished stairs, lace curtains, and huge ferns in china bowls ran on butter.

And Hilde was happy. It was a safe existence where everything was in its place. God ruled the world. Her father ruled the house. Her mother ruled her. But all three were kind and might be pleaded with prettily for favors. Which they would then grant. God was especially amenable: "Let me not have freckles, like Angeline," and God did not allow Hilde to become freckled. (Her father did not care for freckles.) And her mother would let Hilde buy sweets once a week. Her father permitted Hilde to try a sip of wine at dinner. "It's good for the child's blood."

But Hilde had a secret life. It did not occur to her to share it, let alone confess. It had to do with darkness and her narrow bed, the touch of the linen nightgown on her bareness, and of her hair in a long plait that she might undo, always to the consternation of her maid in the morning: "However did this happen?" And Hilde would be innocent and surprised. For in her heart she knew that her undone hair was not a crime, nor what sometimes happened to her in the dark. They were silly childish things, very pleasant, like playing with the doll, or eating a sweet. Somehow, not so public. A game of childhood out of which, of course, as a woman she would grow, ascending into a cold clever angel, the peerless wife, and adorable admirable mother, in her turn, of other little children.

But the dark … The dark was lovely. A special thing she could do. A sort of present. She doubted anyone else in the world was able to.

And strangely, sometimes when she did this marvelous thing, which left her whole body ringing and tingling, beautifully composed for sleep, she had an incoherent image of some weight that pinned her to the bed, and that the hands upon her were not her own. And now and then, she would kiss the pillow, but not as she kissed her mother or papa. She wished the pillow then was more like a fruit, sweeter, and more moist. Once she had dreamed that it was, and in slumber the lovely thing happened on its own. She was amazed and gratified. Truly, it was a gift, and she was sorry she would have to grow out of it.

She had feared slightly, when the corset had been compressed about her and the long dress put on and her hair raised up, that this might be the end of her game.

But it was not. Oddly, in some curious way, it actually heightened her enjoyment. How lucky. How sad for Mama and Papa that they had never known such a thing and never, now, would.

The Koster house was one of a group of elegant mansions high on Clock Tower Hill. Smart carriages drawn by satin horses speeded up and down the street, and trees overhung the pavement. In the mornings, maids might be seen scrubbing the steps, and gardeners toiled over the flowers against the railings.

Two months after the putting up of Hilde's ginger cloud of hair, Madame Koster descended the steps of the house with her daughter. Their carriage stood ready on the street with a man holding open the door. The lady and her child were going to see a play at the Goddess of Tragedy. It was an epic from an era before the Revolution, poetic prose, three hours of it. A stern moral tale, incidentally full of drama, passion, bloodshed, and terror. The afternoon performance had therefore been thought most suitable.

Everyone in Paradys who might be said to be anybody was to attend at some point. Wishing to go, Madame Koster had assured monsieur the play was a classic, and should be part of Hilde's education.

Hilde, as a girl, had been tutored at home, and these classical plays were sometimes gone through by a pie-faced governess with a high squeaky voice. Something of their power was therefore lost on Hilde, who accordingly did not look forward to the jaunt, save that it was the theater. For this, since her earliest pantomimes, she had cherished a beglamored enthusiasm. She was too, so far, a patient girl. She had been trained to be. It had also occurred to her that while the play went on, if it was very boring, there would be the audience to scan (surreptitiously in the gloom) and thoughts of other things to be gone over – her doll's new wardrobe, a patch of garden behind the house that was hers, and so on.

The Goddess of Tragedy towered white and tiered above the streets. Many mothers and daughters, and some young sons, were assembled. "Why," said Madame Benoit to Madame Koster, "have you not heard of the actor who is playing the Roman?"

"No not at all."

"Well, he is quite astonishing. He has brought the part to life. They say it's frightful, his moment of death."

Soon Hilde was installed in the plush Koster box. Her mother had not agreed to bonbons or chocolates. It was not that sort of play.

Hilde sat quietly, and having viewed the fashionable afternoon gowns, she saw the gas lamps lowered, and the heavy curtain rose.

For twenty minutes it was very dull. So dull that even obedient Hilde felt a faint jab of rebellion.

But then. Then, *he* came out. Out of the wings onto the plateau of the stage.

Stage light is always miraculous. It is a magical spell that breathes on things and changes them, *remakes* them. Besides, the creatures who people this universe have, very often, a psychic, extraordinary power. How else can they do what they do?

The man who characterized the Roman wore a costume of black and silver, the notion of the time as to what the garments of a Roman commander might have been. But he was tall and slender, with wide shoulders. He had a priest's face, and the arrogance of a priest, officiating at his altar. His hair was black as ravens. His eyes, blacker.

From the instant he emerged from nowhere onto the stage, Hilde understood, just as a bird grasps abruptly how to fly, that here was the reason for her instinct and her life. She did not have to question herself, or any other. She did not have the temerity to say to God: *Why?* Let alone, *No, no.*

Her body felt light as cobweb. Her heart was engorged and beat like a gong.

She floated somewhere just above the ledge of the box, and oddly, her mother could not see this. And Hilde knew quite well that the man below, so near, so far, the Roman, she knew that he must also be intensely aware of her. For she blazed like a lamp, and he, being what he was, must see all things exactly. He would sense her, and look up. And so he did. Up to the box, his eyes flaming like stars, over and over. And then Hilde burned, and she must look away. But only, each time, for a moment.

The play, forgotten parts of which the squeaky governess may even have read to her, this time fixed itself into Hilde's mind. She was conscious of every iota of it, every histrionic, profound, and adult emotion. As if a door had been flung open before her, revealing a new world.

When it came time for the Roman to die, Hilde's gonging heart stopped. She felt herself die, too. And thereafter, what could she be save reborn?

She saw him again briefly, the actor-priest, taking his bows at the end of the play. He did this coldly and magnificently, as if to show them he had elevated the Host already, what more could they want? Only one further time did he raise his face toward Hilde's balcony. One ray (like a lighthouse). Then gone.

Hilde went home in the Koster carriage and in a dream, a trance. She had been ensorcelled.

"Hilde, eat your food."

"I'm sorry, Mama, I'm not hungry."

"What is the matter with the child. Are you unwell?"

"No, Mama."

They had not noticed how silent Little Hilde had become because she was generally a quiet, abstemious daughter, what they preferred.

"It's the weather," pronounced Monsieur Koster, "Eh, Hilde? Too hot. Take her for a drive, Lysette."

"We had a drive this morning, Solomon."

"Then probably the carriage was too stuffy."

"The carriage was perfect."

They lost interest in the carriage and Little Hilde, and Hilde was able to leave her unwanted luncheon for the maid to clear away.

As Hilde sat presently, her hands resting on an oval of unseen embroidery, she heard her mother speaking to a servant in the hall.

"We must have flowers there and there. And I shall want to see Cook. Some special light dishes that they can peck at like birds."

Hilde's mother was arranging an evening of guests, as she sometimes did. Madame Koster flowed back and forth and so into the sitting room, where she came to inspect Hilde's work. Hilde stitched at a rose.

"How listless you are," said Madame Koster. "Is it your time?" She was referring to Hilde's cycle of menstruation.

"No, Mama."

"I thought not. Well, you must liven up. You're becoming depressing. Tomorrow afternoon you must have a fitting for your new dress."

"Yes, Mama."

"What do you think?" said Madame Koster, a touch flustered all of a sudden. "Some of the theater people are coming to my little evening."

Hilde's hand stayed mute upon the rose.

"Well, you might show some interest, you tiresome girl. All lost in a world of your own. I don't think you need to meet my guests, but your father insists. You look so young and charming – why, you might only be eleven, except for your hair.... Perhaps we will have it dressed down for the night. It's so pretty that way."

Hilde's mother always saw Hilde as very young, and Hilde did not ever question this, nor why it was an extra delight to her mother if Hilde should remain very young. At this minute, in any case, she was not thinking of that.

"Who – will be coming to your party, Mama?"

"Oh, the two leading men of the company, Monsieur Roche and Monsieur Martin. And a couple of the ladies, I believe. But of course you've forgotten all about that important play. What a disappointment you were. Everyone else bubbling over and not a word out of you. I half think you slept right through it."

"Oh no, Mama."

"Well, then, who are Monseur Roche and Monsieur Johanos Martin?" demanded Mama, bridling. She was flushed, but exclaimed, "And well you should blush, Hilde, You've quite forgotten."

Hilde lowered her burning face.

"Monsieur Johanos Martin played the Roman."

"One out of two then," snapped Madame Koster.

She was a tallish woman, curvaceous, with fashionable apparent mounds of hair built up over padding on her skull. Her maid knew many of her secrets. The coiffeur, the rouge, the manner in which madame sometimes lost her temper as the corset refused to reduce her waist below twenty-four inches. Hilde's waist, uncorseted, was eighteen inches, and in its cage of bones became a flower stalk. Her hair grew in lush masses, her skin was fresh as if the dew were on it.

Sometimes the maid privately wondered if madame allowed Hilde so many sweets in hopes of extra girth, or blotches. Hilde had not wanted sweets this week.

"Your new frock is very lovely and young," said madame. "You'll grow up too fast. And you're such a baby."

In the dark ...

Hilde woke. She had been dreaming.

In the dream, the party had begun, and through the crowd of guests Hilde had found herself moving, not dressed as she should be, but in her long white nightgown, and her hair loose on her shoulders. No one had appeared to notice, and after her first terrifying shame, she began to think that perhaps she was dressed quite properly.

Then, by the open door that led onto the little terrace, he was standing. He wore black clothes, she could not make them out, not his costume from the play, certainly, yet neither anything everyday. A sort of soutane, perhaps, a priestly robe, belted close at the thin hard waist.

He had looked straight at her, Johanos Martin, the actor. And, impossibly, she had met his gaze, although her ears roared and her heart choked her.

Everyone else was gone. It did not matter how or where.

He held out his hand, which was ringless, beautiful, and Hilde went to him at once. He drew her out of the door onto the terrace.

Night had fallen, very black, yet with a sort of silver glow along the tops of the trees, and far away a light was shining that might have been the moon reflected on a window – such detail, in this dream.

"You are mine," Johanos Martin said to Hilde. "I promise I will be with you."

And in that exquisite second, she woke. She woke.

She lay stunned, not knowing, or caring, where she was, out of situation and time. And her body was alive, glowing and spangled by feeling within and without.

She had not, since she had seen him, somehow – she had not dared to touch. But now her hands stole to her body. She laid them on her breasts. And in the dark, eyes shut, she thought of his hands lying on her in this way, firm and cruel, capturing her breasts like birds. And then she thought that she would be afraid, half fainting, and he would hold her up, easily, and crush her mouth with his, as in a book she had once seen, a book of her mother's that perhaps she had not been meant to find, the drawing of a man kissing a woman fiercely in this way, holding her swooning and bent back as if he preyed on her.

Hilde trembled violently. Her stomach churned and sank and melted. Her fingers ran lightly down and touched her there, at last, in the secret place.

"I am yours," she whispered to Johanos Martin, as he bent her back, supporting her, his mouth on hers. And shivers of fire ran upward through her body, familiar and yet unique. Her loins seemed to rock at the impact of deep, rare blows. And the door that had opened in her brain flew open in her womb, showering her with suns and comets, shaking her end to end. She cried out before she could prevent it.

Two minutes later her maid came in with a lamp.

"What is it, Mademoiselle Hilde? You do look hot."

"A dream," muttered Hilde. The first time she had had to practice true deception.

"There, there. Well I must get on if you're better."

"Quite better, thank you."

The maid removed herself. Hilde wept. She did not know why. But she was racked again by tears silenced in the pillow that once, misunderstanding, she had kissed.

The magic art of the night sprang from him, then. He had sent it ahead of him. He too had always known. He and she.

Her innocence was gone, not her naïveté.

She scarcely slept again that night. The doll lay on the floor.

Madame Koster stood in her upstairs sitting room, turning about to regard her dress of ivory satin. From beyond her windows and their cumbersome drapes, the ripe westering light of the late summer evening flattered her with its glow.

A knock, and Little Hilde's maid entered.

"What is the matter with her?"

"She's been sick again, madame."

"Really. Such a stupid child. Well, I can't attend a sickroom now. She must be put to bed."

"Monsieur gave orders that Mademoiselle Hilde be given a glass of white wine."

"Did he indeed? How will that help? It will make her stomache worse."

"No, madame. He said it was very cooling, for the stomache, and that her vomiting was all nerves, so the wine will do her good."

"Nerves! What nerves? I am the one with nerves. She's just a child."

Along the passage in her room, Hilde sat pale as death on a sofa, staring at the glass of wine on the tray as if it were poison.

"Take a sip. It can't hurt."

The maid too was irritated. Madame took it out on her when the daughter did not turn out right.

"But I feel –" Hilde broke off, swallowing rapidly, like a cat before it pukes.

"Well, madame wants me downstairs, so I must go."

Hilde was only relieved to be left alone.

This was the hour of her most awful trial. She had longed for and dreaded this festivity of her mother's, not realizing her emotion would build to such a pitch that she would be made sick by it.

Suddenly she got up, and seizing the wineglass, she put it to her mouth. Like a despairing damsel in a play, she dashed the potion through her lips and swallowed all of it. Then she stood amazed.

Almost instantly her sickness swelled to an orchestral tumult – and perished. It was gone, leaving her light and slightly afloat. A pulse beat in her temples. Hilde laughed. This too was part of the magic. Her dear wise papa had helped her to safety. She had been lifted above the demons and made whole. For him, the one who would soon be with her.

In her turn, freed now, Hilde moved about to regard herself, her clothes and her hair.

Her mother had aimed for a veneer of complete childishness, but the dressmaker had maliciously somehow done something to the frock, so that it was merely very simple, very fresh. And the effect of the loose, slightly coiling amber hair gave, rather than the impression of a little girl, the look of one of the mysterious beauties of current paintings, maidens from legend, standing in bowers, as knights rode by.

Hilde was happy at herself, guessing this, not understanding. Happy to be lovely, not realizing that she was.

He would recognize her. As she had recognized him.

Half an hour later, she descended to the salon.

The event had already begun, and Madame Koster was at its hub. She looked at Hilde askance a moment, as if not knowing who she was. Perhaps sensible: Does one ever know another, or who they are, let alone a "child?"

But monsieur had not yet come in. He was, in fact, rather at odds with the party. It meant he must dress up very stiffly and parade his grandeur to impress them all, and this was onerous on such a hot evening.

There were many people in the salon. They drank from glasses of champagne. And since the servant came also to Hilde – again, was it some sort of conspiracy? – and offered her the drink, Hilde took it wonderingly, and sipped.

Then the crowd parted, and she saw the window that led out to the garden. No one was there. *He* was not.

Hilde sighed, and a fearful intimation of darkness crossed her, like the shadow of a huge, transparent crow.

Would he not come? Why should he come? Never before had actors been invited to these show gatherings. Why had her mother done it?

Oh, but it was all part of the starry plan, of destiny. It must be.

Three women approached Hilde. They were ladies she had met before, acquaintances of her mother's. Her heart slid down as if to hide itself.

"Why look, who's this? Is it Little Hilde? A young lady at last."

"What a becoming dress. How clever of your mother. And the hair's an exact copy of *Ygraine Waiting for Uther*."

"Do you have it brushed every night? One hundred strokes are essential."

A wing lifted off the room. Everything shifted slightly, an earth tremor.

Hilde's mother skated across the chamber. She met in the door the two tall actors from the Goddess of Tragedy. They were unmistakable. And all at once the crowd broke into applause.

Hilde thought: *For him.*

Fanfares of trumpets and showers of petals.

She drank all the champagne in her glass, the magic potion that, rather than make her invisible, would allow her to be seen.

She watched Monsieur Martin enter the salon.

Her mother deferred to him even more than to Monsieur Roche, who, walking behind, looked down the slope of his long face. No, it was Monsieur Martin that Madame Koster drew into the very core of her house, and kept there, so the wine could be rushed to him and the guests flutter up like greedy moths.

How cold he looked. Cruel, but one would not call it cruel, not if one wished for his kindness. Cold and cruel and closed and *set.*

Seen in life away from the stage, his face was pale, and the eyes were not black but a glacial gray. Nor was he handsome, yet there was that in his face which magnetized, some affirmation.

He did glance about him, but saw no one. Then he spoke graciously, and even smiled a little at the ones who clustered around him. He drank the champagne, several glasses of it.

Hilde remained at the edge of the congregation, like the shell in a story, left behind by the ghost of a primordial sea at the foot of the Temple-Church.

He would see her now, or now. And she waited for this finding gaze, this instant of pure acknowledgment, stretched taut as the string of a lyre. But it did not come.

And gradually something gave way a little at the center of her physical and etheric frame. Only a tiny derangement. It should have warned her. But how should she know it?

Presently they went into the supper room. Madame Koster sat at one end of the dainty table, and the actors sat either side of her, Monsieur Martin to her right. Monsieur Koster, who had blustered in after all, too late to be properly noticed, thumped down at the table's opposite end, and in the upheaval, no place had been allotted Hilde. So she sat among some of the men and women who knew her, in the bars of the trap of their patronage.

She could not eat a thing, but she sipped the wine. Some of the ladies noticed and disapproved. "That girl is taking too much. What is her mother thinking of?" "Of Johanos Martin," whispered another lady behind her fan.

Hilde did not hear this. She watched the lord who had given his promise to her in a dream, but carefully. It was not subtlety or care that made her careful. Rather she sensed the fire of herself, so bright, so piercing. She dared not be obvious.

He never looked her way.

Never.

After the supper, Monsieur Roche, a little tipsy, agreed to give a speech from the play. This was second best, but of course Johanos Martin would not perform. He had modestly and arrogantly refused.

Monsieur Roche, though the worse for wine, was very good.

The night had dropped like velvet on the garden. The lamps were lit along the paths, and up against the two small statues Monsieur Koster had had imported.

The guests walked in the soft air.

Madame Koster was arm in arm with Monsieur Martin. However had she achieved it? He looked disdainful, faintly amused. She seemed to take this for his interest.

Monsieur Koster was arguing about business in the salon with three gentlemen from a famous bank.

Hilde walked out between the hedges.

It had taken all her nerve, all the six glasses of wine she had consumed.

Unlike Monsieur Roche, Hilde Koster was not drunk. She was a maenad, given over to the god, and balanced in his hand. But had she mistaken the wrong god for the real one? For the real god of the wine is the god of self-knowing, dark twin of Apollo, black sun of opening and rebirth. Dionysos offers often painful truth with the wine, but he does not actually *lie*. Hilde's god, maybe, was all a lie, and that was what the look of affirmation was, a wonderful, successful sham. Like acting itself.

"Oh –" exclaimed Madame Koster. She was caught in the state known among mothers and daughters. Here was the fruit of her body, which she had loved, and perhaps still did love. Only not now a joy, but an interruption. Worse, a reminder.

And Johanos Martin looked from his height. And noticed Hilde.

She was very beautiful. Better than the poor little mutilated classical statues. Better by far than the women of the house. He did not want her, for he had already what he wanted. But still, he looked. At last, he saw.

"My daughter," said madame. "My little girl. Hilde. This is the great actor Johanos Martin."

Hilde gazed up, for a while half blinded by his eyes. Then she glanced down. She held out her hand because she had long ago been taught to do so. All sense had left her, it was automatic.

"Mademoiselle," said Johanos Martin. And he bowed.

That was all.

"Come," said Hilde's mother, "your glass is empty, monsieur." And she led him back toward the terrace by the window, where the servant had appeared with long glinting goblets.

"I'm afraid, madame, I must take my leave," said Monsieur Martin.

"But no – such a lovely night – this garden air is so good for you after –"

"Ah, madame, you must permit me to know what is good for me."

Madame Koster was speechless. Unfortunately, she had got used to people who rarely said what they meant.

And so he slipped from her clutches like the sea.

The two women, one middle-aged and sour, one young and blighted, stood on the walk and watched the cold priest stride away, back to his church of Tragedy.

In her room, Hilde became hysterical.

Naturally, she had not meant to. It was a reaction to the wine, and to grief. (Was Ophelia only drunk?)

She wept in the way one screams.

The maid ran for tired, soured madame.

And madame came like a storm.

"What is the matter with you? Ridiculous noisy child! Be *quiet!* Here I am with a migraine and all this racket."

Hilde tried to stay her tears, her shrieking sobs, for she was accustomed to obey.

But the grief was new. It ravaged her. She was torn. How, with her entrails ripped from her body, could she be calm and quiet?

"Well – what is it?"

"Oh, Mama –"

But Hilde did not say what it was. There is a knowledge beyond knowing. Besides, how to speak of the unspeakable? Persuaded to the throne of love, and pushed aside.

"Hurry – three drops of my mixture, quick. Give it her; for God's sake."

The drops were administered. On top of the wine they worked wonders. Hilde was violently sick again, and eventually, exhausted by these humiliations, tumbled into sleep.

Is death this? To wake in a vault and swim slowly upward, and there to meet the blows of memory?

O God – O God – But God had gone deaf.

In her virgin's bed, Hilde wept. Softly now, as after the ecstasy in the dark. Must not be heard. No one must find her. For who would help?

Her maid chided her for not arising. Then for not touching the invalid breakfast.

Madame came, and chided too.

Hilde lay like a wounded snake, spineless, broken.

Then she heard a woman, some gypsy, singing in the street. Servants from the houses chased her off. And Hilde wept again.

But then she thought, *He bowed to me.*

And she recalled how his eyes had, finally, seen her.

But her mother had been by. And all the people. And the lights.

Perhaps ...

Hilde got up and went to her mirror. She was so young, even after the outburst of anguish and tears, still she was what she had been. And somehow her youth infallibly told her she was not yet destroyed.

Of course, there were concerns surrounding him. In the story, the knight must win the notice of the lady. And she, Hilde, she must win his notice.

What could she take to him? Only herself. Surely he must see. Surely, surely, he must know.

She would die for him. That was enough. She must be brave. She must seek him out. Alone. Alone he could not fail to find her, as she, amid a crowd of hundreds, had found him.

Hilde washed and dressed and put up her hair and went down.

Monsieur Koster was at home, and beholding her, he beamed. He had heard she had been naughty, but now she was only his pretty, nice little daughter, his very own, that one day he would sell for a high profit in the marriage market Babylon of Paradys.

"Well, Hilde, got over your sulks?"

"Yes, Papa. I'm sorry, Papa."

"You mustn't be a bad girl. You worry your mother and then she worries your poor papa. A young lady must be demure and gentle. Loving and giving. Docile. Not these unbecoming tantrums and noise."

Hilde drifted past a mirror, and some radiant, true, but deceiving part of her called in her soul: *No one can ignore this. This youth and bloom, this being and nature.*

Loving and giving.

THREE

Paradise

Who put the "art" in heart, the "pain" in paint,
and the ice in Pardise?

John Kaiine

Smara walked through the night mist of the City, under her floating lamp. One hand she kept against the rough and stony, dripping surfaces of walls. In the other, she carried a long and slender knife. This was her left hand. She was naturally right-handed but had trained herself to left-handedness. It had been her first curtsy to the craziness of her world.

She was on the path beside a canal. A snake, perhaps, glicked and eddied through the water, but she could not see it, only the blurred ripples picked up by the lamp.

Then, footsteps.

Smara waited, and a man came from the mist. He wore graceful gray garments, and a mask like a black bird.

"Beloved – how extraordinary to meet you here," he exclaimed. And held out his arms to Smara.

She went to him, and plunged the knife slantwise into his throat. Blood sprayed like thick drops of jet, some hitting the lamp in the air, but it quickly shook them off.

The man soon fell dead on the towpath, and Smara bent over him. She removed from his finger a ring of twisted bronze, and then dragged the bird mask from his face. Beneath he too had the face of a bird, beaked nose, tiny mouth, protuberant sideways eyes. Smara held her breath in dismay.

She stood up and hurried away, having only paused to wipe her knife on the bird man's sleeve.

The third bridge had long ago collapsed into the river. It was feasible to go halfway across it, and then to jump into the mercury-colored water and swim for shore. To those who sat in the bar above the strand, the intermittent splashes of these jumps were broadcast spasmodically.

577

A woman danced naked on a table to the tune of a comb.

Felion sat drinking from a jug of water drawn out of the river. It was highly toxic, more inebriating than any liquor.

Smara went to him and gave him the ring. There was a trace of blood on it. He put it on, and handed her four brushes of wonderful springing hair.

"He was painting shells on the ground in the porch of the church. A shame it was a painter I killed. He was quite talented. But the shells will stay. He didn't smudge them as he convulsed all over the stone."

"Mine wore a bird mask," said Smara.

She drank some water and closed her eyes. She was very pale.

A man came by with a tray of lizard-scaled, fanged fish snared from the river. Felion bought one, and put it into his drink. It revived and swam about. He threw it from an open smashed window, back into the river.

"What are we to do?" said Smara. "Oh, what?"

"Let's go into our uncle's labyrinth."

"No," she said. "No."

"Let me remind you of his will. He had accrued property and funds in the other city – the *sane* city. These riches would come to us. We could live there."

"But to walk through the ice …"

"Don't be afraid," he said. His face was beautiful with compassion. "Smara, what can hurt us worse than *here*?"

"I must kill again," she said abruptly.

"All right. Let's finish the jug, and then we'll go together."

Now she nodded. He refilled her glass twice, thrice.

A woman came by selling human eyes set into rings.

"How lovely," said Smara.

"They won't last," said the woman. "I'll sell you one for a kiss."

"Then kiss me."

The woman kissed her, briskly, and gave her one of the rings. The eye in it was pure, a crystal spherical gray.

"How much better than the ring I brought you."

Felion took her hand. "When we go out, you can throw it away."

She nodded. Two silver tears ran suddenly from her eyes. "I try so hard. It's as if I must. Do you remember Mother?"

"She's dead," he answered absently.

"I wish –"

"No, you don't wish that. Let's live. Come on, we'll kill."

They left the bar together and walked along the pebbly strand. From the banks of the City, gleams and glares spilled into the water. Someone leapt off the bridge and drowned.

"This way," he said. He led her up, onto the embankment, and then they turned into the upper City.

Out of the charcoal fog of nighttime Paradise, the open doorways gaped, shining. Here and there processions of citizens passed, chanting and banging gongs, or weeping, or utterly silent.

"Where are we going?" she said.

"To the Clock Tower Hill."

"Dogs run in the streets there," she said.

"Yes," he said, "and when we kill, it will feed them."

So they climbed up the heights of Paradise.

A bell was ringing in the cranium of the cathedral, but when they reached Clock Tower Hill, only the ticking of ancient apparatuses, mimicking clocks, was to be heard, and an occasional snarl.

Felion and Smara found people dancing around a bonfire and lured them off one by one, and sliced them to death in the shadows.

After about an hour of this, only two were left dancing by the fire. Felion and Smara joined them briefly, then stole away.

"Where now?"

"You know where, Smara."

"No, I won't."

"*Please.*"

They stood beneath a street lamp that still burned with a cold luminescence. Smara's personal lamp had faded.

"I won't enter the labryinth of our uncle."

"Then I must do it by myself."

Smara turned from him.

Lightless, she moved away like a ghost, down a slim alleyway under broken casements, into the fog.

As he climbed back up the hundred steps to his uncle's mansion, Felion experienced a partly irritated excitement.

When he gained the house, and it had let him in, he went at once to his uncle's study, or workroom, on the second floor. The room was built into a sort of tower and jutted out over the abyss of the steps. In the darkness, anything might have been below, a cliffside, even some sluggish silent sea.

Felion activated the mechanical lights, and then, sitting at the great black worktable, he reread portions of the rambling letter his uncle had left for him. (Smara, of course, had never consulted it.)

All about lay bizarre machines that did not now work, and which perhaps never had, and arrested experiments involving vials of glass and transparent plastic, coils of metal, balances, and fluids that had solidified. Over these the damp dust formed a second skin, in parts thick and vegetable as moss.

"... I am a scientist who has always longed to be a poet," said the sonorous and self-indulgent letter. "Where, after all, is the difference? Scribbling down on scraps of paper equations and potential formulae, or snatches of mystical words, couplets that rhyme. My labyrinth is also a sonnet. It has its own meter, its own intrinsic meaning. One must reach the heart, and then the farther side, and so new knowledge. This requires concentration, but not necessarily courage. Nothing mechanistic can be taken into the maze. No watch or other timepiece, no devices for measuring. Not even a gun, should you or your sister have come across such a weapon on your karma-collecting activities of murder. No mechanical lamp. You may use one of the torches I have prepared and left for you; each needs only a match to light it. As you pass through the ice of the labyrinth, the torch may melt it a little, but that is to the good. There will then always be a limit on the number of occasions you may go in and out. This isn't a game. You will have to decide whether you want your inheritance, a life in the second city beyond the maze."

Felion glanced about the study. One of the unreliable lamps fluttered, as if winking at him. He turned the page, and read:

"I myself am not in fact approaching death. But I am going away. I won't confuse you by attempting to explain. My first identity I established through a connection – false – to a pair of people in the partially rational City. Metal, which as you know is valueless in Paradise, is almost priceless here. With such a fortune I have done much as I liked but mostly kept to myself. The half-sanity of this second world is in some ways disturbing. I have, obviously, left a will in this place that recognizes such things, and it names you both. I am also the (spurious) uncle or guardian to many persons here, but only one might have proved an obstacle. She is a painter and will find my cash useful. You need not fear she is in your way. Probably she will drink herself to death quite soon. Her madness attracted me to her, although she is not insane in the manner of Paradise, would get no glances there."

The flirtatious lamp went out. Felion shuffled the pages of the letter and held them toward another light.

"The exit from the labyrinth is always subjective. It is controllable only by will. Maybe you won't be strong enough to operate journey's end with any skill. I must warn you, too: The labyrinth, because it is modeled on a brain, and therefore inevitably upon mine, may open randomly to show you one other particular place, or time, where I have gone, or am going. For time slips in the labyrinth, and it is possible to travel into the past. I have never attempted the future, in case the future of the second city should be as dismal as the present of Paradise. You would do best to ignore these latter past excursions. The place involved would not appeal to you, although I have seen its potential and indeed, because I am insane, found it in my destiny to go there. Avoid it yourself, however – it is not for you. Keep your mind on the present parallel world I offer. The woman painter will soon die, and then you can do as you wish. You can even kill in the second city, if you want. I myself have done so, although only once. It was the day that my two introductory people became curious about me, quite suddenly, after a drinking party. On the pretense of playing with their vehicle, I destroyed something in its engine, and an hour later both of them were killed on one of the vast highways that now run over this city. I may add that in the past of the City, I have slain no one. But I believe, even so, there will be death there."

Felion skimmed through the final pages of the letter. They were repetitious and increasingly disordered.

But a little later he found the antique torches in a cupboard, and above on a shelf a box of matches, with some eccentric items, among which were two wooden dolls of Smara's, a necklace, and half a brown glass bottle with a shattered neck.

When Felion had got down to the basement and walked along the track, he reached the cavernous hall that housed the labyrinth, and now he looked at it wryly. That it should truly be the route to another world, and to other planes of time, seemed unlikely. And yet how horrifying it was, this wall of ice, shimmering, and drily wet, in the torchlight.

Like the prince in the legend, he could go in, holding up the torch, and knife in hand. (Smara should have been the priestess who stood to guard the entrance.) And in the maze, at its heart, would be a monster.

Felion listened and heard a faint roaring, like the quake of ocean captured on a screen. But it was only the blood sounding in the shells of his ears.

Suppose he went in, and it was a reality, and he could not get back? He considered Smara, alone in Paradise. In childhood, when they had begun to kill, they had formalized the slaughter, devising a ritual of changing implements. Blades, then cords, then poisons, before blades again. Of these means, Smara found the use of cords, the method of strangling, the most difficult. Generally she needed his help. And if he were not there, she might not manage the act efficiently, and die in turn.

He could burn his uncle's letter – even burn down the mansion, if necessary. Or he could merely leave at once and never come back.

But he was sane, surely, that was the whole trouble, and his sanity insisted he investigate the maze. Smara would not need to begin to kill again for some days. Even if it took him a week to return … And then again, would he not anyway reemerge into Paradise at the hour, minute, or moment he had left it? Pieces of the complex wandering letter had seemed to tell him this.

Felion walked across the floor, toward the white wall. It came nearer and nearer. And then he was against it. He touched the surface with his finger, and it was *cold*.

Holding the torch high, the knife in his right hand – he had been left-handed but trained himself otherwise – he entered the arched opening.

At once, everything was altered. Became absolute. Although he could still see the entry point behind him, the wall of ice towered up and up and disappeared into an indescribable nothingness above that was not mist or space – or anything.

The labyrinth was freezing, like a winter, described to Felion in bits of rotten books. The ice breathed out a faint vapor that swirled around the nasturtium tatter of the torch.

There was a smell he recognized, if only from a laboratory. Not chemical. What had it been called?

The ground was like muddied glass. (He was reminded of the shattered bottle.)

Sounds came, rushes, like seas, like … blood moving in the ear. And he felt a slight vertigo. But then that would be proper, if the balance of matter had been disturbed.

He moved forward, following the left-hand turnings of the wall.

He believed in the labyrinth now, as he had not done when outside. He believed that it was real, and apt, and led to somewhere. His thoughts of Smara dwindled. The archway had vanished out of sight.

The first specter – hallucination, vision, element of elsewhere – spun suddenly at him, it seemed from the wall. He had not anticipated this, and despite his uncle's warning (*The labyrinth may open randomly to show you one other place or time*) had not understood what the notation might mean.

It was like a surge of the fog that clung about Paradise, but in this fog were lights, shapes, voices. Felion heard a frightful shriek, but he had grown used to shrieking. Then the sight of women was before him, ugly women and one very beautiful in a dark fur cap, or else her hair was fur. Another of the women had been struck down. She lay full-length, and the beautiful one bent abruptly to her, touching gently – and then the mirage was gone.

Felion had stopped. He shouted, "Ah! Uncle!" And then, softly, "O my prophetic soul!" And then he grinned. And saw his grinning shadow reflected from the torch into the ice wall.

Stupid to hesitate. He had had the warning and not heeded it. But the *thing* had done him no harm. No, this was not the Minotaur of the labyrinth.

Felion strode on. He whistled a tune of the bars and dives of Paradise. The walls obligingly caught it up hollowly and it echoed back to him.

The second vision came quite mildly. It was like an aperture, filling the area between the walls, the ice-rink floor, and the illimitable ceiling. He saw a dry, tawny lawn, grass, without mist, rising up to a weird house of glass. And in the glass an enormous vine was growing with bursting black fruit.

He moved toward it, and wondered for an instant, if this was the exact exit point, but certainly he had not come far enough.

And the picture smeared, crumpled, and gave way. And there the labyrinth of ice went on.

"Smara," Felion said.

He looked back. Could he *turn* back now?

Then he cursed his uncle, an awkward obscenity, for Paradise no longer had a God, a religion, or any regularized views of sexuality, to form the substance of oaths.

Felion walked on. He did not whistle.

He came around a turn, and a silver insectile web hung across the labyrinth. In the web a woman sat, her tongue protruding, and snakes for hair.

She was gone in three seconds.

And instead, he found he had reached the heart of the maze.

The heart was empty.

An oval region, with one way in from the convolutions of the ice, and a second way out.

In the floor was a stealthy mark, but it only looked as if something had scratched the surface, without intent. It was not a rune, a message, a cipher.

Felion raised the torch high again.

He recalled the woman who painted and would drink herself to death. He did not think she was one of those he had glimpsed in the hallucinatory visions. But now, standing in the womb of the ice, he credited that other world beyond, which his uncle had named, as if jestingly, *Paradis*.

Felion spent a few minutes at the core of the maze (the empty heart), and then he went on through the outleading arch, and continued, keeping to the left-hand wall.

Felion was primed now for further demons, but nothing occurred.

Nothing occurred until he came around one of the twines of ice and saw in front of him an arch of purest nothing.

It was not like the etheric tapering-off of the ceiling. It was a sort of omission from sight. He did not like to look at it. He looked away.

Here was the end. The *egress*.

Perhaps it was all a joke. A hoax.

Perhaps the labyrinth opened into hell, whatever hell was. Or heaven. Or into colossal snows. Or the sea.

The exit could not be relied on. His will might not be able to control it.

Felion's will was strong. He and Smara had wills of iron and flame.

He glared again at the vacant arch and said aloud, "Her house. The painter who inherited from my uncle. *There*."

And as he said it he thought, *Maybe, in this other world, there are no houses. Maybe they drift in the air –*

But the archway convulsed. It filled.

He saw a room, in shadow.

And with a howl, Felion ran between the walls, and out into that room. While as he did so, the torch puffed into darkness.

The house of the artist.

He had made it be, at the tunnel's end.

Everything about the room (he deduced it was a room) was totally uncanny to him. It was not that the furnishings and accoutrements were so alien. But no mist hung over it, and above a skylight showed rich, black night.

An easel of metal stood in the room. And elsewhere were stacked canvases, and there, a long table littered with paints, and all an artist's accessories.

He had accomplished his objective.

Felion kept still, and felt after the psyche of the house. The house of the woman who painted and drank. Who was the heir to his uncle's fortune in this other world.

And the house was like a casket, chock-full of nothing. Empty, like the labyrinth's heart.

Felion looked up.

And in the black pane of glass, he could see – *stars*.

Stars.

Felion kneeled on the floor of the studio in the parallel world of Paradis. He prayed to something that had no name.

Later, he investigated the room, but only superficially. He did not move anything from its appointed place.

When he eventually looked around for the way back into the labyrinth – this first time he was quickly satisfied, entirely overwhelmed – he could not see it.

But when he beat his head against the wall, crying, "Smara – Smara –" the wall gave way, and there it was.

As he stepped through, shuddering and hot with fear, the great cold came, and the dead torch – which all this time he had kept in one hand, the knife in the other – mysteriously revived.

He ran through the labyrinth, then. He ran through the heart of it, up against the right-hand wall.

And when he sprang out again into the cavern under the mansion of his uncle, he screamed.

Every stone reiterated his cry. He lay on the ground beside the track, hearing it, and the torch guttered out once more.

The initial killing had been a little like this. But then he had had no additional puzzlement. He had gone to Smara with a severed hand, and shown her, and they had marveled together over the whorls of its fingertips. But now, how, how to tell Smara of *this*?

FOUR

Paradis

Mary, Mary, quite contrary,
How does your garden grow?
With silver bells, and cockle shells,
And pretty maids all in a row.

Nursery Rhyme

Leocadia remained calm.

Like any sentence of death, she did not believe it.

Even after she had taken up her new life, her food and music and drink supplied, books delivered, as she wished, paints and canvas, drawing materials, notebooks, clothes, powder, everything, even then in the hermetic environ of her prison she did not believe in it. Not wholly. Not with her mind.

Was that, after all, a form of madness, then?

Even after she had sorted the pieces, grasped the plot. Accepted that her very calm itself must come from minuscule tasteless particles in her food, and in the air itself, which did not restrain her creative flair or her energy, or ability to concentrate, but which must be controlling her. Not even then.

And as she went to and fro from her room in the daylight summer hours, having found she might, and met in the corridor and garden other inmates of the Residence, who were genteel and well-mannered, sometimes bemused, excitable, but never abusive, loud, or agonized, not then either.

Until in the end even her mind knew, and it was too late, she had accepted it.

For, though powerless, she should have resisted. In some fashion, however oblique or useless.

Her asides to the doctors – *I'm anxious to leave, I'll tell visitors how you torture me* – were not protests or shields, let alone missiles. It was almost a repulsive flirtation, her acid quips, their smirking refutations.

And how did her life differ? She did much as she had always done. She spent a vast amount of time alone. She painted. True, the elegant dinners were gone, but had she ever really enjoyed them? True, she had no lovers, but surely it might be possible, if she were desperate, to seduce some person or other, their bizarre quality or nasty appearance offending her not at all in the onslaught of needy lust. And then again, if she could not be bothered with such unappetizing creatures, this must mean her sexuality burned low, she had had enough.

She missed walking in the City. But then, too, months had sometimes passed without her venturing more than two streets from her house.

Now she did not explore the asylum grounds. A low fence lay across the grass and trees the far side of the gravel walk, beyond the broken hothouse. It was easy to climb the fence, and now and then some inmate might scramblingly do so. But they returned from wandering among the old buildings of the madhouse disconsolate, once or twice crying.

It occurred to Leocadia that she kept the blocks of the madhouse in reserve, making of them something mystical and bad, against the ultimate rainy day of terrifying ennui.

"Oh dear, you're too late, I must go down now," Mademoiselle Varc had said to Leocadia when Leocadia first left her room and found the white woman in the corridor. "If only you had come sooner." And then she scurried to the elevator.

Leocadia then did not see Mademoiselle Varc for several weeks.

Instead she confronted Thomas the Warrior, who might once have been a wealthy old soldier, that in his youth had conceivably seen action in some small foreign war, tanks and carrier planes, and the threat of worse. Now he puffed about a flowerbed he was in charge of, below the summerhouse. It was a wonder of blooms and stone slabs, on top of one of which stood a stone head of Medusa poking out her tongue.

Thomas was elderly, thin and stooped. He paid Leocadia no attention, only speaking to his flowers. Doctor Saume had informed her of his name.

Three or four more went about the garden regularly, and some of the other older ones would bask nervously in the summerhouse. Males and females, they were sad and frequently decrepit, moaning with stiffness that even contemporary medication had not been able to alleviate.

The most immature of those she saw was a young man, possibly twenty-five years old, who crouched along like a dismembered spider. He frowned at unseen things, but meeting humans he usually brightened for a moment, telling them how well and lovely they looked. But of Leocadia he seemed afraid, and ran away and hid behind objects as she approached, even behind Thomas the Warrior and his Medusa, if nothing else were available.

Only Mademoiselle Varc actually greeted Leocadia, now thinking her her maid, her niece, her nurse, and once or twice some kind of empress or queen that she had perhaps been introduced to long ago. On these latter occasions Mademoiselle Varc curtsied, and Leocadia had felt a sudden compulsion, in case Mademoiselle Varc fell over. This was the first compassion Leocadia had ever experienced for a being other than an animal. And so Mademoiselle Varc amused Leocadia, and Leocadia was careful, in her contrary way, always to attempt to be the one she was mistaken for.

Probably the strangest time had been when Mademoiselle Varc had taken Leocadia for an old schoolfriend, and both women had then seemingly become adolescent girls. They had sat under the summerhouse in the shade of the trees, and Mademoiselle Varc had confessed she had no idea what a man and a woman did together. Leocadia had told her a carefully constrained amount, and Mademoiselle Varc had giggled girlishly, even blushed, though Dr. Duval had revealed that Mademoiselle Varc had borne six children.

When she had returned from the sun-fallen garden, kindly driven in with Mademoiselle Varc by the warden in his dark uniform (before the trees could come alive and eat them), Leocadia stepped into the dusk of her room and heard the door shut with its final click, which meant her little freedom was gone until tomorrow.

There was autonomy in the way of lamps, and she switched them on in the sitting area of the room, and going to the refrigerator, she drew out a bottle of white wine and a narrow glass.

Then she moved into the painting area and turned on the working lights.

On its easel, the picture of the ship, the beach, the spillage of oranges.

Leocadia studied it coldly.

Was it some response to the other thing upon an easel? Asra, raped and choked with orange paint, her bare flesh adorned by islands.

The doctors who had oozed charm over this painting had seen it as such; they must have done.

But she, what had she been doing?

The ship was not Asra, and yet the ship was feminine. And the sea had split her, and she ... bled.

Leocadia drank her wine. A swirl of panic rose deep within her like a beast in a bottomless lake. How long before it would reach her surface?

She tossed the glass against the wall, where it broke. Later the wall would suck up the bits.

But not quite yet.

So interesting, the knives for her food, the glasses that might be smashed.

Leocadia went close to the painting. Yes, it could well be seen as some expression of inner horror at Asra's murder, which murder she had performed, and then forgotten.

Massed sky, the vessel with its snapped wing. And the little shells she had added. And there – what was *that*?

She leaned nearer. She could not make it out. Something white on the sand, a small distance from the shells. But not a shell.

She had not painted it. She did not know what it was.

Then again, it was done in her style, in tiny feathering brushstrokes, half its curve delineated as if cut.

Of course, they could copy her.

Leocadia crossed the room and turned about the two paintings she had previously executed here.

One a scene of a mountain, smoking over a peaceful valley. The other, a road leading into a wood. Both were dark, lowering, sinister. Neither contained a hint of orange, or any image she did not recall putting into them.

Leocadia dreamed not of distant bells but of screaming. It was full-throated and savage. It echoed and swerved through the building of the Residence. On Thomas's stone the Medusa poked out her tongue farther.

Leocadia woke up, and got out of the bed, which squeaked its incontinence plastic at her.

She went to the worktable and picked up a tube of orange paint, which she had employed without thought, as if to prove her innocence.

She uncapped it, and squeezed.

The tube screamed.

It screamed in her hand.

Leocadia kept hold of it. As her fingers relaxed, the scream stopped.

She put it on the table and pressed down on the tube with her whole hand.

Now the scream came vivid and awesome, rocking the room, dizzying her ears.

As it faded, she heard an afternote, like the boom of a massive organ in the Temple-Church twenty miles away.

Not me, Leocadia thought, concisely. It was the drugs in the food and drink, and in the light and sound and air. Or could it even be some other trick, like the orange that bled, the white ball entered in her painting?

"Or is it me?"

She seemed to stand above herself on a height, looking down into her soul, not with brief compassion, as she had gazed at the curtsying Mademoiselle Varc, but despisingly, as if at an expensive, once-reliable machine, which failed.

"Come along, Lucie," cried Mademoiselle Varc. "I've found such an interesting place. It's rather dirty, but you won't mind, will you? You're always braver than me."

Leocadia had been sitting on the hot lawn near the empty birdbath, and now Mademoiselle Varc came up and filled the bath with cold tea from her breakfast pot.

Lucie was the adolescent friend, but she and Mademoiselle Varc seemed to have grown even younger.

Leocadia was not in the mood now for role playing.

"Not today," she said, as if to a fractious infant.

But Mademoiselle Varc took no notice. She put down her alabaster hand and caught Leocadia's arm.

"Come *on*. Before they catch us."

Leocadia guessed correctly from this expression that although it was not in fact barred to them, Mademoiselle Varc wanted to go over the fence to the madhouse.

"No."

"Oh, yes. Oh do. It's really fascinating. There's all sorts of things there. I found it last week, but I didn't tell."

"No one will prevent you, if you go," said Leocadia.

"But they will. They'll spank us. It's an awful place. You know something terrible happened there. You're not scared? I dare you, Lucie."

"Of course, something terrible," said Leocadia. "What else, there?"

The old lunatic asylum. Not like the modern Residence. There had been a story about it, but then was that not the other story about the shells – that the sea had washed in over the building? No, this could never be right.

Leocadia got up as Mademoiselle Varc tugged at her like a ferocious moth.

They hurried by the summerhouse, passing Thomas the Warrior. The young spider man was creeping along and raised his face in delight to Mademoiselle Varc, saw Leocadia and lolloped away.

They rushed across the walk, and over the grass. Oak trees and gray cedar towered above them. Then there was the dilapidated fence.

It was like a boundary in a dream. But Leocadia reasoned she had perhaps already, the previous night, crossed whatever boundary there was.

Mademoiselle Varc tottered over and sat abruptly in the uncut grass the far side, but laughing.

Leocadia followed more easily.

The sun burst on the ruined hothouse and the raisin vine, black, as if mantled with bursting tarantulas.

"We have to go among the old buildings," said Mademoiselle Varc.

"Very well."

Marigolds grew wild in the long grass (and Leocadia thought of the marigolds in ice, which had prevented nothing) and pure white daisies.

Mademoiselle Varc stumbled, but she was a little girl again, only about ten, and she made nothing of it.

"Do you believe in ghosts?" she asked Leocadia. "If you look at the windows you might see them. Even by day. Women in a row."

Leocadia shrugged. She raised her eyes to the foul blank windows, seen closer now than ever before, but they were dead as ever, the optics of corpses.

Pipes thick with rust coiled from the walls of the buildings like flexible bones which had pierced the skin.

They came onto a paved place sprung with weeds. The buildings loomed above.

"This way. Down here."

Mademoiselle Varc led Leocadia toward a sort of alley between the light biscuit walls.

There was no sound. That was, one heard the sizzling chorus of cicadas, and the tweets of passing birds; insects buzzed among the rogue flowers. High, high in the sky, a plane purred almost silently over, a silver cigar with fins. All these ordinary noises. And yet, it was like the loud singing in the ear of utter soundlessness. And everything so still, as if, rather than stunned by heat, the area had been frozen.

The alley was drowned in shade.

Mademoiselle Varc darted along it in quick marsupial spasms.

Above, the ranks of corpse windows, black with grime and weather and time. From the pipes hung cakes of filth.

The alley opened in a square, around which the buildings of the madhouse reared and onto which the windows continued to stare without sight. Three big doorways seemed shut like the gates of hell.

And in the center of the square was a great heap of rubbish, stretching up five meters or more, as if constructed over some more solid base.

"See – see –" Mademoiselle Varc sprang at the garbage mountain eagerly.

Noises were fainter here, and though the sun splashed in between the roofs, it was like being in a new block of bright, thick atmosphere.

Mademoiselle scrabbled at the grisly pile.

"There!"

Leocadia observed.

She saw Mademoiselle Varc was holding up a gleaming rope of syrup, a necklace of amber beads.

How bizarre. How could such a delicacy have been overlooked? Unless Mademoiselle Varc herself had deposited them here, in order to "find" them.

Leocadia glared into the coalescence of rubble. And as she did so, she felt the eyeless windows watching, as if sudden specters had gathered behind their masks.

A pile of garbage. Old newspapers, a destroyed chair raised high as a throne. And lower down, slabs of tin and wool and corrosion.

"Look!" squeaked Mademoiselle Varc.

She raised a wooden doll with jointed arms and legs and black cotton hair.

How was she finding these things? She must have placed them here, her treasures.

"Here's another," said Mademoiselle Varc, and pointed Leocadia into the heap of debris. A wooden limb poked out, and sure enough another wooden maiden emerged into Leocadia's hands. This one had flax hair and cool glass eyes.

"I wonder what else we shall get?"

It was a festival. It was a barrel of goodies into which you must plunge your fingers.

Something was dislodged from higher up and swiveled down the rubbish with a frantic sound.

It fell at Leocadia's feet.

"Oh just see. It's given you something."

Leocadia bent down and raised the artifact.

It was an old brown bottle, curiously shaped, square, with a four-sided neck and a four-sided mouth. On the front, a label. It showed clearly a weird landscape of ice and glaciers, and before them a black and white penguin with a marigold flash beside its beak. Above, the name. *Penguin Gin.*

Leocadia examined the bottle in a trance. It was very old. It was clean, and bright. The penguin pleased her, for it was realistically portrayed, and into her head came the thought: *I have a model now. I can paint penguins.*

"Yes, I've heard of it," said Mademoiselle Varc, peering over. "There was a slogan for that gin." She held a wooden doll in either hand, the amber beads about her neck, along her whiteness. "Penguin Gin, it eases pain."

"Not in your youth, surely," said Leocadia.

"Oh no. Long before. Long, long ago."

Something shuddered in the pile of rubbish. A thin black smoke uncoiled from it.

"That's enough," cried Mademoiselle Varc. "We must go."

She sprinted back into the alley.

Leocadia turned slowly, watching the deadly walls above. Nothing was in the windows.

But she would take the bottle. She would paint penguins.

Someone knocked on the door to Leocadia's room, the way the female attendant did when she brought a hot meal.

"Yes," said Leocadia.

The door was opened.

It was eleven o'clock in the morning, and the doctors, when they came, arrived at five in the evening. Yet here was Van Orles, all alone.

"What do you want?"

"Why, to see you, mademoiselle."

Leocadia wore her cream housedress, which had so generously been sent to the asylum for her. She had no makeup on. She had been about to don her working smock and prepare a canvas.

Van Orles looked at her insidiously.

"Here I am, as you see," said Leocadia.

"Well, shall we have a little talk?"

"If we must."

"Always so bristly!" merrily chided Van Orles, and he came bouncing into the room. He wore another of his pasty cravats. Sitting down on the couch he lit a pipe. Leocadia opened the second window. "You never ask for cigar-ishis," said Van Orles. "Don't you miss them?"

"I seldom bothered with them. They had no effect on me."

"Yet still you drink."

Leocadia propped up a canvas on her table.

"And you began to drink when you were eleven years old, I understand."

When Leocadia did not reply, Van Orles puffed away at his pipe as if considering her silence an answer.

Leocadia was irritated. She did not like to work with anyone near her, as all her lovers had soon discovered. She went to the dressing table and began to brush her curling hair with harsh strokes.

"What a lovely girl you are," murmured Van Orles. "Don't you miss other things? Companionship? Dalliance?"

A faint livid light was ominously blooming up from nowhere. She tensed. The distasteful man seemed to be making a pass at her. Leocadia swung slowly around and smiled at him. Van Orles appeared taken aback. Leocadia lifted the brown bottle off the dressing table where it had lain through the afternoon and night.

"Look at this, Where do you think I got it?"

"I've no idea."

"In a junk heap in a yard of the old building."

"Which building is that?" he inquired innocently.

"The madhouse."

"Ah. How quaint. The lunatic hospital. Really, that place should be walled off. The masonry isn't safe."

"Don't you think it's a pretty bottle?" said Leocadia. "Quite old itself, I should say, from its shape."

"Very likely." Van Orles got up carefully and came to stand over Leocadia. "And you are interested in such items?"

"Oh, yes. Why don't you tell me about the madhouse?"

"Now, we shouldn't call it that. They were awful days. The poor sick people weren't treated well. Sometimes they were even displayed to the public, to make others laugh. Immorality and disease ran rife –"

"But what happened?" said Leocadia.

"How do you mean?" Van Orles crouched closer.

Leocadia hit him quite hard on the hand and stood up. She moved away.

Van Orles looked happy. He presumably thought he was being teased, a preliminary.

"I mean," said Leocadia, "something curious took place, didn't it? The madhouse was suddenly closed down."

"Oh, there is some story – a warder was killed, and someone disappeared. Perhaps the inmates attacked the staff for their brutish treatment. But one shouldn't set too much store by tales."

Leocadia held the bottle labeled *Penguin Gin* up to the window. For a moment a screaming and contorted face seemed to writhe inside it, but it was only the action of sunlight and the shadow of ivy on the wall.

"Is that all you know, or all you'll say?" asked Leocadia.

Van Orles chuckled. He seemed to think Leocadia's prurient intriguement was a form of foreplay. Gruesome details of the lunatics might arouse her.

"There was a rumor of a ghost. A great dark thing. Very tall, gliding through the corridors. And something about a bad winter. I can't recall."

"Then," said Leocadia, "I think I'll go out for a walk."

"Now, now, not yet. I must perform a small check on your physical well-being."

Leocadia turned from her worktable, the palette knife in her hand. The glare of light was around him like a halo, the warning phenomenon that had come before.

"But I am violent," she said. "And I might not care for this small check."

"Ah –" Van Orles stepped away. He was still smiling, the smile a daisy left behind by a retreating tide. "Now, Leocadia –"

"If you touch me," said Leocadia, "if you come in here again alone, I will set on you." She was tepid, easy. She had had to threaten others. Generally they accepted her terms. And so did Van Orles.

"You are being most unreasonable, Leocadia. Merely because I can't satisfy your ghoulish curiosity about the lunatics."

"But *I'm* a lunatic," said Leocadia. "How can you trust yourself with me? What would the other doctors say if they knew?"

Leocadia walked to the door ahead of Van Orles and opened it. She went into the corridor. Van Orles stood lost in the middle of the room. Leocadia threw the knife back there, so it whirled past his head. He yelped and ducked low, and his pipe fell on the floor.

"I shall have to report this," said Van Orles.

"And also, of course, that you came to me by yourself, for how else did it happen?"

She did not want to leave him in her room, and sure enough, when she stood right back, he came hurrying out.

"You've turned nasty, Leocadia."

He hastened away.

Probably, she had been ill-advised. She was not free now, and doubtless to make such an enemy was unwise.

Outside, it was hot, the sun going up to the zenith. In the summerhouse the old ones lay like spoilt seals. Thomas was not at his garden. No one was anywhere.

Leocadia looked across the grass and gravel, between the trees to the buildings.

Cries in the night – of course. The sheer misery and abjection of that place had been recorded in its stones. But she, had she now come to the hiatus, the point where she must, even physically, pass over into her new life? The low fence symbolized this.

She could kill herself. They must mean her to, leaving all the handy knives and glasses for her. But first, there was the landscape with the penguin to paint.

Leocadia walked along the fence, not crossing it.

Large chestnut trees arose, and under their canopy she came upon the spider man sitting, looking where she looked, toward the madhouse.

Seeing her, he jumped up.

"Wait," snapped Leocadia.

He gave a wild cry. He ran, not like a spider now but a wounded hare. He rushed at the fence and sprawled across it and charged on toward the madhouse walls.

Leocadia got over the fence also, and holding up her long skirt, she ran after him grimly. Her legs were long and slim and strong; she was soon close.

"Stop," she commanded, but he shrieked and bolted away.

He chased along the paved space under the windows.

Swearing, she caught him in both hands, letting her skirt go.

He hooted, went down, and crawled at her feet.

"I won't," he said. "I won't."

"You will," she said. "Why are you afraid of me?"

"Weasel," said the young man. He touched Leocadia's sandaled foot, tore back his hand as if she burnt.

"I am not a weasel. I wish I were. Or are you supposed to be? You're a spider."

He glimpsed up at her face. He said, experimenting, "You look well today."

"I am. Tell me something about that." And she pointed at the madhouse.

"All gone," said the young man. "They went in a night. All the doors were locked. A great wave." He got up and bowed to Leocadia. "Your highness is so powerful. Do take care," he said. Then he flung himself off again, racing back at the fence, away from the buildings.

Leocadia looked up at the rows of dead windows. They were now familiar. She thought she could hear a bell ringing somewhere, but perhaps this noise was only in her ear.

The crickets were silent, and the birds. The marigolds had scorched in the grass and the daisies withered.

Gone in a night. A great wave.

Shells left behind, but that was the other story.

What had gone on here?

Leocadia turned down an alley between the buildings. It was not the way she had come with Mademoiselle Varc. Yet the alley looked just the same, the deep shade, the walls and pipes.

And sure enough, the alley led into a courtyard. Here there was a stone block. It was featureless and gave no indication of its use. Three doorways (hell gates), as before.

Leocadia crossed the yard, which had no rubbish heap, climbed a short stair, pushed at the black door. It was shut, forever.

The madhouse of Paradis.

Something fluttered on the edge of her eye.

Leocadia turned and stared up. Above, in a window, stood a feminine form with bright marmalade hair.

Leocadia's blood seemed to sink through her. A great wave … it hit her feet and vertigo made her drop her face into her hands. Then it was gone, and looking furiously up again, unsteady and sick, she beheld the window empty.

As she came back over the gravel, Leocadia saw Thomas the Warrior sitting under his Medusa, in the flower bed.

"Wait, mademoiselle."

"Everyone talks to me now," she said.

"You have been *there*."

"There. Where?"

"What did you see?" asked Thomas. He was elderly and gnarled and his voice was cracked.

"What could I see? Some deserted buildings."

"Once full," said Thomas the Warrior.

"Gone in a night," said Leocadia.

Did she imagine it? Was the tongue of the Medusa longer?

"You must understand. In your great-grandfather's time. The doors were all shut. The inmates packed in for the night. But in the morning, all the lunatics had gone."

He stopped. He looked like old men from her childhood. This annoyed her. She said, "Aren't we all lunatics?"

"Oh, no, mademoiselle. *You* are only mad."

"What's the difference?"

"One day you'll know. Or perhaps not."

"Tell me anyway," she said, "about the madhouse."

"They vanished," he said, "But not the warders. There were twenty of those. I can see them now – in my mind. All were found dead. Some were in corners and some pressed up against the ceiling like flies, stuck fast. Can you see it, too?"

"Dead," she said.

"Yes, mademoiselle."

"How?"

"They drowned. And they were drunk to a man. Drunk and drowned."

"But meanwhile," she said, "these may be lies. Why did you tell me?"

"You asked."

"That's no reason."

"True. I told you so that you can see all the way around the great circle, of which you are now a part. My congratulations. Now you're one of us."

"No," said Leocadia.

"Then," said Thomas, "what are you?"

He rose and came to soldierly attention as she walked away.

The new canvases were gone. That must be the doing of Van Orles, his repayment.

The rest of her equipment – paints, brushes, knives, and rags – were still there. Even the easel. Even the brown bottle with the penguin.

Penguin Gin, it eases pain.

Nothing to paint on.

Her frustration was boiling and immense.

In one of her notebooks – on the surface of which it would be impossible to apply paint – she wrote down what the spider man had said to her, and the words of Thomas. But not what she had seen in the window, the maiden with orange marmalade hair.

Penguin Gin, Penguin Gin, drink it up –

She poured vodka slowly.

The walls of the Residence seemed to be breathing. The gray screens of them must try to shift, and other barriers pass behind them, through them …

Beyond the window, in the sunset, the madhouse flamed.

Drunk and drowned.

She could hear the screaming, and it was night. And she knew, if she left the bed and walked to the door, it would be open. An oversight, an act of malice.

As she went across the cool floor, she was surprised that she heard the screaming still, and yet she thought, *It's not me. I'm not mad. I hear only what is.*

She went into the corridor, belting her night robe as she walked, and got to the elevator. It worked soundlessly. Had someone fixed everything just so? Was Van Orles lying in wait? And if he was, would she kill him?

But the lift went down to the garden and no one was there.

The night was soft and fragrant, without lights except for a few vague glims high up about the Residence. And the stars, sharp as pins and claws, brighter than eyes. No moon. Leocadia could not remember seeing the moon for a long while. Had it gone away from her?

She went down the lawn, the grass crisp on her bare feet, going by the birdbath with the dregs of tea. The summerhouse was ghostly, the hothouse like a fiend, its vampire vine and smashed edges.

Across the grasses the ancient blocks were white now, as if after all a moon shone on them, or within. Yet the windows had stayed blind.

The fence was difficult – perhaps she had chosen a more awkward spot. It tore her robe.

Through the high grass, pleased, like a lion in the park. She got onto the paving and moved toward the alley she had taken last, and so reached the square with the stone block, and the girl phantom in the window.

Nothing now. Nevertheless, she located the particular pane, marked it out. Then she went up the steps, still warm from the summer day, and she thrust at the door.

Which opened.

Leocadia stole into the deserted halls of old madness.

She could see very clearly, a sort of night sight.

She could make out long passages, and rooms that led off them, and stairs ascending.

She did not mean to lose her way.

She chose a left-hand stair and moved up it. These steps were not warm at all. No, they were cold as marble. She shivered. And then she gazed upward.

High over the stair, high on the wall, a mark. A tide mark. Fluid had risen, and stood, and then drawn away. The wave. The wave that drowned. It had been here.

At the stairhead, she turned aside. She was going toward the place where, from the outside, she had seen the girl.

How cold, the building. How silent and – *stopped*. Like a clock that had used up all its time.

Everything was the same. Passages and doors opening into rooms. Bare, polished as bones.

And here was the one, the room that she had looked into from below.

Leocadia crossed the shining floor.

At the window, no one. And yet, the windowpane – She went near and examined it.

Upon the casement, like the play of winter frost, were two fine and narrow shapes, the prints of two hands. Formed in ice. A little moisture trickled from them, but only a very little.

If I'm dreaming, I can wake up now.

But she could not.

The cries and screams had faded. There were only the handprints and the print of high tide on the walls, and the freezing stillness out of time.

She left the room quickly. She ran toward the stair and rushed down it. Fear had almost caught her up. Below too she ran, for the doorway, and dashed through it and down the steps.

Too cold.

Up the alley Leocadia flew. It was as if the madhouse might collapse on her, masonry unsafe –

She grazed her feet on the paving, and among the long grasses she fell once but jumped up and ran on.

As she managed the fence, she felt her heart beating pitilessly.

The gravel hurt. It was hot now, after the coldness. She entered the Residence and found the elevator, and it went up with her, up and up, and it took too long, but here was the corridor, so modern and pristine, without the marks of tides. She came to her room, and the door gave without fuss. She closed herself in. She stumbled to her bed, and as she lay down on it, she woke up.

Her eyes opened. She was stretched out full-length. She had been dreaming, then. But she was so cold, so chilled.

She pushed herself off the bed, and stepped over her night robe, which was lying on the floor, with a tear in it. Her feet were sore, yet numb. She got to the door and tried it – fast shut. She had never been out.

Leocadia went into the alcove with the refrigerator. Shivering with cold, she wanted a drink, the revitalizing vodka.

She opened the refrigerator. A gust of delicious warmth poured out on her.

She saw the ice packed in, but like feathers from some glorious bed. She touched it. It was soothing, smooth, like the stone hot-water bottles that had come back into fashion. It gave off heat.

She took out and poured the vodka. Cold, as it was meant to be.

She stood by the refrigerator for warmth. It was wonderful, like a summer meadow.

She turned, to warm her back in its depths, and saw across the room a great shadow. Over two meters in height, like a black column with an aproned core of whiteness. Its elongate and fearful head was moving. Horizontal, elliptical. Daggered.

The glass dropped from Leocadia's hand, and as it broke, she touched the light switch beside the alcove.

The lights roared on. She could not see. And then she did, and the room was empty. The night was warm and the refrigerator cold. Her feet were not sore.

But across the floor, she could still see it, the tear in her night robe the fence had made.

FIVE

Paradys

■

Georgie Porgie, Pudding and Pie,
Kissed the girls and made them cry.

Nursery Rhyme

"Very well, you may go. Anything to shake you out of this silly mood."

So Madame Koster pronounced, hearing that Hilde was to go over to spend the afternoon with Angeline. Madame did not inquire into this. She was drawn and ill-tempered, had headaches. Normally she would have asked to see the invitation.

Hilde went in the Koster carriage.

Let off at Angeline's house, she loitered until the carriage was gone. Then she found her way, with some difficulty, but with the glow of purpose on her, to the street of the large theater.

She had not thought any of her adventure through. Had not considered that one day, conversing, her mama might mention to Angeline's mama the afternoon the two girls had been together. But then, what did that matter?

Hilde approached the theater diffidently but proudly. She had the pride of youngness, and its abashment, too.

There was an old doorkeeper by the actors' entrance.

"What can I do for you, mademoiselle?"

"Monsieur Martin –" Even to pronounce his name was like a stab of fire to her.

"That's right, mademoiselle. But there's no performance. Not until later tonight."

"I have a packet for Monsieur Martin."

Hilde did not really grasp from where her invention had come. Some novel? But there it was. And, oddly, the doorkeeper responded. Not by asking after the packet (for example where was it?) but by looking at Hilde cunningly and crudely.

"Yes? Well, monsieur never said. Remiss of monsieur."

"I must see him," said Hilde, one minute a flame, and then the white of ice.

"Yes. Well. Monsieur does see a lady now and then. But usually," — The doorkeeper rapped his coat.

Hilde did not know why. She, or her actor, should have tipped the old man, this overseer of indiscretions.

"I must –" repeated Hilde.

"Yes, yes. He's there. Go in, then." The overseer spat past Hilde's pretty skirt. "I suppose he'll settle. Later. Or not. But then, mustn't speak ill of *Monsieur*. Oh, no. Up you go. Up all the stairs, then left at the top. Perhaps he'll be waiting."

Hilde did not comprehend any of it, not even that *Monsieur saw ladies*. She did not know, of course, that Martin had come for some adjustment of costume, and that, liking his dressing room for its ambience – the cloister of the cathedral of art – he sometimes lounged about there, looking over his lines and exquisitely twisting them, pacing around and smoking. It was not often that a woman had come there to him, but once, or twice, they had.

Now Hilde climbed the horrible stone stairs, on which lay cigarette corpses, flakes of broken glass, dead flowers, clouded stains – all the evidence of vile prediction. But why should she guess?

As she rose a smell grew more dense. It was of the greasepaints the actors used and the creams whereby they got them off, also of dusty clothes that somehow stank of the history they faked. And there was alcohol and tobacco, and the incense of inner things. It *was* a church, in its way.

Half there, Hilde felt faint and leaned on the wall. But then she braced herself. She too was holy. Possibly it was some emanation of his that had made her into an acolyte. He had not meant it to.

She reached the top of the dark tower.

There had been other corridors, but here was one that was black even in daylight. Had she been older, some intimation of death might have held her back. But she had too recently come the other way. She did not identify.

Hilde walked softly into the corridor and so, as if in some dream, came to a line of doors.

She moved down them, lost. And in that second two men rolled from a corner wheeling a costume hamper between them. They stared at her, and so she said, "Monsieur Martin?" Her password.

One of the men grinned. He directed her. It *was* the helpfulness of the spider in the web: *This way.*

When she had gone, he turned to his mate. "That worm. He gets it all. Nice young bit like that."

"Maybe his sister."

"Oh, for *sure*."

As Hilde went between the doors and so reached the proper one, the hamper descended to the enormous wings of the stage, where it was left. Here the hollow cutouts of scenery rested like vampirized dinosaurs, and ropes and pulleys, chains and spars were stranded, as if on the decks of a ship.

Cleaners had been sweeping the stage.

"Johan has a girl again," said one of the descended men.

"Poor bitch. What do they see in the bugger?"

"Why, he's an actor," said one of the sweepers, striking a pose with his broom. "Glamour. That means magic."

Storeys up, Hilde knocked on the door.

His beautiful voice (it was beautiful) spoke brusquely. "Yes? What?"

She could not speak, could not, for her life.

But soon, half angry at being disturbed in his meditations, he flung the door open.

So he noticed her again. And she him.

"Yes? What do you want?"

She gazed at him. Speech, strangely, came.

"To find you."

"Oh, very well. What is it?"

But then, but then, he *saw* her once more.

He saw her now as a woman, though young as a new moon. He saw her as lovely – that is, *attracting*. He saw that she was there. Some vague remembrance arrived, too. She was an abject subject of his, a convert. Some well-off sempstress of the streets, probably, who had stitched her fine dress herself and put it on to impress him, for who else would seek him in this way?

And she was charming. Skin like lilies, hair like apricots. Eyes cast down. And trembling.

His art fired him also, Johanos. It aroused him, and he had been viewing his art, here in the cramped room with its piles of stale clothes, and cluttered screens, and a bottle of brandy, and cigarettes, and manuscript, and *his spirit* crammed in everywhere. The room that led to the high altar.

Not merely acolyte. Sacrifice.

Down on the stage a mile beneath, the cleaners were mock fighting, being the Roman and his Foe, with brooms. Blobs of dust and waves of sawdust were stirred, it was like the parting of a sea. And behind stood the movable walls of the scenes, a hundred countries, other worlds.

But Johanos Martin said to Hilde, "Yes, I understand. Come in."

And as she entered his cell, the priest took her between his hands.

Hilde looked up at him. She could not see the error for the exactitude.

"Johanos –" she said.

"Oh, are we on familiar terms? Perhaps we are."

He did not admit though, that, this being the case, he had forgotten. He bent his head and kissed her lightly and Hilde slid against him, becoming only soul, dissolving.

So then he kissed her more deeply, this offering. She was fragrant and delicious. Obviously, one must have more.

To Hilde it was the dream come true. It was the truth, reality.

Below on the stage one broomer stabbed the other. Handle jutting out beneath his armpit, this other howled. "Oh! I die! I die! What cities and what lands fall down with me."

"Bastard," said another, "I'll take my bet he's dying on her now."

He had drawn her to the rickety little couch and there undone her bodice and slipped in his hands. She cried now with shame and pleasure. He had never had a girl so young, took her for seventeen, pulled up her skirt and touched between her melting thighs.

She did not know anything beyond his touch. She had given herself over to the service of the high altar. She was the sacrifice. He wanted her and by some extreme telepathy had extended his need to her innermost mind.

One of the broom men fell "dead." The other straddled him, and then all looked up into the soaring flies.

They cursed Johanos Martin, whom they hated, for he was stingy and rude, imperious, mean, and frozen like old winter.

And just then he thrust into Hilde's body, tearing her so she screamed with shock and hurt and some mad outrage that was not only of the flesh.

She tried to fight him off. He struck her white face, leaving a lurid mark that faded quickly, for he had not, gentleman that he was, struck very hard.

He finished in twenty seconds. A breach, a ramming motion, the explosion of a passion cold as heat.

"Silly girl," he said, getting up, turning his back, adjusting his male dignity. "I'm sorry I was rough. But you shouldn't entice and then be coy. We've done it before." Even her virginity had gone for nothing. He thought her tight and awkward from inexperience and perversity.

Hilde, too, somehow got to her feet. She stood, drooping, almost bent right forward, like a snapped stem.

Up the stairs a cleaner boy was running. He was bringing Johanos Martin the Hated a gift from the street, but Hilde did not know.

"What have you done?" she said.

"Oh, come now."

"Why have you done this to me –"

"Now, don't be stupid. For God's sake. You'll be asking for money next."

Hilde straighened wearily. She was in pain, as if she had given birth. She had. The birth of terror.

"Please, help me," she said. For in this Ultima Thule of life, still she looked to him, her lover, to offer her hope and help.

But Johanos Martin was disgusted.

"For God's sake, get out. How can I deal with this? Get out, you little whore, or I'll send for the police."

Hilde was numb, and now speechless again. She had entered the world of nightmare, which she would never leave. Or not until another nightmare woke her. Despair had occurred suddenly. As such things do.

She tidied her clothes reflexively, and went to the door, which he was now theatrically holding open for her. As she went forth, the door banged.

So she saw and smelled, outside in the corridor, the shovelful of horse's dung collected for him from the street, and spread out carefully on the ground.

She was beyond fainting, as the starving man is beyond hunger. There were no escapes.

She stepped over the dung and slowly went down through the building.

She would never afterward remember doing so, only the reek of the feces of a grass-eating animal, fed on stuff that was not natural to it.

In a country that has no justice and logic, it is useless to behave normally. Hilde did try. In the nightmare world, she attempted to sleep, to get up, to eat, to dress herself and go about with her mother on the endless trivial errands of their house. But Hilde was passionate. It had been kept closed up in her the way a flower is closed in a bud. Once open it can only bloom and blow, and then the petals fall. The fall had come.

Hilde did not sleep. She wept all night and rent the sheets and bit the pillows from agony. Her maid saw what had happened to the linen and told madame, and madame shouted at Hilde. Was she a wild animal from the zoo?

Hilde did not, and perhaps could not, say what was wrong with her. Neither could she swallow food. She found it impossible to get up from her bed. If forced to do so, she sat in her robe before the mirror, unable to proceed further.

She stared at herself. Who was this?

She had hidden the doll in the wardrobe, that it might not see.

And God – Hilde called to Him but He had not regained His hearing.

The doctor was fetched instead. He said these foolish vapors afflicted young girls, and prescribed a tonic, rest, and exercise. Hilde drank the tonic, which tasted of hot iron. Her mother drove her out, accompanied by the bored and resentful maid, to walk in the parks of Paradys.

Hilde began to suffer from fits of searing rage. She flung a bottle of cologne across her room and it broke. Sometimes she would stand before her mirror and shriek at herself wordlessly.

Her father spoke sternly to Hilde. Hilde sat before him like a dead doll.

Hilde's mother shouted at Hilde and slapped her hands with a narrow silver bookmark. Hilde started to wail and cry.

The truth was expelled from Hilde by the tiny irritant pain of the bookmark on her knuckles, one last straw.

"I can't bear it – I can't! I love him. There's nothing else. He – he killed me."

"What? Who? What are you talking about, you uncontrolled and wretched girl?"

"Johanos –" said Hilde. And at the name, the fissure was soldered shut again. It had let out everything that was necessary.

And now Madame Koster slapped her daughter across the face, as Martin the priest had done.

"What a lying little beast. Are you mad? You've seen him only once, in this house. These idiotic fanstasies. Such a man is far beyond you. And besides, unsuitable. A common actor. Don't let your father hear a word of this."

But Hilde turned and ran about the room, up and down, like a dog in a cage. She beat the walls with her fists, and her cries were so loud now they might be heard in the street.

Her mother rushed at her and slapped her hard again, two or three times, until Hilde fell on the floor.

"How can I live?" said Hilde. Her words were unintelligible. "How can I bear it?" She was, of course, too young to know that much of life involves the bearing of what cannot and should not be borne.

And Madame Koster, who did know, being seasoned enough, and who had the passion of a small gnat in her heart, imagined that her self-control was due to her superior type, and that Hilde's lack of it was proof of Hilde's revolting weakness and unworthiness. As Hilde lay there, madame her mother would have kicked her. For being all madame was not. Therefore an insult, a challenge, and a threat.

All love was gone. Dream love, and motherly love.

Hilde was locked into her room, where she lay in a stupor, not caring.

And then madame brooded. And presently she summoned her husband home.

The Koster house was built of respectability, of reasonable sane ambitions, formats and rites. Hilde was a spy of chaos who had got in, masquerading as a daughter.

Two doctors tested Hilde's mind carefully. They conferred with monsieur. Madame shed a few dryish tears.

Only thirteen days had passed since Hilde's return from the Goddess of Tragedy.

"It seems she is the victim of – monsieur, forgive me – a sexual delusion and a frenzy. It affects certain unlucky young women in this way. Such women are feeble, unformed. They are not meant for physical ardor and can't withstand it. The proper female votive of sacrifice and tenderness becomes warped into obsession. She's a danger to herself, and to others."

The Kosters had put it about that their daughter was gravely ill, and when word came that she had abruptly died, there was speculation but no disbelief. Death did descend in this way, and the young were vulnerable. That the parents were secretive and sorrowful was only to be expected. The funeral was very private, indeed, clandestine.

A headstone appeared in the graveyeard. Those who discovered and read it were sometimes struck that it was a little odd. "Our dear daughter, Hilde, strayed from our lives ..."

Massively drugged, insensible, Hilde was taken away in a closed carriage at three in the morning. It was all managed very discreetly. If people saw, they did not understand.

The carriage wheeled sedately through Paradys, along the cobbled lanes and up the wide paved roads, under the churches. Our Lady of Sighs, Our Lady of Smokes. Beneath the Temple-Church. Reflected in the river. It went up into the hills to where the last of the dark trees were, beyond the outlying architecture of the City, and came to a big brick citadel, sometime before dawn.

The walls were high, the gate was straight.

It was the lunatic asylum of Paradys. The madhouse.

The door slammed shut again, on Hilde.

SIX

Paradise

We are outside the Labryinth now. Searching,
only finding. Staring headlong into a ghost's
looking-glass.

John Kaiine

In the garden room of her apartment, Smara had been working the clockwork cat. The clockwork, however, was wearing out, and the cat was no longer friendly, as it had been in Felion's and Smara's youth. It would pad a few meters, and then stop.

The garden room had plants made of black velvet and rubber, and sometimes Smara dusted them. Their mother had spent many hours here, before one day she flung herself off a high tower in the City. Their father was unknown to them.

When Felion arrived, they drank sweet wine and talked about ordinary things. Smara had killed a woman in a cemetery, managing to lasso her as she knelt over a grave.

Finally, Smara said, "But you went into the labyrinth, didn't you?"

"Yes. Shall I tell you?"

"If you want," said Smara. Her face was sharp and anxious.

Felion told her what he had seen in the passages of the ice, the visions of women, the glass building, the being in the web. He spoke of the empty heart at the labyrinth's center, and how nothing disturbed him on the farther side, until he emerged into the studio of the artist their uncle had made his inheritrix.

Smara listened, but she kept moving about. She began to dust the plants, and the stone head that stood on a plinth against one window.

"And will you go back?" she inquired when he had ended.

"I think I will. There were stars, I saw them, Smara, through a skylight. The sky was a deep black, and there they were. I want you to see them too. And the sun. And the moon."

"Oh, but I've seen that," she said. "In pictures."

Felion began to persuade her, to nag her and wear her down.

She allowed him to talk, but soon she got up and wandered from the room, and so from room to room of the apartment. Felion pursued her, still talking, nagging.

It grew dark, and the opaque gray blanks of the windows changed to ebony. Sometimes a light might shine out there from some height or other, and tonight there was one, quite fierce, and fluctuating. Probably something was on fire.

Felion was hoarse. He left off and only sat looking at Smara. There was nothing to eat in the apartment.

"Shall we go out and find some food?"

But now Smara said, "Why must I come into the labyrinth?"

"To reach the other city."

"Is it so wonderful, then?"

"It must be." He added, "You mustn't be afraid of the ice. It's not like winter." This was a lie. "And I'd be with you."

She did not reply then, but as they walked the wide smoggy streets, she said, "I've been thinking of it, the other city." Then, as they ate burned potatoes in a café, she found a round rock, of course, cooked in with the vegetables. She said, "I asked for bread, and into my hand was put a stone."

Felion flung the rock at the cook, who had appeared in the café. The man shied, laughing, and the rock only broke another window.

"We can go tonight," said Smara. "Yes, I'll try."

He took her right hand at the entrance. In her left he had seen she carried her killing cord. He held up the torch, and the ice wall gleamed.

She looked frightened, but she did not hold back now.

They went in together. They were inside.

Then they walked forward, keeping to the left, not speaking.

The sounds came, the dim roar like oceans. Smara made no comment, asked no questions. Her hand felt as cold as the ice.

Felion waited for the visions, but nothing stirred.

Suddenly Smara said, "Oh, look!"

But Felion could see nothing at all.

"What is it? I don't –"

"That old man in a garden … Isn't it our uncle? He's dressed as he was in the photograph, the one taken during the war. And look – oh, *look*! There are flowers – just like the ones the screens show."

Felion could make out nothing, but Smara's white face was alight with interest. Then she blinked. "It's gone."

"I didn't see. But it must be one of the elements he said we'd find here – time slips, images of some other place. He said he went there, as well as to the city. He went there or would be going there ... And so. Probably you saw him."

"There was a glass building," she said. "It had white and brownish panes."

They went on. Smara moved quickly now.

No images unfolded before Felion, and Smara apparently saw nothing else. Quite swiftly, they reached the center.

Inside this icy oval, Smara hesitated.

She stared about her, and drew her right hand from Felion's grasp.

"This is a terrible spot," she said. "*Something's here.*"

"No, nothing at all. It's empty."

"Yes, there is something. Something horrible and dangerous."

"*No.*" Felion put his head on her shoulder.

Smara darted her head upward and pointed, into the height of the ice wall.

And something was there. A kind of hump bulging out in the ice. It had not been present before.

He said, "Smara, you must control yourself. You're making this happen. It's *you.*"

She covered her eyes with her hands.

The bulge in the ice did not go away, but it had now a fixed, inert appearance.

"How much further?" Smara whispered.

"I don't know. Not far."

All at once she broke from him and ran off.

He shouted after her, and also ran to catch her up, but although in the City he could have done this easily, here something prevented him. And so she was gone, flying ahead, vanishing. He called that she must keep to the left of the walls. He remembered how he had told her over and over that will had projected him through into the second world, and where they would be going: the studio of the woman artist.

Then, running, he reached the exit point, and saw, with hardly any forethought, the studio outside.

He rushed into it – but Smara was not there.

Again, as before, the house in the second world was vacant.

At first, he barely noticed, searching about in it, uncaring and unthinking, for his sister. Who mattered, what counted, but she?

But Felion did not find Smara.

Instead, he found other things.

The rooms were quaint, some orderly and clean, others jumbled. Dead flowers (flowers!) in a vase, the butts of cigarettes with a scented smell, books – intact – cast about lying on the carpets. There were glasses with the phantoms of alcoholic perfume, but no dregs.

On the walls hung interesting pictures. There were persons in them with the heads of beasts Felion recognized from the screens and portions of books in Paradise.

The furnishings were not so dissimilar to those he knew. That was a chair, and this a table, a cupboard, an ashtray, a cup.

But.

The windows.

It was dawn, he thought, and he saw a sun come up. It was an orb like a lamp, but quickly it became too bright to regard. Then the whole sky flooded with brilliance and color.

Did Smara see this? Where was she?

He hunted through the house of windows, and piece by piece the strangeness, the volume, of what he saw overcame even his concern for Smara.

He did not leave the building. And yet, outside, he beheld streets. There were old trees, growing and real. It was possible to see a long way, because there was no mist.

Felion wondered, if anyone entered the house, what he would do. But no one came to the house, and outside the calmest day went by. Vehicles passed now and then, and sometimes people walked along, in costumes that, as with the furniture, were not so unlike the clothing of Paradise, although he noticed no masks.

He could not find a cooking area, or anywhere to come on a drink; he longed for water. There seemed to be mechanisms that worked for the maintenance of the house, but he could not activate them, for the panels that apparently related to them were incomprehensible.

In the hallway at the bottom of the house there was some evidence of the passage of many people. He noticed that something had been done to the door, externally, which worked to secure it. A spangled woman's shoe lay on the stair.

The day went with the passage of its sun, and bars of light and shadow roamed over the chambers, fascinating him. The whole house was like a clock.

At length, he went back to the upper attic room, the painter's room.

He realized now, something seemed to have happened here, too. He was uncertain what. Some tubes of paint were stuck to the floor. With distaste, he found that someone had vomited in a corner.

As previously, the exit-entry point had disappeared, and in a sudden rage he crashed his fist against the wall.

"Let me through. I want Smara."

It was what they had called *dusk*. He could hardly believe he had spent so much time here, when she –

The wall gave way. It was as much emotion, then, as will that caused the labyrinth to operate.

The tunnel of ice curled before him, and idiotically he glanced at the ground, to see if Smara had left lying there one of her shoes, to guide him. But there was nothing.

He stared around the attic again. He had looked at some of the canvases that were stacked against the wall. One had a blond man standing on a roof, high above a city that was devoid of mist.

Inside the maze, he walked backward, watching the aperture, until it abruptly dissolved.

As he came into the center of the labyrinth, Felion paused.

His heart beat heavily; he was conscious of great fatigue and mental enervation.

It was now incredible to him he had lingered so long in the parallel house of a painter (whose name his uncle had never bothered to tell him) when his sister had vanished inside the maze of ice.

He looked up, and there the bulge still was, in the ice wall. It had changed.

Above, the ice had sunk to a type of darkness, almost like some view of the misty night of Paradise. And in the space thus supplied, the frozen tumor had gone to a blocked and incoherent shape. But it was tall, and had a birdlike head –

In that moment, Felion heard light footsteps on the floor of the ice, tapping toward him. His blood leapt, he looked down, and saw Smara.

She stepped into the heart of the maze nearly indifferently. She was not pale, but nearly luminous, as he had seen her after a particularly fortuitous murder.

She too looked at him, and stopped.

"Here you are," she said.

"You ran away," he said. "Where did you go?"

"Into the painter's studio, where else?"

"But – I was there. I explored the house. I didn't find you."

"Nor I you." She frowned. "Somehow that seemed to be all right. I knew I'd find you *here*."

"We must," he said, "have gone into the studio on different planes of time. Did you see her, then?"

"No, The room was empty."

"What hour of day was it?" he asked. He trembled with relief at discovering her, did not mind what they said, or where they were.

"Day, I think. There was *sunlight*. It fell across the floor from the two windows."

"The window in the roof?"

"No, one in each wall. One gave on a bank of vines. The other window had a view. A lawn and trees, some buildings ..."

"We weren't in the same place," he said.

Smara scowled, as if he had accused her of some misdemeanor, as had sometimes happened in their childhood. "It was her studio," said Smara. "There was an easel with a painting on it."

"Of what?" he asked darkly.

"A ship," said Smara.

"Do you recognize a ship?"

"... Yes, from a picture. It had a sail. Things were spilling out of it. I don't know what."

"The bitch must have two studios. What did you do in this room?"

"Very little. I was only there a few minutes. Then I came back to look for you."

"How?"

Smara lowered her eyes. She seemed angry also. "I cried out your name at the wall. I'd got in there."

Felion swept his arm upward.

"What's that?"

Smara glanced. She became pale again and distressed.

"I didn't do it."

"It's your fear. It's some sort of bird of ice. It's formed itself there."

"I won't stay here," she said. She was immobile.

He went to her and took her hand. She still held, limply, her strangler's cord.

"We'll go back, then."

They walked away into the convolutions of the labyrinth. He said, "Don't be afraid of birds."

"You used to flap with the sheet and say –"

"I was horrible. Please forgive me and forget it. We were only seven."

"I saw the picture of a bird once. It was black and white. It had a terrible beak."

"I looked for it in the books," he said, "specially. It was a totem of the peoples of the northern ice waste. A spirit fashioned as a bird, with a black head and a white breast. And it was a good spirit, which they invoked to bring them help. It cured the sick."

"Are you pretending?" she questioned.

No visions came, the ice walls slid curving around them. They did not run.

"It's true," said Felion.

"In her room" Smara said, "I did something."

"What?"

"Will it hurt?" she said.

"I don't know. Damn her, who is she? Who cares?"

"I painted in something white on her picture. I don't know why. A ball of ice."

"How?" he said, again, curious and unnerved. He had done nothing.

"One of the brushes you gave me," she said, "from the man you killed. I had it with me. I used her paint. It was as if I'd always meant to, and –"

"Yes?" he said.

"I hid her spare canvases. The ones she hadn't used."

"Why?"

"I don't know. I hate her. She lives *there*."

In the winds of the ice, he turned his sister toward him and kissed her forehead.

"Forget her," he said. "Then she won't be in our way. Did you like the sun?"

"Yes."

"Wait," he said, "until we see the moon by night."

Smara had shut herself into her apartment. Felion knew that she was there, although she would not answer his signal at the door. She had not been out for days, save for one night when, turning into her street, he saw her gliding up the steps of her home. By the time he had reached it, she was inside.

He too killed desultorily, with the strangler's noose. But he was not interested in the activity now.

The idea of the labyrinth, and the city beyond, had come to obsess him.

He thought about the parallel endlessly, visualizing for himself how it might look, its heights and depths, its river – for surely, like Paradise, it had one.

His own room was in a hovel. He preferred this, he disliked possessions, for they seemed to gain a hold over him. To the clockwork cat, for example, he had had a loyalty, insisting on trying to make it work, to carry out its old antics of play and purring. But the cat was stubborn. It had "died." Smara only used its leftovers for a distraction, it did not disturb her.

In Felion's room, which was in a ruined building near a quay once known as Angel, Felion kept a hammock to sleep in and a steel safe in which lay his weapons, a few fragmented books, and some clothes. Across the door, which was itself off its hinges, stretched an electrical device that kept out intruders. One day, probably, this too would break.

Felion stayed in his room or walked by the river.

Gigantic rats, quite beautiful, but savage, prowled the edges of the water. Sometimes Felion fed them with parts of bodies, but not often. He did not want the rats to become a responsibility.

After two weeks, when Smara was still locked away, he returned to his uncle's labyrinth.

As he walked forward, he counted the turns of the ice wall. He was just inside the fifth turning when the first vision appeared.

Felion stopped, staring.

Like Smara, or as Smara had claimed it, it seemed to him he saw his uncle. But not in a garden. The old man was shambling through an alley, an alley of the elsewhere place, with no mist, and only a light on him that came down from the sky. Felion looked up, and so he saw it, the moon by night.

It was the moon – round as the perfection of all circles, russet as parchment, *bright* – it was the moon, not his uncle, that pulled Felion into the vision.

And the image did not burst or fade. It stayed whole about him.

He was brave, blasé. He thought, *I can get back, in and out as I want. I'm somewhere he told me not to go. So what?*

Felion followed his uncle along the alley in the moonlight and so up onto higher ground.

It seemed to Felion his uncle was younger, but that might only be an effect of the amazing darkness. Felion heard his uncle's feet on the cobbles and in slicks of mud. Heard his *own* footfalls.... But the uncle of Felion did not turn. He seemed, the uncle, immersed in some dream, now and then gazing up at the moon. Just as Felion did.

Smara, you should have seen – you will see.

There was a bar or drinking shop up the slope beyond the alley, and Felion's uncle went in there. Felion stalled. Then he, too, made to go in. There was a sign hung over the door: A half-transparent figure hurried over a hill, under which was a rim of light; a ghost fleeing the dawn, as in Paradise, maybe, it would not have to? On a wall in the picture curled something with the black head of a bird. Felion did not understand this sign, nor the writing beneath. The letters of it were like those of Paradise, but not the language. His uncle had not warned him that in Parad*is* they would have to learn to speak a foreign tongue.

Inside the bar, under the beams, Felion's uncle sat drinking and writing on a tablet of paper.

The clothing of the people here was not quite like the garments Felion had glimpsed from the artist's house. It was, evidently, a different time.

From another table, a gang of evil-looking humans raised their glasses to Felion's uncle.

"Here's health to you, poet!"

Felion withdrew, back into the street.

In the alley a women was selling herself to a man. As Felion went by, she smiled at him, over her customer's bowed skull. "Only wait a moment."

It came to him that after all he understood their speech, only their writing was incomprehensible.

Felion reached the end of the alley, and walked back, as he meant to, into the labyrinth of ice.

How easy. He must assure Smara again of how straightforward the adventure was.

No other visions come.

He reached the heart.

He made himself look up, and there that bird thing was, still shaped out of the ice.

Across the murky floor had been scattered some scraps of brown sugar, or glass.

Felion turned around. He did not want to go on without his sister. He would have to bully her again. He wanted her to see the moon.

He walked back out of the maze, and nothing happened. It was as if he had cheated or mocked it, and he expected trouble, but there was none.

Below the hundred steps leading to his uncle's house, Felion found a woman and, with a kind word, strangled her abruptly. He took her earrings of pearl for his sister and put them through the receptor of her door, impatiently, when still she would not let him in.

A day after, they met by accident in the nave of the cathedral. No one else was there but for a corpse lying in a side chapel, unknown by sight to either of them.

"Come back into the other city."

"I went there," she said, "in a dream."

"That isn't the same," he said.

Smara shook her head sternly. "How can we know? I saw *her* studio again, by night. I was outside and I opened the door. Someone was sleeping there, but I didn't go in. I stayed outside. There was an elevator.... Downstairs there were lawns and tall trees. In a lighted window was a man peering out at me. I ran back again. There was," she added, "a house of glass with a vine of fruit in it. But the vine was dead and the glass had broken."

"Was the glass brown?" he said.

"I don't think it was."

"Come with me," he said.

Smara said, "Not today. Not yet."

SEVEN

Paradis

The north wind doth blow,
And we shall have snow.

Nursery Rhyme

Hot summer light: The room seemed arid, and larger than before, and Leocadia sat with her robe across her lap, examining the tear at its hem. She must have got out of the bed and wandered around the chamber, and caught the silk on something. On what? Some shred of broken glass the mechanical device had not cleared? (During the night the second broken glass had also been cleared up, the glass she had dropped when she saw a black pillar with a beaked dagger of head standing there across the room.)

The panel that supplied music and told the time had also a small button to summon the attendant.

Summoned, the girl in the dark uniform now knocked and entered. It was always the same girl. Or could it be that they simply employed a number of girls who closely resembled each other, sisters perhaps?

"Yes, mademoiselle? Would you like a cooked breakfast? There are some excellent rolls, just made –"

"No, I don't want breakfast. I want to see one of the doctors."

"I understand, mademoiselle. Are you feeling worse?"

"Worse. You mean, I'm always ill, so now I must be worse. I'm neither. Duval will do. Or Leibiche. Even Saume, probably. *Not* Van Orles."

The maid – one thought of her as a maid, rather than a jailor – smiled. "Very well, mademoiselle. I'll take your message. But I can't promise anything. The doctors are always very busy."

When she was gone, Leocadia went to her refrigerator. She opened it quickly. Chill air smoked out, winter in little.

Last night the refrigerator had been warm and she had basked against it.

Now she poured out vodka, and drew forth a long sliver of white cheese.

If the temperature of the refrigerator had failed, the food would be spoiled, and it was not.

Had she still been dreaming? The warmth, the apparition? No, for another of the glasses was missing, the one she had dropped in startlement.

Leocadia glanced aside. Nothing was disturbed, no shards of glass on the floor. Her canvases, removed by Van Orles when she was out, were still missing.

He must be amused, gratified. All her painting materials left to her, and no means for their use. Of course, even such a fool would know what this would do to her.

If one of the other doctors came, doubtless he would have been told Leocadia herself had demanded the subtraction of the canvases, or made some threat having to do with them. It would be unwise to accuse Van Orles of anything, let alone report his graceless lechery.

How many, trapped here, had submitted, to him or to some other? And would she have to prostitute herself to get her canvases back? After all, anything could be taken away from her, a reason could always be found, since she was insane.

All afternoon, no one had visited. Nor at five o'clock, the usual time.

Leocadia went down into the garden.

No one was there, either.

The summerhouse and flower bed, empty. A pigeon flew away from the Medusa's head at Leocadia's approach.

The lawns and walk were vacant, and across the grass, through the trees, the buildings of the madhouse were like old rocks in a desert.

Penguin Gin, Leocadia thought, *Penguin Gin. Drink it up, it will* –

Leocadia could not recall, out in the garden, where she had left the antique bottle with its square neck and top, its label of ice floes and bird.

She felt almost afrighted, a kind of pang.

Leocadia made herself move slowly back toward the Residence – someone might be watching.

When she gained her room, the bottle was standing on her worktable. Had she put it there? Had it been there all the time?

Leocadia picked up the bottle and examined it, an archaeologist with a flask of Egyptian pottery, some tiny god incised upon it.

Drink it up, it will –

Maddening, a rhyme that did not conclude.

Maddening.

Of course, possibly they watched her in her room, in the same way that unseen sounds and unheard lights threaded through it. But then again, if they had decided to keep clear of her – some campaign of theirs, or else some ploy of *his* – probably they would monitor her response but not interfere.

She felt a consoling violence as she prepared the wall beyond the book alcove.

The best of the light fell here, almost as good as the spot where the easel balanced.

There would be difficulties, but they must be met in the nature of challenges rather than of barriers.

The walls had always annoyed her. The pale gray surfaces without texture, against which she saw the motes in her eyes.

To change the wall, smother it in shadows and densities, illusions and images, that was a fair return.

And whatever else, unlike canvas and oiled paper, the plaster, the bricks and mortar, could not be taken away from her.

She covered a large area, larger than any canvas she had ever attempted.

Then, leaving it to dry, she took the gin bottle to the ivy window and studied it again.

The next day, Leocadia walked around the asylum grounds and across to the old buildings.

She patrolled their alleys and looked up at their windows. She paused in their courtyards, listening.

She did not come on the great teetering rubbish tip – either it had vanished, or she had chosen the wrong entry.

Leocadia saw and heard nothing.

There was no one else about, as on the previous day, except that, coming back, she beheld Thomas the Warrior in his flower bed.

She spoke to him.

He took no notice.

"The silence is broken," said Leocadia. "You talked to me, at some length."

Thomas paid no attention.

In the summerhouse, Mademoiselle Varc lay sleeping, and Leocadia did not try to wake her.

Returned to her room, Leocadia drew across the white expanse of the prepared wall the guideline of a horizon. Here the snow would end against the silver of the glaciers. And here, below, a penguin would stand, comic and baroque, like one note of music played too loud. She began to sketch it in. It was tall.

Van Orles had not thought to remove the finished canvases, although she might have painted over these. How had he known she would not? Was he clever after all?

She stared at the ship that spilled fruit, and on the sand beside the shells the white thing lay, which now she recognized. It was a snowball.

The hot light made the snow of the wall very rich and enticing. And in the same way the brown glass showing through the label of the bottle made that snowscape also alluring and warm. Warm as the refrigerator.

White snow gentle as a young summer.

Leocadia drank wine, and let fly a tuft of darkness on the drawn penguin's daggered head.

EIGHT

Paradys

But had I wist, before I kissed,
That love had been sae ill to win,
I had locked my heart in a case o' gowd,
And pinned it wi' a siller pin.

Ballard

Every day about noon, Dr. Volpe toured his kindgom, the lunatic asylum. This gave him a feeling of uneasy and strange power, which he confirmed for himself as the sense of duty. He always hoped that nothing had gone wrong, that none of them had become violent or terribly ill. He liked them to be docile, sitting or wandering about in the straw of the large white rooms. Some nodded or rocked or swatted invisible insects, some sang quietly. These aberrations were normal and he found them almost soothing. The bad smell of confined bodies or those who had messed themselves he was accustomed to. Snuff taking had dulled his nose; he brought with him a scented handkerchief. Now and then there would be an upset. One would not eat, or had set on another, or banged his or her head against a wall. These inmates were restrained, and the sight of their tethers, and the mad-shirts confining their arms, calmed Dr. Volpe.

Sometimes more drastic treatment was required, the Swing or the Waterfall. Doctor Volpe disliked these measures, as he disliked shutting his patients in the upright coffins that permitted only their faces to be seen. He preferred where possible to administer huge doses of opium. As the raving creature sank into oblivion, Dr. Volpe felt an iron clutch slacken on his own muscles.

After his noon perambulation, he would return to his apartment in the adjacent block. Here, when the door was shut, he might, aside from the occasional interruption, have been in some luxurious flat of the City, a gentleman of leisure. There were his shelves of books, his piano, his plants, his various collections – of birds' eggs, butterflies on pins, and so forth. He could potter about all day, and in the evening, the housekeeper brought him his dinner, after which he would drink a bottle of fine brandy.

625

It was another concern of Dr. Volpe's that some of his warders drank inferior liquor. Although it was, of course, reasonable to drink large amounts of a decent vintage. Amid his brandy Dr. Volpe played scherzos at his piano. His thoughts ranged. Finally he slept well, indeed late into each following day. But to drink all one could afford of a cheap and dreadful gin, which, it was said, was actually poisonous ... He did not berate the warders. They were curious men and women, bound to their profession by ties Dr. Volpe did not always care to consider. One must not cross them, or one could not exact service. But nevertheless, he had once or twice glimpsed the terrible gin bottles, brown and queerly shaped, with a peculiar label.

Dr. Volpe let out his inner excellence at his piano, and every six months it was carefully tuned.

Playing, he knew a faint loss, for he could have been a great pianist. Misfortune and the pressure of his bourgeoise upbringing had led him where he was.

In fact he did not play very well, fumbling and bluffing works he should not have attempted, firing off like explosions or farts cascades of horrible wrong notes. Besides, and worse, he lacked expression. There was no tenderness, let alone the delicate neurasthenia so often called for. At his most fiery he was at his most appalling. This he did not know.

He was dreamily thinking of his music now as he passed along the galleries above the pens of white rooms.

The women and men were to have been kept separate, but ultimately it was easier to enclose them together. They were scarcely human after all. One woman warder and two men kept watch today, or rather were playing cards at a table.

Dr. Volpe moved over the room like a visiting meteor. All was well. A couple were tethered, the rest moved freely about, or sat in arrested attitudes on the ground. One of the females kissed her hand to the doctor up in the air. He had always liked her gesture, and saluted her gaily. He did not know who she was. Only the troublemakers became, temporarily, known to him.

"Judit is frisky again," said one of the doctor's attendants.

"Judit?"

"The bitch who kissed her hand to you. Better be careful, monsieur doctor."

"Oh, now, now," said Dr. Volpe.

"There is the new female patient," said the woman attendant somberly.

"Ah. Yes."

"She's in the cells."

The "cells" were the place to which newcomers or desperates were assigned. Until their especial malady had been glanced at, they were not herded out with the rest of the prisoners of the asylum.

"Then, I must interview her. Is she lucid?"

"Not very. She's young. About fourteen."

"How tragic," said Dr. Volpe, who was wishing that the cells were unoccupied. He had begun a Russian novel of vast import the night before and longed to get back to it. "What cause is known?"

They shrugged.

"She's crazy. A girl of good family. Suddenly afflicted with *melancholia* and *hysteria*." (The words he would approve of were stressed.) "Her parents were vague."

Dr. Volpe pursed his lips. This kind of mania particularly offended him. Perhaps the woman attendant knew it. Her face was like a wooden box with a nose, and twinkling eyes. She drank the perfidious gin, he knew.

"Well, shall we go along now? I'll see her."

They crossed the last of the gallery and were gone from the rooms. (None of the beings below now seemed aware of them.) They descended stairs and went through a door, and so across a yard where sometimes the mad people were pushed out for exercise. There was a stone block in the middle of the yard. It had been put there for a statue. The statue had been going to represent Madness, with snakes for hair, but in the end this had been thought too strong, and also a waste, for mostly only the mad would see it, and not understand its significance.

The doctor and his warders entered another block, went up a stairway and along other corridors. Below were rooms of treatment, containing the Swing and the Waterfall, and a sample of other apparatus. Above was a set of offices, and near these were the cells.

The wardress unlocked a door. They went in.

Beyond a lattice was a place with a bed, a sort of pallet having one pillow and one blanket. Here someone lay.

Her eyes were open, but they might have been closed. Long bright hair rayed over the pillow. She was dressed in ordinary garments of the City, for she had not yet reached the level of an inhabitant.

"I'll wake her up," said the male warder. His name was Desel. Dr. Volpe believed that he was cruel, but efficient, perhaps necessary.

Desel strolled over, and came into the shut-off portion of the cell. He stood over the bed, and then he slapped the feet of the girl with his stick.

She was still wearing shoes, which had not yet been removed. Nevertheless, the shock boiled through her, and she sat up like a jack-in-the-box. She did not cry out.

"Sleeping Beauty wakes. Doctor's here," said Desel, smiling.

The girl looked at him with utter disbelief. As if he, the warder, were entirely mad.

"Get up, you. Get up and be respectful."

And the girl got off the bed and stood, looking around her, the way a doll would if someone unwisely brought it to life.

"What is your name?" called Dr. Volpe through the lattice. "Do you know?"

"Hilde."

"Good, good. You know your name."

"What is this place?" she asked faintly. "Is it hell?"

"Oh, hell." The doctor laughed. "No, it is to be your heaven."

"I was thrown down. I was held! They struck me," said Hilde. But she seemed bewildered.

"It was for your own good. No doubt you were irrational."

"What is this place?" repeated the girl.

"A hospital. You'll soon be better."

The girl began to cry. This was like a demon coming on her.

A second demon: The warder Desel, started to chuckle with enormous amusement. And the girl, looking up at him, screamed until her throat cracked.

"Go in, comfort her," said Dr. Volpe.

"I? She's dangerous. She tears things," said the woman, Marie Tante.

"Well, then. What do you think?"

"The Waterfall," said Marie Tante. She added mildly, "That will sedate her."

Dr. Volpe grimaced. The Waterfall did not, he had long reasoned, half-kill. It softened, eased.

"She's so young."

"A savage case. Look at that hair. A tricky color. She was vicious with her own mother."

The girl with orange hair had gone on screaming, and they had been forced to shout.

Desel stood by, waiting only for the girl to rush at him. But she did not. She fell suddenly down and lay on the floor. Silence.

"There, the fit's passed."

"Better be sure," said Marie Tante.

"Prepare her," said Dr. Volpe. These people were indispensable. He must follow their advice.

They led Hilde Koster to a large white room that was somehow like a giant's bathtub turned upside down. There was another partition, this time of glass, and beyond it a terrible little black chair, the highchair of a malign child, with bars.

In this chair they put Hilde, Desel and Marie Tante, who, now the girl was to be "subdued" did not seem to fear handling her. The bars of the chair were fastened, across the throat and lap and ankles.

Hilde put out her hands, and Marie Tante slapped them back.

"What are you doing?" Hilde asked.

"Ask no questions," said Marie Tante cheerfully.

"A little wash," said Desel, and grinned.

Hilde seemed embarrassed, confused. All violence had deserted her, run away and left her at their mercy.

The two warders came out of the area with the chair and joined Doctor Volpe behind the glass.

From the ceiling of the room, above the chair, hung a black tube, large and coiled, a sort of serpent.

Dr. Volpe peered through the glass.

"Is she quite ready?"

"Of course. She can't get away."

The doctor stretched out his hand to a lever, then hesitated.

"You shall do it, Desel."

Dr. Volpe had an air of conferring a favor. And Desel was pleased, Marie Tante almost jealous. In fact, Dr. Volpe did not like to perform the action. He would have preferred not to watch.

The warders, though, were avid, and Desel, taking hold of the lever, plunged it down.

In the ceiling the serpent suddenly snapped straight, and out of its headless mouth there rushed an avalanche of water. Its weight was unimaginable, although it had been precisely gauged. It crashed upon Hilde in the little black monster chair and she vanished. Her first shriek of terror was cut off in a frightful choking. Then all audible sound was crushed under the gush of the Waterfall.

Desel's face was now a picture of content, and Marie Tante's was pale with some sort of oblique arousal, pinched and pointing. They stared through the glass, and Dr. Volpe stared too, but with his hand up to his face, shielding his eyes.

For ten minutes the onslaught of the water raged.

"That will be enough," said Dr. Volpe.

"Surely," said Marie Tante, "a few minutes more."

"Oh, yes, then."

"To be sure," said Desel, helping him.

Dr. Volpe thought of his Russian novel. This would soon be over now.

It was over. Marie Tante pushed up the lever, and the incredible Waterfall slackened to a pulse, a flickering tail, a few harsh drops.

The girl sat still in the chair, impossibly not smashed and flushed away.

Yet she was colorless, her clothes like rain, her skin like white paper. Even her vibrant hair, though darkened, seemed diluted out.

Marie Tante now managed Hilde alone. She undid the bars of the chair and dragged the drowned creature out of it. Hilde's eyes rolled, yet she was still conscious. Water ran from her mouth. Marie Tante thrust the girl along before her, holding her up by the back of her sodden dress.

Dr. Volpe was more sunny. He shook Desel by the hand before hurrying away to his sanctuary. He had done all he could.

In another cell, Marie Tante and the woman Moule stripped Hilde of her soaked clothing. When she was naked, they prodded at her, saying she was too soft. Marie Tante tweaked Hilde's nipples and asked if she had been a bad girl. "Push your finger in and see," said Moule, but neither she nor Marie Tante did this. The girl, unable to stand, lay on a pallet. They hauled her up. "We should cut her hair," said Moule. Marie Tante scraped back Hilde's wet and deadened tresses and, holding them in her fist, hacked them through with a pair of scissors. Hilde gave a faint cracked cry, the first since the treatment, but she did not seem to realize what had happened, even so. "Shorter," said Moule. "That will do," said Marie Tante. "Look at it," said Moule, "all that hair, at least a meter of it." "It can be sold," said Marie Tante, "but not for much. If it had been black, now. But some ginger cat will buy it in the slums." "Don't forget I helped you cut it," said Moule.

They dressed Hilde, then, in the uniform of her prison. A coarse seamless petticoat and over that the death-white dress of the asylum, tied at the waist with a black cord. On her legs were gartered woolen stockings, and her feet were shoved into heelless cloth shoes.

Hilde was ready now, for the ball.

She was just able to walk, though not to speak, and probably not properly to see or hear.

They conducted her from the building and out across the yard with the stone block. In the shadow away from the sunlight, Moule drew a glinting brown bottle from her pocket. She gulped some liquid down and smacked her lips, then reluctantly passed the gin to Marie Tante.

"They say the vats are all corroded," said Marie Tante. "The rats die that drink the dregs."

"And someone has poured acid in it, too," chortled Moule. "Penguin Gin takes away your pain."

It was almost autumn, and as they crossed the last stretch of yard between the black doors and window-eyed walls of the madhouse, an intimation of fall sweetness drifted from the air – the low sun, the smolder of the trees outside. But the two wardresses did not heed, and the girl was past knowing what it was.

Beyond the asylum, an apron of untended garden ran off into a wood, the trees of which were sometimes cut down. There, over the barricade of an outer wall, lay the countryside, impossible as a foreign land. Even the warders took no notice of it. They too lived in hell, going out rarely, and then in a sort of disdain.

Back inside the first building, Marie Tante and Moule bore Hilde through into the succession of white rooms, where the mad people were.

They moved her out into the middle of the floor, over which the ill-smelling straw extended, giving the space a peculiar farmyard touch. They left her there, like a landmark, and drew back, the two women, to see how the indigenous population received her.

But nothing happened. No one went near.

The mad continued at their insanity quietly, not bothering with the new mad one.

"Here, here" — Moule took hold of a man who kneeled on the ground, swaying,—"there's a new girl, go and give her a kiss."

The man who swayed began to cry. He curled up on the floor and Moule kicked him with her booted foot.

"Useless," said Marie Tante. "No spirit. Slugs."

One of the male warders had come in, and seeing them, walked up.

"A new lovely for you," said Marie Tante.

"None lovelier than you," said the warder. "Do you have a drink on you?"

"No," said Marie Tante. Moule twitched her pocket uneasily.

Hilde stood alone in the middle of the room. She looked down into the straw, and presently crumpled and slipped over.

"No trouble with her," said the man.

"She's been swimming in the Waterfall."

All around the white forms with cropped or shorn heads bobbed slowly at their antics, like leaves on a pool.

"They make you sick," said the man, "this filth."

They went on into another room, where there were one or two tied up who could sometimes be tormented into noise.

Hilde lay on the straw, and a roach with transparent copper wings crawled over her wrist but did not hurt her.

A woman sat on the straw by Hilde.

Although her hair had been cropped, her head shaved, a dark shadow downed over her skull, which was exquisitely shaped, so that it did not mar her beauty. She was very beautiful, a face of bones and eyes and lips, the thin body of a damask lizard having breasts. Some kind of sphinx?

As Hilde raised her fluttering lids, the woman spoke. "I'm Judit, Queen Judit. I come from a distant country, where I rule. Barges of metal with silk sails go about on my river, and palaces of marble rise. But here I am."

Hilde gazed, her sight returning, into the face of a mother, for the mother to the tiny helpless child is a goddess, infinite and gorgeous, inexorable, yet kind. And all this Judit was. Queen Judit, the mad, who had been a whore in the alleys of Paradys.

"Help me," said helpless Hilde.

"Of course," said Judit. "You mustn't be afraid. This is a great trial. We queens are born to it, and grasp its syntax. But you are only a little angel fallen into the beastliness. Don't be frightened. I'm here."

"Oh," said Hilde.

Judit held her wrist, over which the bracelet of the roach's running had gone. Judit kissed Hilde on the eyebrow.

"Now you're my handmaiden," said Judit. "All will be well."

"But," said Hilde.

"Forget the past, my dear," said Judit. "This is like death. Of course, it will end and we shall go back, in victory. But would you rather come with me to my own country? The mountains embrace the sky. Hawks feed from my hands. I've had a hundred thousand lovers, great kings and lords. Each brought me a fabulous gift, and my house is seventeen stories high."

"How do you reach the top?" asked Hilde, stirring a little, like a wounded bird.

"A flying carpet," said Judit. "How else?"

Pleased, for she had an answer to every question, and liked to display her skill, Judit laughed.

Her teeth were flawless, but for one eyetooth that had been struck from her mouth by a warder (Desel) long ago. She did not recall this. She knew she had lost the tooth in a fight, when she had defended a king who had lain with her, a long dagger in her hand. Judit's beauty had grown with her delusions of beauty, and her strength too. Never, as a starveling harlot, had she had this excellence.

"How did you come here?" asked Hilde.

"A trial. Didn't I say?"

"But why?" Hilde, only half in the world, at once revealed her sense of the truth of Judit, for how should a queen, of Sheba, Egypt, or Andromeda, be *here*?

"There was a face of bronze," said Judit, "which I killed." She was satisfied. "That is why. And how. But I'll triumph over all ruin. One passes every day to whom I blow a kiss. He doesn't know that each kiss is my power; he'll fall under the spell of it."

"Will you help me?" said Hilde, sleepily. The fortitude of Judit had lulled her.

"Poor child. You are mine now. Fear nothing."

And Judit drew Hilde into her lap and held her, stroking the crinkled apricot hair, all that was left of it.

In a hovel Judit had slain a man who had tried to mutilate her for his pleasure. And Judit had gone mad. Mad with anger and justice, to escape the foulness of her world. Now she dwelled among shining thoughts, remembering always she was a queen.

Her fingers were like honey after the horror before. Judit was fire to heal the blows of water. She smelled unclean, but not impure.

The man who had cried had also crept to her, and Judit had not thrust him off. He lay with his mouth against her skirt, asleep.

Judit sang softly of her palaces, of the lions that drank from the river, and the curtains of spun light, and the flowers of her garden, which were fed dead murderers. Her song sounded like gibberish, but this did not matter.

After a time, Hilde told Judit what had happened to her, and Judit listened carefully, her perfect head turned a little to one side. Judit wept, her tears were flames. Hilde saw this, but she was not afraid.

Twice a day, the inmates were fed. In the morning a gruel was brought, and in the evening a type of stew without meat. Both these meals were slops. Bread was served with them that had, as often as not, gone a little moldy.

The cauldrons of food were brought through the rooms on a contraption like a four-legged stretcher with wheels. Certain of the patients were recruited to dole out rations, overseen by the warders with their sticks. To every patient, rounded up and herded to the cauldron, was given a small bowl. There was no cutlery, as even a spoon might be put to dangerous use. They ate with the bread and with their fingers and mouths.

Those who would not eat were watched, and after the third day taken to a room the warders had nicknamed the Banquet Hall. Here a tube was thrust down their throats and they were force-fed on a kind of ant food or sugar water. Sometimes a patient had died from these feasts, from mere shock, or because of the carelessness of the operative, who had inserted the feeding tube into the air vent rather than the esophagus, and so flooded the lungs and drowned them. (These poor patients were always found to have choked while eating too greedily.)

Of such things Judit warned Hilde as she drew her gently to the cauldron.

While they waited their turn, a male warder came to Judit and was familiar with her, putting his hands on her buttocks. Judit laughed in his face. Her
body had no scruples and no modesty, and she was, besides, a queen.
But when the warder turned to Hilde, as if to extend the treatment to her, Judit
came between them, smiling. "Get off, you old whore," said the warder, and
backed away, menacing Judit with his stick.

In the bottom of the cauldron, under the soggy vegetables, something
glittered.

"There are spikes there," said Judit.

Once a small man, a dwarf, had hidden in the tureen and so got to the
kitchens, where he took a knife and attacked some of the warders. Now the
spikes were in the pot to prevent another such attempt.

Hilde did not want to eat, but Judit urged her to take a little, especially the
disgusting bread. The warders had not realized, it seemed, that the fungus on
the bread helped keep off infections. Judit's grandmother in the alleys had
taught her this, but she had forgotten, and now explained a great physician
had exposed the fact to her.

After the cauldron was removed, most of the warders went off to their
own dinner of meat and potatoes in another building. Only four were left on
duty, two playing cards in a central room and two patrolling.

"What is it they drink?" asked Hilde.

"A venom," said Judit. "I, too, have tasted it. Unlike the wines of my own
country."

Judit took Hilde by the hand through the many large mirror-like white
rooms, on which now late afternoon was gathering from the high barred windows that showed nothing but the closing sky.

Hilde stared at the mad people in still wonder. She was so shocked, so
wrecked, that now her capacity for fear was virtually gone. She had entered
a translucent state, as human things sometimes do when they lose their per-
sonalities. Everything that had happened to her seemed to have happened to
another. All the world was alien and illogical and this piece of it no more so
than the rest. She wanted nothing, except perhaps eventually to sleep. She
was glad of Judit's company and seemed to have known her countless years.

Several of the mad acknowledged Judit, and some even bowed or curtseyed to her. But others were too busy. One was an insect and waited in her
web for flies and another was talking to spirits or invisible people. One
crawled in a circle around and around.

In perhaps the third room a man had been tied to the wall by a thong about
his throat. He wept ceaselessly and his neck was raw from trying to pull free.
Judit went to him and wiped up his tears with her long hair, which no more
existed. A second man was in a mad-shirt, and he rolled along the floor, bit-

ing at the straw and making strange hoarse barks. The warders had beaten his legs on their patrol.

In a fifth room there was an arrangement of old broken furniture that rose in a hill higher than the gallery that ran along the wall. The hill was some distance from this, and from all the windows. At its top sat a skinny man, looking out like a gull from a roof.

"There's Maque," said Judit.

She began to climb the structure, her firm legs, bare of stockings, revealed up to the white knees. Hilde did not follow, for though she was no longer able to be afraid, some physical nervousness remained. But then Judit turned and beckoned her, and Hilde did go up the stair of furniture, which was actually quite solid, its uneven places simple to avoid.

Aloft, on a table, sat Maque, and here they joined him.

The glory of the height was its view through a window. Although about six meters away, unreachable, it showed sections of burning sky and the crowns of burning trees. The sun was setting there, as if it had never before done so, and meant to make the world pay attention.

They stared at it, their faces lit like potter's clay.

Maque was extraordinarily thin, and in his ears were tears from which the rings had been torn years ago, on his arrival at the asylum. Elsewhere now, in the City, his ill-omened earrings were worn; they had got free.

"I've sailed the sea," said Maque presently. "I had a pet monkey that died of old age when he was twenty-three. I've seen Eastern ports where women dance naked but their faces are veiled in black. I've smoked hemp under the shelter of an elephant and eaten powdered pearl for the pox, which cured me." His conversation, or rather monologue, was somewhat like Judit's. He said, "Ten men gone overboard in a tempest. We came to an island. There were unicorns there, but our mate said they were only a kind of goat. A virgin may capture a unicorn."

The sun went under the window, and the bars stood on thick burnished sky. Shadows spread among them. Below the hill of furniture some of the mad people made small sounds.

"This child can never," said Judit, "capture a unicorn. She's been violated."

Hilde was not shamed. She nodded, distantly.

"Yes," she said, as of another, "that happened to me."

"She went to him in love," said Judit.

"Look," said Maque. And he got up on one knee and pulled from under his right thigh a brown glass bottle. "Empty, of course," he said, "Thrown away near the latrine."

"A gin bottle," said Judit. She took it and gave it to Hilde. Hilde had never seen such a thing. On the label was a great black and white bird with a flush of amber next to its head. Behind was whiteness.

"I never saw a land such as that," said Maque the sailor. "A cold country with mountains of snow. But I heard of them. The freeze forms vast cliffs of ice that float into the sea, and when they meet they clash like glass. These birds live there. Penguins, they're called. They can't fly, but stalk about like kings."

"Are they little birds?" asked Hilde childishly, for this was her protection now, between Judit and Maque.

"Some, maybe," said Maque. He pointed at the bottle. "But not this fellow. Look at him. He could be seven feet high. And his beak's a knife."

Below the furniture, many of the inmates had gathered close, and looked up at Maque. Maque rose, and taking back the bottle, he raised it. One last spark of sunlight came in at its top and shot a ray from sky to ground.

"And they said," said Maque, "the snow is warm, there. So warm you can lie down and sleep in it like a feather bed. And flowers grow when the sun shines on the ice. The sun never sets but hangs low, so it's always dawn or sunset. That is Penguin Land."

"I'd do without my country, to see that," said Judit.

"But," said Hilde, some dim rationality struggling deep within her. Yet she had no use for it any more, and abruptly let it go. "You could play at snowballs in Penguin Land," she said, "and never burn your hands on the snow."

"You would never be hungry or thirsty," said Judit. "Fruit and sweets grow on the trees and wine runs down the ice."

The light ray melted from the bottle and went out.

The room was very dark.

And through the doorway stamped three wardresses, jingling their keys.

"Get down, you bitches," shouted one at Judit and Hilde.

"What is it now?" asked Hilde.

"Now they lock us into our dormitories," said Judit. She smiled, "After dark, we're sinful, so they must separate the women from the men."

When they were near the bottom of the furniture, Marie Tante seized Hilde and pulled her off, bruising her. "Not quiet yet? Perhaps you'll need more subduing."

The women were marched away by women, and men came in a crowd, toting their sticks, to get charge of the male inmates.

Darkness was full now in the asylum. One of the female warders carried a lamp, and the outer corridors had been sparsely lighted.

They passed up a stair, and a door was unlocked. Into the women's dormitory they went.

The beds lay along the floor. They were straw pallets covered by thin blankets and having each a soiled and impoverished pillow. Every place was foul, and a worse smell came from buckets of necessity set at intervals and doubtless not frequently emptied. On a wall facing the beds and buckets was a wooden cross. This was ignored by one and all.

The women went where they wished, or where they felt they must, and sat or lay down.

Marie Tante drove Hilde the length of the room to a pallet apparently unclaimed.

"Here, my lady. Your couch."

Hilde got onto the bed and crouched there. After all, fear remained of this woman who seemed grown to a preposterous size. (Why not then a giant penguin?)

"You'll have lice by tomorrow," said Marie Tante. "What a stink in here. We must hose these beasts down."

"That one's been wetted already," said Moule.

The third wardress giggled and swung up her lamp, to make the room career and spin. The madwomen gazed at this phenomenon silently.

The wardresses left them, locking the door.

The room was black, and in the black the women rustled and whispered. One moaned over and over.

Hilde sat in dull dismay, for Judit was far off. The awful smell oppressed her, but then she sensed a current of cleaner air. Some tiny panes of glass were missing from the window above, and now a night breeze blew. It would be cold in winter, not warm as the snows of the Penguin Land.

An hour later, the moon entered the window. And so the room.

On the space of black floor below the powerless crucifix, the milk-white squares of the barred window appeared.

One by one, two by two, the madwomen left their verminous beds and came down to the pool of light.

Here they moonbathed. Some washed in the moonlight, rubbing their arms and faces, or lifting up the whiteness between their legs. Others lay down and swam among the squares. The woman who moaned tried to prize the shadow bars away and could not, and crept back, made dumb, to her bed.

Judit stood up in the center of the reflection, her face raised into the light, which tinted her like snow.

But the moon passed over, and total darkness returned. And in this dark, the door was unlocked, not brashly now, but with stealth.

The male warder who had come after the moon sought Judit the whore among the women, and mounted her. They heard her say, in a voice of velvet, "What, are you here again, oh my king? What an honor." And then they heard the man strike her. It was Tiraud, who would drink to capacity and then seek out the queen of harlots. Soon finished, he called her filthy names and exclaimed now over the fetor of the dormitory.

At the door another chuckled. And away along the corridors there started a wild whooping and screaming.

Hilde sprang up, and Judit was by her, for even so soon she knew Judit's touch.

"They do things to the men they don't dare try with us."

The awful crying went on, and the women huddled off their beds. They congregated around Judit, as they had gone to the moon pool. Her skirt was sticky, but she was yet a queen.

When the cries stopped, there came instead a crazy clatter in the air, and at the door the jailers laughed raucously.

Something flew against Hilde, leather and fur, and she shrieked in turn. No, fear was not all gone.

All about, the women gurned in panic. Into the dark it was not possible truly to see, only to hear, as they burrowed and howled and ran at the walls. The other thing also did that, swooping from side to side.

Judit had stood up again, and she raised her arm, and mysteriously she was half visible as if faintly luminous from within.

So, by Judit's shine, Hilde saw the bat the warders had let go in the room. It whirled overhead and dipped suddenly down, settling on Judit's fingers as the hawks did in her dream country.

A demon with a fairy face, the bat folded its wings.

Judit carried it to the wall, and put it there, and the bat detached itself and crawled upward, into the high embrasure of the window. Here it found a broken pane and slipped through.

"Very good, very good," said the men at the door. "She's clever, is Judit."

As they locked the door behind them, the cries began again across the building. Dr. Volpe, two blocks away in brandy sleep, would not hear them. And if he did? Lunatics were noisy.

Hilde lay back. She pushed the crying from her and thought of the bat in the cool sky, and of the warm snow.

The mandarin leaves fell slowly and sparingly from the trees on the lawn and in the wood. Gray geese passed over.

An extravagant hothouse built for Dr. Volpe on the lawn outside the asylum blocks began to burgeon with harvest, black grapes on a vine, apricots, toasted roses.

The mad people were never allowed as far as the lawn, and never beheld it from the windows.

There had been plans for a summerhouse too, maybe a small lake. But these things had never come to be.

One evening an agent brought Dr. Volpe a wonderful new prisoner, a dead butterfly with huge bright wings.

Hilde did not cause any trouble, and Marie Tante had lost interest in her. One of the men had taken to shrieking, and was conducted to the Swing, where, in a sort of box, they rotated and reeled him until he vomited and swooned. Thereafter he sat quietly in his mad-shirt on the straw.

Hilde came to recognize her fellows, though usually not by any name.

Judit showed her the poet Citalbo, who had gone insane from reading drama and writing verses. Citalbo walked solemnly from room to room, sometimes scribbling on small pieces of paper that the warders allowed him, as Dr. Volpe had decreed. The warders often stole the papers, however. This did not appear to matter. What Citalbo wrote now was nonsense, frequently illegible. He never seemed to miss his former works, or anything that was stolen, as if, once he had put down an idea, God had it in safekeeping.

During the days of straw, Judit occasionally told stories, histories perhaps, of her queendom. At night also, now and then, for they would not always sleep at night in the dormitory, as by day sometimes they would. Maque sat upon his hill. They did not speak or approach him again. The brown bottle had vanished – confiscated? No one mentioned the Penguin Land.

One morning the warders beat a man in front of all the others. He had been running to and fro and the warders caught him suddenly and threw him down, kicking him with their boots and striking him with their sticks. The noise rose in the madhouse then like a storm in a cage of parakeets. The screams and cries of the mad did not quite overcome the oaths and grunts of the male warders or the shrill giggles of the three wardresses who were present.

The beaten man was left lying, and somehow recovered, or at least did not die.

When Dr. Volpe went along the galleries at noon, the lunatics were generally very still. Some tried to hold their breath. Most did not know who Dr. Volpe was, only that he appeared rather like a clockwork toy, at a certain time, also that he presided over the worst tortures.

There were other incidents: The shaving of a woman's head, the force-feeding of another, a drunken song the warders indulged in without warning. The afternoon that something was added to the slops which gave the inmates pains in their bellies, and how Judit raved about the healing tinctures of her land, and between calmly told Hilde this had occurred before, and would soon pass. By night, intermittently, Tiraud, or others, came into the women's dormitory, to use Judit's body. She did not resist these rapes. Once or twice some other woman was violated as well or instead. In particular darknesses, outcry resounded from the men's cloister.

The moon came often to the women's barred window, at different hours, and laid its light along the floor. The women did not always go down to it. And one night Hilde stood alone in the midst of the pool, staring up at the window, its source, above. She had lost all comprehension of the place she was in, she did not look for rescue, if she ever had. The image of Johanos Martin had long since withered from her, as had her night game, the sweet masturbation of her innocence. In a manner, the asylum had done what it had promised, driving out the devils that had brought her here, but only to replace them with others.

Judit, who had been preyed on three times that night, lay sleeping. Hilde went to her and curled up by Judit's feet. It was cold. Hilde thought of the Penguin Land.

Dr. Volpe dusted the leaves of a palm, and standing back, surveyed its effect against the autumnal window. He could see down toward the hothouse, and the chestnuts and oaks of the wood. This was a pleasing view and might be that of any country retreat.

A knock on the outer door alerted him and he pulled a child's sulky face. His housekeeper entered.

"The gentleman from the theater, Dr. Volpe."

Dr. Volpe had forgotten.

His face of distaste became harder and more adult.

"Very well, you may send him in."

Dr. Volpe paused beside the case with the new butterfly in it. He would linger just long enough to show the visitor what was important, and proper.

But the visitor, the blustering gentleman from the Goddess of Tragedy, launched at once into a speech, not waiting to be asked.

"We are delighted that you'll do as we desired, Dr. Volpe. This will render my actors a great service. And in the course of art –"

"It is a disgrace," said Volpe, his face swollen now. "To bring sightseers here. As if into a zoological garden. These people are my patients."

"Quite, quite." The visitor brushed Volpe's words and stance aside. "But as you're aware, the minister has overridden your objection. I'm sure you don't set yourself above him, doctor."

Volpe was ruffled. He was at the mercy of upperlings and underlings.

"If he thinks so. I'm not certain the minister was correctly informed."

"Oh, *quite* correctly."

"To have your troupe here, staring at these poor deranged souls."

"What harm can it do?" said the agent from the theater. "And so much good. The lunatics won't notice, I expect. And for my actors, an invaluable help in the preparation of the mad scene for our next production."

"I dissociate myself from the proceeding," said Dr. Volpe.

"Of course. I suppose your warders are capable of overseeing the affair."

Dr. Volpe imagined his warders poking the mad people with sticks, forcing them to caper and wail to interest the actors. But they would do it, too, if he was present, and then there would be the shame of it. The warders would expect to receive large tips.

He did not offer the agent refreshment, and when he was gone, Dr. Volpe walked among his birds' eggs, caressing their smoothness (each a tiny coffin, but he did not consider that).

Soon after dawn, the dormitory was unlocked and the women were hustled out again, down to the common rooms. Today it was not the same.

Marie Tante, and the wardress Bettile, stood at the doorway. They took hold of Judit at once. "This one," they said, "she's much admired."

The other women, thinking Judit had been singled out for some therapy (punishment), shied away, all but Hilde.

Marie Tante reached and gripped Hilde's arm.

"This is a pretty one. Look how quickly her hair's grown back. You'll have to be shorn again, my lady."

Hilde hung speechless in her grasp. But now Bettile grabbed two other girls from among the women.

"These will do. For the *pretty* ones."

"Hah! They'll pass."

The four chosen women and the one other Bettile hauled out, who whimpered and then sobbed, they led away along the corridor to a big tiled area.

Hilde felt again the invasion of terror. This was like the white room in which she had been tortured. She could recall very little of it, but she had thought that she died there, and came back very changed.

"Don't be afraid," Judit said sternly.

The warders told them to take off their garments. Judit removed hers almost blithely. Despite her captivity, she was still very beautiful, and though her breasts were not those of a girl, they were full as two blown roses.

Marie Tante jeered at Judit: "Not bad for an old whore."

But Judit laughed, and Marie Tante turned her attention to the other women.

These were malformed and undernourished, or oddly fatty, their bodies blemished by moles and pimples, inner subsidences of the flesh.

Hilde was ashamed to bare herself, and Bettile charged at her and ripped the clothes off her body.

"Too proud, eh? What have you got to be proud of, ugly little runt?"

When all the women were naked, hoses were turned on them. The water was icy cold but not extremely violent. Some fell down. Hilde dropped to her knees. Yet, since the water only occasionally covered her head, it did not completely recall the former horror. Almost, she missed the landmark of it.

When the sluicing was over, rough sheets were flung to the women, and those that could dried themselves. Two could not, and these Marie Tante saw to with harsh buffeting swipes.

They were given new tunics, and white sashes, bundled into them.

The warders mocked the women. "Just need a spot of powder." "Some flowers for the hair."

They were removed next to a narrow chamber, and awarded some of the breakfast gruel. One of the women spilled the fluid on her new robe, and Bettile cuffed her. "Dirty sow. Do you think you'll get another washing? You'll have to go as you are."

"What will they do to us?" Hilde whispered.

Judit said, "Sometimes ladies and gentlemen pay to look at us."

Hilde relapsed in apathy, but when they were presently taken out again, she stayed close to Judit.

The women were then put into a long room that faced onto the yard with the stone block, and here they were left some hours, with Bettile to watch them, but Bettile drank her gin, set out her cards, and fell asleep.

Two of the women sat down on the floor, where one wept until the snores of Bettile, perhaps taken for a reprimand and threat, silenced her. Judit and Hilde and the fifth woman went each to one of the three windows that looked onto the courtyard. There they stood in a row.

Outside it was a fine, still fall day, the misty sunshine soft as gauze. At the center of the court, about the stone, was a curious structure, in fact a makeshift stage Tiraud and some of the warders had put up. It was only a foot or so high, and composed of trestles, over which some sheeting had been draped.

On the far side of the court was something even more incongruous. An awning had been erected and armchairs put under it. And there was a table with a white cloth on which now began to be laid plates of food under napkins, dishes of fruit from the hothouse, coppery pomegranates, oranges and apricots, and black grapes. Into buckets went slabs of ice. Judit said, "That will be for the champagne. Someone has looked after them. Perhaps they're princes," and she spat abruptly on the floor.

"Ice from Penguin Land," said Hilde, to please her.

"No," said Judit, "the ice from there would never melt. The ice there is warm."

And Hilde was humbled by her mistake. She put her hand on the warm glass of the window.

Her back had begun to ache from standing immobile so long. But the draw of the courtyard, a view it was possible to gaze at, kept her there. Besides, she waited nervously to see who had come. She had forgotten people – she and the inmates of the asylum were not people – and so in turn human things from the outer world had become like wild beasts. What would they do, or require? Would they sniff and paw, or rend? She dreaded that she would have to show herself to them, but not because of the state to which she had been reduced, only because they were so alien.

Now she said, to please Judit again, for Judit was real, "What is the name of the Penguin Land?"

"Maque will know," said Judit. She added, "They'll display Maque. He's a model patient, controlled and articulate. And Citalbo, perhaps. Because he speaks poetry."

There were sounds below. One of the black doors opened, and Desel came forth. He was taking on the role of guide that Dr. Volpe might have assumed, and Desel had dressed up in suit of clothes and a high collar. He looked fearsome and terrible, like some species of poisonous insect that has adopted the gaudy wings of something it has recently killed. The fifth woman at the window groaned, and going sadly away, sat down on the floor with the other two.

Out of the doorway after Desel came the beasts who were people, the beasts who had come to visit the zoo.

There were a couple of ladies in flowered dresses, with hats and parasols, and a group of men, two rather tall, each smartly dressed.

Hilde drew back from the window.

Hilde pointed.

Her fingertip touched the glass. Now it was cold.

And Bettile awoke.

"Oh, are the bastards here? I expect Desel will give you bitches autumn crocuses to hand to those fine, jumped-up ladies, to show how well we've trained you."

Judit turned her shaven head on her white neck, like a snake, looking at Hilde, then turned back and looked down again into the yard.

Hilde moved even farther back, her arm still outstretched, as if frozen.

"What's up?" said Bettile. She rose, taking as she did so a swig of gin.

"Johanos Martin," said Hilde. Her face suffused with an appalling embarrassment.

"Oh, the great Martin," said Bettile. "Fancy, you know the name. When were you at the theater?" She elbowed Hilde's shrinking body aside and peered out. "Well, so that's the bugger. The tallest one, I've heard he's tall."

The gray eyes of Johanos Martin passed smoothly over the windows, seeing nothing. He was accustomed to looking up, from a stage, blind to those who hung above.

Hilde ran into a corner and curled herself together. Bettile swung round and marched toward her.

"Get up, slut. Get up, I say."

She pulled Hilde to her feet and Hilde screamed. She forgot who Bettile was, and fought with her, and Bettile felled Hilde with a single blow.

In the gilded day, ten lunatics were let out on the platform.

In the awning shade, drinking freely the wine their theater had sent them, picking at segments of chicken and orange, the actors watched. It made a change for them, someone else putting on a show. They did not completely like it, you could see. And they stared acutely to tell how much better they would be able to do it, to act the insane.

Desel did not have his stick now but a cheap florid cane he had bought in the City. With this he poked at the madmen, making them whine or snort or shy. Sometimes they did not respond at all. Some crawled, others walked in a curious apelike way. The more interesting specimens were directed to the front of the trestles.

The ladies made disapproving sounds over the one who drooled from his permanently grinning, tooth-barricaded mouth. His smile was a rictus that never went away, his lips dark and his teeth long and sallow. His eyes were thick with pain he no longer considered.

"The man who grins," said Desel, as if he had invented all ten lunatics, carefully, in a laboratory. "He never speaks, and forces food between his fangs only when we make him. His grin goes on while he sleeps. What a happy sight to keep before you. Imagine this one in your sitting room." He was a touch impertinent, Desel, for now he was dressed up as gentleman, and they were only actors.

After the grinning man, a man came who seemed to think he was a dog. He moved on all fours, panting, and now and then he licked his own hands.

And after this one came the one on a tether, led by Tiraud. When Tiraud jabbed the tethered man with his stick, the madman began to sing in a shrill voice songs that were just recognizable as old ballads of love.

Presently they drove forward the man who was surrounded by a swarm of invisible wasps, at which he beat wildly. Tiraud struck this man's ankle, and the man fell upon it, biting and snapping at his own flesh, trying to pull something not there away from him.

Others were left standing in the background, where they drooped or padded about in small circles.

After these first men, some women were brought, shaven-headed and in matted gowns. The wardresses, notably Marie Tante, shouted at them, and the women moved about with a hobbled gait, like lost cows that do not understand but know the smiting of sticks.

Desel stepped into the middle of the stage. He commenced giving a lecture on the types and attributes of madness. He sensed the actors had become bored and saw that they grew restless. He did not like them. Nobodies risen to fame by dint of luck, and whoring. Look at the actresses – strumpets. And the men, doubtless lax of morals, perhaps given to unnatural vices.

The tallest man, the one called Martin, looked at Desel with icy and expressionless eyes. These eyes flustered Desel. He wished for a moment Martin had been in his power.

But it was the other man, Roche, who called out, "Ah, come on, come on."

Desel concluded his address hurriedly. Turning, he struck one of his charges so the man squeaked and leapt over the stage, making the trestles creak ominously.

The crowd of male and female lunatics was herded aside, and some, the most troublesome, were removed from the court. (A couple had soiled themselves from fear or need.)

Now the women came who were supposed attractive, and fairly docile. Desel had thought the ginger girl, Hilde, would be among them, but she was missing.

Bettile led the women forward.

"Curtsey to the gentlemen and ladies," said Bettile, and swung her rod at the backs of legs. Two women curtsied, and one tumbled to her knees. Judit stood. "This one won't," said Bettile. "Tell the people why you won't."

Judit glanced at Bettile, then she gazed at Roche. Her dark eyes passed through him, and Judit murmured, audible and sorrowfully, "A queen does not obeise herself."

Roche stood up and doffed his hat. He bowed.

His eyes were not at all full of mockery. He said, "I believe she is."

But Judit only smiled forgivingly, and raised her eyes to the sky above the buildings.

Soon three or four more men were brought to be shown off. Among them was Maque.

"This man was a sailor," said Tiraud. "It was the sea sent him crazy. Now he invents lands that don't exist."

"All lands exist," said Maque.

"How true," said Roche. "In the world and out of it."

Roche was drunk perhaps. Most of the champagne bottles were empty. The actresses were flushed. Even Martin had a slight trace of color in his face.

"Tell the gentlemen about your travels, Maque," said Tiraud.

Maque said, "My last voyage was to this place. Here they tore the metal rings out of my ears. I was locked in a room no bigger than a hutch, and later in an upright box. I could not move my hands. I was fed on rotted bread and stale water."

"He attacked a warder," Desel explained carefully.

Tiraud said grimly, "Speak of your sea trips, sailor."

Maque closed one eye. "I forget."

"The Swing for you," whispered Tiraud in Maque's mutilated ear.

Maque said, "I saw a land once, covered with snow. And on the trees grew bottles of gin."

Tiraud hit Maque across the spine.

Maque did not turn. He stared away, as Judit had done.

All the champagne was gone; the actors had become instead the receptacles. And the warders were full of spirits.

They brought Citalbo, the poet who had gone mad.

He stood on the stage, and spoke to Johanos Martin in a sonorous voice of leaden silver.

"Why," said Roche, startled, "he's saying your lines from the play – the Roman –"

"He speaks very well," said Martin, and gazed up the short distance at Citalbo.

"Empires shall go down like suns," Citalbo said. "And ships beach in the bays as locusts do, on the firm corn."

He inclined his head, and waited courteously.

Johanos Martin laughed. He got up, and said, ringingly and perfectly, "So it was, and so it shall be always," and paused like a coquette.

And Citalbo went on: "Until the earth is a dry husk and the sky falls, and in never any house –"

"A girl sits," Martin said, "to braid her hair. Or a warrior stands –"

"To buckle on the brass of war. But then," Citalbo said, "we shall be dust, and thus –"

"Who cares for those that do not think of us?" Martin finished.

Roche applauded. The other actors and actresses were caught up, and put their gloved and bead-garlanded paws together.

"Monsieur," said Martin, for Citalbo had dared to speak his lines with great beauty and skill, "as I am, you are: an actor."

"Then you, sir," replied Citalbo, softly, carryingly, "must be as I am. Mad."

Martin's face closed. His eyes were steel. He drained his glass, and turned away as Maque and the others had not been able to.

"Let's leave. We've seen enough."

"Oh," said one of the actresses, with whom once Martin had made unsatisfactory love, "his lordship is suddenly squeamish."

"Not at all. I consider you. The sun can be harsh on the complexion at your age, Susine."

Dismayed, Dr. Volpe had stepped about his room. His books gleamed and he read their titles, remembering *I have this, and this*. He examined eggs and ornaments (*and this*). Across the blocks of the asylum things went on, but he might pretend they did not. This was his apartment, his country retreat. The palm in the window, the autumn woods.

He went to the case where the new butterfly was displayed, and stopped – in revulsion, distress.

The pinned specimen, which had been like flame and night, was crumbling. Its wings were showering off in soot and embers. Its body had twisted as if tortured, into a corkscrew.

When they brought Hilde from the tiny box where they had locked her, the "coffin," her head was shaven like a bronze ball. She was shut now into a straitjacket, a mad-shirt, her arms secured across her body. One of her shoes had been subtracted.

They put her in the straw. She could barely move.

The women came.

As animals softly nose at each other in the winter fields, just so they approached, not actually touching, but mute, reserved, at one. They knew her. She was themselves.

And then Judit was there, and sat by Hilde.

Judit spoke of the land of snow, where the lovely fruit grew and the dawn-and-sunset sun poured out its jasper radiance. Birds sang and far off the sea glistened, waters that were not cold and into which the wine streams cascaded.

Hilde listened.

When Judit ceased, she said, "Judit, I'm dying."

"No, poor child. You must simply endure."

"But I am. You see, my blood's turned to water."

Judit stroked Hilde's face. "Why do you think so?"

"Because my time hasn't come. Not for weeks."

"Your time? Oh. The female cycle … Once, I too." Judit frowned. "My womb's burned out. Yours also? Be thankful. They shame us here, when we bleed."

Hilde bowed her head. "Then this is good?"

"Oh, yes," said Judit strongly. "Be glad, dear."

NINE

Paradise

Love that moves the sun and the other stars.

Dante Alighieri

Months had passed, but Paradise had no seasons, as it had no sun, no moon.

They had killed with cords, but then came poisons. This often called for a particularly intimate attack – besides, they tried to find new types of bane. It taxed their ingenuity, and this time Felion and Smara put off the task. They did not poison anyone. They told each other, when they met, of their oppression at shirking the labor. Both had come close to it. Smara had even lured a man to her apartment, meaning to put some of the acid from the clockwork cat's leaking panel into a glass of wine. But then she had not done it. The man had left resentfully; obviously he had expected something. "He may only have anticipated sex," Felion told her.

They did not talk about the labyrinth, or the City beyond.

The mystery was like an ache that never went away.

Smara dreamed that she was moving through a pale warm building. An elderly woman in white was hurrying down a corridor, and when she passed Smara, the woman said, "Go away, Lucie. Go to your nurse."

There was a long room that gave on a flagged patio, and here some men sat at ease, drinking tea. They did not seem to see Smara, who prowled about them, half wondering if she might drop poison in their cups. One man smoked a pipe and another toyed with an eye glass. They were elegant, and one very handsome, with longish silken hair. Smara took a fruit or vegetable from a bowl on a table. She threw it past them, out onto the lawn. There it rolled like an orange snowball, away and away, until it hit a low fence in the distance.

Smara did not tell Felion about this dream, in which there had been clarity, daylight, and no mist.

Felion did not dream about the other City, or its environs.

They walked the broad fogbound boulevards, that sometimes echoed at their voices or rang with unknown laughter.

One afternoon, they came, seemingly by chance, to the foot of the hundred steps.

They stood for some time, as if awaiting another person.

Then, in fits and starts, frequently stopping to stare away across the blank of Paradise (the cathedral tower was invisible today), they climbed the steps.

On the Bird Terrace they did not pause. Felion opened the door with the chant of numbers. They went into the house, through, and down.

In the basement a small machine had woken and was bustling about, moving little metal boxes, cogs, and bunches or wire from one place to another, apparently without logic.

As they walked along the track, it skittered after them, then veered away, twittering angrily.

"It believes we're intruders," he said.

"Are we?"

"Yes, but we were meant to be."

Then the ice wall was ahead of them.

Felion picked up the torch he had left lying, and lit it.

"We can run through," he said. "Keep hold of my hand or we may be separated again."

"I'm not afraid," she said. "And that seems wrong."

"They've done something to the door of the artist's house," he said. "That may make it difficult to leave the premises. We must break through *outside* the house. You must *will* that, too."

"I don't know how."

"Demand it then, aloud, of the labyrinth. How else did you get in and out before?"

"It seemed … easy," she said.

"It is easy. Yes," he added, "of course, it must all be wrong. The heat of the torch will finally spoil the ice – what then? We have to decide, Smara, where we want to be."

In the labyrinth they did not run, but walked briskly, she striding and he slightly checking his pace, to stay in step with each other.

A glowing thing bloomed in the wall.

"Look!" she said.

He saw it too, presumably the same vision. A child watching a tiger in a cage. It was a horrible child, sneering at the incredible and flawless animal, which, if the bars had not been there, would have destroyed the child fastidiously and at once.

Then the image dispersed.

They had come suddenly into the oval heart of the labyrinth.

On the floor was a fruit, an orange fruit.

Felion let go of Smara's hand, bent down, and picked the fruit up. But Smara was gazing at the bird-headed thing that had risen above out of the ice. If anything it was now more clear, more like the statues on her uncle's terrace.

Felion tossed the orange fruit up at the ice statue. The fruit struck it a weightless blow and sailed on, and over into nothing, whence, surely, it had come.

"I'm not afraid of that now, either," said Smara. "It's only a shape."

Felion took her by her hand again quickly.

"Let's go on."

A sound rose, the oceanic breathing roar of the labyrinth.

Smara moved reluctantly. "I thought it would crumble a little, when I said it didn't frighten me."

Beyond the heart, keeping to the left, they strode forward.

"Remember," he said, "the *outside* of the woman's house. The street there."

"Are you still holding my hand?" she asked.

Felion hesitated, and as he did so, the torch flickered as if a wind rushed through the maze. And Smara slid away from him.

It was as though she were moved away on runners. She did not seem to notice. When he called out in alarm, she only nodded. "*Outside* the house," she repeated.

And then she was furled aside into the ice wall.

Perhaps Felion had been pulled aside in this way as he followed his uncle, or the man who resembled his uncle, those months before when he had come back here alone.

Felion was appalled nevertheless. He tried to approach the wall, but it was solid, ungiving, and Smara had gone.

He had no choice, it seemed to him, but to proceed to the labyrinth's extremity. Maybe, anyway, he would find her there.

When he reached the end of the tunnels, the torch was fluttering sickly. Ahead, in the opening, lay a cloudy void.

Felion spoke aloud to it, telling it harshly what he expected it to become, the street outside the artist's house. But even when he walked right up to it, the exit from the labyrinth showed nothing but formless clouds, save far away, he seemed to glimpse a shape like a mountain.

"But it's easy," he said. He dropped the torch by the exit point, and plunged his hand and arm out into the cloudy aberration.

Perhaps the tiger's cage was there, and his hand had gone in through the bars.

Felion drew his arm back. It was whole.

Then he shut his eyes, lowered his blond head, and jumped through the gap straight into the cloud.

Smara stood on the golden bank of a malt-dark river. She was not distressed. She had not been so before, when she had lost Felion and arrived in another world. Not to be distressed was possibly distressing.

And this was not the other City. Assuredly not.

The air had an exceptional brightness and lucidity. Distant mountains embraced the sky.

Below, on the honey strand, tigers and lions were feeding on something among the onyx boulders.

Above, a city did line the bank. High, white, pillared buildings, glistening with metal. Huge trees which might have been palms, but their fronds curved to the ground.

Around Smara was a garden, and everywhere in it girls in white were watering the flowers. Probably Smara had not been noticed for this reason, for in her hand was a bronze dipper filled by water. Smara went quietly up the slope of the turf and came out on a walk. On the horizon was a marble palace of extreme tallness. Nearby, a queen or empress was seated under a white sunshade. She was beautiful, more beautiful even than Smara's mother. Around her throat was a rope made of twenty or so chains of enormous pearls. Her black hair fell from a starry coronet to her feet.

A man sat at her feet.

He was tanned almost to leather, and in his ears winked diamonds. He was telling the beautiful queen boldly about a voyage he had made in a timber ship. He showed her on a map that was stretched over the grass.

"But she ran aground, Majesty. We lost the strange fruit and the priceless glass vessels. I was there ten days, with my men, before the king of the land heard what had befallen us and sent his chariots to our assistance."

"I have never known luck like yours," said the queen. "Maque, you know you're worth more to me than any cargo. But who," she added, "is that girl, listening?"

"Your favorite handmaiden, surely."

"No, she has hair like ginger spice. This one has hair like cream. Who are you, young girl?"

"Smara," Smara said, and she bowed. But then the dipper spilled all over her skirt.

"She's in search of some other country," said the queen. "Be careful," she added, "not all of them are good."

"Madame," said the sailor, who had been called Maque, "in a way, it's true of us all – that we search for other countries. Of the mind, the heart, and the soul. And sometimes even we search for hell on earth."

The queen smiled. She laid her hand on his arm. "Where are you going?" the queen asked Smara.

"To Felion, my brother."

"Do you love him?" asked the queen.

"Yes."

"Love can do anything," said the queen.

Smara turned, and a cloud was there behind her. She dropped the dipper on the grass, and then –

And then it seemed she was her mother, falling, falling from the whirling tower, into the stony mist.

The sun was beginning to set, and for a while he forgot even his sister.

Felion was high up, above the City, the wonderful City that had not been corrupted by mist. He could see all of it. The scales of its million roofs, like plates of a crocodile's back, its towers and domes, and far off the loops of its river, tiger's-eye, catching the rays of the extraordinary sun.

But then he wanted her to see this, this fabulous City, beautiful beyond any dream or wish. Oh, he wanted Smara to be here with him. He wanted to live with her, here.

A flight of pigeons passed over the disk of the sun.

Tears streamed down Felion's face, and dried. He had never before, not once, known such joy.

And then Smara came walking toward him, out of a brick wall just down the street, which was not the street outside the artist's house. She looked about shyly, but when she saw him, her face lit with more than the glory of the sun.

He took her hand again, and not speaking they stood together on the height, and watched day move down below the curve of the earth.

Every architecture rose black against its shining. And then the disk was drawn away, and a wonderful softness closed the air, and a magical nocturne of dark, and stars burned up as if nowhere, not in a thousand worlds, had there ever been stars before, or eyes to see them.

"Smara – where did you go?"

"A garden. Not here."

"And I came out miles from that house. Who cares? What does she matter, our mad uncle's artist?"

Hand in hand, they walked the streets as the night filled them. Lamps lit on poles. A breeze blew, sweet with the smell of blossoms from a spring that maybe had not yet begun.

Higher up, they reached the cathedral. The great door was carved with saints and devils, and stood open. An owl flew over their heads.

They entered, and the church was like the stomach of a cliff, it went up for miles. Some service (they had heard or read of such things) must have taken place, for hundreds of candles had been left alight. In the aisle, paper flowers had been scattered.

Felion and Smara separated and went about the body of the cathedral, where no one else was.

Above the altar, a book lay spread on a stand, but when she approached it, Smara could not read the prayer.

Felion, however, found another book in an alcove over a granite tomb. And somehow he read this: "*And the names of the three, who are jointly this demon, are OBLATIC, SAMOHT, and TOLEHCIM.*" Which for some reason made him laugh. And after that the words blurred over and became nonsense, he could not make any phrases out of them.

He and she kneeled under the altar.

"What shall we pray for?" he whispered.

"What is 'pray'?"

He could not answer. He said, "I love you. I always have. If we stay here, we can be lovers."

She turned to him with a look of wonder and happiness. "Could we? Oh Felion, how I'd like that."

They got to their feet and left the cathedral.

Outside, the night was as black as ink now, and the stars had paled before the street lamps, but the big white moon was up, horned, asking only a sky to find its way.

"Where shall we go?" she asked.

"We can go where we like," he said.

So they walked the City.

Paradis has been many things, but seldom heaven on earth. No, Paradys is a venue of shadows, its own books tell us so. But not now, not for these hours. That is the madness of Paradys. It can be also holy, benign, bountiful, and tender.

Outside a café lit by lanterns, Felion and Smara are randomly but charmingly summoned to join in a bridal feast. Delicious food and drink are given them, gratis, food without stones in it or serpents – and wine, not hemlock.

Later they stray up into a park, and here there is a masquerade. Beings with the heads of beasts and birds, deities, and imps. Smara is given a mask of black feathers tipped with nacre, and Felion a sun mask ruffed with gold. They discover that though they cannot read as yet the writing of Paradis, they know its dances, as if taught in childhood.

All night they drink and dance, and later, under a panther black cedar tree, they kiss like the lovers they wish to become, timidly, sensually, carelessly, caressing each other's hearts in surprise.

"We can stay here now," he says.

But Smara is abruptly startled. Perhaps the nightingale singing in the tree has interrupted her thoughts.

"But – not yet."

"Why not? What do we leave behind?"

"We must go back, one last time."

"Why?" he says. "Why?"

"I don't know. But don't you feel we must?"

"Yes. I feel it."

"How can we live there?" she says.

"This City takes care of us."

"Tonight it has," she says. "But will it, afterwards?"

They stare across the park, from whose grassy floor one or two absorbing graves rear up their slabs. (Those of whom Paradis has not taken care?)

"Our uncle," Felion says, "trusted himself to this City. I think, in more than one time. He gave himself to it. Let it be cruel, and kind to him. As it wanted."

Smara sat up. She shivered. "I want to go back."

"To what?"

"We were born there."

"All right. Yes. We must."

They left their masks lying, the bird and the sun. There on the grass among the graves.

It was cold before the dawn, the stars were going out.

"Look," he said, "down there, there's the bitch's street after all. Do you see?"

Smara frowned.

They did not, now, touch at all.

On the grass a cloud had formed, showing them, like a temptation, the way back into hell. But they knew hell. They had got used to hell. They went into the cloud.

The labyrinth was freezing and both of them ran through it.

It took a long time, it seemed like hours, to reach the oval heart. And there, panting and dismayed, they halted.

"Has it gone?"

"The ice bird? No, still there."

"I don't mind. It's nothing."

They stood on the glacial floor and he let the guttering torch droop.

"I know how we can be safe in the other City," he said. "We're the heirs of our uncle. And so is she, this artist. We must kill her, Smara. Then we'll have her place."

"Yes," Smara said. It had seemed to her they would never kill again. But she had been in error. "We'll poison her," Smara said, deciding.

Through the labyrinth something roared, and sighed.

They went slowly now, Smara walking just behind Felion. Not careful, not afraid. They were exhausted. The banquet, after starvation, had been too much, for there are those who have died from something like that.

TEN

Paradis

●

What's the use of worrying?
It never was worthwhile,
So, pack up your troubles in your old kit-bag,
And smile, smile, smile.

George Asaf

Brassy chrysanthemums were bursting from the flower bed. Black ivy had climbed the pedestal of the Medusa, but not reached, or had avoided, the neck and straining mouth, the protruding tongue of stone, and the petrified snakes.

Thomas the Warrior was tying up flowers to sticks.

Leocadia stood over him. Suddenly, intrusively, he reminded her of her infantile memory of her Uncle Michelot.

"On your feet," she said briskly. "Soldier."

And Thomas rose, and stood to a stooped, cramped attention, his chin raised, hands quivering.

"Madame."

"I want a report, Thomas."

"Yes, madame. The chemical attack is over. The losses were slight. The suits held up."

Leocadia raised her brows. Chemical weapons were illegal. Where had they been used and what was he recalling? But it was not this past that mattered. Perhaps he was trying to sidetrack her.

"That's good. Now tell me about the asylum."

Thomas relaxed a little, and looked down at her.

"When I was very young," said Thomas, "a child was eaten alive in the zoo, by a tiger. No one knew how the tiger escaped. Its bars, they said, seemed to melt. It was supposedly destroyed, but not in fact. Someone took it away, it lived in a private house. God knows what meat they fed it. Children, perhaps."

"That's marvelous, but not what I asked you, soldier."

"I am," said Thomas, "a voluntary patient. This is my cage, but I don't mind it. I need a cage. I went mad in the service of my country."

(Oh! Uncle!)

"But *are* you mad?"

"Yes. I have a paper to prove it."

"And I'm mad too, am I?"

"Don't you have a paper?" asked Thomas. "You should ask for one. Then you know where you are."

"I know where I am. In the madhouse."

"Not at all. And anyway, that doesn't make you, madame, a correct candidate. Although you may be," Thomas amended, respectfully.

"I believed you thought I was."

"Well, madame, my opinions alter. Part of my condition, of course. Everything does change, here."

"Yes?" Leocadia scented some element of interest, tart as the tang of citrus zest.

"The buildings, for example," said Thomas the Warrior, "move. As the continents do. Slowly. But now in one direction, now another. The hothouse, for example. I recall it was farther off." He indicated the elder asylum. "Gradually, it crept this way. Perhaps to evade capture."

"Capture by what?"

"Who knows?" asked Thomas.

She saw suddenly through him, how he had been young once. And had he ever been a tiger of a man?

"Tell me about," said Leocadia, "the gin bottles. The brown glass ones with the penguin on the label."

Thomas smiled. His teeth were good.

"Penguin Gin," said Thomas. "It's an old rhyme. A corruption of the original slogan of advertising."

"And how does it go?"

"Penguin Gin, Penguin Gin, drink it up, it'll do you in."

"Ah," said Leocadia softly. "And did it?"

"I expect so. Poisonous, apparently. Lead and copper in the pipes, if such there are in the making of gin. Modern gin is completely wholesome and without additives."

Leocadia said, at her sweetest, "So it poisoned them."

"Oh, there was a story I read once," said Thomas, untying a flower from a stick. The stick but not the flower fell down. "An actor, quite famous, from the era of the gin. His name – Martin. He visited the asylum and charmed the patients with recitals from the plays of the great. But later his brain was curdled from the experience. He began to drink gin in low dives of the slums over the river. One evening he died, in a shocking way." Thomas did not look shocked. Nor did he elaborate. He retied the flower to another stick, and breaking the stick that had fallen, he tossed it over the lawn. Then checked. "I always forget. My dog grew old. Have you ever kept pets, madame?"

"Animals are too good for me," said Leocadia.

Thomas seemed pleased by her reply.

He said, "Johanos Martin was killed by Penguin Gin."

Leocadia said, "You're a mine of information today, Thomas. Tell me some more."

"Today I am," said Thomas the Warrior. He pointed at the Medusa's head. "That was a statue of Madness, once. It crawled or hopped here from the old asylum. I found it in the flower bed one morning. The dew was on it."

"Oh, the dew," said Leocadia. "I've not seen it often. And the leaves are falling now. Will there be snow?"

Thomas stared at her, and through her, and away to his chemical battle-ground which ought never to have been.

"I remember black snow," said Thomas. "Go away. Our conversation is over."

Leocadia said, "Just one further thing. What do you know about the doctors? What can you say about them?"

"Enemies," said Thomas, "who are friends."

"Van Orles," said Leocadia, with distaste.

Thomas turned and walked off along the lawn. The spider man was coming from the other direction, and pawed at Thomas, murmuring he had a good color.

She felt a momentary great loss.

Why had she not thought to paint Thomas, or the head of the Medusa which was not. It was too late now.

She returned uneasily to her room, but her paint had not been removed, her brushes lay where she had left them, and the dangerous bottle, now associated properly with death. The wall of nascent images had not been touched either, yet she was dissatisfied with it and might wish to make changes. (Suitable to the changeable asylum?)

Then again, it was a risk to attempt anything, until she had dealt with her enemy-friend, Van Orles.

Leocadia went to the refrigerator and opened it. Cold.

Leocadia used the button to summon the attendant.

The girl – or one of the girls who all looked the same – arrived.

"I said, I must see the doctors."

"They are so *busy*, mademoiselle."

"I must have Van Orles. It's urgent. It must be Van Orles."

The maid considered her, then went out.

Leocadia drank the pure, cold vodka.

Then she took off her clothes and donned the cream silk housedress.

If parts of the old asylum moved, then too the Residence would move, sliding bits of itself surreptitiously in among the ancient buildings. And the old asylum slunk up over the new, covering it like a rampant animal.

Leocadia left the neck of the dress loose. She brushed her hair viciously. But then there was a noise at the door. She laid down the brush. Her face was smooth as an egg.

Van Orles came in, shut the door. He was all alone, as before, pale and puffy and agitated, trying to be bold and lofty. The warning light around him was like a dry white neon.

"Now, now," he greeted her. He sounded more silly than she had ever heard, like a caricature of himself. He did not light his pipe. He glared, and Leocadia laughed. At that, he backed away. "No violence!" he squawked. "I have warned them, you may be out of control. Someone will come with an injection."

"And spoil our fun?" asked Leocadia.

Van Orles' silly face became a pudding of startlement.

"At least," she said, "you came back alone. I expected you days ago. What a man. What a tease."

Van Orles looked uncertain. He blinked.

"You were unhelpful," he said, "contrasuggestive, previously. You misunderstood my intention and became hysterical."

"I understood everything," said Leocadia. "It was you who made the mistake. Letting me chase you off, when all it required was a little strength. A little manly firmness."

"Your meaning?" demanded Van Orles. His voice was indeed stronger. He sat down on the couch, took out the pipe, and began to toy with it.

"Why should I explain? Are you simple?"

"Be more respectful, Leocadia. In my position –"

"Oh, hush. Such nonsense. Your position is, you're a man, and I am a woman. Do you agree?"

Van Orles assented.

"I was – playful," said Leocadia, sadly, "and you took fright and ran away. He will return, I thought, sweeping all before him. What did you do? You stole my canvases."

"I –"

"Naughty man."

Leocadia offered the unsuspecting Van Orles a grin she had seen displayed in the painting of a famous whore of bygone times. To her irritated unsurprise, Van Orles mellowed immediately, and smiled upon her. What a fool, there in his orb of almost blinding, radioactive light, the light that showed her where the danger was, brighter by the second.

I shall try to see him, she thought, *as a pie with legs and a head*. Just so she would have painted him, if she had been forced to paint him.

"I meant to make a miniature of you," she said. "I meant to paint it on my thumbnail."

Van Orles sniggered.

"What a woman you are, Leocadia."

"Instead I have to paint penguins on the walls. Will it be allowed?"

"Whatever you want, dear Leocadia." Van Orles patted the couch. He slipped the pipe lasciviously into his pocket. "Let me take your pulse."

"Once you brought me a clockwork cat," said Leocadia. "And a fruit that bled."

"Did I, dear Leocadia?"

"Then you won't tell me why."

"Oh, Saume," said Van Orles, "his little experiments. But truly. I don't recall a fruit that – bled, you say?"

Leocadia allowed a button of her cream silk bodice to come undone. Van Orles was riveted.

"My pulse as yours," said Leocadia, "keeps temperate time."

Another button.

"My pulse," said Van Orles, grinning now like the whore, "is quite fast, Leocadia."

And another button. Van Orles puffed, without aid from the pipe. His small eyes bulged.

Leocadia let slip the silk, inch by inch, along the contour of her breast. She waited, and Van Orles made a tiny sound. Then the silk slid over and the globe of whiteness appeared entire, round and pointed too, with its tawny nipple like a sweet or nut.

Leocadia cupped her breast in one hand.

"Do you think," she asked, "I'm losing my looks?"

"Oh – Leocadia –"

Van Orles got up like a stuffed chair on two legs and blundered toward her.

She allowed him to catch her, to rub his face into her naked breast and rub at the other with his hand. In her turn she caught deftly at the fuming doctor. Through the material of his clothes, the familiar bulge amused her experienced fingers.

Van Orles writhed in her grasp. "Ah – no, Leocadia –"

"And here is the other breast, not a stitch on it. And what is here. Look.

My legs are long, don't you think? I've been told they are. And white. But all this bad black hair …"

"Ah – Leocadia – I can't –"

"I can feel you moving. What a strong man. You can't resist me, can you?"

Van Orles struggled now, but Leocadia held him firmly in her clever hand, caressing, goading. He stared down between them at her loins, screwed up his eyes, and made a spluttering noise.

"Alas," said Leocadia.

In horror now, Van Orles peered down at the wetness spread upon his upholstery.

"Such is your effect – er – this is – I –" Gravely embarrassed, annoyed, cheated, and overheated, he limped toward her bathroom. "Excuse me."

Leocadia wiped her hands with turpentine and did up her dress.

When Van Orles emerged he was in a worse state, the wet patch now a soaking extravagant monument to vast incontinence of apparently every sort.

"Hurry and hide, before anyone sees," said Leocadia. "If you were noted in your present state –"

"But I –"

"I'm afraid," said Leocadia, "you do look such a sight."

Van Orles' face was now florid. He perambulated about the room in total confusion, staring at things wildly as if they might assist him. Reaching the door he flung himself on it and bolted out.

Leocadia glanced at the wall of ice crags, the dark glimmer of the penguin. Had she shamed Van Orles sufficiently to safeguard her work?

She walked to the wall, and taking up her brush, loaded it with whiteness whiter than a breast. She was exhilarated. She smiled in a painful rictus, and created mountains.

During the night, Leocadia dreamed that Asra, her hair full of bleeding orange paint, stepped out of the refrigerator. Nothing else happened in the dream, but the next morning, a visitor was shown into Leocadia's room. It was Nanice, her ugly cousin, the inheritrix who had ousted her, put her into the madhouse, *cunning* ugly Nanice, who had had Asra murdered.

Nanice was a picture.

Not that she had grown beautiful, but someone had dressed her as though she might be. Her lusterless hair had been permitted to grow and it had been curled. She had put on a long "artistic" frock, patterned stockings, and un-usual shoes. From her left ear dangled a second ear, made of silver, from which, in turn, hung a single polished diamond. Nanice spread her hands in a theatrical way. On her fingers were silver rings shaped like fingers wearing rings.

"How are you?" asked Nanice, beaming.

"Not dead yet. My apologies."

"Always so tragic," said Nanice. "I can't stay long. It was my duty to see you. I've tried before, but they said you were violent. But here I am. Though my friend is below. *She* hates to wait."

Leocadia deduced that Nanice was implying her friend was a female of the intimate sort.

"Art," said Nanice, savoring, "is very freeing. I understand you now so much better." And she removed from her bag a flask, and drained it. Nanice hiccuped.

"And what do you want?"

"To show you how well I am," said Nanice promptly, like a precocious child – and with such a true and perfect malice that it was both naïve and blameless.

"Yes, you're well. But who runs the firm of assassins you hired to dispose of Asra?"

Nanice blushed. She said, "How can you speak so lightly of that terrible crime?" She added, "Artistic license can only go so far."

"It was clever of you," said Leocadia, "in a filthy, muddled way. And then, did you wait in the street until Pir and Jacqueline and the others had broken down the door? How much were *they* paid?"

Nanice flounced and the silver earring danced. "Your horrible uncouth friends burst in your door for their own edification. Pir was howling that you ruined his dinner, and that woman Jacqueline said you had run out with a knife in your hand and must be stopped. They hated you, and were impossibly drunk – drunk in the wrong way. They're vandals. But yes, we were on the street, Monsieur Saume and I. I told you, you were being watched. I too was afraid for you." For a moment, Nanice looked her old pious self. Then she smiled, kindly.

Leocadia cackled.

Nanice said, with the air of a canny child changing the subject tactfully, "Robert has been sick in your studio. Robert is always sick, isn't he?"

Leocadia felt a dim rush of fury, but she held herself against it and it sank.

"I have an urge," she said, "to pull off your ear."

"Isn't it wonderful? This jewelry is very fashionable." Nanice was not ruffled. She said, determinedly, "It was such a pity Robert was sick in the studio. I've begun to paint there."

Leocadia now felt wooden, almost lifeless. She had never fainted, but perhaps this was what the sufferer experienced in the instants before awareness went out. Hollow, adrift yet fixed, immutable and flowing. She could not explain this. She said, stiffly, "I suppose you paint little images of pretty ladies you think are yourself."

"Oh no. Not at all. I'm painting a woman with the head of an elk, riding on a horse on wheels."

Nanice did not, as she had vowed, stay long. Her visit had been improbable, as if maybe the friend-enemy doctors had requested her to come: one more test. Or – and for a minute or so after the visit, Leocadia seriously considered this – had she hallucinated Nanice? But would a mad woman conjure something so trite?

Yet the creature who was Nanice was no longer precisely trite. Nanice had taken over the role that Leocadia had played so well and so diligently for thirty years, in the City of Paradis: The bad woman, the eccentric, drinking artist.

Leocadia sat on her couch, turning her brushes in her fingers. On the wall the penguin stood amid the snow, large and three-dimensional.

Leocadia thought about Van Orles coming stupidly outside her body, and the warning light, which had faded as he rushed out of the door. She thought of Thomas, who had begun to look so like Michelot, her uncle, who had been kind to her. And of Asra, of course of Asra, whom she had never really liked.

But Nanice had taken Leocadia's life from her, her persona, her obligations of thought and deed. Her memories? And if Nanice had done that, was Leocadia relieved of Leocadia? No more duties to Leocadia. Leocadia, like a bundle of heavy clothes, rolled up and packed away.

Who am I?

She, whoever she was, rose and went to the refrigerator and took out the tall bottle of vodka. Then, with a sigh, she put it back. She did not really want it. She did not have to drink it.

Who *was* she now?

Strange, she must still paint. The painting on the wall drew her like a window full of light and air. Perhaps, then, like Mademoiselle Varc, and Thomas, she was now a conduit for the madhouse. Whoever she was, she smiled at that. And anointed her brush.

ELEVEN
Paradys

Penguin Gin, Penguin Gin,
Drink it up, it'll do you in.

Popular corruption of an advertising slogan

At the Cockcrow Inn, the blackish scum of the alleys had risen to the surface. Outside, the hovels of Paradys clung and clustered to the rainy bank, dark mounds with slitted, small, dull eyes. The interior of the tavern was raucously alight with oil lamps and thick with the smoke of pipes and the foulest cigars. When the tall man entered, heads lifted up into the avaricious glow. They knew him, he had come in before, several nights now. They knew him also as a confidence trickster, a deceiver like themselves, but honored in his profession, as they were not. An actor.

He had not spoken to any of them. Those few who had recognized him had informed the rest. This did not make them like him, or his silence.

When the bar girl had initially told him, pertly, there was no brandy, but only the popular drink, raw gin and sugar, he had taken that. He drank a great deal, and when he was drunk, sitting in his corner, he had muttered things from plays.

Citalbo the poet had once drunk at this inn. It was an old inn, and had had other names.

Perhaps Johanos Martin had been curious about the madman who had given line for line to him. Perhaps he had meant to visit the inn only to see if some essence of Citalbo, or of Citalbo's ultimate fate, had lingered there. Or maybe Citalbo had put a spell of magic upon Martin that had driven the actor down into the inn as another might be sent into Tartarus.

On this sixth night of Johanos Martin's appearance, two of the other deceivers got up from their places and went and sat with him.

"You're the great actor, aren't you? Martin, of the Tragedy."

They spoke of it as if it were a sort of jest, something he might laugh at. But Johanos the priest looked down upon them from the high altar of lamplight and gin and said calmly, "I am Martin."

"Well met," said the bigger of the deceivers, a robber who had once slit

665

throats as regularly as two a night. "Allow us to buy you another drink, monsieur."

"Very well," said Martin. "But what do you want?"

"Oh, the pleasure of your company, monsieur, before we go off on our evening's labors." And with a whistle the cutthroat summoned the bar girl, and bought from her a brown bottle with a penguin on its label. "The best drink in Paradys. This will add fire to your turns on the boards."

"He doesn't lack fire," said the other man, who was only a runner for the squadrons of robbers, capable enough with a club, but mostly good at racing the alleys and climbing up to roofs. "No, it'll cool him, this will. Mixed with snow, this beverage is, and hence the label of ice and freeze."

But Martin was not interested in the bottle. Not yet – he would come to be. Now only the contents had his attention.

They saw to the drink for him themselves, and the runner stirred in sugar. Then all three drank.

The eyes of Johanos Martin were as ever cold and clear and far away, yet he did betray now a slight nervousness. He said, presently, "You gentlemen are generous. But I hope you don't believe you can rob me. I'm not such a fool I brought any valuables into these slums."

"Rob you? Why, monsieur, what do you take us for?"

Martin smiled faintly.

"This inn," added the big man, "is a kind of fellowship. You're safe enough here. Although, I might say, your great-coat would be worth a little trouble to one or two, if they were to catch you before you reached the bridge."

"Are you threatening me?"

"Indeed not, monsieur. In fact, since you're seen drinking with us, I think you can be easy on your way."

"*He* is the important man," said the runner, indicating the cutthroat. "Like yourself, monsieur. A star in the dark."

"Oh, yes," said Martin, so disdainfully his companions laughed.

And then Martin made a slight move, as if to get up, and a third man who had come into the corner from another table slapped him on the shoulder.

"We like you, monsieur," said the cutthroat. "Don't go. Have some more gin, and then do us a recitation from one of your plays."

Johanos Martin had already been fairly drunk when they first approached him. (And afterward it was speculated upon that he might have been insane, that the jaunt to the asylum had sent him so, or why else had he risked his person in this sink?)

Martin said, "If you wish."

And possibly he was willing to perform, unfed, for a table of creatures such as these, where he would not for the supper tables of the upper City.

But it did not come to reciting. For something in the gin thickened Martin's tongue, as his other tipples had not. Thickened his tongue, and paved his brain with luminous crystal thought that told him he was not in jeopardy, just as all men know they can never die.

Near midnight, they led him out, the cutthroat and the runner and the robber, and two or three others, and together they went along the worm trails of the low bank, through places very old, built over again and again, like some terrible painting that could never be finished.

It was winter, and cold. Above, only occasionally hindered by lamps, the stars were pocks of snow in the sky, the footprints of something, going somewhere. But Johanos Martin did not look at these. He was a great actor but he had no true spirit. Besides, he could not, after all the gin, properly see.

They led him into a house above a coil of the river.

It had not been planned, at least, not in their conscious brains. They let him lie down on a bed, and then they ripped off his precious coat, and then they tied him to the iron bed frame.

When they took from him other clothes, they found his body was pale and hard, in better condition than their own, from his exertions on the stage.

Although drunk, he cried out when, one by one, they invaded him.

In prisons, orphanages, aboard ships, in gloomy watches of the soul, they had found out this means of sodomy, which now they brought and worked out upon Johanos Martin. They raped him many times. Without a single kiss.

And finally it was the runner who thrust into Martin's body the empty gin bottle. Who worked with that upon him.

Inside the anus of the helpless man the four-sided glass neck shattered. (Normally, only orgasm would be sufficiently strong to break such glass.)

Much later, after the deceivers had left him, he was found. And thus, later still, five days later, in a paupers' hospital, Johanos Martin died of a bottle of Penguin Gin. The death was disgraceful, and hushed up.

No last words, or quotations, remained, for in a delirium of agony, such things did not arise.

No one mourned him in particular, yet the spectators of the City did so, for he had held many in thrall that he had not met. The love of strangers.

All that escaped was the rumor he had died of drink.

They did not mind that. It was romantic, tragic: usual.

Hilde woke, weeping in the darkness. Hearing her, some of the others began to cry, and the woman who made sounds made them, over and over, like a bell.

Judit came to Hilde across the moonless black.

"You must be brave. One day, we'll be free. We will go to my country. Or into the heaven of snow, Penguinia. For that is the land's name. Yes, I asked Maque. Don't you recall?"

It was winter, and the room was icy. Hearing Judit's voice, the women whispered and were mute.

"Think of the warm snow," said Judit, "warm as feathers. And the sweet wine."

"I'll never see it," said Hilde.

Judit touched her gently, her head, her neck, her shoulders and hands, Hilde's stomach. There, Judit hesitated.

Like all the beings of the madhouse, Hilde was ferociously undernourished, and she had become very thin. Her hair they had let grow, but it was not as strong as it had been, not springing or bright. The woman Moule had said she doubted it would be worth trying to sell Hilde's second crop of hair. Hilde's belly, where Judit's hands had paused, was hard and round, like the gut of a terrible hunger.

The warders had not noticed, for they did not investigate their charges once novelty wore off, and Hilde, so slight, looked only swollen in the way of malnutrition. But to Judit's fingers, the fact of this pathetic taut belly now became apparent.

Judit, who had been a whore, sat back in queenly stillness. Within the black, Judit closed her beautiful eyes.

"We must prepare."

She bowed her head in a gesture of acceptance and mourning.

Hilde said again, "I'll never see the Penguin Land. The Penguinia. Never. It isn't real."

"Yes. And you will see it, child. Before I do. Penguinia is the country of joy that lies behind this place of pain."

Far off, from the men's dormitory, came the lonely hyena calling of despair.

It was not true that Maque had named the Penguin Land. Judit had done that. After the day the actors came to look at them, Maque had been punished in various ways, and he had grown silent. He did not climb on top of the hill of furniture, and one morning the warders dismantled it. They threw the old chairs out into a yard of the asylum.

Citalbo had become quiescent too, and no longer wrote his snatches of verse. The noise from the male dormitory reminded Judit of these silences.

While inside Hilde, a bud had formed, even as the hair grew from her shaven skull. After a few weeks, Marie Tante and Bettile had ceased fastening Hilde into the mad-shirt. As well, for otherwise, they might, even they, have seen.

But the child in Hilde's womb was without quickness. Judit had felt such things before, in her previous existence.

So she prepared, not for the arrival of life, but the advent of death.

Hilde Koster, in the madhouse, carried the dead child of dead Johanos Martin for a little more than five months. Any symptoms of her pregnancy she mistook easily for the constant malaise due to ill treatment, and the minor poisonings to which the inmates of hell were subjected, the lack of any care. And Hilde, who had once been "Little Hilde," was ignorant of biological fact.

So she walked about in the straw of the white chambers, and sometimes in the stone court of exercise, and she slept in the room of the moon, stunned by the horrible cold, a dummy of flesh closed tight around this small lump of mortality.

At the beginning of the sixth month, about fifty days after Martin's death in the paupers' hospital, an incredible quiet sank on the asylum.

The warders prowled the rooms, sometimes slashing at the mad people with their sticks.

"What are they up to?"

Even the ones who crawled in circles or beat at flies did so in utter noiselessness.

Into the yard had been shunted a few of the men and most of the women, among them Judit and Hilde.

The day was frigid, like gray quartz, and up into it the biscuity walls rose, gray also in the stasis of the light. Hilde's ruined hair was like a beacon, the only brilliant thing visible, a drop of autumn sun, the splash of a summer fruit. But under the trails of this hair Hilde was a white shivering Madonna of death, who suddenly dropped down, her mouth shaping into the grimace of a mask, a shock too vast for sound.

Figures of ice, the other women stood about, a chorus in a play without words, and without motion.

"Damn the pigs, why don't they make a noise?" demanded Bettile. "Go over, Marie, and hit one of the bitches. Pull that fat one's hair."

The air was stony and silence hurt their ears.

Bettile took a step toward the group of women. And at this instant Hilde screamed in agony.

"Ah, there goes one. Again, again, you slut. Let's hear you!" cried Moule.

And as all the women began to shriek, and inside the block the men yowled like dogs, the warders shook themselves and passed back and forth the brown bottle that only a shameful convulsion could shatter.

Like a hedge, the mad women solidified around Hilde on the ground, and unseen, Judit kneeled by her.

There was no time for Hilde to question or protest. Death broke from her in a shattering spasm of water, and of blood.

Hilde screamed, and the women, her chorus, screamed.

The wardresses congratulated them. They smote one or two across the legs. These women skipped and grunted, and then resumed their outcry.

"Old Volpe will hear," said Moule, with satisfaction.

They were tickled.

If Volpe heard, up in his apartment on his country estate, he pretended to himself that these were the cries of winter geese blown inland from the river miles away.

Something tiny and dreadful was squeezed from Hilde's broken body, and lay on the stone ground, linked to her by a silvered cord.

It was if her soul had been squashed out in the shape of a monster.

The warders had gone in, it was too cold for them in the yard. The women stared down on the death that had been born of Hilde.

It was a child, a child in parenthesis, not wholly formed. In color – in color it was like the skin of a pumpkin. An orange child, the product of wronged blood or a damaged liver, the product of a flame that had burned out.

Judit took Hilde's hands.

"It's over," said Judit, as in the back streets of her past she had said it to this one or that, silken girls murdered by reproduction, the task devised of a male god, or demon.

Hilde could not speak. Behind her eyes the sea was drawing away. She lay aground upon the beach. Hollow, adrift yet fixed, immutable and flowing.

"Don't be afraid," said Judit. "You ask me where you are going to? Now you'll see Penguinia."

For a second a light lit in the tidal windows of the eyes. Was it so? After this interval of the impossible, the redemption most human things hope for? Then the light flickered and faded. So swiftly, so clumsily and unbelievably, we must leave.

They were all dead now, the father, the mother, and the child of a cursory act one had wrought on the other.

Only the force and sorcery of the appalling event remained, and hovered there like the smolder of the blood, and was breathed in, through lips, through stones.

The women drew away. There was no more they could do. The ghastly orange gnome of the stillborn must be left for the warders to discover and remove, as the corpse of Hilde, the last door of all slammed on her, must be come on and tidied, roughly and with oaths. A piece of earth somewhere on the premises was kept for such debris. Dead lunatics were cast into sacks and so into quicklime, that there should always be space for the next one.

Outside the walls, about one hundred and thirty meters along the road, and among some desolate somber trees, Tiraud and Desel stood in the dusk before dawn.

Tiraud was grumbling that he had hurt his back, lugging "that bitch." Desel was sullen, in the grip of a sort of agoraphobia that often came on him when he had to go beyond the asylum precincts.

The burial of the dead female lunatic and her stillborn infant had been gone through on the previous evening. Dr. Volpe had not attended, and it was Desel who spoke the prayer over the dead – which consisted of a drunken burp. The warder had botched up some evidence of the correct event, and then laid the two corpses together in a stout sack. It had been more difficult in earlier years, when Volpe had nerved himself to oversee all obsequies. Frequently then there had been nothing to salvage for the sinister carts that came up the road, with the morning star.

"Here it is now," said Tiraud, as he gave over the gin bottle to Desel, the Penguin of Joy. "Are they going to haggle again? He's lucky to get it. Such a fresh one, and only a girl. And the abortion's grand for study. Some doctor will delight in it."

Such was the security of the house of madness that they had easily been able to carry out the pitiable sack between them. Those that saw knew and approved their errand.

The cart came rolling up the road, a bundle of shadow, the lean horse pulling it, like some medieval image of Death.

But it was a cheery, leering individual who craned down.

"What have you got for me, eh? Something nice?"

"A young girl of fifteen, only a day old. And a premature child of unnatural coloring," said Desel. "Do you want to see?"

"No, I trust you, *gentlemen*. You know there'd be trouble if you lied."

One bag was hoisted up into the cart. Another, lighter, plopped down.

"It's not enough," said Tiraud. "You promised more."

"Ah, but there, you see," said the carter, "you think this is a rare treat for me, this young lady and her calf. But they're harder to dispose of, these oddities. More questions are asked. And some of my clients turn shy. They'll take a strapping great man without a qualm. But a maiden and a monster baby – who can tell? Why, I may have to tip the lot in the river."

"You bloody liar," said Tiraud.

"Don't waste your breath," said Desel. He took the money bag and began to walk up the road toward the loom of the asylum, which, from this juncture, looked like a weird mansion or fortress, probably romantic, in the half-light and mist.

Tiraud made after him, as if afraid to be left alone and standing in the world.

The carter eyed their retreat.

"Mad things," he said to his horse. "Madder than their charges."

As he turned the cart, the sack rattled under the cover. It lay amid sacks of potatoes and swart cabbage, and once he would have taken more care to ensure it was jumbled, the unvegetable death, among his other goods. But this did not matter much now, for the way he went by, into Paradys, was watched by those with whom he was on friendly terms.

It was a winter morning, and the dawn star was very radiant, sending fine shadows away from the standing things of the landscape. A bleak scene, the road and the black trees that periodically flanked it. Here and there a shorn field. Presently there would come gaps where the earth swept down, and the City might be glimpsed, curled around its river and smoking as if deadly on fire. The morning fog preempted the sense of smoke. A silence pushed in against the cart.

"Mad people," said the carter of cabbage and death. "The world's mad. Take me. I could be snoring in bed. Take you, horse, letting me fasten you to this cart."

Something moved in the cart's interior. It might be potatoes tumbling through a sack.

The carter cocked an ear. He knew the noise of potatoes.

"What's that, eh?" He did not look back. In his particular trade, he had heard the stories, the corpse that sat up, perhaps wearing the face of a loved one. But the carter had no loved ones. "Better keep still," he wheedled. "I'm taking you somewhere lovely. I am. To help in the pursuance of knowledge."

There was a sound now like a knife slitting a sack.

The carter mused.

"Just stay quiet," he said.

Then something rose up in the cart, and dislodged the cover. Because the dawn star was behind it, its shadow fell across the carter and his lean horse.

"Christ, now," said the carter.

He turned slowly, and looked back.

As he did so, a darkness fell through the air, and then a pallor, and something stung his cheek. It was a snowflake. And in the cart, on top of the sacks, was a huge rock of a bird, black-caped like a nun, with a breast of ice, and an amber blaze against the blade of its beak, which resembled – or might have been – obsidian.

The carter did not know what this creature was, although he had seen it represented somewhere.

In the silence it towered over him. A smell came from it, the odor of spirits, killingly sweet. During those moments, before the carter could in any way respond, the reins jerked in his hands – the horse began to run.

As the carter clung to the reins and shouted, the darkness seemed to swirl about his head, and the only picture that was with him was of that stone beak like a dagger plunged between his shoulders. Yet he had no choice but to strive with the running horse.

Snow dashed in his face like pieces of a broken moon, a moon made of dead white flesh.

The horse grew tired suddenly and stopped still, the cart juddering and slewing to a halt behind it. With a loud cry, the carter turned again then, and saw the fearful bird thing had vanished from the cart. There instead strewn on the sacks, were the corpses of the dead girl and a little swathed thing that might have been anything small and once alive.

"Now," said the carter, "now, now, now."

He glanced over from the cart, through the flurry of the snow, and saw a hollow place into which they had almost fallen; the horse had stopped on the very brink. Below was a black pool not much larger than a well.

Touching the dead did not bother him, but now he would rather have not. Even so, it must be seen to. The money was lost, but he had cheated them anyway.

He hauled the girl and her fruit off the cart and flung them over into the hole of water. They went without a note, the water closed, and they might never have been.

When he was a mile farther off, the snow ceased. He gazed back and saw it falling still among the uplands and the raped fields. The trees had the shapes of birds waiting motionless, but for what?

Marie Tante moved with her lamp along a night corridor. She was searching for Moule, who always had gin upon her person. Sometimes Moule would slouch up to the room beside the chamber of the Waterfall, and sit behind the glass partition. Marie Tante had often come this way to find her. There beside the lever they would stare into the dim inverted bathtub, with its hanging serpent and the horror chair beneath.

At the unlighted corridor's end, Marie Tante found that she had lost her way. She was not where she had believed she would be. For years she had come in this direction and by this route. She checked in surprise. Here she was on the other corridor, which led to the little cells where newcomers were confined. How could this have happened?

Marie Tante had no imagination. Cruel things stirred her obscurely, but most of the nooks of her brain were closed up, or vacant. It might have been said she was a being who should never have been allowed to live but rather sent back at once to be refashioned, for her life had never gained anything for her, and to others, often, it had been the cause of atrocious evil, misery, and pain.

Lacking intuition, Marie Tante did not consider that something bizarre had occurred, although she knew she should not be where she was. She did not think anything had misled her, let alone that sections of her plane of existence had *shifted*. No, she merely retraced her steps, and got again onto the path toward the Waterfall.

Then however, as she was turning the corner, her lamp cast up a gigantic shadow on the wall high above her head.

Even Marie Tante was arrested.

She stopped, holding the lamp, and looking.

Then she looked back, over her shoulder.

Far off, at the passage's other end, something moved. How its shadow had come forward, and so through her lamp, was a mystery. No other lights burned in these corridors when they were not in use.

Marie Tante could not be sure what she had seen. She took it for another warder, a tall man, and called. But the shape was gone now and the shadow also.

She went on and opened the door into the room that overlooked the Waterfall.

Something black rose up in a lump from the floor.

Moule balanced in Marie Tante's lamplight, hugging herself, pulling faces. On the ground was a smashed bottle. So much for the gin.

"What's up, you fool?" said Marie Tante.

"*Something's out there.*"

"Yes, old Big Feet wandering about, or that other one, Bettile's fancy."

"Oh yes," said Moule, "oh yes."

"What did you think it was?" demanded Marie Tante, irritated by the lack of drink. She toed the shards. In a pool of liquid, the label floated, sodden.

"Do you remember," said Moule, "when we cut off that girl's hair?"

"What girl?"

"The one who died."

"The ginger slut? What of it? You got your share of the money."

"That baby. It was a strange color. Like her hair, the color."

"Tiraud and Desel will have seen to that."

Moule mumbled. She glanced into the chamber of the Waterfall, and squeaked. "Look, Marie."

Marie Tante looked through the glass, where her lamp vaguely shone, and saw that fluid was running from the hose above the chair.

"You dolt. Why work the lever now?"

"I didn't. See, it's in place."

"Some fault in the apparatus," said Marie Tante. "I'll report it."

The smell of the spilled gin was very intense.

"Let's go away," said Moule, spinning about like an unwieldy top.

She clutched at the lamp, but Marie Tante kept a firm hold on it.

"It's the drink," said Marie Tante, "it's addled you."

"Oh, it could be. Let's go back, where the others are."

"Yes, they may have some gin."

Moule followed Marie Tante closely as a scared child, along the dubious, quiet, and unlit passageways.

Down in the courtyard, they passed a pile of furniture, wrecked chairs and parts of tables. Marie Tante seemed to remember it had been stacked up elsewhere, but she did not dwell on this, for obviously the pile had been moved.

The night was bitter cold.

"It'll snow," said Moule, staring up at the bright black hardness of the sky.

"So what? We'll keep warm."

The lunatics had been propelled, for the period of the dark, to their segregated dormitories. In one of the annexes off the vacated rooms of straw, the warders had a fire going. Into this area Moule darted and went shivering up to the hearth.

Desel and Tiraud sat among the men, smoking their pipes and gambling with the cards. Some of the wardresses too had a game, but Bettile was making a shawl, working the smoky wool cleverly, with harsh sharp twists. The hands of Bettile, which had inflicted so many blows, so much hurt, which had struck down Hilde when she would not parade before the actors, and later held her while another shaved the girl's scalp, now forced into the shawl some awful psychometry. Only she, on a holiday, could have borne to wear it.

Tiraud got up abruptly. He had been uneasy since this morning's transaction over the sack.

"Ah, he's off to his harlot," said one of the men. "Give Judit my kiss. Tell her I'll be by."

Tiraud spat. "Judit? That vermin. I'm only going to stretch my limbs."

"Don't take cold. The women's pen has ice hung from the windows."

Tiraud was away, removing in turn the lamp Marie Tante had brought in with her.

The room was sunny with firelight, a merry picture, dear friends gathered at a hearth.

There was the drink also. They portioned it out, starving predators with a kill, who must protect each other for the strength of the pack.

The fire described them, their faces and their hands, the angles of their bodies.

And one by one, it described how they flinched and touched at their cheeks or necks, and then gazed up.

A faint whiteness … fell softly through the room.

"Snow," said Bettile, shaking it from her shawl. "The roof's leaking. A fine thing."

"How can it leak? There are the rooms above."

The snow fell. It fell thickly now and swiftly. They got up. It sizzled in their fire and in the lamps, which flickered.

Then the snow stopped, and only the wet spots were on them, like the marks of God.

"Volpe must be told. Some crack in the wall –"

Marie Tante took a swig from her mug. The gin was hot and laced with sugar from the can on the table.

Moule crouched over the fire. She was thinking of a sister she hated, who lived north of the City, and how she might go calling on her very soon.

"Judit, you filthy cow. Open your legs."

The queen of lands beyond Sheba and Babylon lay under Tiraud. Her face of a damask sphinx was exposed to the ceiling of the women's dormitory, and so she saw the snow begin to fall at once. Judit smiled.

"Like it, do you?" said Tiraud. "Dirty whore."

Judit raised her slim hands into the snow, and Tiraud finished in her with a series of unmusical grunts. As he left her, he stood up into the snowstorm.

On all sides the women were sitting up or getting on their feet. They made little noises like birds greeting the morning sun.

"What is it?" said Tiraud. His eyes were wide. He knew perfectly that the snow was falling in the room, out of the ceiling itself.

"Penguinia," said Judit calmly, also getting up, her unclean skirt dropping to hide the vulnerable wound of her body. "The country of ice is coming."

The women were romping now, in the snow, holding out their hands to catch it, rubbing it on their cheeks and eyes. The snow gleamed with its own light, defining the room with a beautiful silver deception, so that the meanness and foulness disappeared, the perspective of pallets and buckets and walls went on forever, becoming hills and distant tumuli. And the women looked young and fresh, lovely, tender.

Tiraud tried to flail the snow away from him like a swarm of wasps. He heard Judit say, "It's warm as roses." He rushed toward the door, grabbing up the lamp, flinging himself outside.

"What is it? It's some trick. Some insane trick of theirs –"

And he heard, from the men's dormitory, a sudden ululation, not the howls of distress or terror that generally went up there, but a full-throated, gladsome baying.

"Desel –" said Tiraud. He ran down the building, down a flight of stairs. A few lamps burned below, and he raced toward the light, for the darkness was not safe.

The snow had not been warm, not to him. He shuddered and sucked his frozen fingers as he ran. Of course, it had only blown in through the broken windows. What was the matter with him? Crazy as the stinking mad people.

He stopped at the bottom of the stairway, amazed at himself. And from the shadow just beyond the lamps, came a statue, walking.

Tiraud identified the creature at once. Laughable and absurd. And yet. It carried with it the soul of the darkness, and all the fearful majesty of some god of the Egyptian underworld. It was the spirit of the gin bottle, and only through that could Tiraud, ignorant of all things but self, have identified it: The Penguin.

It moved as a penguin moves, in a lurching waddle, but very slowly, ponderously, like a juggernaut of the East, a mechanism that had the power of ambulation. It was seven feet in height, perhaps taller. On its white breast the smudge of foxy color. Its head black as stone, black-eyed, and its beak was made to be a weapon of death.

From the dark it came, bringing the dark with it, and went across the space, not heeding the man who watched it, paralyzed, and away again into shadow.

Tiraud's legs gave way and deposited him on the lowest step. Here he flopped, not able for some while to recollect motion.

Then at last he rose, cuddling the stair rail, and next shot himself staggeringly off into the passage *It* had left alone.

And as he wove and sped, Tiraud screamed. The scream burst from him uncontrollably, like steam from a kettle.

He reached the dayrooms of Madness, screaming like this, and screaming he thrust back among his brothers and sisters, the warders. So, being used to it, and to a particular reply, they took him, beat him, knocked him to the earth.

"What now? Are you cracked like the rubbish upstairs?"

"I saw –" said Tiraud, lying at their feet.

"Saw what?"

They did not seem skeptical, but as if they had anticipated this messenger out of the web of the building.

Yet even now he did not dare to tell the truth. He sat and nursed his knees. "Give me a bloody drink." And then he thought of the image on the bottle and pushed the liquor aside. "Someone's out," said Tiraud. "One of them's escaped. Wandering in the corridors." That was all he could say, to them, and to himself, to justify what he had seen. For what he had seen was not real. Then for a moment, he thought of the dead body in the sack. So he reached for the drink after all.

The warders became ferocious, accusing one another. How had one of the lunatics evaded the nightly shutting-up? (And Tiraud, drinking, realized he had not relocked the women's dormitory. He had left them scampering about there and the door had only to be tried –)

And all at once, miles high it seemed, the bacchante cries of women flew through the upper air of the building and unravelled away.

"The beasts are out – all of them," exclaimed Marie Tante, Her eyes lit, and Bettile put down her shawl.

There, in their cave of firelight, they listened. The vision seemed conjured in the room, the mad people in their white rags, flying along the upper corridors, down the steps, across the yards, and up into the other blocks, figures painted by a strange white light, like the moon, with streaming hair and outstretched arms.

Desel strutted forward.

"Idiots! Some of you – you and you, you three there – go to the men's place and see to them. Use your sticks. And you women, you go after those bitches. You'll be sorry, Tiraud, screwing your brains out on that trollop and forgetting the door. I know. Go and alert Volpe now. Why should *he* sleep, the bastard?"

In his downy bed, within his luxurious flat, Dr. Volpe, full of dinner and brandy, was dreaming.

He performed on the piano to a vast audience, up on a great white stage. He felt his genius flood from him.

But it was very cold. His fingers were losing feeling. They stuck to the keys, burning. It came to him, the piano was made of ice, and the stage also was ice. In horror he stared about him, and found he was adrift on the ice floe in the midst of a coal-black sea by night. And from the sky rang hammering blows.

These blows woke him. He lay huddled, the warmth slipping back into his body, gradually understanding that someone smote on the door. His housekeeper had gone to the City on some errand. He would have to attend to the door himself. And what could it mean, this nocturnal racket, but only trouble?

Still shivering, he lit his lamp, and fumbling himself into his dressing gown, he sought the door.

The warder Desel and some other man stood there.

"The lunatics have escaped, doctor, and are running all over the buildings, perhaps the grounds."

"What?" said Dr. Volpe.

Desel repeated his cryptic news. Volpe sensed, correctly, that even in agitation, Desel drew enjoyment from Volpe's fright.

"They must be caught," said Volpe superfluously. "They may damage things – they may harm themselves."

"The others are going about, doctor, trying to capture the wretches. They will, of course, be as gentle as they can, but restraint or blows are probable."

"No, no," feebly said Volpe.

Desel glowered with authority.

"They're violent. Suppose they get out on the road?"

"Ah ... yes."

Volpe drew back into the room. He strained his ears but heard nothing at all, not the faintest cry.

Desel said, "We'll inform you, doctor, of events."

"Yes," said Volpe. "Good, trustworthy men. I can leave this – in your hands."

When he had shut them out, Volpe bolted and locked the door. He hurried to the window.

Something pallid flitted among the chestnut trees – or did he imagine it? He was sensitive and now his nerves were bad. He could no longer see anything moving there.

A loud crack caused him to jump. He gazed transfixed at the hothouse. Some panes of glass had given way, he could not see them, yet he felt the hiss of coldness coming in upon the winter fruit.

Because he had been woken, the brandy he had drunk was affecting him uncomfortably. His heart beat in a rattling way in the midst of his frame.

There was an impure and acid smell in the room.

Dr. Volpe turned, tracing the smell at once to the ewer of water standing beside his plants. He went to the ewer, sniffed at it. He recoiled. One of those men must have played a joke on him. It was in bad taste, and besides he could not think how it had been done, since neither of them had entered the room. The ewer, however, was full of their disgusting gin.

Volpe wanted to open the window and pour the muck out but was afraid to. Perhaps the mad people were on the roof and might, somehow, reach down –

And perhaps one of the mad people had got into his apartment as he slept, and contaminated the water.

Volpe was immobilized by terror for some minutes.

Finally, trembling, he lit the other lamps in the room, and then in the bedroom, and armed with the poker from the dead fire, he stole around, parting curtains and peeking into closets.

No one was there, and nothing but the ewer had been disturbed.

A dreadful compulsion made him go at last to the ewer, dip in one finger, and lick it. The flavor was like venom; it made him gag, as he had known it would. He raised the jug and bore it into the bath chamber, pouring it away through the drain of the bath. Then he employed the tap, and from its nozzle ran a stream of stuff that stank just like the gin, that surely *was* gin, although how could it be?

Volpe shut off the tap and panted back into his sitting room.

In the lamplight, the birds' eggs and the growing plants glistened oddly, as if they had been coated with moisture or frost. And on their pins the butterflies flamed, and the remains of the butterfly that had crumbled were like metallic dust.

Reaching the male dormitory, the three men found the door was shut and locked. The calling of the women had faded, and they had seen none of them. Marie Tante and her crew would take care of this.

There was no longer any noise, either, from the male dormitory.

Armed with their sticks, and certain other implements, iron hooks, and so on, the warders decided to go in and effect a lesson on the madmen who had howled of their own volition.

The door was undone.

The long room, substantially exactly the same as that which housed the women of the asylum, was undisturbed. But by their pallets the men stood, every one of them, voiceless and intent, as if ready. Even the worst cases, who seldom kept still even asleep, were poised and altered. The man worried by insects did not hit out at them, the swaying man scarcely moved. On the grinning face of the man who grinned, the pain had been mitigated by a curious attention.

"What's this row, then?" asked one of the warders, irrationally, of the silence, and a couple of others hefted their sticks and hooks.

Thin as the thinnest rope, the mad sailor, Maque, walked forward from his bed place.

"I've sailed the seas," said Maque, "but I never saw the cold country of the snow."

"Shut up, you," said the foremost warder. "Or do you want a bit of this?"

Maque leapt up in the air, straight at the warder. Maque's bony hands and nails like claws tore furrows in the flesh of throat and face. And as the warder raised his stick, shrieking, his fellows roiled forward. But in that moment a colossal sound passed through the building, through atmosphere, through stone, and through every atom in between. It was the resonance of an enormous organ, or perhaps the music of the arctic wind that threaded some hollow pipe of ice floating in eternity.

After the sound, the wind itself rushed across the room. It blasted against the warders and threw them back, and they careered about with their eyes starting, yelling at the cold savagery of it, the sticks and iron ripped from their frozen hands.

Where they fell, the lunatics sprinted by and over them. As if at this signal, the prisoners darted out to freedom.

Of the felled warders, the two that could got up and pursued the madmen, shouting and cursing. One man, whose leg had been snapped, pulled himself along the corridor, begging his comrades not to leave him, but when he reached the turn of the passage a huge shadow went by and the warder buried his head in his arms, gibbering.

Marie Tante, Bettile, and their sisters could not find the madwomen. In small groups, they spread out through the buildings, searching. They too carried lamps and sticks, and a few had brought mad-shirts, in preparation.

From outside the blocks of the asylum, it was possible to see these lamp-lights passing up and down the windows of the buildings, and now and then over the yards, which gave the bizarre impression that parts of the masonry were shifting about, going from spot to spot, crossing over one another.

Sometimes a shout would echo down the night, but it carried no meaning except alarm or rage.

No snow had fallen on the outer ground, or if it had, it was invisible. Only the great cold was there, and the moonless shine of stars.

In the last block, Dr. Volpe's apartment burned with frantic light. Once or twice he appeared at the window. He had heard a peculiar sound but now believed it was only his overwrought nerves that had caused it, inside his own head.

Small pieces of glass from the hothouse lay on the grass like fragments shed from the duller stars.

The captives of the asylum strayed down, maybe from force of habit, to the rooms of straw to which they were herded by day. They had never been there in the dark.

Citalbo met Judit, and Maque appeared with blood under his nails. The rest followed them.

Uncoerced, they went into the annex where the warders had been sitting at their fire. This room was warm and magical, and the people called lunatic wandered about in it, examining the things their jailors had left lying, the cards and pipes, and the hideous shawl, which Judit cast suddenly into the flames of the hearth.

They sipped, too, at the abandoned mugs of gin. But their systems had been denied alcohol so long they did not like it, indeed some wept and spat the gin onto the floor.

All about them, the madhouse was rife with searchers and destroyers, but here in this firelit heart they were in sanctuary. Had their warders returned here, they would have found these freed slaves easily. But they did not return. Only darkness and whiteness, with a flash of amber, came and filled the entry.

Then the people were afraid.

But Citalbo said, "No. This is the hour."

And Maque said, "They're mild birds. They don't do harm."

And Judit said, "He's like a king, a great monarch. We must go with him."

And so, as the Penguin moved from the entrance way, they went out, all of them. And in their path, right across the rooms of straw, there was a wall. And on the wall was a painting. It was of ice floes and sheets of ice, and beyond the ice were mountains. A marigold glow hung over it, and there before its face the Penguin was, as if it had been painted too, onto the wall.

"Penguinia," said Judit. "I'll give up my land, to be there."

There are instants of immeasurable beauty. They evolve and are and cannot be argued with.

Out of Penguinia came the organ note that shook the asylum to its roots, and next came the wind of the snow. But it was not cold. It was warm as the fire on the hearth and much, much sweeter. And as this happened, as Penguinia breathed upon them, the wall of the painting opened, and became actual, like the gateway into a garden.

So they saw the soft, warm snows, and the trees blooming up from them with their apricot and orange fruit, and the sun purred on the ice, and a stream bubbled like champagne. Flowers grew in Penguinia, and beyond the slopes of white, a golden sea sparkled.

Some broke away at once and ran and ran through and ran out into the landscape of this country of heaven.

"I dare," said Citalbo. "Let's go there."

And Maque and Judit and Citalbo walked up to the edge of the snow and stepped over among the flowers.

Then the others came after, all of them, the ones who slouched like sad apes, and the ones who shook and the ones who had cried alone in the night for years. And as the soft ground of Penguinia received them, they looked up in wonderment.

Judit bowed to the spirit, the great Penguin, and then alone hastened over the snow toward the sunlit sea, where the seals were diving and descending like mink ribbons.

"Worlds set like suns," Citalbo said, "and rise like suns. That's mathematics."

"There'll be huge white bears," Maque said, "and little white foxes."

"But kind," Citalbo said, "here."

Behind them the rooms of straw had become only a hole of darkness, which was dissolving.

Maque looked back.

Through the aperture, some of the warders appeared. They had blundered into the lower building from the yard. Marie Tante was there, and Tiraud. They gaped at Penguinia.

"Close the gate, quick," said Maque.

On the platelike faces of the warders was a look that had nothing to do with reason or duty. It was a gaze of fury and jealousy, of wicked, blind human bestiality, which had been cheated.

But then the hole back into hell went out, like a momentary flaw in sight. It was gone, and the world was gone, and there was simply *here*, which would be kind.

Only Tiraud ran at the empty space and smashed at it with his stick. Only Tiraud roared.

Marie Tante had already dismissed the mirage. As what? She did not have the wit to specify.

Moule sniveled, thinking she had gone mad.

While all across the buildings of hell, the others bounded up and down, with their lights and instruments of hurt, seeking, stumbling, and in his flat, the collector of murdered birds and butterflies, Dr. Volpe, tapped at his piano in objectless fear. And the walls and planes, the walks and yards and lawns, slid and shifted this way, that way, and abruptly froze to stillness.

"What's that noise?" said Desel, pausing on a stair.

"I smell gin," said Bettile suspiciously.

Dr. Volpe stared inside the piano lid.

There was a trickling, and then a flow, like a thousand taps. That was all. And then there gushed from every pipe and drain, from every cup and bottle, out of every crevice and pore and tiniest crack, the Wave.

It reeked. It reeked of gin. It was gin.

Iridescent and limitless, it crashed through all the lower chambers, and up all the stairs. It plowed across the rooms like a liquid wind of steel. The lamps sizzled out.

They heard and saw it come, and *smelled* it come. This climax of poisonous despoilment.

There was a handful of seconds, during which not one moved, but everything in them lunged and boiled in an attempt to keep its life. But the very smell of the jolly fluid, on which they had sustained themselves, was vilely overpowering. Tears ruptured from their eyes and nostrils and dribbled, salivating helplessly at the onset of death. For death came, it swept in on them like the tsunami, the tidal breaker of an ocean. The putter-out of light.

Then they screeched. Each and all of them. They had been made one.

Drooling and retching, tears and snot running down their faces, they tried to get away before it, but the Wave caught them, effortless, and swallowed them. They were lifted off their feet, turned over, bobbed up to the very ceilings and peaks and slammed there.

Full. They were filled. Bellies, sinuses, lungs, arteries, blood. Brains. Spasms uncontrollable and useless convulsed bodies, drowning in liquid fires, everyone trying to heave inside out and so expel the invasion. Mindless, soundless sneezing, spewing, acrobatic in the wet globe of rushing spirit. *Drowning.* Gin skins.

They gave up their ghosts through their mouths, and there came then the last squeezed fistful of seconds, during which hallucinations settled on them, devils and nightmares, the beasts of the labyrinth of an alcohol-drenched mind, the children of the Minotaur.

And so Marie Tante was skinned in slices by bald, taloned things, and Moule was choked with skeins of hair, and Bettile beheld swimming toward her the net of her shawl, which tore off her breasts and reached in for her heart, and Tiraud lay on a dissecting table, conscious, while his organs were prized out of him, and Desel was stretched on a rack until he broke.... And in his apartment, Dr. Volpe was trying now to burst open his window, and it bit at his hands, and so he witnessed his plants had hold of him like things of the sea, and as they held him the eggs hatched, and out erupted prehistoric birds to peck his eyes and liver, while the butterflies flew in the flood of gin and scratched him with their pins.

When the twenty-one overseers of hell were dead, the Wave sank swiftly down, leaving only its tidemarks on the walls, and here and there a body, stuck against the plaster, or on the stairs, or the floor.

The Wave melted and only the night replaced the Wave. And presently the moon rose over the pristine buildings, and the lawns and the hothouse, which had grown cold. The moon was round, and white as snow.

The penguins waddled and preened on the flowery ice. The people played.

The man who was tormented by insects held out his hands, and the butterflies that now flighted around him sat like fiery papers on his fingers. The man who swayed was dancing. The woman who mourned, sang. The man who grinned was solemn, not a trace of a smile, as he paced beside a small pale fox. Citalbo walked with bears. Maque sailed the golden sea.

On Judit's head was a starry crown.

It was dawn forever. And a day.

TWELVE

Paradise

See, the Minotaur has two daughters; call them
"Left" and "Right." Sometimes.

John Kaiine

"Do you remember our uncle's dog?" Felion asked Smara.

"No," she said. "He can't have had a dog."

"Yes, a feral dog from Clock Tower Hill. It lived with him to a very old age and died in its sleep."

Smara laughed. "I do remember now. He said it could purr."

They sat facing each other, over the woven carpet they had brought to sit on. They were at the heart of the ice labyrinth, had been there most of a day, picnicking on bottles of river water, fried lentils, and dry bread soaked in wine.

Above, the shadow of the ice bird hung as if against a starry night. Both of them had noted this. The torch burned steadily. It did not seem the ice had melted at all.

"When we were born," said Smara, "we were energy. But it became flesh. It became *us*. If we'd died at birth, where would it have gone?"

"Back into our mother."

"But she might have died too."

"Why do you ask?" he said. "We didn't die."

"I dreamed someone dropped our mother into a well," said Smara softly.

"She threw herself off a tower."

They drank the water of Lethe, and stared at the patterns in the carpet.

Each of them recalled the hours in the other City, the amber light, the sun and moon and stars. But all this seemed far off. And what they had to do – that was farther still, perhaps unreachable. Both had killed so often, it was nearly a commonplace, a piece of work that required cleverness, quickness, application, and toil. But simple. Now, eventually, they had arrived at a killing that would be momentous: the murder of their uncle's heir, which would cement their chance in the world beyond the maze.

687

Sometimes Felion, or Smara, would have got up, but some laxness or nervous gesture of the other's put them back again.

At last he said, "Shall we do it now?" Smara said, "Suppose she isn't there?"

"We must want her to be there. We must want to meet with her. And if she isn't, we must wait in the house, for however long it takes her to come back."

They rose.

Smara wore the earrings Felion had recently brought her, and he the ring she had awarded him.

They had agreed. They would use, since it was the term of poison, the means they found to hand in the artist's studio, for these would surely be unique, unlike anything they had employed ever before.

They left their carpet and their picnic lying, and walked out along the left-hand way, into the labyrinth.

"If we're separated," he said, "we must each try to find the other. By thinking of the other. That seems to be the way. We always do find each other again."

"And we're always parted."

They did not touch, they did not hold hands. They carried nothing with them save the torch.

The labyrinth seemed, now, very silent. No visions had assaulted them when they first came in, and none flowered out on them now. They might have been in an ordinary cold, weird corridor, some vein of their uncle's house, going nowhere very special.

And then they turned a turn and found the exit point before them.

"Can you see anything out there?" Felion asked Smara.

"No," she said, "just darkness."

"Yes, only darkness. No moon. No stars. We'll have to trust it. It seems to demand that. Don't be afraid."

"I'm not," she said. "Only cold."

He put down the torch. They went forward, without faltering, side by side. And side by side they passed through the exit of the labyrinth. And were parted from each other as day from night.

The woman was there. Before him. In the studio. She had her back to him, and she was naked.

Felion kept entirely still.

Overhead was the skylight. Black, moonless. And the lights in the studio were so bright he could not see the stars.

But the woman was clear. Her white body and long fleecy hair.

And as he watched she turned about. She saw him at once, but in a misty way, amused rather than amazed. She was drunk or drugged. In her hand was a tube of orange paint, with which she had been daubing her slim, smooth body, shapes like islands.

"Well, hallo, hallo," she said to Felion. "Have you been hiding here long? Have you enjoyed the show? My, I thought the door was only set to recognize *me*. And all the while she's had another secret lover." The girl paused. "I'm glad I told them all those lies now, about her. About her violence. What a cat. She deserves it." She shook her hair. "But you're a real beauty. Oh, yes. Who are you?"

"Felion," he said.

"Felion. What a pretty sound. And I'm Asra."

"So that's your name," he said.

She wiggled the tube of paint down her skin, leaving a glowing trail like a snake of alien blood.

"Do you like my canvas? It's a new gimmick, edible paint. It tastes of *oranges* – yum. I thought she might like to lick it off. But now that I've seen you, perhaps you'd like to? Just think, if she comes back and finds us together. You know what a beast Leocadia can be." Asra, Felion's uncle's heir, the artist in her studio, dipped the edible paint against, between, her loins, and squeezed. "Won't you try a little?"

Felion moved toward her, and reached on the way the table with its paraphernalia of materials.

Another tube of the orange paint was there.

"And is this edible," he asked, "or toxic?"

"Oh that's the real stuff. No, leave that alone. Look, there's plenty here. Why don't you let me put a little on you?"

Felion left the table, the other tube of toxic paint in his hand. He came up against Asra, against her satin body, smearing it slightly, and then stepped around her, behind her. He slid his left hand about her silky throat and up over her lower face. In a second he had blocked off all her air, and she was kicking and writhing, her feet off the floor. He let her drunkenly struggle for half a minute, not exerting enough force to choke but only enough to stifle.

Then he slapped away his hand from her and pushed instead the opened tube of toxic paint between her lips. As her mouth gaped wide to gasp the air, he compressed the tube strongly.

The finesse of many murders had made him more than competent.

He held her as she convulsed, as he had never held a woman in the death throes of love.

When Asra, his uncle's heir, was dead, he raised her and hung her over the easel in the middle of the room.

He stood a moment, taking in the picture that she made.

Then he walked over against the wall.

"Smara!" he called.

The wall opened, and there, simplistically, was the way back into the ice. Smara must be there. Or she would meet him there, as before.

He glanced behind him, but the studio was already reeling away, swaying and bucking, on a chain of light. He seemed to have lost hold of it, all connection to it. He had a sense of panic – but then he only stepped over into the labyrinth; he had done what he came for. He must find Smara. Then they must return at once, outside the house. They must go back to this City for good, the City of the sun and moon, and nothing would stop it. They could never be separated again.

Even as he emerged into the heart of the ice (so quickly he got to it), Smara ran into the space after him, as if she had only been concealed somewhere in the wall, and it was a game. She was giggling.

"I did it!" she cried. "Without you."

"What did you do?"

"I killed her," said Smara, happily. "And then I came here, to look for you."

Felion said, "Wait. You killed her?"

"I went straight into the studio. The room you described, with the skylight. I think it was afternoon. She was blind drunk, going about in front of a canvas smothered in daubs of paint. There was a bottle of white spirit I knew was poison. I ran at her and tipped half of it down her throat before she realized what was happening."

"But Smara," he said, "*I* killed her."

"You?"

They stood as if frozen in the heart of ice, in the silence, and in the shadow, for neither he nor anything had bothered with the torch, which had gone out. They stood and stared at each other.

"If we both," he said, "killed a woman in that room, which of us killed *her*?"

Smara said quietly, "Or did neither of us kill her?"

"We must go back," her said. But they started together as if magnetized.

And from above came a huge crack of noise, like the thawing of a frozen sky. Stars rained over them, but they were stars of ice.

Felion and Smara looked upward, and framed by a smothered darkness, like Paradise, they saw the bird of ice, a column with a great beaked head, leaning over on them as if it meant to speak. Neither of them uttered a sound. They flung their arms about each other, and through their skulls swirled the images of their lives, bright as sparks, and over these a closing curtain thundered like a wave.

The ice statue crashed directly onto them, crushing their bodies together, so that the bones of each broke through the other's skin and mingled, and next mashing them down deep into the ground surface of muddy glass, from which their picnic had vanished. The bird beak of white obsidian went through their hearts, and pinned them one to the other, and pinned them to the earth. The bulk of the bird thing cracked on them like a boulder, covering them, stoppering them beneath into the floor of the labyrinth.

When the silence came again, it was imperfectly. For it was full of a faint tiny sound, like dripping water. The shadow and the cold wavered and dulled, and a sort of rain began to fall, but there was no one to see or hear it. No one to wonder what it might be. If it was anything at all.

EPILOGUE

Paradis

Boys and girls come out to play,
The moon doth shine as bright as day.

Nursery Rhyme

Between waking and sleeping, twilight illusions would come to her, not really dreams. As she grew older, she liked these times, and sought them out. From them she had garnered much of the material that now she painted, but always the backdrop of these pictures was the same. She had come to love and want to paint the same vision, over and over, only subtly altering it here and there, adding, as years passed, the diamonté trees and glimmering fruit and bonbons, the animals, the ship on the sea, and the dancers on the shore.

There had not been an exhibition of her work for two decades, and *then* they had said, "Leocadia's senile. Does that still happen? Look, how repetitious and trifling."

Nanice's one great masterpiece was still at the academy near the Observatory, the modern building with the dragon of bronze on its roof, and antique graves paving the garden at its foot.

Leocadia would cackle when she though of Nanice. After all, Leocadia was now ninety years of age, and to cackle, finally, was quite becoming. Her gray hair was still thick, and still kept its obstreperous curl. She wore it loose to her waist. The rest had gone the way of all flesh, shrunken and fallen. And yet a young photographer who had come to visit in the autumn had obviously found her beautiful, not sexually, but spiritually, in her second youth before the coming of age of death.

Leocadia did not miss sex, she had had so much of it – precisely enough, in fact – in her earlier years. Only during her sojourn at the Residence had she been celibate, and that omission had only lasted nine months, the length of a pregnancy.

The scales had dropped from her eyes. And what scales! After she had painted the penguin and the ice floes on the wall. A day, two days, ten, went by, and gradually, softly, it came to her that everything had been a delusion. She discovered her canvases then, stacked up among the books in the alcove library, where she must have placed them, hidden them from herself, pretending that Van Orles had done it as a punishment. Indeed, it was Van Orles who congratulated her on the wall painting. He had followed her work for years, and this, he said, was an honor for them, and a great pleasure, to have an original landscape by Leocadia le Vey to enhance the room. It would be therapeutic for whoever was lucky enough to be put in here.

Van Orles was not ugly. Nor were any of the other doctors. Saume's teeth were even and white, Leibiche did not have pimples, only one coy beauty spot beside his mouth. Duval was extremely, nearly stupidly handsome. What had she been seeing? She asked them.

"Ah, we were your enemies, posing as friends. Beware of Greeks bearing gifts. Your line of defense, mademoiselle, was to remake us as monsters."

When she told Duval she had found him ugly (which she could not resist doing), he blushed, like a plain woman complimented on loveliness. Obviously, no one could ever have said this to him before.

When Leocadia had not drunk anything alcoholic for seventeen days, they urged her to take a little wine. Her system was not ready for such drastic deprivation after the influx that had gone before. So then she had a glass of wine with her dinner, and a little gin in the afternoon. She fancied gin. It was totally pure, colorless, not like the liquid that had been in the mysterious brown bottle.

They were intrigued by the bottle. Sometimes, they said, the Residence guests did find things of historic interest. Did she wish to keep the bottle? Leocadia kept it.

They began to let her go for walks in the countryside, and presently to journey by car to the City. A doctor always went with her. When she could, she chose Van Orles. She had begun to find him very attractive, better than Duval, who was like a classical god, a sweet too pretty to eat. Van Orles was muscular and brawny, with thick dark hair. He did not speak in the peculiar threatening way she had believed, and when they talked, answered her freely, offering his past among a family of cooks, and how he had made his way with difficulty into his profession. No white neon, like a rampant moon, shone around him now, nor did it with the others. She did not know what the light had been, save it was a warning – of her own misjudgment, presumably. She could not be sure how much she had only imagined, although evidently many scenes had not occurred at all. She thought this entertaining rather than unnerving. Perhaps things had taken place on some other plane, in some parallel world. There Van Orles had harassed her, and there she had made a fool of him. But not, certainly, here. Now Leocadia did try to seduce Van Orles. And she began by telling him of the delusion, what she thought she had done, baring her breast and forcing him into a premature ejaculation that had spoilt his trousers. Van Orles lowered his eyes. "Naughty Leocadia," he said. And then, when she kissed him, gently, "You're a wonderful woman, and I'll admit I've had a crush on you for years, before even we met. But how can I now? You've been, and still are, my patient. I'm selfish. I'd lose everything. And you'd only laugh." He did kiss her back. She never forgot his kiss. It was strong, courteous, amorous, frightened. "Of course I'm afraid," he said, "Look what could happen, out in this field." For she had made the car stop on the way to Paradis. She did not do so again.

She briefly hated the City. It looked unfamiliar, as if it had been up to something while she was away.

"For a long while," he said, "you've been out of touch with yourself, and everything."

She insisted she had not killed Asra. But recalling the episodes of accusation swathed in light, she did not think he would say that she had. And he said, "No. Unfortunately the murderer has never been found. But it wasn't ever thought to be you. You seemed to think so, from time to time. But even your cousin, Nanice le Vey, was quite belligerent on the matter of your innocence."

The pastel cravats suited him, mild on his tanned, bold shyness.

She had misinterpreted everything, but something in the painting of the penguin and the snow had released her. Why and how? They spoke to her of projection, of unknown country being the cipher for death and so of rebirth. She knew the moment she had begun to be reborn – or at least the moment of death. Nanice had done that for her, by taking Leocadia's role. They would not admit they had tried to use Nanice as a catalyst, only that she had been an insistent visitor they had at last allowed to call.

Leocadia herself experimented with the others, the bizarre people of the Residence. Mademoiselle Varc had reached the end of her treatment, which she had been receiving for a premature senility. She was now quite sane. Soon she would travel far away. She sat in the summerhouse with the white and cinnamon windows, and held Leocadia's hand. "You were so patient with me. Do you know, I'm a journalist? It's almost a surprise to me, I can tell you. I can't wait to get back, I've missed so much. Thank God, they've made me myself again. And did I call you Lucie? She was a dear child. No, not my friend – my daughter, who died. But yes, there are five others. Each has a different father, and all are fascinating. But there, the proud mother."

Leocadia mentioned the wooden dolls and the amber necklace Mademoiselle Varc had drawn from the rubbish tip in the yards of the old asylum.

"But I believed *you* put them there – for *me!*"

Leocadia said, "Oh. You've found me out."

It was then that truly she began to slot together all the pieces. Having no guide, she did not know for sixty years what they formed.

She only said to Van Orles, then, "The asylum itself is mad."

"What else?" he said.

Thomas the Warrior would no longer speak to her, and perhaps never had. Van Orles explained that Thomas was a war hero from a campaign seldom spoken of, erased from government files. He was almost unreachable, but he feared dogs. He would never reveal why. He also feared high towers, apparently.

The spider man, too, was not as Leocadia had thought him. His odd way of moving was due to a spinal injury that had proved incurable. He was afraid of anyone who walked upright – almost everyone – and Leocadia found that if she sat down immediately he appeared, he would come and talk to her. He was a poet, and the most exquisite phrases poured from his lips. One evening, before the sun had quite gone and they were expected to go back to their rooms, Leocadia lay in his arms under a cedar tree, out of sight of everything but the biscuit blocks of the old madhouse. Nothing happened, but she knew she had made him glad. She knew, greedily, he would put her into a poem.

For by now she was greedy. She ate roast chicken and potatoes with cream, mandarin tarts, orange caviar.

They let her go in the very early spring, before anything but bark was on the trees.

She had by then heard about Nanice.

Leocadia's cousin, who had taken on Leocadia's life, living in Leocadia's house, adorning herself as an artist, painting in the studio, drinking in Leocadia's style. She had been infected, as if the house were full of a plague called Leocadia. Poor Nanice, she had led such an exemplary and careful existence until then, incarcerating Leocadia from moral concern, or was it moral jealousy and wild hunger?

Nanice, in her Leocadia role, was painting in the attic one day, dead drunk. Her works were a disaster, she had no talent, but Nanice had not noticed this. Nor did she notice in her inebriated confusion that the bottle she gripped contained white spirit and not vodka. She had drained it. There was no hint she had intended suicide. Her lover, a young woman of slight mind, had told how Nanice was full of life. By which it was thought she meant full of money.

In the death seizure, however, Nanice fell headlong onto her current canvas, and the resultant chaos, when it was peeled from beneath the corpse, had become a sensation of the City.

It was exhibited at the academy, and popular acclaim kept it there. In its queer and ragged runnels, its smears and gobs of color, Paradis read impassioned and macabre secrets. Dead, Nanice became one of the most famous artists of her era, far eclipsing Leocadia le Vey.

Even so, the house near to the old wall was left vacant, and Leocadia moved back into it, and her inheritance returned to her without hindrance. There had been no plot. Asra's death had driven her out of doors from an already wavering mind. Though why was in some ways a dilemma. Again, sixty years would need to elapse before it would seem that possibly she had

had to go mad, had been needed to go mad, in order that she enter the Residence, and there perform the magical spell upon the wall.

Emerging from the asylum was far worse, more uncomfortable than emerging from insanity. Now she must leave her true friends who were not her enemies. She did so. She shut them all out.

She scoured all trace of others from the house. She made it white, with sofas and drapes of snow, carpets of simulated polar bear fur, mirrors like glaciers. Her studio she filled with treated ice sculptures that did not melt, holding ivory daisies, marigolds, lilies, ivy.

It was said in Paradis she was still mad, had got worse.

Although she took lovers and ate dinners and strolled in the City, she closed herself in, every month more and more. She painted huge canvases of a land of ice, with mountains of ice. And as she picked her way across this snowy id, she reached the sea, and there she painted the meeting of a black-haired queen with a young girl who carried in her arms a child. And Leocadia painted also ships with carrot sails, and seals, and dancers, and butterflies. And still, she did not know why.

The photographer who came to Leocadia in what she supposed must be her old age was in love with her painting (like Van Orles – now, alas, long dead) and with a little novel she had published, about a land she called *Penguin.*

They sat in Leocadia's white salon, drinking orange-flower tea and tiny goblets of crystalline gin.

She showed him the brown bottle with the four-sided throat and the label.

"Is it awfully old?" he asked.

"Older than I am."

"Oh," he said, "but you're young."

"It was the time I went mad," she said. "I found it in the grounds of the lunatic asylum."

He said, "You're one of the truly sane."

She showed him the pictures, all the views of *Penguin,* some with proper penguins stamping humorously about the ice. And sometimes there was a tiger-colored moon, very bright.

"Have you heard about the penguin spirit, Koodjanuk?" he said. "I think you must have. The ice peoples invoke him to heal the sick."

"Yes, I must have," said Leocadia. Something clicked loudly inside her skull. One of her elderly bones shifting, perhaps. "Also a vengeful spirit," she said vaguely.

"Maybe all spirits are, if you go against them." He smiled at the penguins, which were small and playful. "And who is this girl – may I ask? – with ginger hair?"

"I saw her once," said Leocadia firmly. "She must have died, because she was a ghost."

And Leocadia thought, *How wise and elegant I've become, with ninety years.* And again, click.

"But here she is too," said the young photographer, "and here, dancing with a young child – it's charming."

"God knows who she is," said Leocadia. She thought, *But I know her really. She's the young virgin at the Sabbat, before the cocks crow. Through her the power comes, to remake things.*

She thought, *And through me. Something I did. I made a world. I gave it life. And the sun and the moon.*

Leocadia dreamed that one day she would be painting among her solid statues of ice and flowers that did not die, and a touch would come on her shoulder, or something harmless would be thrown at her neck. And she would turn to find the path into *Penguin*, which she had earned, and which was, presumably, only the afterlife.

When the photographer went away, bubbling with fizzy youth, to write a whole book about her, Leocadia went up to her studio, unhaunted by the deaths of Nanice and Asra.

She stood among the canvases and considered. Possibly death did not matter. Possibly stupidity and cruelty, banality and rheumatism (which even the best drugs could not quite dispel) did not count.

What counted, then?

Why, what we want. What we truly desire.

"Write," said Leocadia, "in the great fat tome of time. Real desire, of any sort, is what counts."

And when she was one hundred and five and a half, Leocadia was painting the Penguin Land in her studio, slowly, because her hand was stiff. When in the ice sculpture before her, beyond the picture, she caught an image.

It was of a girl – two girls, but one not long ago a child. And both had marmalade hair.

She heard their laughter like distant bells.

Leocadia imagined that behind her the wall had opened, and there lay heaven, with snow and flowers, a sea of golden wine, a penguin king and a queen in a crown of ice.

If she means it, the minx, she'll throw a snowball at me. Then I'll look round and it will be there, and I can go in.

And Leocadia would be young. And though it might not be forever, it would be, at least, for one long, shining day.

And then the snowball, which was warm as toast, struck her shoulder.